HARVEST IN TRANSLATION

Open Heart

A·B·YEHOSHUA

Open Heart

Translated by Dalya Bilu

A HARVEST BOOK
HARCOURT BRACE & COMPANY
San Diego   New York   London

Library of Congress Cataloging-in-Publication Data
Yehoshua, Abraham B.
[Shivah me-Hodu. English]
Open heart/A. B. Yehoshua; translated by Dalya Bilu.
p.   cm.—(A Harvest book)
Previously published: 1st ed. New York: Doubleday, 1996.
ISBN 0-15-600484-4
I. Bilu, Dalya.   II. Title.
PJ5034.Y42S5513   1997
892.4'36—dc21   97-2507

Text set in Sabon
Book design by Paul Randall Mize
Printed in the United States of America
First Harvest edition 1997
A C E F D B

To Gideon, who returned from India

Contents

Set thy heart upon thy work
But never on its reward.
Work not for a reward;
But never cease to do thy work.

—*The Bhagavadgita,* Chapter 2, verse 47
(Translated by Juan Mascaro, Penguin Classics, 1962)

PART ONE

Falling in Love

One

The incision was ready for stitching now. The anesthetist slipped the mask impatiently from his face, and as if the big respirator with its changing, flickering numbers were no longer enough for him, he stood up, gently took the still hand to feel the living pulse, smiled affectionately at the naked sleeping woman, and winked at me. But I ignored his wink, because my eyes were fixed on Professor Hishin, to see if he would finish the suturing himself or ask one of us to take over. I felt a tremor in my heart. I knew I was going to be passed over again, and my rival, the second resident, was going to be given the job. With a pang I watched the movements of the scrub nurse as she wiped away the last drops of blood from the long straight cut gaping in the woman's stomach. I could have scored an easy success, I thought bitterly, by completing the operation with a really elegant suture. But it didn't look as if Hishin was about to hand over the job to anyone. Even though he had been at work for three straight hours, he now rummaged, with the same supreme concentration with which he had begun the operation, through the pile of needles to find what he wanted. Finally he found the right needle and returned it angrily to the nurse to be sterilized again. Did he really owe it to this woman to sew her up with his own hands? Or perhaps there had been some under-the-table payment? I withdrew a little from the operating table, consoling myself with the thought that this time I had been spared humiliation at least, even though the other resident, who had also apparently grasped the surgeon's intention to perform the suturing himself, maintained his alert stance beside the open abdomen.

At this point there was a stir next to the big door, and a curly mane of gray hair together with an excitedly waving hand appeared at one of the portholes. The anesthetist recognized the man and hurried to open the door. But now, having invaded the wing without a doctor's gown or mask, the man seemed at least to hesitate before entering the operating room itself and called out from the doorway in a lively, confident voice, "Haven't you finished yet?" The surgeon glanced over his shoulder, gave him a friendly wave, and said, "I'll be with you in a minute." He bent over the operating table again, but after a few minutes stopped and started looking around. His eyes met mine, and he seemed about to say something to me, but then the scrub nurse, who always knew how to read her master's mind, sensed his hesitation and said softly but firmly, "There's no problem, Professor Hishin, Dr. Vardi can finish up." The surgeon immediately nodded in agreement, handed the needle to the resident standing next to him, and issued final instructions to the nurses. He pulled off his mask with a vigorous movement, held out his hands to the young nurse, who removed his gloves, and before disappearing from the room repeated, "If there are any problems, I'll be with Lazar in administration."

I turned to the operating table, choking back my anger and envy so that they wouldn't burst out in a look or gesture. That's it then, I thought in despair. If the women are on his side too, there's no doubt which of us will be chosen to stay on in the department and which will have to begin wandering from hospital to hospital looking for a job at the end of the month. This is clearly the end of my career in the surgical department. But I took up my position calmly next to my colleague, who had already exchanged the needle Hishin handed him for another one; I was ready to share in the responsibility for the last stage of the operation, watching the incision close rapidly under his strong, dexterous fingers. If the incision had been in my hands, I would have tried to suture it more neatly, not to mar by so much as a millimeter the original contours of the pale female stomach, which suddenly aroused a profound compassion in me. And already the anesthestist Dr. Nakash, was getting ready for the "landing," as he called it, preparing to take out the tubes, removing the infusion needle from the vein, humming merrily and keeping a constant watch on the surgeon's hands, waiting for permission to return the patient to normal breathing. Still absorbed in the insult to me, I felt the touch of a light hand. A young nurse who had quietly entered the room told me in a whisper that the head of the department was waiting for me in Lazar's office. "Now?" I hesitated. And the other resident, who had overheard the whisper, urged me, "Go, go, don't worry, I'll finish up here myself."

Without removing my mask, I hurried out of the shining darkness of the operating room and past the laughter of the doctors and nurses in the tearoom, released the press-button of the big door sealing off the wing, and emerged into the waiting room, which was bathed in afternoon sunlight. When I stopped to take off my mask, a young man and an elderly woman immediately recognized and approached me. "How is she? How is she?"

"She's fine." I smiled. "The operation's over, they'll bring her out soon."

"But how is she? How is she?" they persisted. "She's fine," I said. "Don't worry, she's been born again." I myself was surprised by the phrase—the operation hadn't been at all dangerous—and I turned away from them and continued on my way, still in my pale green bloodstained surgical gown, the mask hanging around my neck, the cap on my head, rustling the sterile plastic shoe covers. Catching the stares following me here and there, I went up in the elevator to the big lobby and turned into the administrative wing, where I had never been invited before, and finally gave my name to one of the secretaries. She inquired in a friendly way as to my preferences in coffee and led me through an imposing empty conference lounge into a large, curtained, and very uninstitutionally furnished room—a sofa and armchairs, well-tended plants in big pots. The head of the department, Professor Hishin, was lounging in one of the armchairs, going through some papers. He gave me a quick, friendly smile and said to the hospital director, who was standing next to him, "Here he is, the ideal man for you."

Mr. Lazar shook my hand firmly and very warmly and introduced himself, while Hishin gave me encouraging looks, ignoring the wounding way he had slighted me previously and hinting to me discreetly to take off my cap and remove the plastic covers from my shoes. "The operation's over," he said in his faint Hungarian accent, his eyes twinkling with that tireless irony of his, "and even you can rest now." As I removed the plastic covers and crammed the cap into my pocket, Hishin began telling Lazar the story of my life, with which he was quite familiar, to my surprise. Mr. Lazar continued examining me with burning eyes, as if his fate depended on me. Finally, Hishin finished by saying, "Even though he's dressed as a surgeon, don't make any mistake, he's first and foremost an excellent internist. That's his real strength, and the only reason he insists on remaining in our department is because he believes, completely wrongly, that what lies at the pinnacle of medicine is a butcher's knife." As he spoke he waved an imaginary knife in his hand and cut off his head. Then he gave a friendly laugh—as if to soften the final blow he had just delivered to my future in the surgical department—reached out his hand, placed it on my knee, and asked gently, in a tone of unprecedented intimacy, "Have you ever been to India?"

"India?" I asked in astonishment. "India? Why India, of all places?" But Hishin laughed, enjoying his little surprise. "Yes, India. Lazar's looking for a doctor to accompany him on a little trip to India."

"To India?" I exclaimed again, still unable to take it in. "Yes, yes, to India. There's a certain sick young woman who needs a doctor to accompany her home to Israel, and she happens to be in India."

"Sick with what?" I asked immediately. "Nothing terrible," said Hishin reassuringly, "but a little tricky nevertheless. Acute hepatitis, apparently B, which got a little out of hand and led to deterioration. And even though her condition seems to have stabilized, we all decided that it would be best to bring the young lady home as soon as possible. With all due respect to Indian medicine, we can still give her the best care here."

"But who is she? Who is this woman?" I asked with rising petulance. "She's my daughter." The administrative director finally broke his silence. "She left on a tour of the Far East six months ago, and last month she caught this jaundice, and she had to be hospitalized in a town called Gaya, in East India, somewhere between Calcutta and New Delhi. At first she apparently didn't want to worry us and she tried to keep it a secret, but a friend who was with her there came home two days ago and brought us a letter with a few details about her illness. Even though everyone's assured us that there's no danger, I want her home before any complications set in. We thought it would be a good idea to take a doctor along. It shouldn't take more than twelve days, maximum two weeks, and that's only because she's stuck out there in Gaya, which is a little off the beaten track as far as trains and flights are concerned. To tell you the truth, I tried at first to entice your professor, who's never been to India and could have done with a rest, but you know him as well as I do, he's always too busy—and if he has got any time to spare, he prefers to go to Europe, not to Asia. But he promised to provide us with an ideal substitute."

Ideal for what, I asked myself gloomily, to drag a girl with hepatitis around India on dilapidated old trains? But I held my tongue and turned to look at the secretary, who came into the room with a story about someone who had been waiting a long time to see the director. "Just don't move," commanded Lazar, "I'll get rid of him in a minute," and he disappeared, leaving the Hishin and me facing each other. I knew that Hishin had already sensed my disappointment and resentment of this strange proposal, because he suddenly rose to his feet and stood towering over me and started talking to me gently. "Look, I can see that you're not enthusiastic about the idea of suddenly dashing off to India like this, but in your place I'd accept the offer. Not only for the sake of an interesting free trip to a place you might never have the chance to go to again, but for the opportunity to get to know the man himself. Lazar is someone who can help you if you want to go on working at this hospital, in internal medicine or any other department. The hospital is run from this room, and Lazar holds the reins. Apart from which, he also happens to be a nice, decent man. So listen to me and don't turn him down. You should go. What have you got to lose? Even if all you get out of it is a pleasant adventure. And besides, there's not much to do for hepatitis. I don't believe the young lady has managed to do any real harm to her liver or kidneys, but even if she has, it's not the end of the world—the body will heal itself in the end. All you have to do is watch out for sudden hemorrhages, prevent the glucose level from falling, and of course keep her from becoming febrile. I'll collect a few good articles on the subject for you, and tomorrow we'll consult Professor Levine from internal medicine. Hepatitis is his baby—he knows everything there is to know about it, including things nobody needs to know. And we'll put together a nice little kit for you as well, so you'll be ready for anything that might crop up. And another thing, you can say good-bye to them in Europe if you like and take a vacation. I couldn't believe my eyes when I saw your file—in the whole year you've been with us you've only taken one day's leave."

So he can't wait to get rid of me, I thought miserably. He can't even wait one more month till the end of my trial year. It was unbelievable. And then Lazar came back. "Well?" he asked with a broad executive smile. "It's agreed?" But Hishin immediately and sensibly slowed him down. "Just a minute, Lazar, what is this? A man has the right to think things over."

"Of course, of course," replied Lazar, and glanced at his watch. "But till when? There are so many technical arrangements to make, and I planned on leaving the day after tomorrow, to catch the Tuesday flight from Rome." But he must have sensed the threat of refusal in my continuing silence, since he stopped pressuring me and invited me to his home that evening to talk over the details and to give me time to make up my mind. It would have been churlish to refuse the invitation, and besides, I felt that these two assertive men wouldn't allow me to start resisting them now. As I was making my way out of the room, address and directions in hand, Lazar called after me, "Wait a minute. I forgot to ask, are you married?" When I shook my head, his spirits immediately soared; he turned to Hishin with raised eyebrows and asked, "In that case, what has he got to think about?" and the two of them laughed good-humoredly.

The afternoon turned very rainy, and as I hurried from bed to bed in the intensive care unit, battling to stop a sudden hemorrhage in the young woman who had been operated on that morning, I made up my mind to refuse. If it was only for the sake of some weird trip to India that I had suddenly become ideal in the eyes of the head of the department, why should I give up the last month of rounds to which I was entitled? Every day I was learning new and fascinating things, every minute in the operating room thrilled me, even if I was only watching. What could I possibly gain from a sudden trip to India in the middle of winter? But as dusk descended and I arrived at my apartment wet and tired, prepared to call Lazar and give my decision, I had second thoughts. Why insult a man who might be useful to me one day? The least I could do was listen politely to the details before finally turning him down. I hurried to take a shower and change my clothes. At eight o'clock I rode north to an apartment block standing in a broad avenue of oak trees rustling in the wind and the rain. I covered my motorcycle with its tarpaulin, but when I saw that the rain was coming down harder I changed my mind and dragged it under the foundation pillars of the building. On the top floor, in a large, elegant apartment, I was impatiently greeted by Lazar, dressed in a loose red flannel shirt which made him look bulkier and older. "But how could I have forgotten to tell you to bring your passport?" he greeted me plaintively. "Is it valid? When was the last time you went abroad?" The last time I had been abroad had been two years earlier, on a short trip to Europe after graduating from medical school. I didn't have the faintest idea whether my passport was still valid, and I tried with an embarrassed smile to fend off his enthusiasm and to indicate that although I had kept the appointment, I was still very undecided and had come only to hear him out again and think it over. "What's there to think about?" cried Lazar in astonishment and a kind of childish anger. "But if you insist, come and see where I want to take you, and don't panic; even if it looks like the end of the world on the map, we can make it there and back in two weeks, and even take in a few sights on the way, because I don't want to turn the trip into one long *via dolorosa* either." And he pulled me into a large, attractive living room. A boy of about seventeen in a pale blue school uniform shirt, very like his father except that his hair was long and soft, immediately stood up and left the room.

On a low glass table lay a large open atlas, with photo albums and travel guides scattered around it. "You're not the only one who was taken by surprise," Lazar apologized. "It fell on us like a bolt out of the blue when that girl knocked on the door yesterday with the letter. But first come and see where we're going. Here's New Delhi, here's Bombay, here's Calcutta, a kind of triangle, and here's Gaya, a remote but holy town surrounded by temples. Tomorrow I'm going to Jerusalem to meet someone who spent several months there a few years ago, and after that I'll have a clearer picture of what to expect. But just a minute, before we go any further let me introduce you to my wife."

A woman walked into the room, a plump brunette of about forty-five, of medium height, her hair gathered into a rather untidy knot on top of her head, her eyes flashing me a frank, vivid smile behind her glasses. I stood up and her husband introduced me to her. She nodded affably and immediately sat down opposite me with a regal movement, crossing long legs that didn't match the heaviness of her arms and shoulders, and began watching her husband, who went on drawing lines on the map of India and calculating times. As I tried to follow the route he was mapping out I sensed her appraising me, and when I looked up at her, her eyes suddenly lit up again in the same warm, lively, generous smile, and she nodded her head slightly in a gesture of approval. Then, as if she sensed my gnawing doubts, she suddenly interrupted her husband and addressed me directly. "Do you really think you'll be able to leave your work at the hospital and go abroad for more than two weeks?" Her husband, who was very put out by this question, answered crossly in my place. "First of all, why do you already say more than two weeks? Where do you get that from? It'll be less. I have to be back on the Sunday after next, don't forget. And second, why shouldn't he be able to leave the hospital? He can leave it for as long as he likes. Hishin gave him carte blanche—he can take it as leave due to him, if he likes, or as ordinary working days and we'll find a way to make them up." But his wife immediately protested. "Why at the expense of his leave? Why should he sacrifice his vacation for us?" And again she looked directly at me, and said in a clear, firm voice, which did not suit her plump, soft looks, "Please find out what payment you're entitled to for your services on a trip like this. We will gladly compensate you for your efforts."

Suddenly I felt stifled in the elegant, spacious apartment. The two middle-aged people sitting opposite me looked powerful and influential. "It's not a question of money"—I began to blush—"and it really is true that I've got a lot of leave coming, but if I go away now, even for two weeks, it's as if I've already finished my trial year in surgery, and I don't want to miss a single day there."

"In the surgical department?" asked the woman.

"Yes," I replied, "I started in surgery, and that's where I want to continue."

"In surgery?" said the woman, looking at her husband in surprise. "We thought you were transferring to internal medicine or some other department, because Hishin told us that you weren't going to continue in surgery." A tremor of real pain passed through me on hearing the final verdict on my future spoken so casually by this strange woman. It wasn't even a question of a position being available, I now realized, but a clear professional judgment against me. And Hishin's tall figure seemed to loom up behind the woman, who never stopped examining me with her smiling eyes. "Who said I wanted to be an internist?" I burst into a bitter snort of laughter. "Even if Hishin has reservations, I'm still not giving up surgery. There are other hospitals, if not in Israel then abroad—England, for instance—and you can get excellent experience there too."

"England?" repeated Mrs. Lazar, and her friendly smile disappeared. "Yes. My parents came here from England, I'm a British citizen, and I won't have any problems doing my residency there." Lazar, who was uninterested in the argument between me and his wife, suddenly beamed. "So I was right. I saw in your file that your parents were born in England, and I wondered if you were a British citizen too. That will help you on the trip to India. I suppose your English is perfect."

"Perfect? I wouldn't say so," I said coldly, again trying to rebuff the single-minded enthusiasm of the man. "I was born and educated here, and my English is the same as everybody else's—in other words, far from perfect. I usually speak Hebrew to my parents too, but of course, since I often hear them speaking English to each other, I'm fluent—not perfect, but fluent." Lazar appeared more than satisfied with fluency and gave me a smile of undisguised gratification; it seemed that nothing could now detract from my virtues as a candidate for the trip to India, and he turned to his wife and raised his eyebrows. "What's this? You haven't offered our guest anything to drink! We've been talking so much we've forgotten our duties as hosts." But the woman made no move to rise from the sofa. Instead she smiled at her husband and said, "Why don't you make us some strong Turkish coffee? We're all exhausted."

Lazar jumped to his feet. "You don't object to Turkish coffee?" His wife turned to me, as if to dare me to object; then she took out a slender cigarette and lit it. When her husband disappeared into the kitchen, her eyes flashed again with the same bright smile, and she leaned toward me and began talking intimately in her soft but very clear voice. "I feel that you're still having doubts. That's natural. Because really, why should anybody be ready to drop everything from one day to the next and go to India? And if you feel that we're trying to put pressure on you and it offends you, you're absolutely right. But try to understand that we're upset too. We have to bring our daughter home quickly; the disease—as you know better than I do—is exhausting and debilitating. According to the girl who brought the letter, her condition has already deteriorated, and everyone who's been consulted strongly recommends taking a qualified doctor with us. Before you arrived, Hishin phoned and warned us not to let you wriggle out of it, because in his opinion you're the ideal candidate."

"Ideal again." I interrupted her with an angry laugh that welled up inside me. "Hishin's exaggerating. In what sense ideal? Ideal for what? Maybe, as your husband said, because of my British passport." The woman laughed in surprise. "Of course not! Naturally, it won't hurt to have a British passport in India, but that's not what Hishin meant, he's really very fond of you. He spoke of your quiet manner, your friendliness, your excellent clinical perception, and especially of your deep concern for your patients." She spoke warmly, passionately, her words clear and eloquent, but I was aware of a certain hypocrisy and exaggeration too. It was impossible to tell if Hishin had actually heaped all that praise on my head or if she was inventing compliments to seduce me. I lowered my eyes, but I didn't know how to stop her. In the end I let my hands fall wearily to my sides and asked, "How old is she, this girl of yours?"

"Girl?" The mother laughed. "She's not a girl. She's twenty-five years old. She has spent two years studying at the university. Here, this is a picture she sent two months ago, before she got sick." She picked up an envelope of coarse green paper, from which she extracted two snapshots of a young woman with a pretty, delicate face. In one of them the woman was standing alone against the background of a vast river in which naked figures were crouching, and in the second she was near the entrance of a building which looked like an Indian temple, a boy and a girl on either side of her, their arms wrapped around her.

When I got home I decided, in spite of the late hour, to phone my parents in Jerusalem and ask their opinion. To my surprise, both my mother, who was still awake, and my father, who was awakened by the ringing phone, thought that I should on no account turn down such a proposal from the head of the hospital. "He's only the administrative director," I kept explaining, but my father was adamant. "All the more so," he insisted, beginning to speak English in his sleepiness. "Those are the people with the real power, because they're permanent fixtures, and the others come and go around them. Even your Professor Hishin might disappear one fine day for one reason or another, and it won't do you any harm to have the support of the administrative head of the hospital in the future."

"That's not the way things work, Dad," I complained wearily. "It's not so simple." But my parents were resolute in their enthusiasm. "Just don't be in such a hurry to refuse—the hospital's not running away, and you've worked so hard this year that you deserve a vacation."

"In India?" I said sarcastically. "What kind of a vacation can I have there?" But now my mother began praising the country. She had an uncle who had served there between the two world wars, and she remembered that he was in love with India and never stopped describing its charms. "That was a completely different India," I said, trying to cool her ardor, but she persevered: "Nothing in the world ever becomes completely different, and it was once full of magic and beauty—something must have remained, and for such a short trip it will be quite enough." I was surprised by my parents' reaction. I had assumed that their constant anxiety would make them try to talk me out of the idea, and instead they were joining in the pressure to make me go. "I can't see what kind of vacation I'll have on a trip like this," I grumbled into the phone, "and I don't need a vacation now, either. My work at the hospital's so fascinating I don't want to miss a single day. In any case, I'll think it over tonight. I promised to give them a final answer tomorrow morning." I tried to put an end to the conversation. But my parents wouldn't let me go. "Even if the idea of the trip doesn't attract you at the moment," argued my father, "people here are asking for your help—it's an opportunity to do a good deed."

"A good deed?" I laughed. "There's no question of a good deed here—they want to pay me a fee for the trip. It's got nothing to do with good deeds, and anyway, why me? They've got the whole hospital at their disposal; they could easily find some other doctor to go with them and bring their daughter back for them."

But of this I was not certain. When I had promised the Lazars a final answer early in the morning, they had repeated that if I refused, they wouldn't have time to find and persuade another suitable doctor from the hospital.

"This is a chance for you to experience another world and refresh yourself," said my mother. Recently she and my father had been worried about how absorbed I was in my work, fearing that I was in danger of becoming a slave to it.

"Another world? Perhaps," I replied heavily, pulling the telephone onto my lap and falling exhausted onto my bed, "but will I be able to refresh myself there?" My parents were silent, as if I had finally succeeded in conveying to them across the distance that separated us the full weight of my weariness. "When would you have to leave?" my mother asked gently. "Right away." I closed my eyes and covered myself with the blanket. "They want to fly to Rome the day after tomorrow."

"The day after tomorrow?" repeated my astonished mother, who had not realized the urgency of the trip. "What did you think? It's serious. There's a very sick girl out there. Who knows what really happened to her? That's what I've been trying to explain to you, it's not exactly a pleasure trip." And suddenly I felt the pressure lifting on the other end of the line. "In that case, we really should think twice. Perhaps you're right. We'll all sleep on it, and talk again in the morning." Now I was sorry that I had called them. I knew that their short night's sleep would be even shorter tonight, because of their inexhaustible appetite for discussing me and my plans. In the first place I was their only child. Now, more than ever, I'd begun to worry them as an icicle of lonely bachelorhood had begun to grow inside me. I was only twenty-nine years old, but I noted with pity their attempts to steer me toward a life outside the hospital walls, prompted in part by their guilt for having put so much pressure on me to devote myself to my studies. And sure enough, early the next morning when I called, my father said, "We stayed up all night thinking about the trip to India, and we've changed our minds. It will only exhaust you, and you don't need to go." But to their astonishment I told them that only half an hour before I had agreed to go, and asked them to find my British passport and take down a good suitcase for me.

Instead of pleasure and satisfaction, I now heard only tension and anxiety in their voices, as if all that talk the night before had referred not to an actual journey but to a theoretical one. Was it because of them that I had changed my mind? my mother wanted to know. I reassured them that I had thought it over again myself and decided that I should go. Then I gave them the unpleasant news that Hishin preferred the other resident to me. Who knew, maybe his hands really were better than mine. There was silence on the other end of the line. "Hishin prefers the other resident to you?" my father said incredulously. "How can that be possible, Benjy?" And my heart contracted painfully at their certain disappointment. "You'd be surprised at how possible it can be," I said with deliberate lightheartedness. "Never mind, it's not so terrible, and actually this might be a good time to go somewhere far away, where I can think about what to do next." The truth was that I actually felt relieved, as if something had been liberated inside me. From the minute I had agreed to join the Lazars, at six-thirty in the morning, it was as if the excitement of the journey had swept the anger and the envy out of my heart. Lazar's wife had answered the phone, and for a moment I failed to recognize her voice, which was younger and fresher than she had seemed the night before, and although she did not seem surprised by my decision—as if she had known that I would come around—she thanked me repeatedly, and asked me if I was quite sure. But then her husband lost patience and snatched the phone from her and began shooting out instructions with terrific efficiency. He was going to Jerusalem to meet some India expert at the Foreign Office and to get letters of recommendation and introduction, leaving his wife and me to conclude the necessary arrangements. "And what about the hospital?" I asked. "They're still expecting me in the operating room this morning—there are operations scheduled." But Lazar was unequivocal. As far as the hospital was concerned, I could leave it to him; it was his turf, and Hishin had given his express consent. "No," he rebuked me firmly, "from this minute on, please stop thinking about the hospital and devote yourself exclusively to making arrangements for the trip. Time is short. This afternoon we'll find time to sit down with the doctors and the head pharmacist and discuss the medical aspects. All that's no problem. The main thing—I almost forgot to ask—is your Israeli passport valid?"

No, my Israeli passport wasn't valid. I had checked it the night before. Lazar gave me instructions on how to get to his wife's office in the center of town. His wife, a lawyer by profession and a partner in a big law firm, would take care of it. I barely recognized her when she came out of her office to meet me, dressed in black, wearing high heels, her face made up. Again she thanked me for my decision, with a friendliness that struck me as artificial and exaggerated. I handed her my passport, and she immediately passed it to one of the girls sitting in the frenetic front office. Then, she took out her checkbook, signed a number of blank checks, which she gave me, and said, "Here, this is Hannah, who's going to devote herself to you this morning and get you ready for the trip." In the travel agency, surrounded by posters of glorious tourist sites, I sensed a sudden joyful wanderlust burgeoning inside me. Two of the travel agents put themselves at our service to speed things up. First of all, they informed Hannah and me that travelers to India had to present certificates of vaccination against cholera and malaria to obtain a visa, and told us not to forget to tell Lazar and his wife. "His wife?" I asked in surprise. "Why his wife?" But the travel agents' records clearly showed that the previous afternoon Mrs. Lazar had asked them to book her on a flight too, with an open ticket. "She probably wasn't sure if I'd agree to go," I tried to explain, "and so she asked you to get a ticket for her just to be on the safe side."

"You may be right," they replied politely, "but don't forget to tell her about the vaccinations anyhow." It was then I sensed the first shadow falling on the happiness that had just begun to awaken in me. I had been imagining a vigorous, perhaps even rather adventurous expedition undertaken by two men, who in spite of an age difference of twenty years might still be able to enjoy the kind of fine friendship that grows up in a small army reserve unit. But if Lazar's wife was going to tag along, I reflected in concern, mightn't the whole thing turn into a tedious, leaden trip with a couple of middle-aged parents?

❧❧

But could I still back out? I wondered, sitting late that morning opposite a bank clerk and waiting for the foreign currency, my now valid passport in the slim, strong hands of Hannah, who had spent the morning leading me efficiently from office to office and organizing everything for me as if I suffered from some kind of handicap. Why on earth was Lazar's wife going? Was it really out of concern for her daughter's health, or did the situation require the strengthening of a parental delegation for some reason? I still hoped that Mrs. Lazar would decide not to go at the last minute. I didn't like her constant concern and warm smiles. She could only be a drag on the speed and ease of our travels, I thought as I parted with her office clerk, taking back my passport and rejecting, with some mortification, her offer to accompany me to the Health Service to receive the necessary vaccinations, and perhaps to pay for them too.

I mounted my Honda and rode to the place, where I found the door of the vaccination room sealed shut because of a nurses' strike. As I wandered around the corridor looking for a solution, I was recognized by an old friend from medical school, who had dropped out in his fourth year because of an involvement with a girl he later married and who was now working here as the medical secretary of the district physician. He bounded gleefully toward me, and when he heard about the trip to India, he was very much in favor of it. I told him that I would be paid a fee on top of my travel expenses, and he became so excited that he slapped me on the back in congratulations and said with undisguised envy, "You're a clever bastard, a quiet, clever bastard. And you're a lucky bastard too—you always have been. What wouldn't I give to change places with you?" Immediately, he rushed off to find the key, ushered me into the nurses' room, opened a big glass cupboard, pointed at the rows of rainbow-colored vaccine bottles, and said jokingly, "Our bar is at your service, sir. You can be vaccinated here against any disease you like, the weirdest and most wonderful diseases you ever heard of." And while I studied the exotic labels on the little bottles, he took a sterile syringe out of a drawer and offered to inject me himself; he was two-thirds a doctor, after all. "You're not afraid of me?" he cried with incomprehensible hilarity, waving the syringe in his hand. But I suddenly drew back; the empty room filled me with an inexplicable anxiety, as if I missed the reassur-

ing presence of reliable nurses, whose quiet and careful movements always calmed me. "No," I said, "you'll only hurt me.
Give me the syringes and I'll find someone to do it for me at the
hospital. Just stamp the certificate." And he gave in unwillingly.
He found a yellow vaccination certificate, stamped it, and began
dragging out a long, boring conversation, trying to recall the
names of erstwhile fellow-students, wallowing in nostalgia for
his wasted student days, inviting me to go and have a cup of
coffee. When we got to the dreary little cafeteria and sat among
the indolent government clerks, next to a big window which
raindrops were beginning to streak, I thought about the exhausting day ahead of me and how I was going to find time to say
good-bye to my parents. I listened absent-mindedly, with uncharacteristic passivity, to my companion justifying his academic
failures with all kinds of tortuous arguments and complaining
about the unfairness of his teachers. Finally I pulled myself together, cut the conversation short, and stood up, saying, "Listen,
I really have to run. Let's go back to your 'bar' for a minute." We
returned to the vaccination room, where I opened the cupboard
myself and collected additional bottles of vaccine against cholera
and malaria and also against hepatitis. I added a few syringes in
sterile wrappings and asked my companions to stamp two more
vaccination certificates without filling in the names. He agreed
generously to all my requests, but in the end he couldn't resist
saying somewhat sourly, "I see the travel bug has really bitten
you hard."

Indeed, I was already burning with travel fever, a dull, somewhat sullen fever, and when I reached the hospital on my motorcycle, wet from the rain, I felt alienated from the place that I had
served so lovingly and faithfully for the past year. In spite of the
nurses' strike, which had been declared that morning, everything
seemed to be functioning normally, and I hurried to the ward
only to find no doctors present—just the usual shift of nurses,
who seemed surprised to see me. "You?" They giggled archly.
"Hishin's been telling everybody that you're already winging
your way to India." I put on my white coat, with the name "Benjamin Rubin" embroidered in red on the pocket, and went to
look for Hishin, but he, it appeared, had been urgently summoned to the operating room. The young woman he had oper-

ated on the day before had developed complications. My first impulse was to hurry there after him, but I knew that the other resident, my rival-friend, would be there too and I might have to face rejection or be painfully ignored again before saying good-bye. Accordingly, I decided to let it go and to pay a little private visit to the patients in the ward instead. However, the senior nurse, a noble-spirited woman of about sixty, who was sitting in her corner dressed in ordinary clothes in order to express her solidarity with the strike without actually striking herself, stood up and stopped me: "What do you need to make rounds for, Dr. Rubin? You've got a long, difficult journey—you should go home and get ready. Don't worry, we'll take care of everything for you here." What she said made sense, and I was so touched by her sympathetic tone that I couldn't resist putting my arm around her and giving her a little hug before I slipped off my coat. Without another word, I took two little bottles of vaccine out of my pocket and asked her to give me the shots, which she did with such a light touch that I didn't even feel the prick. I threw my coat in the laundry bin and set off for administration to look for Lazar. In the office the girls recognized me immediately, even without my coat, and greeted me in a friendly, respectful manner, saying, "Here's Dr. Rubin, the volunteer doctor." They called the head secretary, Miss Kolby, who said that Lazar had phoned a number of times from Jerusalem to ask about me. "He's still in the Foreign Office, looking for India experts?" I exclaimed in surprise. But it turned out that he was in the Treasury, not about the trip to India, but about the nurses' strike. However, he had still found time to instruct the head pharmacist of the hospital to put together a kit with the appropriate medical equipment, and also to remind Hishin to prepare a medical brief for me. In the meantime his wife's office had left the message that my ticket was ready. So there was nothing to worry about. "Is his wife really coming with us?" I asked the secretary in a tone of annoyance, and I saw her hesitate, as if taking refuge in uncertainty, perhaps for fear of antagonizing me and giving rise to some new resistance. For a moment it crossed my mind that because of the nurses' strike Lazar might have to stay behind, and his wife was getting ready to go in his place, and instead of having a male traveling companion I would have to negotiate the complicated routes of India with two women, one of them middle-aged and the other very sick.

I ordered the secretary to get my mother on the phone, so that I could prepare her for the possibility that I might not be able to get there before evening. My mother, who thought that I was already on my way to Jerusalem, was not upset but instead tried to calm me down. "Never mind, Benjy, don't worry; you'll sleep at home tonight, and we'll drive you to the airport tomorrow. I've already told your father to take a day off."

Now I was impatient. I had already agreed to travel to a completely foreign and remote world the next day—so why was I still hanging around the hospital, which suddenly seemed gloomy and stifling? I hurried to the surgical ward to look for Hishin and get the article about hepatitis from him, but since I wasn't wearing my coat the new guard outside the entrance failed to recognize me and refused to let me in. On a bench in the corridor I again saw the two relatives of the young woman who had been operated on the day before. They recognized me but for some reason ignored me, as if they too had already realized how weak my position was here and how false my promise about the patient's rebirth had been. I wanted to go up to them and ask them how she was, but I stopped myself. In the space of one day I had become superfluous here. I decided not to wait and made my way to the office of the head pharmacist, Dr. Hessing, a bald old German Jew, who immediately dropped everything and led me into one of the cubicles in the depths of the storage area, where he showed me a large knapsack. He immediately opened it to display the wealth and variety of the medical equipment it contained and the snugness and efficiency with which it had all been packed—drugs, ampules and syringes, thermometer and sphygmomanometer, stethoscope and test tubes, scissors and little scalpels, and of course infusion sets; like an entire miniature hospital. Maybe the pharmacist had been so generous because his budget depended more than that of any other department of the hospital on the personal whims of the administrative director. But at the sight of the overflowing knapsack, my spirits fell. "Why do I have to drag all this with me?" I protested. "I'm not going on a climbing expedition to the Himalayas." I demanded that he take out some of the equipment, but he stubbornly refused to remove a single item from the kit, which he had evidently prepared with loving care. "Take it," he coaxed me. "Don't be foolish, who knows what you might need there. You're going to one of the filthiest places in the world, and if you decide you don't need something once you're there, you can always give it away."

And so, carrying the knapsack, I returned to the surgical ward to look once more for Hishin. To my surprise, the operation was still going on. Something's gone wrong there, I thought to myself, trying not to meet the eyes of the woman's relatives, who were still sitting on their bench in the growing darkness, rigid with anxiety. Now nobody stopped me at the entrance to the ward, and with the knapsack on my back I stood outside the big door of the operating room, in exactly the same spot where Lazar had stood waving his hand, and through the same porthole I saw the same team as the day before; only I was missing. The other resident's back was bent in a tense and supple arch next to Professor Hishin, who I guessed by his movements was struggling to solve a serious problem deep in the woman's guts. All I could make out from the porthole was her delicate white feet, shining out from under the sheet at the end of the table. Nobody noticed me, apart from Dr. Nakash, who hurriedly whispered something to Hishin. Hishin immediately raised his eyes and waved, and a few minutes later he came out to me, the scalpel in his hand, his gown covered with bloodstains, looking tired and upset. Before I could open my mouth, he silenced me and said in his ironic Hungarian accent, "Yes, yes, forgive me, I know I'm keeping you waiting, but you can see for yourself, I'm not taking part in an orgy here." And I knew immediately that for the past hour he had been battling against death itself, because whenever he felt death near he would refer in one way or another to sex. I felt a pang because I was not participating in the dramatic battle taking place on the operating table, not even as an onlooker. "What's going on in there?" I asked accusingly. "Why did you have to operate on her again?" But Hishin waved his bloody hand in my face, refusing to talk about the operation, and with unaccountable emotion he put his arm around me and hugged me and said, "Never mind, don't worry about it. Just some stubborn woman who keeps on hemorrhaging from unexpected places. But you stop worrying, you have to keep your head clear for the journey. You have no idea how grateful Lazar is to me on your account. They've fallen in love with you already, him and his wife. So what do you need now? Ah, you want to know what to do about our hepatitis? As a matter of fact, nothing. Yes, yes, sorry, I forgot to bring the article. But it doesn't matter. I see you've already been given equipment and drugs. And the truth is, there isn't much to be done in these cases. Just reassure them all psychologically. Everything's psychological nowadays, isn't that what everyone says? Soon we'll be able to do without surgery too. So don't worry, you won't have much to do. I told you, hepatitis is a self-limited disease."

When I left the hospital, I looked up at the sky to see what to expect on the way to Jerusalem and whether I should take my Honda. How had I got mixed up in this crazy journey? Suddenly I wanted to hurry home to my parents, so that they could cosset me with warmth and concern and help me to get ready for the trip, which I now felt approaching at a gallop. At my small apartment I quickly washed the dishes in the sink, made the bed, and packed clothes, underwear, socks, and toiletries in a sturdy old suitcase. I disconnected the electricity, shut the water, and phoned my landlady to tell her I was going abroad. Then I tied the suitcase and the knapsack onto the pillion of the Honda and drove to the Lazars' apartment to arrange for our meeting at the airport and to get my ticket, as well as the dollars that had been withdrawn from the bank in my name but had been pocketed by Mrs. Lazar's little clerk. In the spacious apartment, now glowing with the rosy light of sunset, the preparations for the journey were evident: a suitcase lay next to the door, and by its side was an open bag. "Here you are at last," cried Lazar from the living room. "We've been asking ourselves where you disappeared to!"

"I disappeared?" I asked, insulted. "In what sense did I disappear?"

"Never mind, never mind," said his wife, emerging immediately from the living room in a velvet jump suit. I could already see that she had an overpowering desire to be present everywhere, and she looked different to me, maybe younger but also uglier, short and thick, her hair a little rumpled, her face pale, and the radiant smile in her eyes faded behind the lenses of her glasses. "Don't pay any attention," she said. "Lazar's always worrying, he thrives on worry, you'll have to get used to it, but come in Dr. . . ." She paused then, uncertain of how to address me. "Call me Benjamin, or Benjy, if you like."

"May we really call you that? Benjy? Good. Then come in and sit down. We've got Michaela here, Einat's friend who brought us the letter. Come and hear what she has to say about Gaya and the hospital there." But I declined the invitation. "Sorry," I said. "It's late and I'm in a hurry to get to Jerusalem to say good-bye to my parents and organize my packing."

"And will you sleep there tonight?" asked Lazar in a disappointed tone. "What a pity. We thought of asking you to sleep here, so that we could all go straight to the airport early tomorrow morning."

"Don't worry," I said, "my parents will get me there in time." But Lazar was evidently unable to stop worrying, and he immediately ran to fetch a pencil and paper to write down my address and phone number in Jerusalem, while his wife—I was still asking myself whether she was coming on the trip or not—urged me again to come into the living room. "My mother's here with us, and she's eager to meet you."

"Your mother?" I said in confusion. "All right, just for a minute," and I entered the living room, where I stood amazed at the view of the roofs of Tel Aviv spreading out in every direction before me. When I was here the night before, the curtains had been drawn and I hadn't guessed what a commanding position the penthouse occupied. On the sofa sat a frail old woman in a dark wool suit, and next to her a boy dressed for some reason in a white cotton dress. But when I went closer I saw that it was a sunburned young woman whose shaven head threw her big light eyes powerfully into relief. "Mother," said Lazar's wife in a slightly raised voice, "this is Dr. Rubin, the doctor who's volunteered to accompany us to India. You wanted to meet him." The old lady immediately held out her hand to me and nodded, and a very faint echo of her daughter's automatic radiant smile flickered for a moment in her eyes. Now I could no longer restrain myself. The possibility of Mrs. Lazar joining us began preying on my mind more disturbingly than ever, and while I inclined my head toward the young woman with the shaven head, who discreetly made room for me at her side, I turned to Lazar's wife with uncontrollable annoyance and said, "Excuse me, I don't understand. Are you coming with us?" But Lazar cut in before she could reply. "It hasn't been settled yet; we'll decide tonight. But why do you ask?"

"I just wanted to know," I mumbled, looking at his wife, who was no longer smiling at all, although her head turned with an almost imperceptible, slightly threatening movement in her husband's direction. And then, against my will, I sat down in the place vacated for me by the shaven-headed woman, who gazed at me curiously, as if to take my measure with one look. With the sofa cushions around me still fragrant with warmth, I reached out to take the cup of tea that the grandmother had poured, and through the big window I watched the great, silent fan of an approaching rainstorm spreading over the horizon of the sea. It was then I felt a certain annoyance and anger. I had to get going; my mother and father were waiting for me. What was I doing sitting there like a member of the family? As if I wouldn't be seeing more than enough of them for the next couple of weeks, whether I liked it or not. I stood up quickly, without tasting the tea, without even saying a word to the slight young woman, whose ostentatious Indianness made me anxious, but also newly eager for the journey. "Did you have a chance to get the two vaccinations for the visa?" I remembered to ask my host on the way to the door. "What vaccinations?" asked the astonished Lazar, who was sure that he had everything connected with the journey under control. It turned out that his wife had forgotten to tell him. "How could you have forgotten?" he cried in despair. "Where are we going to find someone to vaccinate us in Rome?" But when he heard that I had brought the vaccines and sterile syringes with me, as well as two stamped vaccination certificates, and that I had them all in my pocket, he recovered immediately. "You're the best," he said, and gave me a hug. "You're the best; now I understand why Hishin was so determined to have you." He demanded to be vaccinated on the spot and led me to their bedroom, which was also elegant and spacious. There he removed his shirt, exposing his hairy arms and heavy back, closed his eyes, and made a face in anticipation of the prick of the needle. Outside the big window next to the double bed, on which lay a large suitcase surrounded by scattered items of clothing, the sheet of rain sailed slowly eastward in the glow of the setting sun. "Don't make such a face," laughed his wife, coming into the room with cotton wool and alcohol while I filled the syringes, "it's not an operation." And she stood next to me, watching carefully. When I finished vaccinating her husband, he put on his shirt and prepared to accompany me to the door. "What about me?" she said in offended surprise. "Shouldn't we wait and see what we decide tonight?" said her husband tenderly. "Why be in such a hurry to get shots you may not need?" She flushed deeply, her face darkened, and she turned to me sharply and demanded to be vaccinated too. First she tried to roll up her sleeve, but her arm was too thick and she couldn't get the sleeve past the elbow. She went up to the door and half closed it, as if to hide herself, then slipped off the upper part of her jump suit and stood there in her bra, revealing very round breasts and heavy shoulders spattered here and there with large freckles, and smiling with charming shyness. I hurried to give her the shots, and she thanked me with a nod and pulled on the top of her jump suit. It was then I knew for sure that she was indeed coming to India with us, and my heart tightened. What had I let myself in for here? I said good-bye to her and went down to the street with Lazar, who had decided to transfer the medical kit to his car. The spreading rain now darkened the city and a fine mist sprayed the air. Lazar took the knapsack from me and examined the big motorcycle curiously. "Are you really going to ride that to Jerusalem in this rain?" he asked, with fatherly concern mingled with admiration. When I was sitting on the Honda, with my foot in position to start it, something stopped me. I couldn't hold back any longer. "Excuse me," I said, "I understand that your wife is coming with us." Lazar moved his head in an unclear gesture. "But why?" I asked in a kind of quiet despair. "Two escorts are already more than enough, in my opinion. Why three?" Lazar smiled and said nothing. But I was determined to pursue the matter. Perhaps I would succeed in persuading him at the last minute to stop his wife from coming. "Is there some special reason that she has to be there—something I don't know yet?" I asked. "No, nothing like that," replied Lazar. "She just wants to come along."

"But why?" I insisted, with a bitterness whose intensity I couldn't understand myself. He looked straight at me, as if he were paying attention to me for the first time, trying to make up his mind if he could trust me, and then he spread out his hands and smiled in embarrassment. "It's just that she doesn't like being separated from me, she doesn't like being left alone." And when he saw that I was still determined not to understand, he smiled at me again with a kind of sly satisfaction. "Yes, she's a woman who's incapable of staying by herself."

Two

Is it possible to bring up the word "Mystery" yet? Or is it still too early even to think of it? For none of the characters moving at this wintry dawn hour from east or west toward the airport knows how thoughts of mystery are born, let alone what it is made of, and how it flows. Not even the great India awaiting them can stimulate thoughts of mystery, for it is not yet a different dimension of being in their eyes, only a place they wish to reach quickly and efficiently, in order to collect a sick young woman and bring her carefully home. And that sickly yellowness, clouding the whites of her eyes and surrounding the greenish irises, flickering between the gray sheets in the little room in the monastery on the outskirts of Bodhgaya, can that ignite a spark of mystery? No, certainly not. Because in the imaginations of the people now dragging their suitcases through the departure lounge, that sickly yellowness toward which they are directing their steps holds no portent of mystery, it is only the symptom of a disease, which has a name and is described in books and articles, and which, according to Professor Hishin, is self-limited, even if the return journey holds a turning point, where it will hover desperately between life and death. But even in that terrible crisis there is no mystery, and now it stands still in the time and place appointed for it, among wicker furniture smeared with bright purple paint, waiting for the precise moment of time, which always arrives with an astonishing simplicity and naturalness.

In other words, the sense of mystery is still as quiescent as the point of the pencil delicately poised on the white sheet of paper between the characters. Or the travelers and their escorts, who are sleepy and somewhat excited in the departures hall, sending tentative signals to each other in the tired smiles of resignation

with which they answer the predictable questions of the girl car-
rying out the security check, who is dressed in a spotless white
shirt with a tag fastened to its pocket with a safety pin. A drama
student in the evenings, she interrogates them one after the other,
in a dry, monotonous voice, about the contents of their luggage.
But their detailed replies do not save them, in the end, from
opening their suitcases and exposing their personal belongings to
each other, and handing over the big medical knapsack too,
which astonishes one and all with the wealth and variety of its
contents, the sheen of its instruments, until it seems that disaster
and disease will be sucked into it willy-nilly. And the morning
mists that pursued the young doctor and his parents on their way
from Jerusalem filter into the great hall, hovering over the keys of
the computers which eject the boarding passes, and the white-
haired parents now hand over their only son, even if he is already
twenty-nine years old, to the care of another pair of parents,
total strangers, but faithful to the solidarity of parenthood as a
self-evident human value. Perhaps it is precisely here, in this act
of handing over, that the mystery originates. But if so, where
does it lead?

It leads nowhere, for that is its nature. It has no direction, for
the goal disappears once the cause has been forgotten. And in the
tireless turning of the earth the ancient mystery suddenly appears
among us, like a forgotten relative let out of a mental institution
on a short vacation, despite its continuing delusion that the earth
is eternally still, and every hour is sufficient unto itself, and noth-
ing in the universe is ever lost; and after it comes to visit us, and
sits among us pale and emaciated, and sets forth its fantastic
views, it suddenly stands up, careful not to spill the tea we have
placed before it, and begins wandering like a sleepwalker be-
tween our bedrooms, to meet people and events concluded long
ago.

And so, even if a drop of mystery has fallen here, there is still
no one capable of sensing it. Certainly not the young doctor's
father, Mr. Rubin, a tall English Jew wearing an old felt hat
purchased five years before on a trip to Manchester, the city of
his birth, who has been listening for some time in profound and
patient silence to the lively explanations of the hospital director,
whose hands, now that his luggage is sailing away on the con-
veyor belt, are free to sketch the map of India over and over in

the air, pointing out the possibilities of various alternative routes, while his plump little wife, dressed in a loose blue tunic, her eyes no doubt already smiling behind her big sunglasses, listens calmly to the polite small talk of Mrs. Rubin, a lean, bony English Jewess, who steps ahead of her toward the guard, who in a moment will separate with a gesture of his hand the passengers and the people seeing them off, but who will not be able to separate the common thought, new and pleasant, that has begun spinning itself secretly—yes, secretly and without a word—between the two middle-aged women, each of whom is now imagining to herself a possible love story between the young doctor-son, who still sees the journey as something that has been forced upon him, and the sick daughter, waiting thousands of miles away in a state of total debilitation.

§2§

To my great relief my seat on the plane was not next to the Lazars, but several rows distant from them. If they had arranged it that way on purpose, I thought, it was an encouraging sign. They too wanted to avoid excessive intimacy, which would make us get on each other's nerves right at the beginning of the trip. And indeed, for the first three hours of the flight I saw them only once, on my way to the toilet. They were sitting in the last row, in the smokers' section; their breakfast trays had not yet been removed, but the curtain on the window was drawn. Lazar's wife was sleeping, the dark glasses clutched in her fist, her head buried in the chest of her husband, who was studying some papers. My parents, who were only a little older than they were, would never have dared to display such intimacy in public. I intended to slip past without their noticing me, but Lazar took off his gold-rimmed reading glasses and asked me affably if I had managed to sleep. "I didn't even try," I replied immediately. "I've decided to tire myself out in anticipation of the flight to New Delhi tonight." I could see that this practical answer was to his liking. "Do you find it difficult to fall asleep in the air too?" he asked. "Yes," I said. "So you're like me," he pronounced happily, as if he had found an ally. "I've never been able to sleep on a plane. We'll see what happens tonight." His wife raised her head; without her glasses her eyes looked red and puffy with sleep, but they immediately lit up in that mechanical, indiscriminate smile of hers. "What nice parents you have," she said unhesitatingly, as if she had just seen them in her dreams. "Yes," I nodded in agreement, and added without knowing why, "They're not hysterical." But she understood. "That's right," she said. "Your mother told me that they actually encouraged you to make the trip with us."

"Yes, India has apparently kept its charms for Englishmen of the older generation."

"You won't be sorry you came with us," she said soothingly, as if she still felt that she had to overcome the vestiges of my resistance. "You'll see." I didn't answer, only smiled faintly. It was on the tip of my tongue to ask her about the foreign currency the girl from her office had withdrawn from the bank in my name and for some reason pocketed herself, but I restrained myself and continued on my way to the toilet.

We reached Rome at eleven o'clock in the morning, and had about ten hours until the night flight to New Delhi. During these ten hours we had to get our visas for India, and Lazar decided that we should drag our luggage with us in order not to lose precious time, so that we wouldn't have to come back to the airport in case of any delay with the visas, should we miss our flight and have to sleep over in Rome. But his wife was in favor of leaving the luggage at the airport so that we could get around more freely. They immediately plunged into a heated argument, which Lazar, with his practical pessimism, seemed on the point of winning, but suddenly, without any warning, she gained the upper hand, and the three of us went to look for the baggage check. We walked up and down corridors, confused by misleading directions, with Lazar grumbling at his wife all the time, "You see what a mess you've gotten us into now?" until in the end she stopped smiling and hissed, "Stop whining, get a hold of yourself," and he shut up. Finally we found the place, which seemed to be located in a very out-of-the-way spot, but when we remarked on this to the baggage handler, he protested indignantly and pointed to the nearby elevator, which reached the heart of the airport. Once more we were obliged to undergo the tedious process of opening our luggage and having it inspected, and I was forced to contemplate for the second time their intimate belongings—far too many, in my opinion, for a short trip with a serious purpose to a poor country. Lazar collected the claim tickets and we emerged unburdened into a large plaza to look for a cab. His wife smiled happily, and said with a note of self-congratulation, without any animosity, "There you are— now we can move freely." But although Lazar too seemed pleased, he didn't want to admit it. "We've wasted the whole morning on the luggage, and who knows if those Indians go back to work at all after their lunch break." But it transpired that the Indians worked without a break. When we arrived at the consulate building, which was surrounded by shrubs and ornamental trees, we found a long line of waiting Indians, and we lost no time in joining it. But Lazar soon expressed doubts as to the purpose of the line and wandered off to make inquiries, returning to announce triumphantly that we were in the wrong line: this one was only for Indians, the line for foreigners was around the back. And indeed, behind the building, in a little annex, we found an office with only a few European youths waiting in front of it. Lazar took my two passports, deliberating whether to present the Indians with the Israeli one or the British one, which seemed to interest him greatly, for he kept turning the pages to see how it was organized. In the end he gave it back to me, saying that we had better not present them with a passport that we would not know how to defend if it turned out to have flaws we had not noticed, and handed the three Israeli passports to the quiet, dark-skinned clerk, who refused even to look at them without the airline tickets and vaccination certificates. Lazar whipped out these documents, which he had ready, and smiled modestly. As a bureaucrat himself, he knew how much damage and delay could be caused by one recalcitrant official at a pivotal point. But the official wasn't in the least hostile. The visas were quickly stamped, and we returned to the Roman street with eight free hours in front of us.

It was one o'clock, and Lazar's wife, whom he called Dori, announced with a gleam in her eye that before anything else we had to find a good restaurant. But although I too was very hungry I decided that if I didn't set limits right away, I would soon begin to find the pressure unbearable. I therefore informed them that I preferred to do without lunch at the moment and would wander around by myself instead, slightly stressing the words "by myself." They were taken aback. "Aren't you hungry?"

asked Lazar with fatherly concern. "That's not the point," I answered frankly. "I just don't want to waste any time. I've never been in Rome before, and I want to look around a bit on my own." Again I gently stressed the words "on my own." His wife's automatic smile suddenly vanished. Her face grew grave, and she touched her husband's sleeve lightly, as if to warn him. But Lazar didn't feel her touch. "Just a minute," he cried in alarm. "Where do you want to go, and where will we meet?"

"Where will we meet?" I thought aloud. "At the airport, of course. I've got my ticket, and if you'll be so good as to give me back my passport and the claim checks for my suitcase and knapsack, I'll go straight to the airport in time for the flight." Lazar was still upset by this sudden independent plan. "Just a minute," he cried, "where in the airport? And why the airport? You saw how complicated it is there. Perhaps we should meet somewhere in town, at least, so we don't lose each other just before the flight." But his wife, who had grasped my clear intention of drawing a definite line between us, hastened to reassure him. "It's perfectly all right. Why not? We'll meet when we board the plane. What's the problem?" And he was obliged to take my passport as well as the checks for my suitcase and the medical knapsack out of his pocket, asking as he unwillingly did so, "But where do you want to go in Rome? In what direction?"

"I don't have a direction, I don't know yet," I replied, careful not to mention any specific place in case they found a way to join me after all. And then I saw a flicker of offense in his eyes, but he suppressed it immediately, and confined himself to asking me if I had enough money. "No, I've got hardly any money," I answered quickly, and directed a look of silent rebuke at his wife. "The girl from the office withdrew my foreign currency from the bank yesterday, but then she took it with her." Mrs. Lazar blushed. Lazar took her purse from her and rummaged in it for the envelope with the money. He counted the bills, reflected, and gave me half, two hundred dollars, and then changed his mind and added another hundred, saying, "You see, it's a good thing I asked you. But I don't understand," he said, confronting his wife, "why she didn't give him the money, and how come you didn't notice it was there. Didn't you even look in the envelope she gave you?" But before she could reply he dismissed it with an impatient "Never mind, never mind," and turned to me. "Let's not waste any more time. But you see, it's a good thing that I'm something of a worrier, otherwise you would have gone off without any money, and if you got lost we would all be in a real mess. And from now on, please don't be shy with us, tell us if anything's bothering you or if you need anything, and that way there won't be any misunderstandings. Now, where are you thinking of going?" He seemed determined to get it out of me, and I said without thinking, "Since I'm here, I may as well pay a short visit to the Vatican," and the two of them chorused in evident relief, "An excellent idea."

※)ぬ

And I, bound by my promise, set out to look for the Vatican, even though I knew that we would see plenty of holy places in India, and according to Lazar the town of Gaya itself was full of ancient temples. But at least I would have something in my recent memory to compare with all that, I thought to myself, maybe even a subject to talk to them about. As soon as I got off the bus at St. Peter's Square, I found a mobile pizza stand and bought two hot little pizzas and ate them standing up, taking shelter from the raindrops under a convenient awning. In spite of the gray light, I wanted a photograph of myself against the background of the famous gray dome. I noticed a group of elderly tourists nearby, standing under a canopy of umbrellas and listening to the explanations of a tour guide who was wrapped up tight in a raincoat. Judging by their unperturbed attitude to the rain, and also by the battered felt hat—like my father's—which one of them wore, I guessed that they were English, and I was drawn to them. I took advantage of a momentary pause in the guide's lecture and asked one of the women, whose gray head was wrapped in a big woolen scarf, to take a photo of me in front of the dome in two different poses. After she returned the camera, she explained that they were a group of pensioners from England on a European tour, as I had guessed, and for most of them it was their first time abroad. When I told her that I was flying to India that very evening, to a remote town in the east of the subcontinent, to bring a sick young woman home to Israel, her eyes lit up with curiosity, and for a moment she didn't want to let me go. At first I thought that it was the idea of my immi-

nent flight to India which appealed to her, but it quickly transpired that it was the idea of a young doctor flying to the ends of
the earth to heal a sick person that caused her excitement. She
called her friends to tell them about me and my rescue mission,
and one of the old men immediately stepped forward to say that
he had served in India himself and was very willing to tell us all
about it. The young Italian guide, too, nodded at me affectionately and invited me to join the group for the rest of their tour of
the Vatican, and although I was afraid that joining this geriatric
group would eat up the few hours I had to spare until the flight—
for I had already noted the extreme slowness of their pace—I
thought it might force me to take Hishin's advice and split off
from the Lazars on the way back from India, in order to spend a
day or two sightseeing in Rome. And this way I'd have at least
finished the Vatican. Which was, indeed, exactly what I felt when
I parted from the English pensioners in the big, empty square at
half-past five in the evening, in the darkness and the rain, my
mind crammed with historical explanations and detailed descriptions. At first I thought of going straight to the airport and getting rid of my hunger there, for I guessed that Lazar would be
there early, and even though we had agreed to meet between
seven and eight, he would soon begin to worry about me. But on
second thought I decided that for the sake of our future travel, I
had better start getting him used to trusting my reliability, and I
wanted, too, to enjoy my last hours away from this couple, with
whom I would undoubtedly be forced into ever closer proximity.
I therefore sat down in a modest restaurant on the corner of one
of the streets leading out of the Vatican and ate a full meal,
which did not prevent me from arriving, complete with suitcase
and medical kit, at our charter-flight counter two full minutes
before the deadline agreed to with Mr. Lazar.

In the distance I could already see his grayish mane sticking up
between the brightly colored saris. The two of them sat side by
side next to their two suitcases and newly acquired parcels,
among the colorful crowd of passengers gathering near our flight
counter, which had not yet opened. Lazar was very pleased by
my punctuality, even though he had no cause for concern, because it had already been announced that our flight would be
two hours late. He made room for me next to him and asked me
to put my luggage with theirs. "From now on we should stick

together," he declared, in case I might be contemplating some new adventure. His wife inquired about my visit to the Vatican. They themselves had not seen anything of particular importance, only strolled along some beautiful streets and bought essential presents. "Do you have to bring back presents even from a trip like this?" I asked in surprise. "Why not?" asked Mrs. Lazar with a smile, and a somewhat reprimanding look which was apparently directed at her husband too, who explained that she still suffered from the old Israeli guilt at the very fact of leaving the country, which had to be covered up by expensive gifts for those left behind. "Guilt?" I persisted. "For this trip?"

"For every trip," his wife said quickly, turning to her husband and adding, "Perhaps we should buy something to eat, sandwiches and snacks. Who knows what kind of meal they'll serve on this peculiar flight, if they serve one at all." He immediately rose to his feet, but she got up quickly too, saying, "I'll come with you." This woman really can't be alone, I thought, smiling to myself. "We're a little past the age for these charter flights," apologized Lazar, who seemed put out by the character of the crowd gathering around us, which consisted mainly of teenagers with huge backpacks. His wife offered to bring me something from the buffet too, but I politely declined. "I've already eaten a full meal," I said, "and I think it will last me until we reach India." I suggested that they go and sit down in the cafeteria and eat a decent meal, while I stayed behind and looked after the baggage. I had already noticed that they suffered from a chronic anxiety about remaining hungry, and that they were constantly sucking candy or chewing gum. And indeed, they were both obviously overweight, although Mrs. Lazar was more disciplined about the way she carried herself and succeeded to some extent in disguising the roundness of her belly. They quickly vanished, and I put a couple of parcels on the chairs they had vacated to keep their seats for them. In the meantime the commotion about the delay increased, although someone from the airline had arrived at the counter and started negotiating with problematic passengers.

Suddenly, through the display window of a small, fancy shoe boutique opposite me, I saw her silhouette. Sitting on a little armchair in her skirt and blouse, stretching one long leg toward the gentleman who was lightly supporting her foot in order to demonstrate the virtues of the dainty shoe to Lazar. He examined it closely and compared it with another shoe he was holding in his hand. A pale green light, faintly reminiscent of the lighting in an operating room at home, shone from the little display window and lent an air of secrecy to the picture of the plump woman stretching her long legs out to the two men. Passersby stopped to look. They were really a strange couple, these two, caught up in their pleasures to the last moment, seemingly indifferent to the difficult journey awaiting them, and perhaps even to thoughts of the condition in which they would find their sick daughter. When the flight was announced over the loudspeaker at last, they hurried up excitedly, carrying wrapped sandwiches in a bag and two cardboard shoeboxes. "The shoes here are so cheap that it's hard to resist the temptation," explained Lazar, "and they're so beautiful too." He went on apologizing while his silent wife, who seemed embarrassed at his apologies, opened the two suitcases, the contents of which I was already becoming only too familiar with, and stacked the Roman purchases one on top of the other, trying to leave the shoes in their boxes. But Lazar immediately jumped up in protest. "You'll burst the bag with those idiotic boxes," he warned her. But she refused to give in. We both watched hostilely as she stubbornly tried to cram the shoeboxes into the suitcases. One of them disappeared into the depths of the case, but the other rebelled. It seemed that she would be obliged to give up and bury the naked shoes among the clothes, and then, I don't know why, I suddenly felt a strange compassion for this middle-aged woman's childish disappointment, and I offered her my suitcase as a temporary lodging place for her new shoes. Lazar still objected, and started scolding her for her stubbornness. "Why on earth do you have to drag that damned shoebox all the way to India and back?" But his wife didn't even look at him. She raised her head, shook her collapsing hairdo out of her eyes, and looked at me with a flushed face, not even troubling to smile her familiar smile: "Are you sure you don't mind?"

On the flight to New Delhi, which took off at eleven o'clock at night, I read a few pages of Stephen Hawking's book *A Brief History of Time,* which my father had bought at Ben Gurion Airport when he discovered I didn't have anything to read, then sunk into a deep sleep, the sleep I had been looking forward to since morning and for whose sake I had been tiring myself out all day long. It fell on me sooner than I had imagined, but it was also shorter than I would have wished. When I woke up after three hours, with my seat belt still fastened, I didn't know where I was, and for a moment I imagined that I was on night duty in the hospital. It was very dark in the plane, and the passengers were all asleep, sprawling in the seats and also lying in the aisles, as if they had been struck down by a sudden plague. Beyond the swaying wing of the plane I tried to discover in the darkness of the sky the first hints of dawn, which by my calculation should have appeared long ago if the plane had followed a logical course. Now I saw that Lazar or his wife had visited me in my sleep, for one of the sandwiches they had bought at the airport, in addition to a large bar of Italian chocolate, was stuck in the pocket of the seat in front of me. They must have noticed that I had missed my supper when I fell so swiftly and soundly asleep. I wrapped myself in a blanket and greedily devoured the sandwich and the entire bar of chocolate, delighted at this welcome manifestation of their concern. And suddenly I was seized by the desire to see them both, or at least to know where they were sitting, but I decided to wait until dawn, which I was sure was about to break soon.

I didn't have to wait long, and in the pale golden light I stood up and went to look for them. But I had a hard time finding them. Indian children lay huddled together in the aisles, as if in solidarity with their little friends sleeping on the sidewalks at home. The number of passengers seemed far larger than the number of seats, but nevertheless, it felt strange to me that I was unable to discover the whereabouts of the two Lazars, as if something had gone wrong with my sense of reality during my deep sleep. The plane began to sway in the wind, and Indian flight attendants emerged and instructed the passengers to return to their seats and fasten their belts, with the result that the aisles were gradually vacated, and here and there blankets which had been hung during the night to create sleeping nooks were taken down and hidden corners exposed. I returned to my seat, wondering if the Lazars had for some reason been seated apart and I had been mistaken in searching for them together, but I immediately dismissed this impossible thought. My parents, if unable to find seats side by side in waiting rooms or buses, would sit down separately without any hesitation, but not these two. When the wind died down and the passengers were released from their seat belts, I suddenly saw Lazar's gray mane looming up in the front of the plane, and then I remembered that I had sometimes come across him in the hospital during the past year, but without knowing who he was. He started advancing down the aisle, and when he reached me he bent down and said in a tone of mild complaint, "You slept and slept and slept," as if my sleep had somehow deprived the rest of the world of theirs. "And you?" I asked. He ran his fingers through his curly hair, closed his eyes wearily, and answered in a strangely complacent tone, "Me? Hardly ten minutes. I told you, I'm a lost cause, I've never been able to sleep in something over which I have no control." "And Dori?" I asked, blushing slightly at my inadvertent use of this pet name but reassuring myself with the thought that it would have been strange to go on saying "your wife" after twenty-four intensive hours of their company. He laughed. "Oh, all she needs is something soft to put her head on and somebody to keep watch in the background, and she sleeps like a lamb." And he suddenly leaned right over me to look out the window. "Where are we now?" I asked him. "Don't ask," he laughed. "Probably flying over some crazy country like Iran." There was a silence, after which he couldn't resist saying, "I hope you found the sandwich and the chocolate we left for you. We saw that you missed supper."

"Yes, yes, it was great. I wanted to thank you, but I couldn't find you."

"Listen," he said with a suddenly serious expression, "it doesn't matter if you can't find us in the plane, but what will happen if you lose us in India? We'll have to lay down a few rules for keeping contact. In the meantime, you should know our private whistle, which has stood us in good stead ever since our honeymoon." He whistled it a few times so that it would stick in my head.

❧❦

On a soft and hazy afternoon we landed in India, and for a moment I had the feeling that we were entering not a living reality but a vast screen on which a Technicolor movie about India was being projected. Already I found myself squeezed against the two of them, next to the knapsack with the medical supplies and the suitcases, which looked clumsy and almost superfluous in the small space of the ancient cab and in the face of the Indian poverty bombarding us through the car windows in a whirlwind of color. Lazar's face was pressed against my shoulder, very tired and wrinkled under the stubble of his beard, while the plump and lively face of his wife was made up and scented and radiant with childish excitement. Every few minutes she broke into loud cries of admiration, exhorting me and her husband to look at all kinds of passing Indians who seemed to her worthy of special attention. But Lazar refused to raise his head. Worn out, his eyes closed, he grumbled, "Enough, Dori, not now, I haven't got the strength, we'll have plenty of time to look later," while I actually tried to respond to her cries, despite their annoying loudness and enthusiasm, and turned to see where she was pointing, repeating a silly sentence that I couldn't get out of my head: "I feel as if it's not real yet, as if it's only some English movie about India, and we've become a little English ourselves." And she smiled at me kindly, as if I were a child trying to be original. But when we reached the hotel recommended by the travel agency, within the walls of the old city, her enthusiasm suddenly plummeted, which confirmed my objections to her joining us. Although the hotel was quite ancient, neither I nor Lazar could see anything wrong with spending the night there. But as we neared the reception desk, her face fell and she began whispering to her husband, demanding to see the rooms before we handed over our passports. Lazar grumbled at first but finally gave in to her, and they left me in the lobby with the luggage and went up to examine the rooms. On their return the argument between them seemed to have grown sharper. Her face was flushed and determined, and he looked very annoyed indeed. "I don't understand," he repeated, "I simply don't understand. It's for one night, at the most two. I haven't slept for thirty hours, I'm falling off my feet, and all I want is a simple bed. That's all. Where are we going to find a better hotel now?" But she gripped his arm tightly in an angry, distraught gesture, as if she wanted to shut him up, and sent me an automatic smile when she saw me looking at her, perhaps in order to shut me up too. "One night is worth something in life too," she said, rebuking her husband, and she gave me a reproachful look as well, even though I hadn't said a word.

We had no alternative but to leave the hotel, and the minute we hit the street two Indian boys pounced on us, relieved us of the knapsack and suitcases, and led us to see other hotels. And since we now felt light and liberated after the long, cramped flight, and the weather was soft and mild, we walked as if floating on air to not one but five hotels. The travel agent's warning that we were due to arrive in India at the height of the pilgrim season proved true. The hotels Mrs. Lazar approved of were full, and the hotels which could take us were rejected by this impossible woman, who went up by herself to "smell the rooms," as her husband remarked with a helpless smile, in which to my astonishment I also sensed a hidden admiration. And thus we wandered around the streets of the old city in the company of the two boys, who were enthusiastically prepared to lead us farther and farther, until after an hour of searching we finally found a hotel which was "at least possible," and whose prices turned out to be no higher than those of the ones that had been rejected. Our two rooms were next to each other, quite small but clean, or at least colorful. The windows were draped in curtains of pale green silk, like saris, and there were heavy chains of bright yellow wilted flowers hanging over the beds. After a day and a half I was really alone at last, and the welcome solitude wrapped me in its sweetness. It was already four-thirty in the afternoon, and I wondered whether I was too tired to do anything but take a shower and get into bed or whether I should go out now, before it got dark, into the new world beyond the door. In the end hunger gained the upper hand, and since Lazar and his wife had uncharacteristically failed to mention their plans for our next meal, I decided to go out and get something to eat on my own. I wasn't sure how frugal I needed to be since the financial arrangements between us had not yet been finalized. All I had to go on was the vague and general statement of intent made by Lazar's wife on the first evening in their apartment. The arguments over the choice of the hotel, which was situated in a far from elegant quarter, indicated that in spite of her indignant protests, expense was a factor to be taken into account, at least as far as Lazar was concerned. It wasn't going to be a luxury trip. And indeed, why should it be?

There was no restaurant in the hotel, only a small, dim bar in which a few guests in white turbans and old-fashioned European suits sat paging through newspapers and conversing quietly in

English, as if they were actually Britons who had been left behind when the Empire was abandoned and whom the years had darkened into old Indians. I changed a hundred dollars into rupees at the reception desk and emerged into a little street full of soft, dry sunlight, still clad in the thin skin of the English identity in which I had been pleasantly and secretly wrapped since landing in India. Unwilling to station myself, like an avid Israeli tourist, in front of the trays heaped up on the many food stalls, in order to nibble something sticky and mysterious, I decided to go back to the first, rejected hotel, where I had caught a glimpse of a large restaurant. I succeeded in retracing our footsteps with surprising ease, and entered the restaurant, where I examined the food lying on the tables before choosing the dish I fancied, a portion of roast meat buried in a thick black chapati resting on a large yellowish leaf. My hunger satisfied, I felt an urge to go upstairs and take a look at one of the rooms, to see what Mrs. Lazar had found so offensive. An Indian servant took me up to the second floor to show me the only vacant room left in the hotel, possibly the same room they had shown her. It was, in fact, a spacious room, with a view of a large, reddish fortress in the distance. I concentrated on the details, trying to see them through her eyes and understand what had put her off. The bed was large and covered with a gray blanket, clean but torn at the edges. One of the walls bore long thin stains, as if someone had thrown a drink at it. I took a step into the room in order to smell it. The Indian smiled at my side. I couldn't smell a thing, apart from a faint, sweetish whiff of mold. What, then, had made her recoil? I wondered, thinking of the pampered woman with a new and unfamiliar anger.

I left the room, but instead of returning to our hotel, although I was tired and sticky, I set out for the fort I had just seen through the window. I didn't want to waste a minute of my time in this fascinating place. We had already been told at the airport that we would have to travel from New Delhi to Gaya by train or bus, since at this time of year, with so many people on the move, we had no chance of getting onto a plane, or even perhaps of obtaining an air-conditioned compartment on the train. I assumed that Lazar, in a hurry to get back to Israel for his important meeting, would not want to hang around in New Delhi, and in spite of his promise about the fine sights we would see on the way, he would probably insist on setting out tomorrow, or at the most the day after tomorrow, in order to reach our destination as quickly as possible. And since I had a feeling that we would find the hepatitis patient in a worse state than her parents imagined and that from the minute we arrived I would have to be at her beck and call, because practical people like the Lazars didn't drag a doctor to the ends of the earth at their own expense for nothing, I had better make the most of every chance I got to take in whatever I could of the magic of this place, which was already beginning to draw me to it.

And so much the better, I reflected, that I was sticky and dirty from the journey; it would make me freer in my first contact with the reality of India, which seemed to be flowing and pouring and thickening around me like colorful lava; while at the same time my secret English identity would protect me from getting into trouble. And so, after writing down the name of the hotel on a piece of paper, I allowed myself to roam the filthy, crowded streets at will, proceeding slowly and steadily in the direction of the reddish stone fortress. By twists and turns, without asking anyone the way, I finally reached my goal, and discovered that my attraction to it had not been in vain. A wall stretched for hundreds of yards in the same reddish color which had initially caught my eye, and to which the light of the setting sun had now added a special charm. For a moment I searched for English tourists again, so that I could join them and rub up against the sounds of my parents' language. But the only people standing at the gate were a few hesitant Indians, who were being urged by the guards to go in quickly before they shut the fort, which was indeed, with surprising simplicity, called the Red Fort. Although it was too late for a comprehensive tour I went in, almost the last to do so. I passed through an arcade of elegant shops selling antiquities and souvenirs, and from there to several exquisite little pavilions, particularly the one called the Painted Palace, which were already growing dark in the gathering dusk and which had been almost deserted by the tourists. I was still trying as hard as I could to feel like the hero of a movie with definite values and a clear plot, as if this were the only way to give some meaning to the trip that had been suddenly forced on me and to console me for the loss of my prospects in Hishin's department at the hospital.

When I emerged from the gates of the fort with the last of the tourists, my soul stirred by the little I had managed to see, the sun had already set, darkness was rapidly falling, and there was a new chill, accompanied by soft raindrops, in the air, apparently coming from the direction of the broad river which I had glimpsed from one of the windows in the fort. I thought that it was the Ganges, until the guide corrected me and said that it was called the Yamuna, and it only joined the Ganges at a distance of some six hundred miles from here. And even though my weariness had hardened into what felt like an extra organ inside me, I told myself that if I had already come so far and enjoyed so much, I should go and see the river too, for even if it wasn't the famous Ganges, it would have some spiritual significance which could teach me something new. Because by tomorrow evening my independent ramblings would all too quickly end, and I would be sitting in a bus or a train, squeezed between Lazar and his wife, with their anxiety about their sick daughter growing more overpowering the closer we got to the hospital. I continued eastward in the direction of the river in spite of the encroaching darkness. With my father's sturdy old windbreaker to protect me from the cold and occasional snatches of English, local or otherwise, rising from the darkness to encourage me, I began making my way through rows of wretched hovels whose inhabitants seemed quite friendly, or at least not actively hostile.

In spite of the chill and the fine drizzle, the animated voices of women doing their washing or even bathing rose from the river, and from time to time the bobbing light of a lamp revealed their lively movements. I stood there for a long time in the fragrant rain, until I heard a long-drawn-out hoot and a very long illuminated train moved out of a nearby station and began crossing the river on an invisible bridge, as if it were floating between heaven and earth before sinking into the black horizon. At that moment I made up my mind to reconcile myself to this enforced journey and to stop inwardly protesting against Hishin for giving in to Lazar's manipulations, and I allowed my profound weariness to turn me in the direction of my waiting bed, festooned with its chain of yellow, slightly wilting marigolds.

But who could have guessed that the heavy darkness had fallen not only on the river and its environs but on large sectors of the old city as well, despite the streetlights scattered here and there, whose dim light only succeeded in blurring the landmarks I had memorized in order to lead me back? I thus had no alternative but to repeat the name of the first, rejected hotel to passersby, who were usually full of goodwill but also confusing and misleading. To my dismay, I found myself recognizing shops and stalls which I had already passed, until I realized that I had been going around in circles without anyone's warning me that the streets here went around a square and led nowhere. I immediately lost all confidence in the directions I had been given and began accosting people lying on the sidewalks and demanding explanations, even if I had to wake them up. Somehow I eventually found my way to the rejected hotel, which to my surprise was brightly lit and full of the sounds of music and singing because of a wedding celebration, which I stood and watched for a while as if spellbound. From there I remembered the way to our hotel, which looked dark and silent.

I hurried up to the second floor, wondering whether the Lazars were angry with me for having disappeared for so long without even warning them, or whether they had already resigned themselves to the fact that they had no control over me or right to expect anything of me, except for the performance of my medical duties when the time came. But if I came in for a mild reprimand, I decided, I would bow my head and accept it in silence. After entering my room and discovering that it had no electric light but only an oil lamp, which had been brought in my absence and suspended over my bed, I hurried out again and knocked lightly on the door of the Lazars' room, to announce my return and hear what they had seen and done in the meantime. Lazar opened the door, tousled with sleep, barefoot, short and clumsy in old-fashioned flannel pajamas, his eyes red and narrowed. Their room was smaller than mine, strewn with their clothing and possessions, and illuminated by a soft, weak light coming from the oil lamp hidden under their bed, which was not much larger than mine and which held the outline of Mrs. Lazar, curled up in a blanket with only her little feet sticking out. Her capacity for sleep was apparently as great as her capacity for smiling, I thought, again with a strange anger. And in fact, it transpired that no sooner had I left them than they had both fallen into a prodigious sleep, ignoring the great Indian city about them, and accordingly they had not even been aware of my absence. I couldn't contain myself, and standing on the threshold like an excited child, I told Lazar about the Red Fort, the little palaces, and the river too. He listened with his head bowed, swaying slightly. The true master of our great hospital, according to Hishin, stood before me now like a weak, bewildered old man. But I went on whispering nevertheless, and as I did so I saw two smiling eyes shining brightly from the outline on the bed. "I see that you enjoyed yourself," Lazar finally stated. "It's a good thing you didn't wait for us. I don't know what made us collapse like this," he began to apologize, "but it was stronger than we were. Don't forget we spent a few sleepless nights even before the journey. Ever since that girl brought us the letter, we've both begun coming apart at the seams, even if we don't look it."

He accompanied me to my room and obtained two sleeping pills. Then he told me with his characteristic practicality and foresight that he was determined not to let sleep slip away from him, in order to charge his batteries for the arduous journey still ahead of us. And indeed, when he knocked at my door and woke me up at ten o'clock the next morning, I noticed immediately that the limp exhaustion of the night before had been replaced by an energetic wakefulness. He apologized for waking me up, but explained that there were a few "urgent administrative matters." At ten o'clock that night we were continuing our journey on the night train to Varanasi. A long journey of seventeen hours. And we had to vacate our rooms at noon and leave our luggage downstairs. "So we're leaving tonight?" I asked in disappointment, even though I knew that his eagerness to reach his sick daughter quickly and get her and himself back to Israel as soon as possible would outweigh any promises made in his living room. Regrets welled up in me, for I had planned to go back to the river and see it in daylight, and also to visit a few places which had caught my interest when I walked past them in the dark. But it seemed that we had no alternative; it was impossible to get seats on a plane for the next two weeks, and even the express train, on which we had pinned our hopes in Israel, was full. It was only by the greatest ingenuity that he had succeeded in reserving us seats on a train that was slightly slower and less luxurious but reliable and reasonably comfortable, for otherwise, who knows, we might have been forced to rattle our bones in a dilapidated old bus as if we were characters in an adventure movie. "Yes, that's the long and the short of it," he apologized again, but actually he looked rather pleased with himself and his ability to cope with administrative difficulties, even in India. "We've arrived at the height of the internal tourist season in India. But we didn't choose the timing of this trip, it chose us. At least there's one thing in our favor—the weather's fine, and we don't have to worry about savage monsoons coming down on our heads."

His wife emerged in sunglasses, ready to go out. She had changed the blue tunic for a colorful Indian scarf, which she had purchased that morning and immediately draped round her shoulders. On her feet she wore flat walking shoes, which made her look short and clumsy. When she saw me at the door of my room, she put her hands together and bowed her head mischievously in the Indian greeting and said, "We owe you our thanks for the Red Fort. After your stories last night we ran to see it this morning, and it really is exquisite."

Lazar rummaged in his pockets, took out my train ticket, and said, "Here, you'd better keep it yourself." Then he took out a pen and wrote the name of the station on the back of the ticket, and said that we should meet at the hotel at eight o'clock before leaving for the station together. "Eight o'clock?" his wife protested. "Why so early? The train leaves at ten. We'll never get back from that place everyone says you should see at sunset. Why don't we meet at the train station? He's already proved himself."

I felt a sudden surge of resentment at the way she was calmly laying down the law. I fingered the stubble of my two-day beard and said with a provocative smile, "And if we do get separated? What happens then?"

"But why should we get separated?" she asked in genuine surprise, this woman who was only here with us because she couldn't bear being left alone. But Lazar immediately backed me up. "You're right, everything's possible, and if you really do get lost here, there isn't even anyone to inform." He rapidly wrote down the address of the hospital in Gaya on a piece of paper. "It's over a thousand miles from here," he said, smiling, "but at least it's a clear and definite address. I've already given you money and paid for your room in the hotel. And tonight we'll meet here, just as I said, at eight." He turned to his wife with a frown. "You always think you can play with time. But not now. So we'll all be back here by eight. And until then you're free," he added, turning back to me. "I see you like to roam around by yourself. Just see that you don't get into trouble. And we won't get on each other's nerves."

But they still didn't leave. Now they were waiting in the corridor for a dark, very delicate boy who came to take their luggage down, and I slowly closed my door on them. In spite of my tiredness, I didn't go back to bed but immediately began to shave, and suddenly the thought flashed across my mind, Yes, those were the right words exactly. This overweight couple was really beginning to get on my nerves, though I didn't yet know how or why. Maybe I'm too sensitive, I said to myself, but something about the strong, deep bond shining between them, slipping to and fro with sly efficiency between Lazar's dry, practical concern and his wife's warm, phony charm, with her sudden, superfluous smiles, was beginning to irritate me profoundly. In spite of their openness, they weren't frank with me, and I didn't know what was going on in their heads, which undoubtedly worked like one constantly coordinated head. I still didn't even know something as simple and straightforward as how much they were going to pay me for the trip. It was hard to tell what their real attitude to money was, their calculations between themselves and their calculations regarding me. And wasn't there something strange about the fact that they were both here and dragging a doctor with them? Surely one person would have been enough to bring this sick daughter home? Suddenly it struck me that they were a little afraid of the meeting with their daughter and they had brought me along as a kind of go-between. Had Lazar been telling me the truth outside his house when he said that his wife couldn't be without him? And if so, in what sense? It was insane. I could already sense the powerful nature of this smoothly oiled conjugality, which was only a little younger than the one between my parents, but how different they were. It would never occur to my father in a million years to take my mother's hand like that and squeeze it in order to make her stop talking. My father would never embarrass a strange young man watching them like that. But perhaps, I said to myself as I lathered my face for the third time in anticipation of the long journey beginning tonight, perhaps I really was too sensitive, without cause, perhaps because in my heart of hearts I was still lamenting this trip imposed on me by Professor Hishin, who at this early morning hour in Israel I could see stepping, fresh and cocky, into the operating room, where the nurses, together with the anesthetist and the second resident, are waiting for him. I could even imagine Hishin's jokes, as he teases the patient lying on the stretcher, sedated, and pale with fear, ready for the "take-off." Perhaps he even makes a few ironic remarks to the operating team about me and the fantastic trip he has graciously bestowed on me, although he and all the rest of them know very well that all I ever wanted was to stay at his side, next to the operating table, looking and looking deep inside the human body, in the hope that one day the knife would be placed in my hand.

Three

Is it possible to bring up the word "Mystery" yet? Or perhaps as of now it can only be thought of? For our three characters (three? for the time being) are not seeking mystery; the relative stability of their personalities, the reasonable rationality of their thinking, has set before them a well-lit goal and a clear road to reach it. And if they only remain free of the tyranny of the imagination, of its arbitrariness, they will arrive by their own powers at the simple heart of the matter and return safely to their homes, after parting from each other without acrimony or pain.

For what will they gain from a mystery that leads nowhere? And this young doctor, a rather reflective and solitary hero, abruptly cut off three days ago from Professor Hishin's surgical department, which has filled his life for the past year and on which he pinned his hopes for the future, is now, owing to the sudden trip to India, left without even the possibility of any other hope to cling to. He finishes shaving, washes his face, and begins packing in a mood of sullen resentment. But before he finally parts from the dim room where the colorful silk curtains are still drawn and prepares himself for a day of intensive sightseeing—so that he will not be shamed by friends and acquaintances at home for having traveled all the way to New Delhi and failed to see the things you have to see there—he goes to check that the door is locked, quickly takes off all his clothes and lies down naked on the bed, and masturbates heavily and without recourse to fantasy, in order to feel freer and lighter for the long journey ahead, since he knows that the next bed offered him by his purposive companions will be very far away.

But the young doctor had no hidden desire to imagine this bed as in any sense mysterious, even though as he emerged from the hotel, erect and slightly dizzy, straight into the heart of the rosy

Indian light floating over the streets stinking with stunning, colorful humanity, a twinge of anxiety entered his soul, whereas the day before, in these very same streets, even in the darkness of night, he had felt quite relaxed. Because the English movie in which he imagined that he was taking part in order to protect himself had completely vanished during the night, and now he was exposed without any barriers to the alien and powerful reality. And this anxiety was so new and sudden to the doctor that he stopped the first available rickshaw, even though it was drawn by a bicycle and not a motorcycle, and threw himself onto the soft seat, and said, Take me first to Humayun's Tomb. And the rider-driver, a serious Indian of about fifty who wore dark glasses and spoke better English than his passenger, turned out to be an excellent tour guide and spent the rest of the day guiding the young tourist intelligently and efficiently about the city, so that he would see not only the sights the guidebooks defined as not to be missed but also those listed as optional. Thus, after they had visited Humayun's Tomb, the Qutab Minar complex, and even the National Museum, and after the guide had noted that his tourist was not a dawdler but looked quickly and walked briskly, he suggested that the tourist pay a visit, perhaps in his capacity as a doctor, to a unique site—a hospital for birds, not far from the Red Fort. There, on the second floor, in a dimly lit room, opposite stinking cages in which lay sick and wounded birds—some of them with their legs in splints, among them crushed and mangy birds of prey who would suddenly shriek horribly—the doctor's anxiety deepened, until his soul trembled and he asked to leave. "What a crazy idea," he argued outside, but when he saw his guide's disappointment, he corrected himself and said, "Maybe the idea of a birds' hospital is original, but shouldn't human suffering come first?"

And then the guide removed his dark glasses, revealing slightly bloodshot eyes, and spoke of the reincarnation of souls, and the doctor secretly clenched his fists and bowed his head in silence, and after the guide concluded, he paid him the exact sum agreed on between them and sent him away without a tip, and instead of going down to the river again to see it in daylight, as he had planned, he turned slowly, feeling rather depressed, in the direction of the hotel. It was five o'clock in the afternoon, and the softness of the fading light was suffused with unfamiliar scents.

By now he was already in possession of a map of Delhi, and he could find his way without having to ask anyone directions. He sat down in a restaurant and looked at the throng streaming past, and to his astonishment, among the many tourists he suddenly recognized Lazar and his wife, who was still wrapped in the morning's Indian scarf, walking past him at a distance of a few paces away, as if it were the most natural thing in the world, and vanishing into a shop that sold textiles and rugs. How strange, he thought, to bump into them of all people in a city of millions, in this little alley of all places. How strange, he repeated to himself, quickly gulping down his tea, waiting for the moment when they would emerge and he would go up to them to dispel his gloom with her smile, and to compare what they had managed to see today with what he had seen, and to find out if there was some additional sightseeing obligation that he might fulfill in his last hours in Delhi. But they didn't come out of the shop. The cup stood empty before him, he had already paid the waiter, and he smiled to himself at the insatiable lust for shopping displayed by this fat middle-aged couple. In the end he went to look for them in the shop. But they weren't there, even though the shop was not a large one and there did not appear to be any other way out. Here was a riddle: suddenly they appear and then they disappear again? This story is beginning to get mysterious, he whispered to himself, not yet pronouncing the word itself but only its adjective.

He reached the hotel at seven, a whole hour early; he figured they must have emerged from the shop and slipped out of his sight when he was paying the waiter and checking his change. He positioned himself on a soft leather sofa in a corner of the lobby not far from the reception desk, with his suitcase and knapsack next to him. Now he could survey the guests going in and out at his ease, paying special attention to the Indian women, never mind their age, in an attempt to discover the point at which a Westerner, with a rather shy sexuality, like his own, could connect with them. And then he thought of his parents, and he decided to call them, not because they would be worried, but simply in order to hear the reassuring sound of their voices, for they too were to some extent responsible for his being here. But the reception clerk was unable to put through a direct international call from the hotel phone, and told him to go to a post office

*some distance away. The young doctor had no desire to forfeit
the sofa he had taken over and decided to postpone the phone
call. It was already eight o'clock, and the dusk had deepened, but
the Lazars had not yet appeared. He felt no anxiety or anger, but
only a gentle wonder. The street visible through the hotel entrance did not sink into silence and darkness as it had the night
before, but took on a festive appearance; many new oil lamps
were brought into the hotel lobby, and people walked past in
festive attire. With a strange pleasure he said to himself, those
two are crazy; their daughter needs them, she's lying sick hundreds of miles away from here, and they're strolling around and
enjoying themselves like a couple of provincial tourists, looking
for bargains among the Indian shmattes. But at nine o'clock he
realized that something really had gone wrong. He remembered
Lazar's slogan, "So we won't get on each other's nerves," but
still he felt no bitterness or anger, only a sense of profound wonder. His return ticket to Israel was in his wallet; he had all the
documents he needed with him. If they really disappeared, he
would be his own boss again, and he would even be at liberty to
go home.*

*At five past nine he picked up his luggage, left a message at the
desk, and took a rickshaw to the train station. Perhaps they
would make it at the last minute, even without their luggage. But
from the minute he entered the heart of the storm in the old
station—where the quintessence of travel fever raged in its
purest, most hectic form, flooding the place in a dim yellowish
light full of smoke and smells, swarming and groaning in the cars
crammed with people, which belched out and sucked in bundles
and mattresses from every possible opening—the doctor felt the
last vestige of hope of finding the couple draining out of him.
Nevertheless, he resolutely elbowed his way through the crowd,
passing from platform to platform and finally reaching the right
train, and the exact compartment, which turned out to be handsome and modern, with the air-conditioning lending a European
chill to the air. The four seats looked comfortable, ready to be
converted into narrow bunks for the night. The dark, opaque
windows turned the travel fever of the station into a scene on a
television screen. Was he going to wind up traveling into the
depths of India on his own and against his will in order to meet a
sick and unknown woman for an undefined medical purpose? he*

*asked himself with the mild irony he had inherited from his En-
glish father. And the wonder and loneliness he had been feeling
all day welled up in him with a new intensity and washed away
the remnants of his anger and disappointment. Now his soul was
flooded with a sweet wave of mystery.*

*This is not yet the mystery itself, but only its sweetness, which
has now been born not from the external reality existing outside
the dark window but from the inner depths of this young doctor
himself, who was introduced by Professor Hishin to his friend as
the ideal person for the journey. For only the superficial eye of a
tourist would seek to find mystery in the Indian train, for instance, which suddenly begins puffing and moving slightly to and
fro, presumably in order to take on additional cars, toward
which tall Tibetan monks in orange robes hurry, gently but
firmly rebuffing obstreperous beggars, some of them real lepers
with amputated limbs, thrusting themselves between the legs of
porters carrying enormous bundles of rolled-up mattresses for a
group of merry pilgrims passing along the platform. Delicate
women flit among the throngs like moths, an intelligent third eye
shining in the center of their foreheads and guarding them from
bumping into Sikhs with wild black beards and carrying daggers,
who are obliged—even they—to impatiently circumvent the solitary white cow which has innocently found its way into the station and is now nibbling the sparse grass growing next to the
platform, indifferent to the savage looks of the lean, half-naked
Indians clambering over the cars and struggling with the train
officials, who are trying to force them down from the roof of one
of the ancient trains, where they are strapping their bundles and
themselves between the iron railings and settling down for the
night.*

*No, in all this feverish activity in the old train station of Delhi
the young doctor sees no mystery, nor even the faintest shadow
of its sweetness. He sits quiet and still, five minutes before the
train departs, in the right compartment on the right seat (he has
repeatedly checked and asked), his suitcase and medical kit on
the shelf above his head. In this serenity, which is almost joyful,
submitting to the task to which an invisible hand has appointed
him, a clear and genuine sign comes to him, and he cannot resist
whispering to himself, as the train starts slowly gliding from its
place, It's not possible, they really have disappeared, those two,*

and it's a real mystery. And now a thin-faced old Indian nods to him as he enters the compartment, dressed in a light-colored European suit spotted with ancient stains and carrying a shabby little suitcase in his hand, and makes him a little bow, careful to avoid the cup of tea that the train steward placed on the tray a few minutes before. He sits down shyly, takes a pair of cheap metal glasses with one cracked lens out of his pocket, and opens a Hindi newspaper. And anyone who now hears the ineffable word whispered naturally and spontaneously in his ear is finally at liberty to put it carefully down on the paper in front of him.

Two or three minutes after the train left the yellowish hell of the station and, as if suspended in the air, began crossing the pitch-black river, the door of the compartment shook with a violent knock, which so alarmed the Indian passenger that the newspaper fell from his hands. Through the little round window in the door I saw Lazar's familiar gray mane again, and I hurried to open it and found both of them squeezed into the passage with their two suitcases. Lazar's face was gray with exhaustion, and his eyes guiltily evaded mine. Even before stowing the suitcases on the racks, he admitted his failure. First of all he clasped my shoulders, then he clutched his head between his hands and began shaking it. "I don't know what happened to us," he said despairingly, "I don't understand how we could have lost our way like that." But his wife burst into loud, uninhibited peals of relieved laughter, astonishing the elderly Indian, who now folded his newspaper and put his cracked glasses away in his pocket in order to gaze at this boisterous woman. Her topknot had unraveled completely and her hair was falling onto her flushed, heavy face, from which all traces of makeup had vanished. They had apparently suffered an hour of extreme anxiety and were now overjoyed at having found me. Lazar kept on apologizing; as someone who knew how to blame others, he now seemed eager to take the blame upon himself, but also to explain exactly how and where they had gone wrong and to apologize again for the worry they had caused me. It turned out that they too had tried to call Israel, but nobody had warned them about the length of time it would take until the connection was made. "Enough already, what does it matter?" his wife interrupted him, annoyed by his repeated apologies. "The doctor wasn't worried, believe me. He would have gone on ahead and we would have arrived a day later. I've already told you, he's not the type to get lost." She said this in a gentle but slightly mocking tone, and began combing her hair in front of the little mirror in the corner of the compartment, smiling at Lazar indulgently as she did so. When she had finished combing her hair, she bestowed a warm smile on the old Indian too, who hadn't taken his eyes off her, picked up the cup of tea standing on the tray by her seat, and started to sip it with her eyes closed. Only now did Lazar begin to calm down. He started rearranging the luggage on the racks, tugging and pushing, and a little while later, when the steward brought us the ready-packed meals included in the price of our tickets, he sat down and ate heartily.

☙❧

In the meantime his wife was already discreetly questioning the Indian about the purpose of his trip, and he responded willingly in reasonable English and also gave her his card. He was an official in a government department in New Delhi who had recently retired and was on his way for the first time in his life to Varanasi, in order to bathe in the Ganges before he died and to take part in the cremation rites for his eldest brother whose body would be taken there from the south by his sister-in-law and nephews. Every time he pronounced the words "before I die," Mrs. Lazar's eyes lost their smile and her face clouded, as if she refused to countenance his thoughts of death even by listening to them. But she was wrong; the thought of death only gave the old Indian pleasure. Since nothing in the universe was ever lost, all that was left for him to do was to ensure his rebirth in more advantageous conditions, which he was now about to do by bathing in the holy river.

"Unbelievable—this man is actually convinced that someone is going to bring him back to life again after he dies!" Lazar exclaimed in Hebrew, his hunger satisfied and a good-humored smile on his face, which was still gray and exhausted. His breathing sounded heavy, and for a moment I was afraid that his heart wasn't functioning normally. The Indian passenger fell silent, as if he sensed that he was being made fun of. Outside it was already completely dark, there was no light to signal any passing reality, and for a moment it seemed as if the train were standing still, even though its wheels were turning. Soon the Indian was listening with interest to Lazar's wife as she explained the purpose of our trip. He did not seem surprised to hear that three people had come specially from Israel to take the sick girl home. Perhaps she has sunk into Nirvana, he said, absolutely seriously, and it will take much strength to pull her out of it. Toward midnight a young boy came to remove the dirty dishes, to pour tea, to distribute blankets, and to help us convert our seats into bunk beds. Lazar's wife and I climbed into the upper bunks, and Lazar and the Indian lay down in the lower ones. We switched off the light and covered ourselves with our blankets, but I was afraid I would not be able to fall asleep with so many people surrounding me. Strangely enough, the presence of the old Indian official below me seemed to reassure me. My face touched the dark blanket. I strained my eyes until I began to make out the outlines of the reality beyond the window—poor peasant houses and desolate dirt roads. Here and there I thought I could see a man plowing in the fields, and I asked myself whether a new day had already begun for him or the old one had not yet ended. From time to time the train slowed down at little country stations, gliding silently past the shadowy, blanket-wrapped figures that crouched next to the tracks and avidly examined the passing train. Lazar's wife fell asleep immediately and began to snore, but Lazar was still tossing and turning on his narrow bunk. Every now and then he got up and put his hand on his wife to stop her snoring, but his touch only succeeded in interrupting her snores for a few minutes, after which they began welling up again, gently but strongly. Finally he woke her up. "Dori," he whispered firmly, "Dori, you're disturbing everybody." She woke up, raised herself slightly, looked around in confusion, saw me, nodded at her husband as if agreeing with what he had said, and sank back into a deep sleep, carrying me off with her.

Lazar was clearly as resistant to sleep in trains as he was in planes. When I woke up at dawn, stunned by the clamor of the wheels, which my deep sleep had succeeded in suppressing, I saw him sitting heavily on his low bunk, sad and lonely without his smiling wife at his side. The moment he sensed that I had opened my eyes, he tried to latch on to me. Although I would have been happy to go on snuggling into my warm, narrow bunk, I felt his distress and climbed down to talk to him. It transpired that he had spent most of the night sitting up in bed or prowling around the train. He had even managed to wash and shave. He was too tense to fall asleep, or even to read. Worry about the state in which he would find his daughter was eating him up, and he was preoccupied too by interrupted business at the hospital. I took the opportunity to ask him about his work, and he responded willingly, but suggested we continue our conversation in the corridor. There was no need to disturb those who always managed to sleep in spite of everything, he said with a smile, and I didn't know if he was referring to his wife or if he also had in mind the old Indian, who had curled up into a little white ball on half his bunk, as if rehearsing the fetal position in anticipation of his rebirth. In the corridor of the train, which was now racing through reddish hills, I began interrogating Lazar about the hospital, discovering through his administrative point of view new and surprising things even about the surgical department, which I thought I knew so well. Although he was not familiar with the professional medical aspects of our work, he had a surprisingly good grasp of the way the department was organized, and he was astonishingly well informed about the personal lives of the doctors and nurses. He had something to tell me about everyone whose name I mentioned, and was quick to express an opinion or assessment of them as well. Sometimes he added a story about a power struggle which had ended in success or failure. I suppose he knows all about me too, I thought to myself, and perhaps he even has an opinion of my abilities, which he got from people whom I would never have imagined took the trouble to think about me, but he's too discreet to drop me a hint. I asked him about plans for the future, hoping to hear of new openings, but he sighed and began throwing out figures about budget cuts, which were doubly painful in the light of his desire to expand by constructing buildings with two operating rooms and up-to-the-minute laboratories, for example, whose future location he sketched in the air with broad movements.

❧❧❧

In the meantime the first light of morning broke in the hazy sky, and a large round sun rose from an unexpected direction. Thus the day of the long journey to Varanasi began, in the glow of dirt roads, huts, and villages slipping slowly past the dark windows and the radiant, aromatic dimness of the big stations where we suddenly stopped among trains of various kinds and colors with droves of passengers getting in and out. During the few minutes of the stop, Lazar would sometimes hurry out to the stalls crowding the platform and bring us sweets or chapatis or bottles of unfamiliar effervescent drinks. His wife, if she didn't join him, would stand at the window so as not to let him out of her sight. I had noticed their craving for sweet things in Rome, and even in India they didn't hesitate to suck and chew all kinds of candies whose names the Indian passenger taught them to pronounce. He himself had already changed his spotted old suit for a kind of white robe, which gave rise to a pleasant, intimate feeling, and indeed he was soon deep in conversation with Lazar's wife, who seemed amused by his views on life and the world, but who was careful to question him in a tactful, friendly manner. This won him over to such an extent that he soon opened his little suitcase, took out an old deck of cards illustrated with all kinds of gaudy gods and demigods, and tried to teach us a kind of Indian poker, whose peculiar rules made her laugh so merrily that it seemed she had completely forgotten the purpose of our journey.

In the afternoon the Ganges appeared in all its vastness, flowing slowly not far from the train tracks, and the Indian's dark face glowed in the abundant yellow light. Overcome with awe of the holiness flowing next to him, he stopped playing cards and chatting to Lazar's wife, rose to his feet full of power and vitality, and retired to the corridor to sink into meditation opposite the holy river. But while the Indian was evidently growing stronger in anticipation of the baptism awaiting him, the sleepless Lazar was growing weaker; his eyes kept closing, his head nodded, fell, and jerked up again. "Try to lie down and rest for a while, don't be so obstinate," his wife urged him, but he was unable to let go of his tension: "It's too late to sleep, we'll be there soon." Finally she succeeded in persuading him to take off his shoes and lie down on the seat, and even to overcome his embarrassment at my presence and lay his head on her round stomach, while she held his head firmly between her hands as if to absorb his anxiety into herself. And it worked, for after a few minutes of vacillating and grumbling, Lazar plunged into a deep sleep, his breathing very relaxed, as if he had fallen out under the hands of a practiced anesthetist. His wife tried to engage me in conversation, but I stopped her. "We shouldn't disturb him," I whispered, "now that he has finally fallen asleep." My reaction surprised her, and for the first time I noticed an offended blush spreading over her cheeks, as the faint down covering them glinted in the sunlight. But she obediently took off her glasses and closed her eyes, and an hour later, when the train slowed down in preparation for its ceremonious entry into the last smoke-shrouded station and Lazar emerged from the abyss of his sleep, he discovered that his wife had fallen asleep with him.

The elderly Indian passenger, who had been so friendly and talkative during the long journey, had now become estranged and remote in anticipation of its ending. His relatives, dressed in white as he was, were already waiting for him on the crowded platform, and they immediately swallowed him up without a trace. The three of us were left staring, dumb and paralyzed. The crowds we had seen on the streets of New Delhi looked sparse and quiet compared to this one. We were obliged to stick close to each other and hang on tightly to our suitcases, which seemed to have taken on a life of their own as they jerked about in the frenzied crowd. We had to stop at Varanasi to make our connection to Gaya, but we had had no idea how many tourists and pilgrims would be engulfing this major attraction at the height of the tourist season. While Lazar was haggling with a lively, dwarfish porter who had attached himself to us, one of the Lazars' two suitcases was carried away by the crowd. At first Lazar gave way to despair and seemed on the point of tears. But then he recovered and plunged into the crowd, pushing and shoving in search of the thief, refusing to resign himself to the loss even though his wife was already trying to comfort him. In the end they left me in a corner in charge of the cart piled with the rest of the luggage while they set out with the dwarf to search for the suitcase. Again I found it ridiculous that they had to do everything together.

But perhaps precisely because of this, they succeeded in accomplishing the impossible, fishing the suitcase out of the stormy sea of people into which it had been swept, not stolen, and loaded by mistake onto another porter's cart. Now it reposed on the back of the diminutive porter, dusty and battered, as if in the short time of its disappearance it had traveled across an entire continent. And the same thing, it seemed to me, had happened to us. New Delhi had given us the illusion that we understood the rules of India, but in Varanasi we were all gripped by a feeling of anxiety, and Lazar, whose deep sleep on the stomach of his wife had restored his alertness and vigor, instructed me in no uncertain terms to stick closely to him and not to start dreaming now; for indeed, with astonishing perceptiveness, he had caught me in the kind of dreaminess that sometimes took hold of me in the hospital at dawn, after a night on call, when I crossed the borderline into a new working day. "But what makes you think that he wants to dream now?" said his wife in surprise. "The dream is what's happening here around us." But Lazar didn't answer her, because at that moment it seemed to him that one of the suitcases was about to fall off the cart racing ahead of us, and he rushed forward to catch it, only to trip and fall onto the platform himself. He sprang up immediately, an expression of wounded pride on his face, and also of offense, as his wife exploded into merry peals of laughter, which continued as she asked him if he had hurt himself while helping him dust off his clothes. "It's not a dream, it's madness," he said, smiling at himself. "What's going on here is total madness. Let's get out of this station at least." But the madness was waiting for us outside the station too, in the seething streets of the dusty, humid city, where the air was full of sweetish, colorful, unfamiliar stench. Without waiting for instructions, the porter hurried ahead, accompanied now by a flock of barefoot children, who stretched out filthy little hands to finger the smooth leather of the suitcases. "But where is he rushing to, that crazy little dwarf?" asked Lazar in astonishment. "To the hotel," replied his wife. "The hotel?" echoed the bewildered Lazar. "What hotel?"

"He told me about a nice hotel overlooking the river, with a view of the bathing ghats the man in the train told us about."

"But what hotel, Dori?" repeated Lazar in alarm, unable to believe that his wife had already come to an agreement with the little porter. "A hotel in the old city," she replied, "next to the river."

"Have you lost your mind, to follow a character like that to some hotel in the old city in the middle of all the muck? What's come over you? I don't understand."

But his wife was unperturbed by this outburst. "What harm can it do to try? We've got plenty of time. The Indian in the train said it's the only place to find a hotel, and since we're stuck here, at least we'll be able to watch their ceremonies from the window."

"What window?" cried Lazar. "No, no, Dori, we're not running from one hotel to the next to smell the rooms this time. No," he announced firmly, "it's out of the question, Dori. We're not starting to look for a hotel in the old city; even here, in the new city, it's barely tolerable. We'll find a decent, civilized hotel—we're completely exhausted already, and I don't care how much it costs," and he hurried forward to catch up with the porter.

The little man tried to argue, but in vain. He appealed to Lazar's wife, as if she had made him a definite promise, but Lazar cut through his pleas with a wave of his hand, and the porter, no doubt disappointed at the loss of his commission, his feelings hurt by the broken promise, turned back and began trudging through the streets until he brought us to a very fine hotel, which met with general approbation but had only one vacant room. Since Lazar had no intention of allowing us to split up in Varanasi, we set out to look for another hotel, but there were no vacancies anywhere, until we reached a brand-new hotel called Ganga Mata, which had rooms but must have been very expensive, for I saw Lazar hesitating, in spite of his previous declaration that expense was no object. In the end, however, while his wife maintained a serene silence, he said, "Never mind, it's only for one night," and signaled the porter to hand over the luggage to the splendidly uniformed doormen. But then I saw his wife hold out her hand to stop the porter and grab hold of her husband's arm. "You're so obstinate. If we're only here for one night, why should we stay at an ordinary hotel, just like thousands of other hotels all over the world? This porter knows about a special hotel, overlooking the river. Why shouldn't we try it?" she said very gently and persuasively. And Lazar raised his hand hesitantly, as if to stop the doormen, who had already taken down two suitcases, and then laid it on his head with a curious gesture, as if to show the pain of his thoughts. "You decide," continued his wife, "not because of the money, because of the view." And suddenly, without any warning, Lazar gave in, announcing as he did so, "It's your responsibility, Dori. If you don't like the hotel there, don't you dare say you want to come back here." But his wife made no promises. "Trust my intuition," she said. "This porter knows where he's taking us. And besides, why shouldn't we wander around a bit? You don't have to carry anything. It's still early in the day—we have time. And you're not so tired now. You had a really good sleep in the train."

❧ ❧

The little porter, who had been following their conversation intently and guessed which way the wind was blowing even before anything was said, became filled with happiness and energy and began pulling the suitcases out of the hands of the elegant doormen and replacing them on his cart. And I said to myself, I'm nothing but a piece of luggage here myself, or a child. It doesn't even occur to them to ask me what I think; maybe I'm very tired and I'd rather stay in this hotel. I returned the smile beamed in my direction with a sullen look, and hoisted the medical knapsack wearily onto my back as if to say, What choice do I have, I'm just a hired hand here. I saw that my sullen look had upset Lazar's wife, and as we set off she turned to me and said, "Perhaps you would have preferred to stay here?"

"What does it matter what I prefer?" I replied with a bitter smile. "I have no say in the matter." And I saw that this domineering woman was hurt, as I had intended her to be. She blushed. "Why do you say that?" She spoke in an offended tone. "Everybody says you should be close to the river—that's where all the rites take place. And since we're here for such a short time, we should be close to the main thing, or at least in a position to get a good view."

But before reaching the River Ganges, with the view of the heavy, gray ghats lapped by its waters, we had to make our way through winding alleys so narrow and jammed with people that our agile porter had to leave his cart in one of the little shops and hire two of the barefoot children who had been following us ever since we left the train station to help him carry our luggage. It was almost four o'clock, and there was a chill in the air, which took on a pinkish tinge. A steady procession of pilgrims, singing and playing on musical instruments, streamed purposefully toward the river, and scattered among them were young backpackers, rubbing shoulders with us on the right and the left and sometimes even smiling at me in a friendly, inviting way, as if I were one of them, for they had no way of knowing that the pack on my back was filled with medical supplies and that I was not free like them but tied to two heavy, middle-aged people in travel-creased gray clothes. Lazar looked tense and worried, jostling and being jostled as he hurried a few steps ahead of us in order not to lose contact with the band of children hot on the heels of the dwarf, who because of their smallness sometimes vanished completely in the crowd. The river was apparently close, for the dust of the alley turned muddy and the crowd tightened around us. From time to time a slender dark hand would touch my shoulder, asking me to make way for a corpse wrapped in white or yellow winding sheets, which would be carried past, raised up on steady hands, until it seemed to be floating of its own accord over the sea of heads surrounding us. I stole a look at Lazar's wife, who was trailing behind us, picking her way fastidiously between the sewage canals and the slippery cowpats, slow but light in her low-heeled shoes, looking unsmilingly at the corpses floating through the alley to be burned on the banks of the river. She must be regretting her obstinacy now, I thought, and perhaps because she noticed the mocking smile on my face, she stopped for a moment, wiped the indiscriminating smile off hers, and called out to her husband to slow down. But Lazar was too intent on not losing the porters, who were now crossing courtyards, passing alcoves concealing gaudily painted statues and wild-haired ascetics, and finally leading us into a back alley where a very old but rather attractive country house stood, surrounded by dusty trees with tiny vegetable gardens planted between them. At the entrance to the house, which was decorated with dark little statues that were nothing but variations on male sexual organs painted red and black, at which Lazar stared in nervous amusement, a small group of Indians clustered, apparently waiting for the dwarfish porter and the new guests he was bringing from the train station. Without asking our permission, they rapidly sent the children on their way, took the suitcases, nimbly relieved me of the knapsack, and led us up three flights of stairs covered with a torn old carpet, passing rooms full of people on the way. On the third floor they ushered us into a big, dim room carpeted with colorful straw mats and containing two very large beds, a closet, and wicker chairs, and without losing a moment, they flung open a curtain and took us out onto a little balcony full of flower pots, which in the eyes of our hosts was the justification for our coming and the fulfillment of the promise made by the porter on the station platform. And who indeed could have imagined that we would emerge from that labyrinth of narrow, winding alleys to stand before this rich, spacious view, open from horizon to horizon, with the great Ganges flowing through its heart, glittering in the reddening light of the approaching evening.

Lazar's wife uttered a cry of admiration and praised the view enthusiastically to the Indians. Lazar leaned silently on the balustrade, sighed, and smiled faintly to himself. Suddenly I understood his wife's hidden power, and why he had been prepared to give up the new hotel so easily. He had a deep faith in her intuitions about people, and since she believed in the little porter and his promises to lead us to a high place overlooking the river, he gave in to her. And perhaps the fact that he would be saving a considerable sum of money had something to do with it too, for I had already noticed that in spite of the emergency that had precipitated the journey, he was not indifferent to its cost. A great deal of money had already been spent, and there was no knowing how much more would be needed on the way back, when the patient would be with us. It would be impossible to drag her through narrow alleys to a simple hotel, however unique the view from the balcony—which Lazar's wife continued to praise extravagantly, to the delight of the hotel owners.

But it was only now that they realized we needed two rooms. The little porter had taken us for a family, perhaps imagining me to be their son on holiday with his parents. Even now, when they heard that I was only a doctor accompanying the Lazars to Gaya, they couldn't understand why we needed another room. They would bring another bed right away, and set up a screen in the middle of the big room. Lazar looked at me. I could have refused immediately, but I wanted him to be the one to demand another room. The thought of spending the whole night in the same room with them seemed too much to cope with. They too seemed uneasy at the idea. "No," said Lazar, "we'll take another little room for him." But it appeared that all the rooms in the inn were full, and the only solution was to put me up in a kind of shed next to the building used as a dormitory for backpackers and solitary pilgrims. Suddenly I felt very bitter toward Lazar's wife, who had dragged us here, but I said nothing and picked up the knapsack, since I would rather sleep in the shed than share their intimacy. But she, feeling guilty and embarrassed, objected vehemently. The idea that they would remain here, with the spectacular view of the sacred river, while I was relegated to a kind of dormitory seemed to her so unjust that she began coaxing me to stay with them. "What does it matter? It's a big room, we won't take up a lot of space, they'll bring a screen. Why should you miss the view of the river and the ghats? That's what we came here for in the first place. I don't like to think of you down there alone."

"I don't mind being alone," I said, with a faintly contemptuous smile, but she didn't understand what I was getting at and continued enthusiastically. "Once in a lifetime you get to see something this amazing. The room's not important—it's what you can see from it, the wonderful view, the river, the ghats, the pilgrims, and the night falling. Why should you sleep in some mean, wretched place? You deserve better." And then she suddenly added, "Why should it bother you? Last night all three of us slept squashed up with the Indian in one little compartment."

Lazar remained silent and gloomy, also apparently angry at his wife for complicating things. But she appealed to him helplessly to persuade me, touching his hand lightly to convey her request. And Lazar said quietly, "He'll decide for himself where he wants to sleep, what do you want of his life?" And she said, "It's not fair for him to sleep downstairs with all the vagabonds." And suddenly, without warning—her conscience must have really been bothering her—she threatened that we would have to go and look for a new hotel unless I agreed to share their room. Now Lazar gave me a despairing look. "Why shouldn't you sleep up here with us, really? There's no problem as far as we're concerned, if you don't mind. We're leaving tomorrow morning, and the air's better up here, and there's such a special view." His eyes were hollow, and his skin looked so gray that for a moment I felt concerned about his health again. In the meantime the Indians had decided for us, and two boys with gleaming white smiles brought in a folding bed and a red screen decorated with paintings of snakes, and without further ado Lazar's wife indicated a place next to the window, where they opened the bed and set up the screen, and only then did she turn to me and say, "Put your suitcase behind the screen. Don't worry, we'll be quiet as mice, you won't even know we're here."

I gave in. The view from the little balcony with its flower pots was so stunning and exhilarating after the long cramped train trip that I couldn't bring myself to refuse the offer to remain in the room with them, especially since I knew Lazar's wife wouldn't give up until she'd searched all the nearby hotels for a decent room for me, and I felt sorry for the exhausted Lazar. But even though I had to sleep with them that night, I didn't have to stay now and sit behind the screen on the folding bed until they had undressed and bathed, being careful not to expose themselves to my eyes. Though my clothes were also damp and sticky from the journey and the walk through the alleys and I too would have liked to wash and change, I immediately announced that I was going out for a little walk, to see the pilgrims dipping in the river and perhaps, before it got dark, the cremation rites at the famous "burning ghats" referred to in the guidebook. Lazar, who had already taken off his shoes and shirt and was busy massaging his big stomach, said with a tired smile, "Even though you've already proved that you're not the one who gets lost and we are, please do me a favor and watch where you're going, because there aren't even any streets here, it's all one big confusion, and if you get lost here you might as well be reborn as somebody else, because you'll never find your way back." And we all burst out laughing in a spirit of reconciliation, and we even forgave the stubbornness. I agreed to return by a certain time, as if the Lazars were my parents. When I went down into the little garden in front of the inn and looked at the maze of passages and courtyards surrounding me, for a moment I was afraid that I wouldn't be able to find my way back. I decided to find someone, a boy or a girl, to guide me. Under one of the trees I saw the little porter sitting with his friends and eating his supper, and although his English was almost nonexistent, I asked him to lead me to the river, because he had already impressed me, not only with the enterprise that had attracted Lazar's wife but also with his delicacy and tact. I knew that he would return me safely to the inn, which for a reason I could not explain suddenly tugged at my heart.

Indeed, he led me nimbly to the riverbank and to a ghat he called Lalita. There we descended many broken steps, making our way through the strong smells and colors of the pilgrims, Brahmins, and beggars. And then, without even asking me, the porter installed me in a boat which already contained two young Scandinavian backpackers, and we embarked for the center of the river to observe the rites from the sacred water. We saw women in saris descending the steps slowly and gracefully, cupping their hair in their hands and dipping it in the water, and half-naked men diving deep into the river and disappearing for a long time before they reemerged, purified. In the distance, all along the riverbank, we saw many more ghats teeming with pilgrims, all performing their religious duties in a tumultuous silence. And then, in the gathering dusk, loudspeakers began hoarsely chanting long prayers, and many of the bathers came out of the water and stood on the riverbank or the steps to pray and perform complicated yoga exercises. The boatman abandoned his oars and kneeled down to pray while the boat was swept toward the next ghat, where spirals of white smoke rose from a big red funeral pyre. The two tourists and I sat riveted by the sight of the boatman sunk in his prayers while the boat changed direction and floated aimlessly into the middle of the river, and now we could see that while one bank was teeming with people and activity, densely strewn with ghats and temples, the opposite bank was empty and abandoned, with nary a house or a human figure to be seen, evaporating into the void of the sky as if all that crowded holiness dissolved in the middle of the river and turned into nothingness. When the chanting finally stopped, the boatman rose from his knees and picked up the oars with a dreamy look in his eyes. I said to him in a friendly tone, "Shiva," because I had read in Lazar's guidebook that Varanasi was the city of the god Shiva, the Destroyer. His dark face immediately filled with interest, and he nodded his head, but corrected me: "Vishvanath," and, dropping the oars, he spread out his arms to embrace the whole of the universe. "Vishvanath," he repeated, as if to stress that this name was bigger and more important than

that of Shiva. Gently placing my finger between my eyes to sig-
nify the place of the third eye, I repeated softly, "Shiva, Shiva?"
while the two Scandinavians stared. But the boatman stood his
ground, even though he seemed pleased by my knowledge. He
corrected me again—"Triambaka, Triambaka"—and repeated,
"Vishvanath, Vishvanath." When he saw that I was disappointed
by these names, however, he eventually acquiesced and said with
a sly smile, "Also Shiva, also Shiva."

❧❦

When darkness fell, the little porter took me to one of the ghats
where bodies of the dead were burned. First I saw how people
threw flowers and sweets into a well; then, from a little distance,
for the dwarf warned me not to go too close, I stood for a long
time watching a body burn on a funeral pyre while the members
of the family sat in a circle and chatted quietly. I waited until the
fire went out, and in the dark, by the light of a torch, the family
stood up and slowly circled the ashes, and one of them cracked
the skull to liberate the soul into the river, and they gathered up
the ashes to sprinkle them on the water. Only then was I able to
return to our inn, which was already mostly shrouded in darkness. I gave the porter a few rupees and he put his hands together
in thanks, but he did not leave me, for he was afraid that I would
go to the wrong room, so he led me up the pitch-dark steps until
I was standing in front of the door to our room. I knocked lightly
to announce my return, but when there was no reply, I carefully
opened the door. The room was dark and the big beds were
empty. The Lazars appeared to have moved them closer together
in my absence. On the balcony I made out the two heavy silhou-
ettes. When I approached, I found them in their bathrobes, their
hair still wet from the shower. All that was left of the spectacular
view was deep, empty darkness; the temples and the ghats had
completely vanished, and only a few solitary torches still burned
on the banks of the Ganges, with mysterious shadows stirring
around them. Next to the Lazars stood a stool covered with an
embroidered cloth, with plates holding the remains of their supper. They did not notice my arrival, for they were deep in a
conversation. I knocked lightly on the balcony door, and they
both immediately turned their heads, smiling and very pleased to

see me, like parents who had awaited their son. It turned out that in all this time they had not left the room but remained by themselves on the little balcony, content with the distant, general view. "You've been sitting on the balcony all this time?" I marveled. "We're not as young as we used to be," said Lazar complacently, "and this balcony is an experience in itself." He was in a good mood, and he seemed pleased with me too, for succeeding again in not getting lost. His wife invited me to sit down beside them and tell them about my experiences on the river, but Lazar stood up and asked if I had had anything to eat. For a minute I couldn't remember, since I felt no hunger, but when I replied in the negative he urged his wife to get up and clear away their leftovers. "We thought of leaving something for you," he apologized, "but we know you prefer eating alone." His wife said, "Never mind, we'll go down now and get something for him. What would you like to eat?"

"What would I like?" I repeated. "What have they got here?" And when they tried to tell me I interrupted them and said, "It doesn't matter, just something light, whatever you bring. I'm really not hungry, I don't know why."

"Maybe the soul of an Indian fakir has already been incarnated in your body and from now on you'll be satisfied with a starvation diet," Lazar said with a chuckle, still diverted by the idea of reincarnation, which now, given the total darkness and the soft Indian tumult rising from the courtyard, seemed to me correct, even if impossible.

They both said at once, "Go and get washed, and we'll go downstairs and get you something to eat. Maybe you've forgotten, but it's Friday night," and they went out to allow me to get undressed and wash myself in peace and quiet. In some strange way I didn't feel dirty and sticky, even though my trousers had got wet in the river and cow dung had stuck to my shoes; it was as if the boat trip had dipped me in the river too, and the long contemplation of the cremation and the cracking of the blazing skull had purified me with a sense of profound mystery, which had made me forget my hunger and reconciled me to the dirt. But I didn't want to embarrass the Lazars. I washed myself quickly in cold water before they came back. I had a long wait before they returned with a basket of fruit and candies and fresh-smelling chapatis, as well as a big bowl of steaming rice mixed with pieces of boiled mutton; and strangely enough it was Lazar, not his wife, who encouraged and coaxed me to eat, with a tender, absurdly fatherly air, trying to arouse my lost appetite and insisting on adding more and more to my plate, as if the whole great hospital in his charge had now been narrowed down to a single person, on whom he could focus the full strength of his control and concern. His wife sat opposite me, her stomach swelling, her long legs crossed, smoking a slender cigarette and examining me. When I described the cracking of the skull in order to liberate the soul, her face twisted in dismay. "How terrible—why did you look?" But Lazar understood me. "It sounds fascinating, I wish we could have seen it ourselves," he said, as if he were actually sorry we were leaving the next morning by train for Gaya. "Tomorrow?"

"We should have stayed in New Delhi and insisted on getting a direct flight. That's what we should have done," said his wife. "So what do you say?" she asked, as if I had a say in anything that went on here, and she threw the burning cigarette butt over the balustrade. Lazar jumped up to reproach her. "Dori, are you crazy? There are people down there, you'll burn somebody."

"People don't burn so easily." She laughed, but at the sight of my gloomy face she said gently, "I see that you're disappointed." Her glasses glinted in the dark. "A little," I said, "but it doesn't matter, I understand. But still, it seems to me," I stammered, "for your own sake, you should have come down to the river, because from the balcony you can't feel what you feel on the river, inside the thing itself."

"But what is the thing itself?" She sat up with a strange anger. "Burning corpses?"

"No," I answered her, "there's something very strong here. It's hard to explain. Something very ancient—not like historical ruins in Israel, it's not historical, it's real. If you go down, you'll feel that what's happening here, the purification rites and the cremations, has been going on for thousands of years, as if that's the way it's been forever . . ." Now a different smile crossed her face, not the automatic one but a thoughtful smile, as if she were wondering not about what I had said but about me. I felt that I had made a mistake in exposing my feelings to them, and in so doing giving them, especially her, permission to invade my privacy, now that she had talked me into sharing a room with them, something my parents had never done. And in order to stop her I decided not to give her another opportunity to interrogate me but instead to ask her about their sick daughter, about whom nothing had been said up to now, as if we had a kind of tacit agreement not to talk about her. Had she ever suffered from any serious illnesses in the past? I asked. Had she ever been hospitalized?

When the time came to go to bed, we moved the screen between us and I lay down in my pajamas on the folding bed, which was very narrow, intended for a skinny Indian with a wish to mortify himself during his sleep. They made some noise, presumably pushing the beds closer together, and in the end they switched off the little light, and she called out suddenly, "Good night," and her husband said, "Shh, he's already asleep." But I answered in a weak voice, "Good night," suddenly afraid that they might make love in the middle of the night. On the balcony they had seemed close and loving and attracted to one another. And even though I said to myself, They wouldn't do that to me, I remained agitated, and I began tossing and turning in the dark on my narrow bed, until a soft rhythmic snoring reached my ears, and I knew that they were her snores, which I remembered from the train. I waited for him to stop her, but he just got up and went to drink a glass of water and out onto the balcony. Before he returned I fell asleep, but only for a few hours, since a band of musicians passed very close to the inn just before dawn, beating drums and clashing cymbals. One of them broke into song, and when the music faded away I knew that the Lazars too had woken up. Suddenly I heard Mrs. Lazar whispering to her husband in a surprisingly childish, pampered voice, which I wouldn't have imagined her capable of, "Do you love me?" and he replied with a strange decisiveness, "No." But she did not seem upset, and in the same soft, wheedling tone she continued, "Then you should."

"Why?" he replied in affected astonishment.

"Because."

"But why?"

"Because I'm nice."

"But you're terribly obstinate," he said sternly.

"I'm not terrible at all," she answered archly, but he insisted,

"Yes, you're terribly obstinate. You talked us into this room, and the poor boy has to sleep here next to us like a dog."

"Why a dog?" Now she was taken aback, but she didn't lose her self-confidence. "What kind of a way is that to talk? Can't you see that he's perfectly happy and pleased to be with us, even though he's a cold type who doesn't show his feelings?"

"Shh . . . Shh!" Lazar suddenly seemed nervous. "He can hear us."

"Nonsense," she said. "The way those youngsters sleep, nothing wakes them. Come and hold me. Let's go to sleep—I'm afraid of what's waiting for us tomorrow." They must have started kissing, or so I assumed, and I immediately turned over in bed in order to stop them, and they evidently heard something, because the rustling stopped at once, and soon her faint snoring rose again. It suddenly stopped, but I couldn't go back to sleep. And after a long time I got up and walked barefoot, careful not to look, past the two beds, which were indeed a little closer together and bathed in the light of the huge moon slowly rising over the far bank, desolate and a little frightening, of the Ganges.

❧

In the morning they woke me ruthlessly and pressed me to eat my breakfast, which was already laid on the balcony table. Their suitcases were packed, and they had also managed to go down to the river at dawn to see the pilgrims taking their first dip. Soon two elderly Indians arrived to take our luggage, loaded it onto a pushcart downstairs, and led us to the train station through a flood of fresh pilgrims, who had apparently arrived on the night trains and were now on their way to the river. Again I had the feeling that I was in a very ancient place, as if precisely here, in this muddy swarm of humanity, between the large cows stubbornly stuck in the middle of the alleys, the world had been created, or at least begun to bubble. When we entered the frenzied station, I spotted as if by magic the diminutive porter of the previous day in the distance, a suitcase on his back as he led two elderly female tourists in big straw hats, probably to the room we had just vacated. I could not resist the impulse to rush up to him and say good-bye. To my surprise, Lazar's wife hurried after me. The little porter was so moved by our gesture that he removed the suitcase from his back and almost knelt in the middle of the dung and the mud, putting his hands together in the Indian greeting and pleading with us in the little English at his command, "Come back to Varanasi. You didn't see anything."

On the train traveling east we shared our compartment, this time with two brothers in white suits who were returning home to Calcutta after cremating their father's body. At ten o'clock in the morning, after the train left the station, they presented Lazar and me with their cards, and when we saw that one of them was a doctor, Lazar quickly told them about the object of our journey and asked if they knew anything about the hospital in Gaya. Immediately filled with interest and curiosity, they began showering us with advice and ideas. They had never seen the hospital in Gaya, but they knew by hearsay that it was small and poorly equipped, for it sometimes sent specimens to the private laboratory the Calcutta doctor was connected with a consultant and a partner. Accordingly, they advised us to take Einat as quickly as possible to the big hospital in Calcutta, where everything was more reliable. At this point Lazar informed them that I too was a doctor, that we had brought medical equipment with us, and that we had no intention of wandering between Indian hospitals but were going to take the girl home to Israel as quickly as possible. This idea seemed to them basically sound, and they wished us luck and asked if they could peep at our equipment. Now that we were approaching the patient, Lazar too was curious to know what we were bringing to save his daughter, so I opened the knapsack and displayed its contents, explaining what everything was. The Indians listened attentively, as if eager to learn from me, and Lazar took each instrument and examined it carefully, questioning me as to how it worked, as if he believed that by mastering such details he could penetrate his hospital more deeply and strengthen his control over it. His wife sat in absent-minded silence, her liveliness and gaiety extinguished, as if the approaching meeting with her daughter filled her with dread. I measured Lazar's blood pressure, at his request, and found it to be very high, 170 over 110, but I didn't want to upset him before the meeting with his daughter and gave him lower numbers. The Indian doctor asked for the sphygmomanometer and measured his own and his brother's blood pressure repeatedly and at length, but since I didn't ask for the results, he saw no reason to tell me what they were.

When we got off the train at the Gaya station that afternoon and said good-bye to the two Indians—who presented us with their cards again and reminded us that they would be waiting for us in Calcutta if we needed them—we felt that the last part of the trip had passed comfortably enough, and congratulated ourselves on the ease with which we had reached the point that had seemed so remote when we looked at the map lying on Lazar's living room table. "So this is Gaya. What a hole . . ." muttered Lazar as we stood outside the station, contemplating the strange, absolutely un-Indian emptiness around us. All around us were low yellow hills, and the earth was dry and hard. An apathetic porter approached us slowly, but when he heard where we wanted to go he drew back and beckoned to a more energetic friend, who took us to the hospital, which was a rather small three-story building plastered with pale brown clay. "You go in, and I'll wait outside with the luggage," I said to the Lazars, "and don't tell them you brought a doctor, or you'll make the medical staff nervous." Lazar looked at me sharply and said, "You're right. Quite right. Very good thinking." And when I saw his wife's face, rather pale, tired, and ugly, without any makeup, dark glasses covering her unsmiling eyes, I added, "And don't be frightened if she's yellow or even greenish—it's hepatitis, and the color isn't dangerous." They nodded their thanks and went inside. I sat down on the ground next to a ruined fountain, leaned against one of the suitcases, and prepared myself for a long wait. Well, I thought, I'm on duty at last—if I had a time card here, I'd have to get it punched. But fifteen minutes later they emerged from the hospital in a state of extreme agitation. It appeared that their daughter was no longer there; the week before she had been transferred to Bodhgaya, about ten miles from Gaya, since there was no reason to keep her in the hospital any longer, whether because her condition had improved or the opposite neither of them had managed to understand.

In a panic they hailed a passing auto-rickshaw, and we hurried to Bodhgaya over a rough country road winding through soft fields. A sweet breeze caressed our faces, and in the distance, at the end of the plain, poised gently and motionlessly on the horizon, a big yellow Indian sun refused to sink. In just half an hour we were at Bodhgaya, which turned out to be a pleasant religious retreat full of leafy trees, with a broad dirt road leading from one Buddhist monastery to the next. There were no tourists or backpackers to be seen. We seemed to be the only Westerners in the place, but we had no difficulty in finding the right monastery, luxuriant entrance where green creepers twined around a big door. We were welcomed by several Thai monks, who were expecting us and even looking forward to our coming, since the telegram sent to the hospital from Israel had been attached to the patient as a kind of guarantee that she was not anonymous and somebody would soon come to claim her. Here too I stopped in the courtyard and suggested that I should wait outside with the luggage while the Lazars went in, but Lazar's wife insisted that I go in with them, as if she couldn't face meeting her sick daughter without a doctor on hand to calm her. So we went in with all our luggage, since Lazar was unwilling to part from it even in a Buddhist monastery, and we were led through corridors decorated with tattered carpets and statuettes of gods into a dim chamber strewn with big backpacks and rolled-up sleeping bags. Two Japanese girls who were sitting next to a gas burner and drinking tea stood up as soon as we entered the room and stayed in the corner bowing their heads politely and respectfully. The patient, a blonde with cropped hair, lay exhausted in a fetal position on a sleeping bag covered with a gray sheet, a mosquito net folded at her side. Her skin was dry and as green as the bark of a tree, and there was a grubby bandage on her right leg. Her parents went up and knelt down next to her, talking in low voices, stroking her hands and cheeks, trying to joke, but taking care not to kiss her. Lazar's wife tried to flash her automatic smile in order to cheer her daughter up, but in the circumstances her would-be cheerful gesture came out as a strange grimace. The girl was silent and remote, and for a moment she seemed angry with her parents, either because they had come late or because they had come at all. And then I saw the despairing looks as Lazar and his wife turned mutely to me and invited me, the doctor, to approach. I stepped up and bent down next to the patient. Her father introduced me by my full name, and the girl turned her pale green face, whose features I immediately saw to be pure and fine, toward me. Even though I was a stranger to her, she tried to give me the smile she had withheld from her parents. And the flickering light green irises, drowning in the dark yellow, almost orange whites of her eyes, were very like the eyes not of her mother or father but of her grandmother, who had been sitting in their living room and longing, according to Mrs. Lazar, to meet me.

Four

Is it time to speak of falling in love? For the lover is not yet
aware of his state, although in the middle of the night it steals in
and clutches his heart and he wakes up stirred to the depths, as if
falling in love is only a new dominance and not also a servitude
which is liable to drag anyone who persists in it to his doom.
Already he can't go back to sleep, and in his happiness he has to
get out of bed, still not believing that it has actually happened to
him, and, dazed and heavy, he propels his agitated being through
the dark rooms of the house, trying to understand what it is that
has shattered his sleep. And there in the kitchen, next to the
dining table, he discovers her—a strange little girl, left in his
house without his knowledge by one of the neighbors, or perhaps
the cleaning lady, and forgotten there. Still wearing her school
uniform, with a simple childish badge pinned to her chest with a
safety pin, she bends over her books in the faint light of the
moon and a streetlight, merging and filtering together through
the window bars, and does her homework. He whispers to himself, somewhat ironically, It can't be possible that this has really
happened to me, that I've simply fallen in love; I know hardly
anything about her. But he goes on advancing soundlessly
toward the back of the girl, who has been waiting in his heart
and who now ignores him and continues bending over an old,
ink-stained atlas, a chewed-up pencil between her teeth. And already he is gazing breathlessly at the back of her neck, which is
pure and stalklike but also rich in mature delights as it descends
into the school-uniform shirt, which after a long day of study is
still sweet and fresh. Only when he clenches his fists, careful not
to touch her, does she turn to look at him, and with a brisk,
simple movement she tosses her curly head, and her serious,

beautiful face shows no surprise at the stealthy approach of the silent intruder with the knife twisting in his heart.

Even as the pain stuns his heart he tries to reassure himself. It isn't serious, it's a midnight madness, it will pass, it's already passing, it's a bizarre, absurd, superfluous, almost criminal, and also hopeless infatuation, in a minute someone will come and take her away. But the little girl gives him a frank, open smile that does not suit her tender years, as if in the few seconds he stood behind her and lusted after her neck she grew up and understood—understood so much that he panics and tries to cover up his sudden infatuation. He bends coolly over the open atlas, leafs through an exercise book, and asks in pretend irritation, "Haven't you finished yet? Do you have any problems? It's late. Why don't you leave it now?" Her pure face grows even purer, and she places her little hand freely on his pajama sleeve and says, "Shh . . . he's here." And in the long corridor between the dark rooms of the house, the funny old glasses glitter on the nose of the mystery, that skinny, humorless mental patient who is still stubbornly seeking people and events that came to an end long ago.

❧❦

Still without touching her, judging only by the way she lay limply curled on the gray sheet in the corner of the room, I concluded that the young woman's clinical condition was not good and that she may, in Hishin's words, have "managed to do herself real liver damage." I had already noticed how she was hugging herself with both arms, and how with weak but incessant movement she kept scratching and rubbing herself, a classic symptom of accumulated bile salts penetrating the skin. But I smiled, trying not to reveal to her parents, who were standing right behind me, any sign of anxiety or panic. I knew too that there was no point in undressing her now, in front of her parents and the Japanese backpackers, and trying to auscultate her heart and lungs. Obviously I had to perform a blood count and sedimentation rate quickly and obtain the exact bilirubin and glucose levels and liver functions. I had to see the color of her urine and have it tested right away. In the meantime I bent over her on my knees and covered her forehead lightly with my hand to feel her temperature, which seemed worryingly high, and I put my other hand onto her cropped blond head, wondering momentarily whom she had inherited this blondness from, for both Lazar and his wife had dark hair. Then I slid my hand down to her nape and her neck, to feel if there was any swelling in the neck or the thyroid gland, and at the same time I asked her the kinds of meaningless routine questions I usually asked patients in order to gain their confidence and encourage them to reveal, even if unintentionally, additional truths about themselves.

I was glad to see that despite her weakness she seemed eager to cooperate with me, for my main fear when I had begun this trip had been that I would find her so far gone in that she would be completely apathetic, or even resist my efforts to arrive at an exact diagnosis of her condition and take the right steps to bring her home quickly. In contrast to the resistance she seemed to show toward her parents, she answered my questions willingly, if hesitantly, and recalled how it had all begun and what she had felt and where it had hurt most, and she was even able to describe the changing color of her urine since then, and of course what hurt her now, apart from this itchiness that was driving her crazy—for which I was prepared, because after Hishin had forgotten to bring me the articles he had promised, I had managed to read up on the disease in an old English medical encyclopedia I found in my parents' house the night before we left, where the itch was particularly vividly described. "Apart from the itch, what is giving you pain?" I pressed her to go on complaining to her heart's content, and she did so, and although I noticed that she was confusing symptoms associated with the disease with independent symptoms, such as pains in her legs and a heavy feeling in her back, I said nothing and just nodded my head in agreement with everything she said, still stroking her neck, where I felt a slight swelling on the trachea. Perhaps, I thought, the swelling was natural to her, and I dropped my hand in order not to confuse myself with superfluous speculations before I obtained the results of the crucial tests, which had to be given and rushed to the hospital in Gaya immediately. But I couldn't forget the remark made by the Indian doctor in the train, about the unreliability of the laboratory in the Gaya hospital. It was a pity we'd met him, I reflected bitterly, because if we had to start checking up on how reliabile the Indian laboratories were, we would never finish. But I immediately suppressed this idle thought. Even if Hishin had exaggerated my qualities greatly, mainly in order to get his friends off his back, he was well acquainted with my scrupulous thoroughness, and he had trusted it to guide me without making any mistakes that might eventually be discovered in the hospital in Tel Aviv, where malicious professors and sycophantic doctors would lick their lips over them. I was only too familiar with the fact that in medicine everybody always has to have the last word: what should have been done, what shouldn't have been done, and what did more harm than good.

But I knew that here I was in sole charge, and I had to make an immediate decision. Even though it seemed strange to me for a moment that the director of a big, modern hospital, with the best medical minds at his disposal, should be standing here anxiously with his wife in a dark little chamber in a Buddhist monastery at the end of the world, completely dependent on the professional opinion of an inexperienced young resident, who had not yet examined the patient properly but only touched her lightly on the forehead to feel her temperature and felt her neck a little, I stood up to announce my decision.

"We have to perform some essential tests immediately," I explained, "so we'll know where we are and where we're going. Even though her condition's not great, she can be moved. But before that we have to find out a few things, such as the bilirubin and glucose levels, in order to learn how much damage has already been done to the liver. But there's no need to return her to the hospital; we can obtain the samples on the spot and take them to Gaya. In the meantime, I suggest we find a better room and move her into it. She shouldn't be left in this squalor."

A smile now hovered on Lazar's wife's face—not the familiar smile, which still confused me by its ready appearance, but a more inward and personal smile, as if she were wondering at the authoritative tone I had suddenly adopted (which, to tell the truth, originated with Professor Hishin, who always used the first-person plural when he came across a patient or the relative of a patient who appealed to him particularly). The two Japanese girls came out of their corner, bent over the gas burner, and offered us some of the pale tea they had brewed. Lazar's wife hesitated, but Lazar declined the offer, in a hurry to rush off and obey my orders by finding a decent place for us to stay. "You can all wait for me here," he announced. His wife seemed upset by his urge to depart, quickly stiffened, and said, "Just a minute," and Lazar said, "What's the matter?" and she replied, "Perhaps I should come with you."

"But why?" asked Lazar. "There's no need."

But she insisted: "No, I think I should come along to help you." She was already bending over her daughter to kiss her, and promising, "We'll be back soon." Then she turned to me and said, "You stay with her, and if possible start your tests, and we'll be back right away." So saying, she went off with her husband, evidently unable to remain alone not only with me but even with her daughter.

Einat was still lying hugging herself with both arms, scratching and rubbing, sending me a quiet look from eyes as yellow as a tiger's or a hyena's. But in spite of her obviously poor physical condition, I felt no pessimism, for I knew that I had already gained her confidence by the way I laid my hand on her head and felt her nape and neck. From the minute Hishin told me about her, I had harbored the suspicion that I was being sent to an apathetic patient who had lost the will to recover and might even resist my efforts to help her. But it didn't look as if the young woman lying here would be able to mobilize any resistance; she was too absorbed in her frenzied scratching, and she was eager too for strange hands to touch her and even to take part indirectly in the frantic scratching. But I didn't want to hurry to work yet, and although it was beginning to get dark, I first drank the bitter, scalding tea offered by the Japanese girls and asked them to tell me about themselves. They told me that they had arrived in Bodhgaya two days before, directly from Japan, to take an advanced course in meditation in the nearby Japanese monastery, and since there had been no room there they had come here and been given a place to sleep with the sick girl, on condition that they look after her a little. They had tried to take care of her needs without getting infected, and wore cloth masks when they touched her. Yesterday they had taken her into the inner garden of the monastery and fed her the rice gruel that they had cooked for her. But her itch was severe, and the ointments the monks had given her didn't help, and had I brought some good medicine with me? they asked, as if I had come all the way from Israel to treat an itch. "Maybe," I said, "we'll see," and I opened the knapsack and began emptying its contents onto the blanket they spread out for me, angry with Lazar's wife for not staying to help me undress her daughter. But the Japanese girls were very helpful; they brought me a big flashlight to supplement the dim light of the bulb, and then they sat Einat up and helped me take off her stained white robe, and supported her thin white back while I knelt and passed the stethoscope inch by inch over her back and chest to auscultate her lungs and see if they were clear and free of liquids, and of course to listen to her heartbeat, which was completely regular. The two girls watched my examination, pleased that somebody had come to relieve them of the responsibility for the patient, who had been entrusted to their charge maybe as a kind of religious test imposed by the monks. I nodded my head in satisfaction and said to my patient, "Everything sounds fine, Einati," adopting the pet name used by her parents, and then I laid her slowly on her back to feel her abdomen, which was hard and covered with red marks from her incessant scratching. To my surprise, her inflamed liver, which should have been enlarged, appeared to have shrunk so much that it was difficult to palpate in the flat, hard abdomen, as if it had already begun to degenerate. At first I was alarmed, but I immediately said to myself that degeneration couldn't possibly have occurred only two months after the outbreak of the disease. The gall bladder did seem enlarged, and was apparently also inflamed, for the slightest pressure from my fingers was enough to make Einat scream so loudly that the Japanese girls averted their faces. Footsteps were quickly audible in the corridor, and a shaven-headed monk in a robe the color of the setting sun came hurrying up to discover the cause of the scream, which had echoed through the quiet monastery. He spoke no English, and I asked the Japanese girls to explain that I was a doctor from Israel who had come with the girl's parents to take her home.

But the monk remained standing in the doorway, as if he were unable to grasp the connection between my words and the scream of pain uttered by the woman lying half naked on the floor. I felt suddenly disheartened at the possibility of losing my patient's confidence, and rage at Lazar's wife's desertion welled up in me for her. I decided to interrupt my clinical examination and postpone the palpation of the spleen and kidneys to another time. I would have plenty of opportunities later, I said to myself,

and so I changed the dressing on the wound on Einat's leg, which
seemed to me infected but not serious. I put her stained white
robe back on and tried to reassure her. "Don't worry, it's only an
inflamed gall bladder, which is quite natural in hepatitis."
Among the medications I found a tube of cortisone ointment,
which was supposed to relieve the itching, and allowed her to
rub it on her arms and abdomen herself, warning her not to
expect anything more than temporary relief, since the unexcreted
bile salts accumulated under the skin and the itching could be
relieved only from inside. But she thanked me gratefully. While
she smeared herself with the ointment, assisted by the Japanese
girls, I asked one of them to bring the flashlight closer and prepared to draw blood. I have to admit that it gave me a kick to see
them all, including the Buddhist monk, frozen in their places as I
tightened the rubber tube around Einat's thin arm, looked for a
vein, and gently and slowly extracted a syringe full of blood. Not
content with one, I took another one and filled it too. As long as
she's lying here quietly, I thought to myself, I might as well get
two—who knows, a test tube can break or become infected; the
blood's flowing now, and who can tell what might happen tomorrow?

❧✦☙

Now we waited for the Lazars to return. The monk went away,
and one of the Japanese girls took Einat to the toilet with two
transparent sterile containers I gave her for a urine sample and if
possible a stool as well. I remained with the other girl, and made
no bones about asking her for a fresh cup of tea, which she was
happy to give me, adding a little dry cake as well. Since she
seemed intelligent, I asked her what she was looking for in Bodhgaya, and she told me about a local course in a kind of meditation called Vipassana, whose main feature was abstinence from
speech for two weeks. "For that you have to come all the way
from Japan?" I asked with a smile. "Couldn't you keep quiet for
two weeks at home?" But it transpired that silence next to the
Buddha's sacred bo tree had a significance that was different
from silence anywhere else. Then I asked her to tell me something about the Buddha and what his teachings could mean to a
rational, secular man like myself, who had no inclination to mys-

ticism or belief in reincarnation. She tried to explain to me that Buddhism had nothing to do with mysticism but was an attempt to stop the suffering that came from birth, illness, old age, and death, or even the mental suffering incurred by the presence of a hated person or the absence of a loved one. And the way to stop the suffering was to try to become detached and free and thus to attain Nirvana, which was the end of the cycle of rebirths. "Is it really possible to stop the cycle of rebirths?" I inquired with an inner smile, in Hindu irony, and as I asked, Einat returned from the toilet supported by the Japanese girl, who was carefully carrying the two little receptacles, which contained a faintly pink fluid, the color of the tea I had just been drinking. And although my heart froze for a moment at the obviously pathological appearance of the urine, which suggested the presence of blood, I said nothing and betrayed no sign of anxiety. On the contrary, I congratulated Einat on the success of her efforts and took the two little containers and placed them with the test tubes of blood in a padded leather pouch which could be fastened to someone's belt for safe conveyance during a trip. Good for our head pharmacist, I thought admiringly; I mustn't forget to praise him for his foresight and ingenuity when I get back. I went on talking to the Japanese girl about the Buddha and his followers, drinking my third cup of tea while Einat dozed in the fetal position, as if the loud cry she had previously produced had calmed her. I was beginning to feel astonished at the procrastination of her parents, and thinking angrily of Lazar's wife, who even at this difficult hour was no doubt looking for somewhere original to stay.

They finally returned, agitated but also proud of their achievements. Suddenly the room filled with a number of half-naked young Indians, who before our eyes put together two stretchers from bamboo poles and mats, like the ones on which dead bodies were transported to the river. One of them was quickly loaded with our luggage, while the sick girl was carefully lifted onto the other and covered with a floral cloth. In a soft, beautiful twilight hour, our little procession left the Thai monastery with two stretchers held shoulder-high and made its way through the tree-shaded streets of Bodhgaya, passing shacks made of cloth and wood, under the sympathetic gaze of locals and pilgrims. Our destination was a hotel not far from the local river, surrounded by lawns and flower beds, where the Lazars had found a bungalow consisting of three small rooms connected by a passage and a rather dirty kitchenette with a sink and a stove in one corner and a table in the middle, which someone had already heaped with fruit and vegetables, cheeses and chapatis in anticipation of our arrival. For a moment I stood amazed at the transformation of my simple request for a decent room into this massive domestication. Before even asking about the results of the examination I had carried out on their daughter in their absence, both the Lazars burst into a frenzy of organization. Einat was put to bed between clean white sheets in a little room of her own, and Lazar's wife fussed over her and pampered her and went to fetch a vase of fresh flowers from the hotel manager, while Lazar himself attacked the clutter and disorder with a vengeance, opening the suitcases and putting the clothes away in the closets as if he had forgotten all about his hospital and his promise to conclude the trip in ten or twelve days. It was as if all he wanted was to settle down in this little bungalow in the charming Buddhist village, which in comparison to the Indian reality we had seen up to now was a veritable paradise on earth.

But I still hadn't opened my suitcase, only put it on the bed in the little room set aside for me. I was uneasy, not only because of the color of Einat's urine, and the blood, which at first sight looked diseased and saturated with bilirubin, or the enlarged gall bladder, which had made her scream with pain when I touched it, but mainly because of my failure to palpate the liver, as if it had shrunk or degenerated in an alarmingly accelerated process of cell destruction. In which case, I thought, there was a good chance that before long she might develop a sudden internal hemorrhage. The thought terrified me, because if that happened here, in this remote village, all we would be able to do was pray to Buddha. As Lazar stood in the doorway with a strange-looking apron tied around his waist and invited me to come into the kitchen, I pulled myself together and decided to return immediately to Gaya and hand the samples over to the hospital laboratory and at the same time have a look at their equipment, so I would know what would be available to us if we needed it. If, as I feared, the results were bad, it would make no sense to settle down in this funny little bungalow with its dirty little kitchen and big dining table—we should go straight to Calcutta and take her to the hospital recommended by the Indian doctor on the train, so I wouldn't have to cope with any possible deterioration on my own. Strangely enough, the Lazars did not seem worried; perhaps they had expected to find her in worse condition, or perhaps they had put their faith in Hishin's pronouncement that in the last analysis hepatitis was a self-limited disease, and accordingly, after collecting their daughter and transferring her to the bungalow, all they sought was rest. The holy village too appeared to have had a calming effect on them, and they seemed perfectly happy to putter about in their little kitchen with its knives and forks and plates and even a pot bubbling on the stove.

I decided to sow a few seeds of anxiety in the cozy domesticity that was taking over here, and, declining to sit down at the laid table, I announced without undue gravity that I felt obliged to go straight to the hospital at Gaya with the samples I had obtained. I placed the ointment to relieve Einat's incessant itch on the table, between the fruit and the chapatis, and also a few Valium tablets and paracetamol to bring down her temperature, and warned the Lazars not to mask her symptoms by exaggerating the dosage. But I wasn't sure that I had conveyed my anxiety to them, for Lazar greeted my announcement with astonishment. "Are you sure that it's really necessary to go to the hospital now, in the dark?"

"I'm positive," I replied immediately, and added that I might be delayed there until the next morning, because if it turned out that the laboratory was closed at night—something inconceivable in a serious hospital—or even that it couldn't be trusted to give me reliable results, as the Indian doctor from Calcutta had warned us, I would have to look for another. "But where will you find another one here?" asked Lazar with a smile, surprised at this new, stringent side of my character. "I don't know, I'll ask. If I could, I'd go to Calcutta, to that Indian doctor's private laboratory. I trust him, and we have his address on his card."

"To Calcutta? Are you mad?" Lazar leapt up as if he'd been bitten. "How will you get there? It's hell on earth, and it's hours from here."

"Yes, it's far away, but maybe there's a flight from Gaya."

"A flight?" repeated the stunned Lazar. "Are you trying to tell me that you want to fly to Calcutta just for those tests?"

"No, of course not," I stammered. But Lazar wasn't satisfied.

"I don't understand what's gotten into you. What exactly are you looking for?"

"Nothing," I said, "I just want reliable results."

"Reliable." He sighed. "Here, of all places?" And when I said nothing he added, "Perhaps we should just let Einati recuperate here for a few days and go straight home, and they'll do all the necessary tests there." Now I had to protest, although I was still careful not to worry them too much. "Those tests are important," I stressed. "If you say no, that's your right—but then you'll have to explain to me why you dragged me here with you in the first place." And Lazar's wife, who was sitting opposite me with a gray face and slightly untidy hair, wearing a lightweight white blouse which revealed small new freckles on her neck, smoking her slender cigarette in silence, and examining me intently with an expression that I felt radiated a new sympathy toward me, suddenly burst out and said to her husband, softly but firmly, "He's right. Trust him. And if he wants to fly to Calcutta to get reliable results, why not? We can wait; that's why we made ourselves comfortable here. Do whatever you think best"—she turned to me—"and we'll wait here patiently. But have something to eat before you go."

I sat down at the big table, ate quickly, and stood up immediately to get ready, because I still hoped to return the same night. I removed everything except a few drugs and bandages from the knapsack and filled it with a clean shirt, a sweater, underwear, and toiletries, hung my camera around my neck, and was instantly transformed into a wandering backpacker. I fastened the pouch with the samples onto my belt, and took three hundred dollars from Lazar for expenses. His wife made me sandwiches with the chapatis and put exotic fruits in a brown paper bag for me. Before I left I decided to take another look at my patient. She was sleeping, her beautiful face peaceful, only her hands still clutching each other and making sleepy scratching movements. For a moment I was loath to wake her, now that she had finally found rest in a decent bed, but I didn't want to leave without taking the opportunity to palpate her organs. Lazar's wife helped me wake her up and raised the light flannel pajama jacket they had brought from Israel for her. The yellowish chest, the small breasts, and the scratched stomach were again exposed to my fingers, whose special palpation technique had once even aroused the admiration of Hishin himself, who ever since then had called me "the internist." I could now clearly feel how shrunken the liver was, compared to the enlarged gall bladder and spleen. But I was very careful not to hurt her again, because I wanted to regain her confidence. I concluded my examination and covered the thin body. I still wanted to get a stool specimen from her; it wasn't essential, I explained to her parents, but if at all possible, it might prove very helpful. Just as I was about to leave, standing in my green windbreaker, Lazar's wife came out and handed me a little parcel wrapped in newspaper, which I couldn't resist removing so I could look at the color of the stool. It was suspiciously black, as if it contained occult blood. But I said nothing and wordlessly rewrapped the container, which I enclosed in another receptacle. Lazar and his wife accompanied me outside, where a gaudily painted auto-rickshaw was waiting, hired for me by Lazar, who had already begun to exert his organizational gifts on Indian life. "The driver will be at your disposal all the time. I've already paid him there and back, don't worry," he said dryly, as if he was angry with me for giving them new grounds for anxiety instead of reassuring them. Leaning against one another, embracing without an embrace, they stood and watched me as I sat down in the open rickshaw, behind the elderly and grave-faced motorcyclist, who was wearing a towering white turban on his head and who immediately began pulling me into the dark night, as if we were orbiting in a black void.

He took me to Gaya by strange shortcuts, dirt roads winding through fields and orchards, and if there were any houses or shacks in the vast, flat plain, I was unaware of them, for their lights were buried deep inside them. Since the sky was shrouded in a dense gray mist and there wasn't a moon or a single star to be seen, the only sign of life was the white turban floating before me. Nevertheless, I felt quiet and confident as I held tightly to the edges of the swaying seat, the knapsack at my feet, and I was no longer troubled by attempts to decipher the Indian reality. My mind was now occupied by a practical medical reality, at the center of which was the need to diagnose correctly the condition of the sick woman I had left behind, whom I could still see in my imagination, lying in her little room with her parents—who, I now, in the darkness of the night, sensed were afraid of her— tiptoeing around her bed. When the rickshaw began to slow down, I strapped the knapsack onto my back and checked to see that the pouch was snugly fastened to my belt, and the moment we stopped outside the hospital, which I recognized even in the dense darkness, I jumped down and said to the turbaned Indian, "Don't move from here." I ran eagerly up the steps: it had been more than a week since I had been in a hospital, and I missed even the smell.

But the smell that greeted me here was utterly different from the familiar one of Lysol and feces, or of drugs and ether, sometimes mingled with the smell of boiled vegetables. And it wasn't the smell of the dead either, with which I was also familiar, but simply the smell of rot that violently assailed me. I stopped in the doorway, took a large gauze pad out of the knapsack, sprinkled it with iodine, and tied it onto my face with a bandage, like a surgical mask, and then I was able to enter the corridors to look for the laboratory. It was possibly thanks to this orange bandage on my face and not to the fact that I announced myself to be a doctor that someone paid attention to me and led me to the laboratory, which was situated in a courtyard at the back of the hospital, in a big, old hut besieged by silent patients, mainly women squatting on the bare ground with ragged children by their side. There nobody was impressed by my orange-stained mask, and I had to push my way to the head of the line and force my way into the hut, toward a very dark-skinned but noble-looking middle-aged woman, tall and thin as a slab of black marble, dressed in a flimsy rainbow-colored sari, with a big red third eye painted between her eyes. She was the lab supervisor, perhaps a clerk or perhaps a technician, slow in her movements and apparently also very disorganized, because her desk was untidily heaped with dozens of cards and lab results in different colors, among which she rummaged for the test numbers in order to give the results to the people crowding around her. At first she persisted in ignoring me, even though I had already removed the mask and explained that I was a doctor, but at last she turned to me and asked me what I wanted, and when I told her and added that I was prepared to pay double if the tests were done at once, she looked down at me from her towering height and said with a faintly contemptuous expression that a hospital belonging to Buddha, who was also the god of beggars, did not take payment, but if I wanted to make a donation there was a box for this purpose at the main entrance. "Certainly, I'll make a donation at once," I promised, and hurried to take the test tubes and containers out of the pouch. At first she recoiled. "Not here," she said, waving me away, "not here, there's a special counter. Go and stand in the line." But finally she gave in and told me to write down which tests I wanted on some hospital notepaper. I wrote it all down, and added a request for liver-function tests; I signed my name and gave the number of my Israeli medical license, and needless to say, I avoided mentioning the fact that until a few days before my patient had been hospitalized in this very hospital, in order not to give rise to any unexpected bureaucratic complications. She glanced at my list, put a big red question mark next to "liver-function tests," said that she was not sure if they could do them here, casually wrapped the blood and urine samples in the notepaper—without even bothering to secure it with tape or rubber rings—and threw them into a big cardboard box full of dusty test tubes, some empty and others full of strange-colored fluids. I thanked her, but repeated my request to have the tests done as quickly as possible; if necessary, I said, I was willing to step into the laboratory myself and help. "My patient," I said, "is burning with fever in Bodhgaya, and as soon as we know the results we can begin to treat her." But then the noble Indian woman suddenly flared up. "Everyone here wants to know, everyone here is waiting, everyone here is sick, everyone was sent by a doctor, nobody comes to have blood tests for fun," she scolded me angrily, as if I were a boy. Why did I think I was entitled to an answer without waiting my turn? Was it only because the people standing here had darker skins than mine? And with a long, slender hand she waved me contemptuously away.

Without understanding why I felt so deeply insulted by this woman, I had a momentary impulse to ask her to return the samples so that I could take them somewhere more reliable. But I kept quiet. Feeling both mortified and at a loss, because I didn't know where else to go, nor when to come back for the results, I left the laboratory hut. For some time I hung around in the courtyard, pacing to and fro among the Indians waiting in the dark, peeping through the window at the tired lab technicians sitting crowded together in the dim light, big bottles of serum at their sides, peering through ancient microscopes at the blood and urine samples that had been brought there in little blue glass jars.

In the end I got fed up with this aimless hanging around and returned to the place where I had left my rickshaw, but it was now surrounded by many similar vehicles and I couldn't recognize it. I had to go from one rickshaw to the next and examine the sleepy drivers curled up on their backseats before I found my driver, who, luckily for me, had kept his regal white turban on in his sleep. "Take me to the river," I instructed him, for from the day I had arrived in India I had found myself drawn to rivers. But the sleepy driver smiled at me with his gaping, ancient, toothless mouth and tried to explain that there was no river in Gaya now. "There's no river now?" I said in bewilderment. "But there's a river on the map in the guidebook." There was a river but there was no water in it, he tried to say, helping me in the meantime onto the seat, still warm from his sleep, covering me with a tattered blanket, and pulling his rickshaw silently out of the heap of rickshaws surrounding it. He drove me to the bank of the river, which was indeed there, where the guidebook said it was, but almost entirely dry, even in this winter season. In the depths of the dry riverbed a fire was burning, and by its shape I guessed it was a funeral pyre. The figures squatting around it in such celestial serenity were presumably the relatives of the dead man, helping to liberate his soul.

I got out of the rickshaw, opened the knapsack, and took out my sweater, for there was a chill in the air, and began carefully descending into the broad, dry riverbed, drawn to something whose nature was not clear to me and with the tall, thin Indian woman's reprimand still burning inside me. But why did I feel so insulted? I tried to examine myself. What was happening to me? Was I hurt because she had made light of my concern? Lazar and his wife did not appear worried; they did not seem aware of the fact that their daughter was really sick, that she was in real danger, that her disease was not simply going to run its course and cure itself. A wave of pity for the sick girl and her doctor surged up in me, and as I climbed down the bushy bank toward the funeral pyre, little tears stung my eyes. What the hell was this? Why was I really so hurt and angry? Hishin had the right to choose not to keep me in his department, but what right did he, a doctor I had always admired, have to say contemptuously "a self-limited disease"? What did he know, that Hishin? And I trembled as if he were standing before me. But I didn't stop; I went on advancing between the bushes and over the pebbles lying on the dry bed of the creek, between the rampant wildflowers, colorless in the dark, picking my way carefully past the sleeping bodies of pilgrims or beggars covered with blankets and cardboard boxes, wiping away the unexpected tears, scoffing at myself for turning into a crybaby, here of all places, in a place that was supposed to make us pampered Westerners calm and humble in the face of real suffering.

The Indians sitting around the fire apparently sensed that I was making my way toward them, and they started getting up to welcome me, but also to prevent me from approaching the pyre and desecrating the sacred rite by my alien presence. Judging by their attire, they were urban Indians of quite a high class, and they behaved with both firmness and tact. They surrounded me, putting their hands together on their chests in the traditional greeting, apparently intent on barring my way. I joined my hands in an imitation of their gesture, to signal my sympathy and good will, and then I felt someone touching me lightly. It was my rickshaw driver, who had secretly followed me to see that I didn't get into trouble. He spoke favorably of me to the people, but he too tried to prevent me from approaching the pyre, which was burning brightly and cheerfully, as if nothing was lying on top of it. I took the knapsack off my back and sat down on a big, damp boulder. The remnants of the river were gurgling nearby, and the night was cold and misty. Now that the Indians saw I had given up any intention of breaking through to the fire itself and had seated myself to one side, they calmed down, and one of them offered me a cup of scalding tea, perhaps as a sign of thanks for my restraint. I took the cup gratefully, but before I raised it to my lips I saw in astonishment that the body lying wrapped up next to the pyre and waiting to be burned was not yet dead but that of a mortally sick or dying man, who had apparently been dragged here in order to die in the right place. Every now and then someone would bend down to examine him, to stroke him, or to whisper to him, to encourage him with hopes for the waiting fire. Now I understood why they had been so insistent about barring my way. I could no longer drink the tea, and after a while, when the sound of an airplane overhead made all heads turn upward, I quickly poured the yellowish liquid onto the ground. Bright red lights now appeared in the mist, and a large old plane, whose propellers made a pleasant purring sound, came down very low, right over our heads, and continued flying along the riverbed until it landed. The Indians began talking about this night flight from New Delhi, which stopped at Gaya and went on to Patna and Calcutta. "Calcutta?" My excitement flared. They all knew the old plane and spoke affectionately about the night flight, which in an hour or two would take off for Patna and would reach Calcutta at dawn. Without another moment's hesitation I stood up, returned the empty cup, and said to my driver, who was sitting there in his tall turban, looking pleased with himself and drinking his second cup of tea. "Take me quickly to the airport. I want to go to Calcutta." "No chance," he said without budging from his place. "That plane is always full." But I insisted. The possibility of ascertaining not only the bilirubin level but also which liver functions had been impaired, especially with regard to the glucose level and clotting factors (a deficiency which could cause an internal hemorrhage), was so crucial that it justified an attempt to get to Calcutta, even if Lazar, who had never been there in his life, called it "hell on earth." I congratulated myself on having had the foresight to take double samples of everything from Einat, so that I wouldn't have to go back to the tall Indian woman in the laboratory.

The flight was indeed full, just as my rickshaw driver had warned me, but after I had repeatedly explained to the clerks at the airport that I was an English doctor who needed to take urgent medical tests to a laboratory in Calcutta—I even displayed the blood and urine samples as evidence—they agreed to provide me with a little folding seat at the back of the plane, apparently meant for the attendants, whom I paid for the ticket, which seemed very cheap. I gave the rickshaw driver a few rupees and a note to take to the Lazars in Bodhgaya, in which I outlined my plans to take the samples to Calcutta and return the next day, by train or plane, with reliable results. Don't worry, I concluded ironically, I'll come back from hell too—you know that I don't get lost. I added quotation marks to the word "hell," to show that I was quoting Lazar but also to alleviate my own anxiety, and signed "Yours, Benjamin." It was almost midnight. I took one of the three large sandwiches Lazar's wife had prepared out of my knapsack and ate it with relish, and I thought about the two of them and how compatible they were. Even their attitude toward their daughter was the same: a strange, detached compassion, and something like fear of her as well. Would Lazar's wife also have called Calcutta hell? And what did Lazar know about hell? He must know sinister places in his hospital, like the morgue. Let's say that Calcutta was hell—the doctor and his brother whom we had met in the train looked perfectly cheerful, and they lived there. And even if the poverty and suffering were worse than anything we had seen up to now, so much the better. On my return to Bodhgaya I would have a certain advantage over the Lazars, which would establish my authority as a doctor if the dire circumstances I feared arose. They were too sure of themselves; the deep bond between them made them smug. And when, after midnight, the propellers turned and the plane took off with an ease that was surprising in view of its age, I saw the takeoff as a sign of the rightness of my decision and fell asleep at once.

I dreamed that I returned to the bungalow, which was no longer in Bodhgaya but in some other town, still in the east but not in India. The kitchen was much larger than in reality, and the wooden table had given way to the glass table in the Lazars' living room in Tel Aviv, with other furniture from their apartment too, and also furniture from my parents' place in Jerusalem. The motorcycle I had left in my parents' yard stood covered up next to the sink. Only my patient was missing. The Lazars were both sitting sadly at the dining room table, waiting for me to return from Calcutta with the results of the tests, and I suddenly realized that I was very late, and that instead of returning the next day, as I had promised in my note, I had returned after a few weeks, perhaps even months. But they were still waiting for me, faithful to the promise they had given my parents to look after me. Where's my patient? I asked in boundless distress, and they looked at each other, and Lazar remained seated. His wife stood up and led me to the corner, where a strange little girl was lying wrapped in a gray sheet. He's arrived, her mother whispered.

With the first signs of light the plane began the descent to fog-enshrouded Calcutta, where solitary lights glittered. The city looked like a huge ancient factory where work had stopped but which still had a cloud of smog hanging over it. Although it was very early in the morning, aimless crowds were already milling around, and the people looked as if they were floating, as if the law of gravity had been abolished here. The thought flashed through my mind that if I wanted a sign that I had indeed descended to the lowest rung of human suffering, this was it. In New Delhi or Varanasi even the beggars and cripples had some kind of direction, but here all direction had been lost, and people were milling around together in a vortex into which I too was soon swept, unable to find my way out. Naked beggars clung to me, leprous and limbless, and it was impossible to shake them off. I was thirsty and tired from the flight, but I vacillated between having something to drink here, in the heart of the commotion, next to maimed and dying people lying next to the walls, and waiting until I reached the city itself. In the end my thirst won and I went over to one of the stalls and asked for tea with milk, the way my English mother made it. I chose two postcards with stamps already printed on them, and took another one of the sandwiches prepared by Lazar's wife out of my knapsack and ate it standing up while I scribbled a few affectionate words to my parents in my small, neat handwriting, telling them why I was in Calcutta. The stall-keeper showed me where to find the mailbox, which was red and big and very British, inspiring me with confidence that the letter I dropped into it would indeed reach its destination. The other postcard I put away in my pocket, and feeling somewhat recovered, I extricated myself from the human swarm. Without hesitating I chose not a rickshaw but a proper cab, which took me straight to the laboratory whose address was printed on the card.

The dream I had had on the plane disturbed me but also served me a warning: I must not get lost here. My purpose was to ascertain the liver functions, the two transaminases, the clotting factors, and the glucose levels. I had full confidence in the Indian doctor and his brother. They were connected with the University of Calcutta. But when the cabdriver dropped me outside a regular apartment building in a little alley, without any sign of a medical laboratory, my spirits fell, and I would not release the cabbie until he led me to the doctor's door. To my surprise, the shabby apartment building, which was only a few stories high, possessed a little elevator, but it was impossible to tell if it was working, for there were a number of people sleeping in it, huddled together like a tangle of black snakes. At this early hour the stairwell too was full of sleeping people. The cabbie immediately removed his sandals and stepped over them barefoot, and I too took off my shoes and tried to glide over them in my socks. In that way we reached my doctor's flat, where we found a card like the one in my pocket pinned to the door. The cabbie was not content with leading me to the door but went inside to drag the doctor out of bed. The doctor, with only a narrow loincloth on his smooth, slender body, which looked like that of a boy, was not at all surprised to see me standing before him. He cried joyfully, "All the time I've been saying to my brother, Dr. Benjamin will have to come to us in the end if he wants to know the truth. But who would have believed that he would come so early?" He laughed and ushered me into a big, dim room full of carpets and ornaments, where two little girls were sleeping on the couch. He removed them quickly to the next room and returned after a few minutes in a pale European suit. He immediately took the samples from me, listened attentively to what I had to say about my patient's condition and my suspicions, and in a clear firm hand wrote down the particulars of the tests I wanted performed, with which he appeared to be thoroughly familiar. Nothing seemed to him either impossible or superfluous. Finally he stood up and said, "Give me half a day and my brother and I will have all the results ready for you. If you don't make the afternoon flight, you can always take the five o'clock train, which reaches Gaya at dawn." He then spread a thin, colorful rug on the couch where the little girls had been sleeping, beat the cushions lightly, and turned them around. He scattered a few joss sticks in an ashy incense bowl, lit them to banish the smells of the night, and said, "You can rest here and even sleep, and return tonight refreshed to the patient for whose sake you came all the way to Calcutta."

❧❦

I found myself in a rather pleasant room, with chains of flowers and little statues of gods with elephant and monkey faces. The subtle scent of incense pervaded my senses. There was no sign of hell here. I immediately sat down on the couch in my socks and thought how strange my journey to this place had been, and wondered whether it had really been purely out of concern for my patient or whether I wanted to prove to Hishin what a devoted and determined doctor I was and how far I was prepared to go to obtain all the relevant data about my patient's condition. I took the second postcard out of my pocket and wrote in a rather lighthearted vein: "Dear Professor Hishin, Regards from Calcutta, which is the lowest of the low as far as human suffering and poverty are concerned. I arrived here alone to obtain a reliable and detailed diagnosis for our patient, whose condition is more worrying than you thought. The Lazars are nice and India is interesting. Yours, the 'ideal' man." I wanted to add, "whom you seduced," but I stopped myself. What would he understand by it? Even the word "ideal," which I had put in quotation marks, seemed superfluous. What if he didn't remember? I put the card in my pocket. It would reach him after I arrived home, so what was the point? I took off my sweater and heard light footsteps behind the door. Did the doctor's wife know who I was and what I was doing here? But the couch was soft, and I stretched out on it in profound weariness, thinking to myself, This is a little paradise in the midst of the hell which I haven't yet really felt, and maybe I won't feel it at all, and in any case I have no intention of boasting about having been in it.

But in spite of my tiredness I couldn't really fall asleep, but only dozed, because the sleepers on the stairs began to wake up, and the residents tried to chase them away, and the elevator, which had apparently been relieved of its nocturnal refugees, began creaking up and down on its cables, and the doctor's two little girls opened and shut the door to peek at me, trying to wake me up, until I finally had to invite them in. They hesitated, but in the end came shyly into the room, dressed in their school uniforms, which consisted of flimsy pink saris, with blue ribbons in their hair and satchels on their backs. I tried to get them to talk to me and to amuse them by making funny faces, but they didn't laugh; maybe they thought my grimaces were natural to a Western face. In the end their mother came to take them to school, but she was hesitant about leaving me alone in the apartment. "In that case, perhaps I should go out and walk around the town a little. Is there a river here?" I asked. And of course there was a river, which was called the Hooghly River, with ghats of its own, and there was a fort here too, called Fort William, which was situated in the beautiful Maidan of Calcutta. It would be a pity not to see the sights, I thought, and said good-bye to my hostess. When I went downstairs I counted the stairs and made a note of their number, so I wouldn't have any problems finding the right apartment. I went outside and noted landmarks to help me identify the alley too, and walked up and down to practice remembering the location of the building, but when I left it and turned into the main street, I was immediately surrounded by the milling crowds and realized that I was the only foreigner there. I felt suddenly weak, and I remembered my dream. I had to be careful not to go too far, to watch myself, because I had to get back; Lazar's wife had placed her trust in me. I wasn't a tourist, I was a doctor on duty, and I had to get back tonight to my patient, whose delicate jaundiced face came into my mind from time to time, accompanied by the meaningless smile flashing in her mother's eyes. I decided to forgo the river and its ghats, as well as the important fort and the beautiful Maidan, and to confine my movements to a safe, narrow circle, without losing touch with the street. Every half-hour or so I would return and stand in front of the building, and sometimes I would go upstairs and knock on the door to see if the results had already arrived. In one of the nearby streets a building with a big crowd jostling in front of it attracted my attention. At first I thought it was another temple, but when I went closer I saw that it was a big old cinema, covered with colorful posters. On the sidewalk lay an old woman who appeared to be dying, with some lepers sitting next to her looking with burning eyes at the people going into the cinema. Perhaps I had better see India in a movie, I thought. I bought a ticket and entered a big, dark hall with crumbling carvings on its many pillars. Rows of heads greeted my eyes, some of them turbaned and others bare—smooth-shaven, wild, or curly. As I walked in they almost all turned, as if there were something unique and strange about my smell or footsteps. I selected a seat in one of the middle rows, and they all stood up eagerly to let me pass and smiled at me encouragingly. But before long an usher with a badge pinned to his chest arrived and started persuading me to move to another seat, apparently a seat of honor. At first I tried to refuse, but he pointed to the people around me and said, "Bad people, bad people," and they all smiled at us. Again I tried to refuse, but he insisted, coming all the way down the row and gripping my arm forcibly, pointing once more to the people around me, who never stopped smiling. In the end he led me to an armchair upholstered in red velvet, which had grown pink and stubbly over the years, like the pelt of a mangy old animal. And on the seat which had perhaps known guests more notable than myself, I sat and watched a movie without subtitles, in which a lean young Indian movie star suffered the pangs not of hunger but of love.

When I returned to the apartment at midday, I found not only the little girls and their mother but also the doctor and his brother, waving the results of the tests. My suspicions were right. There was liver damage. The coagulation system was impaired. The bilirubin was very high, nearly thirty. The ALT had risen from 40 to 180, and the AST was also elevated. Hypoglycemia was causing the extreme fatigue. The patient needed an urgent injection of glucose, and perhaps also something to replenish the depleted clotting factors, the simplest thing being a unit of fresh blood. They also showed me results of tests I hadn't requested. There was no doubt that they had done a thorough job—spent the whole morning running from one laboratory to the next and squeezing the maximum information out of the samples I had given them. Now I had to get back to my patient as quickly as possible; I didn't have a minute to waste. I took out my wallet and gave them a hundred dollars, a very generous sum, not only in their eyes but in mine. However, I added a condition: that they wouldn't leave me to get back by myself but would put me on the right train for Gaya, since there was no hope of getting on a flight. They were astonished and delighted by the fee and promised to make a generous donation to charity with part of it, and they said that of course they would put me on a good train to Gaya, but first they wanted to know if I had seen anything of Calcutta. "Very little," I replied. "It's a rough place, but it's not hell on earth." They burst into hearty laughter, but insisted that parts of the city were indeed hellish, as if being a hell on earth constituted a major tourist attraction they were reluctant to give up. On the way to the train station they would show me places that would really depress me, but on condition that I first sit down to feast. I wasn't hungry, and my anxiety for my patient was beginning to overwhelm me, but I couldn't refuse the blandishments of my genial hosts. In the meantime a lot of little dishes arrived, full of every possible kind of food in a variety of original shapes and colors. The doctor and his brother sat down next to me with the little girls in their arms, and they all watched to make sure that I didn't miss tasting a single dish. I soon felt full and slightly nauseated. The grave looks of the dark little girls added to my anxiety. I stood up and announced apologetically that the results of the tests had deprived me of my peace of mind. "I beg you, my friends, in the name of God, let's go, and if you want to show me something on the way, maybe you can drop me next to the river, because I don't know what's gotten into me, but ever since I arrived in India I've been drawn to rivers as if I've fallen in love with them." Although they were sorry at the interruption of the feast, they quickly did as I asked and took me to the Maidan, a vast green expanse overlooking the river, at the northern end of which stood a tall column, where they took a photograph of me with my camera and posed for me to take one of them. But I wasn't satisfied with looking at the river, I wanted to go right down to the water. They took me down, and when they saw me suddenly bending over and dipping my fingers in the chilly water, they bowed their heads in gratification. This private and independent dip reinforced their opinion that I was worthy of seeing hell from within, and not only from the window of a speeding car but very slowly, in a man-drawn rickshaw, through terrible alleys full of vast piles of stinking garbage, in some of which decaying human beings were crawling, dying from the moment they were born, cast-off humans twitching like broken insects squashed beneath a giant boot. For an entire hour they led me through streets that had apparently once been pleasant and civilized, in which fine houses had once stood, and that now looked as if they had been ravaged by a terrible leprosy, and the pain was even greater because of the vestiges of beauty that were still evident. And so we advanced in the clear winter sunshine, I in the slow rickshaw and my two bearded escorts in their white suits walking beside me, occasionally taking a coin out of their pocket and placing it in the palm of a dying man or a child, seemingly pleased by my interest. "Could hell be worse?" they asked, turning to me in the end with a strangely triumphant expression as we entered the station.

Although the train trip lasted nine hours, I couldn't sleep a wink. The sights of Calcutta mingled with the gnawing anxiety about Einat had turned into a single entity weighing on my heart. In the end, when sleepiness almost overcame me, I went and stood in the corridor, afraid that Gaya might slip past in the night. After midnight I was ejected onto the platform, which looked like the last station at the end of the world, and picked my way carefully through the rickshaws standing outside in the hope of finding the rickshaw driver with the white turban, but he wasn't there. Another, younger driver took me to Bodhgaya on a country road winding through pleasant hills outlined by a slender crescent moon. The hotel by the river was closed and dark, and for a moment I forgot where the entrance to our little bungalow was. On my last legs, I walked around the building, and for the first time on this trip I felt my composure collapse, and a painful, unfamiliar sob escaped my lips. Would I really have to stay outside all night in the chill rising from the river, just because I wanted to be ideal not only in the eyes of the Lazars but in my own eyes too? I sat down under one of the large trees to recover, and remembered I still had one sandwich left, which I ate in order to ward off sleep. Then I stood up, heartened as if by a glass of good wine, and walked around the grounds again until I recognized the bungalow. I knocked lightly and the door opened at once. It was Dori, without her glasses, her hair loose, in a thin nightgown that outlined her full body and her big, firm breasts. I saw that her slippers had high heels. At first she seemed about to bestow only one of her automatic eye-smiles on me, but her emotions got the better of her and she spread out her arms and embraced me with forbidden warmth. For a moment we lingered in the gloomy kitchen, where dirty pots stood on the stove, but Lazar immediately appeared and gripped my head in a powerful embrace of both anger and deep affection. "What's the matter with you? Where did you disappear to? In a little while we would have left without you! Just don't tell me that you took those tests all the way to Calcutta!"

"Didn't you get my note?" I questioned him with a strange pride. "Was it really necessary to go all the way there?" said Lazar as if he hadn't heard me. "Yes, it was necessary," I replied with a new firmness. "I got all the results possible in a reliable form, and now I know where we stand."

"Where?" asked Lazar, who seemed offended by the way I had spoken. "In a minute," I said. "I'll tell you in a minute. Just let me check on Einat first." And just as I was, without washing my hands, I went into the room where a yellow light illuminated the sick girl, who was still scratching herself in her restless sleep and who had no idea of the dangerous time bomb ticking inside her. I crouched down by her bed and laid my hand on her forehead. The fever was the same as before. Lazar and his wife looked at me impatiently. Her condition in the past twenty-four hours had not been encouraging, and now I had come back with the results of the tests and I was bending over her in such concern. I have to worry them, I said to myself, otherwise they won't cooperate with me; otherwise the authority I'm going to need here will be compromised. I held her limp wrist to take her pulse. Her green eyes opened wide in her thin, beautiful face, but she didn't smile like her mother. "Well?" said Lazar, irritated by my performance. "In a minute. Just let me wash my hands," I said, and went into the kitchen. Lazar's wife handed me a towel and soap, and I smiled at them, turned to Lazar, and said, "As far as Calcutta's concerned, you were right. But there are good people there, and you won't believe it, I actually saw a movie."

Five

But even supposing that he has really fallen in love, what can he do about it? he says to himself with a gloomy smile, his eyes caressing the supple back of the little girl bending over the atlas and gnawing her pencil. She has to belong to somebody, he reassures himself, somebody who will come to fetch her. But the thought that the little girl has been abandoned in his kitchen goes on percolating in him, and with a new and pleasant lust, which can still, he believes, be controlled, he lays his hand lightly on her slender shoulder, in order to encourage her. He leans over the tablecloth spread out in front of him in its blue, green, and yellow, sweetly reading the names of towns and countries, and says to her in a tone of mild rebuke, "But what else is there to look for here, if this is the place?" And he lays his finger on a greenish stain crossed by the blue lines of rivers and announces firmly, "There, that's the right answer. That's enough studying now— it's late." And while a sharp little knife twists in his heart, he closes the atlas and the workbook, opens the safety pin, and removes the school badge from the pocket of her blouse, feeling at the tips of his fingers the outlines of the childish breast, and now he has to ask himself what she's feeling, and what she's capable of understanding, and if he can kiss her without endangering himself.

He plucks up the courage to lay still lips on her forehead, listening to the lonely noise of the refrigerator in the silence of the night, and he goes on, kissing her eyes, licking the tip of her earlobe, and says to himself, So far and no further, otherwise you're doomed. But the little girl doesn't sense his desperation; she closes her eyes wearily and opens her mouth wide in a little yawn, until he can't stop himself and pokes his burning tongue into the pink mouth, to lick the residue of candies sucked during

the day. But this can't possibly be love, he explains to himself,
only a momentary, passing infatuation. Will she understand? His
hand clutches her between her legs, and suddenly he swings her
up to the ceiling, feeling the lightness of her childish body, so
that she can enjoy gliding through the air after such a long day of
study. And he believes that this strenuous effort to amuse her will
prove the purity of his intentions.

But to his annoyance he feels the lust rising in her light little
body as it swings through the air, for otherwise why, instead of
bursting into uninhibited childish laughter, is she closing her
eyes, and parting her lips in a soft spasm of pleasure, and grow-
ing heavy in his hands, and dropping down and wrapping her
slender arms around his neck, and kissing him warmly, blinding
him with her curls? Can it be possible, he asks himself in sur-
prise, for such a little girl to possess lust? And very gently he lays
her on the big kitchen table, and in his mind a new thought
flashes. Perhaps she is sick, perhaps she is dying, and this will be
the last happiness he can give her. How can he withhold it from
her? And he steps back, takes off her sneakers and her white
socks, which in the depths of this marvelous night, after the long
day of study, have inexplicably preserved their freshness. Breath-
lessly, he bends down and cups two plump feet in his hands to
warm them with light kisses, even though they need no warming,
for they are blazing with lust. And even if she isn't dying yet, he
goes on reflecting painfully, perhaps she is an orphan who is
about to be sent away into some distant exile, and it is the place
of her exile that she is seeking in the ink-stained atlas. And so he
carefully removes the pale blue blouse, noticing the little moles
sweetly spotting her shoulder next to the straps of the childish
white undershirt, which is all that is covering her now, and he
says to himself, who could blame me now if I just washed her
with soap and water before she goes to sleep? But the delicate
navel, opening in front of him like a third eye, casts him into
confusion, and he turns around in despair to look for help.

But is there really any help to be had from the lean and serious
mystery, which finally emerges from his hiding place behind the
old refrigerator humming in its loneliness, and puts on his cheap
metal glasses, one of whose lenses is cracked from top to bottom,
the better to see with his somber, humorless gaze the disheveled
little girl sprawled out on the table, who—the would-be lover

now realizes in his despair—is apparently his delinquent little daughter, who waits at the end of the school day next to the gate of the mental institution, in case he is released, and then she can trail behind and accompany him on his sudden visits, which are all subject to the same obsession: that the earth stands still, and every hour is eternal and sufficient unto itself, and nothing is ever lost.

彩

After washing my hands well, I injected my sleepy patient with 100 cc's of glucose, because if there was real liver damage, even normal functioning of the alpha cells in the pancreas would fail to produce enough glucose to overcome the deficiency. The change was rapid, almost dramatic, and before long there was a marked improvement in Einat's mood. She got out of bed and, yellow and emaciated, joined us at the kitchen table, where Lazar and his wife had already prepared a surprisingly lavish midnight feast. At first I wanted to tell them frankly about my concern over the findings I had brought back from Calcutta, centering above all on the coagulopathy, which might cause sudden internal hemorrhage. But a soft and wondering look from Einat, as if she had only just been struck by the actuality of my presence next to her parents, held me back. In any case, I assumed that in spite of his rich hospital experience, Lazar would not be able to understand the subtleties of organic processes, especially those associated with the coagulation system, which are somewhat obscure even to us doctors. I therefore buried my concern for the time being, and in spite of my exhaustion I tried to sample the food on the heaped plate set before me by Lazar. His wife's eyes kept beaming at me, as if to let me know that not only was she happy at my safe return, but she also understood and perhaps even approved of my trip to Calcutta. Lazar hastened to announce that he too had not been idle in the meantime, and he already had an almost complete outline for our return journey: the day after tomorrow a flight from Gaya to Varanasi, and from there, after a wait at the airport, on to New Delhi, in the hope of getting onto the direct flight to Rome on Thursday, and from Rome the Friday afternoon El Al flight to Israel. He and his wife had managed to get all this worked out at the travel agency they had found in Gaya, which luckily possessed a fax. "You went to Gaya with him?" I asked, turning to Dori, unable to believe that her inability to be alone had led her once again to desert her sick daughter. "Only for two or three hours," she answered quickly, blushing slightly in embarrassment, as if she had heard the underlying rebuke in my words, "and we left a nice Indian maid we found in the hotel with Einat."

"I'm exhausted," I announced, narrowing my burning eyes, and I began getting out of my chair and propelling myself toward my bed before I collapsed on the big table itself. The two of them jumped up, alarmed by the intensity of the fatigue that had suddenly overtaken me, and rushed to support me, and they must have helped me to undress and take off my shoes as well, because when I woke up twelve hours later—buttoned up in my pajamas, wrapped in a white blanket, with reddish light strewn around me like pomegranate pips, signaling with its pleasantness the last hour of the afternoon—I didn't remember having done these things myself.

But I did remember Lazar's wife laughing long and loud, either because of my sudden collapse into their arms or because of my objections to their undressing me. Now it was quiet in the dark little bungalow. The two Lazars were absent, and their sick daughter, and also perhaps her doctor, had been left in the care of a gentle Indian girl in a blue sari, who when she saw me getting out of bed stood up straight in my honor and put her hands together in the traditional greeting. In reasonable English she told me that Lazar and his wife had gone to Gaya to arrange for our flights. I felt strangely insulted: it hadn't occurred to them to consult the doctor they had brought all this way, as if one shot of glucose were enough to solve the whole problem. I dressed and shaved quickly before going in to examine my patient, whose limpness told me that her condition had deteriorated again even before I reached her bedside. I was accompanied by the Indian girl, who did not realize that I was a doctor and apparently took me for a family relation. The effect of the glucose shot had been short-lived. Einat's temperature had risen, and her skin was even yellower than before. But even more worrying was the possibility that she had not passed a good amount of urine for several days. I began questioning her as I changed the dressing on her leg, and she answered rather vaguely: the hepatitis had already lasted a month, and the borders between health and sickness had grown hazy. I helped her to take off her shift and asked her to lie on her back, so that I could feel not only her shrunken liver but also her kidneys, which were a little enlarged. The Indian girl watched me curiously as I avoided touching her exposed breasts, which in comparison to her skinny body were actually rather full. I had already heard young doctors complaining about the harmful effects on their sexuality of intimate contact with sick women, and although I myself had nothing to complain of in this regard, I did not take their complaints lightly; and here in Bodhgaya, in this cool, bare room, the strong presence of the attractive Indian girl standing behind me merged with the enjoyable sensation passing through my hands kneading Einat's bare stomach, and I felt a faint flare-up of lust. I reminded myself to masturbate tonight when I went to bed, before we began the long trip home the next day—a trip I still considered rash, and perhaps even dangerous. Given with the blood profile I had brought back from Calcutta, the correct procedure would have been to keep my patient in bed for a few days, until I was sure that there was no chance of relapse and that she was on the road to recovery.

"Your parents are in a hurry to get home," I said to her while I gave her another shot of glucose, but I refrained from saying anything about my opinion of this haste. "Yes," replied Einat weakly, as if she too were afraid of starting off. "Daddy has to be back at work on Sunday."

"But why?" I inquired. She didn't know, or else she didn't want to give me a clear answer, as if she had no desire to be her parents' interpreter. I therefore decided to forget about satisfying my curiosity, and suggested a short walk outside. "I know you feel weak," I said to her, "but if your parents insist on leaving tomorrow, you might as well take your first step home this evening, in the open air and without any pressure." A timid smile crossed her face, hesitant, a little agonized, quick to efface itself under the pressure of some inner anxiety. At first she wasn't interested, but then she agreed and got up, swaying on her feet. She didn't know whether to change the long white Indian shift she wore as a kind of robe. In the end she decided to keep it on, adding a faded jean jacket, which emphasized the yellowish tinge of the whites of her eyes. I slung my camera over my shoulder and asked the Indian girl to accompany us so we could get back safely if we got lost, although there was actually no danger in this calm, tranquil place, which in spite of its simplicity I still insisted on thinking of as a kind of little paradise, perhaps because of the eternal sun, immense but soft and ripe, poised motionless on the flat horizon.

And in its yellow light I first posed the two young women next to the little golden gate in the stone wall surrounding the Buddha's sacred bo tree, which was festooned with strips of colored cloth. Then I asked the Indian girl to photograph Einat and me in the same place. But when I asked Einat to take a photo of the Indian girl and me next to the nearby lotus pond, I noticed the camera trembling in her hands, and I immediately took it away from her and asked a passing Oriental pilgrim to photograph the three of us. This is what paradise must look like, I kept thinking as I lightly supported my patient, giddy from the walk I had imposed on her after she had spent so many days in bed. "Look how steeped in spirituality everything is here," I said encouragingly, and pointed to the flourishing gardens surrounding the big Tibetan monastery farther down the road. "This is what paradise must be like, full of spirituality. It's intended for the soul, not the body, after all." And again I took my camera out of its case and asked passersby to photograph us at various points along the road that wound among the different Buddhist monasteries, each of them belonging to a different nation. "After I die, perhaps my soul will peep into the photograph album and remember where to fly to," I said in English to the Indian girl, but my joke did not raise the ghost of a smile. On the contrary—she bowed her head and confirmed that it was right and proper for a young man like me to start thinking seriously about his death. "It's really a shame that your parents insist on leaving tomorrow," I repeated to Einat, who said nothing. "If your father's in such a hurry," I added gently, "let him go alone, and we'll stay for a few days, until you feel better." But she maintained her strange silence. Was the idea of her parents' separating for even a few days impossible for her to contemplate, I wondered, or was her debilitation making her apathetic? But precisely because I wanted to go on interrogating her about her parents, I refrained from pressing her for an immediate answer, especially since in the distance, at the end of the broad road, it was already possible to see the dumpy figures of Lazar and his wife, trailing a pinkish light from the river behind them and picking their way gingerly through a big crowd of young backpackers who had just arrived from Gaya. Presumably they had been told at the hotel that we had gone out for a walk, and they had come hurrying to find us. "I'm suddenly beginning to like India," I announced to the Indian girl, feeling that "like" was a temporary word, until I found a better one, to describe the strange sensation of freedom that was welling up in me. Then I noticed the blood beginning to flow from Einat's nostrils, without her being aware of it at first. I not only put my arm around her, I even swung her up in the air to seat her on a stone wall, with her head thrown back and resting carefully on my knee as I sat beside her, using my handkerchief to soak up the stream of blood, which was a small but clear sign of the correctness of my medical intuition. So, I said to myself, it *is* too early to start the trip home.

But it was already too late to change anything. Lazar and his wife had come back from Gaya with plane tickets for all of us for the next morning, and Lazar reacted with considerable annoyance to the sight of the blood-soaked handkerchief. "What on earth made you go out for a walk?"

"If you want to leave tomorrow morning," I replied in a tone that I knew contained both complaint and rebuke, "she has to get accustomed to the open air." But only his wife was aware of the rebuke. Lazar, looking at his daughter, who was beginning to raise her head, was even more determined to leave for home before things got worse. "Never mind," he said, as if he were the expert here, "it's only a little nosebleed, and it's already stopped. Let's go back to the hotel—we have to eat and start packing." I took my camera out of its case again and snapped the three of them a couple of times. Then I called the Indian girl to join them and I took a photo of the four of them, and after that I asked Lazar to take one of the four of us, but I still wasn't satisfied. I took the camera again and posed him and his wife opposite the soft sun, and took a picture of the two of them by themselves. "We might as well finish the film," I said. "The light's so pretty now and the place is gorgeous, and tomorrow we'll be on ugly roads." Lazar looked too tired to take any further part in my sudden lust for photography, but Dori cooperated gladly. It was evident that she liked having her photograph taken. There was suddenly something captivating about this middle-aged woman—in the way she drew herself up to her full height, crossed her long legs, tried to pull in her protruding stomach, and then looked straight at the camera and shot out smile after smile, even before the button was pressed. And for the first time on this journey I felt a slight pang of regret and longing. I had come so far but seen so little. Would I be able to come back here one day?

Although I guessed that the sudden bleeding was related to Einat's general weakness, and perhaps also to the onset of her period—as sometimes happens, but usually with young girls—I couldn't avoid the nagging thought that there might be a small hemorrhage somewhere which refused to stop because of the coagulopathy caused by the viral hepatitis. So I didn't take my eyes off Einat, who was now leaning on the Indian girl. Lazar's wife supported her too, and the three of them walked slowly behind Lazar, who hurried in the direction of the hotel. Who could tell what other surprises she had in store for me on the way home? I thought to myself, adopting the cynical tone beloved of Hishin, who sometimes talked about his patients as if they were cunning opponents whose only aim was to trip him up. And while I quickly changed the film in the camera and insisted on snapping one more shot of the four of them outside the entrance to our hotel, which was now suffused in a strange purple-yellow twilight, like a huge bruise remaining after the sun refused to set, I also inquired casually, and without explaining why, about Lazar's and Dori's blood types. I had guessed right: the only possible donor if an emergency arose would be Lazar's wife.

❧❀❧

In the night I tossed and turned in my little room. I was still angry at the decision to leave in the morning. Was it only the insult of not being consulted that was bothering me? Maybe it was the nagging thought that I was about to return home without a job, and even though I had spent a whole week, twenty-four hours a day, with the administrative director, I still had nothing to show for it, and it was very much in the air that on my return I would have to start looking, without much hope, for a residency in the surgical department of another hospital. When I realized that I wasn't going to fall asleep, I got out of bed and began to pack. I switched on the light and started putting the medical equipment back into the knapsack, carefully examining every item as I did so. The pharmacist was a genius; he had thought of everything. And the imagination, precision, and economy of his preparations had a particular radiance shining next to me in the silence of the night. I made a mental note to express my appreciation as soon as I got back, as I folded everything up and packed it in the knapsack, trying to remember exactly where each item fit. In the end, even though a red glow was already beginning to appear between the palm and coconut trees, I decided to try to snatch a couple of hours of sleep before the journey, and from a little glass jar with three words written on its label in the pharmacist's handwriting—"Effective Sleeping Pill"—I fished out a smooth blue capsule and swallowed it.

The pill was so effective that Lazar had to shake me several times before he succeeded in rousing me, and his wife, who was busy cleaning the kitchen as industriously as if it were a friend's borrowed apartment, flashed me a look which seemed to express astonishment at my voracious capacity for sleep. "I didn't sleep all night," I explained spreading out my hands apologetically to them, but Lazar wasn't interested in apologies, he wanted rapid organization. Three swollen suitcases stood ready—two older bags and one new one, which had swallowed up their daughter's sleeping bag, backpack, and other possessions. Einat herself was sitting on a chair outside, very pale, wearing the simple flowered dress and red cloth hat that her mother had brought from Israel—a sad and pensive tourist, carrying away only the hepatitis B virus, testimony to the fact that her independent backpacking trip to the stormy, colorful subcontinent had ended in failure, requiring an emergency rescue by Mommy and Daddy. Without examining her again before leaving, I hurriedly dressed and ate the sandwiches prepared by Lazar's wife, who for a moment also seemed uncertain of the wisdom of starting off on the return journey so soon. But at this point the rickshaw driver in the white turban arrived, and when he saw me he came hurrying up to shake my hand enthusiastically, adding a little bow to express his satisfaction at my safe return from Calcutta. This time he had brought a bigger rickshaw, which easily took the four of us and our luggage aboard, and transported us rapidly to the dirty little airport in Gaya, which the light of day stripped of its mystery.

The flight from Gaya to Varanasi was not long, and the plane did not climb to any great altitude; nevertheless, a spurt of blood burst out of Einat's nose again. I was absorbed in the window, sleepily watching, with a mixture of depression and admiration, a silvery flash apparently emanating from our plane, which streaked ahead of us, gliding over the fields and roads, vanishing into woods and canals and little lakes, then unexpectedly appearing again, darting quick and silver over another part of the landscape. Lazar's wife was sitting in a window seat two rows in front of me, and during the flight I noticed her bun unraveling. Suddenly Lazar rose from his seat, a blood-soaked towel in his hand. I jumped up, but when he saw me he signaled me to sit down again. I ignored him and hurried over to them. Einat was lying with her head on her mother's lap. "It's stopped," Lazar announced immediately, as if to send me away, but his wife looked uncertain. Her automatic smile had vanished. "What is it?" she asked me in real anxiety. "It's probably weakness from the hepatitis," I said without thinking, "and maybe a result of the change in atmospheric pressure too. Let's change places for a minute," I suggested to Lazar, sitting down in the seat next to his wife and looking straight into Einat's eyes. She raised her head to me; she seemed a little pale, but mainly unhappy. In spite of the inconvenience to Lazar, I insisted on remaining next to the two women until the landing, which from the window was spectacular and startlingly beautiful. The plane circled over the two banks of the Ganges, the deserted east bank and the swarming west one; then it began gliding past, temple after temple, ghat after ghat, rocking in the air over the tiny black figures as if it too wished to bathe in the holiness of the golden river. I began talking to Einat, to distract her. Had she ever been in Varanasi? I asked her. She shook her head. "It's a pity your father's in such a hurry," I said, "otherwise we could have squeezed in another day here. The little we saw when we were here only whetted my appetite for more," and I smiled at her with the automatic smile of her mother, whose eyes were fixed on my face in profound concern.

It reminded me of those times in the operating room when we noticed that the glint of irony usually present in Professor Hishin's eyes had vanished. We had to stop; it was my responsibility. This new thought began to torture me as we sat with our suitcases and knapsack in a dirty corner of the Varanasi airport, surrounded by Indian children who had come to stare at me and my patient, leaning against me with her eyes closed, too exhausted even to look at the big basket a few feet away, from which rose the alert head of a large snake. We had three hours to kill before the flight to New Delhi, and although Lazar and his wife had brought sandwiches and bottles of soft drinks from Bodhgaya, they made their usual tour of the shops, returning from these expeditions with a relatively clean-looking pastry or a glass of hot tea. I took my patient's hand in mine to feel her pulse. It was rapid, a hundred per minute, and then, in the absurd despair of a doctor whom nobody believes, I found myself praying that she would begin bleeding again, because this was my only chance of asserting my authority and putting a stop to the dangerous journey, which Lazar and his wife were conducting with such feverish zeal. "Do you feel nauseous?" I asked. She thought a little and then nodded her head. "Then come along with me and let's get it up." I helped her to stand and led her into a corner, where I held her shoulders and gently pressed on her abdomen. She didn't vomit much, but blood was evident. Wherever it was coming from, there was no doubt that the damage to the clotting factors was exacerbating the bleeding. I led Einat back to her seat and told her to lie down across my seat, after which I went to stand guard over her vomit, to make sure that nobody effaced the telltale signs until her parents returned and saw with their own eyes. At that point I was finally able to confront them quietly but firmly: "I'm sorry, but it's impossible to continue to New Delhi. She has to have a blood transfusion immediately. You're in too much of a hurry to get home, and you're putting her at risk unnecessarily."

Lazar was flabbergasted. But I stood my ground, and in the quiet, firm tone that has powerful effects on patients and their families, I insisted that we could not continue our flight, that we had to reach some decent hotel—perhaps the Ganges, where we had almost stayed last time—and there, in a quiet atmosphere and hygienic conditions, I would give Einat a blood transfusion, which would require complete bed rest for twenty-four hours for proper recovery. "Of course," I continued, "we could put her in a local hospital. But even without the problem of dirty needles and contaminated blood supplies you'd have to be insane to hospitalize anyone in this 'Eternal City,' where nobody cares about anything but reincarnation and cremation." Lazar still tried to protest. "Let's go as far as New Delhi, at least," he begged. "It's only a two-hour flight. We can stop there—because who knows when we'll be able to get onto another flight, and traveling sixteen hours by train will be more dangerous for her than postponing the blood transfusion for a few hours."

"No," I stated quietly, "it would be more dangerous to postpone the blood transfusion," and I looked directly at his wife. But when she remained silent, as if unwilling to come out on my side, I raised my hands in a dramatic gesture, as if a hidden pistol were pointing at my head, and, closely surrounded by a ring of Indians who had gathered to see the little drama taking place in their midst, I burst out a tone of pain and grievance which surprised even me with its intensity, "Okay, she's your daughter, but just explain one thing to me—why did you drag me here with you?"

Perhaps it was these words that defeated Lazar's wife, who now threw her weight decisively onto my side, until Lazar too gave in and immediately began organizing the postponement of our flight, looking for porters, and thinking about a suitable hotel. And then Einat fainted and fell to the ground, and for the first time I was overwhelmed by a real fear that she was going to slip out of our hands. Passersby helped to lift her up; the characteristic Indian expertise in carrying the sick and dying soon proved most helpful as we were provided with a stretcher improvised from a blanket and two bamboo poles, and with a great hullabaloo we were led out of the airport building. A ramshackle minibus took us on board and with un-Indian speed covered the twelve miles between the airport and the town. We soon reached the Ganges Hotel, and although Einat had already recovered from her faint, the managers apparently thought it best to isolate us from the other guests, and instead of showing us into the hotel itself, they led us to an annex in the rear, a kind of pilgrims' lodge, where they installed us in two simple but very clean rooms furnished with wicker furniture lacquered a bright purple. After washing my hands and face and taking the extra precaution of putting on a little surgical mask, I turned quickly to my medical kit to collect everything I would need for the blood transfusion, which I had decided to perform as an emergency procedure, as described in the first aid manuals of the Magen-David-Adom station where I had worked night shifts while I was in medical school. In other words, a direct transfusion, where I would have to approximate the amount. I asked Lazar to push two beds together and lay the two women side by side, and Lazar helped me to take off their shoes and undo their belts. I measured their blood pressures, which were good, both about 130 over 80, and asked Lazar's wife, who was studying me with a rather ironic expression, to take off her glasses. "Why?" she asked in surprise. "It's not important," I said in embarrassment. "I just thought you might be more comfortable that way," and without insisting I found the vein for the intravenous line on Einat's slender wrist and connected it to the small infusion set. When the needle went in she let out a sharp cry of pain, and I immediately stroked her head and apologized, even though I knew that with the thinness of her arm and the irritated state of her skin the pain was unavoidable. I passed the tube over the table lamp standing between the two beds and began looking for her mother's vein, which was buried in the plumpness of her flesh. I tied a rubber tube around her upper arm, and since I felt no fear emanating from her, I found it easy to plunge my syringe quickly and painlessly deep into the vein. As the blood began slowly pumping out and I noted the time on my watch, she smiled at me and began joking lightheartedly. I asked Lazar, who was prowling around me not like the head of a hospital in which complicated operations were performed day and night but like a frightened husband and father, to raise his wife a little and prop her back against the pillow, to allow the blood to flow unimpeded between her arm and her daughter's according to the law of equilibrium. His wife's hair had come loose and partly covered her face. She tried to encourage her daughter, who was lying with her eyes closed and an expression of pain on her face, as if the blood flowing into her hurt her. Now there was a long silence. Lazar was still examining my actions with a mixture of anxiety and suspicion. Was I keeping an eye on the amount of blood? he suddenly asked in a whisper. I nodded my head. I knew that everything I did here was being registered in his sharp mind, down to the last detail, and that when we got home he would waste no time in asking Hishin and the rest of "his" professors if it had really been necessary to perform the blood transfusion so urgently and to cancel the flight. But I was calm and sure of myself, ready not only to justify the urgent transfusion to all the professors in the hospital but also to demand the respect due to me for my diagnosis and ingenuity in a medical emergency. They had wanted the ideal man for the trip—I suddenly felt a surge of elation—and they had found him!

After the transfusion of approximately 450 cc's of blood, according to my estimation, I removed the intravenous line from Lazar's wife's vein, applied alcohol to the spot, and gently folded her arm. Again she smiled sweetly at me. If not for Lazar's needless haste in catching the tube, not a single drop of blood would have been spilled in vain, but he was careless, and a bit of his wife's blood splashed onto my clothes. "Never mind," I said, and disconnected the tube from the infusion line in the wrist of my patient, who had calmed down and slipped into a doze, which I wanted to turn into a real sleep. I therefore took a Hartman's infusion bag, hung it from a nail in the wall, connected it to the infusion line which had just been thirstily and efficiently drinking in the blood, and went over to the window to draw the curtain and darken the room. But before I did so I stood still for a moment and relished the golden moment to the full. "And now we all need a rest," I said, facing them, "especially you, Dori," and I blushed, for this was the first time since the beginning of the trip that I had addressed her directly by her husband's pet name for her. But they both smiled at me affectionately, and Lazar put his arm around me in a conciliatory gesture. "You need a rest too," he said, but I was as alert and full of vitality as if I myself had received a blood transfusion. I packed the instruments in the knapsack and put it in the other room, and since I knew that the pair of them were perpetually hungry, I offered to look after our patient while they went to have lunch, and then, if everything seemed to be going smoothly, I would go down to eat myself, and perhaps have a look at a nearby museum.

But I knew that I wouldn't be going to look at any museum. It was the Ganges River and the swarming steps leading down to it and the vast, mysterious, dark brown temples which I hadn't managed to see before that called me. After eating a late lunch by myself in the hotel restaurant, encouraged by the clear signs of recovery in Einat—who, after absorbing the entire contents of the infusion bag, woke up and even tasted a bit of the food her parents brought her—I allowed myself to go out to the river before darkness fell. A warm, fine rain sifted through the air, and a stench rose from the town like incense. Who could have guessed that I would return here, I mused, as once more I made my way through the narrow alleys and the tireless, endless crowd until I reached the riverbank, which in spite of the rain was full of bathers. I hired a boat by myself and asked the boatman to row me to the southern ghats, so that I could view the great temples from the heart of the river. The dusky air merged with the river and the boat glided calmly over the water, but I did not succeed in drinking in the mystery. I was still preoccupied with all that had just passed: the argument at the airport with Lazar, the sudden faint, and especially the successful blood transfusion, which had been so elegantly performed. The smile that had gleamed from his wife's eyes as I took her blood now floated pleasantly through my thoughts. It seemed that I had succeeded in impressing them, and when we returned to Israel, as the cunning Hishin had hinted, Lazar might be able to help me stay on at the hospital. But I soon realized that it wasn't Lazar I was thinking of but his wife, who couldn't stay by herself. And in the final analysis, I thought with satisfaction, it was a good thing she had joined us; how would I have found a suitable donor in the eternal crowd? And who would have helped me persuade Lazar to interrupt the journey?

As illuminated launches sailed past us and our little boat rocked in their wake, I began thinking affectionately of Einat too. How sad for it to end like this, a trip that perhaps was intended to be more than just a trip, a little rebellion or an escape. And in bringing me along, hadn't Lazar and his wife had some hidden intention to put her in touch with a young doctor, an "ideal man"? She was only four years younger than I was, but she seemed a little bit of a lost soul; why hadn't she even finished her B.A.? The oarsman called out to me to look at the ghats we were passing. Sensitively he had noticed that I was preoccupied with irrelevant thoughts. I smiled my thanks and raised my eyes to the brown stone temples. Vishvanath, I said softly, getting the name right this time, Vishvanath, and the oarsman's face lit up and he immediately put his hands together in a gesture of acknowledgment. But the magic had somehow been dispelled, and at the end of the tour of the ghats, when we returned to the bank,

I did not linger but hurried back to the hotel, stopping on the way at a small telephone booth, next to which a number of backpackers were clustered. To my surprise I got through right away to my parents, who were overjoyed to be awakened from their sleep by the sound of my voice. We're already on our way back, I announced, and everything's going well. And I told them briefly about the day's events.

Outside the door to our rooms I heard loud voices, and when I entered I found the two parents sitting on the purple wicker chairs and arguing with my patient, who was sitting up in bed, very yellow and scratching but wide awake. Lazar was in high spirits, having succeeded after strenuous efforts in getting four tickets on the plane to New Delhi the next night. He still hoped to be able to change the flight from New Delhi to Rome that we had missed because of the stop in Varanasi for one the day after, so that we would be in time for the El Al flight home on Friday. I had finally learned the reason for his haste. He had an important meeting with a delegation of big donors from abroad, whom he had persuaded to devote their Sunday morning to our hospital. "You wanted a twenty-four-hour recovery period, and now you've got thirty hours until the flight," he said aggressively, as if the recovery were meant for me instead of his daughter. But I only smiled. His face was very gray, his little eyes were sunken, and if I had been as close to him as Hishin was, I would have hospitalized him for a few days in the internal medicine department for a comprehensive checkup. But his wife was apparently used to the grayish hue of his face, as were the many doctors with whom he came into daily contact. It was still early for bed, and for a moment I was loath to part from them; I didn't know if they intended to move the patient into my room, or if Lazar intended to move in with me for the night. In the end Lazar asked me to help him move one of the beds from my room into theirs. What did you think, I said to myself with an inner smile, that his wife would agree to spend a night without him?

At eight the next evening we arrived in New Delhi, where Lazar was in for a bitter disappointment. There was only one seat left on the Thursday morning flight to Rome. And flying home via some other European city would mean forfeiting the tickets, which had cost a lot of money. "Why don't you take the available seat and fly back alone?" I asked Lazar, who seemed plunged in despair. "The three of us could fly to Rome on Friday and get a flight home on Sunday or Monday." He looked at me but didn't react, and then he glanced at his wife, whose eyes were fixed anxiously on his face, with no trace of her usual smile. "That's impossible," he blurted out in the end, exchanging another glance with his wife, who stared at me tensely, ready to reject any additional suggestions. So we had no option but to ride into New Delhi, which after Varanasi, Calcutta, and Gaya looked like a normal, civilized city. With uncharacteristic absentmindedness, the Lazars let the rickshaw driver take us to a big modern hotel, with large and apparently very expensive rooms. And once again the three of them had to crowd into one room, while I was sent to the floor above, to a room that was not large but very pleasant and grand in its own way. For the first time on the journey, I felt the kind of mild, vague guilt toward them that I sometimes feel toward my parents when I think that they are doing without on my account. Accordingly, I went downstairs and knocked on their door, and despite the lateness of the hour and the disorder of the room, they welcomed me in like a member of the family and listened in surprise to my offer to look after our patient the next day by myself, so that they could take advantage of our enforced stay in New Delhi and go on a tour to Agra, 125 miles away, to see the Taj Mahal. "How will you face your friends if you come back from India without having seen the Taj Mahal?" I said with a smile, and offered to let them take my camera with them. "And how will you?" laughed his wife, whose hostility toward me had vanished without a trace. "I'm still young," I said tactlessly. "I'll return here one day." To my surprise they accepted my offer, as if they were entitled to some form of compensation from me, and early in the morning they set out in a tour bus to see the mausoleum built by the Emperor Shah Jahan in memory of his wife, while I spent most of the day with Einat, sitting in the armchair or lying on her parents' bed and trying to read *A Brief History of Time,* although I didn't understand much. The blood transfusion I had given her turned out to have been vital; for one thing, the sudden nosebleeds had completely ceased. However, she was still febrile and exhausted by the relentless itching caused by the accumulated bile salts. She hadn't slept properly for weeks, and she kept dozing off as I changed the dressing on the wound on her leg, which looked much better. When she roused from her sleep, I showered her with questions, first about her trip to India, and then about her experiences in the hospital in Gaya, which she answered briefly but frankly. In the boredom of the lengthening hours, I began questioning her about things unconnected with her illness—first about her traveling companions, especially the shaven-headed Michaela, with the huge light eyes, who had brought the news of her illness to her parents, and then, as if I were about to become her family doctor, I began slipping in little questions about the family, asking about her younger brother and her charming grandmother. Then I questioned her eagerly about her parents, of whom she was obviously not too fond, and asked whether there was any truth in the strange complaint her father had made to me, that his wife was incapable of staying by herself.

When dusk began to fall, Lazar and his wife showed up at last, full of impressions from their day. Lazar returned my camera and thanked me for the idea of taking the trip. In addition to the sweetmeats and silk scarves they had bought for themselves, they had brought me a present, a model of the Taj Mahal the size of a small foot, made of pink marble. Lazar's wife described the sights they had seen enthusiastically. Lazar too appeared relaxed, amused by the strange Indians he had encountered on the way, as if he had only now begun to wonder about their true nature. His face had acquired a tan during the day and no longer had its sickly gray tinge. They were about to order a big meal for the four of us to be brought up to the room, but I suddenly felt trapped and restless and got up to go out for a walk and say my good-bye to India. As I had done ten days before, I began walking around the dark streets of New Delhi, this time in a more affluent district, mingling and moving easily with the crowd whose bodies had a strangely ethereal quality in the darkness. And suddenly I sensed that in spite of my youthful boast to the Lazars, I would never return to India. As long as I lived, I would never see the wonderful Taj Mahal which they had both seen today, and this strange certainty began pressing sorrowfully inside me.

I went into a fabric shop for the first time since I'd arrived in

India, to buy something for my parents. Entering the fragrant darkness, which rustled with flowered fabrics, I thought of my parents' two very separate beds and wondered if they would consent to having anything so bold and blazing in their bedroom. In the end I bought two lengths of brightly colored cloth which seemed to me suitable for bedcovers; I wanted to go on and buy something else as well, because everything was so amazingly cheap, but suddenly I was fed up with wandering around alone and decided to go back to the hotel and chat for a while with Lazar and his wife; maybe she too would thank me for the enjoyable day I had given her. When I got back they had apparently gone to bed, for there was no sound in their room, not even a crack of light under the door. There was nothing left to do but go up to bed myself, and as on the last night in Bodhgaya, I tossed and turned for hours in search of sleep, which usually came to me the minute I put my head on the pillow.

We arrived in Rome in the afternoon, and of course we missed the El Al plane, that always left exactly on time so it would reach Israel before the beginning of the Sabbath. We had to wait until Sunday, but Lazar had not yet given up hope of arriving in time for his important meeting. No sooner had we settled into a big old-fashioned hotel in Via dei Coronari than he went off, to his wife's obvious annoyance, to find a cheap flight that would get him back to Israel the next day. When I returned to the hotel in the evening, after strolling around the Roman Forum and the Colosseum, I found the two of them in the hotel lobby, a new sadness on his wife's face. It appeared that in spite of his age, he had succeeded in getting himself onto a cheap student flight that left early the next afternoon and arrived in Tel Aviv via Athens late on Saturday evening. Delighted with his own ingenuity, he now tried to appease his wife, who saw the whole thing as vanity and caprice on the part of a man who believed that he was indispensable. The next day at noon we said good-bye to him. He seemed tense, and adopted a slightly mocking air toward his wife, who to my surprise looked really upset, as if what was at stake were not a parting for twenty-four hours but total desertion. Although I was standing next to them he embraced her and kissed her again and again, smiling as if he were secretly enjoying the anxiety that stemmed from some deep and obscure source within her, and over which she had no control. Then he turned to me, as if I were a member of the family, and said, "Take care of her until tomorrow." I saw that these innocent and half-joking words intensified her anger and her stress, and she immediately extricated herself from his embrace, gave him a little push, and said, "Go on, go, and be careful on the way and phone the minute you get home."

For a moment I felt a desire to try and calm the childish anxiety of this middle-aged woman, who was only nine years younger than my mother yet so strangely bound to her husband, who seemed conversely unable to tear himself away from her. But as soon as he was gone, before I had a chance to think of something suitable to say, her eyes gleamed with that smile again, as if her pride would not allow her to look miserable in my presence. She asked me if I had any plans, and when I hesitated, she asked if I would be kind enough to stay with Einat for a little while, because she had to go and have her hair done, since she too had to go straight back to the office on Monday. For a moment I was flabbergasted. I had baby-sat for them for an entire day in New Delhi, and now she had the nerve to expect me to stay stuck in the hotel again, as if I really were their hired hand, even though nothing had yet been said about the fee due to me for the trip. Her confident assumption that she would be returning to work on Monday, too, with the mental image it brought back to me of the self-assured woman in the short black dress and the high heels who had greeted me with such aplomb in her legal office, infuriated me. And who was going to take care of Einat on Monday, and take her to have the tests she still needed? Did they mean to turn me into their family doctor and nursemaid? But before I could say anything, I saw that my silence had been taken for consent, and she turned away and disappeared around the corner, as if she knew exactly where she was going. I returned unwillingly to my room and picked up my book, no longer interested in questioning Einat. Then I knocked lightly on her door, but there was no answer. I knocked again, and called her name, but there was dead silence on the other side of the door, and for the first time since meeting her I felt real panic. I hurried to the reception desk, introduced myself and explained my connection with the Lazars, and asked them to open the door. At first they refused, but I insisted, and eventually I was able, with the help of my doctor's ID, to infect them with my alarm. But when the

bellboy attempted to open the door with the master key, it transpired that a key was stuck in the lock on the inside of the door,
and the door refused to open. We banged on it, but there was no
reply. I tried to reassure myself that Einat's condition had already
shown signs of steady improvement after the blood transfusion;
she was even strong enough for me to think of giving her a whole
diuretic pill later in the afternoon to accelerate her kidney functions, since I was still worried by the small amount of urine she
passed. But by now the Italians were panicking, and they began
to talk excitedly among themselves. In the end a solution was
found. Another young bellboy, who looked like a North African,
was summoned, and he immediately entered the adjacent room
and with the agility of a monkey succeeded in entering the
Lazars' room through the window. When he opened the door
and let us into the room, we found Einat sound asleep—after
many sleepless nights she had finally succeeded in falling into a
deep, restful sleep.

"Everything's okay, everything's okay," I reassured the disappointed Italians, who were anticipating a big drama and didn't
want to go away. I sat down next to my patient; even her hands,
which hadn't stopped their incessant scratching since we arrived
in Bodhgaya, were now lying quite still on the bed. I lit a small
lamp and began once more to read Hawking's book, which according to the blurb on the cover had already been bought by
millions of readers, who had no doubt thought, like me, that they
were about to have the secrets of the universe explained to them,
only to discover that these secrets were extremely difficult and
complicated, and above all, controversial. Nevertheless, I went
on reading, turning pages and skipping to more comprehensible
passages and thinking crossly of Lazar's wife. Even though my
presence at the bedside of my sleeping patient was not really
necessary I didn't budge, in part because I wanted to see how she
would apologize to me when she finally returned. And when she
walked into the room with her elegantly styled hair, her face
made up, her hands full of parcels, her high heels tapping, blushing at her lateness, I felt not anger but a strange, frightening
happiness, which flooded me as if I were in love.

My face turned red and I immediately sat up in the armchair.
She would never be able to guess, not even in her wildest dreams
. . . All she did was apologize, and apologize again. She hadn't

thought that I would still be sitting next to Einat, who for some reason woke up as soon as her mother entered the room, assumed a suffering expression, and began furiously scratching herself again. When I told Lazar's wife about Einat's long sleep, she looked worried and asked me to examine her again. I therefore went to fetch my stethoscope and sphygmomanometer, and palpated Einat's flat stomach, trying to feel the damaged liver. There did not seem to be any change for the worse; the kidneys still seemed somewhat enlarged, but I decided against intervening at this stage with any additional medication, and left them after agreeing to come back to the room later for dinner. Outside it was raining, and the display windows of the European shops which had taken the place of the Indian temples gleamed with colored lights. I walked along the sidewalks, getting wet, amazed at my sudden new feeling for this impossible older woman. It's completely idiotic, I scolded myself, but nevertheless I soon retraced my steps and returned to the hotel, went up to my room to shower, put on the shirt I had washed in Bodhgaya, and joined the two women for an excellent Italian meal. In spite of my excitement, I tried to joke with Einat, whose deep sleep had brought a fresh, rosy color to her cheeks. Her mother laughed a lot all evening, and when the phone rang and Lazar announced his safe arrival, she sounded loving and tender and not at all angry. She asked him about the flight and assured him that all was well with us. They spoke for a long time, as if they weren't going to meet again in less than twenty-four hours. I looked at her legs, which for most of the trip had been hidden by slacks. They were youthful and very shapely, but the overflowing belly and full arms spoiled her appearance. Nevertheless my excitement persisted, not without the accompaniment of an inner nervousness, and I stayed with them longer than they expected me to.

In the middle of the night I woke up, opened the closet, stood in front of the mirror, and examined my reflection in the dark. I suddenly whispered her name, Dori, Dori, as if by the mere act of whispering her name I was exorcising her or secretly taking possession of her. This is too weird, this is insane, I chided myself. The room was heated to boiling point, and in spite of the high ceiling I felt stifled. I got dressed and went downstairs to see if I could get a glass of milk. But it was two o'clock in the morning,

and the hotel bar was still and silent. Even the reception clerk—
perhaps the same one who had helped me to break into the
Lazars' room that afternoon—was asleep on a bed hidden behind
the desk. I wandered around the big, dark dining room, where
the tables were already laid for breakfast, and before going back
upstairs I opened the door into the kitchen, as I was in the habit
of doing when I was on call in the hospital at night, in the hope
of finding something there. And indeed, the big kitchen was not
in total darkness. In its recesses a faint light flickered redly on
great copper saucepans, and I heard low laughter. I advanced
past the neat tables and gleaming sinks. Next to a big dining
table I saw three people sitting and talking in a foreign language,
not Italian, eating soup from pottery bowls decorated with pink
flowers. They were foreign workers, perhaps refugees. One of
them immediately rose from his seat and asked me what I
wanted, in Italian and with a friendly expression on his face.
"Milk," I said in English, and I laid a heavy hand on my stomach, to signal the burning pain of my sudden fall into love, while
with my other hand I raised an imaginary glass to my lips and
drank it to the dregs. He understood at once, repeated my request to his guests in their language, and went to the refrigerator
to pour me a glass of milk. Then I saw that next to the giant
fridge, whose motor was humming like a small plane's, sat a little
girl with a waiflike appearance, looking at the screen of a small
television set. And next to her a thin bespectacled man with a
very sickly appearance sat paging through a school workbook.

PART TWO

Marriage

Six

Lazar received special permission, apparently on medical grounds, to meet us in the arrival lounge immediately after passport control. Even before his wife and daughter noticed him, I saw his stocky, broad-shouldered figure in a wet raincoat standing next to the guard at the end of the barrier, anxiously inspecting the people walking past him as if he really doubted our ability to get home without him. Next to him, his long hair soaking wet and a distracted expression on his face, which resembled his father's, stood Lazar's son, whom his mother hurried to gather lovingly to her bosom, as if he were the dangerously ill child who had to be brought back home. But Lazar had no intention of allowing anyone to waste time on hugs and kisses. He handed his son a big black umbrella and instructed him to lead his sister, draped in a raincoat, straight to the car, while he himself hurried to seize an empty cart and began to collect the luggage. "Wait till you see the storm raging outside—you'll wish you were back in India," he warned us. "Was it really necessary for you to get back in such a hurry?" his wife asked him, her tone still showing vestiges of her anger at having been left alone for twenty-four hours. "Not only necessary but essential," he replied with a triumphant smile, and when he saw me looking at him somberly, he reassured me cheerfully, "Don't worry, your parents are here too, waiting for you outside."

"My parents?" I was astonished. "What on earth for?" Lazar seemed taken aback. "What for? I don't know—so that you won't have to go home by yourself in the rain, I suppose. My secretary got hold of them on the phone this morning, and they promised to be here to take you back to Jerusalem." But I didn't want to go to Jerusalem now, even though I had left my Honda there; I wanted to remain in Tel Aviv so as to report back to the hospital at the crack of dawn. Lazar had kept his promise; the whole trip had lasted only two weeks, and here, next to the luggage conveyor turning emptily on its axis, the length of our absence shrank to its natural proportions. Nevertheless, I was afraid that significant changes to my disadvantage had taken place in the meantime. "Did you have time to tell Hishin about what happened?" I asked, dying to know if Hishin had already been told about the blood transfusion I had performed in Varanasi. "No," said Lazar, with his arm around his wife's shoulder, as if he still had to appease her. "Hishin's not here, he took off for Paris a few days ago. That's why he didn't want to come with us himself. He kept the real reason from us. Never mind, we managed very well without him." He smiled at us complacently, as if the medical responsibility had been shared equally among the three of us. He seemed elated now. The meeting with the group of donors had been a success. I saw that underneath his raincoat he was elegantly dressed in a suit and tie. His wife started to fawn on him, the abandonment of yesterday suddenly forgiven. I looked at her and found myself blushing. She looked tired but happy to be back home. Had I really fallen a little bit in love with her, I wondered, or was it all some strange hallucination?

But there was no time to go on thinking about it, because the luggage started arriving, and soon it would be time to say goodbye. My suitcase, which had already been separated from theirs on the plane, turned up first, and Lazar saw no reason to keep me waiting. "You still have to drive to Jerusalem—you'd better get moving," he said firmly, and while I was still wondering how to say good-bye to them, he remembered something and grabbed hold of my suitcase. "Just a minute, let's free you of the silly shoe box we dumped on you before you go." To my surprise, Dori tried to stop him. "It's not important, not now, don't trouble him with that now, his parents are waiting for him. He'll give it back when he's got time." But Lazar could see no reason why I should have to drag his wife's shoes to Jerusalem and back. "It won't take more than half a minute," he said, and he helped me to undo the straps and open the suitcase, and without even waiting for me to assist him, he inserted his hands as delicately as an experienced surgeon into my belongings and quickly extracted the cardboard box, which I had carefully avoided opening throughout the trip. He said, "There you are, no trouble at all," and smiled good-bye. "Then I'll see you at the hospital tomorrow," I said in an effort to keep the thread of a connection between us. "At the hospital?" Lazar seemed puzzled, as if this weren't the place where we both worked, but he immediately remembered and said, "Of course."

"Then I won't see him again?" said his wife, examining me with surprise but not with sorrow. Locks of her long hair had fallen onto her face and neck, her makeup had faded during the flight, and under the white neon light, her wrinkles were once more revealed. She didn't know how to say good-bye to me, and a sweet wave of pain trembled inside me. "The photographs," I stammered in embarrassment, and my face began to burn as if I were playing some trick on them. "The pictures I took of you are still in my camera. When they're ready, I'll bring them." Lazar and his wife remembered the snapshots and exclaimed happily, "Right, our pictures!"

"Yes," I promised, "maybe I'll bring them around to your place, because I should check up on my patient anyway and see how she's getting along."

And perhaps because of the promise that we would meet again we parted casually, as we had parted from time to time in India, without shaking hands or embracing. Still I refused even to wonder whether Dori had been touched by a spark of that absurd nocturnal fantasy of falling in love, which would no doubt vanish as soon as I got through customs and emerged into the night, where the stormy rain and hail had gathered the people loyally waiting into a dense huddle under the scant protection of the shelter—a huddle that still managed to display the traditional Israeli enthusiasm, embracing every returning citizen of the state as if his absence warranted a gentle hand to guide him home. This at any rate was apparently the attitude of my parents, who had waited for an hour at two different observation posts in order not to miss me when I came out. My mother spotted me first, and we had to go to some trouble to find my father, who was standing calmly under his umbrella in the pouring rain, after giving up his place under the shelter with his natural gentlemanliness to two elderly women who had been reduced to hopeless despair by the storm. "You look well," said my mother as we followed my father in the dark to the parking lot, trying to shelter me under her little umbrella. "You're a little thinner, but you look happy. So you weren't disappointed by our India." My mother was always afraid of disappointments and disillusionments that might come my way, afraid of those states of emptiness that threaten to overwhelm the young. Consequently, as the person who had encouraged me to accompany the Lazars on the trip to India, which she felt entitled to call "ours" because of her uncle's memories, she was on tenterhooks to know how I had managed. And although I hadn't yet had a chance to say anything of substance, she sensed that I had returned satisfied. If not the rain, which forced us to step carefully between the puddles of water, she might have sensed something of my feelings for Dori as well, and of the pain of parting which had already started to bubble inside me.

My mother thought that I should do the driving as the storm gathered force around us, but my father refused to forfeit his place at the wheel. "It will be all right," he reassured her. "I know the road, it's plain sailing," and she had to make do with seating me beside him to guard against possible mistakes on his part. He took off his coat, cleaned his glasses, and as usual overheated the engine. He hadn't yet spoken to me. Only after he had brought us calmly and carefully out of the parking lot into the heart of the storm, and turned onto the main road, did he turn his face to me at last. He looked at me affectionately and said, "So, it was a success."

"A success?" I said, startled. "In what sense?"

"In the sense that you had to prove yourself," my father replied in his characteristically calm tone. "Lazar's secretary said that you had performed the correct medical procedure and saved the situation over there." I quickly turned my head to my mother, who was sitting in the backseat. She did not seem pleased that my father had blurted out the story, stealing my thunder, so to speak. However, happiness surged up in me. Had Lazar already managed to tell one of the professors about the tests in Calcutta and the blood transfusion in Varanasi, and was that how the news had traveled to the administrative office? Or had he said something in all innocence to his secretary, and she, full of goodwill but without really understanding anything, had sung my praises to my parents when she called to tell them when the plane was due to arrive? I would find all that out tomorrow, I said to myself, but in the meantime my father, who was eager to hear every detail, and in the right order, was already forcing me to describe the medical part of the trip from both the practical and the theoretical point of view. He drank in my explanations thirstily. He possessed the virtue of being able to learn something from everyone, which was why he was such a silent man and such a profound listener. Now, as he sat erect and slightly back from the wheel, silently contemplating, like an objective judge, the concerted efforts of the car, the wipers, the headlights, the windshield, and the road itself as they battled the savage storm threatening to drive us off the road, he wanted to learn from my lips the full extent of the salvation I had brought to the Lazars. He was afraid that the modesty he attributed to me, which he regarded as an unfortunate inheritance he himself had bequeathed to me, would make me belittle the importance of my achievement. Likewise, he had still not resigned himself to the fact that the second resident had been given the longed-for post we had all been hoping for. My mother too listened in silence. From time to time she slipped in a brief question, ultimately succeeding in picking up my lack of enthusiasm for Einat, for whom she had cherished secret hopes. She was trying to hear the inner story, which I was attempting to disguise as I spoke. In the end she blurted, "You keep saying Lazar's wife, Lazar's wife, but what's her name?"

"Her name's Dorit, but her husband calls her Dori," I replied, and a sweet pain gripped me. "And what did you call her?" my mother stubbornly demanded. "Me?" I wondered momentarily why she was so insistent, staring wearily at the road which loomed up through the rain. "I called her Dori too in the end," I admitted. "And what kind of a woman is she?" my mother kept on. "A spoiled woman," I answered at once. "In the beginning she made a big fuss about the hotels." And I closed my eyes in exhaustion, seeing the plump little woman advancing along the alleys of Varanasi with her slow, pampered walk, stepping carefully in the mud and smiling absentmindedly at the Indians crowding around her. And a wave of warmth suddenly engulfed me and almost choked me.

And I realized at that moment that I had to be careful when I was talking to my mother, because she sometimes succeeded in seeing into my soul with astonishing accuracy, and she was liable to sense something of the strange feeling I had brought back with me from the trip, and it was only natural that this feeling would offend and upset her and give rise to the wish to do something to nip this ridiculous infatuation in the bud. If that was the right word for my thoughts about this woman, which now included a lust that I was just becoming aware of, sitting cozily next to my father as we drove through the night from Lydda to Jerusalem. I looked at the road climbing between the hills, from which the rain and mist had cleared, giving way to lightly falling snowflakes. It would be a shame, I said to myself, if my mother had to suffer even for an instant because of a feeling that was absurd and hopeless by its very nature. It would be better not to talk too much about the trip to India, in case I unintentionally let slip some hint that would embarrass us all unnecessarily. Accordingly, I suggested to my father, who was a little offended, that I take his place by the wheel, because the airy flakes were turning the journey home into an adventure that might become dangerous. And in fact the light, shining flakes, which had begun flying through the air a few miles after Sha'ar-Hagai, turned into a heavy snowfall as we approached the city, and for the next two days I was stuck in Jerusalem, because my parents, who generally trusted my driving, implored me not to return to Tel Aviv on my motorcycle on the snowy roads. Since I felt a great weariness rising in me, the fruit of the unexpected excitements of the trip to India, I agreed to settle down again in the old bedroom of my childhood and relax into a delicious sensation that had nothing to do with food and drink—for my mother had never distinguished herself as a cook—but with the silent stirrings of a ghostly British presence in the apartment, which gave me the feeling that even when I was lying in bed that I was participating in an old black-and-white family movie full of stable, kindly values, whose happy, moral conclusion was guaranteed in advance. Thus, hidden at home, surrounded by a blanket of snow, I tried to cool and perhaps even to kill my infatuation with Lazar's smiling round-limbed wife, and I tried to stop thinking about her, so that here, in the faithful room of my childhood and youth, she would sink into the depths of the darkness, dragged down by the weight of her years.

❧❧❧

But the smiling middle-aged woman refused to sink, and blended instead with the familiar furniture and curtains of the room to which I had been brought at the age of two, when my parents moved to Jerusalem from Tel Aviv because of my father's government job. And so I escaped into sleep, careful not to leave traces of my lust on the spotless sheets provided by my mother, who marveled together with my father at my sudden craving for sleep. They had grown accustomed to seeing me as a serious student who burned the midnight oil, a hard worker who got up early in the morning, and more recently as a doctor on call, capable of going without sleep for twenty-four hours at a stretch. "You're taking us back to your days in boot camp," said my mother with a slightly worried air when I entered the dim old kitchen at twilight after sleeping the whole afternoon, feeling a pang of intense longing for the bright colors of the Indian temples. "It's the soporific effect of the snow," explained my father, in English, and he got up to give me my old place at the table, which he had taken for himself when I left home. "Yes, yes, you sit in your place," he insisted when I tried to refuse, at the same time checking on my mother as she poured my tea and set it before me with a slice of crumb cake, on which I immediately spread a layer of jam to take away the dry, slightly moldy taste, which had depressed me even as a child.

"While you were asleep, your father went to town and had the photographs you took in India developed," my mother said with a slightly embarrassed air as she handed me two envelopes crammed with pictures. "My photographs?" I turned to my father almost with a yell, refusing to believe that this quiet, aristocratic man had stolen into my room on his own initiative and taken the two rolls of film lying next to my bed while I was sleeping. In fact, it turned out that the initiative was my mother's—she had gone into my room to check if I was warm enough, noticed the two rolls of film, and sent my father to have them developed in the center of town. She must have wanted to find out more about the trip to India, since I was too busy sleeping and too preoccupied with my thoughts to tell her. I suppose she can sense that something happened to me over there, I

thought, hanging my head and avoiding her eyes, but even her
native intelligence would never dare to imagine what had really
happened. "Don't you want to see how your pictures came out?"
she wondered, as I went on gripping the two envelopes tightly in
my hand. "But they're not all mine," I explained quickly. "Some
of them are the Lazars', I lent them the camera when they went
on a trip to the Taj Mahal." My parents were astounded to hear
that the Lazars had gone off together and left me by myself with
their sick daughter, and even after I told them that it had been
my idea to send them to see the Taj Mahal, they went on criticiz-
ing the Lazars for accepting my offer, though they were proud of
my generosity. "Well, why don't you show them to us already,
and tell us all about them," said my mother as she stretched out
an eager hand for the envelopes. "Of course," I said, "but I
thought you'd already looked at them." And a little panic took
hold of me at the thought of confronting her image here, in my
parent's sad kitchen, and I stood up at once and put my cup and
plate in the sink and went to the bathroom to wash my face and
brush my teeth again, and when I returned the kitchen was
flooded with light and the table was covered with colored pictures glowing with India's reddish brown light, and already from
a distance I saw her figure, which had miraculously managed to
insert itself in more pictures than I would have imagined possible, and not only those taken by Lazar at the Taj Mahal. Was it
her innate serenity and automatic smile that enabled her, in spite
of her abundant plumpness, to look so natural and photogenic in
every picture, even when she was surrounded by Indians in rags
or sitting on a rickety bench in the twilight next to the Thai
monastery in Bodhgaya? My father passed one picture after another before his eyes and requested detailed explanations, but my
mother fell silent, and a new pallor covered her cheeks. "She
certainly likes having her picture taken," she said at last, and
there was a note of complaint in her voice. "Who?" I asked
innocently. "Lazar's wife—or what do you call her?" My mother
kept her head lowered, as if she were afraid of meeting my eyes.
"It's her husband, it's Lazar. I lent him my camera," I said in
self-justification, my voice muffled by the wave of excitement
that surged up in me again at the sight of the woman strewn in
bright glossy squares all over our gray kitchen table.

That evening the snowstorm intensified, but I went anyway to visit Eyal, a childhood friend who had studied medicine with me, and who was on call tonight in Hadassah Hospital, where he was doing his residency in pediatrics, after having been turned down by the surgical department. We sat in a little room with pictures of children stuck up on the walls, surrounded by the racket of sick children running up and down the corridor pursued by their harassed parents. We drank tepid tea from plastic cups and as usual compared conditions in our respective hospitals before discussing anything else. Then he asked me about my trip to India, of which he had already heard about from my mother, and at the sight of his friendly eyes fixed on mine, I felt an impulse to tell him immediately about the most important thing that had happened to me on the trip. I thought that Eyal, who had been living with his widowed mother for the past few years, would understand better than most people. But at the last moment I stopped myself. I had plenty of time; this wasn't the right moment. And I began telling him about the medical aspects of the trip. He was very impressed by the night flight to Calcutta with the blood and urine samples, but seemed doubtful about the blood transfusion I had performed in Varanasi. "I hope that in your enthusiasm you didn't infect the mother with the daughter's virus," he said with a smile. "Nonsense," I replied, "how could I have infected her? I was careful to place her higher than the patient too."

"That doesn't make much difference," he said knowingly, "but there's no use crying over spilled milk. The main thing is for you not to lose touch with this Lazar—and don't take any money from him, so he'll remain in your debt and maybe he'll influence Hishin to let you have another year in his department." While Eyal was showering me with practical advice, he was urgently summoned to the emergency room to examine a boy who had tried to kill himself. It was late, but I was curious to see how they would manage the case. The patient was about thirteen, tall for his age, jerking violently under the hands of the nurses brutally pumping his stomach. Since I was wearing civilian clothes, they took me for his brother or some other relative and kept ordering me out of the little treatment cubicle. In the end I decided to leave in spite of my curiosity. Eyal, who had thought that I was going to spend the night keeping him company, suggested that I postpone my return to Tel Aviv and come to lunch at his house the next day. I hesitated. The commotion of the

Hadassah emergency room made me homesick for my own hospital. But Eyal began urging me through the curtain separating us, holding on firmly to the arm of the boy, who had already begun spewing out the sleeping pills through the thick tube which had been inserted into his stomach. "Come on, you have to come—I've got an amazing story for you."

"What story?" I asked suspiciously, unwilling to commit myself. "You won't believe it, but I'm getting married," he announced loudly and shamelessly to the frightened, unhappy people filling the emergency room.

The road from Ein Kerem back to town was very clear now; the crowns of snow on the branches of the trees and the rocks at the roadside lent a new magic to the night, and I was cheered by the thought that after lunch tomorrow, in exchange for the story of the wedding, I might gather the courage to tell Eyal about my own unexpected falling in love. Why not? If not Eyal, who would be able to understand me? My mother was waiting up for me, sitting in the dark in the living room in her old woolen robe. "It's because of the snow, only because of the snow on the roads," she apologized, and immediately got up to make us a cup of tea. "I already had tea with Eyal in the hospital," I announced, and made for my room, refusing to linger and risk a nocturnal interrogation. And as she retired, disappointed, to her bedroom, I caught a glimpse through the door of my parents' beds standing in an L-shape under the two moonlit windows. "You won't believe it, Mother," I blurted out in a whisper, "Eyal's getting married."

"Why shouldn't I believe it?" she cried. "It's high time. For his friends too." And my father poked his head out of the blankets and chuckled. "You're opening a battlefront in the middle of the night." But my mother had already calmed down, and she only asked curiously about the bride. "I didn't have a chance to hear," I said, "but tomorrow I'm going there for lunch, and maybe I'll even see her."

"So you're staying tomorrow too," said my mother with a certain relief. Even if I wasn't getting married, at least I was staying with them for one more day.

When we were both students at the hospital, I often ate at Eyal's place, because we preferred studying in his house, which was big and quiet. His mother, who lived alone, didn't like being by herself in the house at night, and she would cook up tasty meals to ensure that we always studied there. She was a sad woman, with some of her former beauty left, and she liked talking to me in English, since she was hoping to find work in the tourist bureau. From time to time she received visits from middle-aged men, but she refused to become involved with any of them. Now the two of them sat looking politely at the photographs of my trip. "A pretty girl, but obviously neurotic," Eyal said, dismissing Einat. "I doubt if she's worth investing in." He went on to study Lazar's broad face with evident enjoyment. "It's obvious," he pronounced, "that he's a strong man, but also friendly and humane. If you've already become close to him and his family, it would be a shame to lose that."

"His wife's very nice too," I said suddenly, and felt myself blushing. Eyal examined the snapshots again. "Yes, she's always smiling," he agreed. "You can see at once that she's pleased with herself." I was so delighted by these perceptive words that I wanted to go on talking about her. But his sad mother, who had grown very fat lately, didn't want to leave us alone together. "Are you glad that Eyal's getting married?" I asked her carefully. "She's overjoyed," Eyal answered for her. His mother said nothing, and after a pause she asked if we were ready for lunch. Eyal suggested that we wait for his girlfriend, who was due to arrive soon.

But his mother said the food would get cold, and in a surly tone, which I had never heard her use before, she demanded that we eat right away. And then, when we sat down opposite each other at the elegantly laid table and she disappeared into the kitchen, I lowered my eyes and said with a miserable smile, "You're suddenly getting married, and I, I don't know what's happening to me, but I've suddenly fallen in love with a married woman."

"A married woman?" Eyal's little eyes filled with a sly smile, which showed that my frank statement hadn't taken him by surprise. "Yes, a married woman." I nodded my head sadly. "Don't tell me that you're talking about the director's wife," Eyal said, looking at me with a pitying smile. "Lazar's wife?" I laughed in astonishment. "What an idea!" And I immediately went on, "Can you really see me falling in love with a woman twenty years older than me?" But Eyal did not seem put out by my

indignant protests. He shrugged his shoulders and went on smiling. "I didn't mean anything—it doesn't matter. It's just that I
saw you couldn't stop taking pictures of her, and besides, she
really does look nice. But it doesn't matter. If not her, then who
have you fallen in love with? And what's more important, who's
she married to?" But at this point his mother returned and set
two bowls of soup carefully before us, after which she sat down
beside us and placed her beautiful white hands on the table.
"Aren't you eating with us?" I asked her sympathetically. "No,"
she said hesitantly, "I'm not hungry," and her face, which was
turned to her son, grew very red. Eyal reached out, laid his hand
gently on her shoulder, and said affectionately, "Yes, Mother has
to watch her weight."

Toward the end of the meal, when the bride-to-be, Hadas—a
vivacious, good-natured girl, with a fresh, wholesome look about
her—arrived and shook the snowflakes gracefully off her hair,
Eyal's mother retired at last to her room and left us alone. I made
up my mind not to say any more to Eyal, who immediately began
questioning me again about the "married woman," who had apparently sparked his imagination. Hadas, who radiated goodwill
toward me, was surprisingly well informed about my trip to India. It turned out that the shaven-headed girl, Michaela, who had
brought the news of the hepatitis to the Lazars and whom I had
taken at first for a boy, was from the same kibbutz as Hadas. I
stood up suddenly, though I had planned to leave, as if thrown
off balance by the excitement caused by the discovery of this
unexpected coincidence. I wondered whether I should go to
Eyal's mother's room to say good-bye and thank her for her
hospitality or leave her to rest. Eyal, maybe eager for me to leave,
stood up and said, "So, Benjy, don't say it's too far for you to
come to Ein Zohar for our wedding."

"Have you already set a date?"

"Of course," they chorused, and they told me the exact date
and made sure that I wrote it down in my calendar, and that no
night shift in the world would prevent me from being there. Then
Eyal insisted that I go in and say good-bye to his mother, who
was so fond of me; why not give her a little pleasure? I followed
him cautiously into the large, dim room, where we had played
when we were children and where she was lying, large and very
white, covered only by a sheet, which revealed how much weight

she had put on in the past year. "Benjy wants to say good-bye to you," whispered Eyal, gently waking her up. "Yes, I wanted to say good-bye to you," I said, "and also to thank you for the meal, which was even more delicious than usual." But she didn't smile at me, she only nodded her head and said, "Give my regards to your parents, and don't forget to come to Eyal's wedding. It's important for you to be there, not only for our sakes but also for yours."

"I'll be there, I promise," I said, and to reinforce my promise I put both my hands together over my heart in the Indian salutation.

I had every intention of going to the wedding. Eyal had been my best friend since we had been in school, after all. But in truth, I also held out hope that the boyish Michaela, a friend of Eyal and his future bride's, might be there, and perhaps through her I'd be able to make indirect contact with Einat, and through her with her parents, in case my connection with Lazar proved short-lived. As I strolled down the Jerusalem street, marveling at the great heaps of snow piled up along the sidewalks, the pleasant feeling did not leave me, nor did the mild envy I felt at Eyal's approaching marriage, nor the thought that any hopes of my own in that direction would have to be postponed for the time being owing to my feelings for Lazar's wife. Nothing could stop me from wishing to let myself go on falling into the abyss of the sweet new feeling. I got home and told my parents, who were waiting for me with their usual eagerness, that the roads were now free of snow and there was nothing to prevent me from returning to Tel Aviv; they knew very well that I had to get back to the hospital in order to fight for the continuation of my residency in the surgical department. My father suddenly burst out with uncharacteristic vehemence, "Why do they leave it up to Professor Hishin to decide by himself who to keep on in the department and who not to keep on? In these matters there are always hidden motives at work, and perhaps precisely—listen to me for a minute before you jump in with a ready retort—perhaps precisely because you're so hardworking and dedicated he wants to push you out. Why don't they let other people in the department decide? It's not only nimble fingers that count, but also loyalty and dedication, like you've given the hospital over the past year. Why don't they remember that?" It was hard for me to hear my father talking like this, perhaps because I felt the same smarting injustice. "But, Dad," I said, trying to calm him down, "you're talking as if it's the only hospital in the world. I can find a place at another hospital in Tel Aviv."

"Not on the same level as the one you're at now," he pronounced, and he was right. "So maybe I'll come back to Jerusalem," I said. "To Jerusalem?" said my father in disgust. "You're thinking of returning to Jerusalem and perhaps coming back to live at home? Then you'll really never get married." I burst into strange laughter. It had never occurred to me that my father too was worried by my single state. Now my mother broke her glum silence. "Don't keep him," she scolded my father. "It gets dark quickly. He should leave while it's still light." But my father grabbed hold of my shoulder. "Listen to me, Benjy, you fight for your place. Now you've got allies with influence in the hospital— Lazar and his wife."

"What's his wife got to do with it?" I asked in pretended surprise. "What has she got to do with the hospital?"

"She's got something to do with Lazar," my father insisted, "and he might be able to provide an additional post in the surgical department for you. He saw what a good doctor you are if not for you, they would still be stuck in India with a dying girl."

"Nonsense," I said, "you're exaggerating. All I did was perform a simple blood transfusion."

"I don't interfere in matters I'm not an expert in," said my father, "but listen to me. They haven't paid you anything yet?"

"Not yet," I said apologetically. "They didn't have a chance; we said good-bye at the airport."

"Never mind, it doesn't matter," explained my father. "They don't have to pay you. All they have to do is keep in touch and help you stay on at the hospital, so that you can stay in Tel Aviv, a town with a bit of life in it, at least." And he turned a wonderful, tired smile on me, illuminated by the bright blue of his eyes, trying to soften his words, because he knew very well that all his anger stemmed from his dream of returning, when he retired, from his Jerusalem exile to live near me in Tel Aviv.

My mother looked out the window and raised her eyes worriedly to the sky, as if to keep the blue expanse from clouding up. "If you've made up your mind to go back today, then you should start now," she urged me, using her common sense. I went into my room and saw that my bags were ready, crammed with freshly laundered clothes and underclothes, and peeping out of one of them I saw a tin of the Scottish shortbread I had loved as a child, which my mother continued to ply me with even though I had lost my taste for it long ago. I hadn't brought a single thing back from India for myself, apart from the accursed infatuation which continued to preoccupy me even here, in the shadowy room of my childhood. I put it on, and although my parents didn't like me to wear my crash helmet in the house, I put on the black helmet and fastened the strap, pulled on my old leather gloves, and went to start my Honda, it started with the first kick, emitted a spurt of bluish smoke, and was ready to go, as if my prolonged absence, the cold, and the snow made no difference to it and its clean white streamlined body were unaffected by external circumstances. I strapped the knapsacks to the pillion and covered them with canvas. My father stood by my side in a light flannel shirt, admiring the motorcycle. My mother stood behind him, shivering under her shawl. "Call us when you arrive," she said before I lowered the transparent visor over my eyes and revved the engine, and she went inside—but my father stayed where he was, unwilling to miss a single detail of the maneuvers that led me slowly along the sidewalk, against the direction of the traffic in the one-way street, and took me quickly and efficiently onto the main road.

You'd better drive carefully, I admonished myself at the first turn on the descent from Jerusalem, as the Honda went into a serious skid on an invisible layer of ice on the road. I immediately reined in the fast, powerful engine, shifted to second gear, and with a muffled roaring sound rode slowly down the middle of the road, slowing the cars behind me, whose drivers felt confident on the snow-free road and even had the nerve to honk at me. But I had no intention of picking up speed, and raised my visor so I had a better view of the slippery black pavement. As I proceeded at this leisurely pace, I noticed the coppery Jerusalem light, which the white snow had shot through with noble shades of purple. At first I thought that this light was given off by the

snow-covered rocks at the side of the road, but when I raised my
eyes and saw that the horizon of the white mountains all around
was full of the same strange light, I felt as if the heavy snowfall
had penetrated the very soul of the city, and for a moment I was
seized by anxiety and I slowed down even more, as if this new
light had it in its power to rob me of control over my bike. In the
next lane the drivers passing me were looking at me uncom-
prehendingly and even angrily, as if the fear I was betraying by
my slow driving were not only incompatible with my heavy black
crash helmet but also objectively unjustified. Even on the broad,
majestic three-lane ascent to the Castel, which was entirely man-
tled in snow, I did not increase my speed much and only went
into third gear, although the Honda was easily capable of flying
up the hill in fifth and devouring the distance in a single roar.
The strange light suffusing the familiar coppery pink of Jerusalem with such a sad, mysterious hue was still preoccupying me so
much that I did not want to hasten its inevitable loss in the abundant stream of clear, cheerful light that would come pouring in
from the open western horizon when I passed the summit.

But the horizon of the plain, which first appears as a solemn
promise at the summit of the Castel, then it gradually disappears
again on the steep descent separating the new stone houses of
Abu Gosh from the springs of Aqua Bella, was now stained not
only by the big round sun going down in the west but by the blue
lights of police cars surrounding a huge, showy motorcycle that
had crashed on the road and the large white helmet lying next to
it. Drivers slowed down and turned their heads, trying to figure
out from the exact position of the helmet what was left of the life
of the wretched rider, who was already being borne toward the
awesome Jerusalem light. And now the cars behind me and next
to me expected me to slow down even more on the dangerous
multilane descent. But I stayed in third gear as I sailed down to
the little valley of Abu Gosh, thinking not of the motorcyclist but
of myself. If it had been me, would Lazar's wife—whom I still
hesitated to call Dori to myself—remember me and my name,
let's say in one or two years' time, when the trip to India was
already forgotten?

But could a journey like that be forgotten? I wondered, as the
Honda began eagerly devouring the short, straight ascent that
divided the blue-branched pomegranate orchards of Abu Gosh

from the white houses of an Arab village whose name I had never succeeded in learning, and which still looked to me like a Jewish settlement onto which the minaret of a mosque had been grafted. After all, India wasn't Europe or America, buried in identical airports and brightly lit avenues of churches and giant department stores. Could the golden Varanasi, with the sweetish smoke of its dead, or the temples of Bodhgaya, with their statues of animals and birds, be forgotten just like that? And was this woman, whose nickname I tried to whisper against the wind, doomed to go on remembering the journey to India even when she was an old woman in her nursing-home bed? What a pity that she would not be able to add to this memory, which from now on would become absolute, the strange passion that the young doctor accompanying them had conceived for her, a passion which gave an unexpected sexual value to a woman approaching her fiftieth year. Strange, I thought to myself as the motorcycle began picking up speed on the pleasant curves of the Sha'ar-Hagai road and I had to lower the plastic visor against the stinging, pine-scented wind, strange that I still didn't know the date of her birth, even though her passport had lain open more than once before my eyes.

And thus, full of tender thoughts of love in spite of the savage roaring of my motorcycle behind my back, I emerged in fifth gear from Sha'ar-Hagai into the Ayalon Valley, crossing the last border of Jerusalem, which had steeped me in rest but also in enforced idleness, with a feeling of relief. Before I could enjoy the orchards and broad fields, and the large water reservoir which had recently been built here, a first quiet flash of lightning appeared on the horizon, which was the greenish color of a computer screen, signaling a warning that the big cloud floating merrily toward me like a dirigible, ignited by the rosy glow of the setting sun, was already preparing to burst not into fire but with water. I had to hurry, I said to myself, and increased my speed to over sixty-five miles an hour, noticing too late the police car parked on the other side, which caught me in its radar trap. The blue light began to blink and the car started to move, which forced me, even before the policeman decided on his policy, to shoot up to a hundred miles and disabuse him of even the glimmer of a hope of catching up with me. And at a really wild speed, foreign to my nature and also to my values, I ate up in a

few minutes the twelve miles separating the Trappist monastery
from the interchange leading to the airport, the thought of the
passenger terminal filling me with intense longings, and by side
roads and detours I entered the heart of Tel Aviv, which seemed
to me, in spite of the nagging, miserable rain, full of a secret new
promise.

Once home, with my bags crouching in the middle of the room
like a couple of wild, wet animals, I phoned Lazar's house immediately. It wasn't only my right, I thought, but also my duty to
check up on my patient, who to my surprise answered the phone
herself and sounded more confused and lost in her own home
than she had in India. But perhaps thanks to the trust I had
inspired in her on our first meeting, when she was lying on a
sleeping bag in the Bodhgaya monastery, she soon bucked up and
shed her listlessness, and gave me a few details about her physical
condition, at least insofar as she understood it. The head of internal medicine at the hospital, Professor Levine, had come to see
her the previous morning and had wanted to hospitalize her immediately in his ward, but her parents had decided to wait for
their friend Hishin, who had returned from Paris this morning.
Hishin had come straight from the airport, given her a long examination, and recommended that she remain at home, even
though her temperature had gone up again. Her temperature had
gone up? I was profoundly disappointed, because I had presumed
that the blood transfusion would also eliminate the liver infection, which was apparently the cause of the ongoing dysfunction
in the immune system. "Did you tell Hishin about what happened in India?" I asked. "Of course," replied Einat. "My
mother and father told him everything."

"And what did he say?" I inquired anxiously. She thought for
a minute, and then said, "He said that the main thing was that it
turned out all right."

"What turned out all right?" I sneered, offended, but Einat
was unable to explain Professor Hishin's meaning, and so—with
a pounding heart, tightening my grip on the receiver—I dared to
ask to speak to her mother for a minute. But her parents weren't
at home. Lazar's wife had gone to work after Hishin's visit, and
Lazar had gone out on errands shortly before I phoned. "And
you're at home alone?" I said in a tone that surprised even me by
its anger. "Yes," she said, presumably also taken aback by my

inexplicable rage. When she saw that I had fallen into a strange silence, she asked if I wanted her father to call me when he got back. "No, it doesn't matter," I said quickly, "I'll see him tomorrow at the hospital." I hung up, undid the buttons of my leather jacket, threw it onto the floor, and immediately phoned the surgical department, to get hold of Hishin and hear from him directly what he thought of the blood transfusion. But it transpired that Hishin, who had only just arrived, had gone to the internal medicine ward to talk to Levine. "What for?" I asked anxiously. But the nurse didn't know. "What did you come back in such a hurry for?" asked my rival-friend, the other resident, grabbing the phone from the nurse. "We all thought that you would take advantage of the trip to do a little sightseeing on your own." He sounded friendly. Had he heard something from Hishin about the transfusion I had performed in Varanasi? He wanted to hear my first impressions of India, but I didn't have the patience to talk about my trip, and I asked him what had happened in the department during my two weeks' absence, inquiring about one patient after the other, mentioning their names, which I remembered perfectly, and asking about the results of the operations at which I had been present. He was surprised by my detailed questions, but he tried to answer them as fully as possible. Then I suddenly remembered the woman who had been lying on the operating table when Lazar came to call Hishin to his office. "How is she? How is she?" I asked in unaccountable agitation. "You sewed her up yourself." He sounded slightly embarrassed when he replied, "She died of an internal hemorrhage a day or two after you left."

"An internal hemorrhage?" I repeated, suddenly struck by real sorrow for the young woman, and for her husband and her mother, who had been waiting outside the door of the ward. "Why should she have hemorrhaged?" I went on with a twinge of anger. "I remember every minute of that operation, I haven't forgotten anything, I thought about it again in India—it was a simple benign operation."

"Yes," he confirmed in his deep voice, "that was our mistake. We thought it was a simple operation, but it wasn't simple. The bleeding flooded and infected everything, and Hishin still hasn't discovered the source."

"And what about the postmortem?" I demanded.

"Nothing clear, a complete mystery."

"Mystery?" I pounced in scorn and despair, as if he were personally responsible for this death. "What mystery? To call something a mystery, you don't have to be a doctor."

Seven

Has the time already come to consider marriage? If so, the author responsible for imposing the ideal of marriage on this chapter will have to begin melting the hard gray shell of bachelorhood in which he has wrapped his hero, who at this hour of wintry dawn is skillfully and responsibly maneuvering his motorcycle through the stream of Tel Aviv traffic, casting occasional sidelong glances at a woman sitting behind the wheel of her car and smoking a cigarette, no longer in the normal wish to enjoy the sight of a pretty face but in the new hope of encountering a familiar one.

But how will it come about, a marriage, which can sometimes be seen as an easy and self-evident thing, with a natural flow of its own, but is also liable to be difficult, demanding, and recalcitrant? It may, with the same justice, be called an unnatural and even absurd act, like two big, strong birds led on a chain by the rather irritable and myopic character who appeared as a mystery in the first part of this book and has turned, in the second part, into marriage without losing any of his original and delightful mysteriousness, or his nasty habit of paying brief, unexpected nocturnal calls in the guise of an ancient, forgotten relative, appearing suddenly from the bedroom closet, dragging behind him two predatory birds, who may appear to be stepping tamely and obediently in his wake but on closer inspection turn out to have been bound together.

"Maybe you should free them and let them fly?" we suggest with friendly compassion. "Free them?" he replies in surprise, in disappointment, even in annoyance, and tightens the chain in his hand. "How can that be possible? They're married." "Married?" We can't help bursting into short peals of merry laughter in the silence of the night, bending down slightly to observe the curious

couple standing in happy indifference, their tails touching. "In
what sense?" We burst into laughter again. But we're too late,
and we can no longer obtain an answer to the question which
our rash laughter has rendered superfluous, for the pair now
draw themselves up gravely, shedding a golden feather, and with
a silent, crooked gait they continue on their way, dragging the
mystery of their marriage behind them, its deep purpose, its anx-
ious bond, its dumb loyalty, its achievements, and its frustra-
tions. Now the mystery passes before us, stern-faced and sad-
eyed, bowed beneath the weight of a responsibility which is not
always comprehensible, which is not always justified, and the
chain wrapped around his hand trembles and chimes like a little
bell.

๛๛

When I arrived at the ward, Hishin was already doing his
rounds. At first he seemed to be trying to avoid me, and he
slipped into his office, and then he changed his mind and
emerged and came at me from behind and embraced me warmly.
"I heard all about it," he said in a loud whisper. "A great success—I'm proud of my choice. I saw Einat too, and examined her
thoroughly, and I'm with you a hundred percent. Not only in the
diagnosis, but also in the emergency blood transfusion. I told the
Lazars, it was the brilliant idea of a doctor whose insight is
deeper than the sharpest knife. And if there's a slightly different
opinion, like that of my good friend Levine, who regards the
transfusion as a frivolous and superfluous procedure on your
part, take no notice—he's a strange, proud man who thinks he
invented hepatitis. Don't be upset by what he says to you—he's
already said he wants to talk to you. Listen to him patiently, nod
your head politely, but know that I'm behind your idea, especially from the psychological point of view, and as I've often told
you, psychology is no less important than the knife in your
hand," and he gaily brandished an imaginary knife. But I wasn't
interested in hearing again about his belief in psychology. I
wanted to clarify immediately whether behind that sly, jocular
manner he really did support my blood transfusion, because I
still thought with strange longing about the thin, transparent
tube silently pumping the blood between the two beds in

Varanasi while crowds streamed into the Ganges below. "But what's Professor Levine's problem?" I asked in despair, and before he could reply, I rapidly and angrily hurled the test results at him, all of which I still knew by heart. The two transaminases which rose from 40 to a 180 and to nearly a 158; the bilirubin level of nearly 30; the suspected damage to the coagulatory system. "Where's my mistake?" I demanded. But Hishin was already waving his hands impatiently. "Please, my friend, don't try to convince me, I'm already convinced, altogether I'm your greatest fan." And he winked at me and at the nurse standing next to us, and joined his hands on his heart in a new, Indian gesture, which astounded me with its cunning. "I beg you, don't start throwing those numbers at me now—I've never really understood what they tell us about the state of the liver. That's what we've got Professor Levine for, he's the one who understands the liver, I only cut it up." He burst into laughter and hugged me again. "No, Dr. Rubin, don't waste your energy, because I really am a great fan of yours, otherwise I wouldn't have sent you to India, and I'm glad to know that others have now joined me in my good opinion."

I knew at once whom he meant, and the feeling of happiness was so sudden and overwhelming that the blood rushed to my face. I lowered my eyes and said nothing. But now Hishin decided to talk, and with the same speed with which he made his initial precise, elegant incisions, he seized me by the shoulder, dismissed the nurse, and led me into his office. He shut the door and seated me on a chair and said, "What do you think, that I don't know what's eating you all the time? But what can I do? There's only one position available in the department, and I have to choose between the two of you, and it's a very difficult choice, because you've each got a lot of virtues and only a few shortcomings. Lazar and his wife have also asked me if you're going to continue as a resident with us."

"Lazar and his wife? Why his wife?" I muttered, but the thought that she had shown an interest in my future at the hospital sent a powerful thrill through me. "Why did you tell them about me?" I asked in offended innocence. "But they were the ones who asked," Hishin justified himself. "They both wanted to know what your chances in the department were, and I saw that it pained them to hear that I hadn't chosen you, so I said to Lazar, you dare complain? The number of positions available are up to you; give me another position and I'll keep him on for another year, even though"—and he raised an admonishing finger—"it's not really his natural place. He'll be an excellent doctor, but his true aptitude is in his soul, not his hands. Not because his hands aren't good, but because he thinks too much before he cuts or stitches, and in the meantime time passes, and time in an operation isn't just very precious but also very dangerous. So why insist on playing with knives when his feeling, his deep understanding, his bright ideas are needed elsewhere? So we both decided to speak to Professor Levine about you, because there's a place for a substitute doctor for six months in his department. In the meantime take that, hang around there for a while and learn what you can—you'll always find someone, if it's really so important to you, to take you back to the operating table. But for God's sake, get the business of that blood transfusion you performed in India out of the way first. Go and tell him why you thought it was necessary, so he won't agitate himself for nothing, because he's not a well man."

And thus the final clarification of my position in the surgical department was concluded. There were only two weeks of the trial year left, and I tried to get the most out of them and not to miss a single operation. Sometimes I would stay in the hospital in the evening, after my shift was over, just on the off-chance that I might be able to take part in an emergency operation and look deep inside the human body again before my enforced banishment from surgery began. And now that I was about to leave, everyone was generous. From time to time I was allowed to finish minor sutures by myself, or even to begin primary incisions. And I did it well, or at least I thought so. Senior doctors in the department, who knew that I was soon leaving, nodded their heads in satisfaction, and Hishin himself would say, "Very good, excellent stitching, what a pity you're leaving us," and wink at me. But we never had a real talk. Once, when we were standing and waiting in the operating room for the results of the lab tests, he asked me to tell him about India, but I answered with deliberate dryness and blandness, and then he said nastily to the nurses busy with the instruments, "What do you think of Dr. Rubin? We sent him to India and he keeps all his experiences to himself. You could show us a few pictures, at least. The Lazars were at my place yesterday and they complained that you were still hanging on to all the photographs of the trip."

Indeed, I was still hanging on to all the photographs of the trip, including the ones of Lazar and his wife. The pictures were lying on the little table next to my bed, and I would often look at the two of them, study the way they stood together in front of different views of the Taj Mahal, which I was now sorry I had missed owing to my exaggerated generosity. Again and again I examined her face and her body and the way she stood and the way she managed to smile spontaneously in all the pictures, and in my heart I insisted on calling her "my love." I knew that if I gave the photos to Lazar, I would run the risk of finally parting from them, whereas I was busy racking my brains all the time for ways to renew my contact with Lazar, in order to reach her through him. The idea of secretly developing pictures of her by herself and keeping them struck me as immoral, even though I imagined that in the end I wouldn't be able to resist the temptation, at least with regard to one picture in which she looked particularly charming in the reddish brown Indian light. I wondered what they had in mind regarding the financial arrangements between us. Were they going to give me a fee or not? At the beginning of the month I received my full salary from the hospital, and I saw that there was no mention on the slip of a vacation or absence from work. As if the journey to India had taken place only in my imagination. Had the administrative head of the hospital issued secret instructions to the financial department to ignore my absence, or had it simply not been brought to their attention? For the time being I didn't go to Lazar to ask him about it, so I wouldn't have to remind him of the remuneration his wife had promised me in our telephone conversation on the eve of the trip. The knapsack with the medical kit was still in my apartment too, and for a few days I wondered what I should do with it. It occurred to me to confiscate it as compensation for my trouble, but I was afraid that Dr. Hessing, the head pharmacist, who had prepared it with such loving care, was still waiting for it. Finally I decided to hand it back to him personally, and to my surprise he was disappointed that I had seen fit to drag it back from India with me instead of donating it to some institution there, as he had suggested. "We were in an emergency situation there up to the last minute," I explained to him. "I didn't know whether I might need it until we were actually on our way home, and I could hardly leave it standing in the middle of the airport."

"I would simply have written the word "Israel" and the name of our hospital on it and left it with one of the airport guards," said the pharmacist regretfully. And he unpacked the drugs and dressings and threw them all away without even looking at them, and put the instruments into an old cardboard box. I wanted to say something to him about the resourcefulness and imagination with which he had prepared the kit, and tell him about how I had used it, but he was already shaking his head at me with a certain hostility, as if I had spoiled his intention of taking advantage of our trip to make a private gesture of humanity toward the true sufferers of this world.

After this I made up my mind to give the photos to Lazar, and thanks to the good education I had received at home, I refrained at the last moment from duplicating for myself even one of the pictures in which she was alone and contented myself with the more distant family photos I had taken in Bodhgaya. If I was to liberate myself from the thoughts enslaving me to this woman, I warned myself, it had better be sooner than later, and a good, clear picture like the one in which she was standing and smiling (albeit only a faint smile) with the entire Taj Mahal floating miraculously behind her head, shining in the rosy light, would only delay the desired liberation. Although three weeks had already passed since I had seen her, things kept on happening to complicate my feelings toward her. For example, there had been Hishin's casual remark about how it wasn't only Lazar who took an interest in my future in the hospital, and the sudden suspicion, idiotic but persistent, that Hishin too was secretly in love with her. Thus, in the afternoon of one of my last days in the surgical department, I went to the administrative wing to give Lazar the photos, to ask about the welfare of my patient, and at the same time to give my regards to his wife. But the secretary, who immediately recognized me and remembered my name and greeted me with genuine heartiness, informed me regretfully that Lazar had just left his office for his lunch break. A devil must have gotten into me, for just as I was, still in my white coat, I hurried to catch up with him or, more accurately, to follow him.

For I was sure that he was on his way to meet the woman I persisted in secretly calling "my love." He didn't like leaving her alone, I thought with anxiety and a spurt of lust, which hastened my steps and sharpened my senses so that I was soon able to identify the big head with the mane of curly gray hair in the distance, among the people streaming toward the hospital parking lot. And as I walked I took off my white coat, which I bundled into the Honda's black box. I took out the crash helmet and quickly put it on, and although I didn't have my leather jacket with me and it was quite cold outside, I started the motorcycle. Since I knew the make of Lazar's car, which we had discussed on the long train journey from New Delhi to Varanasi, I was able to identify it as it pulled out of its reserved parking place. From the movies I was familiar with the advantages of pursuing an automobile on a motorcycle, but I had never considered the absolute advantage of the helmet visor, which allowed the pursuer to tail the target so closely as to be almost intimate. It was one o'clock in the afternoon, and Lazar's car wove confidently and cleverly among the traffic, aiming for the center of town and the street where Lazar's wife's office was. There was no parking, and he had to leave his car on the sidewalk, apologizing to the owner of the store whose display window he blocked, and wait for his wife there. She finally came out, after a few minutes of waiting which seemed interminable to me too as I sat at a little distance on my Honda, getting damp from the fine drizzle filling the air. When I saw her hurrying on her high heels, this middle-aged woman in a short skirt—perhaps too short for her age—draped in the velvety blue tunic that she had taken all the way to India but hardly worn at all, her plump face laughing, a bundle of office files tucked under her heavy arm, insisting on opening an umbrella to protect her bare head during the short distance between the office door and the car, I realized that there was no mistake about it, it wasn't a delusion or a mirage: I was really in love with her.

❦

I could have stopped my pursuit then, got off my bike and taken shelter in one of the building entrances until the rain stopped, and then returned to the hospital; or I could have approached them as if it were an accidental meeting, given them the envelope with the photos, said a few words holding out a promise for the future, and gone away. But instead I remained on the bike in my light jacket, masked by my helmet, and waited for them to start off so I could go on following them—this time from a greater distance, for I was afraid of her turning around. I rode behind them, saw them stop at a bakery, and watched her go in and come out with a rectangular white box tied up with a blue ribbon, which reminded me of the shoe box I had voluntarily stored in my suitcase. From there they continued to a fruit-and-vegetable stall, where they stopped after an apparent argument, and an Arab youth came out and loaded bursting bags into the car. So they're still cultivating their round bellies, I thought sarcastically, and although I was already soaking wet I kept on their tail, because I wanted to see them with my own eyes arrive at their apartment in Chen Avenue, get out of the car, help each other carry the bags and boxes, and disappear through the big glass door. So she won't be left alone during her lunch break, I thought, and I felt a kind of relief.

But I didn't hand over the photographs that day, even though Lazar returned to his office at four o'clock. And I didn't take them to him the next day either, but set off to follow him again, to see if this time too he would be careful not to leave his wife alone at home during her lunch break. It was pouring, and instead of the short skirt and high heels she was wearing boots and tight trousers, and a black cape which gave her a new profile. How is this going to end? I scolded myself in despair, returning to the hospital drenched to the skin after they had disappeared into the door of their apartment building. It was my last day in the surgical department, and since nothing had yet been agreed with Professor Levine, who had been absent for two weeks with some mysterious disease, I felt, perhaps for the first time in my life, up in the air, without a patron or a framework. I therefore decided that in the afternoon, when Lazar returned, I would go to his office and give him the photographs and ask him one or two questions about the rights of a temporary, substitute doctor. But this time, although the secretary, Miss Kolby, was friendly, she was unable to find any free time in his tight schedule of afternoon appointments. Only when darkness fell, as I was going from bed to bed on a private final round of farewells—without telling any of the patients that this was my last visit, because I didn't want them to feel abandoned or betrayed during the long, hard night ahead of them—did the secretary phone the ward to look for me and tell me that Lazar had finally finished all his appointments and that he would be very glad to see me in his office.

Once more I found myself in the large, elegant room with its flowered curtains and flourishing plants, which now, at this late hour, looked very different from all the doctors' offices in the hospital, like some cozy domestic interior, protected from all the diseases, the smells, the drugs, and the medical instruments, remote too from all the paperwork, the forms and the files, as if it were not the center from which the hospital was run but a refuge in which to escape it. Lazar sat behind his vast desk, his curly head, which had served as an effective signpost among the heads of the Indian crowds, wagging against the high back of his executive chair as he conducted an animated conversation with Miss Kolby, his devoted thirty-five-year-old secretary, who was standing beside him. "Aha!" he cried in friendly rebuke. "At last! Where did you disappear to?"

"I disappeared?" I repeated with a surprised smile, for during the past three weeks it had seemed to me that he and his wife had been my constant companions by day and by night. "I've been here all the time, in the hospital." "I know you've been here," he said with genuine friendliness, "but we haven't seen you. Dori is already convinced that you must have taken offense at something, because ever since we parted at the airport you've shown no sign of life."

"But I phoned one evening," I protested, filled with joy at this new proof of her interest. "Didn't Einat tell you? She said that Hishin and Professor Levine had already seen her, and I understood that I didn't have anything to worry about anymore."

"You've still got something to worry about." Lazar laughed jovially. "But I'm not talking about Einati, even though she's not completely out of the woods yet, and Levine, who wanted to hospitalize her in his ward and run further tests on her, is sick himself. No, I mean you should worry about yourself, because we've still got some outstanding business to clear up between us."

"Business?" I asked innocently. He folded his hands on the desk and looked right at me. "The fee we owe you for the journey to India."

"There's no need for any fee," I said immediately, and lowered my eyes so that he wouldn't sense any hesitation in them. Lazar tried to insist and I repeated firmly, "I don't want you to pay me anything." I looked into the bright, penetrating eyes of his secretary, who was still standing next to us. "The trip was payment enough." And then I felt a pang, not only because of the payment, which I had finally waived, but also because of the brevity and haste of the trip. "I only came to bring you these," I added weakly, holding out the envelope with the photographs. "Ah, our pictures," he cried happily, and snatched the envelope from my hand and took out the photographs, which he glanced at rapidly, smiling and immediately passing them on to the secretary, who took them reverently and studied them slowly and thoroughly. "Dori always comes out wonderfully in photos," she said in an intimate, familiar way. "Yes," Lazar agreed with a sigh, "that's because she's serene inside herself, not like me. And that always makes the lines sharp and clear," and he nodded his head at me as if to apologize for having to praise his wife in front of strangers. "But how much do I owe you for the pictures?" He whipped out his wallet. "Nonsense," I said, shrinking. "Why nonsense?" he protested. "I can't let you refuse everything here. Tell me how much they cost or I won't take them." And he took out a fifty-shekel note and put it on the desk. With my heart aching at the thought of parting from the pictures, I shook my head firmly and explained that my parents had paid for the two rolls of film to be developed. "It's a present from them, to both of you." This persuaded him to accept the photographs without paying for them. "A present from your parents?" he repeated, as if to obtain my confirmation. "Mind you don't forget to thank them," and he made haste to return the money to his pocket, and turned to his secretary. "Dori'll be thrilled to get them—she loves photographs, and now we'll have something to remind us of the trip, which, believe me, we've already forgotten completely." Then he glanced at his watch and said with an air of surprise, "But she should have been here by now." When he saw me beginning to edge toward the door—and maybe he also sensed my inner turmoil—he stood up to stop me. "Wait a minute and say hello to her. She asked about you." I looked at my watch. It was a quarter past seven. My last hour in the surgical department was already over. "I don't know." I hesitated. "I still have to get back to the ward."

"The ward?" exclaimed Lazar. "But today is your last day there!"

"You know that too?" I cried in genuine admiration. "And even smaller and less significant details too," said Lazar with a sigh, and closed his eyes in agreeable weariness. "That's what I'm here for. I also know, for example, that Professor Levine might employ you as a substitute in his department until June." "July," I said, trying weakly to correct him. "No, only until June," he stated decisively. "The position's only available until June. But what does it matter—June, July, we'll cross that bridge when we come to it. In the meantime we'll have to wait until he gets better, because he insists on clarifying some little thing with you." "Clarifying?" I whispered. "It's no big deal," said Lazar dismissively. "Didn't Hishin tell you? He's bothered by the blood transfusion you gave Einat."

"Yes, so I've heard, but I don't understand what bothers him about it."

"I don't understand what his problem is either. Hishin didn't get it either. So you'll have to talk to him yourself and explain exactly what your intention was. He's a fair man, but impatient."

"What's wrong with him?" I asked. "Something or other," said Lazar, smiling faintly to himself. "But what exactly?" I persisted, consumed with curiosity about my future employer's mysterious disease. Lazar exchanged a glance with his secretary, who apparently knew the secret of Levine's disease but warned Lazar with a look not to reveal it to me. "Never mind, never mind." He waved his hand to silence me, and all of a sudden he cocked his head in a gesture of profound attention. "Here comes Dori, I can hear her footsteps." Neither I nor the secretary, who also inclined her head slightly, could hear any footsteps—on the contrary, the silence in the wing only seemed to deepen. But Lazar insisted that he could hear his wife's footsteps in the distance, by

virtue of the strong bond between them, which had upset and
excited me during the trip to India. And sure enough, we soon
heard the sound of footsteps, soft but self-confident, and joy
flooded me as I discovered that I too was able to recognize them.
She hesitated slightly outside the door of the next room, but then
advanced briskly toward the door of her husband's office, which
she opened quietly but without any hesitation, smiling her warm
smile. She entered the room, dragging her left foot slightly and
definitely surprised to see me, but greeted the secretary with an
affectionate hug and kiss before she turned to me and asked,
repeating her husband's formula, in the same tone of mild rebuke, "What have you been up to? Where did you disappear
to?"

"Where did *you* disappear to?" Lazar interrupted her angrily.
"What took you so long? You said you'd be here by six and it's
already twenty past seven!" "Don't get excited." A tender smile
spread over her plump face. "You can't tell me you didn't have
plenty to keep you busy in the meantime."

"That's not the point," he said petulantly. But he was obviously pleased by her answer, and he stood up to collect his belongings. "Tomorrow I've got a crazy day. But look at the nice
present we've got for you here." He handed her the photographs,
which she snatched from him with a childish cry of delight, and
still without meeting my eyes, she slipped her cape off her shoulders and said enthusiastically, "And we thought that we must
have overexposed the film by mistake." She immediately opened
her umbrella to dry in a corner of the room, sat down calmly in
the armchair between the two giant plants, took off her glasses,
and began to examine the pictures one by one, at the same time
gladly accepting the secretary's offer of a cup of tea and overcoming Lazar's objections that they were in a hurry to get home
with a smiling protest: "Just a minute, let me me relax for a
minute, I'm freezing to death." The secretary, who seemed happy
to wait on her, now turned politely to me to ask me if I would
join them, and although I was already standing poised on one
foot, ready and perhaps also eager to leave, I couldn't refuse, and
suddenly I felt the full power of the hypnotic mystery riveting me
to this woman, clumsy in her winter clothes, her freckled face
flushed, her bun coming unraveled again, crossing her legs,

which the black boots made even longer, and studying with open enjoyment and occasional soft laughter the pictures of herself and her husband on the trip, which according to him they had already almost forgotten.

The quick-thinking secretary, who judging by her bare fingers and the time she had on her hands was presumably single, brought in a tray with three cups of tea and slices of a cream cake left over from some private party in the administrative wing. Lazar's wife thanked her in her usual enthusiastic and exaggerated style. "You've saved my life, I'm completely parched. All afternoon I've been running around with my mother making arrangements for an old-age home."

"Your mother's going into an old-age home?" the secretary asked in surprise. "Why? I met her in a café a month ago and she looked wonderful."

"Yes," said Dori complacently, as if she were personally responsible for her mother's appearance, "she's just fine, she manages by herself, but when we were in India she heard that a place had become available in an old-age home she had put her name down for a few years ago. We'd almost forgotten about it, because nobody seems to die there, and even though she's independent and she could go on living alone in her apartment, she's afraid to lose her place there. What can I do? We have to respect their wishes." She turned her face to me, as if surprised by my silent presence, and in the almost intimate tone which had come into being among the three of us in the last days of the trip, she repeated the question I had not yet answered: "Well, what have you been up to?" When she saw that I was groping for an answer, as if I weren't sure what she had in mind, she went on to ask companionably, "Have you recovered from our trip yet?" Although I was gratified by her use of the word "our," I was still unable to come up with a graceful reply, and I stammered awkwardly, "In what sense?"

"In what sense?" she repeated, perplexed by my pedantic question. "I don't know . . . You looked a little sad and depressed at the end."

"Depressed?" I whispered, completely taken aback, and somewhat hurt by the fact that my secret love had transmitted not warmth but depression. But I was nevertheless pleased that she took an interest in my moods. "Sad?" I smiled at her with faint irony. "Why sad?" Her eyes immediately looked around for her husband, to have her feelings confirmed. But he had lost patience with this idle chatter, and after clearing the papers and files off his desk and snapping his briefcase shut, he stood up and ostentatiously switched off his desk lamp and sent a look of open hostility in the direction of his wife, who was still eating her slice of cake. "We thought you were sad," continued Dori, "because of losing your place in Hishin's department." Lazar, who was already putting on his short khaki raincoat and briskly pulling a funny fur hat onto his head, interrupted confidently, "Don't worry, we've found him a temporary job in Levine's department."

"The internal medicine department?" said his wife enthusiastically, and turned to me: "Well, are you pleased?"

"Yes," Lazar answered for me, "why shouldn't he be pleased? You heard for yourself what Hishin said about him all the time: he's a born internist, and he'll be able to do a good job there." And when he saw that his wife was still slowly sipping her tea, he said impatiently, "Come on, Dori, you've had enough, we have to get home."

But she went on sipping the last drops of tea in her cup, as if intent on stressing her independence and showing that she could be satisfied with herself and cope very well with the world around her, as long as she wasn't left alone. Finally she stood up slowly, draped the long black cape negligently around her shoulders, took a blue scarf out of her pocket and then a sheet of paper, which she held out to the secretary, who appeared to hesitate between her natural loyalty to Lazar and her admiration for his wife. And Dori gave her a friendly smile and asked, "Do you think I could leave this medical report for my mother's old-age home with you for Professor Levine to fill in? I'll phone him this evening and explain."

"It will have to wait," Lazar intervened, with what sounded like a note of malicious satisfaction in his voice. "Levine isn't here. He's sick."

"Levine's sick again?" cried his wife, who judging by the faint alarm in her voice apparently knew the secret of his mysterious

disease. "So what will we do? We have to return the questionnaire the day after tomorrow."

"Nothing terrible will happen if your mother goes to the
Health Service doctor for once," said Lazar firmly. "She pays her
dues every month and she never goes near the place."

"Out of the question!" His wife dismissed this possibility angrily, turning to the secretary for support. "How can she go by
herself to the Health Service? And whom will she see there? She
hasn't seen a doctor there for years." But Lazar seemed too tired
after a hard day's work to deal with this problem, and he
grabbed his wife's umbrella, collected the empty cups and put
them on the tray, quickly cramming the remains of his wife's
cream cake into his mouth as he did so, and hurried toward the
door, where I was waiting for an opportunity to take my leave.
"Perhaps some other doctor in the internal medicine department
could do it instead of Professor Levine," suggested the secretary
carefully. "I can't ask anyone to do it," snapped Lazar. "This
isn't my private hospital, and the doctors aren't my servants.
Levine is a friend of mine, and he looks after her mother out of
friendship. Nothing terrible will happen," he said, turning to his
wife again, still in a faintly spiteful tone, "if your mother goes to
the Health Service for once. It won't kill her." And he switched
off the light in the room, even though the two women were still
in it; and I, having already advanced into the illuminated secretaries' office, looked back and saw the heavy shadow on the wall,
trapped between the shadows of the foliage of the two big plants,
and once again my heart was struck with bafflement at this inexplicable attraction, and still I hesitated, waiting for the right moment to say good-bye without making it final. They were leaving
through the brightly lit office cubicles, stepping between computers and gray-covered typewriters, and I waited politely for her
to pass me. To my surprise, I smelled the sharp, sweet scent of the
perfume she had bought at the airport when we arrived at New
Delhi, where she had asked our opinion of it. Now she was listening to the secretary telling her some long, complicated, personal story which Lazar had apparently already heard during the
course of the day, and I went on trailing behind them—a young
doctor whose position in the hospital may have deteriorated recently, but whose participation in the trip to India nevertheless

gave him the status of a kind of distant member of the family, if not in the eyes of the devoted secretary—to whom it had not even occurred, for example, to propose me as a substitute for Dr. Levine, to spare that nice grandmother the misery of going to the Health Service the next day in the pouring rain and waiting for hours in line in order to coax a medical certificate out of some rigid bureaucrat of a doctor. But as we were standing in the corridor, about to say good-bye, my heart suddenly pounded with joy at the thought that I didn't need any favors from the secretary: I could offer my services myself, and thus wind a flimsy thread—for I was well aware of the flimsiness of all these threads—around this impossible woman.

And so, just before parting from them in the dimly lit main corridor, I stopped and in simple, straightforward words offered them my help in filling out the medical report required by the old people's home. I saw Dori's eyes shine, although she said nothing, waiting for Lazar to respond first. He seemed to hesitate, unwilling to owe me yet another favor, and then he put his arm around my shoulder and said, "You really mean it? That's a wonderful idea. And you'll be free tomorrow, too." But he immediately added a condition to the wonderful idea, that this time I would accept a proper fee for my services, not like the trip to India, which in the end I had given them as a present. At this his wife was very surprised. "How come we didn't pay him?" She turned to her husband indignantly. "He refused to take it," cried Lazar angrily. "Go on, you tell her yourself."

"That's not right," she went on, working herself up to the kind of tantrum I knew she was capable of throwing. "That's not right," she repeated. "We can't possibly let it all come off his vacation."

"It hasn't come off his vacation," replied Lazar in embarrassment. "It's been left as if he were at the hospital all those two weeks. For the time being. Until we decide what to do."

"But that's impossible," she scolded her husband, "and it's illegal too." All of a sudden, amused and excited by their agitated exchange, I leaned toward her, and in the yellowish light of the corridor I looked straight through her glasses into her brown eyes, around which her automatic smile had etched many little lines. "Madame Solicitor," I said in a new, humorous, familiar tone, which no doubt surprised them as well as me, "what's illegal here? Friendship? Here"—I took hold of the slender hand of the secretary, who seemed delighted by the spirit of levity which had seized hold of me, and reproached the two Lazars—"she can bear witness before any committee of inquiry that not only didn't I obtain any benefits from the director or his wife, but on the contrary, they haven't renewed my residency in the surgical department, and they're barely allowing me to be a temporary substitute in the internal medicine department." I took a little prescription pad out of my pocket and jotted down my telephone number, in case they had lost it or even thrown it away, and took Dori's mother's address and phone number from them, and we arranged that the next day, early in the morning, we would set a time for my visit. "I'll try to be there with you," she promised. "Highly desirable," I said promptly. And they thanked me warmly once more, their arms already groping for each other next to the revolving door, from which they emerged together, wrapped up like a pair of clumsy bears, into the thick, heavy rain flooding the illuminated plaza.

A new thread had unexpectedly been tied, I thought with satisfaction, to reinforce the Indian connection, which had weakened and would soon have snapped. And now that the scalpel had been forcibly removed from my hand and I had been transformed into an internist against my will, I could become their family doctor and treat their sore throats, blood pressure, hot flashes, mysterious stomachaches, perhaps even give them advice on questions of weight, and at the same time feed the fever of this strange, impossible love in my fantasies until it died down of its own accord, as I was sure it would. But as soon as she disappeared from view, short and awkward, trying to hold her umbrella over her husband as he hurried to their car, I felt the strange yearning again. Was what I felt for her, in the last analysis, simple lust? Yes, I felt lust, but it wasn't simple and direct, for I had no desire to undress her in my fantasies, and no need to either, because for a long time I had had an intimate, vague, but nevertheless satisfying sense of her body, which had been acquired not only in the enforced closeness of the trip itself but even before that, in the big bedroom of their apartment in Tel Aviv, when she insisted on my inoculating her, and I took in at a glance her large but shapely breasts, scattered with unusually large moles; and it was these brown moles, rather than the breasts themselves, that I would repeatedly conjure up before me when I was seized with the desire to be engulfed by her innermost being.

I turned back in the direction of the surgical ward to say my final farewells to whoever happened to be there, to collect my few belongings, and to throw my coat into the laundry bag, even though it had my name embroidered on its pocket. And again I began to wonder what I was going to do about my growing attraction to this woman, which was beginning to make me look ridiculous even in my own eyes. Did I really want to conquer her in my fantasies? Perhaps all I wanted from her was the right inspiration, to guide me in identifying the young woman I wanted to fall in love with, the one my parents were dying for me to marry. Perhaps all I really wanted was a certain closeness, which would give me a more accurate idea of the young woman she had once been; to sketch by means of the big beauty spots scattered over her arms and shoulders, as if they were signposts, the figure that had once been slimmer and younger, borne on long legs in its kittenish walk. Then I would have a more accurate picture of the type of woman I wanted to spend my life with. My parents thought that my dedication to my work and my devotion to my patients robbed me of my erotic powers. But this was not the case. Even after twenty-four hours of a grueling shift at the hospital, when I came home exhausted, I could ejaculate quantities of semen in the hot shower which I frequently took half asleep. The problem wasn't my erotic powers but my inability to recognize the girls I should have fallen in love with. Because when I came across old girlfriends with whom I had had pleasant but noncommittal relations in the past, and in the meantime they had married or moved somewhere else—and I discovered that since we had last met they had grown not only more beautiful but more intelligent and mature—the pang of loss was especially painful, since I knew that I hadn't missed my chance through arrogance or emotional sterility but through a kind of lethargy, not physical but spiritual, whose source was apparently my increasing ability not only to satisfy myself in solitude but also to enjoy it. And here I had encountered a woman who was my absolute opposite; whose inability to stay at home by herself, without her husband by her side, was not only ridiculous and annoying but wildly attractive.

The next morning I woke up at dawn, even though I was completely at liberty to sleep late, in a way I had not experienced since graduating from high school. Not only didn't I have to go to work, I didn't have any work to go to, at least not until Professor Levine recovered and conducted his medical clarification with me. And so I forced myself to rest, and decided not to shave, and not even to take off my pajamas, and to stay in bed until she phoned. At first I didn't care if the phone call didn't come for a while, because that would prolong the pleasure of waiting, and also because I had immersed myself again in *A Brief History of Time;* although I had nearly given up on it in the last days in India, where the atmosphere was not at all suited to scientific books of this nature, I had decided that I had to pit myself against a few of its utterly obscure chapters again. After all, it was a popular book, or so it said on the cover at least, and even though the study of medicine is only on the fringes of pure science, it was inconceivable that a science graduate from the Hebrew University High School should be incapable of understanding the mysteries of the big bang and the black holes of the expanding universe. I thus snuggled down under my blanket and abandoned myself to the pleasures of cosmic freedom, which were particularly enjoyable in view of the heavy rain steadily pouring down on the world outside, and hardly noticed that the phone call was taking longer and longer to come. It was nearly three o'clock before I concluded that she had decided to dispense with my services and that the flimsy line I had cast over her had been snapped even before I had given it a single tug. Nevertheless, I refrained from leaving the apartment, even to buy a carton of milk and fresh cream cheese. Nor did I go down to the ground floor to pay the landlady the money I owed her for cleaning the stairs. Instead I turned up the heat in the room and took off my pajama top.

As dusk descended, I began to have various interesting thoughts of my own about the fate of the universe, whose future—when it would contract again into a particle with zero radius and infinite density, at the opposite pole to the big bang—concerned Hawking, although he seemed unable to construct a clear and convincing theory about it. Still the telephone did not ring, but I refused to call her and demean myself in front of them, as if I needed this connection more than they did. I switched on the hot water heater in the bathroom, but I hesitated to take a shower in case the phone rang and I failed to hear it. And when I saw that the day was drawing to a close and it would soon be night, I decided to forgo my daily shave. It had been a day of complete physical rest and clear spiritual pleasure, and now, as I sat down to eat the supper I had prepared, I felt that I had finally succeeded in overcoming the matter of Hawking's black holes, both logically and emotionally, and I contemplated his elderly child's face as it looked out from the cover of his book, full of trust in the ability of the intelligent layman to understand him. Only as night fell, after the nine o'clock news on television, when sadness crept into my soul, did I decide to phone the old granny directly and introduce myself.

Not only did she immediately recognize my name, but it turned out that she too had been waiting all day, dressed and ready in her apartment, because Lazar's wife had incorrectly assumed that I had taken her address and phone number in order to get in touch with the old woman directly and arrange a time that suited everybody for the visit. And even though they had spoken to each other during the course of the day, Lazar's wife had prevented her from calling me, on the grounds that I was a very reliable person, and if I didn't call it must be because I was unable to make it. "I'm sorry, I'm sorry," I repeated several times to the old lady, who firmly rejected any manifestation of guilt on my part and was only angry with her daughter for misleading us both. "Never mind that, when can we meet?" I interrupted her apologies enthusiastically, as if we were talking about a romantic date rather than a doctor's visit. "Whenever you like." The old lady laughed happily. "I haven't got any other rendezvous."

"Tomorrow morning?" I suggested immediately. "Yes, tomorrow morning's fine, or tomorrow afternoon, whenever it suits you—even this evening, if you like."

"This evening?" I repeated in surprise. "But it's already night."

"Not yet," the old lady protested. "The news has just finished, and there are still plenty of programs to see." I hesitated for a moment, and then agreed. "Just give me time to get organized," I requested. "It's twenty to ten now. I'll be at your place by half past ten."

"You'll find me here even if you come later," she reassured me jokingly, "and in the meantime I'll phone Dorit. Maybe she'll want to come too."

"Yes, I think that would be a very good idea," I said, and went quickly to take a shower.

In spite of my haste, I arrived later than ten-thirty; while I had spent the day in bed reading about the expanding universe, a number of the central arteries of Tel Aviv had turned into real lakes, in whose murky yellow waters I had no desire to dip my motorcycle or wet the instrument bag my parents had given me in honor of my graduation from medical school. Accordingly, I chained the Honda to the post of a taxi rank and took a cab to Grizim Street, one of the little streets in the north of the city which despite their proximity to busy main roads are themselves quiet, with pretty, comfortable houses. Lazar's wife had not yet arrived. "But she's coming," promised her mother, who was quite elderly but, unlike Dori, very slim. She was wearing a tailored gray wool suit, and warm slippers on her feet. The centrally heated house was scrupulously neat, although the furniture was old. On a low table next to the couch, a tea service and dishes of candies and nuts were waiting, perhaps since morning. "We won't wait for her," I announced, and I requested the medical questionnaire required by the old-age home, which was packed with questions and demands. I sat myself down at the table and began asking her about herself and her childhood diseases, in order to fill in the first, more trivial items. Then I hurried to remove my sphygmomanometer from my bag, but before I could wrap the cuff around her frail arm the old lady admitted, or perhaps simply recalled, that she sometimes had peaks of high blood pressure, reaching levels of over 200—the systolic—and 110—the diastolic. "We'll soon see," I said, and measured her blood pressure a number of times, one after the other. It changed every time I measured it, but the average was a little high. "Are you excited now?" I asked gently. She blushed, thought for a minute, said, "Perhaps," and smiled with a faint echo of her

daughter's enigmatic smile. I asked her to show me the pills prescribed by Professor Levine, which she didn't like taking regularly because they made her sleepy and depressed. Indeed, they
included a powerful sedative used in the emergency room.
"Maybe I'll give you something gentler instead," I suggested,
"but in the meantime you must take it regularly. Even a half or a
quarter of a tablet a day is sufficient—the main thing is the regu-
larity." I stood up and went to the kitchen and fetched a big
knife to show her how easily the tablet could be divided into
four. As I was returning to the living room a key turned in the
front door, which opened to admit Lazar's wife wrapped in her
cape, her hair wet from the rain, wearing the black velvet jumpsuit which I remembered from my second visit to their house. She
was also wearing clunky white running shoes. She was pale and
not made up, and when she saw the knife in my hand she raised
her finger threateningly and said in a mock-serious tone, "I hope
you're not about to operate on my mother. I don't want any
more misunderstandings between us."

I stayed there until after midnight. We spoke about aches and
pains, illnesses and eating habits. I checked the old lady's medicine chest and recommended a few changes, which I wrote down
on the prescription pad my parents had once had printed for me,
with their Jerusalem address under my name. Then I asked her to
take off her white silk blouse so that I could auscultate her lungs
and heart with my stethoscope. Dori helped me clear the cushions off the sofa and settle her mother comfortably on it so that
I could examine the abdominal organs. Her skin was very
withered, but washed with scented soap, and at a superficial
glance her body looked more like her granddaughter's body than
her daughter's. The map of her beauty spots was completely different. Dori stood next to me, looking at my hands palpating her
mother's stomach. Was she too remembering the dim chamber in
the Thai monastery in Bodhgaya? I wanted to ask her, but I
restrained myself. Finally I completed my examination and sat
down to fill in the questionnaire with scrupulous care. In general
the grandmother's health was fine, but it seemed to me that Professor Levine was keeping her on an excessively rigid medication
regime. His approach was more appropriate to recent hospital
cases than to ordinary patients who led normal lives. As a conse-
quence she occasionally suffered from severe constipation. I sug-

gested ways of obtaining relief and reduced her medication. My long day of rest had made me exceptionally lucid and eloquent, and when midnight approached and my job was done, I agreed to have tea with the two women, who did not seem in a hurry, even though Lazar had already phoned his wife twice. Was he too incapable of staying at home by himself?

The night into which I now emerged was not the same night in which I had arrived. In the new clarity flowing from the star-spangled sky, diamond drops slid separately down the the windshield of Dori's car. Dori drove me to the post where I had chained my motorbike, teasing me about the lake of yellow water that I been afraid to cross, which had in the meantime drained completely. "What do you need a motorcycle for in the first place?" For some reason this question seemed to me too personal, and I felt unable to give her a satisfactory reply. I expressed my admiration for her mother and asked her what she intended to do with the apartment. Would she sell it? "No," she replied, driving slowly but with no consideration for the other drivers on the road, "in the beginning we'll only rent it, so my mother can always go back there if the experiment with the old-age home doesn't work out."

"Have you found somebody to rent it yet?" I asked softly. "No." She shook her head wearily. "So far we haven't even thought about it."

"The reason I ask," I kept on, "is because I'm looking for an apartment." She gave me a quick glance which seemed to hold a mild suspicion of hidden motives. "How much are you paying now?" she asked. I told her. "That's not much," she stated, with justice—the rent I paid was definitely low. Now she fixed her eyes on me. I noticed an incipient double chin blurring her jawline. "We'll want more than that for my mother's apartment," she warned me. "I don't care," I said calmly, with my eyes focused on the road, as if I were the one driving the car, "not only because it would be nice to think of you as my landlady, but also, who knows, I might get married soon, and then there'd be someone to help me pay the rent." And then I saw the smile disappear completely, for the first time, from her eyes, which widened as her face turned a little red in the headlights of an approaching car. "You're getting married?" she asked softly, as if marriage weren't a possibility for me at all. "Not exactly, not yet," I replied with a mysterious smile, full of love and sympathy for her. "I mean, there isn't even a candidate yet, but I feel that she's already marked, even if she isn't yet aware of my existence."

Eight

But in fact, how do marriages come about? Why should two separate creatures wish to tie themselves to each other with one chain, however slender and delicate? Is it the mystery—which in the dead of night smuggles a schoolgirl in a pale blue uniform with a badge pinned to her heart into the house, where she sits bowed over her books and workbooks at the kitchen table, waiting for an empty bed—is it the mystery which clouds their minds and ties them to each other, in order to turn itself into their subject, their willing slave, seeking to take responsibility for something that may prove too much for its powers?

Here they are, sailing serenely down the river while the hidden chain joining them underneath the water is slowly covered with rust, like a film. And even when they step onto the green land and begin combing methodically for invisible seeds and grubs, their free and natural gait still disguises the fixed distance between them, strictly maintained by the figure which has taken off its cracked metal-framed glasses and settled down with its eyes closed on a little mound of hay next to the river, exposing its weak chest to the warm spring sun.

Do they know how to fly too? And who will take care that in the air too they remain unseparated? The pair approaches us; a solemn creature thrusts a long, black, glistening neck toward us, and a one-eyed stare—whether it belongs to a male or a female, we will never know—pierces us. And before the answer we await is given to us, a beak as big and strong as a sword stabs the weak chest which the mystery has abandoned to the warm spring sun, and four great gray wings are opened and stretched as far as they will go, and with one mighty flap they fly high into the sky, to tear whatever held them together to tatters.

I raced back home, cleaving the clear night air with the roar of my motorcycle, which as always was infected by the excitement inside me; I had thrown this woman another thread, which if it indeed lassoed her would not easily be undone. If I were a tenant, the connection between us would no longer depend on occasional medical matters or chance encounters in the hospital, nor would it depend on the wishes or the presence of Lazar; it would be based on a clear legal contract, which she herself would probably draw up, and would include not only payments, promissory notes, and deposits, but also a regular correspondence, municipal taxes, broken boilers, leaking pipes, and perhaps even complaints by neighbors, if I decided to throw a party for my friends, for example. In short, a new and independent bond, which would override the memories of the trip to India and its weakening aftermath, and for the sake of a bond like this it would be worth paying a higher rent and doing night shifts at the MADA First Aid Station, as I'd done in my student days, to make ends meet. After all, I would have more time now, for the enthusiasm and devotion that had tied me to Hishin and his department would not be necessary in the internal medicine department, if indeed Professor Levine agreed to take me on after he recovered from his mysterious disease and we resolved whatever issues lingered between us over the blood transfusion.

But would she want to rent me the apartment after what I had said? If she was thinking about that sentence now, it must be causing her a lot of confusion, and I doubted if she would tell Lazar, who was probably waiting up in bed. It was hard to imagine that after she explained why she was so late and described the thorough medical examination I had given her mother, she would add with a mysterious smile, "Guess what, I already have a tenant for Mother's apartment." Even if there were no secrets between them, not even concerning something as obscure and ambiguous as my parting words, it was inconceivable that Lazar would have remained under the blanket, looking out from the sleepy slits of his eyes. No, he would sit up, rumpling the bedclothes still further, as I had seen him do on the first night in New Delhi when I had peeped into their room, and exclaim,

"Really? He wants that apartment? How come? He really likes it?" imagining instead that all I really wanted was to keep up the connection with him, hoping he could influence Hishin to change his mind. Lazar probably thought that I considered him all-powerful in the hospital, whereas I knew that even if he could do something, he would never interfere in professional appointments, precisely to save his clout for more important things. Then she would undo her bun, loosen her tresses, take off her glasses and put them on the bedside table, and stick her head through the neck of the nightgown spotted with sprigs of pale yellow flowers. She'd sit down to rub cream into her long naked legs and massage her bare feet, utterly rejecting her husband's interpretation in her heart, because she would have already felt that it was she I meant, only she, and in the midst of the astonishment flooding her, perhaps a little wave of pity for me would well up too, as if now she understood that something had upset my balance during the trip we took to India together. Therefore, she'd decide to keep her counsel and not to tell her husband anything about what had passed between us, but to let him go on lying under the blanket, the tired slits of his eyes turning into two little sparks, and she'd prick up her ears to listen to Einat, who was still dragging out the last of her hepatitis and who had now awakened and gone into the kitchen. Then she'd slip in next to her husband, tickle him a little, and say, "Wait, wait, don't go to sleep yet, give me a hug, warm me up," and she'd put two cold little feet onto his warm thighs.

But I was pleased with myself and with the first clear sign of the emotion that I had succeeded in conveying to this woman. Although I knew it was all hopeless and absurd—and even if it had a chance, it wouldn't lead anywhere—I still refused to crush my love with my own hands but wanted this woman, who had appeared after long years of emotional desolation, of lovelessness, to crush it herself, with the same charm with which she crushed those long cigarettes of hers, which Lazar regarded with hostility and sometimes with outright protest. Therefore I said to myself, You have to rent that apartment, come what may. And since I found it difficult to go to sleep anyway after my day of deep rest, and the view from my window showed clearly that the storm was finally over, I could not resist putting on my leather coat and helmet and riding at a leisurely pace back to the street and the building where I already saw myself as a tenant. In the dark I inspected the neighborhood and the shops, and figured out whether I would be able to park the Honda under the building's pillars. I was pleased by everything I saw, including the short distance from the apartment to the sea, which I covered in a few minutes as I drove right down to the beach, where I stood for a long time opposite the waves breaking enthusiastically on the shore, still faithful to the storm which had disappeared without a trace.

Now a period of uncertainty began. In the personnel department of the hospital I was registered as an employee on vacation, but in actual fact I was up in the air, waiting for Professor Levine to recover from an illness whose nature suddenly seemed suspect. The secretary of the department and also the nurses put me off with vague replies on the telephone, until I decided to go to the hospital myself and have lunch in the staff cafeteria in order to bump into someone from internal medicine who would be able to shed some light on the situation. At first I thought of dropping into the surgical ward and retrieving the coat with my name embroidered on it before it disappeared, as personal possessions had a way of disappearing in the hospital. But at the last minute I changed my mind, because I didn't want to bump into Hishin or any of the other doctors, who would ask me questions about my unclear future. So I entered the cafeteria without my white coat, wearing my black leather jacket and holding my crash helmet in my hand. As soon as I walked in I saw Hishin sitting over the remains of his meal with other doctors and nurses from the department, smoking, arguing, and gesticulating. I tried to keep out of sight and took my tray to the opposite corner, where I looked for a familiar face from the internal medicine department. But I couldn't see any internists I knew. I sat down at a little table that was still covered with what was left of someone else's meal, and for the first time I found myself feeling faintly nauseated by the hospital smell rising from the food in front of me. The cafeteria, which I had always regarded as a pleasant refuge, now seemed to me, after the quiet days I had spent in my apartment, noisy and ugly. I left most of the food on my plate, and slowly ate the pink pudding which I had always enjoyed. Suddenly a hand came down on my shoulder, and even before turning my head I knew by the lightness of its touch that it belonged to Hishin. He was standing over me with his entire team, even the old anesthetist Dr. Nakash, all in the green uniforms of the operating room. They looked pleased with themselves, as if they had just successfully concluded a complicated operation. "What's the matter with you? Are you boycotting us?" he asked gently, bending down and looking at me with pitying, sympathetic eyes. And before I could reply, he shook his head sadly and said, "Don't be angry with everyone because of me. They're not to blame." Now I realized that it had been a mistake to ignore them and sit by myself. "And you are to blame?" I decided to adopt a tone of indignant protest and honest surprise. "You're quite wrong. I've got no complaints. The trip to India turned out to be fantastic. Why should I be angry with you when I know that you've got my best interests at heart?" I looked straight into his eyes. He was taken aback by my words; in spite of the seriousness and sincerity of my tone, he was sure that they hid a subtle sarcasm he couldn't quite put his finger on. He looked around at his team, trying to read my intention on their faces, but they all looked away, as embarrassed as he was. Then he apparently decided to take my words at face value, and placed his hand lightly on my shoulder again, nodded his head, and took off with the rest of them, except for the anesthetist, who wanted to talk to me. Dr. Nakash was a man of about sixty-five, thin and bony, whose white hair, clustered around his bald pate, becomingly contrasted the darkness of his complexion. In India I had seen quite a few people who reminded me of Nakash, which gave me a feeling of sympathic closeness with him. Hishin respected him and preferred to work with him, even though he was not the most senior of the anesthetists. "Nakash doesn't always understand what's going on in the operation," Hishin would say behind his back, "but he's always alert, even in ten-hour operations. And that's the most important thing. Because the patient abandons himself not to the hands of his surgeon but to the hands of his anesthetist."

Now Nakash asked me when I was starting work in internal medicine. I told him that I was waiting for Professor Levine to recover. "Isn't he out of there yet?" said Nakash in surprise. "Out of where?" I asked, and Nakash revealed with complete naturalness the secret that up to now everyone had succeeded in keeping from me: "They clean his head out," he said in his direct, simple way, "and he comes out fresh and new, until he gets depressed and commits himself again. What can he do? His patients depress him, and he can't cut them open like Hishin does." After that he asked me if I was interested in having work as his assistant in operations at a private hospital. Lately they had been very strict about the anesthetist having an assistant. The pay was strictly by the hour, without all the extras and under-the-counter payments, but the fee was high, tax-free, and unambiguous. "But I have no training as an anesthetist," I said, surprised. Nakash insisted, though, that the art of anesthesiology was not beyond my understanding; the technical side was simple and could be quickly learned, and the main thing was not to abandon the patient, to think of his soul and not only of his breathing.

While the surgeon and his team concentrate on a small part of the patient, he explained, only the anesthetist is thinking all the time of the patient as a whole, not as a collection of parts. The anesthetist is the real internist, no matter how much the surgeon pokes around in the patient's innermost organs. "And you," Nakash added, concluding his little speech, which surprised me by its eloquence, "want to be an internist."

"Want? Not exactly," I said with a bitter smile. "I haven't got a choice."

"I thought you were being sincere when you admitted that Hishin made the right decision. Believe me, Benjy, I've been through a lot of surgeons in my time. Who knows them as I do? And I'm telling you, I've seen you at work, and it's not for you. Your scalpel hesitates, because it thinks too much. Not because you're inexperienced, but because you're too responsible. And in surgery too much responsibility is fatal. You have to take a risk; to cut a person up and still tell him it's good for him, you have to be partly a charlatan and partly a gambler. Look at Hishin— who, by the way, also performs private operations sometimes, so you'll be able to stand next to him in the operating room again, if you miss it so much." The offer was so tempting that I didn't even ask for time to think it over, and said immediately yes. Nakash was not surprised. "I knew you'd like the idea, and anyway you're at loose ends until Professor Levine gets out and finds time to cross-examine you about that blood transfusion you performed in India. He's a difficult customer; he's always trying to depress his colleagues in the department, and when he doesn't succeed he gets depressed himself. So if I were you, I wouldn't be in too much of a hurry to fall into his hands." I wrote down Nakash's phone number at home, and he wrote down mine. "But it's only temporary," I warned him. "I'm moving into a new apartment soon."

That evening I informed my landlady, according to the agreement between us, that I intended to leave at the end of the month. She was very sorry. I knew that I was a highly desirable tenant in her eyes; the fact that I was a doctor apparently filled her with confidence, even though she had never consulted me on personal problems up to now, but only on general medical questions. "May I know why you're leaving?" she couldn't resist asking. "I need a change," I said, with an honesty I immediately regretted, for I saw a shadow of pain cross her sharp face. "But what change?" she insisted, inexplicably angry. "A change." I stubbornly repeated the word, which I may have chosen by mistake but was now stuck with. "Just a change." I lowered my head and went away without any further discussion. That same evening when I phoned my parents to tell them about Nakash's offer, I couldn't resist telling them about my plans to rent Lazar's mother-in-law's apartment as well. They were immediately worried. The idea of transforming the Lazars into my landlords struck them as a very bad one. "Why go and complicate your relations with Lazar now, after having won him over on the trip to India?" said my mother crossly. "But I'll be reliable as a tenant too," I argued, "and besides, it's not exactly with him, but with his wife."

"That makes it even worse," my mother burst out vehemently, trying as hard as she could to dissuade me from the idea. "If you break something in the apartment, or if you demand money for repairs, she'll complain about you, and that will count against you at the hospital too. And believe me," she added with unexpected venom, "she knows how to look out for number one. Anyway, you should never mix business with friendship." My father lectured me too. "I don't understand," he began in his quiet voice, which revealed signs of emotion. "Are you trying to get a quid pro quo for what you did for them in India?"

"Certainly not," I retorted angrily. "I'll pay more for that apartment than I'm paying now."

"You'll pay more?" said my father in astonishment. "How

much?" When they heard that no rent had yet been agreed on, their disapproval increased. And then a kind of cry of protest burst out of me: "My dear mother and father, I'm twenty-nine years old—do me a favor and trust me to decide what's best for me!" This outburst silenced them. It wasn't really fair of me, because in fact they always trusted me, and their anger with me this time stemmed only from the fact that I had confused them by hiding my real motives. I immediately took pity on them. I didn't know how to appease them without getting further embroiled in lies. "I need a change," I said gently. "I saw the apartment by chance and I liked it. It's close to the sea, it's on a nice quiet street. I won't make problems with Lazar or his wife. You know me." They listened attentively, trying to accept my inexplicable decision because of their love and respect for me. "The fact that you want a change," said my mother finally, "is all to the good, because you definitely need one. Just be careful it's not more of a change than you bargained for."

❧❧

When a week went by without any sign from Lazar's wife, I wondered anxiously if I had been in too much of a hurry to announce the change in my life. Had she forgotten me, or, on the contrary, had she decided to beware of me? I knew that her mother had already moved into the old folks' home. I had called her there myself to ask if the new dosage had indeed given her the hoped-for relief. She was very excited by the telephone call and happy to talk to me. Her chronic constipation had indeed been relieved, perhaps not only because of the change in her medication but thanks to the peace and quiet of her new home, which she spoke of admiringly, inviting me to come and visit her there. "Do you know," I said to her in the end, "that I'm going to rent your apartment?" To my astonishment, she knew nothing about it. Her daughter hadn't said anything. So, I said to myself, it's a good thing I talked to the old lady. Now I can expect a clear sign one way or the other. If Dori has changed her mind, or found some other tenant, then okay, that's it, let her go ahead and crush my love. In the meantime my landlady had found a couple to rent my apartment, whom she agreed to let in without consulting me, to take preliminary measurements. One day she stopped me on the stairs and demanded coldly that I move out before the end of the month.

I was in an embarrassing predicament. Was I now going to be thrown out into the street because of a bizarre and abstract infatuation which had no point or purpose? Finally, I mustered my courage and called Dori to ask her where I stood and what I could hope for. The secretary put me through without asking me to identify myself. Dori picked up the receiver and held it in her hand while carrying on a lively conversation with someone for whom I suddenly felt a faint pang of jealousy. Her voice was loud and enthusiastic, full of confidence and authority. When I identified myself, I could tell she was confused. So, I said to myself, a spark or two has already escaped to her. "There's been another misunderstanding," I began jokingly, "and I'm going to be out in the street with my goods and chattels starting next week." Then I sensed her relief. She no longer had to hesitate about letting me use the apartment as a means of ensnaring her. The situation in which I had landed myself, which I described in terms that were no more than accurate, forced her not only to accept me as a tenant but even to apologize for not getting in touch with me sooner. "The apartment's not ready. There're still a lot of things we don't know what to do with."

"Never mind," I reassured her, "you can leave them there. I don't need a lot of room." After some waffling on her part, we arranged to meet in the apartment on Tuesday afternoon, when her office was shut, so that she could see what had to be removed and what could be left there, and of course to finalize the terms of the lease. When I put the receiver down, I wondered whether she would bring Lazar with her or come alone.

She was waiting alone for me in the apartment. Behind the door I heard soft classical music mingling with the pleasant sound of running water. I knocked, two light taps, because I didn't want to press the bell, whose jarring noise I remembered from my first visit. She opened the door with a somber, serious expression on her face, wearing high heels and with a bright red apron cinched around her waist. Her hands were covered with soap. "You've complicated things for me," she complained, her face flushing slightly. "Look at all the things I have to do here for you now." Her direct, aggressive tone startled me; I was unprepared for it. Her eyes too, which had not yet flashed a single smile, looked hard behind the lenses of her glasses. "But what's there to do?" I began stammering stupidly, trying to defend myself and perhaps also to dismiss her complaint as I stepped weakly into the apartment, in which I immediately felt a change even though I had only been there for a few hours the first time. The apartment was still neat and tidy, but the coziness and brightness that had prevailed on the evening I had examined her mother were gone. Perhaps it was the removal of the embroidered cloths from the little tables next to the sofa and the disappearance of the crystal and silver goblets which had stood behind the glass in the dark sideboard, or perhaps because the big family portraits had been removed from the walls. The curtains were open, and the view from the window consisted exclusively of rooftops, without a single scrap of sea between them. There was no visible sign of the apartment's proximity to the beach, which had made me so happy on that evening. However, I quickly overcame my disappointment as I glanced around and saw how the rays of the setting sun were transmuted into a golden powder, which made the whole interior glow sweetly. On the white marble counter in the kitchen stood a row of delicate long-stemmed goblets crowned with soapsuds. The possibility that she was washing them for me, and not in order to store them, touched me profoundly. For a moment there was an embarrassing silence. My eyes avoided staring too obviously at her straight legs clad in honey-colored silk stockings. She still looked annoyed to me, perhaps somewhat humiliated by the dishwashing that had been forced upon her. "We thought we'd prepared everything," she said, "but there's still a lot left to organize here."

"How long has your mother been living here?" I inquired in a friendly tone. "Not long. Seven years. Since my father died. But she loved this apartment. And she invested a lot in it. It's a shame; she could have stayed here for a few years longer. I still haven't come to terms with the fact that she won't be living here anymore. That's why I wasn't in a hurry to get in touch with you. I hoped that she would change her mind and come back. But now you've forced me to hand it over." The surprising admission that she had actually surrendered to my demands flooded me with such a strong and unexpected wave of pleasure that I had to bow my head and close my eyes, which she interpreted as a sign that she had offended me. "If your mother changes her mind and wants to come back, I'll move out immediately," I said gallantly, in an attempt to make myself into an even more desirable tenant. But she shook her head firmly. "There won't be any need for that. Don't worry. So far she's very happy there." And then I couldn't resist saying, "I know," and proceeded to tell her about the telephone conversation. She listened in silence. A pleasant smile hovered on her lips, but her eyes were fixed in a hard, suspicious expression, as if intent on assessing the precise degree of danger posed by my determination to invade her life.

Meanwhile the apartment was growing dark and the golden powder was losing its glow, fading into shadowy hieroglyphics on dull yellow parchment. She dropped onto the sofa at my side and crossed her legs. Her little double chin sagged. From a shabby cardboard file containing telephone, gas, and electricity bills, she took out a sheet of paper with a few words written on it, and said despairingly, "I have to make an inventory of the contents of the apartment for the contract between us. And I don't have any idea where to begin. We've never rented an apartment to strangers before. Some people write down everything, including closets and sinks, but you're not planning to remove the furniture and sell it, are you? Or dismantle the lavatory and the sink, right?" She spoke without humor, and I shook my head solemnly in reply. I was hypnotized by the rapidly darkening room. "So we'll just list the really important things," she suggested, "the carpet and the more valuable dishes, and one or two pictures. And we'll write down the number on the electricity meter, and get the phone company to read the phone meter, and that will more or less cover everything. As for the clothing and stuff of my mother's that she left here—are you sure you don't mind? At least come and look at the space we've left for you and see if it'll be enough." She stood up, but to my surprise she didn't switch on the light in the apartment, which was growing darker from minute to minute, not only because of the fading light outside but because of the darkness welling up inside the apartment itself. Between the kitchen and the bathroom, from an alcove where the brooms and mops were standing, a fresh, dense darkness was steadily flowing and gradually spreading into the two rooms. When I followed her into her mother's bedroom I noticed that the glass goblets, from which the soapsuds had disappeared, were shining on the white marble with a ruby-colored radiance. The window above the sink was set in the wall at just the right angle to catch the rays of the setting sun. I wanted to draw her attention to this little discovery of mine, but she was already standing next to her mother's double bed, which was covered with red bedspread and piled with fat cushions with flowery covers, and opening the doors of two empty closets to show me the space already at my disposal. Then, with a gesture of resignation, she opened the two full closets too. In one of them I saw gray suits, all alike, hanging, and in the other I found myself standing, as in a familiar dream, in front of stacks of white shoe boxes, in which various objects had no doubt been stored. "There's plenty of room," I said in a whisper behind her broad back, in an attempt to reassure her. "Don't worry, we'll clear it all away. Just give us a little time to breathe," she said in a hoarse voice, looking at me again with that suspicious, hostile look, which, far from discouraging me, turned me on so much that my penis began to swell. If only I could talk to her now about some shared memory from our trip to India, I thought quickly, I might be able to lighten the atmosphere a little. But the lust boiling inside me paralyzed me. Only now I realized that the darkness she insisted on preserving in the apartment was flattering to her. For I no longer saw the creases in her neck, nor the wrinkles around her eyes, and even her little paunch had disappeared, leaving only the impression of a mature, ripe woman. Maybe she wants to seduce me? I asked myself when I saw her turning back in the direction of the living room, where a new stream of light, pouring out of the tatters of a flimsy cloud, was now struggling against the darkness. "Now we have to talk about the rent." She sighed and dropped heavily onto the sofa, crossing one long leg over the other while the silent battle between light and darkness raging in the room drew delicate pale golden arabesques on her stockings. The only thing I'm going to get out of falling in love with this woman, I thought anxiously to myself, is an exorbitant rent that comes from the lack of experience of a new landlady. "What figure did you have in mind?" she asked me unexpectedly. "Me?" I laughed. "I don't have any figure in mind. But don't worry, you've already warned me that the rent will be higher than what I'm paying now."

"Yes." She smiled to herself in satisfaction. "I already warned you. Even though I've already forgotten what it was." I told her the sum. She remembered and looked slightly disappointed, sunk in thought, her face appearing and disappearing in the darkness flowing from the bedroom and coming to join the darkness in the living room. "If we add ten percent to your present rent—would that be fair?" She asked me in her clear voice, which always contained a natural assertiveness. "I still feel guilty that you didn't get anything for the trip to India."

"But I did," I protested, bitterly but also with a feeling of inner satisfaction, since I had feared a far higher rent. "The trip itself, and meeting the two of you. And now this apartment. And you," I added softly, "as my landlady." She didn't answer, only withdrew into the protection of the darkness that she had gone to so much trouble to surround us with, perhaps precisely because of an embarrassing moment like this. I didn't know what to do with it either, except to let it sink into her soul like a little warning from me, like the warning she had given me about the rent, which she had raised by just ten percent. I didn't dare add anything to clarify my feelings, I only knew that in the silence now filling the room, the tension stemming from the age difference between us was slowly, and for the first time, melting, and the fact that she was apparently only nine years younger than my mother and ten years younger than my father, and her daughter was only four years younger than me, had lost its power.

This too could be the meaning of *A Brief History of Time,* I reflected as she finally stood up and went to the kitchen to switch on the light, illuminating the living room only indirectly. Without looking at me and without smiling, she announced that tomorrow or the next day, she would prepare a standard lease in her office, and she wrote down my ID number in a little notebook and asked me to get my parents to sign a guarantee, and we agreed that I would call her tomorrow or the next day to set a date for signing the contract and handing over the key. In the meantime, she promised, her maid would come to clean the apartment for me. "Do you by any chance remember where the valve is that connects the apartment to the water main?" I asked when I was already standing at the door, and a faint tremor of anxiety ran through me at the thought that I was leaving her alone. She tried to remember, going to look for it first under the kitchen sink and then in the bathroom, but she couldn't find the valve, which as in all old apartments was apparently hidden in some unexpected place. "I'll ask my mother; perhaps she knows. And if not, Lazar will find it," she said, and she flashed me one of her automatic smiles, impossible to read, and thus we parted without any response on my part, apart from uttering the word "wonderful," which was all I had to attach this woman to me until our next meeting—at which, I vowed to myself as I slowly rode my motorcycle through the bustling, wintry Tel Aviv evening, I would definitely confess my feelings.

I knew that I should put the confession off until after the lease was signed; otherwise I might be left without an apartment. And even though my current landlady kept putting pressure on me to leave, I was in no hurry to contact my beloved. This time I wouldn't make things easy for her, I told myself. If she wanted to nip everything that had begun between us in the bud, all she had to do was tell her secretary to summon me to the office in her absence, in order to sign the lease and take the key. If she didn't want any further contact with me, if she saw my falling in love with her as something absurd and superfluous, all she had to do was keep away, or set Lazar on me, on the pretext that only he was capable of showing me the plumbing.

But after a few days she called me, and with a new friendliness and none of the hostility she had shown at our previous meeting, she asked me how I was and whether I was enjoying my enforced leisure; she knew, of course, that Professor Levine had not yet recovered from his depression. "If only we had known that you would have to sit here twiddling your thumbs"—a merry laugh came from the other end of the line—"we would have left you to wander around India. Because of us, you didn't even get to see the Taj Mahal."

"Right," I responded immediately, overjoyed that the trip to India had cropped up at last, and turned into a common memory. "Because of your husband's efficiency, the trip passed as quickly as a dream. And that's a shame, because I know I'll never go back there."

"Don't say that," she protested quickly. "How do you know? You're still so young." I didn't answer this, as I had no intention of being dragged into a discussion of my youth at this point, after having convinced myself that the age difference between us had dissolved of its own accord in the darkness of her mother's apartment. She now asked me, in a voice that contained an unfamiliar anxiety, if I was in a hurry to move into the apartment or if I could wait until Tuesday, when lawyers' offices were closed in the afternoon, since she wanted to sign the lease in the apartment so that she could show me not only the whereabouts of the water shut-off valve, but also how to use the stove and the microwave oven, and so that we could go over the inventory that her mother had prepared, and then we could sign the contract at our leisure like civilized human beings. After all, who more than she understood that business deals between friends were always open to misunderstandings and mistaken interpretations. "Will your mother be there too?" A doubt crept into my heart. "If you want her to come too, to explain how to use the household appliances better than I can, I'll try to bring her," she answered naturally and composedly. "No, no." I hurriedly dismissed the idea, aware of the eagerness in my voice. "Why drag her all the way there? It will only upset her to see the apartment at sixes and sevens."

※※※

Even though the suggestion to meet at the apartment for the signing came from her, I was sure that nothing was going to happen between us. She was a mature, realistic woman, basking in the love and admiration of her husband, and apparently of others too. Even if she enjoyed the attentions of a young man, it would never occur to her to think that he had actually fallen in love with her, for a woman who had been dining on a rich feast of love all her life would have forgotten what the obsessive hunger of being in love felt like. Moreover, despite the encouraging smiles she flashed at her reflection in the mirror, she was well aware of the folds of flesh around her waist. Nor did she fail to see the deep creases in her neck, and the blotches on her skin when her makeup faded. And even if she still felt complacent about her straight, slender legs, she wouldn't be able to understand why a young and not bad-looking man like myself, a man at his peak, would suddenly fall in love with her. It would never occur to her that it was precisely her hidden weakness, which her husband had innocently revealed to me, had incited my interest and lust. Nevertheless, I prepared myself for the meeting with a feeling that it would be fateful for me. I decided to wear the checked shirt that I had been wearing when I performed the blood transfusion in Varanasi, even though it was nothing special and faded from many washings, for I hoped that it would give rise, even if only in her subconscious, to the memory of that mysterious hour when I had directed the flow of blood between the two women, and produce some sympathy for me after I delivered my confession, which I knew could only be humiliating and idiotic.

I was determined to unburden myself, and I only hoped that, as before, the apartment would remain shrouded in that golden, dusky darkness which softens, in the natural melancholy of the dying day, everything that is ridiculous and grotesque from the human point of view. But toward afternoon the sky darkened and a hard rain began flooding the town. And I knew that the twilight would be enjoyed only by those flying westward above the clouds, while I would be obliged to stammer my confession in the full glare of the electric lights. Nevertheless, I remained resolute, even though when I knocked on the door I prayed for a moment that Lazar would be there to protect her, and perhaps to protect me too from my imminent humiliation. But there was silence behind the door. She had not yet arrived. After a few minutes I heard her footsteps on the stairs. Was I too beginning to identify her footsteps from a distance, like her husband? She was late, but alone, confident in her ability to deal with me by herself. Her face was covered with a heavy layer of makeup, but the clothes she was wearing were not in the least attractive. On the contrary, they made her look short and clumsy. She had long black boots on her legs, and her body was covered by the black velvet jumpsuit whose sleeves she hadn't been able to roll up when I gave her the vaccination shots. She was brisk and businesslike, and no longer hostile, as on the previous occasion. "It's a good thing you came early." She smiled and opened the door. And I knew there was no longer any need to appease her for my precipitousness. Instead, it seemed that she was already very satisfied with the quiet and undemanding tenant who had forced himself on her. "Isn't Lazar coming?" I asked. "No, he's busy today," she replied, and moved an empty suitcase standing in her way in the passage leading to the bedroom. "But he was here yesterday and insisted on emptying out another closet for you, to give you more room. Come and see how how hard he worked for you," and with a flourish she flung the closet door open to show me how ingeniously Lazar had succeeded in making all the shoe boxes disappear. But he had not been allowed to touch the gray suits, which were still hanging in the other closet. "You shouldn't have made such an effort," I said amicably. "The space was quite enough for me."

"Now," said Lazar's wife firmly, "but how do you know what will happen in the future?" Her eyes twinkled in a smile, perhaps alluding to the marriage I had promised, and she led me into the kitchen to show me a few old electric appliances, which had been dug out of the depths of the kitchen cupboards and were now displayed on the marble counter, decked out in brightly colored covers. But when she tried to tell me how they worked, according to the explanations dictated by her mother, I saw that she was totally at sea. When she began pressing the different buttons, I realized her charming, pampered helplessness, which touched me so profoundly that I could no longer control myself and laid my hand on her little, freckled one to stop her. "It'll be all right," I reassured her. "I'll work it out myself. And if I have any problems, I can always get in touch with your mother directly." Then we entered the living room, to go over the detailed list her mother had insisted on drawing up in her large but almost illegible handwriting, and to try to work out how much the written words matched the actual furnishings of the apartment. After that I read through the lease, which was full of dire warnings and threats to the tenant. But maybe, I reassured myself, this was the standard form in use in Dori's office. Everything was ready except for my parents' signature on the guarantee, which she agreed to wait for until the following week. I signed the two copies of the contract, and as she requested I wrote twelve postdated checks for all the months of the coming.year, so that we would not have to bother each other with additional meetings. She put the checks into her bag without inspecting them and took out two keys, which she placed on the table. Now she was relaxed and at peace with herself, and she lit a slender cigarette, gave me a soft look, and asked, "Have we forgotten anything, or is that all?"

There could have been no better opening than this for my declaration of love, which had been turning around inside me for several days. And without hesitating or stammering, dropping my head slightly so as to avoid meeting her eyes, I began unburdening myself confidently and fluently to this woman who was only a little younger than my mother. "I know that what I am about to say will seem absurd to you, because it seems absurd and strange to me too, but it's still true. If you've sensed it already, you may as well hear it straight and tell me what to do with it, because ever since we returned from India I've been tiptoeing around you and trying to tie you to me with flimsy threads that keep on breaking. And even though you haven't done anything to encourage me, you haven't rejected my attempts to bind you to me either, like this apartment, which I only rented so as to have something to attach you to me, so I wouldn't lose you altogether." I still hadn't raised my head to look at her, because I was afraid that the faint smile in her eyes would throw me off my speech, whose tone seemed just right to me, manly but also touching. "I have to tell you, I don't know what's happened to me." I went on with my head bowed. "That last night in the hotel in Rome, after Lazar left, I fell head over heels in love with you, against all logic, and to my complete surprise, because I've never fallen in love with a woman older than me before. Please don't protest the use of these words, let me tell you that I protest them too, and try to dismiss them all the time, but even if we dismiss the words, the condition won't go away, and it fills my thoughts all day long. And I wonder if I have to fight it and eradicate it from my heart. In other words, is this an immoral love, like that of a grown man who falls in love with a little girl?" For a moment I fell silent, unable to go on talking in my excitement at having succeeded in unburdening myself of the words which had been weighing on my heart for so many days. But I couldn't go on hanging my head and staring at the carpet, which I noticed was a little ragged at the edges—a fact that maybe should have been mentioned in the inventory—and so I raised eyes full of despair to the woman curled up in the corner of the sofa like a soft black velvet ball, whose automatic smile had completely disappeared from her eyes, and who in a gesture I had never seen before had her fist pressed to her mouth, not in amazement or ridicule but in profound attention, which encouraged me to go on talking. "I ask myself if you and Lazar wanted me to accompany you to India not just because I am a doctor but because in the depth of your hearts you hoped that I might fall in love with Einat, as in the plot of some well-intentioned British movie. But reality is a different, incredible movie, and instead of falling in love with the sick young woman you offered me, I fell in love with her mother, and I really wasn't looking for another mother, because the one I've already got is perfectly good. Dori, please don't try to explain my screwed-up psychology to me. It may be screwed up, but not here. Here there's something else entirely, which I call, if you don't mind, mystery. Yes, mystery, a word I've always fought against and that I now find myself enslaved to. And you know what? My heart told me what I was letting myself in for, because the minute I heard that you were coming with us to India, I felt so pressured that I almost decided to change my mind about going."

Maybe this was the right moment to get up and leave her, in goodwill, in friendship, putting my hands together Indian fashion in the middle of my face. I expected nothing of her. But the contract had been signed, the keys had been handed over, and in the apartment where we were sitting, I was the host and she was the guest—and you can't get up and leave a guest to her own devices. So I sat petrified in my place, listening to the rain dripping slowly outside and the strong wind trying unsuccessfully to blow it away. She still hadn't said anything. Was she stunned, or had she been prepared for my confession? Perhaps she was surprised in spite of being prepared, for she went on sitting curled up in the corner of the couch, her fist still pressed against her mouth as if to protect herself from some galloping, inexorable catastrophe. Her plump face was tense and burning, but behind the lenses of her glasses her eyes were full of serenity, if not profound satisfaction. In the end a radiant smile broke through the barriers of her resistance. She took her fist from her mouth and loosened her fingers into a light wave, as if beckoning an obedient pupil or a beloved pet, and whispered, "Come here." I rose immediately to my feet and approached the corner of the couch, but I didn't wait to hear what she wanted, because I knew what I wanted, and I bent down, took her by the shoulders, and raised her to me. Just don't hesitate now, I said to myself. And without asking permission, with the same movement by which I had lifted her to her feet, I began passing my lips over her forehead, her cheeks, her lips, and stroking her soft, creased neck. She began breathing heavily, struggling and trying to push me away, to say something. But I didn't let her talk; I pressed my lips hard against hers, smelling the faint aroma of the cigarette she had recently smoked, and gave her a long, eager kiss, until I felt her hand pulling my hair. "This isn't right," she murmured, trying to push me gently away. "It doesn't make sense, it's just silly." But I only tightened my embrace, because I knew that if physical contact was broken off now, the magic would be dispelled. Nothing had actually happened yet. I had to gather my courage to touch the body itself, to take hold of a few memories for the empty days ahead. I was desperate to hold her round breasts, which I knew were more substantial than any I had ever touched before. With desperate, childish determination I tried to pull off her velvet top, excited by the thought of glimpsing again the map of beauty spots scattered over her pure white shoulders and arms. But my hand, carried away by its own momentum, drove on, seeking a first contact with that beautiful, plump stomach. And when I touched it, I was flooded by a strong sensation of pleasure and satisfaction. Between my fingers I felt the glow of a cushion of natural warmth, which I had been seeking for years in order to lay my forehead or cheek upon it and melt the iceberg accumulating within me.

※♡※

Then, though she had been the one to call me to her, I felt that it was up to me to give her the absolute advantage of the beloved over the lover. I let go of her and with lightning-swift movement took off my shoes and socks, rapidly removed the rest of my clothes, and, indifferent to the cold and before she had time to protest, I stood before her as naked as the day I was born, like a man about to step into a long-sought-after river. I wanted her to see me as I was, and to see that I had no shame before her, so that she could decide whether my love and desire were worthy of her. And despite the astonishment that seized her at the sight of my unfamiliar body, or at my suddenly offering myself to her, I saw her fears dissipate as they were absorbed into her rising desire. But she held up her hand in a quick, nervous gesture. "Not here, not here," she said emphatically, and walked slowly to her mother's bedroom. There she absentmindedly swept my black crash helmet off the bed, where it had for some reason been forgotten when we were examining the closets. Then, sunk in reflection, she cast a backward glance at me as I walked naked behind her, and as if afraid that I might try to undress her myself, she raised her hand in a plea which still contained some hidden anger, and said, "No, please, let me." She sat down on the edge of the bed and slowly and with difficulty removed her long boots, after which she hesitantly and awkwardly undid a few hidden buttons on her unyielding jumpsuit, and began working her head through the narrow opening, emerging flushed, with her hair disheveled, still full of deep shame at the situation imposed on her by my sudden nakedness. With a strange obedience, like a good, loyal wife, she took off her bra, removed her panties, and lay down on the bed, resting her head on a cushion that was still covered with the grandmother's floral cushion cover. Now she was displayed before me like the heavy naked women in art books, posed before baskets of fruit in their dark, shadowy reproductions. But the look she sent me was neither submissive nor indifferent. Still perturbed and even angry, as if I were some inexperienced young animal, she raised her hand again to warn me: "No scratches or bites." I bowed my head compliantly, and full of love, I knelt down next to the bed and began to kiss her plump little foot, in which I discovered a dimple like the one on her face. I immediately sensed that these opening kisses were very pleasing to her, but I was afraid that in my eagerness I might come too quickly, and I stopped myself and stood up to remove the glasses from her eyes, and lowered myself carefully onto her, suddenly aware of a coolness in every limb I touched except for that plump, pampered stomach, which radiated a steady, powerful warmth, as if it possessed an independent source of heat. I kissed her again on her mouth, and on her big breasts, and I laid my forehead and cheek on the roundness of her belly. I still had no idea why she had given in to me so easily, but I suddenly felt that she was losing patience with my love games and was not prepared to let me dawdle any longer, for a confident hand was already grasping my penis, to guide it to the place that was no less on fire than I was.

She was the fourth woman I had been to bed with, but she was the only one who gave me the feeling that I was guiding a great sailing ship into a deep-water harbor. In contrast to the others, who alarmed me with sudden cries and deep sighs, throughout our lovemaking she did not utter a single sound; even her breathing remained quiet and gentle, as if the surprise at her acquiescence blocked any wish for a more intense pleasure. It turned out that this was the first time she had ever cheated on Lazar. This was a fact she felt she had to confide in me the moment she freed herself from my arms and stood up hastily to put on her clothes. I believed her, and in the pride that filled my heart there was also some sadness for what had happened to her. In order to prove to her that she could always trust me, I didn't go to look for my clothes, which were lying on the floor in the other room, but remained naked, sitting on the bed with my legs crossed. "You're like that crazy German pilot who went up in a light plane, penetrated all the radar screens, and landed in Red Square in Moscow," she said suddenly, with a slightly resentful smile, gathering her hair into a bun on top of her head. "I don't understand how you succeeded in penetrating the inner sanctum of my respectable married life." Did she really expect an answer from me? I thought as I drew in my head between my shoulders and held my tongue, afraid to say something that she might interpret as contemptuous of her and Lazar's marriage, the beauty of which I had observed at close quarters during our trip and whose secret I had wished to crack by touching her body. She pulled her boots onto her long, slender legs, and when the telephone suddenly rang she said in a matter-of-fact voice, without a trace of anxiety, "That must be Lazar," and she hurried into the next room. She didn't shut the door behind her, although she spoke in a very low voice. But I had no desire to overhear their conversation as I sat on a corner of the bed alone and naked, like a fakir leaning against a temple wall, and contemplated the darkness spreading through the bedroom of the old lady who might be sitting and drinking tea in her old-age home at this minute, with no idea of what had just happened on her bed. Then she came back, stepping briskly, with her coat on and her face made up. "It wasn't Lazar," she said with a serious expression. "It was a friend of my mother's. You'll have to be prepared to take calls from her friends, and give them her number at the home. Which I don't have to give you, since you already know it."

"But what's going to happen to us?" I asked in a tone of despair, suddenly feeling that there was no heavy gold chain here but only the thinnest of threads, which was liable to snap at any moment. "Nothing will happen to us," she answered seriously. "Forget it. It was an episode. You know that it's total madness for me. There's no future in it. You can afford it, you're still free—I can't. You're a bachelor, and a bachelor is much more dangerous than a married man." I kept quiet, because I sensed that whatever she said now had no power, for if I had begun it—only I could end it. But my heart contracted in pain for her, and I couldn't help reaching out to her. She hesitated, thinking that my lust had overcome me again, and then she gave in and took my hand. "Are you surprised I fell in love with you?" I asked her. She thought for a moment, her head slightly bent at a charming angle, and then said, "Yes. It's strange and it's superfluous. Even though I've heard of similar things happening to people I know. But you're so young, really—what do you need a woman like me for? Tell me, aren't you cold sitting there like that?"

"Yes, but I don't want to get dressed yet and lose the smell of your body." She blushed, but the smile didn't leave her eyes, and she came closer and lightly kissed my eyes and stroked my hair. "If the phone rings now, you don't have to answer. But if you pick it up by mistake and it's Lazar, tell him I left a long time ago, and be very careful not to give me away, or we'll both be in trouble."

As soon as she left I began to miss her. I unwillingly left the empty bed, and in the darkness that had descended on the apartment I went to gather my clothes, still lying in a heap on the carpet, and discovered to my delight, between the roofs and the ugly TV antennas, a modest blue strip of the nearby sea, which I had already given up hope of seeing from here. The fragrance of her perfume lingered on my hands, and I raised them to my face to smell them. The telephone rang, and I knew at once that it was Lazar, looking for his wife. I said to myself, So what, what do I have to fear? I picked up the receiver, and his voice sounded as close and concrete as if he were standing on the other side of the wall. "She's already left," I said quickly, before he even asked about her. "So you finished everything you had to do?" he asked. "I think so." I hesitated, not wanting him to think that from now on they could forget about me completely. "And did she show you that valve you were looking for, or did she forget about it in the end?"

"She forgot about it, of course," I said with a faint sigh, laughing with him at her absentmindedness. He immediately explained to me where to find the valve, which really was hidden in an illogical place. Suddenly I was seized with anxiety. With my free hand I began hurriedly putting on my clothes, as if he could see my nakedness through the telephone. Behind the wall, in the next apartment, there was a sound of footsteps, and a shiver ran through me, as if his ghost were haunting me while his voice kept me talking. Fear and remorse welled up in me for what I had done to him, and I wanted to put the phone down. But Lazar was friendly, and with his natural sensitivity he sensed my embarrassment and wanted to calm me. "Tell me the truth," he dared to ask, "are you angry with me?"

"Angry?" I choked on the word. "Why on earth should I be angry with you?"

"How should I know? Maybe you think I could have persuaded Hishin to keep you on in the surgical department. But believe me, I can't interfere in such matters, and I haven't got any pull where appointments are concerned."

"I know, I know." I hurried to reassure him. "And I've never been angry with you. Just the opposite." But Lazar was not yet satisfied. "Anyway, tomorrow you'll meet Professor Levine, and he may agree to give you the temporary residency in his department."

"Tomorrow I'm meeting Levine?" I said in astonishment. "Has he recovered at last?" Now it was Lazar's turn to be surprised. "But how come Dori didn't tell you? I told her to tell you that you've got an appointment to see him tomorrow morning. She forgot that too? What's the matter with her today?"

Nine

And after they have torn to shreds and smashed to smithereens everything that bound them together, the couple makes haste to part from one another, and with the wild leap of an arrow shot from a mighty bow each of them soars into the depths of the radiant void, to retrieve the freedom stolen from them and to prove that they have always been worthy of it. And it has never been so precious as now, with cool breezes swirling around and caressing their wings, guiding the erstwhile pair gently to the place where each of them wishes to be all by itself, and to gain this end they are prepared to forgo the age-old route marked out by the flames of flying dinosaurs, to reject the safety and warmth of migrating flocks crossing oceans with the help of tried and true ancient codes, and to allow chance winds to carry them to a place where they will never meet the mate from whom they have at last succeeded in separating themselves.

From time to time the bird lands to recover its strength, by the side of a river or in a yellow field, dipping its beak into the fresh water, and with tiny steps it circles in an imaginary ring around the mate who was and is no more, delighting in its absolute absence. But still that pale green eye—whether it is male or female is impossible to tell—calmly inspects its immediate surroundings, to make sure that no one is lurking there to take it by surprise. But there are no surprises, only a peasant plodding heavily between the plowed furrows with a long irrigation pipe on his shoulder, and a little girl in a school uniform with a heavy satchel on her back returning home along a brown footpath. Even if a tiny snake tries to surprise it in the low grass, the snake will be snatched up immediately in an agile beak and disappear.

And so it continues to wander, landing from time to time on a roof or an electricity pole, dipping its head into a fragrant puddle *to fish up a red worm or a trembling gnat, but all the time it keeps its eyes open, to see if someone who was once part of its soul is flapping its wings on the edge of the horizon. For it still does not believe that solitude has truly been restored to it, and that its dead freedom has been resurrected. And so, when the day fades, despite the heaviness it feels in its wings, it soars strongly up into the sky again, to find a west wind which will carry it to the desert, for only there, it believes, will it be able to find a real refuge. It crosses into the twilight at a low altitude, gliding slowly over the pale emptiness in the red evening light. Then, with the same willpower with which it and its mate tore the mystery that joined them, it goes on flying for hours on end over the absolute darkness, occasionally disturbed by the hot breath of a beast of prey. At midnight, tired and content, it permits itself at long last to plummet to a solitary tree or bush in the heart of the plain, there to passionately embrace the freedom which has been fully restored. But immediately it knows that the gleam which greets it in the midst of the foliage is not a firefly or a splinter of broken glass—it is the open eye of its mate, which has been trying to escape it all day long, with the mystery close behind.*

❧❦❧

Even after the conversation with Lazar was over and the receiver had been replaced on the cradle, my sense of alarm did not fade, for I realized that I had penetrated the intimate nature not only of his wife but also of Lazar himself, who was so deeply attached to her. I also knew that what had just happened between us, even if she really succeeded in keeping it an isolated episode, would not liberate me from her but instead would only increase my attraction to her. My feet were already carrying me, half dressed, back to the bedroom, to throw myself yearningly onto the love-bed, which from this moment became my own personal bed, and to imagine my face buried once more in the powerful heat of that solid white stomach. I pulled the uncovered pink comforter which the granny had left me over my head, and in the total darkness I thought sorrowfully about how my chances for marriage, which my parents had hoped for, and which I had wanted too, were receding from me. When I woke up a few hours later and remembered what I had managed to accomplish, my heart flooded with joy. I put the two pairs of keys to the apartment in my pocket and went outside, because I couldn't contain the sense of wonder by myself and wanted to share it with the reality outside of me, which had turned into a wet and empty night. I got onto my motorcycle and rode around the streets for a while, and then I went back to my old apartment, to spend the rest of the night there; and it was a good thing I did, because early in the morning someone from the internal medicine department phoned to summon me to an urgent meeting with Professor Levine. Was it Lazar and Hishin, I wondered, who had urged him out of guilt to lose no time in holding the interview, or was that blood transfusion of mine still bothering him, and now that he had recovered he was in a hurry to confront me with his arguments? With this in mind, I asked to put the interview off till noon and decided to spend the intervening hours in the hospital library, reading everything in the medical computer about hepatitis. I also looked up the article by Professor Levine himself, the one I was supposed to have read before leaving for India, which Hishin had forgotten to give me, but it wasn't there—perhaps Hishin hadn't brought it back yet. In spite of everything I read in the library that morning, I had no idea what direction Levine's attack would come from. On a piece of paper I wrote down in clear figures the exact values of the results of the blood tests in Calcutta, which I still knew by heart. If I had wanted to I could have made the results a bit more drastic, in order to justify myself even further, but anything like that was so foreign to my nature that the thought was banished as soon as it appeared. At midday, armed with freshly honed facts, I entered Levine's office, which looked smaller and gloomier than Hishin's, perhaps because it was so untidy and crammed with books and papers. To my surprise he greeted me with a friendly smile and locked the door so we would not be disturbed. He rolled his chair to the front of his desk and placed it close to mine, as if he intended not just to talk to me, but to perform an internal examination on me with his own hands.

"I understand, Dr. Rubin," he began, speaking quietly and so slowly that I had wondered whether he was still under the influence of psychiatric drugs—maybe anaphranil—or whether this was his normal way of speaking, "that we have a patient in common."

"A patient in common?" I repeated, baffled, until I suddenly remembered. "Of course, the granny."

"The granny?" He looked confused. "Sorry." I blushed hotly. "I must have been influenced by Mrs. Lazar; I just signed a contract with her yesterday to rent her mother's apartment." And I burst into a short, embarrassed laugh, which was evidently superfluous in his eyes, for he did not join in, or even smile, but began to examine me with curiosity and even concern, as if I had surprised him with some shrewd and practical aspect of my character for which he was not prepared. "In any case," he continued, "I spoke to our patient about you this morning, and she appears mostly satisfied with the service you performed for her, just a little anxious about the changes you made in the medication I prescribed for her. And while I failed to understand exactly the nature of the changes you wished to make, I reassured her that it was all right. If the new regime recommended by Dr. Rubin helps you, I told her, we'll all be happy; and if it doesn't, it's no tragedy either—as long as he doesn't intend to give you a sudden blood transfusion, you have nothing to fear from him." At last a faint smile crossed his face, though he had a somewhat suffering look. I nodded my head with a smile, ignoring the heavy hint about the transfusion, since I was eager to explain why I had wanted to change the old lady's medication first. But I immediately understood that he wasn't interested in hearing my thoughts on the question of the medication but wished to go straight to the matter of my candidacy for the position that had become available in his department. First of all, to my surprise, he questioned me about my medical studies in Jerusalem, especially the first year, and he even wrote down on a piece of paper details of the general courses I had taken in the natural sciences, chemistry, and physics. Then he questioned me in detail about my experience as a doctor in the army. In the end he asked about the experience I had acquired during the past year in the hospital, both in the operating room and in the surgical ward. And he asked me a number of times why I thought Hishin had chosen the other resident instead of me. I tried to answer all his questions not only thoroughly but also openly and honestly, being careful only, despite his attempts to draw me out, not to criticize

Hishin, who I knew was a friend of his in spite of the competition between them. But I said nothing about Dr. Nakash's offer of private work as his assistant, since I didn't want him to think that I would have anything to distract me. Finally his questions came to an end, and he crossed his hands on his chest and sank into a long and gloomy silence. For a moment he raised his big blue eyes to me as if he were about to say something, but then he changed his mind and lowered his head, pressing his fingertips to his forehead as if in some kind of conflict. I understood that he was hesitating or even embarrassed to broach the subject of the blood transfusion, perhaps because he didn't want to spoil the good impression I had made on him up to now, especially since I had come with the recommendation of the administrative director, who turned a blind eye to his regular absences from work on psychiatric grounds. I felt a burgeoning pity for this bleak, unhappy man, who was the same age as Hishin but looked so much older and wearier. I wanted to help him unburden himself of his doubts, and if he attacked me, I would have the opportunity to defend my action, which after my visit to the library seemed to me brilliant in its simplicity. Accordingly, when he seemed about to stand up and put an end to the interview, I said in a soft but self-confident voice, "I've been told, Professor Levine, that you have some reservations about the blood transfusion I performed on Lazar's daughter in India, and I would very much like, if you're interested and if you still have a little time, to explain what I did." I saw that I had hit a bull's-eye. First he blushed; then he recovered, raised his head, and unfolded his hands, his eyes lit up in astonishment at my openness and courage, and he began to speak with a new excitement in his voice. "To tell you the truth, Dr. Rubin, I had decided not to mention the incident, but since you've brought it up, I really would like to hear how you justify the blood transfusion you performed over there, which was not only completely unnecessary but also irresponsible and perhaps even dangerous." I had not expected such a vigorous attack, but I resolved to keep calm and continued quietly: "But why not a transfusion? There was a real danger of internal hemorrhage. In less than twenty-four hours there were three severe nosebleeds. I also got very poor results on her liver functions. Just a moment—excuse me, have you seen the data?"

"This may come as a surprise to you, Dr. Rubin, but the data are of no importance whatsoever here," he replied immediately, in a tone that was beginning to sound threatening. "Of course I've seen them. Here they are," and he whipped a folded piece of paper from his shirt pocket and spread it out in front of me. My heart skipped a beat at the sight of the gray Indian paper with the curly logo which I had brought from Calcutta. I wondered where it had disappeared to, and now I knew. Lazar and his wife had kept it to show to their professor friends, to check up on me behind my back and see if my panic in Varanasi was justified. "But why aren't the data important?" I was no longer calm, and sensed that the attack was about to come from a completely unexpected direction. "If there were such high values of liver damage, if the transaminases rose to levels of a hundred and eighty and a hundred and fifty-eight, it's clear that the clotting factors were also impaired. And I'm not even talking about the bilirubin, which reached nearly thirty. So why not strengthen the poor girl with some fresh, safe plasma, from someone as close as her mother, to help her overcome the bleeding? And the fact is, after my transfusion the bleeding stopped."

"It stopped on its own, not because of you." Professor Levine flung these words at me heatedly. "The clotting factors, which you thought you were giving her in your transfusion, are enzymes, not blood cells, and they behave completely differently in a transfusion. They're absorbed and disappear—they're ineffective unless they're diluted in a special serum to bind them and prevent them from dissolving. But this, my friend, not even your excellent teachers in Jerusalem could have taught you, and you simply couldn't have known. I don't blame you, as Professor Hishin has already confessed that he forgot to give you my article, which I prepared specially for you, because I anticipated such complications with bleeding. But, Dr. Rubin, I do blame you for so recklessly endangering the mother, whom you could have infected with the daughter's virus. When they told me in their innocence how you put off the return flight to New Delhi in order to perform a blood transfusion in that city of the dead of theirs, whose name I've forgotten, I was careful not to say a word to betray my horror at what you'd done. It's a miracle that nothing happened. Sometimes God protects people from their doctors. But still, I asked myself, is this young man simply an idiot, who never learned the ABCs of performing a blood transfusion, or did he perhaps have some hidden purpose beyond my comprehension? And then, when I was asked to consider you for a temporary residency in my department, I thought at first, no, not him, I don't even want to hear his name. But Lazar, and his secretary too, and even your Professor Hishin began putting pressure on me, and other people, objective people, said that you were really a conscientious young man, reliable and modest, and I must say, this is my impression too. So, Dr. Rubin, if you want to join our department, even on a temporary basis, I suggest that you spend the coming week in the library boning up on a few elementary laws of physics, such as the law of equilibrium, and consulting a biology textbook about the movement of viruses and how they multiply in the bloodstream, with particular attention to viruses B and C, which are interesting in themselves, and come back to me next week or the week after. There's no hurry—come back and we'll discuss it, so that you'll understand for once and for all what a catastrophe you could have brought down on a perfectly healthy woman we're all fond of, for the sake of your pointless theatrics."

Now I remembered with a chill how my friend Eyal had spontaneously reacted in exactly the same way when I told him about the blood transfusion in Jerusalem. I could hardly suspect Eyal of inventing things for the sole purpose of tripping me up. So what was the truth of the matter? Had I really been so wrong? A shiver ran down my spine at the thought that Dori might believe I had done something reckless to endanger her health, and lose confidence in me as a doctor. But I also knew that I must on no account get into an argument now with this neurotic man. I had better behave in my best "Anglo-Saxon" manner, as my father proudly called it, and avoid a dispute, and not even confront him about the mortifying expression "your pointless theatrics." I rose to my feet, my face burning, humiliated to the depths of my soul, and parted from him with hardly a word, or a promise either. Turning by mistake into the internal medicine ward and walking down the corridor between the rooms, where most of the patients were middle-aged or old and where my eyes suddenly flooded with tears, I thought to myself, No, it's impossible, he's wrong, his fears are imaginary, but I'll never be able to prove to him how absurd his arguments are, because all he wants is to depress me, like Dr. Nakash said—yes, Nakash knows him, all right. And suddenly I felt a powerful desire to see Dr. Nakash, so that he would give me, in his simple, straightforward way, a foothold in the world, because now I felt that I had been finally banished from the hospital which up to a few months ago I was sure would become my true and final place in life. I looked for Nakash in the recovery room, but there I was told that he was in the operating room. Still, I didn't want to give up the idea of seeing him, and I slipped into the wing. Through the window in the door I saw my friends from the surgical department standing there in their green gowns, and Dr. Nakash, dark and skinny, in a short white coat, his head close to the head of the patient. He soon noticed me and sent me a friendly wave, as a sign that I should wait for him. After a few minutes he came out to me. I told him about my meeting with Levine, including the vicious remark about my "pointless theatrics." He wasn't surprised; he only smiled and cursed under his breath. "I told you. He's a difficult man—all he wants to do is depress you without giving you anything in return. Leave him alone. You don't need him. Tomorrow night we've got a big private operation, and at the end of the month two more long, serious operations. I've recommended you to other anesthetists too. Don't worry, Benjy, you won't starve, you'll specialize in anesthesiology, and you won't regret it, because even if you go back to surgery in the end, it will give you a big advantage over your anesthetists. You'll be able to get more out of them."

❧❧

He returned to the operating room to sit at the patient's head while I hurried out of the hospital, which for the first time since I had started working there had become intolerable to me. Above all, I didn't want to bump into anyone I knew from the medical staff and have to justify myself to him. Who could have imagined two months ago, when I stood in the big office between the two strongest, most influential men at the hospital, who saw me as the "ideal man" for the job and succeeded in persuading me to go to India, that things would turn out like this, that in this whole great hospital there was no room for me now, not even a temporary post, and that of all the hopes I'd cherished in the past year, all I'd be left with was a bizarre, impossible infatuation, which would now only make me suffer more? For if it had remained an abstract fantasy, as it had been until yesterday, it might still have been possible to extricate myself gradually, but now that my body had miraculously touched hers, I had committed not only my soul but also my body, which had been seared with pleasure, to go on and prove to myself that it was no passing episode, as she had announced with such confidence while she was quickly putting on her clothes. Because if I was the one who had started, only I could stop. And I didn't want to stop, I didn't want to stop.

So I said to myself as I stepped out into the big parking lot and the strong but sweet light of a brilliant winter's day. I walked over to my motorcycle, which I had recently taken to inserting between the cars of the directors, under their exclusive carport, not only in order to protect it from the rain but also in order to peek into Lazar's car to see if Dori had forgotten anything of hers there. I kicked off and rode quickly out of the hospital grounds, but at the first traffic light, while I was waiting at a red light, I couldn't resist looking back at the yellowish building with smoke spiraling out of its two tall chimneys, and suddenly it seemed to me that it was not I who was leaving the hospital but the hospital that was sailing away from me like some great ship, embarking with its doctors and patients on a journey full of new storms and adventures, which I had been found unworthy of participating in. Professor Levine was right—he had put his finger on something; mental illness sharpened the senses. It was true, there had been something a little theatrical about my actions in Varanasi. There was always something faintly theatrical in the contact between a doctor and his patient, because it was only through acting that you could overcome a total stranger's natural embarrassment at getting undressed in front of you so that you could look into his mouth, feel his stomach, listen to his heart, and finger his sexual organs. But in the hotel in Varanasi, next to the purple-lacquered wicker chairs, it hadn't only been a theatrical show, it had been the beginning of falling in love, a love that I now had to make sure didn't die, didn't turn into a passing episode.

When I arrived at my old apartment, I found the door open and strange suitcases standing in the hall and the landlady hurrying behind me to inform me that the new tenants were already moving in, because they had nowhere else to go and they couldn't wait any longer. Since I had promised to vacate the apartment early, and if my new apartment was ready, why should I delay? I had no reason to delay, but no wish to start packing up my possessions either, which turned out to be more numerous than I had imagined, in front of this couple, fresh out of the army, quiet and in love, who began following me around and inserting themselves softly and insistently into every shelf I cleared. My motorcycle was of course no help in transporting my stuff, and I phoned Amnon, a childhood friend from Jerusalem who was busy writing his Ph.D. in the physics and astronomy department of Tel Aviv University, and supporting himself by working as a night watchman in a big canning plant in the south of the city. At night he had an old pickup truck at his disposal, and I asked him to use it to transport my belongings to the new apartment where I had already been to bed, but not to sleep. I had to wait until late in the evening, when his shift began, and in the meantime the young couple began to push me discreetly but firmly out of the apartment. At first we agreed that I would clear one room for them, where they could put their stuff until I cleared out the rest of the apartment. And at first they confined themselves to the room, giggling in undertones as they put things away in the closets and even hung pictures on the walls. But toward evening, when they saw that I was still hanging around, they grew impatient, and began wandering around the apartment, going into the kitchen to cook themselves supper, and the girl went into the bathroom to take a shower. They were a symbiotic couple, and kept up an incessant communication between them. Even when the girl was in the shower the boy kept going into the bathroom to give her things or get things from her. In the end Amnon called and announced that he would arrive within half an hour. I began taking down the suitcases, blankets, and cushions, and the young couple immediately volunteered to take down the cardboard boxes with my books and kitchen utensils. And even when I was sitting downstairs with all my possessions around me, waiting for Amnon and his pickup, they went on searching the apartment and bringing down all kinds of dirty and forgotten belongings of mine which I had left behind. It was highly disagreeable to have to part in such unseemly haste from my first Tel Aviv apartment, of which I was very fond, and where

I had enjoyed a certain quiet and solitude, and which also preserved the memory of my initial excitement at the hospital, when I would reconstruct the operating table on the kitchen table and practice with a knife and fork and pieces of string, trying to imitate Hishin's quiet, rapid movements.

Amnon arrived very late and found me sitting on the sidewalk covered with a blanket, surrounded by my possessions like a deported refugee. But I couldn't be angry with him, since I knew that he was abandoning his watchman's post for my sake. We quickly loaded everything onto the open truck, and I got onto my motorcycle and rode in front to show him the way. At the new place we unloaded everything onto the sidewalk, and Amnon drove away. "You still have to explain to me what Hawking's problem is with the first three seconds of the big bang," I said before he left. I knew he liked having me ask him questions about astrophysics, so that he could give me a long lecture while I sat and listened like a disciple at the feet of the master. He had been stuck on his Ph.D. for several years now, even though he devoted all his energies to it, and his friends were loath to ask him about it in case a note of incredulity crept into their voices. "Whenever you like—you know I'm all in favor of your taking a break from your quackery and learning a little real science," he said affably. He asked for my new phone number, but I found that I had suddenly forgotten it, so I promised that I would call him that very night and give it to him. But in the new apartment the phone was dead. The thought that my parents had probably been trying to get in touch with me all evening and wondering where I had disappeared to began to worry me. During the past few weeks I had noted a new note of concern in their voices, and there was no reason to add to their anxiety. But what had happened to the telephone? No one had touched it since last night. For a moment it occurred to me that Dori had garbled her message to the phone company when she asked for an interim reading of the meter and had caused them to disconnect the phone by mistake. It was late, and the apartment was alarmingly full of my possessions. Now I had the feeling that it was actually smaller than the apartment I had left, and the closet full of the granny's gray suits suddenly annoyed me. But above all, it upset me that I wouldn't be able to keep my promise to call Amnon, and he would wait in vain in his cold watchman's hut and think that I was trying to get out of meeting him after taking advantage of him and his truck. I left my belongings piled up on the floor and went out to look for a pay phone in order to call him and make a date. As I searched for a phone I thought about the obscurity of those first three seconds of the big bang, encountered by Hawking and others, and in which, according to Hawking's own admission, the theory itself collapsed, owing to its inability to explain how the entire cosmos, compressed into a particle whose density was infinite and whose radius was zero, had begun to expand with such speed. Physics was helpless with regard to these three seconds, for they were simply outside physics. This was the point of transition from spirit to matter. In other words, how could matter shrink back into the single particle from which it was born? Spirit would do it, and not by magic but in a slow and gradual process. In fact, it had already begun. Take the airplane, for example. It compressed matter, canceled distance, and what was the airplane if not a smallish bit of matter in which an enormous amount of spirit had been invested—that is, laws and thought?

When I finally found a phone, I was too tired to engage Amnon in any of my theories and simply asked him to notify the phone company of the problem, and gave him my new number, which I had written down on my identity card. And then, in spite of the lateness of the hour, I phoned my parents, who I thought would be worrying about my sudden disappearance, but it turned out that they were sleeping soundly, without a care in the world, for when they had phoned my new apartment in the afternoon, a recorded voice had informed them that the phone was temporarily disconnected.

"It must be my new landlady's fault," I said immediately, laughing but annoyed. "Instead of asking for a simple reading of the meter, she must have confused the issue somehow, and they disconnected the phone. Terrific. Now what am I going to do?" But my mother calmed me down; she had an inexplicable faith in government agencies, perhaps because my father worked for one of them. "They'll connect it again in the morning, and in any case we won't need it tomorrow, because we're coming to Tel Aviv to sign the guarantee for you and help you organize things in your new place." Suddenly I felt uncomfortable about their coming so soon to my new apartment, where my lovemaking with my landlady still lingered in the air. I was also sure that my mother wouldn't approve of the apartment, which she had been hostile toward from the outset. And even if she restrained herself and didn't say anything against it, she wouldn't be able to resist questioning me about my real reasons for making this sudden change. "No, don't come tomorrow," I said quickly. "The guarantee can wait. I've given her enough postdated checks. Don't come, I won't have enough time to spend with you tomorrow. And tomorrow night I'm taking part in a private operation with Dr. Nakash, who's taken me on as his assistant, and I'll have to go in early to check out the anesthetizing equipment and begin to learn the subject. Why come in the middle of all the mess? Give me a chance to fix things up a bit. Besides, it makes more sense for me to come to Jerusalem on Friday to see you, and I'll bring the guarantee with me so you can sign it there." I concluded on a pleading note, and now there was a silence on the other end of the line. There was no doubt that they were disappointed, especially my father, who had probably planned the visit to Tel Aviv in detail. But my promise to come to Jerusalem for the weekend tipped the scales, and they gave in. "So tomorrow you'll be operating again," said my father, suddenly coming to life. "You see, nothing's been lost. They want you in the operating room again."

"It's only an operation for the surgeon, Dad. For me it's just putting someone to sleep and waking him up again," I said in despair, looking at a young woman wrapped in a winter coat, standing a few steps away in the empty street.

I said nothing to them about my interview with Professor Levine, not wanting to cause them any more grief. I would have to accustom them gradually to the idea that I was out of the hospital. I hurried back to the apartment, and although I had had a difficult, confusing day, I didn't feel tired and immediately began to tackle the task of arranging my possessions in their new places. It turned out that in addition to the granny's closet, the Lazars had forgotten to empty the two little bedside cupboards, which contained mainly documents, old letters, and photograph albums. At first I didn't know if I had the right to empty them on my own initiative, but the thought of having two family archives stuffed with letters and photographs and documents belonging to complete strangers weighing on my sleep at night was too much for me. After some hesitation, I decided to cram everything into some empty shoe boxes I found on the balcony, which I pushed between the gray suits in the granny's closet. At first I thought of keeping one photograph album out, for on paging through it I had found a number of ancient photographs of Dori as a young soldier, a law student, with Lazar and without him, holding a baby in her arms, always smiling, attractive and shapely, a young woman of my own age. But in the end I put it away with the others. I felt alien and hostile toward these photographs. I couldn't connect with her past; nothing here belonged to me, nor did I need it to fire my imagination and fuel my love. I wanted her the way I knew her now, plump, middle-aged, mature, pampered but sure of herself. Until the small hours of the night I was busy putting my things away and cleaning the apartment. I hung my pictures up on the nails which had remained in the walls, not wanting to disturb the silence with the banging of a hammer. Finally I took a shower and made the bed with the clean, fragrant sheets that had apparently been left for my use, and with the disconnected telephone ensuring that no one would disturb me, I sank into a deep, prolonged sleep, with the result that I arrived alert and clearheaded at the private hospital on the Herzliah beach for the operation which began at twilight the next day and lasted until dawn.

It was complicated and dangerous brain surgery, performed by a surgeon of about thirty-five, a visiting professor from America, assisted by a local man, a well-known retired surgeon from our own hospital, who had worked with Dr. Nakash in the past and presumably trusted him to handle the particularly complex anesthesia procedure. For the first time I saw Nakash losing a little of his natural serenity and inner confidence. He was flushed and excited, and after introducing me to the visiting surgeon and his personal assistant, he began addressing me in English, and asked me to answer him in kind, so that we would fit into the linguistic ambience of the place, which from the moment of my arrival had impressed me with its pleasantness. In contrast to the operating rooms I had known up to then, which were always cold, windowless, isolated from the world, buried in the heart of the hospital like the engine room of a submarine, here we entered an operating room that was bright and cozy, behind whose attractive drapes were windows through which an almost pastoral view was visible, with people walking calmly along a well-tended seaside promenade. The instruments were newer than those in our hospital, smaller in their dimensions, light and pleasant to hold. And in the middle of all this was the large shaved skull of a handsome, sturdy man of about fifty-five. Since the days of my anatomy lessons I had not seen a human skull held between forceps and gradually opened up, layer after layer, sawed by the hand of an artist to expose the whitish brain pulsing with its minute capillaries, whose delicate balance between stillness and vitality Nakash was controlling from behind a state-of-the-art anesthesia machine full of little monitors displaying changing numbers. And so the long night began, during the course of which I learned how to stand rooted to the spot for hours at a time in order to follow the movement of the respirator, and especially the changing values of the oxygen concentration, the level of expired carbon dioxide, the volume of air pumped into the lungs, and of course the heartbeats, the systemic blood pressure, the venous pressure, and the state of hydration in the body—all of which make up the drama of anesthesiology, particularly in brain surgery, where the slightest twitch or cough on the part of the patient can cause the exposed brain to bulge.

"If you're getting bored," Nakash whispered to me in the middle of the night in his heavily accented Iraqi Hebrew, "think of yourself as the pilot of the soul, who has to ensure that it glides painlessly through the void of sleep without being jolted or shocked, without falling. But also to make sure that it doesn't soar too high and slip inadvertently into the next world." I had heard him speak like this about his role before, but now, in the depths of the night, a little groggy after long hours of intent concentration on the changing monitors of the anesthesia machine, with the skull and brain not actually before my eyes but only flickering grayly on the suspended video screen, I felt that his words were true. I had turned from a doctor into a pilot or a navigator, surrounded by nurses, who looked like well-groomed stewardesses in this private hospital, coming in every now and then to draw a little blood to measure the potassium and sodium levels, or to pour cocktails of pentothal or morphine into the suspended infusion bags, with special additions concocted by Nakash to ensure the tranquillity of the "instrument flight." And for the first time I saw this work, for all its boredom and frustration, as something that possessed spiritual significance, for the thought and attention of the anesthetist were addressed not to the body, not to the matter, not to the greenish tumor which the two surgeons at our side were battling to extract from the depths of the brain, but to the soul, which I suddenly felt was truly in my hands, in its silence and, who knows, perhaps also in its dreams.

When the operation was over we saw that dawn had already stolen through the folds of the drapes. The two surgeons and the nurses left the room, and the patient was wheeled into the recovery room. Nakash sat next to him for a while and then went to see to the arrangements for us to be paid, leaving me to wait for the "landing"—in other words, to watch the respirator for the first signs that the patient was beginning to breathe independently. I now felt no tiredness. I parted the curtains and let my eyes wander from the respirator to the sunrise painting the sea in soft pastel colors. My hands were clean, without any blood or smell of drugs, without the warmth of the depths of the human body, which I was used to feeling on my fingers after an operation, even if I had played a very minor role in it. And although I hadn't even seen the tumor with my own eyes before it was sent for the biopsy, I felt a sense of profound satisfaction, as if I had truly taken part in the battle. I went up to the patient and raised his eyelids, as I had observed Nakash doing to his patients, but without knowing what exactly I wanted to see there. A new, very pretty nurse, who hadn't been present during the operation, came into the room and sat down next to me and said, "Dr. Nakash sent me to take over from you, so that you can go and sign for the fee." I didn't want to leave the patient; I felt that I wanted to see for myself how the undercarriage of the soul touched the solid ground of the body. The nurse's frank reference to the financial arrangements between myself and the hospital jarred me. But I was new here and I didn't want to step out of line. I thus went to the secretary's office, where a check for eight hundred shekels was waiting for me, together with an elegantly printed page setting out the details of the fee and the various deductions. Nakash examined my check and asked if everything was all right. Then he sent me home. "I'll see that our patient lands safely," he said with a smile. I went to the changing rooms, and even though I had not been soiled by the operation, I couldn't resist the magnificent facilities, and I took a long shower. Then I dressed, tucked my crash helmet under my arm, and prepared to leave the hospital, but before doing so I couldn't help going into the recovery room to see if the landing was over. It was, and the patient was now alone. Nakash had disappeared. The beautiful nurse was gone too. The anesthesia machine had been wheeled into a corner of the room. The soul had returned to the body. The patient was breathing by himself.

I reached my apartment without any problems, leaving behind me rows of despairing cars struggling to enter Tel Aviv. The check was in my pocket, about a quarter of my monthly salary at the hospital. Now I thought about Dori. Should I wait until my parents had signed the guarantee, or should I try to make contact without any actual pretext for doing so? Children in school uniforms were coming down the stairs. Neighbors examined me suspiciously when they saw me standing in my black leather jacket and crash helmet, opening the door to my apartment, but no one dared to say anything to me. I made myself a big breakfast, and then I let down the blinds and prepared for a sweet sleep without any disturbances, not even the chance ringing of the phone. But while I was fast asleep the line was reconnected, and at one o'clock in the afternoon the phone rang insistently. It was my mother, who was glad to see that her efforts on my behalf with the phone company had borne fruit and who asked me when I intended to arrive the next day. "Early," I said immediately, because I knew that I had to compensate them for missing their visit to Tel Aviv. And indeed, I arrived in Jerusalem on Friday afternoon before my father came home from work and told my mother about the interview with Professor Levine and my final banishment from the hospital. At first she listened in silence. Whenever I was involved in a quarrel, she was always careful not to get carried away and blame the other party, and even when it was clear to her that they were in the wrong and had treated me unjustly, she would examine what it was in me and my behavior that had caused them to wrong me. Now, too, she tried to interrogate me tactfully but insistently—was I sure that the blood transfusion had been essential? And how had I felt when I was performing it? I felt sorry for her. She was groping in the dark, looking for something that she could never have imagined was actually there. But I was afraid that she might discover something, so I deliberately increased the darkness in which she was floundering. In the end my father arrived. I wanted to spare him the bad news for a while, but my mother immediately told him. At first he turned a little pale, then he recovered and listened with unseemly gratification to Dr. Nakash's pithy definitions of Professor Levine's mental illness. The fact that Hishin had not challenged the transfusion appeared to him to confirm my innocence of any wrongdoing, and he seemed satisfied. He was also very impressed by my descriptions of the private hospital in Herzliah, and was amazed at the high fee I had received for one night's work. "Dealing with the soul is more important and expensive than dealing only with the body," I said with a smile, "because in the end the legal responsibility falls on the anesthetist. If something happens to the patient, whom will they blame? Who'll have the strength to open up the stomach or the brain again to poke around in there and decide what was cut right or wrong?" My mother sank into a profound silence and gave me a searching look. I felt that for some reason she was dissatisfied with me, but I also knew that she was incapable of putting her finger on the precise source of her complaints.

When my father and I finally finished chatting about the salaries of doctors and possible complications in surgery, my mother held out a white envelope with my name written on it, which contained an invitation to Eyal's wedding, which was to take place in three weeks' time in Kibbutz Ein Zohar in the Arava. My parents had received a separate invitation, and Eyal himself had called to urge them to come. His mother had joined in the request, and even Hadas had taken the receiver and added a few friendly words. It seemed that it was important to them for my parents, who had known Eyal since he was a child, to be at the wedding. "You're not thinking of traveling all the way to the Arava?" I asked in surprise, but it turned out that they had already promised Eyal they would go, and that they intended to drive down in their own car, for after the wedding they intended to continue on to one of the spa hotels on the banks of the Dead Sea and spend a few days there. Their disappointment at the cancellation of the visit to Tel Aviv had apparently only intensified their hunger for travel, for instead of waiting to consult me about their plans, as they usually did, they had arranged it all themselves, and even reserved rooms in a hotel. "What will you do at a wedding for young people on a kibbutz?" I asked with a faint smile. "Why on earth should you travel all the way there, and in the old car on top of everything?" But my mother was determined to go. Eyal had asked them to be present at his wedding, and they didn't want to hurt his feelings. They remembered him hanging around in our house, and there had been times, especially after his father committed suicide, when they had considered him almost a second son. And besides, they had every intention of enjoying the wedding, the trip to the desert, the kibbutz. I would join them in Jerusalem, or they would come and pick me up in Tel Aviv, and we would drive down together to the Arava, and after the kibbutz we would all go to the hotel on the banks of the Dead Sea. They had already booked a room for me, and really, why shouldn't I take a few days' vacation? But I didn't want to meet my old friends with my parents hovering at my elbow, and I immediately rejected their invitation to join them at the Dead Sea, even for one night. I did my best to discourage the whole idea, and told them that they would have to reach the Arava under their own steam, because I intended to ride down on my motorcycle in order to be free to return to Tel Aviv without having to depend on anyone else. "But you have no commitments to the hospital anymore," my mother said, offended by my refusal to accompany them on their holiday. "I have other commitments," I said, without explaining. They were very disappointed by my negative reaction to their plans, especially my mother, who was not enthusiastic about traveling alone on the desert roads and was afraid that my father would get lost, since he had a habit of misreading road maps and was too proud to stop and ask for directions. But when I saw that all the obstacles I put in their way would not deter them from keeping their promise to Eyal, I softened a little and promised to meet them at the exit from Beersheba and ride in front of them to the kibbutz, and also to guide them to their hotel later that night. At this my mother relaxed, and we passed a pleasant Shabbat together. I described the complicated brain surgery again at length, and told them about the new feelings I had experienced as an anesthetist. I also reminisced about India, and this time I was more generous with my stories about Calcutta and the ghats of Varanasi, but I hardly mentioned the Lazars. I didn't say anything about the guarantee either, and it was only on Saturday afternoon, before I set out for Tel Aviv, while my mother was taking a nap, that I got my father to sign it, quickly adding my mother's signature myself.

ஜஜ

I pocketed the signed guarantee with the feeling that I had succeeded in lassoing Dori from a distance with one more slender thread. But how absurd, I thought in despair, that after my daring confession, and after I had succeeded in going to bed with her, I should still feel as if I were standing at the starting point, needing some unimportant piece of paper as an excuse for meeting her. I knew that if I called her on the phone I would give her an opening to evade me, even if she wasn't yet sure herself of what she really wanted. If it was true that this was the first time she had been unfaithful to her husband—and I knew just how deeply she was attached to him—she must surely be full of remorse and self-reproach at what she had done, even if she was a little bit in love with me or felt at least some longing for what had happened between us. Accordingly, I must on no account give her the chance to break off the connection between us before we met again, a meeting I decided to effect by the simple means of walking confidently into her office, like an old client who didn't need an appointment to be granted an interview, however brief. And even though I suspected that she might be startled to see me, I was sure that she would soon realize that my only motive in surprising her in her office was to show her that she could trust me completely, just as I had taken off all my clothes and placed myself at her disposal, giving her the choice to do whatever she wanted with me. Yes, I would meet her on her own territory, where she was protected from any improper gesture or word that might escape me, but I was doing it not just to calm any fears of harassment but also in order to show her that my intentions were not only sexual but deeper than that, as if the guarantee I had come to give her was also a testimony to her tenant's good character. Perhaps precisely because of the significance I attached to my sudden entry into her office, I put it off, even though I had plenty of time on my hands now to haunt the little streets around her building, or to watch her strenuous maneuvers to get in or out of a forbidden parking place—I still delayed my entry, still hesitated to insert myself between one client and the next, to hand over the guarantee and relinquish the sweet thread of hope I held in my hand. Until one day when she appeared in a dream I had in the middle of the day, for now that my time was my own I had gotten into the habit of taking long, deep naps in the afternoon. In my dream she was standing and talking in her friendly, affectionate way to Hishin, who was lying, apparently as a joke, on one of the beds in the ward. And this simple dream for some reason agitated me so much that the same day, late in the afternoon, I bought a brightly colored Indian silk scarf which I found in a little knickknack shop in Basle Street, and I walked straight into her office and asked the dark-haired secretary, who remembered me from the morning when we ran around organizing things for the trip, and greeted me warmly, to let me in to see her for a minute as soon as she was free. But as it happened she was already free, and I went in and shut the door behind me and sat down opposite her, without waiting for her permission, and with lowered eyes I handed her the guarantee with my parents' signatures on it and said, "Here's the guarantee you asked for."

Her eyes lit up in her usual smile, and she seemed quite calm, as if she had been expecting this sudden intrusion, and at that moment I didn't know if she was calm because she was sure that what had happened between us was only a passing episode and it was all over now, or the opposite—she had become calm on seeing that I had not taken her words seriously and that I was bringing her the guarantee in person because I didn't want to give her up. She took the guarantee and folded it as if she were about to tear it in half, but then hesitated and stopped herself, as if the lawyer in her were warning her of unpleasant eventualities in the future. But then she changed her mind again and tore it into shreds, which she dropped into the wastepaper basket, saying as she did so, "Never mind, I trust you." Then she raised her laughing eyes to me and said, "So how are you? Have you recovered?" She blushed slightly, afraid perhaps of what I was about to say, and I said innocently, "From what?" and she said, "You know. From something that is quite impossible and will never happen again." I kept quiet, afraid that my rising lust would cloud the wits I needed for this confrontation, but I looked straight at her. She was wearing a gray suit like the ones hanging in her mother's closet. Her bun was beginning to come loose, and locks of hair had fallen onto her neck. The shade of her hair was darker than I remembered from the week before, and I wondered whether she had dyed it again or whether the light in the room was deceiving me. Her makeup, too, had faded during the day, exposing the cute freckles on her cheekbones. Her breasts looked smaller now, outlined separately under her white blouse. And behind the desk I caught a glimpse of the pampered little paunch. She certainly wasn't beautiful, I thought to myself, and a vague memory of my afternoon dream crossed my mind. But she had a warmth and liveliness and directness that I badly needed now, and if she insisted on thinking that it was over between us, she had every right to do so, for I had not yet succeeded in convincing her that only the one who had started it had the right to end it. And then, in a gloomy silence, I took the gift-wrapped scarf out of my pocket and put it in front of her on the desk, whispering hoarsely, "I got this for you. Maybe because it reminds me of India. I don't know." She was now stunned and overcome with agitation, as if neither my declaration of love nor my standing naked before her had persuaded her of the seriousness of my intentions as much as this little scarf. She closed her eyes tight, and then she pressed her fist to her mouth again, as if she wanted to hit herself for what she had done to me and to herself. She unwrapped the colored paper and spread the scarf out in silence, and then she smiled distractedly and said, "Tell me, Benjy, what do you really want? I'll soon be fifty. I don't understand. What was it there in India that threw you off balance? What happened? True, I made a mistake too. I was flattered by the thought of being desired by such a young man. But that's all. What can it lead to? It's impossible. And you know it."

"Yes, I know," I admitted somberly, and I went on with miserable stubbornness, "but I'm only asking for one more time."

"No," she said immediately and vehemently, without thinking, "there's no point. Even though it was very sweet for me too. It makes no difference. What will one more time give us? It will only make you want more, and you'll come back and pester me again. And why not—you're a free agent, you've got no obligations to anyone. You misled me when you asked to rent my mother's apartment, I believed you when you said that you wanted to get married."

"But I really do want to get married," I replied quickly.

The secretary knocked at the door, and without waiting she opened it and came in and announced the name of a client who had just arrived. "Right away," said Dori, rising from her seat, and carried forward on her high heels, she made for the door, flooding me with a wave of love as she paused by my side. She wanted to say something to me, perhaps to console me, but the client, an elderly, elegantly dressed man who was apparently too agitated to wait, opened the door and stepped into the room without waiting to be asked. She immediately flashed him one of her automatic smiles, and for some reason she introduced me to him, as if to banish any possible suspicion. "This is Dr. Rubin, who's like a family doctor to us. Please come in and sit down." The client nodded his head at me distractedly and sat down. She accompanied me to the hallway and said, "I understand that things didn't work out with Professor Levine."

"No," I said, trembling with excitement. "He's a strange man; I don't understand him. He claims that I could have infected you with Einat's hepatitis when I performed the blood transfusion in Varanasi." She burst into surprised laughter—was she really unaware of Levine's accusations? "Perhaps you really did infect me," she said with a slight smile, and turned around and went back into her room, and through the open door I saw her folding the scarf and putting it into one of the drawers of her desk.

At seven o'clock that evening Dr. Nakash phoned me to ask if I could come immediately to the hospital in Herzliah. In an hour's time an operation was scheduled to begin. It had originally been planned without an assistant anesthetist, in order to reduce the costs to the patient, but the day before Nakash himself had caught a severe cold, and this morning his temperature had risen, and although he had treated himself aggressively during the day, he was still afraid of spreading germs in the operating room, and he wanted me to come and "fly the plane" myself, though he would be right next door to guide and direct me. "Don't you think it's too soon to leave me on my own?" I asked in excitement. "No," answered Nakash confidently, "you'll be fine. I didn't choose you by accident. I've been watching you in the operating room for a whole year now, and I've seen your grasp of internal processes. You understand what anesthesia means. Hishin hit the nail on the head when he praised you that time in the cafeteria. By the way, if you're missing him, you'll be able to see him soon, because he's performing the operation tonight. But for God's sake, Benjy, get on your horse and get over here as quickly as you can." My spirits, which were low after the meeting with Dori, began to soar. I jumped onto my motorcycle, and with the resolution of someone on an emergency rescue mission I began to weave boldly through the heavy traffic leaving Tel Aviv. Nevertheless, I arrived at the operating room after the first premedication shot had already been given under Nakash's supervision. In order to protect his surroundings from his germs he had made himself a strange mask which enveloped his entire head, leaving only two holes for his narrow black eyes. The patient was a woman of about fifty, plump and blue-eyed, whose figure reminded me of Dori's. She had to have abdominal surgery, the correction of a hiatal hernia and a vagotomy—the kind of operation at which Hishin excelled, in spite of the mystery of the death of the young woman on whom he had operated on the eve of the trip to India. I put on a mask, and with the help of the nurses I began preparing the patient for the operation. Since Nakash was keeping at a distance from us, I myself began talking to the patient, asking her about her feelings and sensations, her husband and children, and in the meantime I exposed her chest in order to auscultate her heart and lungs again, to avoid any unpleasant surprises. From the corridor rose Hishin's loud laughter, and Nakash signaled me to hurry up. I gave her the first shot of dormicum, smiled at her, placed the mask on her face, and connected her to the anesthesia machine, and felt her body relaxing under my hands; I gave her the first shot of pentothal, to relax her muscles, and inserted the infusion needle for the anesthetic; she lost consciousness, and I immediately felt her soul asking to be liberated and soar; I took hold of the cylinder with both hands and gave her an initial dose of oxygen; then I forced her clamped mouth open and inserted the small iron blade of the laryngoscope to prevent her mouth from closing, and in the narrow beam of light I succeeded in getting an exact view of the pinkish passage to the vocal cords, through which I slowly inserted the tube into her lungs. Then I turned on the respirator.

The nurse exposed the round white stomach, cleaned it with alcohol, and drew the line for the incision. Nakash, who was standing behind the door with his face masked, like a white mummy with burning eyes, made a V sign with his fingers and signaled me to clear his field of vision, so that from a distance he could watch the monitors of the anesthesia machine piloting the body which had been abandoned by its soul.

Hishin was still delaying his entry, like a conductor waiting for the members of the orchestra to tune their instruments. But when the nurse came in with the X-rays and placed them like a musical score on the illuminated screen, I sensed his close presence and trembled with excitement, for I knew that Nakash had kept my participation in the operation a secret from him. He came in slowly, tall, smiling, pleased with himself, humming under his breath. The mauve color of his gown and mask, which in this hospital took the place of the standard green, gave him a gay, lighthearted air, as if he had dressed up as somebody else. He stopped and stared in playful surprise at the masked Nakash standing in the corner, and then his eyes met mine, which were fixed on the monitors of the anesthesia machine. "What a pleasant surprise," he said when he had recovered. "My friend Dr. Rubin! So you've abandoned the knife but not the operating room. Very good. A very positive direction. When you left us, I myself thought of advising you to specialize in anesthesiology, but I was afraid you would think I was antagonistic to your great ambitions. But I see that Dr. Nakash has succeeded in persuading you. Congratulations, Nakash, you've found the ideal assistant."

Ten

And then at last, the hard, green, open eye—whether it is male or female is still impossible to tell—begins to flicker and dim, until its anxiety is subdued by sleep. And despite the sorrow and the disappointment, for freedom has eluded them again, the caress of a strange but familiar feather brings comfort in the darkness. And when slender spears of light appear between the bald yellow crags and a purple brush paints the sky, the two are already huddled close together, tangled in the branches of a dry, sturdy bush, waiting for the sun to hammer the sky into a bright, unblinking blue. They have penetrated the heart of the Arava in order to learn the lesson that neither of them is capable of remaining alone.

But since they have broken the chain of marriage which joined them, from now on they are doomed to scratch the desert soil for food and to drink the bitter, salty water of the sea of death. Awed by the fatefulness of their meeting, they reverently circle the torn, bleeding remains of the mystery, which never left them and pursued them relentlessly in order to join them together again. Now the ruined, pitiful remains lie before them on the stones, mangled and exhausted but still twitching, as if they want to fly again or to change their form. A severed arm turns into a black wing, a lost leg into a tail, and cracked eyeglasses into a sharp beak, until the furnace of noon welds all the pieces into one, and a glossy black crow rises from the dry ground and flaps its dark wings.

※♋※

For some reason, Eyal's approaching wedding gave rise in me to excitement mingled with a faint anxiety, as if something significant were about to take place. Eyal himself tirelessly drummed up interest in the event by constant consultations about how to increase the numbers of his guests. Since he feared that people would be deterred by the distance and the wedding would be poorly attended, he decided to send out as many invitations as possible, and he kept phoning me to remind him of the names and addresses of forgotten friends from our school days. But even the long list of wedding guests failed to reassure him, and he was constantly on the phone, calling people up to make sure that they weren't planning a last-minute defection. And perhaps it was only the familiar anxiety of my friend Eyal, who ever since he had lost his father was afraid of being abandoned and rejected, that aroused my excitement and expectation, which were apparently conveyed to my parents too, for not only did they buy a handsome and expensive present for the young couple from all of us, but my mother bought herself a new dress as well, and my father took the car to the garage for a general overhaul. The old car and the long drive were now our main concern, and in order to make the long day's drive easier on my father and to avoid unnecessary complications with the meeting in Beersheba, my parents arrived in the morning in Tel Aviv, and after visiting an elderly aunt in an old folks' home, they had lunch with me in a little restaurant and came home with me for a short rest in my new apartment, which to my surprise my mother decided she liked better than the old one in spite of its many disadvantages. "Even though you made a mistake," she said in her pedagogical way, "it was in the right direction." I made my bed for them with clean sheets and blankets, and placed a little electric heater in the room. I insisted that they take off their clothes and put on pajamas and take a proper nap, to refresh themselves before the great adventure. At first they were amused by my insistence, which was uncharacteristic of me, but in the end they gave in. And although my mother emerged from the room after fifteen minutes, my father fell into a deep sleep, which lasted so long that it began to worry us both. It was only when I saw him emerging from my bedroom dazed and confused, more exhausted after his sleep than before it, that I suddenly felt a pang of compassion for them both, and I wondered whether I shouldn't give up the idea of riding down separately on my motorcycle and join them in the car, to help my father with the driving. The problem was the drive from the kibbutz to the hotel on the Dead Sea; I knew that if I left my motorcycle behind, I'd have to drive them there after the wedding, spend the night in the hotel, and take the bus back to Tel Aviv in the morning, a tedious and time-consuming project that I was not prepared to undertake. Especially since I had promised Amnon—who was riding down with his parents, who had also been invited, in a special bus from Jerusalem—to give him a lift back to Tel Aviv on my motorcycle, and during the course of the ride we would finally be able to hold the promised and long-delayed astrophysical debate.

The wedding ceremony was due to begin at half past seven, but Eyal had made us swear to arrive while it was still light so that we could enjoy the long and stunningly beautiful evening. "Don't miss the desert sunset," he repeatedly warned us. However, it was not only for the sake of the sunset that our little convoy set out at three o'clock in the afternoon, but in order to soften the harshness of the 150-mile drive ahead of us. My father was on the whole a good driver, but recently he had begun to experience moments of dreaminess while at the wheel, which would have ended in catastrophe if not for my mother's vigilance. And there was also the question of navigation. Although the road to the kibbutz was straight and uncomplicated, I knew that it was sometimes just these highways, racing automatically ahead, that misled my father, who would wait tensely for the turnoff until he couldn't stand it any longer, and at some blameless and insignificant junction he would suddenly decide that the time had come and turn the wheel. But this time it had been clearly agreed between us that he would turn off the road only when he received a clear sign from me. I began to drive slowly in front of them, as if they were important guests in a foreign land, leading them through the labyrinth of the Tel Aviv streets and onto the right lane of the expressway, where I allowed myself to put a little distance between us, and even to lose them for a while, only to catch them again in the stream of traffic before the interchange leading to the south, whose broad plains were radiant now in the warm light that flooded the inside of my helmet. Even though it was still officially winter, and the young weather forecasters who had become popular media stars during the months of storms and snow were still nostalgically predicting rain and stormy weather, the warmth of spring had already arrived to comfort fields devastated by floods, lawns shriveled by frost, and trees exhausted by strong winds; even the broad asphalt road seemed to be exuding a delightful springlike fragrance. I couldn't resist stopping at the side of the road, and like a grim traffic cop I waved my parents down, to tell them to open their windows and breathe in the fresh new air.

I still nursed a certain resentment and anger in the wake of the disappointing confrontation in Dori's office, but I had not yet given up hope. Still, the determination and decisiveness of her efforts to shake me off had taken me aback. In the beginning I had not hoped for anything, but when she unexpectedly responded to my fervent declaration of love, I realized that I had not suddenly turned into a deluded madman but remained what I always was, a rational, realistic person aspiring to what was within the bounds of possibility. Indeed, reality had proved that even a woman like her, ostensibly so inaccessible, could see me as a possible partner, even though I still didn't know how or why, whether it was only because of the charm of my youth as such, or also thanks to certain inner qualities of my own, which had been revealed to her in the light of India. If she had sent me packing, it was because she was afraid, and rightly so, that I would be completely swept away by the powerful passion of which she had already experienced a small taste. Maybe I was meant to reconsider in a positive light the casual remark she had made about a bachelor's being dangerous in an extramarital affair, and precisely now, in this state of violent infatuation, I should break my stubborn bachelorhood, for it was only in this way that I could protect her from myself, as I was protected from her. Perhaps this was cockeyed logic, but it also held out hope. Perhaps I really should get married. This simple thought began to throb inside me, rolling out in front of me on the black asphalt, awakening my blood, and without my being aware of it, I accelerated the speed of the motorcycle until I realized that my parents' car had disappeared behind me. If they only knew what I was thinking, without of course knowing my secret reason, they would be overjoyed. I knew that they were making this tiring journey to a distant wedding with an expensive gift on the backseat of their car not only to express their affection for Eyal and their joy in his marriage, but also to send a clear signal to their only son, riding ahead of them in a leather jacket and black helmet, about what was really important to them, important above all, and about how his solitude was beginning to alarm them. "Perhaps I really should get married," I said, addressing myself aloud, and turned onto a dirt road and rode up a little hill, which gave me a clear view not only of the road leading from north to south, but also of the agricultural settlements surrounding the housing projects of Kiryat Gat with a belt of pleasant rusticity—green squares of alfalfa, recently plowed fields of rich, brown earth; even the ugly rows of plastic shone in the bright light of the sun like the heating elements of some gigantic stove. The traffic on the road flowed at a leisurely pace, and some time passed before I caught sight of my mother's calm face, with a scarf tied around her head to protect her hair from the wind blowing into the open window. In the backseat sat a young hitchhiker, in spite of my warnings to my father—who liked picking up hitchhikers and listening to their views on the world—not to stop on the way, so he wouldn't disrupt the smooth progress of our little convoy. So they're enjoying themselves, I said to myself, and I let them pass me and get a little ahead before I started my motorcycle and raced behind them to see that my father didn't suddenly turn off in the direction of Ashkelon.

At the gas station at the exit from Beersheba we all agreed that the journey up to now had been very easy and pleasant, and there was no doubt that we would arrive on time, and even earlier than we had planned. But after we passed the Yeruham mountain ridge, which was covered with a green down because of the abundant winter rains, and began to go deeper into the desert itself, the sky clouded over, and the warm reddish light in which we had bathed so enjoyably up to now turned murky and yellow. It would be very strange if it suddenly started raining here, I thought, and in fact the clouds over our heads managed to produce no more than a few big, cold drops, but at the same time an east wind began blowing so fiercely that it threatened the balance of the Honda. I had to slow down, and the distance between myself and my parents shrank. From now on I was no longer simply their guide and leader, but I felt as if they too were watching over me, and when the wind increased I let them pass me and rode behind them so the car would break the sudden gusts of wind that buffeted me and made the motorcycle sway violently. My mother kept her head turned, anxiously watching my battle with the wind and making sure that my father didn't lose me. From time to time she raised her hand in a strange gesture of greeting or encouragement. I had no doubt that she was secretly angry with me for my eccentric insistence on making the long trip on the Honda, but I was also sure that she would control herself and not allow a single word of rebuke or criticism to pass her lips now that the deed was done. And for this self-control I thanked her in my heart, and I waved back at her in a friendly fashion and went on battling with the savage wind. I was sure that at this pace we would only reach the wedding after dark, but when we slowly and carefully inched down the steep thousand-foot descent from the ridge to the Arava junction, I felt the wind subsiding, and immediately after a brief, warm shower, which lasted for a few minutes, gaps appeared in the murky, ugly sky, and fountains of a pure, mysterious, pinkish violet light began to well out of them as if in response to the call of the great sunset which was about to begin far away in the depths of the Mediterranean Sea. My parents wanted to give me a chance to rest after my battle with the wind, but I was impatient to cover the remaining thirty miles, believing in my heart of hearts that keeping my promise to arrive at Eyal's wedding before it got dark would bring me a secret reward. Eyal was waiting anxiously at the kibbutz gate, as if from there he would be able to suck in from a distance any wedding guests who might be deterred at the last minute by the length of the journey. When he saw our little convoy approaching his face lit up, and when we arrived he threw his arms around me and began hugging and kissing me joyfully. But he didn't look like a happy bridegroom. His face was pale with tension, and there were dark rings under his eyes. "Come and say hello to my mother," he said immediately, "she's waiting for you," and he climbed onto the back of the motorcycle to direct us to a little canyon hidden behind the buildings, where a large lawn surrounded a pool whose still waters reflected with delicate perfection the shadow of the wild crag overhanging them in the evening light. Round white tables were dotted over the lawn like giant mushrooms, but only a few people were scattered around them, gazing pensively at the long-haired youth perched on the diving board with a guitar on his knees. As he plucked the strings, perhaps just tuning them, the slow notes, without the benefit of loudspeakers or amplifiers, enveloped the place in a feeling of pervasive goodwill. And it may have been that feeling above all which prompted my decision, which I made before I left that night, to find someone to marry.

❧❦

Wearing a white dress, as if she were the bride, Eyal's mother sat alone in the center of the lawn with a glass of pale yellow juice perched in front of her. Since the last time I had seen her she seemed to have grown even larger, despite the strict diet Eyal had imposed on her, as if she were swollen not with food but with anxiety at his imminent desertion. But I still remembered, even now, her beauty, which had filled me with admiration when I was a child, and her heavy white face, covered with makeup, still preserved its old radiance in my eyes. My parents, though, who had not met her for a few years, hardly recognized her, and when she stood up to hug and kiss them warmly, they were shocked and embarrassed by her appearance. In the meantime Hadas appeared, simply dressed, calm and full of gaiety, and introduced us to her parents, kibbutz members who had not yet changed out of their working clothes and were still busy making the final arrangements for the ceremony. "Eyali's worried that nobody will come," said Hadas with a merry laugh, "but they will, and some of them will surprise you too," and then she disappeared from view. A young woman with big light eyes and curly hair came up to ask us if we wanted anything to drink. My parents wanted their afternoon tea and modestly asked for milk with it, if possible, and while I examined the girl's face and tried to remember where I had seen it before, I asked for a glass of wine, a request applauded by my mother, who immediately exclaimed, "An excellent idea, we'll join you as soon as we've had our tea."

"I don't know what's happening to me," I said to Eyal's mother, keeping my eyes fixed on the young woman as she went to the bar, "but suddenly I feel excited for Eyal."

"May your turn be next, Benjy." She smiled at me lovingly. "You won't escape."

"No, he won't escape," my father promised her and pointed to two big birds gliding over the jagged red outline of the cliff, which had become sharper and clearer as the sun set. He asked the young woman, who had brought our drinks in the meantime,

"Could those be hawks?" But by the time she had placed the cups of tea and glass of wine before us and raised her eyes, the birds had disappeared into one of the many crevices whose black holes were distinctly outlined in the setting sun. And then, like a flash of lightning, I recognized her. "Aren't you Michaela?" I exclaimed in surprise. She nodded her head. "I thought you wouldn't be able to recognize me."

"This is the girl," I said, introducing her happily to my parents, "who was with Einat in Bodhgaya and brought the Lazars the news of her illness." My parents nodded in acknowledgment, and Michaela smiled at them and as if to confirm my words she put her two slender hands together, raised them to her face, and bowed her head in a gesture of such grace and charm that a sweet pain pierced my heart. The vision of the Lazars' large living room flickered inside me, sweeping after it a colorful whirl of scenes from India, among which hovered the warm, vivacious smile of the woman I loved. "How long were you in the Far East?" my father asked her. "Eight months," replied Michaela. "So long?" exclaimed my mother. "That's nothing," said Michaela dismissively. "If I hadn't run out of money, I would have stayed longer. I'm still eaten up with longing." "What is it about the Far East that the young find so attractive?" my father wondered. She examined him closely, weighing up her answer. "Everyone's attracted by something different. I was attracted by the different sense of time. I almost became a Buddhist." She said this seriously, in a way that was impossible not to respect. The three of us were silent, and then she fixed her big light eyes on me, as if her explicit longing had identified my hidden ones, and in a tone of faint rebuke she added, "We were all really surprised that you came back so quickly."

"All of you?" I was astonished by this sudden use of the plural. "Who're all of you?"

"Nobody in particular," she said, retreating, "just other friends who're as crazy as I am about the Far East and who heard about your story."

"My story?" I blushed, suddenly anxious. "What story? I don't understand." But now she appeared to hesitate, smiling faintly to herself and turning with my parents to look at the two buses that drew up at the entrance to the canyon, depositing in the soft silence the many wedding guests Eyal had feared would not come.

Already someone was calling to Michaela to come and help with the new arrivals, and she apologized to us, again with that graceful, precise Indian gesture, and disappeared among the people spreading slowly over the lawn, bringing with them from the north the first signs of darkness. Later I learned that she too, like Hadas, was connected to the kibbutz without being a member of it. Even though her parents had left the kibbutz when she was little girl, she still came back sometimes to work as a hired laborer in seasonal jobs, or as a waitress and kitchen-worker at weddings and other functions. I was still disturbed by what she had said and tried at first to keep an eye on her movements, but my attention was soon claimed by forgotten friends from high school and medical school, and also by a couple of well-known professors from Hadassah Hospital, whom Eyal had succeeded in enticing to come to his wedding and on whom he was now dancing attention, to compensate for the rigors of the journey. Eyal seemed calmer, and the sly twinkle had returned to his eyes. He had agreed to holding the wedding on the kibbutz not only to save money but also because of his plans—unrealistic, in my opinion—to leave the hospital one day and come to live in the Arava, to practice a more "meaningful" kind of medicine and also to enjoy the peace and quiet of the place. And indeed, the wedding was unusually quiet. My parents, who were now sipping the wine Michaela had brought them with evident enjoyment, noticed this and remarked on it to me. There was none of the usual noisy music, only the soft strumming of the guitarist, who had already turned into a dark silhouette on the diving board. Nor were there any spoiled, greedy children running around and making a racket. Eyal's mother had no family left and his father's relations had cut off contact with her after her husband's suicide, so most of the guests were members of the kibbutz or friends of the couple, young people, some of who were still single. The young doctors from Hadassah were on their best behavior under the scrutiny of their professors. The only child there, a boy from Jerusalem, sat quietly between his mother and father. He was Amnon's thirteen-year-old retarded brother, and his parents, like mine, had been invited to the wedding because Eyal had spent a lot of time in their house after his father's death as well, and he was not the man to forget those who had been good to him in the past. Both my parents and Amnon's seemed pleased to have been invited to this desert wedding and delighted at their meeting. After telling each other a little about themselves and reminiscing about the forgotten exploits of our childhood, my father tried to find out where Amnon stood in regard to his doctoral thesis, and to my astonishment I saw my mother, who was always careful not to touch my father in public, reach out and squeeze his thigh in the dark, for with her sharp intuition she had already sensed that Amnon's Ph.D. was stuck far deeper than either he or his parents admitted, and she didn't want to be the cause of any embarrassment.

My father took the hint and immediately cut short his questions, just as Michaela came up with a large tray and offered us warm pies that smelled of meat. It appeared that the protocol was to serve the main meal before the marriage, so that hunger would not prevent the guests from concentrating on the ceremony itself, which was taken seriously here, and conducted in an original style by two Reform rabbis, one male and one female, who came especially from the settlement of Yahel, near Eilat. I was eager to go on talking to Michaela, to retire with her to some remote corner in order to find out exactly what she had meant by referring to "my story." Her passionate longing for India, which she had confessed to us, and her intention to return there as soon as she could, also made me want to refresh my own fading memories with her living ones. And without even finishing my pie, which was surprisingly tasty, I stood up and put my hand on her shoulder before she was swallowed up by the crowd of young kibbutzniks, Hadas's friends, who had just turned up, clean and fresh from the shower after their day's work. "Excuse me, Michaela," I said, deliberately addressing her by name, "could I talk to you sometime this evening?" She blushed, as if my weak hold on her shoulder implied some intimacy of which I myself was not yet aware. "Talk? Why not?" she said. "But when?" I pressed her. "When will you be free?" She looked straight at me with her large eyes. "I'm free already," she replied seriously, unsmiling. "Just let me take the tray back." And she went to the buffet to return the tray. And the great relief I felt at her response suddenly gave rise, as I stood there surrounded by Eyal's guests, forgotten childhood friends, to an idea that at first seemed astonishing and reckless but was also thrilling and compelling. If I really had to get married in order to be considered less of a danger in the eyes of the woman I had fallen in love with, maybe a "Buddhist" girl like this one, gentle and flowing, who drifted free as a bird and full of spiritual longings from place to place, would be ideal for me.

She took off her little apron and hung it on the back of a chair, and said with a pleasant smile, "I'm all yours."

"Then let's find somewhere quieter," I said, trying to hint that I wanted to talk to her about something special. She wasn't surprised by my request, even though the lawn was far from noisy, with people standing and talking quietly, going up to the buffet from time to time to cut themselves additional slices of the delicious pies. At first she led me toward the kibbutz houses, but suddenly she stopped, as if she had thought of a better idea, and retraced her footsteps to the little canyon, where she turned without a word toward the dark side of the cliff, on a mountain path clearly visible between the chalky rocks, yellow in the light of the distant lamps. "Come," she said in a conspiratorial tone. "If you don't mind climbing a little, we can sit quietly and look down on everybody at the same time, so that we can see when the ceremony begins." She wasn't beautiful in my eyes, but very charming and pleasant. Her slim body was too tall and bony for my taste, and her little face seemed too small for her huge eyes, which shone in the light of the rising moon like two blue lamps. I climbed up after her in silence, surprised by her sudden decision to take me up this rocky, winding mountain path which ascended sharply in the utterly deserted landscape where from time to time we heard the rustle of birds startled from their nests and the beating of wings. "Are Buddhists allowed to marry?" The idiotic question burst out accompanied by a light laugh. "They're allowed everything," she replied at once, not surprised by my question. "Buddhism isn't another vicious religion looking for ways to oppress people and frighten them, but a means of alleviating inevitable suffering." She spoke seriously, and the expression "inevitable suffering" came out of her mouth sincerely and convincingly, evoking a wave of affection and sympathy for her in my heart. "It's a pity you couldn't have stayed for a few more days at least in the temples of Bodhgaya," she went on. "There you would have understood for yourself what I could never succeed in explaining to you." And once more I heard in her words a rebuke at my failure to take proper advantage of my unexpected mission to India. "But how could I have stayed there?" I justified myself to her as if I were really to blame. "Mr. Lazar was in such a hurry to get back, and I couldn't leave Einat, who was in bad shape."

"Yes, she was in bad shape," she agreed gently, "and if not for you she wouldn't have made it back home." The path now turned sharply back on itself, and suddenly we were standing as if suspended in the air above the glittering blue rectangle of the swimming pool surrounded by the wedding guests. We were actually quite close to them, but completely hidden and secluded, absorbed in the story Michaela had called mine but which was actually Einat's, and which I had no need to draw out of her, for it flowed from her with the same simplicity and directness with which she spoke about everything, making me feel pleasantly calm and relaxed after months of inner conflict and tension.

She had met Einat with two other Israelis in the street in Calcutta, when Einat, still stunned by the sights, was at the beginning of her trip. Michaela, in contrast, was already an old India hand, after traveling extensively in central India and spending three months in Calcutta, where she had joined volunteer French and Swiss doctors offering free medical services at improvised sidewalk clinics. She had helped these "sidewalk doctors," as they called themselves, in return for two meals a day and a place to sleep. This was how she had met Einat, on the sidewalk, when Einat came to ask for a dressing for a wound on her leg. Michaela had immediately sensed that Einat was in need of her help, that she was very frightened and upset by her encounter with Calcutta, and perhaps even regretted coming to India. But she also realized that Einat's panic was something that she shared with all those who sensed that beyond the poverty and ugliness there was a spiritual power that could suck them in, especially those whose sense of identity was tenuous, who felt unable to achieve their ambitions, and who were always quick to look for a way of escape. And indeed, Einat soon persuaded her two friends to escape from Calcutta and go to Nepal in order to immerse themselves in the glorious scenery of the Himalayas. But after two weeks, to Michaela's astonishment, Einat returned to Calcutta alone and came to look for her. That was how their friendship began. At first Einat worked with Michaela in the service of the "sidewalk doctors," but she soon abandoned the work and joined some other young people who were traveling to Bodhgaya to take the course on Vipassana meditation, not because she was really interested in Buddhism but because she was one of those people who are more interested in escaping than in seeking. "And you?" I asked Michaela sharply. "Me?" She reflected for a while, trying to answer honestly. "I think that I'm actually more of a seeker than an escapist, but I may be wrong."

Now I caught sight of my parents. They were standing and talking to the professors from Jerusalem, glancing around from time to time, presumably looking for me. Amnon stood not far from them, gesticulating excitedly as he spoke to two girls we had known in high school, while his little brother lay on the lawn trying to dismantle a sprinkler. Eyal and Hadas were nowhere to be seen; they were probably getting ready for the ceremony. But Eyal's mother was still sitting where we had found her when we arrived, frozen like a spectacular white statue, a plate of food lying untouched in front of her. Every now and then she raised her eyes to the little crevice where we were sitting, as if she had noticed something. Suddenly low singing rose from a corner of the lawn, where a small group of men and women from the kibbutz were standing holding sheets of music in their hands. "They're beginning," said Michaela. "Should we go down?"

"No, why?" I said unwillingly. "If you don't mind, we can stay and watch the wedding from up here. I'm impatient to hear the rest of your story, especially the part where I come into it. Before you said that Einat was running away, but what from, exactly?"

"What from?" Michaela was surprised at the question. "First of all, from her parents, but maybe from other things too."

"From her parents?" I repeated in mock surprise, full of curiosity and excitement, hoping to hear something I didn't know about Lazar and his wife. "In what sense?"

"You should know in what sense," she broke in quickly. "You spent two weeks in their pockets, didn't you?"

"You could say so," I replied calmly, determined to draw her into an attack on them so that I could defend both the woman I loved and her husband. "But they seemed a very nice couple to me, perhaps a little too attached to one another, in an exaggerated, even pathetic way—the wife, for instance, can hardly bear to be separated from her husband, to be on her own even for a little while. But that's all."

"That may be all for you," said Michaela with inexplicable anger, "but it's evidently too much for someone who has to live with them, like Einat, and be suffocated by that insane symbiosis of theirs. Sometimes I think that if they hadn't taken you with them to India, they wouldn't have succeeded in bringing her back alive. She would have died in their arms on the way back home."

"Died in their arms?" I repeated this dramatic phrase in astonishment, wondering at the profound, if unclear, antagonism toward Lazar and his wife in her words. "You're exaggerating, Michaela. It isn't so easy to die, you know."

The singing below increased in volume, and the simple but unfamiliar tunes became richer and more complex. Two couples dressed in light blue outfits approached the center of the lawn, carrying the chuppah. They inserted the poles into the sockets prepared for them and unfurled the large, richly embroidered canopy, which was big enough for a number of couples to stand beneath at once. After it had been erected, the little choir rose and approached it, singing loudly, as if to encourage the couple, who were embarking on a daring and courageous enterprise, with their optimistic song. And then, from either side of the lawn, the two rabbis appeared, wrapped in prayer shawls; they bowed slightly, with a certain irony, to each other, and they too entered the canopy, while a pretty young girl stepped onto the diving board, walked to the edge, and with a regal gesture invited Eyal and Hadas to come forward and get married.

❧✾❧

"I'm afraid it's going to be pretty ridiculous," I said to Michaela. "Why?" she protested. "I've seen this ceremony before; it always strikes me as beautiful and genuine. If I ever got married, this is how I'd like to do it." And she went very red, as if alarmed by the words that had slipped out of her mouth. But it was precisely this delicate and sudden blush, which was incompatible with the logical and even somewhat dry tone she had adopted up to now, that touched my heart, and I couldn't resist reaching out and letting my hand rest gently on her curls. "Tell me," I said, "the first time I saw you, at the Lazars', just after you came back from India, your hair was completely shaved—for a minute I even thought you were a boy. So how did your hair grow so quickly?" I saw that she made no attempt to free her head but instead kept it very still, as if to wait and see what the intentions of the hand resting on it were. "I don't know." She shrugged her shoulders and laughed. "Apparently it doesn't know how to do anything else. But look—see how they're leading Eyal." And he was really being led, dressed all in white, by two escorts, who were gripping him firmly on either side as he glided between them. One of them was Hadas's father, and the other, to my surprise, was Professor Shalev, the head of pediatrics at Hadassah, whom Eyal had chosen to fill the place of his father. How clever and cunning of him, I thought to myself after the three of them disappeared under the canopy. Making his boss feel emotionally responsible for him certainly won't do him any harm when his permanent position comes up for discussion. From the other side of the lawn, escorted by her mother and a woman who was a stranger to me, Hadas approached, walking with a gliding motion in her floor-length white bridal gown. Eyal's mother apparently didn't have the strength or the will to lead her daughter-in-law into the canopy, and was still sitting in the same place, pensive, set apart from everyone else, raising her eyes in our direction from time to time as if she really were watching us. And then all of a sudden the lights went out, and someone asked the wedding guests to stand up. Two strong beams of light were shone onto the canopy, brilliantly illuminating the rich colors and shapes of its embroidery. The water in the swimming pool, which had been swallowed up in the darkness, began to glimmer. A profound silence descended, in which it was possible to hear the beating wings of the night birds wheeling in the canyon above us.

"Now we won't see anything from here," whispered Michaela in disappointment, and leaned forward in an attempt to see what was happening under the radiant canopy spread out beneath us. Through the opening of her white blouse I caught a glimpse of small, strong breasts projecting freely from her long, lean body. I thought of my parents standing down there with the rest of the guests, enjoying the ceremony but perhaps asking themselves when it would be their turn to lead me under the chuppah. At this moment I wanted to grant their wish and be swallowed up,

like Eyal, under a bright canopy like this one, to stand opposite a
young woman and listen to the kind of thing now being said by
the pair of invisible young rabbis, whose warm words of encouragement rose into the silence of the night. "Actually, I think it's
nicer to watch from up here," I whispered to Michaela, who had
given up on seeing what was going on under the canopy and was
sitting by herself, clasping her knees to her chest. "I wanted to
see them both from close up" she said, without annoyance but
with an acceptance that apparently stemmed not only from her
Buddhism, but also from a basic attitude of cool, clear-sighted
serenity, which, I suddenly felt, might not only accommodate the
strange love in which I was trapped but also appease its pain.
"I'm sorry if I've kept you up here," I apologized, in the polite
British way to which I was accustomed at home, "but we still
haven't reached the end of the story you promised to tell me.
What, if anything, did Einat tell you about me?" A faint smile
crossed Michaela's lips, very different from the one that had captured my heart, not in the least automatic, not brimming over in
all directions, but very skeptical, and at the same time kind. And
while the marriage ceremony below us reached its climax, she
told me that Einat had known nothing about her parents' plan to
descend on her in India and take her home. Someone who had
arrived in Calcutta from Bodhgaya had told Michaela about a
young Israeli woman lying in the Thai monastery there, very ill
with hepatitis. Michaela recognized Einat from the description,
and since she assumed that Einat had been infected by one of the
people treated in the sidewalk clinic while she was working in
Calcutta, she felt morally responsible and went down to Bodhgaya herself to look after her. When she found Einat lying there
in her dark little room, yellow and despairing, suffering and
scratching, she decided that her parents should be informed so
they would come themselves or send someone to get her, but
Einat refused to give her the address, as if she wanted to sink
even deeper into her illness and wallow in it, perhaps because she
was sure that in the end she would get over it by herself. But
Michaela was afraid that if she left her there, her condition might
deteriorate; she had already noticed her friend's hidden desire to
flirt with death in Calcutta, and therefore, in spite of her belief
that everyone was responsible for his own fate, she decided to
move up her own departure from India and insisted on getting a

letter from Einat to her parents. As soon as she arrived home she hurried to the Lazars' apartment in Tel Aviv to warn them about their daughter's condition. But when Einat saw her parents walking into her little room two weeks later, she was not only astonished at the fact that they had made the long, difficult journey for her sake, but also dismayed, since she had no doubt that they would not agree to stay there quietly and look after her till she recovered but would insist instead on dragging her back to Israel with them. Apparently, when she saw a strange young doctor coming in behind them, who dispensed with asking all kinds of irritating questions and knelt down silently beside her to examine her, slowly and thoroughly, her spirits rose, because she immediately felt that she could trust herself to his hands.

"Yes, and so she could!" This sentence may have sounded arrogant, but genuine emotion gripped me as I remembered the dark alcove, the sleeping bag crumpled in the corner, and the two astounded Japanese girls crouching over their little gas burner. "And did she by any chance tell you too about the blood transfusion I gave her in Varanasi?" I asked Michaela eagerly, for there was something in the way she spoke which made me hope that by means of her story I might be able to dispel the mist that still clung not only to my actions but also to my character during the trip to India. "Of course, she told me all about it," said Michaela. "She claims you saved her life." I was very moved. I wanted to keep quiet and let these wonderful words sink slowly into my soul, but I couldn't control myself, and I asked her hesitantly, "And you? How does it seem to you? Like the truth or like an illusion?" She wasn't surprised by my strange question. A faint smile wrinkled her face, which wasn't in the least beautiful, but whose great, shining eyes held out a promise of something that was stronger than beauty. "I think you really did save her," she replied simply, unhesitatingly, and generously, and then I couldn't control myself any longer, and in great excitement I leaned over and took her in my arms, embracing her warmly with those same hands that Einat had found so trustworthy, careful however not to speak a word of love, in order not to desecrate the true love I bore for that other woman. I contented myself with saying sincerely, "I like you. I like you very, very much," and taking her curly head between my hands I carefully placed my lips on her eyes. But she, with a movement whose naturalness belied a lot of experience, slid her lips up to mine and drew a real, prolonged kiss out of me, while below us the singing died down, the lawn was flooded with light again, and cries of "Mazel tov!" greeted the couple emerging from under the canopy.

Now we had to hurry back. But the kiss that had taken place between us seemed to have glued us to each other, and we had hardly begun to descend the path winding down the dark side of the rock when Michaela stopped and invited me into a kind of little alcove or cave. And in the bitter-herb smell of the dry desert soil I encountered no difficulties in removing her white blouse and exposing to the cold moonlight her two little breasts, which I rubbed my face between, not only to feel their comforting softness but perhaps also to smell what remained of the strong Indianness buried inside her. But I immediately realized that her rich experience of men, and the steady honesty of her way of thinking, would not allow me to be content with a dreamy head buried between cool breasts, for her long, rather hard legs were already coiled around my body in a tight grip, pushing me gently onto the dry ground and demanding what a man is expected to provide once he begins rubbing his head between a woman's breasts. So we began to make love, quickly, without great passion but also without suffering or embarrassment, without the words of love which belonged to someone else, with a tenderness and generosity which ensured that we would both enjoy ourselves and also come, quickly and together, and of course silently, for she knew as well as I did that not only my parents but many friends, both hers and mine, were within hearing distance.

"Do you believe in the reincarnation of souls?" I suddenly asked her softly when she had finished putting on her clothes and brushing the dry grass off her hair and turned in the dark toward the path to return me to my parents. She stopped immediately, as surprised as I had hoped she would be. "The reincarnation of souls?" She fixed me with her big eyes, in which a new glint of rebuke had appeared. "I wouldn't have expected you to talk like that."

"Why not?" I asked curiously.

"Because I would have thought a doctor would know."

"Know what?" I asked in confusion.

"That there's no such thing as a soul," she answered quickly.

"There's no such thing as a soul?" I was amused but also a little alarmed by the vehemence of her words.

"Of course not," she said with a new note of impatience in her voice. "The soul is only a figment of the imagination of people who need the idea of having something permanent and unchanging inside themselves, which they have to worry about and keep on stroking and petting." There was something delightful and captivating now in her annoyance, and I therefore kept on at her as we went down the path. "So what is reincarnated then, if it isn't the soul? Isn't there anything that passes from one person to another?" She was silent for a moment, examining me to see if I was mocking her or speaking seriously, and then she started explaining that what was reincarnated was only a bundle of inclinations and aptitudes which underwent constant changes, for human beings weren't permanent, they were just chains of events that repeated themselves, because the energy they used, the energy that was necessary for any material or spiritual action, was not consumed but released at the end of these actions, and then reused. And thus actions or events which had taken place in the past returned in a different guise. Something new in her personality, attractive but also somewhat dogmatic, was revealed to me in the way she delivered her opinions to the accompaniment of strong, decisive gestures. She was so carried away that she paid no attention when we entered the illuminated area, and the guests standing around with little cups of aromatic coffee and glasses of wine eyed us speculatively as we stepped onto the lawn together, probably wondering where we had been secluding ourselves during the wedding ceremony. We parted without a word, by mutual consent, and went off in different directions to mingle with our friends. And suddenly Eyal was in front of me in his white wedding clothes, and I embraced him emotionally. "But where did you disappear to?" he asked in an aggrieved tone. "Michaela took me up the cliff to watch the ceremony from above," I informed him. The sly smile glinted in his eyes again, as if he already knew exactly what had been going on above his head during his wedding ceremony. "So she caught you in the end."

"Caught me?" I said in a puzzled tone. But Eyal persisted. "She asked Hadas a week ago if you were coming to the wedding, and she only decided to come herself when we promised her that you would be here." I was amazed by this news and eager to get more details out of him, but my parents had already noticed me and they now came hurrying up, afraid that I would disappear again. "Where have you been?" asked my father, his cheeks very flushed from the wine. I told them that I had been watching the wedding ceremony from the edge of the cliff with Michaela. My mother stood there silently, her eyes flickering over my face. Can she really tell from the expression on my face, I wondered, what I've just been doing with Michaela? "The ceremony was very nice," I said. "At first I was afraid it was going to be ridiculous, but in the end it was even moving." They both confirmed my feelings. They were very pleased that they had traveled down to the heart of the desert. It would give them something to talk about for years to come. But they were also eager to get started. Although it was only nine o'clock, the journey to the Dead Sea was liable to take more than an hour and a half, and they were accustomed to going to bed at ten. I went to call Amnon, who was supposed to be coming with us. At first it was difficult to pry him away from the excited conversations he was still busy conducting with old friends, but in the end he agreed to come. We began saying our good-byes, and I of course went to look for Michaela. For a moment I thought she had disappeared, but I soon caught sight of her, sitting at a table by herself and eating hungrily.

❧♋❧

Should I tell her before we left, I wondered as I watched her gulping wine from a big glass, not to dismiss the soul so lightly, or should I leave this adolescent argument open till our next meeting? That there would be one, I had no doubt. This girl possessed certain qualities that suited me to the core. Not only the easygoing, carefree lightness she radiated, but also that air of self-containment, the way she had held back, even though she was expecting me, and waited for me to come to her. Yes, I definitely liked her, I thought to myself; even the way she sat alone, eating so heartily, pleased me. She could be the perfect mate for me, precisely because I didn't want to and couldn't fall in love with her, since I was still in love with the woman I had successfully turned into my landlady. This being the case, why should I argue with her and try to persuade her of the existence of the soul, when her view of the world would lead her to give me the freedom I wanted—a free marriage, to banish my landlady's fears that I would overwhelm her with my lust? I went up to say good-bye to her. She did not seem embarrassed, but just the opposite: she looked straight into my face. "You must be hungry too," she said with a smile, and pointed to the brimming plate in front of her. "Yes, I'm hungry, but my parents are in a hurry to leave." And suddenly I couldn't resist adding, "But as far as the soul is concerned, the argument isn't over yet. Because, you know, I'm on the other side of the operating table now. Not a surgeon anymore, but an anesthetist. And to be an anesthetist you have to believe in the possibility of freeing the soul from the body and bringing it safely back again."

"So you've turned into an anesthetist?" she asked calmly, taking a big sip of her wine and trying to grasp the significance of the change, since the world of medicine was not completely strange to her after three months with the sidewalk doctors of Calcutta. "Yes," I replied, and again I couldn't resist adding a phrase I thought would please her, "putting those who've never been awake to sleep." She registered the message and smiled a somewhat suspicious, bitter little smile, very unlike the whole-hearted, generous one that had already captured my heart. We exchanged telephone numbers and arranged to get in touch at the end of the week in Tel Aviv. When I said good-bye to her, I saw my mother standing a little way off and watching us.

Before we set out I decided to offer a little ride to Amnon's retarded brother, who was standing and looking at the Honda with an admiring expression on his face. I put my helmet on his head and rode slowly between the houses of the kibbutz. He was very excited and frightened, and held on to me tightly from behind. His parents thanked me warmly. When we left the illuminated area of the kibbutz for the Arava road, we realized how much light was pouring from the moon, which had risen an hour before from the direction of the Jordan River, enabling us to get up to a good speed on the ruler-straight road. After thirty minutes we had already reached the Arava junction, and after another twenty we passed the white potash works of Sodom, where we slowed down a little on the winding road next to the Dead Sea, not just to enjoy the magnificent contours of the mountains of Edom in the bright moonlight but mainly in order not to miss my parents' hotel, which turned out to be a new, recently opened place set a little apart from the others. It was a quarter past ten when Amnon succeeded in making out the little signpost directing us onto a dirt road, and we found the hotel in darkness. Since my parents had notified the hotel that they would be arriving late, the reception clerk was not surprised to see them, although he was somewhat startled at the sight of the black-helmeted motorcyclist carrying their luggage. "Perhaps we can find a room for you and Amnon to spend the night here," my mother suggested. Amnon received this proposal gladly. He was worn out after the tiring day, which had come directly on top of his night job, and he liked the idea of spending the whole night going over his experiences at the wedding with me. But I refused. I was impatient to get back to my apartment and be by myself, to digest everything that had happened and to think about Michaela and the role she might play in my life. "Don't worry," I said to my parents, "it's a very clear night, and the Honda's running perfectly. The two of us will take care of each other," a beloved phrase of my father's which I always added when I went out at night with a friend. We had black coffee in the hotel lobby, and I bought a small bar of chocolate from one of the vending machines to appease my gnawing hunger. I took a spare helmet out of the black box at the back of the motorcycle for Amnon, and we started off. Meanwhile the moon had disappeared on its westward wanderings, and the sky was now full of an astonishing abundance of stars. The coastal road leading to the Jericho junction was completely deserted, and we could ride right down the middle, as if it were our private road. From the way that Amnon was clutching my waist I could sense his alarm as I kept gaining speed, but after a while he began to relax and lifted his head up to enjoy the journey. The rocky mass of Masada soon appeared on our left, looking in the stillness of the night like an ancient aircraft carrier which had risen from the depths of the sea. A few minutes later the lights on the fence of Kibbutz Ein Geddi appeared, and the buildings of the field school above the creek of Arugoth. The road began climbing steeply to the top of the cliff, and it was all I could do to restrain the motorcycle from flying off it in my enthusiasm at the sight of the steely expanse of the Dead Sea spread out below us. And then came the descent to the shores of the sea, as we coasted past Mizpeh Shalem to a stretch of straight, level road where the motorcycle could easily hit ninety miles an hour. We didn't even notice the turnoff to the Ein Feshka hot springs, and if not for the curve in the road after the Qumran caves we might have raced past them too without even noticing their existence. Only the imposing silhouette of the abandoned old hotel looming up on the Kalya shore told us that we were about to take our leave of the lowest place in the world. And then the Almagor junction was upon us, its green signs pointing us to the west, to the mild ascent leading to the city of our common childhood, Jerusalem.

"But when are we going to get a chance to discuss your astrophysical theory, Benjy?" Amnon yelled despairingly into my ear, realizing that at the speed I was going he would soon find himself on the sidewalk outside his house in Tel Aviv, before he had had a chance to rescue me from my ridiculous mistakes about *A Brief History of Time*. "You're right," I shouted back. "I thought we could go and sit in the Atara or some other café in downtown Jerusalem, but perhaps it's already too late for that—Jerusalem's not Tel Aviv. So why don't I just stop somewhere along the road? Maybe the open sky will help me to explain my ideas." And after Mitzpeh Jericho, in a place called the Mishor Adumim, I left the main road and drove up a short dirt track leading to something halfway between a tree and a bush stuck on top of a little hill, over which the heavens were spread out like a brilliant canopy, infinite but also intimate, gathering even the distant spires of Jerusalem into its folds. I took off my helmet and prepared to expound to my friend in the stillness of the night the theory that had been elaborating itself in my brain over the past few weeks. But first I had to warn him not to interrupt me, however strange my words might sound to him, for new ideas always seemed ridiculous at first. He snickered to himself and sat down on the ground. For some reason he didn't take off his helmet, and he looked like an absentminded space traveler who had arrived here from some other planet. There was a rustle in the branches of the tree next to us, apparently made by birds we had startled from their sleep.

"Hawking himself admits," I began, "that he has two unsolved problems, the problem of the beginning and the problem of the end, which are of course not separate from each other. The first problem is connected to Guth's theory about the inflationary expansion, during which the universe expanded at a rapidly increasing rate in the first split seconds after the big bang. And the second problem is what's going to happen to the universe in the end. Hawking denies the possibility that the universe will go on slowly expanding forever, since the force of gravity, which I was surprised to read is the weakest of all the forces of nature, but which is also strong because it has no antithesis, will increase in the expanding universe until the gravity and the expansion balance each other and the universe stops expanding. But in this case we have to ask, where's the symmetry between the dramatic, mysterious, incomprehensible beginning of the big bang, which from a point of zero size but also of infinite density, gave birth to this whole tremendous universe—between that and what will remain in the end, a kind of static universe without any movement, in which a perfect and absolute balance between gravity and expansion will pertain? What's the connection between the beginning and the end? This is what I ask myself. Are you with me?" He nodded hesitantly. Presumably he was already dying to correct me, but he restrained himself. "It simply doesn't make sense for there to be a beginning that has no identity or connection with the end. Because that would mean that there was a beginning to time and there was some intention in this beginning, and they'll still say there's a God too, which Hawking categorically denies. And in the last chapter he says that we have to assume that just as the universe began with a big bang, it will end in a big crunch, with complete contraction and collapse, and then there'll be a connection between the beginning and the end, which will turn into the beginning again, for this is the only conceivable cycle." A worried, suspicious expression now appeared on Amnon's face, as if he felt that his friend was beginning to say things that were completely illogical, and even childish. But I hurried on, to forestall him until I came to my main point. "In brief, what I want you to think about, because it's possible that there a lot of things I don't understand here, is that the shrinking of the universe will not take place according to the physical laws of expansion and gravity, which Hawking and the others have a problem with, but will be accomplished by the human spirit, because spirit isn't something alien to the universe. Even the first minute particle, which possessed zero volume but infinite density, and from which the big bang began—you your-selves say that not only all the material possibilities we see before us were inherent in it, but also all the laws of physics, chemistry, and biology. In short everything, including ourselves as biologi-cal entities, and of course our thoughts too, and our feelings, in other words the whole human spirit, was inherent in that point of departure. And therefore it's this spirit which will shrink the universe back to the original starting point, which was, in the last resort, what? If Hawking himself says that it was like a particle whose volume was zero but whose density was infinite, what's that? Matter? No, only spirit, or what I call spirit."

"I don't understand exactly what you mean by spirit," Amnon began to stammer. "You know very well what I mean, and don't start splitting hairs with me now," I said angrily. "Spirit. Thought. What we're doing now. What you do in your lab, what you do at your desk. Searching for the law, for the principle behind things. Take this motorcycle—it's built of matter but it has a spirit too, which succeeds in raising this piece of iron from its place and making it race over the road in opposition to the laws of gravity and moving it from place to place in opposition to the laws of distance. And so on and so forth. Nuclear power too, which can explode something and turn it into nothing, into pure energy. And one day we'll have the power to explode a star, or bring it closer, or to destroy an entire galaxy. To make human beings smaller, scale them down into a more compact, more du-rable model, maybe change a few parts—a tiny transistor instead of a heart to supervise the circulation of the blood, and maybe one day in the future we'll be able to get rid of that too and leave only the brain, and reduce even that to a kind of computer chip which will carry out all its functions, and later on do away with individual distinctions, because there's no need for so many peo-ple. A human principle is enough, with everybody's thoughts connected to one pool, and so matter will gradually shrink until it turns into spirit—in other words, until it turns the entire uni-verse into the point from which it all began, where density was infinite and the space-time curve was infinite, which is an attri-bute not of matter but of spirit. Doesn't that sound simple to you?" Amnon finally removed his helmet and began to scratch his curly head. He seemed to have lost touch with what I was saying, which probably sounded like a lot of literary hot air to him. "What you say may be interesting, it may even be possible," he said tactfully, but without any real enthusiasm, obviously disappointed in my words, which he did not even consider worth arguing with. "But believe me, Benjy, it's not relevant to anything said by Hawking or the others. What you're saying is mysticism, and the fact that you're a good doctor makes no difference. I've always said that medicine isn't a science." And suddenly my enthusiasm for my ideas, and for the debate about them, disappeared. "You may be right," I said quietly. "It doesn't matter." And after a pause I added, "It was a nice wedding. I usually hate weddings, but this one was so quiet and pleasant, I wouldn't mind getting married there myself." Then I felt an urge to confess to him, to share something of my life with him in exchange for the disappointment I had caused him with my childish theory. "And maybe I really will get married soon," I added. "You hear me, Amnon? Seriously. I'm warning you, I may get married very soon, and you may have to come down to the Arava again for my wedding." He sat on the ground, tired, his head bowed, without looking at me or taking what I said too seriously, his eyes fixed on a big black crow that had suddenly appeared among the branches of the tree, where it sat with its head cocked, staring at us so intently with its black eyes that it was impossible to tell if it was afraid of us or, on the contrary, was about to dart down and attack us.

PART THREE

Death

Eleven

But I didn't get married in the Arava. My wedding took place in a small hall in the middle of downtown Jerusalem. In spite of the pleasant memory of the kibbutz wedding, my parents could see no logical reason for dragging their guests, some of whom came from England especially for the ceremony, to a kibbutz in the middle of the desert. Michaela's parents, who were separated and who had left the kibbutz many years before, did not have the same emotional ties to their old home as Michaela did, and since they were unable to share the expense of the wedding, they gave my parents a free hand to choose the site as they saw fit. In fact, they seemed somewhat indifferent to their daughter's wedding, for even though Michaela was not as young as I had imagined—she was just a few months older than I was—her parents were not upset by her remaining single, either because they thought that a girl as independent as Michaela did not need a husband to look after her, or because they believed that the moment she decided to marry she would have no problem finding a candidate. Accordingly, when I was presented to them, separately, as their future son-in-law, I was disappointed to see that they both accepted me very naturally and were not in the least impressed by the fact that the man standing before them was a certified physician with a secure future ahead of him, as if their Michaela could go up to anyone she liked and command him, Marry me! Although in this case it was the other way around: I had asked Michaela to marry me, and she had not refused, perhaps in accordance with the gentle Buddhist philosophy that we were not two souls entering into an eternal bond but only two flowing rivers, each secure in the depth and independence of its own current, and would not be endangered if our waters intermingled slightly.

This was how Michaela explained her consent to my proposal of marriage, a proposal that was made even before I had anticipated making it. Although I got in touch with her two days after Eyal's wedding, I had no idea that things would happen so fast. Perhaps because I wasn't in love with her but felt only a deep affection and esteem for her, everything took place that much more quickly. Only three months after Eyal's wedding, to be exact, I too was standing under the chuppah, with Eyal, Hadas, and Amnon looking on in astonishment or perhaps amusement at the young, ultra-Orthodox rabbi who had been sent by the local rabbinate to sanctify our marriage, and who did so at great length and with exceptional thoroughness, as if to overcome some vague, nagging doubt regarding the nature of the union before him. But of course he couldn't have known that Michaela was three months pregnant, because I didn't know it myself until the day after the wedding, when she told me that she was carrying our child in her womb and asked me simply what I wanted—to keep the baby or abort it? Even though I thought I had come to know Michaela in the months before the wedding, I was surprised by this concealment, in spite of the logical and moral grounds she gave for it. Michaela wanted our decision to get married to be taken in complete freedom, untainted by any calculations. "And if I hadn't been in such a hurry, or if I hadn't wanted to get married at all?" I asked my new wife. "What would you have done then?" She thought for a moment and answered honestly, "I would probably have had the baby by myself, because it's not her fault that I didn't take any precautions with you that night on the cliff."

She insisted that this was when it had happened, that she had become pregnant during our first meeting in the Arava—as if it were important to her to create life in the place where she herself had been born and for which she still felt love and nostalgia. Was it only wishful thinking? I think not, for when we made love three days after Eyal's wedding I made sure that she was taking precautions, and added precautions of my own. Because even if Michaela seemed to me the ideal partner in a marriage which would on the one hand give my mistress the protection she required and on the other hand grant me the freedom to satisfy my lust, I certainly had no intention of trying to trap her into marriage by an unplanned pregnancy, a trick that no longer works for women, let alone for men. But when she told me the day after the wedding about the secret buried inside her and explained her reasons for concealing it from me, I realized again that I had not been mistaken in my choice, even though I was a little angry with her for endangering the fetus, and perhaps herself too, by riding behind me on the motorcycle, in which she had delighted from the first moment. For Michaela had turned out to be fearless; if she had any hidden fears I had not yet discovered them. On the first Friday night, when I went to pick her up at the rented apartment that she shared with two other people in the south of the city, I saw by the way she strapped the helmet around her chin how delighted she was at the idea of riding on the Honda. She looked cute in the big crash helmet, which emphasized her huge, luminous eyes. She didn't put her arms around me but crossed them on her chest, and remarked in surprise at how slowly I was driving. When we reached my apartment, she seemed in no hurry to take the helmet off and spent a long time looking at herself in the mirror, enjoying her new reflection, until I was finally forced to take it off myself. The fact that we had already made love relieved me of having to calculate my every move, but our experience was not yet rich enough to enable us to interpret each other's body language with any kind of precision, with the result that she mistook my struggles to get the helmet off her head as impatience to get her into bed. She responded by hugging my head, closing her eyes, and stroking and kissing me, swaying unsteadily and almost losing her balance, until I had to pick her up and carry her to the bed, which for some reason I still thought of as the granny's bed, though it was not the only item in the apartment that belonged to her.

I enjoyed our lovemaking less this time, though it lasted longer, and I even remember feeling slightly giddy at one point. The bright light in the bedroom, too, which we left on, was unkind to the boniness of the naked limbs moving restlessly beneath me, in contrast to the soft, pampered white flesh of the plump middle-aged woman who had lain serenely on the same bed not too long before. Michaela also uttered two brief cries when she came, which reminded me of a throttled bird and disturbed me, because I thought I might have hurt her. But in spite of my slight disappointment, my good opinion of her remained unchanged, and after we dressed and sat down to drink coffee and eat the cake I had bought especially for her, I found myself gazing appreciatively again into her big, intensely blue eyes, which radiated belief and trust in her fellow human beings, as long as they didn't pretend to be what they were not. She began to ask me about my work in the hospital and my new job as an anesthetist in the private hospital in Herzliah. After that she wanted to know if I could identify various exotic diseases she had encountered during her three months on the Calcutta sidewalks. She had an original way of describing the patients and their diseases, mixing descriptions of physical symptoms with penetrating psychological insights of her own in such a lively and vivid way that my living room was soon peopled by the pavement-dwellers of Calcutta in all their colorful misery. As a doctor I was pleased to see that she did not shrink from illness, and this added to her value in my eyes. "It's a pity you didn't study medicine," I said, and she agreed with me. Yes, sometimes she thought she would like to be a doctor, but how could she go to medical school when she hadn't even graduated from high school?

The information that she had dropped out of school in the eleventh grade gave me a pang, especially since I knew that my mother would soon find out and, along with my father, would be disappointed. I had meant to ask her to come with me on a trip to Jerusalem one day the following week and to introduce her to them. But I made an effort not to show the faintest sign of disappointment or to make any disparaging comments about the fact that she was now working as a waitress in a café in the center of town. Since her return from India she had been having trouble finding her place in the world, perhaps because of the longing that was still gnawing at her, and perhaps also because the return from India had been forced on her. "Forced?" I asked curiously. "Surely you're not saying that you came back just because you wanted to tell Einat's parents about her illness?"

"Not only that," she admitted honestly. She had been down to her last rupee, and she didn't have the guts to get involved in something that was beneath her dignity. "Like what?" I asked anxiously, but it turned out that all she meant was begging—an occupation that fit the kind of philosophy she had been flirting with in India. I smiled in relief, even though I had no doubt that she had lived with men in the past, a fact betrayed by the lightness of her touch with me, the naturalness of the way she stood up to clear the dirty dishes from the table and wash them in the sink. I didn't try to stop her; just the opposite. Let her feel like the mistress of the house, I thought, even though she didn't like my new apartment. She couldn't understand why a young man like me would want to rent such a gray, respectable apartment, with an entire closet still full of an old woman's clothes. "Did they reduce the rent at least?" she asked as she stood in front of the sink, with that inexplicable hostility toward the Lazars in her voice again. "Maybe," I said, and told her what I was paying. The sum seemed high to Michaela, who didn't think it revealed any special consideration for the man who had served them so faithfully. "But you can see a bit of the sea from here," I said in praise of the apartment, and described the red ray of light that fell into the sink at sunset. "You'll always enjoy washing the dishes here," I said with a smile. "You think I'll come here especially to wash your dishes?" she said ironically. "Not especially," I replied quietly, "only when you're here," and I brushed her neck with my lips. Her big eyes shone and she closed them for a moment, groping for the marble counter with a cup full of soapsuds in her hand. Again she wound her arms around my head and began kissing me, and by the intensity of her embrace I understood that she wanted to make love again and that she believed it was in my power to give her what she wanted. I did my best not to disappoint her, although this time I refused to go back to the bedroom and get undressed, and insisted on doing it impromptu in the kitchen, which turned out to be big enough to accommodate our lovemaking, but only just, with things clattering around us and at a certain stage in the proceedings the soapy cup falling into the sink and smashing to smithereens. Although I didn't manage to come myself, I had the satisfaction of seeing Michaela come again, this time without crying out but with a deep sigh. "Do you love me?" I dared to ask her when her eyes opened. She thought for a moment. "Just as much as you love me," she said in the end, seriously and without smiling; and this was the policy she adopted from then on—measuring and suiting her feelings to mine, that is to say, to my declarations about my feelings, for I was careful from the outset to keep my love for Lazar's wife a secret from her, afraid that even in the eyes of so liberated and free a spirit as Michaela my infatuation would seem weird, or perhaps even medieval.

After midnight, although an unexpected spring rain had begun to fall, she put the big helmet on her head again and climbed happily onto the motorcycle. She could have stayed the night, of course, but I didn't suggest it. In spite of my sincere desire to speed things up between us, I preferred, after two consecutive bouts of lovemaking, to spend the night alone in my big bed and put my thoughts in order. When I got back I collected the pieces of the broken cup from the sink and put them into a plastic bag, not because I thought the cup could be mended but because it was part of a set and I didn't want to throw it away without first getting the landlady's permission. I got in touch with Michaela the next day even though I knew she worked all day Saturday in the café. I wanted to arrange a couple of dates for the week after, and especially to make a firm date for our trip to Jerusalem together. I was afraid that the longing for India of which she spoke so frequently and the grayness of her life in Tel Aviv might overwhelm her, and she might give in to a sudden impulse to take off for the Far East. If I didn't want to lose her, I thought, I would have to keep in constant touch. But since I was now working a couple of night shifts a week at the Magen-David-Adom station in the south of the city in addition to the private work in the Herzliah hospital, the possibilities for meeting her were limited. I therefore persuaded her to come to the first-aid station after her work at the café to keep me company, and to accompany me on house visits, which she enjoyed very much, since they reminded her of her days in Calcutta. At first the patients and their families were confused by her appearance as she came in behind me like some visitor from outer space, her helmet tucked under her arm, her great eyes beaming signals from an enchanted world. But since I'd immediately introduce her as a nurse (and sometimes she'd even help me conduct the examinations), they quickly got used to her presence. And she too, to my delight, began to get used to me. "Do you like me?" I would ask, testing her. "Just as much as you like me," she would answer immediately, an enigmatic smile passing like an imperceptible ripple over her blank face. But she stopped complaining about her longing for India, as if some of it had been absorbed by our relationship, and some by the sheer fact of my work. I had no doubt that she was attracted to the medical side of my identity, and perhaps this was the secret reason why she had been so eager to meet me at Eyal's wedding. She reminded me of my father in the way she cross-examined me about diseases and symptoms, sometimes even from the back of the motorcycle, in order to understand the vague and tenuous border between sickness and health. And exactly as with my father, she had a pure intellectual curiosity, with no desire to identify personal aches and pains or to draw conclusions about her own body, which seemed sturdy enough, and had preserved the Indian tan I had already noticed on that first brief meeting in the Lazars' living room, when I had mistaken her for a young boy. In fact, this impression of a slight spiritual affinity between Michaela and my father was reinforced by the common language they found on our very first visit to my parents' home, just ten days after Eyal's wedding, which we all still remembered as possessing a spiritual power whose nature we did not really understand.

The visit to my parents was important to me, since I wanted to get a sense of their reaction to Michaela before I made any fateful decisions. If I had known that she was pregnant, however, a fact she was still ignorant of herself, I would certainly not have taken her on the motorcycle but tried to catch one of the last buses to Jerusalem instead. Friday was always the busiest day for surgery in the Herzliah hospital, since on Fridays the surgeons in the big hospitals abandon their public patients to the care of their relatives and take time off for private operations, which sometimes last until after the beginning of the Sabbath. And indeed, by the time I examined the pupils of the last patient and wrapped him in heated sheets to make up for the heat he had lost during surgery, there was nothing left of the waves visible from the windows but faint lines of foam trembling in the dusk. Nevertheless, in spite of how late it was, I had no intention of giving up the visit to Jerusalem, and I called my parents and told them that we would be late and they should not wait for us with dinner—advice they ignored in the hope that we would not be as delayed as I thought, and in fact we left before too long. Michaela was soon ready, and I raced the Honda until it flew over the road, not only because of the lateness of the hour but also because I knew that Michaela delighted in speed and expected me to satisfy her desire. At eight o'clock, with the beginning momentum of the ascent at Sha'ar-Hagai, the road suddenly opened up in front of us, and a full moon rising between the mountains began to sail our way, occasionally dipping behind the cypresses and pines, which gave off a fragrance in the spring air that accompanied us all the way to my parents' house. My father, listening for the sound of the motorcycle, heard it entering the street and came out onto the steps to meet us. I noticed that he was struck, perhaps even startled, by Michaela's enormous eyes. But I knew that their blueness, like the color of his own eyes, would have a reassuring effect on him, and indeed, he immediately began to pay careful attention to her, taking her helmet and chivalrously helping her remove her army jacket, and he began chattering vivaciously, this quiet man, as he did so. My mother was more circumspect, examining my face to see what I expected of her on this visit I had imposed on them.

❧❦

That night, in my old room, Michaela insisted on making love with me—a project that seemed to me not only superfluous but also dangerous, since my mother slept lightly, and presumably her sleep was especially troubled after Michaela's total candor at dinner about her lack of any steady occupation over the past few years. It appeared that the only thing she had done in recent months with any point or meaning was her work with the sidewalk doctors in Calcutta. And for some reason she also took the first opportunity she found to announce to my parents her failure to graduate from high school, without indicating any ambitions to complete her education in the foreseeable future. Even though she radiated her usual confidence and independence, which did not detract from her gentle good manners, I knew that my mother would be upset by the conversation, and that after my father had fallen asleep she would wander restlessly around the house, and I thought it unfair of Michaela to insist on making love in these inconvenient circumstances when the next night we would have my apartment in Tel Aviv to ourselves. "The wine your father kept on giving me is making me horny," she apologized, and she began stroking and kissing my stomach. But I stubbornly refused. "Why?" she said in surprise. "I can come without screaming," she assured me. But I didn't trust her, because recently she had been screaming and moaning a lot, and although I was already used to it, I didn't want my mother hearing even a faint, smothered echo of her cries. In her unsatisfied lust Michaela went on tossing and turning in my narrow childhood bed long after I had already fallen asleep, with the result that she was still sound asleep in the morning when I sat down to breakfast with my parents, who expected me now to tell them my intentions, if in fact I had already clarified them to myself. But what could I tell them? I could hardly hint at my true passion for Lazar's wife, which went on obsessing me even here, in the cool spring air of Jerusalem, with the scent of roses rising from its gardens. I could hardly tell my parents that the marriage I was contemplating with increasing seriousness was also a means of providing the impossible woman who still filled my thoughts with a shield against me.

So, before they had a chance to question me, I asked them to tell me their impressions of Michaela. As I had supposed, my father, who for some reason jumped in to answer first, saw no shortcomings in her, but only her virtues. "She's fine. She's just fine. She'll be a great help to you," he stated with a confidence unusual for him in such matters. "And she doesn't seem spoiled either, in spite of her delicacy," he added, and suddenly blushed. To my surprise, my mother too spoke of her in a positive spirit. "I agree. Perhaps because she's looking for something that isn't clear to her, she still hasn't found her place in the world, and she really is a bit of a drifter. But I'm sure that as soon as she has a baby she'll settle down and be a good mother." Strange that my mother should have immediately pounced on something that was still unthinkable to me, even though on that Saturday morning it was already a substantial fact, to the extent that a two-week-old embryo can be called substantial, in the womb of the woman sleeping in the bed where I had passed so many years of my life. Three months later, after our wedding—when I told my parents about the pregnancy and reminded my mother of her words, and exclaimed at her intuition—she dismissed my exclamations at once. "Intuition had nothing to do with it," she said sharply, "I didn't suspect anything then," and there was a note of annoyance in her voice, because even though she may have tried to understand Michaela's reasons for hiding her pregnancy from me, she could not help feeling that we had behaved irresponsibly toward the baby. "Not only you and your feelings exist in the world. A baby is a human being too." And it struck me as strange that she too, like Michaela, spoke about a tiny three-month-old fetus as if it were a complete, finished being. Yet the truth is that my mother was right. Michaela really had endangered the fetus by constantly riding behind me on the motorcycle and egging me on to recklessly increase my speed. If she had confided in me as soon as she found out that she was pregnant, a month and a half after we met, I would have forbidden her to ride on the motorcycle, and perhaps even exchanged the bike for a car, which I eventually did.

But until we finally parted from my beloved Honda we spent a lot of time racing around on it, especially after I hinted at my intention to ask her to marry me, and soon. This happened on our return from our second visit to Jerusalem, early on a Saturday morning, in the middle of the journey, at a roadside diner near the airport where we had made it a habit to stop. She was sitting opposite the big mirror behind the counter, her head encased in the black crash helmet, emphasizing the radiance of her eyes and artificially enlarging her face, which even in her own opinion was too small and thin for such big eyes. She was not surprised at my proposal; maybe she had already sensed that she had made a favorable impression on my parents, in spite of her failure to graduate from high school, her lack of a profession, and her obscure longing for the Far East. An inner sense told her that my reasons for wanting to get married were not strictly connected to her and that they were perhaps not even entirely clear to me myself, but the air of mystery and the sense of something ambiguous suddenly emanating from a person as rational as I was only added to my attraction in her eyes. I kissed her on her forehead, feeling the hard helmet between my hands, and I wanted to add the words "I love you," but I couldn't get them out of my mouth, and I said something more general: "There's love between us." This was really a more correct and appropriate formulation, because this love, although it was for another and impossible woman, was lying between us on the table like a rich and flavorful dish, which she too was entitled to taste. She listened to me attentively, thought for a while, and then said, "If you really want to get married so soon, I've got no objections. I feel good with you. Even though I don't understand why you're in such a hurry—is it suddenly hard for you to be by yourself? But if we get married, it will only be on condition that you don't prevent me from going back to India for another visit, not too long but not very short either. The best thing would be if you came with me, but if you can't come with me, promise me that you won't prevent me from going, and if we already have a child, then you or your parents will take care of her, because otherwise I'll have to drag her with me to India." I don't know why I suddenly felt such a burst of joy that I couldn't control myself, but I put my face to hers, lightly removed the helmet from her head, and planted a long kiss on and in her mouth, in full view of the few people sitting in the diner at that early Sabbath hour, who looked at us affectionately and encouragingly and seemed relieved that the heavy helmet had been removed at last from the young woman's head.

After that Michaela added another condition to her first: she wanted a small, modest wedding, with only members of the family present. And it was precisely this simple and natural condition, which I agreed with on principle, that gave rise to problems and complications. When I informed my parents of it, their spirits fell, and at first they sank into a grim silence. After a few days they both, each in their own way, began to voice protests about the restrictions imposed by Michaela. As the parents of an only child, they felt not only entitled but also obligated to hold a big wedding reception to which they could invite all their friends and acquaintances and reciprocate for all the similar invitations they themselves had received over the course of their lives. Furthermore, they felt not only a duty but also a desire to take advantage of my wedding to pressure their English relatives to visit Israel at last. I could not help feeling the justice of their arguments, and I asked Michaela to reconsider, but she suddenly revealed an unexpected streak of stubbornness in a nature that up to now had appeared so free and easy in its Buddhist equanimity. A fierce, almost violent stubbornness. She refused to withdraw her opposition to a big wedding. Weddings in big rented halls revolted her, and she stayed away from the weddings of her best friends if they were held in such places. She didn't really like going to the quiet, pleasant weddings at Ein Zohar either, because there were always too many people, and she had only gone to Eyal and Hadas's wedding because she wanted to meet me after hearing about the trip to India from Einat. After I realized that I couldn't budge her, I tried to convince my parents to be content with a large family party, perhaps at the home of one of our wealthier relatives in the suburbs of Tel Aviv. But my parents were offended by this suggestion and showed no readiness to compromise. I began to act as a kind of messenger between them and Michaela, and I would go and eat supper at the café where she worked before my night shifts, simply to try to persuade her to change her mind. Then my parents asked my permission to try to persuade Michaela themselves, and they traveled down to Tel Aviv to meet her without me especially for this purpose. But she refused to be persuaded, as if all her doubts about the marriage were now focused on the question of whether the wedding would be a big affair or a family occasion. At one point in the discussion she even spoke rudely to my parents, and then burst into tears. My parents were alarmed and gave in. My heart ached to see their misery. They were modest people, not at all ostentatious, and if they were fighting for a big wedding it was only in order to both share and reciprocate the many invitations to family affairs they had received. Even though they knew that most of our English relations would not come, they still wanted to let them know that here in Israel they hadn't been forgotten, and at the same time to announce in public that the lengthy bachelorhood of their only son had come to an end. But Michaela's tears upset me too, since she was not at all an emotional type, and if she had burst into tears in front of my parents it meant that something else was troubling her. Perhaps she was having second thoughts about the hasty wedding she suddenly found herself in the middle of, which in the depths of her heart she sensed had hidden, ulterior motives that she could not identify. The mysteriousness surrounding my behavior made me more attractive to her, but it had also begun to confuse her. In spite of her inner freedom and fatalistic view of life, her serenity and confidence were showing cracks. I went and bought a book about Indian religion and philosophy and began to read it, hoping to come closer to her way of thinking and compensate her for my lack of love.

In the meantime my parents' pleas had an effect, and two days after their meeting she called them on her own initiative and said that she would agree to expand the scope of the wedding, which from now on was defined as "medium-sized," on condition that she herself approved of the reception hall. Since the hall had to be medium-sized, the selection was not particularly wide, and from the uninspiring possibilities available, Michaela, who was becoming more alienated from me with each passing day, chose a smallish place in an old hotel in the middle of downtown Jerusalem. The entrance to the hotel was ugly, but the hall itself was attractive and well cared for, full of lush green plants, and the hotel owners boasted of their excellent catering. After Michaela had given her approval, we rode back to Tel Aviv on the motorcycle, stopping as usual at our favorite diner near the airport. She was tense, a little sad; this time she immediately removed her helmet, without flirting with her reflection in the big mirror. Even though I didn't know that she had received the results of her pregnancy test two days before, I could feel her new tension, which came not only from the depressing appearance of the hotel but also from her decision to conceal the fact of her pregnancy from me so that we would be free to cancel the wedding at the last minute if for any reason we chose to do so. Maybe this was what she was hoping for in her unconscious mind, whose workings I tried to follow with interest and concern, feeling that I was conducting my own silent, separate dialogue with it.

❧❧❧

The invitations were finally printed, with English facing the Hebrew, and my parents hurried to send a batch of them off to England, to give the family there time to prepare for the trip. Then we sat down to draw up a list of the local guests. My parents kept strictly to their promise to Michaela, careful not to exceed the limits of a medium-sized wedding. I noticed that my mother's attitude to Michaela had changed as a result of her violent outburst and sudden tears in the Tel Aviv café; she was beginning to treat her with a mixture of apprehension and pity. The problem, of course, was who to exclude from the wedding, and who to invite on the assumption that they would not come. My father prepared three lists of possible guests. First, they asked me for the names of people I thought were "essential." I wrote down Eyal and Hadas, Eyal's mother, Amnon without his parents, two good friends from my army days, and two more from medical school. I added Dr. Nakash and his wife, whom I had never met, hesitated for a moment over Hishin and decided to leave him out, and confidently added Lazar and his wife, and of course Einat, thanks to whose illness I had met Michaela. My mother smiled sourly. "It's funny that we're not allowed to invite good neighbors, people we've been living next door to for so many years, while two total strangers like the Lazars will suddenly be our guests." "Not yours," I said, reacting sharply, "mine. Why not? I have my own reasons for inviting them. But don't worry, they won't come." "Yes they will," said my mother, confusing my father, who was poised to put them down on the list of guests who wouldn't attend. In my heart of hearts I knew that my mother was right. Lazar's wife wouldn't forgo the chance of seeing me standing under the chuppah, not only because of the desire she might feel for me but also because she knew that I was marrying for her sake too.

❧❧❧

And if she didn't know, I reflected, I would have to let her know. With this aim in view, I would have to find a way deliver the invitation to her in person. About the wedding itself she must have heard from Einat, with whom Michaela was still in touch and whom she had even invited to a party to mark the end of her single state. I was a little excited at the idea of meeting Einat again, since I had not seen her since our return from India. "At least you had no trouble finding the apartment," I said when I greeted her at the door and gave her a little hug. She smiled in embarrassment and blushed. Could she have seen me as something more than her physician during the time we spent together in India? She had put on a little weight, and the signs of the hepatitis had vanished, together with all traces of the Indian suntan, which Michaela still had. Now she looked healthy and very cute. She was wearing wide-bottomed black trousers and a white silk blouse with a richly embroidered little red bolero over it. Green earrings, the color of her eyes, dangled from her ears. She was shy, but also a little amused at being in her grandmother's apartment, now taken over by strangers. When she was a schoolgirl, she said, she had often come here straight from school to have lunch with her grandmother and do her homework, and sometimes she had stayed over, sleeping on the couch in the living room. "Were you comfortable sleeping all night on that narrow couch?" I asked. "Why narrow?" said Einat in surprise. "It only takes a minute to convert it into a big bed." The fact that the plain old couch could easily be turned into a large bed had escaped my notice, and if not for Einat I might never have noticed it. Despite Michaela's protests, I moved the chairs and the coffee table aside, and Einat showed me the hidden lever that raised the couch and converted it into a large, comfortable bed, with an old sheet still spread over it and the long-forgotten summer pajamas of the child Einat. "You see, it's a good thing you came," I said to her affectionately. "You discovered your pajamas and we discovered an extra bed. When your mother handed over the apartment to me, she forgot to show me the mysteries of the magic sofa."

"My mother," said Einat in a sneering, hostile tone, "hardly knows what she's got in her own bedroom." And suddenly, without warning, I felt my face flushing and my throat choking up, as if the mere mention of my beloved's bedroom were enough to conjure up a flickering but very vivid memory of her heavy white body and pampered little feet, before which I had knelt in the bedroom next door, from which Michaela now emerged with a plastic bag for the forgotten pajamas to give to Einat, who was standing and smiling to herself in blissful ignorance of what was going on inside me.

In the meantime more guests knocked at the door, and I quickly returned the sofa to its original state. Two "Indian" friends of Michaela's and Einat's arrived. Both of them had recently returned from India after spending more than a year there, and Michaela pounced on them to hear details about new places and especially to hear news of acquaintances, Israelis and others, who had been or were still wandering around the country. Suddenly the great subcontinent was transformed into an almost intimate place, like some big kibbutz full of private corners and friendly people—until I felt that my own short trip to India had not taken place on solid ground at all but in a distant, floating daydream. Accordingly, I sat silently and listened, occasionally asking a brief question. I found it strange that Einat participated in the conversation enthusiastically, mentioning places and peo-

ple as if she too had been a big heroine and not a poor sick girl
whose mother and father had had to come and rescue her and
take her home. I could not take my eyes off her. She was attractive in her way, but there was nothing in her movements or gestures which reminded me of her mother. Her face was different,
bearing more of a resemblance to her father's, but more delicate
and very fair. Had her liver really emerged unscathed? I wondered suddenly, and congratulated myself on still remembering
the results of her transaminases levels. There were a number of
medical questions on the tip of my tongue, but I repressed them,
not wanting to appear in the role of the doctor this evening. In
the meantime one of Michaela's "Indian" friends noticed my
prolonged silence and suggested changing the subject. "But it's
his own fault," Michaela smilingly protested. "He could have
stayed a little longer and not gone home like a good little boy
with Einat's parents. It won't do him any harm to hear a few
stories—maybe it will whet his appetite to go back again with
me." But then the doorbell rang, and Amnon, who had found a
guard to take his place for a few hours, came in with a bottle of
red wine, followed by another two couples who had come to
strengthen our spirits in anticipation of our marriage, and behind
them a few gate-crashers, and the apartment was soon "as
crowded as the Calcutta train station," as I said with a smile to
the "Indian" friends. But nobody heard me, for the group had
already broken up, and some people had went into my bedroom
to sprawl out on the grandmother's big bed. Einat too went into
the bedroom, slipped off her shoes and her pretty bolero, and lay
down on the bed with the others. I sat down next to her and
managed to speak to her quietly in the middle of the din, asking
her first about her grandmother, and enjoying with her the
thought of how the old lady would react to what was going on in
her apartment now; then I proceeded to questions about her parents, casually collecting new items of information about her
mother and tactfully prodding her to reconstruct her feelings and
sensations from the moment we first met in the monastery in
Bodhgaya. Her replies were hesitant at first, but they gradually
began to pour out freely and eagerly. Her face glowed prettily in
the dim, shadowy light. She too considered the blood transfusion
in the pilgrims' hostel as the turning point in her illness. Her
mother agreed with her, and even her father had stopped belit-

tling the decision lately, though he was still a little angry at my hysteria in the airport, when I had forced the stopover in Varanasi.

"Hysteria?" I was astounded to hear this word coming so naturally out of her mouth. "Are you serious? Did I seem hysterical to you?"

"Yes," said Einat, and on seeing my offended expression she added, "A little. But you were right. It's just that when my father makes up his mind to do something, it's hard to budge him. You'd have to have been hysterical to interrupt the flight to New Delhi." But I remained flabbergasted. Nobody had ever called me hysterical before. I had always been well known for my supreme rationality. I had, in fact, been accused of being phlegmatic at times by various women I had dated. Had I really shown signs of hysteria at the Varanasi airport? If so, perhaps they could be considered portents of what had happened four nights later in the hotel in Rome, when I suddenly realized I was in love with the heavy woman who only a few weeks ago had been lying next to me on this big bed, where a bunch of giggling strangers were now sprawling, giving off a faint smell of sweat as they talked softly to each other and looked benevolently at me and Einat. Einat sat with her legs crossed, small and withdrawn into herself, nervously folding the bedspread between her fingers, staring at me intently as if she wanted to say something to me, and finally saying it: "You know, I'm very happy about you and Michaela getting married, I even feel a little responsible for it."

"Of course," I laughingly agreed, "it's all your fault. You were our secret matchmaker." And after a pause I added, "And your parents too."

"My parents?" she said, startled. "How come?"

"Perhaps they infected me with the virus of their relationship—there's such a special bond between them." She laughed, an unpleasant, spiteful laugh. Suddenly I was afraid that she would tell her father that I had called his love a virus. I had to watch the words that came out of my mouth more carefully. "Do they know that I'm getting married?" She shrugged her shoulders; she had left home a few weeks before to live in a rented room. "I'll have to invite them," I said. "Why should you?" she asked sadly. "Because they deserve it," I replied shortly, and her face fell, as if I now had taken away whatever little happiness I had given her.

I still didn't know if my decision to give Dori the invitation personally stemmed from a sincere desire to have her and her husband at my wedding, or whether it was just an excuse to see her face to face again, so that I could say to her, You see, I'm a serious man who keeps his promises; I'm going to get married to protect you from this wild, impossible passion that sets my thoughts on fire, but also so that you'll permit me to be with you from time to time and to lay my head on your soft, round belly. But I didn't want to turn up at her office without warning and be squeezed in like a beggar between one client and the next, so I called her to ask for an appointment. I sensed a slight hesitation in her voice, but also excitement and happiness. She knew, of course, about my marriage, and perhaps she also understood its significance without my having to tell her, but when I suggested that we meet in the apartment, she immediately said in alarm, "No, no, not there." We arranged to meet at her office, after working hours, when the secretaries had already left and the offices of some of her colleagues were already dark. She wasn't alone in her room when I arrived, but with a young couple who were discussing some criminal matter with her, and I sat behind the half-open door and listened to her patiently holding forth in her clear voice. I felt my muscles stretching delicately with the sweet pain of the lust beginning to stir inside my body. This time I restrained myself from bringing a gift, in order not to alarm her again, and when her clients left and she went on sitting silently in the room, I got up and knocked softly on the door, and without waiting for an invitation I went inside, ducking my head so she wouldn't see the violent blush spreading over my cheeks.

Was she blushing too? It was hard to tell, for I found her busy making rapid repairs to her makeup. She certainly looked embarrassed, although not too embarrassed to flash me her famous smile, which I now realized how much I loved. The time that had passed since our last meeting in this room made things harder rather than easier. But she was so much older than me that even if I had wanted to, I could not have saved her from the duty of rescuing us both from our embarrassment and guiding us into an exchange that would consist of more than empty evasions. I saw her hesitate for a moment, uncertain whether to stand up and come toward me, but in the end she remained seated, perhaps to hide the elegant suit which I wanted to believe she had worn for me, or at least for our meeting. Without waiting any longer, I held out the invitation, and she took it with an exclamation of delight that might have seemed exaggerated or even false if I hadn't known in my heart that it was sincere. She really did hope that my marriage would free her from me. She raised the invitation to her eyes to read it slowly and thoroughly, first in the Hebrew version and then, according to the gentle movement of her eyes, in English too. I examined her carefully. She seemed to have dyed her hair recently, for it was much redder. There were two little pimples on her neck, whose creases seemed to have deepened in the weeks since I had kissed it, and her face was a little swollen; perhaps she had her period, or maybe she was taking hormones. Again I confirmed what I already knew: no one would call her a beautiful woman, but nevertheless I was trembling with desire. She couldn't put the invitation down; she read it again and again, and asked me exactly where the hotel was in Jerusalem, and after I had described the place to her, she wanted to know why we hadn't looked for a more attractive place, outside town. I explained Michaela's objections to a big wedding and said that there was no point in holding a small-scale affair out of the city. This explanation appeared to satisfy her, and she smiled and asked, "Is this a genuine invitation or only a diplomatic one?"

"Absolutely genuine," I said quickly. "In that case," she said, "we'll try to come. Why not? I'm really happy for you, and for Michaela too, who still seems a little mysterious to me even though she's been to our house a number of times, maybe because of those astonishing eyes of hers. But Einati always speaks well of her. And she deserves a good husband like you—it was thanks to her that we got to Einati in time."

"And thanks to her that I met you too," I quickly added. She looked pleased, smiled, and held out her plump, freckled hand in a friendly gesture. I bent over and kissed her fingers, and to my surprise she didn't pull her hand away but only laughed and said in a whisper, "Be careful, Lazar's on his way to fetch me." But the light touch of my lips on her fingers aroused me so much that I had to press my knees together to suppress the silent stirring of my erection, which may have also been provoked by the agreeable thought that she couldn't trust herself alone with me, and that was why she had asked Lazar to pick her up at the office this evening. "According to our contract," I said with a smile, "I have to ask your permission to bring another tenant into the apartment."

"Really?" She laughed in surprise, as if she herself hadn't drawn up the contract. "You have to ask my permission? Then I give it." And her face suddenly grew grave, and she added, "But when you have a baby, we'll have to see what my mother says." And for a moment it seemed to me that she expected me to ask her about her mother's health, so that she could boast about the vivacious old lady, but I had no intention of wasting time on such questions or on empty wisecracks about babies—I knew that Lazar was on his way, and I didn't want him to come in before I had said a single real word about the pain of my continuing longing for her. As for the baby, I had no way of knowing that the hypothetical baby she was talking about was already real in Michaela's womb.

I stood up abruptly and went toward her, and in a weak, imploring whisper I asked, "But what about you?" She moved back in her black executive chair and looked up at me with a panic in her eyes that I had never seen there before. Before she could reply, I added in despair, "Because in spite of all this"—I waved at the invitation lying open on the desk—"I think about you all the time." Then the panic vanished from her eyes and the smile returned. "Never mind," she said soothingly. "I think about you too. Never mind. Nobody dies from thinking."

"Are you sure?" I said in confusion, flooded with happiness, and I bent down to kiss her, but she flung out her hand and gripped me by the shoulder to stop me. "Have you told anyone about me?" she asked anxiously. "No, nobody," I replied. "Then please don't, if you want to go on seeing me."

"But why on earth should I tell anybody? Who would I tell?" I said indignantly. And then the hand holding me at bay fell from my shoulder and I could bring my face close to hers and smell her perfume, and kiss her quickly too, and all this was more than I had hoped for from this meeting, even though she protested, rising quickly from her seat on her high heels and pushing me firmly away. "Do you want to wait here for Lazar?" she asked me now in a mischievous tone. "Because he wants to see you."

"Does he know that I'm here?" I asked, extremely taken aback. "Of course," she replied in a matter-of-fact voice. I felt too happy and excited to meet Lazar then, and I said good-bye quickly and rushed out into the street, which was already growing dark.

But then I stopped, because I wanted to make sure that he would come, that he wouldn't forget she mustn't be left alone in this deserted place rapidly being absorbed into the darkness of the spring evening. I hid behind the trunk of an old tree covered with white blossoms until I saw his car, which I recognized from a distance by its headlights, entering the little side street and driving slowly, looking for a parking space. In the end he gave up the attempt and parked on the sidewalk, and instead of the door bursting open immediately, as usual, a few seconds passed before he got out, with an unfamiliar heaviness that didn't suit him, and suddenly I felt a surge of intense curiosity, and I asked myself, What does he want of me? All of a sudden my fear of meeting him fell away, as if the existence of Michaela by my side gave me a new strength and status to face him.

Twelve

Is it permissible to begin to reflect on death? For then we will have to seek the secret door through which it can be smuggled into the soul, so the soul can grow accustomed to its silent presence, as if it were a little statuette brought into the house as an innocent gift or an ill-considered acquisition and irresponsibly set down in an intimate place, let's say on a little bedside table, with a lace doily underneath it, and all this without anyone imagining that what appears to be an innocent inanimate object might suddenly rouse itself one night, kick away the lace doily, and with a swift, stealthy movement choke the astonished soul to death.

Otherwise, how will death be accomplished, with a bevy of doctors determined, in spite of disagreements between them, to fight against it with the most sophisticated instruments and the most efficient drugs at their command? So we will have to find our forgotten old relation again, that ancient retired fellow on leave from a lunatic asylum, the skinny black-clad mystery with the wire glasses on his nose, and prevail on him to sit down beside us and finally drink his tea, which has long since grown cold, and expound to us his fantastic views on the earth, which is eternally still and in which every hour is final and sufficient unto itself. And thus to lull our terror of the death bundled into the inside pocket of his coat in the form of a little bronze statuette.

❦

But at the last minute, although I was only a few steps away from him, I gave up the idea, because I was afraid he would smell his wife's perfume, which I firmly believed was still clinging to me; and also because I knew that he would ask me to go inside with him, in order not to leave her alone there, and I didn't want to confuse her by suddenly reappearing at his side. If he had something to say to me, he would find an opportunity to say it at my wedding, for now I was sure that they would both be there, a thought which filled me with joy. For the first time, though, I felt a kind of jealousy of him, as I returned to my hiding place behind the old Tel Aviv tree and watched them opening the doors of the car and getting into it as they talked with that deep and marvelous intimacy they shared. Even total strangers like my mother noticed their connection and wondered at it when they appeared, because of Lazar's restless efficiency, among the first guests at the wedding, and stood close together, somewhat embarrassed, in the hall of the old Jerusalem hotel, which was decorated with fresh flowers that Michaela had chosen in order to cover up the faintly musty smell. They came without Einat, who arrived later by herself with a fancily wrapped present. The next day, when we opened the gifts and it turned out to be a little clay statuette with many outstretched arms, Michaela was overcome with excitement, and she cried out and covered her face with her hands. When she took her hands away I saw that her cheeks were burning and her eyes were damp. It appeared that a holy man in Calcutta had sold them both identical statuettes, which they had greatly admired. Since Einat knew that Michaela had lost hers on the way back to Israel, she had decided to make her a present of her own statuette. In contrast, the gift brought by Einat's parents—a turquoise bedspread, which made my heart skip a beat— was not at all to Michaela's liking, and she went back to the store and exchanged it for a big cushion. I kept quiet, not wishing to give her any grounds for suspicion.

In general, Michaela was inclined to exchange most of the presents we received, as if by doing so she could wipe out the memory of the wedding, which went on oppressing her for a long time to come, because in the end it turned out to be a very crowded affair, perhaps precisely because of my parents' sincere efforts to hold a medium-sized wedding in a medium-sized hall. Many of the guests my father had listed categorically as guests who wouldn't come, did come, among them, to our amazement, a number of relations from England, who saw my wedding as a good reason to visit Israel. My mother's sister and my father's sister had naturally been invited to stay with my parents, together with their husbands, and my parents gave them their bed-

room and of course my old room, which made it impossible for
Michaela and me to get ready for the wedding there. So that we
would not arrive at the ceremony directly from Tel Aviv, sweaty
and crumpled, Eyal, who saw himself correctly as the catalyst for
this marriage, offered us the use of his mother's house before and
after the wedding. His mother was delighted to have us, and after
serving a rich and delicious lunch, she told us to go and lie down
in Eyal's old room, where I adamantly refused to make love to
Michaela, who I had already noticed was always particularly
turned on in strange places. On no account was I prepared to
risk embarrassing Eyal's mother, who did not go to her room to
rest but sat racking her brains for a way to make Michaela's
simple white dress more festive. In the end she succeeded in persuading Michaela to take two heavy antique silver brooches
which she produced from the depths of her jewel box, and with
the addition of some artificial flowers the dress became, if not
more elegant, at least more original. But in spite of all these
efforts to improve Michaela's dress, which she also ironed twice,
Eyal's mother was secretly planning to avoid the wedding reception. When Michaela's parents arrived, as planned, to take us to
the hairdresser's, and from there to the wedding, she stopped me
from going with them on the grounds that it was not right for the
bride and groom to arrive at the wedding together, and suggested
that I remain with her and go later with Eyal and Hadas. This
sounded reasonable to me, especially since I had no desire to get
involved in possible tensions between Michaela's divorced parents, about whose quarrels I had already heard sensational stories. I therefore stayed to wait for Eyal, and in the meantime
joined his mother for a drink of bitter-tasting herb tea, which
glowed with a dull red color in the Jerusalem summer light, the
sweet light of the long vacations of my childhood. She was still
wrapped in a light bathrobe, her hair untidy and her face not
made up. When I asked her tactfully when she was going to get
dressed, she realized that I understood her intentions, and with a
strange expression on her face, both sad and imploring, she said,
"Let me off, Benjy, I beg you. I haven't been feeling well for
several days now, and I'm afraid I'll feel suffocated there. I know
that hotel—there are a lot of stairs to climb there too. Let me off,
Benjy, and don't be offended. You know how much I love you." I
began to stammer something about my parents being disap-

pointed, but she dismissed that. "They won't miss me. And if they do"—she smiled slyly to herself—"tell them that you gave me an exemption on medical grounds. It's wonderful that you and Eyal are both real doctors now. I remember the two of you as if it were yesterday, such sweet little boys, playing doctor and turning the whole house into a hospital, and making us lie down in bed and close our eyes and groan so that you could examine us and cure us with medicines and bandages." Suddenly she laughed happily, and a wave of warmth engulfed me at the dim but real memory of the two tiny boys bending over the big, beautiful woman, dusting her feet with white powder and wrapping them in bandages. The memory was so deep inside me that I had to close my eyes to bring it up. Then I looked silently at the very heavy woman drawing the edges of her bathrobe together with a slightly mechanical movement. She interpreted my silence as consent, tilted her head to listen, and said happily, "They're here," and as she went to open the door, she suddenly said, "Your Michaela is a very independent girl. Do you really love her?"

"I think so." I smiled, surprised at the question. "Then love, Benjy, and don't think too much," and she opened the door before Eyal had time to turn his key. He and Hadas were dressed up, their hair still wet from the shower. After they had embraced me and examined me from all sides, they both insisted that I put on a tie, at least in honor of my English guests. At first I refused, but finally I gave in, and together the four of us went to his mother's bedroom to choose a tie from the collection left by his father.

Despite the overcrowding in the hall, my wedding was a good-humored affair. The refreshments also, although I didn't taste them myself, must have been excellent, because long after the wedding my parents reported proudly on the compliments they were still receiving from the guests. The guests on Michaela's side, while few in number, were pleasant and polite and mixed well with the many guests invited by my family. Our British relations too turned out to be not only polite but also good-humored and cheerful, and their Scottish accents added a little amusement to their presence among us. Dr. Nakash, who arrived early with his wife—who was also very thin and dark, although a little less ugly than her husband—quickly made use of his oriental good manners and fluent English to make friends with our guests from abroad, and soon introduced Lazar and his wife to his new acquaintances. Although I was very pleased to see the Lazars, I had intended to ignore them until after the ceremony, which was delayed because Michaela was late, but in the constant stream of people pressing forward to congratulate me, I suddenly found myself standing in front of them. Since going to bed with his wife I had not been face to face with Lazar, and despite the friends and relations surrounding me and protecting me, I trembled violently when he threw his arms around my neck. Our trip to India, and especially our sleeping together in the train compartment on the way to Varanasi, had evidently entitled him in his own eyes to an intimacy which included the right to bestow sudden embraces without any warning. "Thank you for coming, thank you for coming," I stammered with my head bowed, not daring to look directly at the woman, whose smile was evidently capable of overcoming any embarrassment or shame. Lazar handed me their gift and immediately told me in his practical way how to exchange it. While I was thanking him and trying to guess what was inside the big soft parcel, my mother's sister from Glasgow, who had undertaken to collect the presents, hurried up to relieve me of it. In order to overcome my embarrassment, I introduced her to the Lazars, and she, who took an intense interest in every detail of my life, not only identified them instantly, but announced heartily, "Oh, we've all been dying to meet you—this wedding is partly your doing, isn't it?"

"Our doing?" repeated Lazar in bewilderment, tilting his head to grasp the meaning hidden behind her thick Scottish accent. But my aunt was not in the least put out. She hugged me affectionately and continued. "He met Michaela at your place, didn't he? And that made up for the position he lost at the hospital because of the trip to India." Extremely agitated, I tried to correct her, but Lazar gripped my hand to calm me and bent over my big-mouthed, tactless aunt again and asked her to repeat her words, which I could see had offended him and gotten me into trouble. "He hasn't lost his position yet," he said in his simple English, but with the confident smile of a director whose power lay in knowing things that other people didn't know—including his wife, who turned to him now with a worried expression. "What do you mean?" I asked him in English, to avoid offending my aunt, who didn't know Hebrew. "First get married," continued Lazar in English, pointing to the very serious young rabbi who had just entered the hall, "and afterward you'll get another present." Then turned to my aunt, who was looking at him admiringly. "Don't worry, we're taking care of him."

Despite the arrival of the rabbi, the ceremony was delayed a little longer, because Michaela was held up by her parents, who had been leading each other astray in the streets of Jerusalem. But it was worth waiting for her. The hairdresser's work had a stunning effect: her face seemed to have grown bigger, her hair was darker and full of new curls, and her enormous, shining eyes were now in proportion to the rest of her head. She looked really beautiful, and her few friends and relations, who so far had been swallowed up by our guests, hurried to hug and kiss her. But the grave young rabbi sent by the rabbinate was already waiting under the canopy erected by the hotel waiters. In my opinion and that of my father, he was much too rigid and long-winded and did not take the spirit of his audience into account. He forced the independent Michaela, of all people, to circle me seven times. His sermon on the meaning and importance of marriage was complicated and full of references to Cabalist sages nobody had heard of. Worst of all, there wasn't a drop of humor in it; he made none of the jokes usually made on such occasions, and for a moment it even seemed that he regarded our marriage as something dangerous, which he had to warn us against. But it turned out that this fanatical Jerusalem rabbi, who annoyed a lot of people with his dry, severe style, pleased Michaela. She did not find the ceremony too long, and the fact that she was obliged to circle me seven times did not cause her any feelings of humiliation but excited her with its exoticism. From the day she had left India she had been thirsty for ritual, and since she had already outgrown, in her words, the childish stage of shallow, petulant protest at every mild manifestation of religious coercion, real or imaginary, she enjoyed connecting the mystery she found in our marriage ceremony with all those rites and rituals she had come across in the streets of India. Her pregnancy, however, she did not include in the mystery of our marriage, and she spoke about it in a rational and logical way. It was just twenty-four hours after the wedding when she told me that she was pregnant, as we sat half naked, taking a sunset dip in the heavy water of the Dead Sea. We were staying at the same new hotel my parents had enjoyed so much after Eyal's wedding; they generously gave us "a few days of honeymoon" there, with all our meals, in addition to their wedding gift. Michaela took most of the blame for our carelessness that night in the desert, and therefore, she repeated, if I decided that this baby was too sudden and too soon, she was perfectly willing to have an abortion. She attached no significance to life at this early stage. She had already had two abortions, and as I could see for myself, no harm had been done. "But it could have been," the doctor in me immediately whispered, overcoming for a moment the astonishment of the new husband, whose head was spinning at the speed with which his freedom was shrinking, and all because of his impossible love for another woman. I don't know how and why Michaela had found out the sex of the fetus after discovering the fact of its existence. But I think that because she spoke of it as "she," a girl baby and not an anonymous fetus, I immediately decided against an abortion. It was clear to me too that Michaela had behaved toward me with true morality, in spite of the complications she had created. Now she also repeated her intention of taking another trip to India, and there was no doubt that a baby would delay these plans, or at least complicate them, and that a secret abortion six weeks before, when she had found out about it, would have suited her better. But since she didn't want to deceive me, for the baby belonged to me as well, she did not terminate the pregnancy, and she didn't tell me of its existence so that I would not feel in any way constrained to marry her.

⚘

I saw this now with absolute clarity, a clarity which was emphasized by the silence and stillness of the desert evening; we were almost alone on the beach in this sweltering summer season. I was excited by the news but also somewhat sad. Michaela's concealment of her pregnancy seemed to me more moral than my own concealment of my impossible infatuation, whose chances of realization seemed even dimmer now, in light of what she had just told me. I felt that I had to make some gesture in honor of the baby, and I bent my head to plant a kiss on Michaela's hard, flat stomach. I licked her navel, and when I saw that nobody was watching I lifted the bottom half of her bikini and went on probing with my tongue toward the place where the baby would emerge when its time came. But Michaela's skin was so salty from the water of the Dead Sea that it burned my tongue; besides, I didn't want to arouse her now and make us both restless before supper. I only said laughingly, "So what do you think? We'll have to call her Ayelet, because we made her at Eyal's wedding!" But Michaela already had another name ready, more significant and compelling, with a special meaning for her. Shiva, the Destroyer; Shiva, which in Hebrew means "return"—a name connected with the person who had brought us together not only in a technical but also in a deeper sense, Einat, whose gift Michaela had brought with her to the Dead Sea shore to fortify her on her honeymoon.

I found Einat standing sadly and absentmindedly next to her parents, with the gift-wrapped package in her hand, only after the ceremony was over, when I began making my way through the crush in search of her father, to hear what he had to say to me. Dori was surrounded by a number of my parents' friends, standing with overflowing plates in their hands. She herself had not yet eaten anything but was smoking one of her slender cigarettes, in spite of the press of people around her, her eyes sparkling and flashing. I warmly embraced Einat, who gave me a gentle, hesitant hug and immediately asked for Michaela, because she wanted to give her the gift, which she firmly announced was "for Michaela, not for you," with her own hands. "Okay, okay." I raised my hands in laughing submission. "But why aren't you eating anything?" I added in the tone of an offended host. "Would you like me to bring you something?" But Einat refused my offer and said in embarrassment, "No, why should you? You've already looked after me enough. I'll get something myself. It looks very good." Indeed, everyone praised the catering. Lazar returned again and again to the buffet, thrusting through the crowd with his head lowered in order to refill his plate with roast beef, which seemed particularly to his taste, while Nakash and his wife, thin and hungry, never moved from the buffet area in case they missed one of the new dishes which kept arriving from the kitchen. Even my shy father, in spite of all

the friends and relations surrounding him, kept finding excuses
to return to the buffet and praise the headwaiter for the excellent
food, ready to be seduced by new offers. Toward the end of the
wedding, when the hall began to empty out, Michaela, who had
not tasted anything up to then, also succumbed to an attack of
voracious hunger. She sat in a corner with her parents and their
respective spouses and sent her little brother to fill and refill her
plate with leftovers. My mother had refrained from eating in
order to be able to give her undivided attention to her guests, and
throughout the reception she had not held even one small plate
of food in her hands, but my loyal young aunt from Glasgow had
not forgotten her older sister, and from time to time she would
squeeze through the crowd with a forkful of "something delicious" and press it on my mother, who at first refused in embarrassment but in the end opened her mouth like an obedient baby
to swallow the tidbit and join in the universal chorus of praise. It
seemed that only Dori and I ate nothing. Dori may have wanted
to eat, but she was too proud to push and shove with everyone
else around the buffet, and by the time Lazar finally took pity on
her and returned from one of his forays with an extra plate for
her, she was so hungry that her fork slipped from her eager fingers and fell to the floor. She stood there smiling with a plate full
of food in her hands, waiting for someone to bring her a new
fork, until one of the waiters, thinking that she had finished eating, discreetly relieved her of her plate. But I had not even approached the buffet, or accepted any of the hors d'oevres from
the waiters circulating with big trays, and with complete indifference, even nausea, I watched my friends and relations diving into
the spread. A great joy was welling up inside me, wave after
wave; the joy of my parents, their excitement at the presence of
their beloved relations who had come especially from Britain; my
own joy in my good friends who had surrounded me under the
chuppah, and in Michaela, who looked so beautiful, and of
course in the secret and thrilling presence of the woman I loved,
standing on her long straight legs and looking at me from across
the room with her laughing eyes, and on top of all this Lazar's
surprising offer, which suddenly held out the hope that I could
return to the hospital via a back door which led through England.

This door was connected with an agreement between our hospital and a London hospital, St. Bernadine's, whose medical and administrative director, an elderly gentile called Sir Geoffrey, had visited Israel a few years before and fallen in love with the country. He had donated medical equipment and drugs to our hospital, and books to the library, and in order to strengthen the connection further he had persuaded Lazar to agree to an exchange of physicians between the two hospitals. In this framework, an English doctor had recently begun work in Professor Levine's internal medicine department, where he had been very successfully absorbed, and our own Dr. Samuel had been about to travel to London with his family to take the place of that doctor. But there had been a hitch at the last minute, for in spite of his assurances, the director of the London hospital had failed to obtain a work permit for the Israeli doctor so that he could be paid a full salary, and to the director's shame and regret, he had been about to bring his doctor back to England, having failed to keep his end of the bargain. But the sharp-witted Lazar remembered my British passport from the Indian consulate in Rome, and he immediately said to himself, Dr. Rubin is the ideal man for the job! It couldn't have come at a better time; it will fall into his lap like a gift from heaven—the possibility of working in a hospital that may be a little old-fashioned but is nevertheless a very decent place, and under the supervision of a director who'll be like a second father to him. And even though the whole exchange was only a matter of ten months, it would still be on behalf of our hospital in Israel, and it would be as if I had come back to it—albeit through a back door, but one which was nevertheless real enough from the bureaucratic point of view. And who could tell, and without making any promises—because even God would be foolhardy to make promises in the State of Israel—perhaps on my return from England a place would be found for me here, in one of the departments.

"But which one?" I asked, beside myself with excitement. "Which one?" repeated Lazar with a forgiving smile, nodding his head at my mother and father, who were approaching us from two different directions, as if they had sensed that important things were being said. "It's too soon to say. We'll see. When we know who's staying and who's leaving," and here Lazar turned affably to my parents, to tell them about the offer he had just made me. My inquisitive young aunt, who saw my parents listen-

ing with deep attention, came hurrying up to take part in the
conversation, which changed its language to English. My aunt
asked the name and location of the hospital, but since she lived
in Scotland the name of the area meant nothing to her, and other
relations, better acquainted with London, were called in to help.
A relative I did not know came up, a tall, very thin man dressed
in black, with small metal-framed glasses whose thick bifocal
lenses gave his long, pale face a strange expression, and this man,
who had no connection with medicine, knew so many details
about the hospital, which was in the northeastern part of London, that I wondered if he had been a long-term patient there.
The term "a little old-fashioned," which Lazar had used to describe the place, turned out to be a typical piece of Israeli ignorance; it was an ancient institution, a historical monument which
had been founded way back in the Middle Ages, at the beginning
of the twelfth century. Some of its wings were still housed in very
old buildings, while others had been rebuilt. My two aunts were
thrilled by the news, sure that my parents would not be able to
stay away once Michaela and I were there and that they would
soon see them again. And Dori, who was standing not far off,
nodding as she listened to someone explaining something to her,
watched the little group clustered around Lazar and me, and
blushed deeply and uncharacteristically when my mother approached her to thank her too, for some reason, for her husband's clever and generous idea.

But had the idea really come from Lazar, who wanted to save
his English colleague from an embarrassing situation and at the
same time give me a consolation prize and a little hope, or had it
actually come from her, because she was afraid and wanted to
get rid of me after seeing how quickly I had fulfilled her implicit
request to turn myself into a married and therefore more possible
lover? Maybe she had had nothing to do with it, and Lazar himself had dimly sensed my feelings for his wife and wanted unconsciously to get me out of the way. All these thoughts were still
running around inside my head when I said good-bye to the last
of the guests, but I could not share them with anybody, including, of course, Michaela, who heard about Lazar's offer only
after the wedding was over, late that night in Eyal's mother's
house. I was sorry I hadn't thought of bringing back a doggie bag
with some of the delicacies served at the wedding, to compensate

her for what she had missed, and also to quiet the pangs of hunger that now assailed me, until Eyal's mother, who had already gone to bed, got up to make me a salad and an omelet in spite of my protests and apologies. Only then did I tell them about Lazar's offer for me to leave within the month for a year's exchange at a hospital in London. Eyal's mother was pleased for us, but in Michaela the proposal lit a veritable fire of enthusiasm. Her weariness vanished and her spirits soared, not only at the idea of going abroad but also because of England's connection with India. And so when we went to bed in Eyal's old bedroom, which still contained some of his childhood toys, Michaela's passion flared, as if the strangeness of the house awaiting us in London had combined with the strangeness of Eyal's room to double her desire. There was no way I could withstand this double desire, especially on our wedding night, but since I was afraid of embarrassing Eyal's mother, who for some reason was still roaming around the house, with the noise of our lovemaking, I kept my lips pressed to Michaela's and inserted my tongue in her mouth to stifle or at least muffle any possible cries or moans during our prolonged intercourse.

But the next night, in the hotel next to the Dead Sea, so seductive in its strangeness, I decided to resist Michaela's tireless lust. I did not want to subject our little English embryo to any additional jolting after all the jolting she had already suffered on the back of the motorcycle and was still to suffer on our approaching trip to England. We both already thought of the baby as an English baby par excellence, with the British citizenship she would inherit from me reinforced by her birth on English soil. Michaela couldn't stop talking about the trip, and since she had been suffering from a mild depression over the past few months due to the loss of her freedom—first by the premature return from India, over which she was still grieving, and then by our hasty marriage, which was now compounded by the baby, who however sweet and good she was would still tighten the collar around Michaela's neck—it was no wonder that the trip seemed to her like an escape hatch to—who knows—those magical and radiant realms, whose fascination I could hardly guess at, for I had flitted past them like distant lightning. In contrast to Michaela, I was more confused than excited by Lazar's unexpected offer. First, because it meant a separation from the woman I could not get out of my thoughts. And even though I knew how narrow the scope of my hopes in that direction was, I also knew that I could always get on my motorcycle at the appropriate time and within a few minutes take up my position in the entrance to one of the buildings next to her house or her office, to watch her going in or coming out, smiling and pleased with herself, stepping lightly, apart from that slight pampered dragging of her left foot. And I hadn't had enough of her mother's apartment yet either, which still held the memory of the marvelous pleasure I had enjoyed on the day I signed the lease, which I didn't know whether to continue or to cancel. Michaela, who had taken an instant dislike to the apartment, wanted us to cancel the lease, so that we could leave for England with a clean slate. She wanted to pack our things in crates and leave them in a warehouse next to the harbor, where her stepfather worked. "They can stay there till we come back," she said, and added suddenly with a mischievous smile, "if we come back." It was no problem for her, of course, because all her possessions could easily be packed in one not very large crate. But I refused to store all the clothes, furniture, books, and other possessions I had accumulated over the course of my life in a dubious warehouse next to the beach, and I couldn't impose them on my parents either. Nor did I want to give up the connection with my landlady, for whose sake I had rented the apartment in the first place. So I suggested to my friend Amnon that he come and live in the apartment and look after our things until we returned, in exchange for a percentage of the rent. To my surprise he agreed, even though the apartment was far from his place of work, and it was hard to find parking there too. Ever since I had started going out with Michaela, Amnon had strengthened his ties with me, because Michaela had more patience with him than I did, and when I went out in the late afternoon to assist Dr. Nakash at the Herzliah hospital, she would invite him to come and have supper with her before going to his night watchman's job. His doctoral thesis was still stuck in the same place, and there were moments when I blamed myself and my confused speech that night on the way from Jericho to Jerusalem, about the relationship between matter and spirit, for his plight, as if my words had actually penetrated his mind and begun to disturb him in spite of the contempt and skepticism with which he had greeted them at the time. Perhaps my philosophical speech had merged in his mind, too, with the warning I had given him that same night about my intention to get married. And when he realized some time later that I was talking about Michaela—whom he liked so much that I suspected he had fallen a little bit in love with her, without admitting it to himself, for his loyalty to me was absolute—my theoretical speculations had joined with her erotic attractions, and he began paying frequent visits to our apartment in order to talk to me, and especially to Michaela, about the way in which matter could be transformed into spirit. I was already getting tired of him, but Michaela had a limitless capacity to sit and listen to him, and to cloud the issue still further by embroidering my own disorganized and primitive theory with all kinds of mystical mumbo-jumbo she had brought back from India.

✦✦✦

I had no doubt whatsoever that we would return at the end of the year. Otherwise I might lose the secret back door through which, according to Lazar and his bureaucratic metaphor, I had already returned to the hospital. He also promised to come and visit us during our year in England. "That would be wonderful," I said with genuine delight. "We'll be happy to put you up, or both of you, if Dori comes with you."

"Of course she'll come," said Lazar immediately. "If she insisted on going along to India, do you think she won't insist on coming to England? You've already seen for yourself how hard it is for her to stay by herself." Indeed I had, and the thought of a possible meeting in England gave me the confidence to notify Dr. Nakash that I was resigning from the remunerative work as his assistant anesthetist. To his credit, Nakash encouraged me to go. "Try to gain experience in anesthesiology there, together with your work in internal medicine," he advised me. "The subjects are connected. It may be an old hospital with obsolete equipment, but you'll always find someone unexpected whom you can learn something from." My parents were of course delighted at our approaching trip to England, in spite of the separation; but when I told them, in Michaela's absence, about the expected birth in six months' time, and tried, not without difficulty, to convince them that I myself had been ignorant of the pregnancy until after the wedding, because Michaela hadn't wanted to influence my decision to marry her, they were flabbergasted, as if they had only now grasped the wild side of Michaela's nature, in addition to the ethical and independent aspects of her character. But their joy at being grandparents soon asserted itself and overcame everything else. They immediately decided to postpone their visit to England. Instead of arriving in three months' time, in the autumn, they would arrive in the middle of winter, for the birth, and they would also stay longer than they had originally planned. The idea that their granddaughter would be born in the land of their birth amused them, but also excited them. "It will be as if we returned to England," said my father, turning red with pleasure and embarrassment at the curious thought. "Exactly," I laughed. "Shiva. Return. That's exactly the name Michaela wants to give the baby, not because of you but because of its Indian sound."

Michaela, flushed from the long walk she had taken to give me a chance to be alone with my parents, came in and gave us a deep, proud, triumphant look. My father couldn't resist hugging and kissing her as soon as she came in, forgetting his shyness now that a part of his own flesh and blood was inside her. My mother too went up to embrace her, even though I knew that she was secretly upset by Michaela's deception. The speed of my transformation from a stubborn bachelor to the father of a child seemed to her unwise, and perhaps too much for me to cope with. But the news flooded her with joy nevertheless. I told Michaela that I had already confided the strange name she wanted to give the baby to my parents, and she was insulted and protested indignantly, "It's not strange at all. That's what we're going to call her, Shiva, whether with a *vav* or a *beth* we'll decide later," and she explained to my parents the mythological meaning of the god Shiva, the Destroyer, and how he complemented the god Brahma, the Creator, and Vishnu, the Preserver. My parents smiled. "Don't argue about it now, it's silly. There's plenty of time to decide. You'll change your minds a thousand times," they said, but I already felt that this would be my daughter's name, and all I could do now was fight for it to be spelled with a *beth* and not with a *vav,* like the Indian god, whose name I remembered calling out to the barefoot boatman rowing me out between the ghats of Varanasi. Meanwhile we had to hide the fact of Michaela's pregnancy from Lazar so he would not relax his pressure on his English colleague to find her a part-time job, not for fear that she would be bored in London, since Michaela always found something to interest her, but to supplement my salary, which would, it transpired, be extremely modest, since it would be calculated according to the shekel salary I would have received if I had remained at the hospital.

But it was too late to change our minds, or even to grumble. We were both young, and our needs were modest. My parents, though, after telephone consultations with the family in England, decided to break into a savings account and give us some cash to tide us over until I received my first paycheck. With the money from the sale of the motorcycle we bought the plane tickets and good winter clothes, and the remainder we deposited in my bank account to cover the postdated checks for my share of the rent. In the plane Michaela was exuberant; leaving Israel had made her spirits soar, even though we were sailing west and not east. She believed that India was spiritually and intellectually closer to England than it was to Israel. I, in contrast, sat next to her in the doldrums, nervous and anxious about the future. Ever since my mysterious infatuation with Dori had begun, my life had been flowing along a crooked, winding course, because of the contradictory and ambivalent signals I received from the impossible object of my desire. Now I was being swept far away from her, and apart from Lazar's promise that they might come for a short visit to England, I had nothing to hang on to. And it was supposed to be all for her: the hasty marriage, the rented apartment, even the growing dependence on Lazar and his schemes. I thought again of all the people putting themselves out for me, especially my parents, who knew nothing of my real motives. It would have been more honest to confess to them and ease my conscience. I looked at Michaela, whose great clear eyes reflected the radiant blue sky shining above the clouds. If I suddenly told her that I had fallen in love with Lazar's wife, what would she say? Would the broad, magnanimous spirit of her Hindu or Buddhist beliefs calm and soothe the pain of this passion and absorb it into the common stream of our marriage?

Because this was how Michaela defined marriage: it was a "common stream," and that's all it was. In the framework of such a tolerant definition, even a sudden confession of the kind I had in mind was entitled to be carried along on the current, like an uprooted tree trunk. But I decided to hold my peace. Nor, in fact, did I have anything to confess, for in the hectic month since our marriage I had had no contact with Dori except for one telephone call, in which I had asked her if we could sublet the apartment to Amnon until we returned from England. About the expected birth I said nothing, not only because I was afraid she might not want to continue the lease, which was intended for a single tenant and not an expanding family, but also because I didn't want to draw attention to my sexual life with Michaela and give her an excuse for breaking off relations with me—as if our marriage were a mere formality. And indeed, although I could hear people going in and out of her office, she was very friendly, and her joyful, tender voice filled me with such lust that when I put the receiver down I felt drops of moisture on my penis, as if it were weeping. She too, like my parents' friends, recalled the wedding as an exceptionally enjoyable occasion, perhaps because of the high spirits of our family from Scotland. Even the strictness of the young rabbi, whose beauty she remarked on, did not seem to her annoying or out of place. "It's a good thing to be serious about the world sometimes," she said, and her laughter flooded the receiver. Then she praised me for taking up her husband's offer and admitted that she had had something to do with it. It was her legal mind that had remembered my English passport when Lazar told her about the complications they had run into with the exchange program in London. "Maybe you just wanted to get rid of me?" I asked in suspense, but without anger. She laughed again. "Maybe I did. But is it possible? I see that you're putting your friend into the apartment to make sure it's there when you come back."

It was true that thoughts of the return to Israel were already occupying my mind during our first few hours in London, where we disembarked into a gray, rainy day. The idea that from now on, because of the unfamiliarity of our surroundings, I would have to cling more closely to Michaela added a disturbing note. Sir Geoffrey himself came to meet us at the airport. He was a rather elderly red-haired Englishman who had remained stubbornly loyal and devoted to Israel in spite of its unpopular policies. It was difficult at first to understand what he was saying, partly because he swallowed his words and partly because of their subtle, often baffling irony. I wondered how Lazar, with his primitive English, had succeeded in establishing such friendly relations with him. Although he was the administrative head of the hospital, he did not seem to enjoy Lazar's absolute authority. His executive style was apparently more diffident and hesitant. For example, when we arrived at the hospital, he couldn't even find a janitor to help us with our suitcases, and he dragged one of them with his own hands into the guest room, which was attached to one of the hospital departments and had been allocated to us for the first week of our stay, until we found a flat. For a moment, when we saw a nurses' station with an old respirator standing next to it at the end of the corridor, we thought that Sir Geoffrey intended to hospitalize us, but as soon as we entered the room itself the hospital was forgotten. It was a charming, old-fashioned room, with a kind of canopy of green material over the high bedstead to make sleep sweeter and more secure. In days gone by the room had been occupied by the nobles and aristocrats among the patients, but it was now used by the hospital's guests, especially those who came for short stays, to conduct seminars or supervise complicated treatments.

A dark-skinned old nurse came in to offer us a cup of tea. We were happy to accept, especially since the forms Sir Geoffrey had brought with him still lacked a number of administrative details, which he was anxious to fill in with our help. He examined my British passport carefully and then turned to the notarized translation of our marriage certificate, stamped and sealed with a red wax rose, to extract the details, which he needed to establish Michaela's status and obtain British citizenship for her, or at least the right to reside in the country and be legally employed. She herself was completely at ease. She took off her shoes and lay down on one of the little sofas in the room, fixing her wonderful, shining eyes with great goodwill on Sir Geoffrey, who would no doubt have been astonished at the ferocity of the lust aroused in this strange young woman by the cold, dim, foreign room—a lust that would oblige me, travel-weary and slightly depressed as I was, to perform my conjugal duties as soon as he left the room. But in the meantime the tea was brought, and in honor of England I decided to drink it as my parents did, with milk. After Sir Geoffrey had finished filling in the forms and folded them up and screwed on the top of his fountain pen, I began to question him about the different departments in the hospital, especially the surgical department, and I told him about my experience as a surgeon, and recently also as an anesthetist, and asked him hesitantly whether I might be able to take part in an operation from time to time. "Yes," Sir Geoffrey replied. Lazar had spoken to him on the phone a couple of days before and told him about the true professional inclinations of the young doctor from Israel, and had also asked him if it would be possible to find a part-time job for his wife, and Sir Geoffrey had begun work right away to fulfill his friend's request. But although the head of the internal medicine department had been willing to do without the services of the Israeli doctor, the head of surgery had no room for another doctor. The emergency room, however, would be happy to have an extra pair of hands, and there too, of course, emergency operations were performed, which were sometimes no less complex than those performed in the surgical department itself. If that was what I really wanted, there was nothing to prevent me from joining their team, either as a surgeon or as an anesthetist, as I wished.

"So he can be a little happy at last," said Michaela in English, in a quiet but mildly rebuking tone, and she went on to explain to Sir Geoffrey how passionately I wanted to stand next to the operating table. Though her English was very basic, she spoke in a correct British accent, which she must have picked up in India, and without a trace of an Israeli accent. Sir Geoffrey listened to her with undisguised interest, apparently spellbound by her great, shining eyes, which added a note of brilliance to the dull gray light in the big room. I was still marveling at Lazar's phone call. Was it simply one more sign of his kindheartedness and concern, or had the hand of my beloved been secretly at work here, to seduce me by means of my surgical ambitions into prolonging my stay in England, or at least to remove any thoughts of an early return? Indeed, I may not have been as happy as Michaela expected yet, but I was definitely pleased and full of hope. The thought that I would soon be allowed to hold a scalpel in my hand and to cut into living flesh in an atmosphere of quiet English politeness, without being exposed to the mocking scrutiny of Hishin or the jealous looks of my rival, excited me so much that I was too late to step in and prevent Michaela from unhesitatingly accepting Sir Geoffrey's offer of a job as a glorified cleaning lady in the little chapel attached to the hospital. The idea of Michaela's doing physical work during her pregnancy, and what's more in a church attached to the hospital where I was working as a doctor, was not at all to my liking, but I held my tongue in order not to embarrass her in front of Sir Geoffrey, who at long last took his leave of us, very pleased with himself at having met the needs of the Israelis he so admired with such unprecedented speed and efficiency.

❧❧❧

I began to unpack the suitcase we had prepared in advance with everything we would need for the transition period, until we found a suitable apartment. Michaela took the Indian statue that Einat had given her out of her knapsack and put it on a little shelf above the bed, where she saluted it with a bow. Then she suggested that we lie down to rest for a while on the big bed before we finished unpacking. But I didn't feel tired, and I didn't want our clothes to become even more wrinkled in the suitcase. She took off her sweater and her socks and undid the buttons of her jeans to relieve the pressure on her stomach, which according to her had already begun to swell a little. Then she sprawled out on the bed, waiting for me to finish putting our things away in the capacious wardrobes and join her. Her eyelids began to droop, and I knew that she was charging her batteries with the lust radiated by the big, strange room. But I didn't feel the faintest desire for sex. I was tired from the journey and excited by the surgical prospects that had opened out before me. "I can't now, Michaela," I announced when I saw her stretching out her arms to me with her eyes closed. But she didn't give up, and with her usual shamelessness she got up, took off all her clothes, lay down again, naked and shivering on the bedspread, which didn't look very clean to me, and said, "Then come and warm me up at least—are you capable of that?" And even though I had no wish to warm her up, I didn't want to hurt her feelings either, especially since I knew how important it was to her to make love in new places, as a sure way of dispelling anxiety and domesticating the unknown. But when I went to make sure that the door was properly shut, I saw that it didn't have a lock or a key but only a slender chain, which made it possible for others to open it slightly and peep in—perhaps to prevent the patients or the medical staff from using the room for illegitimate purposes. "Can't we leave it now?" I said imploringly, afraid not only of an unexpected visitor but also of a cry or moan which might alarm any patients wandering around in the corridor. But Michaela refused to leave it. She was burning with desire. "Don't be such a coward," she said, and pulled me down next to her, taking my head firmly between her hands and placing it first between her breasts and then on her belly, and finally between her legs, so that my tongue could give her the pleasure my prick was too weak to provide. And then there was a light knock at the door, which opened as far as the chain would permit to reveal for a second the blushing face of Sir Geoffrey, who had forgotten to give us the list of apartments for rent in the area which his secretary had drawn up for us. He was too embarrassed even to apologize, and left the list stuck on the door. But later that evening, when we met for supper in the hospital dining room, he seemed even friendlier than before, as if the scene that had flashed before his startled eyes had only confirmed his view of the dynamic, energetic nature of the typical Israeli.

And in fact we both showed plenty of dynamism and energy in the initial stages of our acclimatization, which succeeded more than we could have hoped, perhaps partly because my correct English accent, which I had been making efforts to improve ever since our arrival by remembering my father's speech and taking it as an example, inspired the confidence of the real estate agents and the car salesmen. After only two days we found a suitable apartment for a reasonable rent a short distance from the hospital. The apartment consisted of two large, comfortable rooms, enough to accommodate my parents comfortably during the day but not enough for them to settle in. The small secondhand car we bought also seemed clean and in good running order. And even though I was not officially entitled to a parking place in the hospital lot, which was reserved for the senior staff, Michaela, who had established a slightly ironic, good-humored form of communication of her own with Sir Geoffrey, succeeded in getting permission for us to park in the backyard of the little chapel, which freed us from the need to look for parking places—a daunting task, especially at night, when the area was packed with cars. It was mainly Michaela who used the car, and her knowledge of the streets of London became more intimate and precise from day to day. Although I didn't like the growing proximity between her stomach and the steering wheel as her pregnancy advanced, and I warned her constantly not only to use the seat belt, which she sometimes forgot to do, but also to drive slowly, which was almost an impossibility for her, I had no alternative but to honor her independence and trust her good sense, even when she began haunting the seedy areas inhabited by immigrants from the Far East in an effort to renew contact with her beloved Hindus. I had to rely on her increasingly obvious pregnancy to protect her from harassment. I knew that she had only four months of liberty left until the baby was born, while I myself was being completely swept up in the work at the hospital, which filled me not only with enthusiasm but also with anxiety.

In order to give validity and prestige to the exchange agreement between himself and Lazar, Sir Geoffrey introduced me to all the doctors in the emergency room as an experienced surgeon and anesthetist. My experience as a military doctor also gave me special authority in his eyes. After only one week, before I had time to learn the names and places of the instruments in the little operating room or acquaint myself with the contents of the medicine cabinets, I was summoned to assist at the operation of a small, dark-skinned girl of about ten who had sustained severe stomach injuries in a road accident. Just as the operation was getting started, the senior physician was called to treat another victim of the same accident, who had suffered a heart attack, and without asking any questions, in complete confidence, he gave me the scalpel and asked me to go ahead and conclude the operation, during the course of which it proved necessary to remove the damaged spleen. And so I found myself standing alone in front of the delicate, long-limbed body of a cut and bruised little girl who had just been too vigorously anesthetized and seemed to be losing her pulse. The nurse assisting me was young and seemed inexperienced, but the physician in charge of the anesthesia was an elderly, white-haired woman who inspired my confidence. At first I imagined that there wasn't enough light in the room, because I couldn't see everything I wanted to see inside the deep, open stomach. Perhaps the child's dark skin confused me. But after the nurse tried in vain to increase the light over the operating table, she offered me a little headlamp to strap onto my forehead, like the ones coal miners wear in the movies when they descend into the bowels of the earth. And I felt a little like a miner, bending down and delving into the depths of internal organs which for the first time in my life were my exclusive responsibility.

I immediately discovered that the internal hemorrhaging had not been completely arrested, and I found additional torn blood vessels which had to be reconstructed. I ordered another unit of blood and continued with the operation, which I performed very slowly, waiting for the physician in charge to come back and take the knife from me. But he didn't come back, and I had to continue alone, admitting to myself that maybe Professor Hishin and Dr. Nakash were right when they said that I thought too much during surgery and this hesitancy made me unsuited to being a surgeon. But here, in the English operating room, I believed that my slowness would be accepted in a more tolerant spirit. For although the pulse was regular again, and the breathing was normal, and the dark, slender body was properly relaxed, I was in the grip of a terrible anxiety that something unexpected and unknown would break out in the course of the operation and kill the child under my hands, bringing disgrace not only to me but also to Lazar and his wife, who had sent me here. And so I slowed down the pace of the operation even further and checked and rechecked every cut, and at a certain stage I even insisted on calling in the X-ray technician to take additional X-rays of the spine. It was already long past midnight, and the white-haired anesthetist had taken her eyes off her instruments in order to stare at me, baffled by my slowness. Perhaps it was only good manners that prevented her from asking me what was going on, for she had every right to do so. The young nurse, however, did not hide her anger, and she flung the instruments huffily and noisily into the sterilizing unit, muttering to herself. But I ignored her, and after sewing up the stomach with small, neat stitches that wouldn't leave a scar, I finally, after five hours, signaled the anesthetist to begin bringing the child around. I wouldn't allow her to be removed from the operating room until I had made sure that the words she was mumbling in her peculiar accent made sense, and that there was no brain damage as a result of the operation I had performed from beginning to end all by myself. Without removing my bloodstained gown, I walked behind her bed as it rolled slowly into the emergency room, which at this late hour was completely quiet, and where even the patients who had not yet been sent up to the various wards had fallen asleep. I looked for the senior physician to report to him and discovered that he had retired to his room to rest long before, without even taking the trouble to inquire about the results of the operation he had left in my hands, so great was his trust in the new young doctor. The only signs of life were in the waiting room, where a group of tall, long-limbed Africans greeted me with grateful respect and awe. For them, it turned out, my slowness had been an omen of hope.

Thus I quickly found my place in the work of the hospital, and since I saw that independent operations were likely to come my way in the emergency room, I volunteered to work the evening shift and to be on call at night, to the grateful appreciation of my colleagues, who turned out on the whole to be less ambitious than Israeli doctors. And so I found myself standing in the little operating room attached to the emergency room, sometimes as an anesthetist and sometimes as a surgeon, performing quite complicated surgery on my own, albeit in my own particular way—that is, with the extreme slowness to which the white-haired anesthetist had already grown accustomed; and as for the impatient blond nurse, I got rid of her in favor of a placid, obedient Scottish nurse. At the end of each night, when I saw that nothing more of interest was going to come my way, I would walk home to our nearby apartment and wake Michaela and tell her about my adventures. She would wake up immediately and listen eagerly to everything I had to say, not only because she always liked hearing about medical matters but also because she was happy to see me full of enthusiasm. Her round belly was rising steadily like a little pink hill under the blanket, and sometimes as I spoke I thought I could see a slight movement stirring inside it, proof that the baby too was listening to me. Michaela's sexual appetite diminished greatly during her last months of pregnancy, both because the strangeness of the little apartment had worn off and because of a peculiar notion she had picked up from a traveler who had returned from India: that intercourse could arouse frustrated desire in the fetus. I didn't want to get into theological debates with her about the meaning of life and consciousness in embryos, especially since I was not particularly

keen just then on making love to her. But the memory of the love
I had known on that other stomach, no less large, round, and
white, at the beginning of spring in the granny's apartment, filled
my heart with longings so fierce and sweet that I had to avert my
head to prevent Michaela from seeing the tears in my eyes.

But Michaela had no desire to notice unexpected tears pooling
in her husband's eyes. She was full of happiness at being in London, delighting in her freedom to roam where she would, meeting people connected with India, and dreaming about another
trip there herself. And so when I got into bed after having a long
soak in the bath to cleanse my soul of the blood and pus, I would
find her fast asleep, preparing herself for her little morning job,
her only obligation—sweeping and mopping the floor of the little
chapel and tidying the seats for the congregation coming to pray
or tourists coming to admire the quaint old building. She was
quite satisfied with this simple manual labor, for which she
earned a relatively handsome sum, leading me to suspect a hidden subsidy from Sir Geoffrey, to bolster my low salary. She
would bring home candle-ends from the chapel too, and light
them from time to time to create a festive atmosphere. Sometimes, when I emerged from the bathroom at the gray hour before dawn, I would see that before she had gone back to sleep she
had set a half or third of a candle by my bedside, to dispel my
loneliness before I too fell asleep, and in fact the flickering light
would gradually calm my agitated spirit and lull me to sleep, or
at least show me when it was five o'clock in the morning, when I
would sometimes call my parents before they went to work, at
the reduced nighttime rates. In the beginning I phoned often,
because I hadn't heard anything from Amnon and I was worried
about his paying the rent on time. The two-hour time difference
between London and Jerusalem ensured that I would always find
my parents at home, fresh and alert, ready with news about
themselves and the country but mainly eager to hear about what
was going on in my life, and how Michaela's pregnancy was
progressing, and if there were any signs of an early birth. They
had already reserved their flight and paid for their tickets, and
Michaela had undertaken to find them a room near our apartment. Although they were careful not to drag out the telephone
conversations that I paid for, they couldn't resist asking for more
information about rooms for rent in the area so they could de-

cide what might suit them. They sounded excited, not only in anticipation of the birth of their grandchild and the meeting with us but also because of the long stay they planned in England, to which they had paid only brief visits since they had emigrated to Israel. They were now going to stay for two whole months; it was as if they were coming home, back to the land of their birth.

Thirteen

Sometimes dust collects on the little statuette, until its original color is dulled. And if nobody comes to wipe it off occasionally with a soft cloth, a skinny spider will finally descend from the ceiling to patiently weave a great complex web of dense transparent threads around it, like a delicate lacy dress—until a sunbeam borne on the breeze floating in from the open window transforms the forgotten statuette into a dusty little girl, her shining dress ruffling softly around her, ready to dance with anyone who asks her.

But who will ask her? Who can forget that death is death, however it disguises itself?

❧❧❧

The birth took place on a freezing winter night in our own little apartment, a few hundred yards from the hospital. I still can't understand how Michaela succeeded in persuading me, and especially my parents, to agree. But were we really persuaded, or did we simply give in to her determination to give birth at home with only a midwife present? For what, indeed, could we do? We couldn't force her to have the baby in the hospital. "I'm sorry," she announced with a tolerant smile at the sight of our misgivings, "but it was me, not you, who carried the baby all this time, so I think I have the right to decide where to bring her into the world." And with these words the argument was closed. Nevertheless, I don't think we tried hard enough to change her mind, as if we had resigned ourselves to the fact that she had a few private eccentricities that we had to accept in return for her many virtues, which in London took on a very practical aspect. Not only did she find an excellent apartment for my parents at a reasonable rent, with a separate entrance and a little kitchenette, only a few streets away from us—a room attached to a small house surrounded by a little garden, whose owners were away on a long vacation in Italy—but she also prepared a very warm welcome for them when they arrived. Although she was in the middle of her ninth month, she insisted on going to the airport to meet them and from there bringing them back to our house, where a rich repast awaited them, with all kinds of sausages and cheeses that she knew my father liked. She surprised my mother, who was not a big eater, with a dish that had been a favorite of hers as a child—raspberries and cream, something she had picked up from a chance remark made by my Glasgow aunt. The day before they arrived, Michaela made the beds in their room with fresh, spotless linen, and she added an extra pillow to my mother's bed, which in this room was next to my father's, so that she could sleep with her head raised, as she did in Jerusalem. And on top of everything else she had borrowed two hot water bottles from her new friend Stephanie, in case the English heating was insufficient for my parents, especially since an intense cold had descended on the whole country in the week of their arrival, at the beginning of January.

This Stephanie, a mature woman from South Africa whom Michaela had met in the neighborhood choir and had become very friendly with, was the source of some of her new ideas, including the idea of giving birth at home with a midwife, which apparently was fashionable then among young women in North London, who besides relying on their own sturdy health were looking for some kind of meaning in the simpler ways of former generations. I knew that Michaela was searching for something; she wanted to experience the birth on a basic, elemental level, and if half the human race was still giving birth at home without making a fuss about it, there really was no reason for me to be concerned. Her pregnancy had been absolutely normal, and she herself was a strong, healthy young woman. She had also participated in a Lamaze course, and she knew what to expect; in case of an emergency the hospital was just around the corner, and I myself was a doctor after all, as Michaela reminded me in a slightly mocking tone, for it amused her that a doctor, and a young one at that, should be prey to fears that would never even occur to a layman. It was true that I had accumulated plenty of

experience over the past few months in the little operating room
next to the emergency room, but I had never delivered a baby—
let alone this particular one, whom I was already calling Shiva to
myself, but with a *beth,* not with a *vav.* This was my condition
for agreeing to the birth at home, and Michaela was forced to
accept it, in spite of her protests. "You're wrong, Benjy," she
said. "Shiva with a *vav* is more elegant than Shiva with a *beth.*
And it's also connected to the word *shivayon,* equality, or even,
if you want, to something religious like *Shiviti elohim l'negdi,* 'I
have set God always before me.' "

"But you mean a completely different god," I said immediately. "Why different?" she wondered. "It's always the same
god, Benjy. Why can't you understand? But never mind, let it be
with a *beth* in the meantime, and when she learns to read and
write she can decide for herself how to spell her name. In any
case, in English it's the same, and that's the important thing,"
and this concluded the negotiations between us, with an echo of
her refusal to go home to Israel after the year was over.

My parents had already heard this echo too, on the way back
from the airport, and they remarked on it to me, but their immediate concern was with Michaela's plan to give birth at home. In
the beginning they tried to pressure Michaela tactfully into
changing her mind, as they had tried and succeeded in the matter
of the size of the wedding. But this time I wasn't neutral. I felt
obligated to stand up for Michaela and reassure my parents—
after all, I was a doctor, wasn't I? And that should count for
something. Fortunately, my father's niece and her pale, thin, bespectacled husband, the one with the slightly mysterious appearance, called as soon as my parents arrived and invited them to
dinner and the theater, distracting them to some extent from
their anxieties about the approaching birth, which I intended to
tell them about only when it was over. This wouldn't be easy, for
they were staying nearby, and in spite of their discretion and
promise not to make a nuisance of themselves, they called several
times a day. When I received a phone call at six o'clock in the
evening from Michaela, who was already a few days overdue, to
tell me that her water had broken, I told her not to say anything
to my parents and hurried home from the hospital. There I was
met by Stephanie, who liked taking part in these private births
and who was chiefly responsible for giving Michaela the confi-

dence to go through with it. Michaela was already lying, pale and smiling, on the mattress on my side of the joined twin beds, for her own mattress, soaked with amniotic fluid, had been put in front of the radiator in the next room to dry. I wondered if amniotic fluid had a smell. The first contraction had not come yet, so while we waited I made coffee and sandwiches for Stephanie and myself, but I forbade Michaela to eat, so that she wouldn't vomit later. Even though Michaela had assured me that the midwife would bring "everything necessary," I had prepared myself for the delivery by purchasing at a pharmacy some polydine disinfectant, something to stop the bleeding, and three shots of Pitocin to accelerate the contractions; the Marcaine injections to anesthetize the pelvic nerves, which proved impossible to obtain at a pharmacy, I secretly "borrowed" from the medicine cabinet in the hospital delivery room, in the hope that we wouldn't have to use them. Prompted by a premonition that something might go wrong and that I should be prepared for any eventuality, without asking permission I put a few simple but essential instruments in my bag, such as forceps, scalpels, long, curved scissors, and needles, and as soon as I got home I threw them all into a pot of boiling water to sterilize them. How strange, I thought, that I should be sitting here in our little kitchen, full of fear and apprehension, watching the bubbling water, when only a stone's throw away was a hospital with modern operating rooms to which I had free access. If I really loved Michaela, I wondered, would I have given in to her so easily?

The midwife had not yet arrived, even though she had said that she was on her way some time ago. Michaela showed no signs of anxiety; she was well prepared and confident that everything would go smoothly. Stephanie and I watched as she greeted the first contraction with the special breathing exercises she had learned, without uttering a sound. In the meantime my parents phoned, and guessed by the tone of my voice that something was happening. I made them swear not to come until I called them, and they promised to wait for my permission—but half an hour later I saw them through the window, walking up and down the street as if they wanted, in spite of the bitter cold, to be close to the scene of the event. They were wearing heavy coats, and from time to time they raised their eyes to our lighted windows. Then they disappeared, into a nearby pub as it turned out, from which they phoned to say that they were close by and if I needed them they could be there in a minute. The midwife, presumably stuck in the busy evening traffic, had still not arrived, and I started to become really worried about what I would do if, God forbid, she didn't come at all and it proved impossible to transfer Michaela to the hospital against her will. The rate of the contractions increased slightly, but there was still no sign of an opening. Michaela was quiet, she didn't let out a single moan, and it was a wonder to me that she, who screamed and moaned wildly when we made love, was so restrained in the face of pains so severe that her face went white and she closed her eyes for long stretches at a time. For a moment I felt angry at myself for leaving all the arrangements for the midwife and the delivery to her. But before I took more drastic steps, such as going around to the hospital to fetch someone qualified to help, I decided to bring my parents up to the apartment, not only in order to leave someone more reliable than Stephanie with Michaela, although she seemed quite calm and collected, but also to get encouragement from their presence, and maybe even to get some practical advice from my mother, who had also given birth, even though it had been only once, and thirty years ago at that.

I ran down to the pub to call them. At first I couldn't find them in the crush, because instead of sitting in a corner, as I expected, they were standing at the bar like veteran customers, drinking beer and holding an animated conversation with a group of Englishmen. When they saw me pushing my way toward them, looking agitated, my father had been having such a pleasant time that he thought it was already over and I had come to give them the news. He hurried to introduce me to his new acquaintances, and the friendliness of their nods led me to understand that here too I had been one of the subjects of his conversation. When we left the pub he complained again, as he had done since his arrival, of my poor English vocabulary and the mistakes I kept making, and offered once more to speak to me in English in order to improve my command of the language. But my mother, who sensed my deep excitement, cut him short: "Not now. Let's wait for Shiva to be born first." There was something very agreeable and reassuring in the way she pronounced for the first time the name of the baby who had not yet been born—who was apparently in no hurry to be born, either, judging by the lack of change in Michaela's dilation. My father, of course, did not go into the bedroom and only looked in politely from the door, but my mother sat down next to the bed and began talking intensely with Michaela and Stephanie, who were becoming increasingly concerned at the failure of the midwife to arrive. Three hours had passed since she had been summoned, and there was no sign of her; and they had both been relying on her, not only medically but spiritually.

And then I understood that I would have to delivery my baby by myself, and taking into account the fact that my hospital was only a stone's throw away, the situation into which I had been manipulated seemed to me nothing short of scandalous. Michaela sensed my rage and smiled apologetically. Her face was very pale; there were already black rings under her eyes, and I knew that she was in great pain but that she didn't want to complain, especially after the Lamaze course that she had so faithfully and enthusiastically attended, under the supervision of the very midwife who still hadn't arrived and whose whereabouts were unknown to the people who answered the phone at her house. I brought the instruments and drugs I had prepared into the bedroom, placed two pillows under her legs to raise them, and without hesitation gave her a shot of Pitocin to speed up the contractions. I had never injected anyone with Pitocin before, but since I had studied the formula in advance and read up on its action I had no qualms about administering it, especially since it was simply a weak solution of a substance I recognized as a muscle contractant. My mother watched me respectfully and nodded encouragingly, confident of the skill and lightness of my hand. Even though she was violently opposed to the idea of having the baby at home, she possessed a marvelous capacity for displaying optimism in the hour of need and putting old disagreements behind her. In order to keep Michaela occupied until the next contraction, she tried to remember details of her own delivery, to which Michaela paid scant attention, for now, under the influence of the injection, the contractions were coming more frequently, but still without any signs of the cervix's dilating. The baby's hard skull, too, which I succeeded in palpating in order to ascertain that her head would appear first, was still high up, as if she knew there was no point in approaching the cervix, which was still completely closed. I didn't want to give Michaela the Marcaine yet, in case it caused a relaxation that would delay the birth. I realized that my anxiety was exaggerated and tried to tell myself that it was no big deal; every ambulance driver delivered a baby at least once or twice during the course of his career, and Michaela was showing impressive powers of endurance. She still had not asked me to give her anything to relieve the pain, and she did whatever I told her to without complaining, as if she were ready to press her guts out and tear herself into pieces as long as I left her in our bedroom and didn't take her to the hospital.

❧❧

And when the birth finally came, between six and seven in the morning, after an additional shot slowly but surely encouraged the cervix to begin to open, like a big red rose—and when in the warm intimacy of our bedroom, where at Michaela's request the lights had been dimmed, the head of our baby, covered with wildly untidy hair, emerged together with the first signs of a gray London dawn—I began to understand, if not to endorse, Michaela's stubborn insistence on giving birth at home. Especially since the birth was so smooth and easy. The baby perhaps identifying with Michaela, who had not uttered a single groan of pain all night long, only cried very briefly, and stopped as soon as I cut the umbilical cord and gave her to my mother, who wrapped her in a big towel, her hands trembling with an emotion I had not imagined this logical, unsentimental woman capable of. Afterward, when we recalled these moments, I learned that the emotion which made my mother tremble so much that she almost dropped the baby was due not only to the birth of this baby, with its startlingly hairy, almost devilish head, but also to the distant but vivid memory of the loneliness she herself had felt when I was born, a birth she had not known would be her last. I too was strangely moved by the hairy black head emerging from the bleeding womb, precisely because it was the opposite of the shorn head that had misled me into taking Michaela for a boy when I first met her in the Lazars' living room. As if by some mysterious process a little of my beloved's long, abundant hair had grown on my baby's head, which was now resting dark and shining on my pillow while I waited for the placenta to come out so that I could coolly suture the bleeding tears in the vagina with the needles I had brought from the hospital. I stress the word "coolly" here because even Michaela, who was radiant with joy, could guess how much it had affected me to function as a physician at the birth of my own child. But she had no idea of the price I was soon to extract for having been forced to deal so surgically and directly with her blood, womb, and placenta. And when Stephanie, who had been enthralled by my performance throughout the long night, finally invited my father into the bedroom to see his granddaughter, I didn't wait to observe the reactions of this good man, who had been sitting quietly, wide awake, in the living room all night long, but hurried to the bathroom to wash off what I felt had besmirched the little love I had for my wife.

※

So profound and intense was the weariness that had accumulated between the four sides of my personality, that had been active during the long night—physician, husband, father, and son—that I dozed off in the warm, scented bathwater and failed to register the belated arrival of the midwife, who turned out to be a tall dark woman, perhaps of oriental extraction, with a haughty air and white hair. It seemed that there was a prosaic explanation for her mysterious absence. As soon as she received our summons she had set out, but a car had run into her as she was crossing the street and injured her ankle, with the result that she had to spend several hours in the police station and the emergency room. Since she didn't have our telephone number and we weren't listed in the phone book, she had no way of contacting us. But her conscience wouldn't let her go straight home from the hospital, and just as she was, limping painfully on a crutch, she came to keep her promise, accompanied by her young daughter, and to see if she was still needed. Although the birth was already over, Michaela and Stephanie were happy to see her and made her sit down on the armchair in the bedroom—first of all, to tell her in detail about how the birth had gone and how the correct breathing she taught had helped overcome the pain, and second, to ask her to examine the baby and express her opinion. They woke the baby up and laid her naked on the lap of the midwife, who examined her thoroughly and also anointed her with a special oil she had brought with her, after which Stephanie put her back in our bed, next to Michaela. The baby still didn't have a crib of her own. Although Michaela had purchased all the necessary equipment, she had left it all in the department store, in order not to arouse the jealousy of mysterious evil forces until the birth had been safely accomplished. "I don't believe it," said my father to Michaela in genuine astonishment. "A rational, liberated woman like you, believing in mysterious evil forces?"

"Of course I don't want to believe in mysterious forces," replied Michaela jokingly, "but what can I do if they believe in me?" Stephanie and Michaela praised me to the skies to the midwife, who examined the cervix, praised my stitches, but could not hide her disapproval of the injections I had given Michaela to induce the birth. Why was I in such a hurry? she wanted to know. Nature had a rhythm of its own. If I had not induced the birth, perhaps she would have arrived in time to deliver the baby herself. Who knows whether she was thinking of the fee she had lost or her professional enjoyment, or perhaps of both.

But none of this mattered now. My father's face was crumpled with fatigue, and my mother asked me to call a taxi for them, because she didn't want to put me out. But I insisted on driving them home myself, and I went to get the car from its parking place behind the chapel, trying to engrave on my memory the details of the foggy London street, which looked like a set from an old English movie, so that I could tell Shiva when she grew up about the morning of her birth. Outside the garden gate of the pretty house where my parents were staying, my mother, who was still wide awake, suddenly suggested that she would go back to be with Michaela while I snatched a few hours' sleep on her bed, next to my father. I don't know if it was the somber expression on my face that worried her, or if she was already missing the new baby, but I refused. Although I could have done with a few hours' sleep in their pleasant room, surrounded by the bourgeois quiet of the English house, I didn't know how Michaela would react to my desertion only a few hours after the birth of the baby, and I said good-bye to my parents, who embraced me warmly. I knew that they were very happy now, and the dense fog surrounding us, which reminded them of their childhood, only increased their happiness. They were bursting with pride in my successful delivery of the baby, after all their fears. I too was pleased with myself, and on the way home, as I glided slowly and carefully between the little milk vans, I wondered what to say in the monthly report I sent to Lazar's secretary about my work in the London hospital. Should I mention the fact that I had delivered the baby by myself at home, which might be interpreted by a certain person as excessive intimacy in my relations with Michaela, or should I simply announce the fact of Shiva's birth, so that she, the distant and impossible beloved, would know that the way was open for her to renew our sweet and secret relations, now that she was doubly protected against me?

But when I reached home, I thought that perhaps I should have accepted my mother's offer to go to sleep in their room after all, for Michaela and Stephanie were still deep in animated conversation with the midwife, who in spite of the pain in her ankle was sitting in our bedroom with her daughter, drinking her second or third cup of tea, holding not our baby but the little Indian statuette with its many outflung arms between her hands and speaking now not of births and babies but of life itself, its purpose and meaning, a subject on which I was invited to give my opinion. Stephanie poured me a cup of tea, and I took off my shoes and lay down on the bed, crushed between five women, counting the fingers and toes on my new daughter, who lay next to me blinking her eyes. I discovered that Michaela and Stephanie had good reason for being under the spell of this midwife, who turned out to be an original woman with an eloquent style of speech and strange and diverting ideas. Beyond the practical, competent professional veneer lay a fervent belief in the transmigration of souls, and not necessarily after death but in the midst of the bustle and flow of life. Her idea of the soul was of something flimsier and lighter than the conventional notion, for she removed the heavier parts, such as memory, and left only the anxieties and aspirations, which allowed it to drift slowly around and also to migrate deliberately from place to place and person to person. For example, she said that when her ankle had been injured in the evening and she had been taken to the hospital and realized that she wouldn't be able to reach us in time, she had sent her soul to enter into those present in this room, especially into me. Hadn't I felt, she asked me, that I had done things more easily and confidently than I had ever done them in my life before? "Yes, I did feel that," I admitted honestly. "But if your soul entered into me," I asked innocently, with an exhausted smile, "where was my soul? Surely I didn't have two souls inside me last night?"

"It was in me, of course." The midwife answered my challenge simply and without embarrassment. "I kept it until the birth was over and you returned my soul to me."

"And how did my soul seem to you?" I went on provocatively. "To tell you the truth, a rather childish soul," she replied seriously, blushing as if she had disclosed an embarrassing secret. "A childish soul?" I laughed in surprise but also in pique at this unexpected reply. "In what sense childish?"

"In the strange way it falls in love," she replied. "Falls in love?" I cried in astonishment. "With whom?"

"Me, for example," she replied brazenly, staring at me intently, until her daughter, who had been watching her mother worshipfully all this time, burst into ringing laughter, which immediately infected Michaela and Stephanie too, and in the end also the midwife herself, who stood up and lightly stroked the baby's hair and then laid her hand on my shoulder to placate me.

But after the three females had at long last left the apartment and Michaela had moved into the living room with the baby to give me a chance to sleep for she herself was still too excited to sleep—I suddenly felt, in the fog of exhaustion buzzing in my brain, that perhaps I really was capable of falling in love with this proud, white-haired midwife, just as I had fallen in love with Dori, who soon appeared to me in a muddled dream; and when I woke up and found myself so far away from her—a man with a little family in a gray London winter—I wanted to weep with longing. It was three o'clock in the afternoon, outside it was drizzling, and in the next room I heard my mother talking excitedly to Michaela, who had not yet closed her eyes and was still elated, perhaps because the crib, bath, and baby carriage had arrived from the department store. The baby already had a corner of her own in the world, and since some small things were still missing, my father had gone out into the rain to procure them. At six o'clock that evening I was able to go to my shift at the hospital knowing that the baby was in the safe hands of Michaela and my parents, and that life at home would soon be back to normal. I hastily replaced the borrowed injections and instruments, very relieved that nobody had noticed their absence.

But I was sorry that I couldn't tell any of my colleagues about the home birth, since I was afraid that it would be seen as a vote of no confidence in the hospital. Nor could I boast of delivering the baby myself, for fear of seeming irresponsible to them. So I kept quiet, and since the freezing cold outside kept the number of patients at a minimum, I was free to bask in an inner glow of self-congratulation at my efficient performance of the night before. After midnight, when my shift ended, I went home and found Michaela sitting and breast-feeding the baby. My parents had only just left, evidently unable to tear themselves away from their sweet granddaughter, and perhaps also unwilling to leave Michaela alone. This was the first time we had been alone together since the birth. "You'll collapse if you don't get some sleep," I said to her gently. "Don't worry, I'm fine." She smiled at me affectionately. There was no doubt that the birth had strengthened our mutual esteem. Michaela could not help but be impressed by my skill as a doctor, while the memory of how nobly she had borne her pain filled me with respect for her. I don't know if it crossed her mind that I had refused to give her a sedative or an analgesic not only because I wanted her to be completely lucid during the birth, but also because I secretly wished to avenge myself on her for forcing me to act as her midwife. I had a strange feeling that our growing respect for each other would do nothing to increase the love that was supposed to bring us together, but would have the opposite effect—a feeling reinforced at this midnight hour by my indifference at the sight of her two pear-shaped breasts, which did not give rise to the faintest desire in me, not even to brush one of her nipples with my lips in order to feel what my daughter was feeling now.

During the following week Michaela gradually made up for the hours of lost sleep and prepared herself efficiently to return to her normal life, especially her exploration of London. My mother and father were always at her disposal as baby-sitters, but she was unwilling to rely too much on their help, both because she wanted them to enjoy their vacation, which was coming to an end in two or three weeks, and because we had to start managing without them. She hung a baby sling on her stomach, which had already returned to its normal size, and in it she deposited Shiva, who felt as snug and comfortable there as a baby kangaroo in its mother's pouch. And thus, one week after giving birth, Michaela was already able to return to her little cleaning job in the chapel, with the baby riding on her stomach, and also to visit old friends from India who were now living in East London. Her natural self-confidence began to rub off on the baby, who seemed to be growing to resemble her mother spiritually, for not only did she suffer being dragged around London in silence, she appeared to actually enjoy it. It was still too early to tell whom she resembled physically, in spite of my parents' suggestions. She didn't look like me, and she hadn't inherited Michaela's stunning eyes either. One afternoon when I was alone in the house with her, something about her slightly flattened skull and narrow eyes put me in mind of the pale and faintly mysterious figure of our non-Jewish English relation, the husband of my father's niece, who was very friendly to my parents. One Sunday afternoon, for instance, he and his wife saw fit to invite all our English relatives to a little party in honor of the baby's birth; one of the guests was my energetic aunt from Glasgow, who did her best to persuade my parents to go and spend a week with her in Scotland before they returned to Israel. In spite of her love for her younger sister, my mother hesitated, mostly because she was unwilling to part from the baby, though she wouldn't admit it. In the meantime, we discovered the existence of a semiofficial nursery attached to the pediatric department at the hospital, for the children of the staff. The nursery was not intended for babies as young as Shiva, but Michaela succeeded in persuading the nurse in charge to take her from time to time for a little while. And so my parents were able accept my aunt's insistent invitation after all with a clear conscience and conclude their successful visit to Britain with a return to the scenes of my mother's Scottish childhood.

❧❧

I encouraged them to go, they and my aunt would enjoy it but because I had heard from Sir Geoffrey that Lazar and his wife were about to arrive in London, and I did not want my mother to see the feverish excitement that gripped me as soon as I heard this news. Although Sir Geoffrey said nothing about Dori, I knew that she would never let Lazar go on a trip to London without her. I even told myself that it was because of her imminent arrival that she had failed to acknowledge the announcement of Shiva's birth, which I had appended to my monthly progress report to Lazar's secretary. I asked Sir Geoffrey about the agenda for Lazar's visit, which turned out to be packed with meetings and events, since Lazar intended to set up a Society of Friends of our hospital in London. I therefore offered myself as an additional escort, perhaps to take care of Mrs. Lazar, if she came, and prevent her from being bored. "She doesn't look like a lady who's easily bored," laughed Sir Geoffrey, who remembered her from a visit two years before, hanging on to her husband's arm, smiling and pleased with herself. It was obvious that he liked her, and I had to fight for the right to go and pick them up at the airport, which inconvenienced Michaela, who had to give up her yoga class in South Kensington in order to stay at home with the baby. Shiva, I reminded her, had a slight cold. She didn't protest, although she mocked the practical motives behind my willingness to be of service to the Lazars, and also wondered whether our little Morris would be able to hold "those two fatties" and their luggage. I was already resigned to the fact that Einat had passed on her hostility toward her parents to Michaela, perhaps in their days together in Calcutta, and I didn't bother to respond. My thoughts strayed to the moment when Dori and Lazar would discover me waiting for them at the gate, and to how surprised they would be to see me, although in fact they were used to seeing me in airports.

But as things turned out, Lazar recognized me before I spotted them and immediately embraced me. His wife did not blush with surprise at the sudden meeting either, and, radiant as usual, she held out her arms for a hug with a naturalness that astonished me, and kissed me on both cheeks. And even though I knew it was only a friendly kiss, the result of her excitement at the flight and the landing, and the same kind of reception Sir Geoffrey would have received if he had come to meet them, I couldn't control the violent trembling that took hold of me, as if this simple, smiling kiss, bestowed on me so naturally by my beloved in the presence of her husband, held out the promise of something real and significant occurring in the course of this visit, which began in the soft light of a welcoming London sky. It was presumably these thoughts running through my head, and not her presence at my side, looking for a place to put her long legs in the cramped space of the little car, which caused me to get lost on the way from the airport to their hotel, to the annoyance of Lazar, who was tired and in a hurry as usual. "You were better at finding your way in New Delhi," he remarked sarcastically, sitting in the backseat squeezed next to a suitcase that didn't fit into the trunk, looking at the unfamiliar London streets, which he was sure he would have negotiated more successfully than I was, if he had been sitting at the steering wheel in my place. When we finally reached the hotel and I took the second suitcase out of the trunk, I suddenly recognized it as one of those that had accompanied us to India, and with a mysterious feeling of inexplicable joy I bent down to stroke the slightly shabby leather, which still seemed to be covered with the reddish yellow dust of the dirt roads next to the temples of Bodhgaya. Lazar wanted to open this suitcase in the hotel lobby, to take out the gift they had brought for the baby, but Dori stopped him. "Later, there's plenty of time. We'll give it to the baby herself," she said, and asked about Shiva's unusual name. When I explained why Michaela had chosen the name, she seemed stirred and excited, immediately grasping the deep Indian connection, which included her too. I wanted to tell them my reservations about calling my daughter after a god who wanted to destroy the entire universe, and my preference for a more modest Israeli context and for the spelling of the Hebrew word "return," but it seemed too complicated to explain to two tired people eager to go up to their room and rest after their journey.

When I got home, Michaela wasn't there. In spite of the baby's cold she had decided to take her out. I was annoyed with her for ignoring my medical diagnosis, and I even saw it as a little act of revenge for what she saw as my exaggerated and superfluous favors to the Lazars. The truth was that in spite of the skill I had displayed in delivering the baby, Michaela refused to allow me to extend my medical authority to her. "As far as she's concerned, you're only her father, not her doctor," she warned me in the commanding tone she could sometimes use. It was obviously important to her not to give me any advantage as far as responsibility for the baby's welfare was concerned, and in principle she was right. But I was afraid that wandering around in the cold might make the baby develop an infection and keep us at home now, exactly when I wanted to be as free as possible to cultivate my relations with the woman who, from the moment I had set eyes on her again, I knew I could not give up—could not and would not. Giving her up, even in my thoughts, might damage a vital artery that was sustaining me and giving me strength to cope with Michaela and the baby and even with my parents, who had recently become soft and sentimental, hanging on my every word and doing everything I told them to. And I didn't need much to sustain the obsession that haunted me day and night: all I needed was an occasional smile from her to give me the courage to go into her office again and confess my love with a boldness and desperation that would cause her not only astonishment and remorse but mainly admiration of herself for sending a young man like me into a state of such tender confusion. And that was liable to fire her with a different passion from the kind aroused in her by her devoted husband, who kissed and caressed her without stopping.

But when Michaela returned with the baby, who was healthy and rosy from the walk in the wintry air, without a trace of the morning's cold, I had to admire the maternal instinct that had so confidently and accurately diagnosed the superficiality of the sniffles that I had thought so important. And again I realized how right my mother had been the first time I brought Michaela home, when she predicted that the moment Michaela had a child she would stop looking for herself and find her proper place in the world, so much so that even her lack of a high school diploma wouldn't matter. She seemed so attractive to me now, as she competently changed the baby's diaper and began breast-feeding her, that I hinted at the possibility of a quick session in bed before I had to go to my night shift at the hospital; perhaps it would help to relieve the lust I already felt for the woman who had just arrived in the country, whom we would have to invite to tea soon, with her husband, so that they could have a look at the baby and give her the present they had brought—and give me the opportunity to put out a few feelers about plans for my return to the hospital in Israel, in order to make sure that the English door really led back home and wasn't locked behind us. But Michaela wasn't at all interested. Her friend the midwife recommended refraining from full sexual intercourse for three months after the birth, in order to give all the tears time to mend and allow everything to settle down again after the shock. Although I couldn't

really argue with the midwife's logic, I remained so full of tension that I couldn't sleep after my night shift, so I went back to
the hospital early in the afternoon. I left Shiva at the nursery and
walked up and down outside Sir Geoffrey's office, hoping to
bump into the Lazars. And so I did. I easily recognized Dori's
confident steps in the distance, and soon after that her eyes were
imploring me anxiously, for she realized that I was hanging
around in the corridor outside Sir Geoffrey's office in order to
meet her again. If it hadn't occurred to me on the spur of the
moment to ask her to come and see Shiva, she would no doubt
have followed her husband like a little puppy dog into his meeting with Sir Geoffrey, who intended, as Lazar had already told
me the day before, to offer the Tel Aviv hospital used dialysis and
anesthesia equipment from the English hospital's surplus stock
for next to nothing. I saw immediately that the invitation to
come and see the baby attracted her, and Lazar, who wanted to
examine the offer in depth and make sure that Sir Geoffrey's
good intentions wouldn't lead to more trouble than the equipment was worth, encouraged her to go with me. "But why not,
Dori? Go and see the baby, and if Benjy has the time, perhaps
he'll take you to see St. Paul's Cathedral, which you wanted to
see today. I'm afraid that it's going to take a long time here, and
after that I have to meet the man who's organizing the evening
for the Friends."

"And when will you see the baby?" she cried in a scandalized
tone, as if it were a duty or a pleasure that couldn't be missed.
But I, thrilled at the opportunity to be alone with her, which had
come my way so easily, hastily reassured them on this score.
"You'll still have plenty of opportunities to see the baby," I repeatedly promised Lazar, who didn't seem in the least enthusiastic, and we arranged that I would bring Dori back to Sir Geoffrey's office in two hours' time. Thus, by an unexpected
coincidence, she was suddenly in my charge, albeit for only two
hours, but in a place completely unfamiliar to her, wrapped in
the blue velvet tunic I remembered from India, which apparently
belonged to the category of clothes that could be worn anywhere.
With her high heels drumming a sure and steady rhythm, she
began to walk beside me—a plump, ripe, middle-aged woman,
who by the time I reached her age might have already departed
from this world. This new thought filled me not only with sad-

ness but also with a tender pleasure. In a friendly way, but maintaining a discreet distance, as if we had never lain together naked, I began to ask her about her mother and how she was getting on in the old folks' home, a subject I knew she enjoyed talking about and one that I felt hinted at the intimacy between us as well. When we went quietly into the nursery and I received permission to take Dori into the babies' room for a minute, I wasn't satisfied with pointing out Shiva's crib to her, but I woke the baby up and put her in Dori's arms, so that she would hold something that was part of my flesh and blood.

She hugged the baby very warmly, uttering cries of excitement and delight, which to the nurse standing next to us no doubt sounded phony and exaggerated but which I knew were genuine. Shiva's abundant hair amused Dori greatly, and she clasped the hairy little head to her bosom and refused to part with her, until I had to intervene tactfully and return the wide-awake baby to her crib. I was so moved by Dori's enthusiasm that I couldn't restrain myself, and as I led her through a side door into the hospital's bustling emergency entrance, I told her the entire story of my successful delivery of the baby in our bedroom, in detail. The automatic smile in her eyes was now mixed with immense curiosity. She was delighted with my story. In fact, she seemed so absorbed that instead of taking her to St. Paul's, as I had offered, and risking bringing her back late to the meeting with her husband, I suggested that we take advantage of the rare warmth of the sun and go on strolling around the streets in the vicinity of the hospital, and perhaps venture a little farther, into the nicer neighborhood where my parents' room was situated. Suddenly I wanted to know what this fussy woman who had dragged us from one hotel to another in India until she found one that lived up to her expectations would think of the pretty place Michaela had found for my parents, which she might want to consider for herself during a future London vacation. And since the keys to the garden gate and to the room had been attached to my key ring since I had said good-bye to my parents at the train station a few days before, we would have no problem getting in.

❧ ❧

Behind the small house, which stood in a well-tended garden, was a separate gate leading past beds of roses to my parents' room. There were little bells hanging on the gate, which were evidently intended to give the landlords a measure of control over the comings and goings of their tenants. But they were superfluous now, since the owners of the house were in Italy. After the bells had stopped ringing, I opened the door of the room, which was very dark, and invited Dori to peep inside. Although the windows and curtains had been closed for several days, there was a pleasant smell in the room, a combination of the odor of the floor polish and the lingering ambience of my parents, some of whose familiar clothes were still hanging in the closet. Perhaps because of this ambience, Dori hesitated at first to enter the large, attractive room, but when I insisted on showing it off to her and proving how reasonable the rent was in view of its many virtues, she agreed to follow me into the little kitchenette too, and even into the tiny bathroom, which I knew my mother had left clean and tidy. It was cold in the room. There was a coin-operated gas heater which I wanted to turn on, and I also wanted to draw the curtain so that she could see the pretty garden through the window, but she stopped me with a gesture, sat down on an armchair in the dim light, like that time in her mother's apartment, and stretched her legs out in front of her. All of a sudden I felt a surge of lust, together with profound anxiety. A whole year had already passed, and I didn't know how to go on from here. Was I supposed to declare my love to her again? In the meantime, I offered her a cup of tea, since I knew my parents kept no coffee in the room. Looking surprised but smiling gloriously, she agreed to this strange offer, perhaps because she too wanted a chance to examine her feelings. But when I came back into the room after switching on the electric kettle and putting the tea bags in the cups, I found her standing impatiently, as if she had just grasped how odd, and even perverse, it would be to spend the little time we had left before returning to the hospital sitting and drinking tea in my parents' dark, closed room. She expressed a wish, which seemed to me rather reckless and childish, to see the rooms in the rest of the house. I glanced at my watch; we had thirty or forty minutes left before we had to leave to keep our appointment with Lazar, which I was determined to be on time for so as not to give him any grounds for suspicion. Did she realize, I wondered feverishly, that we would never find a better place than this in which to make love with perfect anonymity and secrecy, or was she put off by the idea of making love on my parents' pushed-together beds? I began to feel the lust churning in the pit of my stomach, but I followed her into a long, narrow passage that led into a dark and surprisingly large sitting room, where all the furniture—armchairs, sofas, and cabinets—was covered with white sheets. I wanted to switch on the light, but the electricity appeared to be disconnected in this part of the house. I thought this would be enough to discourage her from continuing her explorations, but her curiosity knew no bounds, and smiling to herself, without asking my permission as the representative of the subtenants in this house, she went on and opened a wooden door leading to a charming little study paneled in reddish wood, which opened into another passage that led into a room that was unexpectedly light, for one of the curtains was open. The meager daylight streaming in through the window looked bright and strong in contrast to the darkness shrouding the rest of the house. This fine, big bedroom was different in its light, modern style from the other rooms, and it was immediately clear that it had taken the fancy of my companion, for she began to scrutinize it with an inquisitive, proprietary eye, and suddenly pulled the sheet off the bed, disclosing a handsome floral bedspread in various shades of green.

True, it would have been more becoming and more decent to make love on my parents' bed and not to desecrate the room of a couple of strangers vacationing in Italy in complete ignorance of my existence. But I was afraid that if I took Dori back to my parents' room she might regret her impulse, and by the time I succeeded in seducing her we would have to leave. Without wasting time on declarations of love, I went up to her in resolute silence, and put my arms around her and kissed her and felt the heaviness of her body again. This time too she refused to let me take off a single item of her clothing, as if this would undercut her liberty and independence, and as on the first time she waited until I was standing before her naked in the freezing room before she got undressed and lay down on the green bedspread, which in her eyes was evidently not only more beautiful than the plain white sheet but also cleaner. She waited with her eyes closed for me to finish covering with passionate kisses her sweet, full stomach, which had grown even rounder since the last time, as if she were hoarding secrets there in a slow, endless pregnancy. But when I tried to move down to her crotch, she stopped me with a light tug at my hair and pulled me up to lie with her properly, taking hold of my penis and trying to put it inside her with an unclear anger, perhaps because its tip was already covered with a delicate film, like my face, which was suddenly bathed in tears because the pain and pity of this strange love were complicating my lust. In a second I lost my concentration, and I knew that I would not be able to satisfy this beloved woman but only watch as her excitement weakened and died and ebbed away, like a wave returning to the sea. Thus we remained lying in a long, silent embrace until she opened her eyes and glanced at her watch and I saw her surprise at the tears on my face. "But what's wrong?" she said. "Don't be sorry, it doesn't matter. In any case, everything's impossible here." And with uncharacteristic speed she got dressed, watching me with some anxiety as I slowly and feebly collected my clothes and put them on in the strange, cold room. Then we left the house, which she said she liked very much, and if there was time, she said, she would show it to Lazar as a good place to spend a holiday in London. On the way back she chattered gaily and quickened her steps, as if what had happened between us gave her hope of getting rid of me, or at least of warning me off. But when we entered the administrative wing of the hospital her strange gaiety gave way to a mild tension. She preferred to leave me at the end of the corridor and go on alone to Sir Geoffrey's room.

The room looked dark to me, as if nobody were there, and, not wanting to leave her alone, I remained where I was. Indeed, the door proved to be locked, and there was nobody in the secretary's room either. From my position at the end of the corridor I could see that she was very agitated, not only because she didn't like being left alone but also because she was evidently not used to waiting for her husband. She sat down on the bench opposite the office and then stood up and began pacing up and down, until she caught sight of me standing at the end of the hall. "Are you sure this is the place?" she called out angrily, as if I were capable of leading her astray. When I reassured her, she said unexpectedly and somewhat bitterly, immediately giving rise to new hope in me, "So we hurried back for nothing." Then she sent me away, after refusing my offer to go and look for her husband. I went to the nursery, to see if Michaela had already taken Shiva, and saw that the baby was still there. The nurse told me that she had been restless, crying for most of the time since I returned her to her crib, and suggested that I take her home without waiting for Michaela. I put her into her sling, but instead of leaving right away, and despite the fact that I didn't like hanging around the hospital with the baby, I went back to Sir Geoffrey's office to see if Lazar had come to get his wife. From the end of the corridor I saw that she was still sitting on the bench, erect, her legs crossed, smoking a cigarette, and my heart melted with love and concern. I went up to her and asked, "What's going on? Where's Lazar?" She shrugged her shoulders with an unfamiliar melancholy smile, as if she feared the worst. "Don't worry," I said, "he must be somewhere in the hospital. Let me leave the baby with you for a minute and I'll go and look for him." She put out her cigarette and agreed with alacrity, as if glad to have the opportunity to play grandmother for a while. I turned to the surgical wing, since I knew that the equipment Sir Geoffrey wanted to give Lazar was there. But in the surgical wing they told me that the two of them had left half an hour before for the emergency room. "Why?" I asked in surprise, and was told that Sir Geoffrey had taken Lazar to undergo some tests. I rushed breathlessly to the emergency room, to the astonishment of the phlegmatic Englishmen I passed as I ran, who up to now had no doubt taken me for one of them. In the familiar emergency room I immediately spotted Lazar's mane of gray hair. He was lying on one of the beds without his jacket and shoes, his shirt sleeves rolled up, shaking his head and smiling apologetically at the head of the department, Dr. Arnold, a quiet, rather modest man, who was explaining something on the EKG strips to Sir Geoffrey. "Where's Dori?" he asked in Hebrew as soon as he saw me. "She's waiting for you outside Sir Geoffrey's office," I said. "Should I run and get her?"

"There's no need for that. She'll only get frightened. I'll be out of here in a minute," replied Lazar, and added with a smile, "Just imagine, they wanted to keep me here!"

It turned out that when he had examined the dialysis machine Sir Geoffrey had offered him, he decided to check out various electrical apparatus attached to it too, such as the sphygmomanometer and the EKG, and out of curiosity asked to be connected to them. The random EKG showed runs of a rapid heartbeat, which Lazar had not felt at all because of their short duration. The technician immediately noticed the abnormality and hurried to call the cardiology resident, who examined the EKG and wanted to hospitalize Lazar on the spot. But Lazar, who felt no different from usual, and Sir Geoffrey, who suspected that something might not be adequately calibrated in the machine, which had not been used for a long time, asked for a repeat examination on another machine, and those results were better, if not completely normal. A more senior cardiologist who was summoned to examine Lazar suggested that the whole thing could be attributed to the excitement and stress of the trip. This cardiologist was of Pakistani origin—English physicians are far more cautious about confusing the body and the soul. At this stage Sir Geoffrey became fed up with the arguments and took Lazar to the emergency room, where he felt he could rely on the quiet, confident Dr. Arnold, who gave Lazar a thorough examination and decided that there may have been a mistake and that the EKG results were almost normal. Lazar's blood pressure, however, was very high, and he gave him a ten-milligram sublingual capsule of nifedipine, which immediately caused his blood pressure to drop. He also gave him medication for the next few days and instructed him to continue treatment when he got back to Israel. And then he turned to me and began explaining the EKG results, so that I would be able to translate them into Hebrew for the benefit of Lazar, whose visit he evidently saw me as responsible for, in some sense, since I was here at his initiative, after all.

"I didn't feel a thing. I didn't feel a thing, and I don't feel anything now either," Lazar apologized repeatedly to his wife for the little incident, and then turned to admire the baby and try to ingratiate himself with her. Shiva had been removed from her sling and was lying comfortably in the arms of the woman whom I suddenly wanted to drop to my knees before and beg for forgiveness for my earlier failure. Lazar indeed seemed perfectly healthy. And although I could have added something at this stage and shed some light on the medical picture with the little I had understood of Dr. Arnold's analysis of the EKG results, I decided not to add to the general confusion but to leave the Lazars with Sir Geoffrey, for I knew I would be seeing them again later, at the little reception the hospital had arranged for Lazar to recruit Jewish and non-Jewish supporters for the hospital in Israel. And that evening, in a black suit and a red tie, freshly washed and combed, Lazar looked healthy and fit. He spoke vigorously about the problems of our hospital in Tel Aviv, in a heavy Israeli accent and a basic but surprisingly effective English, which reminded me again of our trip together to India. Michaela, who was sitting next to me, listened to him with a mocking smile as she secretly breast-fed Shivi, for whom we were unable to find a baby-sitter.

Fourteen

My parents' visit to Glasgow, which my aunt was looking forward to so much, was somewhat spoiled by a severe cold that my
mother had probably caught from the baby. When my father told
me about it on the phone, I remembered that streptococci in
infants can cause a dangerous abscess in the throats of adults,
and I rebuked myself for not warning my mother to avoid close
contact with Shivi when she showed the first symptoms of her
cold. Although my aunt looked after my mother devotedly and
the two of them no doubt enjoyed reliving their childhood experiences, they were forced to stay at home while my father toured
the wild and beautiful landscapes of the north of Scotland and
the Isle of Skye with my uncle and my bachelor cousin, who was
a physician like me. Because of my mother's illness they had to
stay in Glasgow for an extra three days, and when I met them at
the train station and saw her pale face and heard her dry cough, I
decided that in spite of the help she and my father gave Michaela
with the baby, I should encourage them to return home as soon
as possible, because the damp London air would only make
things worse. From the station I drove them to their room, and
when I carried the suitcase in, I was hit by a wave of longing for
Dori, so much so that while they were hanging up their clothes I
slipped into the house itself and made my way along the route
which she had confidently charted, straight to the bedroom,
which was still illuminated by the pale ray of light coming
through the uncurtained corner of the window. I was startled to
see a large, handsome leather suitcase standing on the double
bed, covering the exact spot of my failure, which now, on second
thought, seemed to me not just human and forgivable but even
attractive in its velvety softness, until I felt a strange desire to fail
in the same way again. I hurried back to my parents, who disap-

proved strongly of my intrusion on the privacy of their anonymous landlords, who as far as they knew were expected back any day now. They're already back, I almost cried, but I controlled myself. "But what were you looking for?" my mother asked, looking very perturbed. "I see that you were here while we were away too." She had spotted the two cups I had set out for Dori and myself and immediately come to her own conclusions. I had given up trying to lie to my mother when I was a child, not only because she had infinite patience and cunning in getting at the truth, but also because I had been taught that the punishment for a lie was always worse than the punishment for the truth. I therefore avoided answering her question directly and began telling them in detail about the Lazars' visit. I described the little medical uproar over Lazar's EKG and told them about the evening for the Friends of the hospital, which had gone very well in spite of Lazar's elementary English, and in the end I told them of the cute little overall for Shiva and the promise he had given me that he would try to arrange a permanent half-time job for me at the hospital as an anesthetist.

"An anesthetist?" asked my father, without disguising his disappointment. "Only an anesthetist? And why only a half-time job?" he continued in the demanding tone he had adopted vis-à-vis Lazar ever since the trip to India. "Because for now that's all that's available," I replied with a smile. "Dr. Nakash is retiring next year, but I'm not getting his job."

"Dr. Nakash is already retiring?" my parents, who remembered him favorably from the wedding, exclaimed in surprise. I too had been surprised when I heard about his retirement. The darkness of his skin and the smooth freshness of his face had misled us about his real age. "But why did you have to bring Lazar and his wife to our room? I don't understand." My mother returned doggedly to the original subject of our conversation. I lowered my head slightly so she would not be able to look into my eyes and said, "Not both of them, only his wife. Lazar was busy checking out some equipment Sir Geoffrey wanted to offer our hospital, and in the meantime, so that she wouldn't be bored, I took his wife to see Shivi in the nursery, and then I showed her around the hospital, and after that I took her for a little walk, and I thought I might as well show her this great room that Michaela found for you. Maybe they'll want to rent it themselves one day." At this my mother pointed out that I had been wasting my time—the house was being sold in the summer, and the new owners would doubtless want to use all the rooms themselves. "So then I misled her," I said, trying on the green cardigan my father had brought me—for the first time in his life on his own initiative—as a souvenir from the Isle of Skye. My mother was silent. Although she was not satisfied by my explanation for Mrs. Lazar's visit to their room, what other explanation could she possibly imagine? She was not a worldly woman, and there was certainly nothing in her experience that might prompt her to guess the impossible truth. She gave up and sat there, sad and exhausted, coughing from time to time. I didn't like the sound of her cough, but since I had never dared to auscultate her heart or lungs with a stethoscope, I could only hope that the cough syrups my physician cousin had given her would help.

But they didn't, and for the last week of my parents' stay in London she refrained from taking the baby into her arms, which I could see was a real sacrifice for her, since Shivi had obviously captured her heart, and not only because she was her grand-daughter. Michaela, who could see my mother's sadness, tried to set her fears at rest. "Take her," she said persuasively. "You won't infect her with anything, don't worry. She's as healthy as an ox." But in spite of my mother's longing to rock the sweet little "ox" in her arms, she was careful not to come too close to her and only gave her sometimes to my father, who looked at the baby in his arms with an expression of playful reproof. We were all sorry for my mother, whose visit to England was ending so sadly. To make up for it to her, a few days before they were due to leave Michaela insisted on inviting them to an Indian night. Stephanie volunteered to baby-sit, and I was instructed to take a day off, for our night began at twilight with a lavish meal at an excellent and far from cheap Indian restaurant, after which we were to attend a performance by traveling troupes of singers, musicians, dancers, storytellers, and acrobats who had been gathered from all over India and brought to Europe by the Parisian Cirque du Soleil, which had taken upon itself the mission of fostering the art of the Third World, in the belief that it was important and worthy of support. This belief was shared by Michaela, who was very excited about the event, not only because of the enjoyment she expected to have herself but also because she was very curious to see how the rest of us would react. Since she had presented herself from the beginning as a missionary for India in the non-Indian world, she felt responsible for the evening's entertainment, which was quite expensive, since the tickets were priced as if it were a charity performance. But as far as the money was concerned, at least, nobody could object, since the whole evening was being paid for by Michaela.

I joined in the general spirit of generosity and treated everyone to drinks before the meal and a bottle of wine to accompany it, which turned out to be a very good thing, for the slightly inebriated state in which we all reached the performance helped us gain a deeper appreciation of things that at first glance, and in spite of our goodwill toward Michaela, seemed completely primitive. Take the opening "act": a half-naked fakir, his head covered with a mane of gleaming black hair which reached down to his chest, emerged from the audience, walked with slow, grave, thoughtful steps through the vast warehouse in the old port of London which had been converted into a hall for the performance, and climbed onto the huge, empty stage, which began to be suffused with the delicate shades of light of an Indian morning, just as I remembered them. He turned a little faucet, and in a profound silence began deliberately and at length to wash his hands, feet, and face. As he began to perform yoga exercises, facing the invisible sun, little troupes of performers entered one after the other, each dressed in a different color and carrying authentic folk instruments. Each group was composed of adults and children of various ages, who were referred to modestly in the program as "pupils," and who, despite the astonishing talents that a number of them displayed, were anxiously attentive throughout the evening to the subtle signals of their adult instructors. Although each troupe was allotted its own performance time and they were grouped separately in the corners of the vast stage, which was supposed to symbolize the map of India, they kept up a special kind of dialogue throughout the evening. While singers from one troupe performed, a child acrobat from another troupe would spring without warning from his place and for two or three minutes turn daring somersaults and cartwheels until he suddenly froze into a many-limbed contortion, like the statuette next to Michaela's bed or like some primeval animal that no longer exists in the world; then he would

unravel himself and go quietly back to his place. Or in the middle
of a dance by three little girls, the ancient magician would suddenly rise from the heights of his podium at the back of the stage,
throw some new magic into the air, and sink back to his seat. It
was evident that a Western hand had intervened in the direction
of the performance, in the attempt to create a meaningful tension
between all the elements, whose power and uniqueness did not
easily lend themselves to collaboration.

The primitiveness of these troupes was evident in the simple
movements of the dancers and in the musical instruments, which
consisted, for example, of two plain boards of wood banged together astonishingly fast, or chains of little bells tied around the
ankles and tinkling with the movements of the feet, or even of a
broken clay jar whose spout could be sucked to produce a sound
resembling the rumble of approaching thunder. It was precisely
this primitiveness that aroused a storm of emotion in Michaela.
She had expected something more stylish, adapted to the "limita-
tions" of the Western mentality, and here she was suddenly confronted, in the middle of gray London, with absolute authentic-
ity, of the kind she remembered so vividly from the dark alleys of
Calcutta or the train station of Bombay. Her cheeks burned, and
tears shone in her great eyes, as if she had discovered something
precious and intimate that had been lost to her and that she no
longer believed she would find again, although in her heart of
hearts she had not given up hoping. I noticed that in her excitement she kept losing her concentration, and her eyes would stray
from the stage to us, as if to test our reactions and see if in us too
the right soul was coming to life. And I think that we passed the
test; not only I, to whom the Indian dancers and singers seemed
to be reenacting the gradual and imperceptible process by which
I had fallen in love the previous winter, but even my father—who
my mother and I suspected would not have the patience for a
performance without a plot—appeared tense and moved by the
silent but clear and touching dialogue taking place between the
"pupils" and the "teachers," which began with acrobatic exercises agilely performed by a hefty Indian countrywoman and em-
ulated by a little girl and boy, who were not daunted by the most
amazing and dangerous tricks, and ended with a tall, gorgeous
Indian woman wrapped in a glittering sari, who told with growing vehemence a long, impassioned story, which according to the

program notes concerned the struggles between the gods. When the performance came to an end, the children in the audience were invited to join the Indian artists dancing and singing on the stage, and the stage was suddenly filled with rosy-cheeked, blond English children, who began to imitate the Indians' movements with such astonishing skill that it seemed as if they must be possessed by wandering Indian souls.

The audience rose to its feet in a storm of applause, including my shy father, who clapped enthusiastically while Michaela actually wept with joy and triumph at the success of her efforts to open closed hearts such as mine and my parents' to the Indian experience. She was still determined to return to India, and she was afraid that since it "seemed to me" that I had already been there, and it "seemed to me" that I had grasped the principle of India, I would have no motive to return. She would repeat this formula with utter seriousness, as if my trip to India hadn't been real, as if I hadn't sailed down the Ganges River in the evening to see the burning of the bodies next to the ghats of Varanasi, as if I hadn't gone into the temples of Bodhgaya and sat in the dark, rotting cinema in Calcutta. No, none of this counted with her, because it had all been secondary to the external aim of taking care of Einat and finding favor in the eyes of her parents. As long as I hadn't been to India for my own sake, to try to purify my soul, which was in need, like all souls, of purification, it was as if I had never been there at all. Although I had given her my promise, after proposing to her in the roadside diner next to Lydda airport, that I would not stop her from going back to India, she now feared the opposition of my parents, whom she had grown very fond of during their visit to London. She knew they would be scandalized if she took off alone for India, with the baby or without her, and it was therefore important to her for me to accompany her, for part of the time at least, perhaps in the context of observing the sidewalk doctors of Calcutta—or the "doctors of the forgotten," as the French called them—and thus take responsibility for her trip vis-à-vis my parents. On the face of things, it seemed strange that a woman as free and independent as Michaela, whose relations with her own parents were tenuous in the extreme, should worry about upsetting mine, but I was already aware that a bond had formed between my wife and my parents—especially my mother, who had apparently decided to

take her daughter-in-law under her wing in the wake of my cold-
ness, which she sensed in spite of my efforts to appear smiling
and attentive and to fulfill all my obligations, real or imaginary,
toward Michaela.

⟡

On the day of my sexual disgrace on the green floral bedspread,
in the light of the pale sunbeam piercing through the half-open
curtain, when I came home with Shivi in my arms, depressed and
upset by my failure and worried by the incident with Lazar's
heart, I felt that I had to compensate Michaela for my unfaithfulness to her. After telling her about the events of my day as she sat
serenely breast-feeding the baby, who had calmed down at last, I
suddenly knelt at her feet and put my head between her strong,
smooth legs and began kissing not only the inside of her thighs
but also the delicate, slightly parted lips of her vagina, which I
had not touched since I had sewed up the tears of the birth over
six weeks before. My lips and tongue now felt my skillful
stitches. Michaela was so surprised by this sudden two-pronged
attack on her privates, with me between her legs and Shivi at her
breast, that she began moaning deeply and uttering loud cries of
pleasure, which would no doubt have put my mother's mind at
rest if she had heard them, and allayed her suspicions about the
weakness of my love for my wife.

⟡

When we said good-bye to my parents in an uncharacteristically
emotional parting at Heathrow airport, my mother agreed, in
spite of her lingering cough, to kiss the baby, whom we had
brought along to soften the sadness of their departure from England. My mother also found a momentary lull in the excitement
to take me aside and praise her beloved daughter-in-law, and
warn me not to let her roam around London by herself too
much, since leaving her to her own devices in this way would
only accustom her to a kind of freedom that would be hard for
her to find on our return to Israel. "I've got no objections to your
going back to India at some future date, especially now that
Michaela has increased our appreciation for the country," she

added in her clear way, "but to go there now would be irresponsible and dangerous for the baby, who's too small even to be inoculated against all the dreadful diseases they've got there, some of which you've already seen for yourself. Wait a few years, until Shivi grows up, and after you've got full tenure at the hospital you can take an unpaid leave and go to India not just as a tourist but as a doctor, and do some good. And who knows, maybe your father and I will come and visit you there too."

On the way back from the airport, with Michaela driving and me hugging Shivi to my chest, we both felt an unexpected sadness at my parents' departure, as we would find it difficult now to manage without them. But while I was sure we would see them in four months' time in Israel, Michaela was cherishing hopes of extending our stay in London by at least one more year, not only because all the Indians she had discovered in various London suburbs helped alleviate her longings for the place itself but also because of the fact that dropping out of high school did not carry the same stigma in London as she felt it did in Israel. In London nobody made any demands on her. Just the opposite: her status had only been strengthened here. Friends of her youth from Israel who came to spend a week in London would call her up from the airport to get instructions about finding things in the city that ordinary tourists didn't even know existed. Sometimes the shoestring travelers among them would be invited to stay with us for a night or two, until they found a suitable place to live. Since I worked nights, it did not bother me to find sleeping figures curled up in the living room when I came home at dawn, because I knew that when I woke up in the middle of the day they would be gone. On one of these occasions Michaela told me, to my astonishment, that one of the sleeping figures I had encountered in the night was none other than Einat Lazar, who was on a one day stopover in London on her way to the United States. "How come you didn't wake me up before she left, so that I could say hello to her at least?" I exclaimed in angry surprise. "I'm sorry," she apologized, "I never thought that you were interested in Einat, or that you made any real contact with her when you were together in India. Besides, it seemed to me that the way you waited on her parents when they were here would be more than enough to promote your career interests in Israel." Naturally I sulked and protested at this cynical remark, but at the same time I was relieved to see that Michaela had no suspicions about my feelings for Lazar's wife, even though the sexual norms of the circles she moved in were broad-minded enough to encompass even the impossible passion that was still filling her husband's heart. But no, Michaela dismissed the Lazars as she now dismissed everything connected with the possibility of our return home. "What's the hurry?" she would repeatedly ask me. Israel wasn't running away, and if we stayed for one more year I would be able to accumulate a wealth of surgical experience, which if it didn't convince Hishin might convince the head of surgery in some other hospital to hire me. "We're happy here," she repeated, her great eyes shining imploringly. "There's nobody waiting for us in Israel except your parents, and to a certain extent mine, and we can go and visit them all next Christmas." But there was somebody else, and I was determined to make up for my failure with her.

I therefore insisted on returning on the original date, at the beginning of autumn, in spite of all Michaela's arguments, which actually made a lot of sense and which were seconded by Sir Geoffrey, who tried to change my mind and persuade me to stay another year. Sir Geoffrey had become fast friends with Michaela and often found time to drop in to the chapel when she was working there. He would sit next to the altar, on which Shivi reposed in her portable crib, and chat to Michaela as she swept and mopped the floor, about Israel, India, and the world at large. Although Michaela's English lacked even the rudiments of grammar, she had a great facility in picking up idioms, which she adroitly inserted into her uninhibited chatter, and she was universally praised for the richness of her vocabulary. It sometimes crossed my mind to wonder whether her relations with Sir Geoffrey were strictly platonic—a bizarre suspicion that was apparently founded on nothing more solid than my wish to balance my unfaithfulness to her in the past and the unfaithfulness I was contemplating in the future. Thus, when I came home from the hospital, I would sometimes imagine that I could detect Sir Geoffrey's smell in the house. But what exactly this smell was, I couldn't say, except that it was the smell of the hospital, which I myself carried on my body and in my soul. In any case, after Sir Geoffrey gave up trying to persuade me to stay for another year, he wrote to Lazar and asked him to send another doctor to replace me. When there was no reply, he phoned his office, but Lazar was never there. In the end Lazar returned his call, agreed to his request, and told him by the way that he was going in for a catheterization soon. He mentioned this not to complain or arouse Sir Geoffrey's pity, which would not have been at all in character, but simply to let him know that the accidental EKG reading in London was evidently not an aberration. In fact, Lazar wanted to tell Sir Geoffrey that the old machines he had offered were in good working condition, and that as a result of the discovery of the asymptomatic arrhythmia he had undergone a stress test in Israel, as well as a stress heart scan, whose poor results had led the doctors to recommend a catheterization, even though he did not complain of chest pains.

But Sir Geoffrey was not happy to hear that his hospital's old EKG machine had been right. He would have preferred it to be wrong. He told me about Lazar's impending catheterization with a grave face, which immediately caused me new anxiety. Even though catheterizations and coronary bypass surgery had by now become such daily occurrences that Hishin, who was not a cardiac surgeon, dismissed them with contempt, the fact that coronary heart disease was apparently associated with arrhythmias in London made the whole case more complicated. I tried to remember if Dr. Arnold had mentioned whether Lazar's was a ventricular or supraventricular arrhythmia, the ventricular being the more dangerous. Who did I think I was, I rebuked myself, trying to diagnose the heart disease of a person thousands of miles away, the director of a hospital who was surrounded by experts in their field and who certainly didn't need the help of a young resident like me with practically no experience in cardiology? But perhaps it was the thought that the incriminating EKG had taken place exactly at the time when one or two miles away I had been committing adultery with his wife that which gave rise to my anxiety and guilt, as if in some mysterious way my actions had caused his heart to fibrillate while at the same time he had made me fail. All these thoughts may have been legitimate in a young man embarking on the kind of adventures you read about in novels, but in my case they prompted me to take action. I went to a pay phone and put through a call to Lazar's office to ask how he was feeling and how the catheterization had gone. Lazar's loyal and devoted secretary was very moved by my interest, and she tried to answer as briefly and economically as possible in order to save me money. It appeared that the doctors thought that it was not a case of simple coronary disease, although they could not be sure until they had the results of the catheterization. The trouble was, complained the secretary, that too many doctors, friends and acquaintances, were interfering and giving advice, so it was a good thing that Professor Hishin was going to take charge. "But how come?" I cried in protest. "He's not a cardiac surgeon!"

"So what?" she answered. "He won't do the operation, but he'll decide on the surgeon, and naturally he'll supervise him during the surgery."

This report from Tel Aviv, instead of reassuring me, only increased my agitation. I say agitation and not anxiety because what was there to be anxious about? If they decided on bypass surgery—with one, two, or even three or more bypasses—this was a routine operation in good hands, with a mortality rate of less than one percent in healthy men who had never suffered a myocardial infarction. My inner agitation therefore stemmed from moral rather than medical concerns. Since we now had only one month left before our return, and Sir Geoffrey insisted that I take the last two weeks as vacation due to me, I decided to ask Michaela, as tactfully as I could, if we could go home two weeks earlier than planned so that I could be present at Lazar's surgery. At first she couldn't believe her ears, and demanded that I explain my reasons again and again. After she had begged me to extend our stay, if only by a month, I was now asking her to move the date up by two weeks. She was stunned. For the first time since our wedding one year before, we began a confrontation that almost turned into a real crisis. Although the argument was conducted in cold and ironic tones, it was fierce and even cruel. Because of the cooling off in our sexual relations, we did not try, as a more passionate pair might have, to take our revenge on each other in bed. Free of any overtones of sexual aggression or calculation, our argument might have seemed to an outside observer calm and civilized, if sharp and penetrating. I did not try to lie to Michaela and invent excuses for my wish to return, but spoke frankly about my concern for Lazar and my need to be there to support him and his wife during the surgery. Since I could not yet admit, even to myself, the true, deep source of my anxiety and agitation, in order to persuade Michaela I had to transfer part of my impossible love for Dori to Lazar himself, as if he had become a beloved friend during the trip to India, even a kind of father figure, to whom I owed my support. "You really think he'll be short of people to support him there? To the extent that you have to go running from England wagging your tail like a puppy?" said Michaela bitterly, narrowing her big eyes as if she could already see in the distance a miserable little dog slinking into the hospital gates and wagging his tail ingratiatingly. "You're right," I admitted frankly, "he won't be short of people there. But how can I explain it to you? I'm not going for his sake but for my own." In the end she grew tired of struggling against my obscure desires and vague arguments and cut short the argument with a surprising suggestion. If I was so desperate to attend Lazar's operation, I could go alone, and she would come later, on the date we had previously agreed on, or even, why not?—a sly, unfamiliar smile suddenly dawned on her face, while her eyes widened again in enjoyment—perhaps she would come later, for if I allowed myself to go home two weeks early, by the same logic, and according to the principles of justice and equality, she could allow herself to come two weeks late. "And the baby?" I asked immediately. "What about Shivi?"

"The baby?" she repeated thoughtfully, with the cunning smile still on her face. "Maybe she'll be the only one to go back on the original date. We'll divide Shivi between us. Fair's fair. I'll find someone here to take her back to Israel, and you'll have plenty of time to organize things for her there, or maybe you can give her to your mother for a while, to give me the pleasure of remaining completely on my own."

And so it was. But after I had advanced the date of my flight by two weeks and the travel agent had warned me that I wouldn't be able to change my mind, because all the flights at the beginning of September were already full, I came to my senses and asked myself why I was doing it. It was as if only then I discovered how warm and pleasant London was, and how full of friendly tourists, and realized how my eagerness to snatch as many opportunities as possible to operate on drunken Englishmen smashed up in road accidents or Asiatics taken sick in the middle of the night had prevented me from enjoying the wealth of cultural opportunities in the great city. Although tickets to the theater were usually beyond our means, there were plenty of other interesting events, such as lectures by famous people, including, to my surprise, Stephen Hawking, who was due to appear at a public question-and-answer session about his cosmological theory in the Barbican two days before my flight. And even though I knew that the hall would be packed with people, I decided to try and push my way in, in order to compensate myself for this premature return which I had imposed on myself in some uncontrollable impulse, as if something important were going to happen at Lazar's operation, or as if by actually looking inside his body I would be able to discover something about myself. I invited Michaela to join me at Hawking's lecture, even though the baby had been restless for the past week, as if the new tension between her mother and me was affecting her mood. But Michaela took no interest in the cosmos from a scientific point of view, only from an emotional one, and since there was a rehearsal of the neighborhood choir in which she sang on the same evening, she suggested that I take Shivi with me to the lecture, on the assumption that the polite British audience would show their consideration for someone, especially a man, carrying a baby and give me a seat. And indeed, little Shivi, strapped to my stomach in her sling, did help me to find a seat in the hall, which was full but not as overcrowded as I had imagined it would be.

Shivi was quiet for most of the evening. Perhaps because she spent so much time strapped to Michaela, who ran around all over with her, she saw her mother as part of herself, whereas I was a separate being, who aroused her interest and in whose arms she could also relax. So it wasn't on her account that I found the evening so frustrating. Although there were some bona fide astrophysicists in the hall, there were also many laymen, interested readers of *A Brief History of Time,* for whom the public evening was intended. But Professor Hawking's hollow, disjointed voice coming from the speech synthesizer mounted on his wheelchair was not as comprehensible to me as it was to the native English-speakers in the audience, and the ease with which I usually understood spoken English, especially after my year in London, failed me now, to my great disappointment. Maybe it wasn't only my trouble in understanding the artificial voice that prevented me from enjoying the evening, but also the fact that it was conducted for some reason in a general spirit of levity and impish humor full of puns and hidden meanings, as if the entire universe, with its black holes and big bang from which everything had begun, and the big crunch in which everything might end, including the poignant question of whether God had a choice when He created this universe, and therefore whether He exists at all—all the theories with which I had grappled that stormy winter day in my old Tel Aviv apartment, wearing my pajamas and waiting for Dori's mother to call me—had turned here in London, on this fine summer evening, into a matter for the amusement and diversion of the stiff-backed Englishman sitting next to me, glancing indulgently at the baby on my lap. And it may have been my serious and agitated state of mind, because of Lazar's impending heart surgery and Michaela's new hostility toward me, that prevented me from sitting back in my chair and trying to smile like everyone else. Accordingly, when Shivi, who had been lying quietly in my lap for a long time, suddenly burst into loud wails—which for some reason gave rise to much mirth in the audience, and led Hawking to make some witty remark—I rose to my feet and hurried out of the hall without having dared to ask a single shy question about the spirit shrinking the universe.

So in spite of all the surgical experience I had accumulated in the emergency room of St. Bernadine's, I left London in a mood of depression, to which was added the unexpected pain of leaving the baby, even though at the end of two weeks I would be seeing her again when I went to meet her at Lydda airport, where she would be accompanied by two English friends of Michaela's, who had gladly agreed to take care of her on the way, and two weeks after that I would be back at the airport again to meet Michaela. I myself was met at Ben Gurion by my friend Amnon, who had been living in our apartment all this time and who had decided when he heard that I was returning two weeks early to borrow a van from the company where he worked as a night watchman in order to help me with my suitcases and various other items of luggage, such as Shivi's crib. I was naturally delighted to see him, but I immediately noticed that he had gained weight and grown his hair and that his whole appearance was sloppy in the extreme. For his part, he was surprised to see that I was wearing a jacket and a tie, as if I had forgotten the end-of-summer heat. As we loaded my luggage into the old van, I noticed that he had adopted a new style of talking, cynical and almost nihilistic—Amnon, of all people, who had always been the most pure-hearted and naive of my friends. This worried me, and as we left the airport and began crawling along in a traffic jam on the Ayalon highway—which made me long for my defunct motorcycle—I began ruthlessly questioning him about the state of his doctoral thesis. He told me that he had changed the subject slightly, or rather expanded it in a more philosophical direction, and he now had an additional supervisor, from the institute for the philosophy of science. The confused ideas I had confided in him that night on our way back from Eyal's wedding were still floating around in his head. "You won't believe it, but I'm still thinking about that nonsense of yours and trying to make something of it from a scientific point of view," he said, with a smile but also a hint of resentment. I told him about the evening with Hawking, and he listened eagerly to every detail, laughing loudly when I repeated one or two witticisms that I had succeeded in grasping. He questioned me again about the reasons for my early return. He couldn't understand how I could leave Michaela, of whom he was so fond, alone in London. "Have you two had a fight?" he asked, with a mixture of concern and hope. When he heard my explanation he seemed surprised, but he accepted it, as I hoped everyone would, at face value. "Nice of you to be so worried about Lazar," he said, half seriously, half cynically. "If you keep on like this you'll end up as the hospital director yourself one day."

The apartment was not as neglected as I had feared, but since Amnon had taken the liberty of switching the furniture in the two rooms around, its whole nature had changed. The big double bed on which I had made love to Dori was now standing in the middle of the living room, covered with the same brown bedspread. Amnon had discovered that from this vantage point he could see the strip of sea beyond the chaotic roofs of Tel Aviv as he fell asleep, and argued that this improved the quality of his sleep. I had to share the apartment with him for a week, while he got himself settled in his new place, but since he worked nights we hardly saw each other, for after a brief and businesslike visit to my parents—from whom I received my father's old car—I spent all my time at the hospital, with the secret aim of getting myself into Lazar's open heart surgery, as a participant or an observer. To this end I went first to Dr. Nakash, to find out what he knew, even before I presented myself to Hishin or Lazar. It turned out that Nakash didn't know yet if he was going to be the head anesthetist at the operation, whose team was being assembled by Professor Hishin. Although the hospital had a cardiothoracic department, headed by Dr. Granoth, a man of about forty who had recently returned from a long fellowship in the United States and was regarded as a gifted surgeon, Hishin, and apparently also Levine, did not see him as the ideal man to perform Lazar's surgery. Perhaps they were afraid that if he operated on Lazar, he would gain the right to a special relationship with the director and threaten the exclusivity of their own deep friendship. In any case, they decided to invite a close friend from one of the big hospitals in Jerusalem, a man of their own age who had gone to medical school with them—Professor Adler, the bypass expert—to perform the operation under their supervision. At first Lazar protested at the idea of bringing in a surgeon from outside for him, as if he himself lacked confidence in the top cardiac surgeon of his own hospital. But Hishin and Levine, working together smoothly and secretly, succeeded in dragging things out and putting the operation off until Granoth would be at a conference in Europe, at which point they would be free to call in their friend from Jerusalem with no hard feelings.

Since the operation had been "stolen" from the cardiothoracic surgery department and transferred to Hishin's general surgery department, it was up to Hishin to select the members of the team. He and Levine, despite their senior positions, agreed to take a backseat to their Jerusalem friend and act as junior or even resident doctors. Naturally Hishin chose Nakash as the anesthetist, but since Lazar did not want to offend Dr. Yarden, the anesthetist from the cardiothoracic department, and insisted on including him in the team, he was invited to join Dr. Nakash, without anyone's specifying which of the two would be senior to the other. At the same time Nakash was given the right to choose an assistant. This was exactly what I had hoped for. It was the sixth day after my arrival in Israel. Up until then I had succeeded in avoiding Hishin, and with Lazar resting at home on the in-

structions of his two friends, I had not met him either. Since my
return to Israel I had spent all my time hanging around Dr.
Nakash, in my capacity as a future colleague in the anesthesiology department, but mainly in order to persuade him to choose
me as his assistant for Lazar's operation. But Nakash, who was
well aware of my professional competence, suddenly refused.
"What do you need it for?" he said in his dry, quiet way.
"There'll already be two anesthetists there, and you'll have
hardly anything to do. And Lazar is in a sense a friend of yours.
Why do you want to be there when his chest is being sawed
open?" But I insisted. Hishin and Levine were real friends, I said,
and they would not only be there during the operation but would
take an active part in cutting him up. And we all had to train
ourselves to maintain our composure in any situation that came
along, whoever the patient was. Dr. Nakash listened to my arguments, his little coal-black eyes glittering in his dark, almost bald
head and his pink tongue licking his lips, as was his habit when
he couldn't make up his mind about something. He was hesitant
because he really was fond of me, in his shy, reserved way. On
the one hand he didn't want to distress me by making me watch
my patron being cut open, but on the other he wanted to give me
what I so eagerly insisted I wanted. In the end he decided to
consult Hishin, who said at once, "Why not? What harm can
Benjy do there? The more the merrier, old friends and new!"

Maybe I was only projecting my own feverish excitement onto
my surroundings, but as the day of the operation neared—it was
set for ten days after my return from England—I sensed that the
whole hospital was in a state of suspense. But perhaps I was
simply not yet acclimated to the Israeli tension and tempo after a
year of long nights in the relative peace and quiet of the ancient
English hospital. After all, the kind of operation that Lazar was
to undergo had become a routine matter in the hospital, and
every week there were bypass operations and valve replacements
in at least ten patients, as well the correction of congenital heart
malformations in babies and premature infants. Nevertheless, I
could feel the suspense in the air. It seemed that the clerical staff,
who were closer in their daily work to the administrative director
and his secretaries than the medical staff, and who were the true
guardians of the spirit of the hospital, were the ones responsible
for spreading rumors and drumming up suspense. The fact that

the operation had been "stolen" from cardiac surgery and transferred to general surgery also added to the drama, and eventually
Professor Hishin decided to schedule the operation for the quieter afternoon and evening hours, so that when it was over he
and Levine would be available for the long hours of their friend's
recovery in intensive care. On the eve of the day of the operation
I decided to drop in to the administrative wing and say hello to
Lazar's secretary, whom I found sitting in her office next to Lazar's, all alone in the dark, deserted wing. When she saw me
standing in the door, she uttered a joyful cry and immediately
rose to her feet, offering me her rather ravaged face for a kiss. I
embraced her, kissed her warmly on the cheek, and sat down to
chat. First of all, she asked to see a picture of the baby and to
hear about England, but I soon turned the subject to Lazar, who
to my surprise was sitting in his office with his two chief assistants, clearing his desk before his hospitalization, which was
scheduled to begin that evening. She too was in a fever of excitement and anxiety about her boss's surgery, and her agitation
pleased me and made me feel that I was not alone in my feelings.
Suddenly she said, "Come and say hello to him, at least." I felt
myself trembling, and blurted out, "Why bother him now?" But
she insisted, knocked lightly on the dividing door, and opened, it
saying, "Dr. Rubin's back from England—he wants to say hello
to you before the operation."

Lazar was sitting with his two assistants next to his big desk.
He didn't seem to have lost any weight in the interim, but he did
look rather pale. With a quick, friendly gesture, he immediately
beckoned me to come closer and said in surprise, "But you were
supposed to come back on the fifteenth of the month. What
made you change your plans?" I was so astonished to see that
there was room in his bureaucratic brain for something as minor
as the date of my return from England, a resident of uncertain
status at the hospital like me, that I was unable to make up a lie
on the spot, and blushing furiously, in front of everybody, I
blurted out the truth, which burst out of me with uncontrollable
force: "I just wanted to be here for your operation. And tomorrow I'm going to help Dr. Nakash with the anesthesia." With
this I succeeded in surprising even the unsurprisable Lazar. "You
came back especially for my operation?" He turned in amazement to his assistants, who were also suitably surprised at my

generous concern. After he recovered he said, "I see that the entire medical staff of the hospital wants to be in on the show. It's a pity they're not operating on me on the stage of the big auditorium." He burst into loud laughter, in which he was joined by me and the two assistants, while his secretary only smiled quietly and somewhat mysteriously. But Lazar soon cut the entertainment short with a wave of his hand in my direction, and I left the room.

Before leaving Lazar's secretary, I asked her how Dori was taking it. As I had expected, she was tense and even more confused than her husband. And soon she would be arriving to spend the night with him in a special room which had been put at their disposal for the first night of his hospitalization. The thought that she couldn't spend even one night alone in her own home and her own bed sent a wave of pleasurable pity surging through me. I was so moved that for a moment I even thought of waiting for her right there in the office, but I was afraid that if she heard the reason for my return from England she would ask Professor Hishin to take me off the operating team, so I removed myself from the scene—but not entirely. In the depths of a side corridor I sat hidden in the growing darkness, waiting for the sound of her brisk, confident steps.

During the six hours of the operation she and her son sat in her husband's office, with his faithful secretary pressing food and drink on them all the time. The granny came from the old-age home to be with the family and give them the support of her natural optimism and experience of life. Hishin and Levine themselves took Lazar down from the ward to the surgical wing at two o'clock in the afternoon, apparently relishing the role of simple stretcher-bearers.

Although Lazar was already dazed and sedated, he had to smile weakly at the constant stream of jokes and witticisms showered on him by Hishin. Professor Levine, in contrast, looked grave and solemn. Perhaps he was silently brewing up the next psychotic outburst, which would save him from his anger. Because of the number of instruments crowding the room for heart operations, the initial "takeoff" was performed in a small induction room where Dr. Nakash and Dr. Yarden were already waiting for the hospital director, and I too was standing in a corner. Yes, it was already clear to me that this would be my place throughout the operation, standing in a remote corner, for apart from the two technicians in charge of the cardiopulmonary bypass machine, and the three nurses, and Professor Adler himself, who was still standing at the basin and washing his hands with compulsive thoroughness, Hishin and Levine would be watching every move with gimlet eyes. In an operation of this nature it was necessary to maintain close communication between the surgeon and the anesthetists, and after the "takeoff" they had been instructed to maintain the "flight" by using a Fentanyl drip, a short-action anesthetic that could be precisely controlled, as opposed to anesthetic gases, whose action was more general and erratic. Nakash just had time to explain this change of plan to me before Lazar was brought in, but the moment his bed was rolled into the room, I noticed something about Nakash that I had never seen before: his hands were trembling slightly. After he had begun to inject the cocktails he had prepared into the two intravenous lines in the wrist, when it was time to insert the tube into the lungs, I saw that he, the most skillful and precise of anesthetists, suddenly missed the exact spot where the tube should have been inserted, and the dazed but not yet unconscious Lazar jerked under Nakash's dark hand as if he wanted to bite it. Nakash went pale, and was obliged to apply force to Lazar's face in order to regain control. It then transpired that the tube had been inserted too deeply so that only one lung was being respirated, and it had to be brought up to above the bifurcation point so that both lungs would be respirated equally. In contrast to Nakash's uncharacteristic agitation, which heightened my anxiety, the second anesthetist, Dr. Yarden, experienced in cardiac surgery, behaved with calm and impeccable professionalism. He immediately bent over Lazar's right leg to insert an extra intravenous line in case there was an urgent need for blood or fluids if something went wrong. All of a sudden Lazar's genitals were exposed to everyone standing in the room. I bowed my head in a sorrowful gesture of respect, but I went on looking out of the corner of my eye at the administrative director's large penis lying there calmly and full of dignity, with no idea that one of the people present had dared to contend with him in the name of an impossible love. After first cleaning the area with Betadine, Dr. Yarden inserted the long, thin catheter into the penis; then he spread a blue, sterile towel over the entire area in order to protect it from the large syringe being inserted into the femoral vein to provide the extra intravenous line.

It was new to me that in complex surgery of this kind auxiliary sites were prepared in various places in the body in order to infuse emergency drugs and fluids. Nakash, who had completely recovered by now, prepared himself to insert a central venous line through the jugular vein into the right atrium of the heart. Hishin, who was watching all these preparations with interest, hesitantly offered to do it, but Nakash, intent on regaining his honor after the slip he had made with the tube, insisted on doing it himself and began to spread the blue sterile towels over the entire chest area of the patient, who was already being ventilated. He put on gloves and with the decisiveness of a surgeon inserted the venous line quickly and efficiently. Then he threw the blood-stained gloves into the bin and indicated to Hishin and Levine, who were watching him as fascinatedly as first-year medical students, that they could take Lazar into the operating room. "Come and hold the ambo, Benjy," Nakash called to me, the way you call to a child when you want to give him something to do, not only to let me know that he hadn't forgotten me but presumably also to justify my presence to the other anesthetist. I immediately began walking behind the bed as it was wheeled into the other room, squeezing the blue ambo between my hands to pump oxygen into Lazar's lungs until he was connected to the respirator next to the operating table. At this table the "ideal" surgeon, Professor Adler, was waiting, wrapped in a sterile gown and wearing a headlamp attached to an electric cable that supplied a special beam of light to help him see through the long, narrow binocular lenses he favored, perhaps because his specialty was correcting congenital heart defects in premature babies. In the argot of the surgical wing this specialty was considered the "penthouse" of cardiac surgery, and even a surgeon as arrogant as Hishin showed respect for the delicate skills required to correct the mistakes and negligence of the Creator Himself. But the patient lying in front of Professor Adler now was not a premature baby with a tiny defective heart but a large and important man, the administrative director of the hospital, who required a very routine operation of three bypasses, two venous and one of the left mammary artery. Thus Professor Hishin, who had apparently decided to do the job of the nurse as well, was swabbing his friend's naked body with Betadine of an almost yolkish consistency, in order to guarantee the sterility that was so essential, before proceeding to make an incision along his leg so the surgeon could extract the long vein which would be cut up to form the bypasses.

The proud and patronizing Professor Hishin, wonder of wonders, seemed not only willing but even happy to act as the junior surgeon to his Jerusalem friend, to whom he and Professor Levine referred by his nickname, Bouma. But Bouma himself didn't seem to be particularly happy with the two professors eager to carry out his orders. If anything, he seemed a little pressured by the crowded succession of tasks imposed on him here. In his department in Jerusalem a master surgeon like himself usually arrived two or three hours after the operation began, after the intensive preparatory work had already been done by assistants and residents while he watched and supervised them on a special television screen installed in his room. When he finally descended to the operating room, he found the chest already opened, the internal mammary artery detached and clamped at its lower end, and the vein destined to become an artery already immersed in its softening solution, ready for cutting. Accordingly, there was nothing left for a head surgeon like himself to do but clamp the aortic outlet from the heart and attach two suction tubes to the inferior vena cava, and then to connect the tubes of the cardiopulmonary bypass machine, say "Bypass on," and warn the two technicians to be ready to drive the entire blood circulation through the wheels of their machine, so that he could begin to work on the still, moist heart. But here he had to attend to the tedious work of preparation too, which there was no doubt he could do in the best possible way but which he hadn't done for a long time. Hishin, who was well aware of the situation, constantly tried to make jokes in order to make the time pass more pleasantly for his friend and prevent him from feeling too exploited. Was he also going to get a special fee from the Lazar family? I wondered. Or would he forgo his fee, like me, in favor of other benefits? To this question I could get no answer, certainly not from Professor Levine, who as an internist par excellence had taken up his position in a more spiritual place, next to the anesthetists. They had hung a sheet between Lazar's face and chest, taped his eyes, and immobilized his neck, gradually decreasing his blood pressure and maintaining a deep and stable sleep in anticipation of the most painful moment of all—the moment when the chest was opened with an electric saw, an operation performed by the Jerusalem wizard with such stunning speed and aplomb that Hishin could not resist a cry of "Bravo!" to which his old friend responded with a faint smile as he bent down to peer at the expressionless face of his patient, whose deep sleep, judging by the stability of the graphs and parameters flickering on the instruments around us, had not been disturbed by the terrible sawing.

Although I was standing very close to Professor Levine, he stubbornly ignored me, as if from the moment I had decided not to go back and be "examined" by him about what had happened in India he had written me off as a moral failure. But knowing as I did that in spite of his mental problems and other shortcomings he was still one of the most thoughtful and intelligent physicians in the hospital, I kept a close watch on his expression, which was stern and grave, as if what was going to happen here filled him with profound concern. Did all this concern stem from the fact that he was an internist, I asked myself, and it was a long time since he had seen the inside of an operating room? Maybe he was worried about his next psychiatric leave, which he was getting ready to take and which his friend Lazar would have to authorize after he woke up, a long time from now. Then the two anesthetists, Dr. Nakash and Dr. Yarden, began to get ready for the second "takeoff," this time into outer space: no longer detaching the body from the spirit, but detaching the body from itself and handing it over to the machine with its five pumps and its gleaming bronze wheels. The three technicians, who had inserted all the tubes into their proper places and who had up to now been running the machine on saline, were ready and eager to receive Lazar's blood from the head surgeon—who began muttering orders to them from behind his mask and binoculars, which all three of them repeated aloud—and to take over the functions of the heart and lungs: pumping, purifying, cleansing, oxygenating, and returning the blood to the body in the right amounts, together with cardioplegia to paralyze the heart. At this moment I saw Levine raising his eyes to the screen in the corner of the ceiling, where he could see Lazar's pulse monitor as a flat, even, horizontal line without any fluctuations, while the systolic and diastolic blood pressure values were equal owing to the uniform action of the silent machine. And then I felt that I could no longer control the excitement surging inside me, and not like an experienced resident doctor but like an inquisitive greenhorn, I tiptoed over to Hishin—who had just finished suturing Lazar's leg and was now standing on a little platform to watch the surgeon deftly implanting the bypasses, and who appeared very satisfied with the way things were going—and asked him if I could join him in watching the master surgeon at work so that I could learn something more, for who knew as well as Hishin did that even if I had been banished from surgery into the exile of anesthesiology, my true and eternal desire was and always would be to get my hands inside the human body? "Of course," he replied immediately and made room for me next to him, to give me a good vantage point. And then, in the middle of the steel frame holding the gaping chest like an open book, I suddenly saw, in its entirety, the still heart of Lazar, and for a moment the pain of my impossible love opposite the silenced love of this strong heart pierced my own.

Fifteen

Very close, yet far away, the brown statuette stands on the little table next to our bed. Can we address our complaints to it? What is it but a bit of inorganic matter torn from nature, lacking any will of its own, indifferent to its painstakingly sculpted human appearance? For the little clay hand flung out toward us is not only incapable of touching us, it can't even let itself drop back into place. And despite the faint, mysterious, Gioconda smile on its face, its threat is only the threat that we project on ourselves, now in the depths of the night, as we toss and turn between sheets that scratch our limbs. Why should the close and intimate statuette of death be any different from the glasses, for instance, or the wallet, or even the keys lying beside it? Nevertheless, in the thick of the night our hand gropes only for it, to take hold of the slender neck and throttle it in the darkness, for in the light of day we might be stopped by the expression on the painted face and the frozen aesthetic movement of the delicate, shapely limbs, which deceive us into thinking that it possesses life and a soul. And then, in the darkness, we hear the sound of the fall, for the groping hand has missed its mark, and as we get out of bed and crouch down to grope for the broken pieces, a sudden but absolute pain jolts our chest and stuns our heart, to tell us that death has indeed come to us and not to the pieces of clay strewn over the floor.

❧❀❧

Now that Lazar's "space flight" had begun, guided by the three agile, swarthy technicians in charge of the state-of-the-art cardio-pulmonary bypass machine—which was connected to many large and small plastic tubes coiling over the operating table and sucking the blood out of the square steel frame of the retractor as it slowly opened the heart like a book, and then streaming it back again—Nakash could leave his post at Lazar's head and go out of the room to pour himself a cup of strong coffee from his private thermos. Although I was ready for a cup of the excellent coffee his wife made for him every morning myself, I couldn't tear myself away, even though Dr. Yarden's supervision of the patient's anesthesia was more than adequate, especially since the respirator was still. Lazar's heart as well as his lungs were paralyzed, and the rate of cleansed and oxygenated blood being pumped into the body and the brain was being determined by the instructions of the surgeon, who kept throwing changing orders over his shoulder. The three technicians would repeat them after him, like a crew of gunners making sure that no fatal misunderstanding should occur. The blood in the tubes flowed freely, with no danger of clotting, thanks to a continuous drip of Heparin, which neutralized the natural clotting factors and ensured an unimpeded flow between the turning wheels. The head of the technical crew enjoyed explaining to me how he pampered the bloodstream entrusted to his charge, warming and cooling it as required, as if it were an independent, sentient being that had to be soothed by an alkaline solution to neutralize the strong acidity produced by the trauma of being suddenly removed from the warmth of the human body and placed into the movement of the alien machine. When Dr. Yarden saw that Nakash wasn't coming back immediately, he took a pack of cigarettes out of his pocket and beckoned me to approach the silent anesthesia machine, which didn't really need an anesthetist but only a pair of eyes to watch the controlled drip of fentanyl and curare, which maintained the relaxation of the muscles and the analgesia. Levine too left the room, and next to the operating table there were now only three doctors, Dr. Adler, Professor Hishin, and myself. I took two footstools and placed one on top of the other so I could raise myself above the net protecting Lazar's head, to give myself a better vantage point from which to look down directly at the implanting of the bypasses. This was now being purposefully performed by Dr. Adler, with the assistance of Hishin, who played the double role of pupil to his friend, addressing various technical questions to him, and teacher to me, generously passing on tidbits of clinical diagnosis or anatomical observations to satisfy the inquisitive gleam in my eye and to ensure that my presence, the reason for which was still not clear to him, would at least seem justified.

That night as I lay in bed, before burying my face in the pillow and trying to fall asleep, I reviewed the six hours of the operation in my mind's eye—Lazar's naked genitals, his exposed heart reposing within the walls of his open chest, the blood coursing through the dozens of crisscrossing tubes, the silent bronze wheels of the cardiopulmonary bypass machine—and everything that had happened there seemed to me more harmonious, calm, and sure than I could possibly have imagined. Including the rather dramatic moment when the blood was returned to the body and Lazar's heart refused to return to its sinus rhythm, a refusal that led Professor Adler to pull two electrodes from the defibrillator, place them on either side of the recalcitrant heart, and give it a few short electric shocks to start it and return it to the right rhythm, which appeared on the screen of the big monitor. Hishin and Levine had been right, I thought, lying in the dark in my bed, to bring in the Jerusalem master, who had worked with awe-inspiring competence and quiet confidence, and who had also dismissed with a reassuring gesture the fears I had dared to express when the operation was over. Although he was so tired after standing on his feet for six hours that he asked the nurse to help him divest himself of all the stuff encumbering him—the mask, the gloves, the headlamp, the sterile cap and gown—he seemed interested and willing to listen, with the patience of a wise physician who is never bored by anything to do with the human body. But Levine, who was still hostile toward me, broke in rudely to point out a mistake in one of the assumptions I had made, and Professor Adler, who had no desire to get involved in an argument, cut the discussion short, murmuring something reassuring about Lazar's heart, and went out with Hishin to inform Lazar's wife and the other members of the family of the success of the operation.

❧

I did not join the convoy taking the sleeping and bandaged Lazar up to the intensive care unit that had been prepared for him in Hishin's department. Hishin had also turned his own office into an improvised bedroom for Lazar's wife, who intended to spend the night there. Now that the operation was over and I had seen what I wanted to see and felt what I wanted to feel, all I wanted was to be by myself. But since it was already past one o'clock in the morning and the rates for overseas calls were particularly low, I decided to phone Michaela to make the final arrangements for Shivi's return in two days, and at the same time to tell her how smoothly Lazar's surgery had gone and how admirably the Jerusalem wizard had performed and how I did not regret my early return from London, even though I hadn't been needed there at all. But in spite of the lateness of the hour—eleven o'clock in London—Michaela was not at home. I found it strange and also annoying that she was prepared to drag the baby around London in buses at this hour of the night.

We had sold our little car, after strenuous efforts, to one of the nurses at the hospital, in order to pay for our plane tickets. Mine and Michaela's, that is, for Shivi flew home free, on the ticket of one of the two sweet young English girls who amused themselves with her on the way. When I met them at the airport, it turned out that Michaela had promised them, without my knowledge, that they could stay in our apartment for their first few days in Israel. I was furious. Only a few days before I had finally succeeded in getting rid of Amnon and all his possessions, and now I had two new guests on my hands—an intolerable nuisance when I was still in a state of inner turmoil stemming from Lazar's operation. Although the operation had taken place forty-eight hours earlier, I had not yet visited Lazar in the special room set aside in Hishin's department, for fear that Dori, or anyone else, would notice the storm raging inside me.

However, I had no option but to keep Michaela's promise, and I sullenly gave the two English girls the key, wrote the address down clearly in both languages, and warned them to be careful in the apartment, since it did not belong to me. I also asked them not to stay longer than one or two days. "You won't want to hang around in Tel Aviv anyway," I warned them gloomily. "It's a filthy place. Go down to the desert, take a bus to Eilat—that's where you'll find the real pleasures Israel has to offer." I strapped Shiva into the special seat I had bought and installed in my father's car, and with her sitting next to me but facing in the opposite direction, I drove to Jerusalem to leave her for seven days with my mother, who had taken a week's vacation as an advance on her next year's leave, since she had already used up all her vacation on the trip to England. On the way to Jerusalem Shivi gave me an inquiring look, as if trying to remember who I was. She was still too young to remember me clearly after an absence of two weeks, but she was old enough not to have forgotten me entirely. And thus, on the border between memory and forgetfulness, she stared at me suspiciously, but so sweetly that I couldn't resist bending down to kiss her whenever traffic permitted, while keeping up a stream of chatter, telling her about my plans for the future and sometimes even bursting into forgotten old songs, to amuse her and also to raise my own spirits. Ever since Lazar's surgery I had been confused, as if the bypasses planted in his heart had somehow wound their way into mine as well, and sometimes I would even feel a sharp pain in my chest, as if it too had been split open with an electric saw.

But when I reached my parents' home in Jerusalem, I immediately stopped concentrating on my inner sensations in order to be free to give all my attention to their concerns. In spite of their joy at seeing their granddaughter again, they were worried about their ability to take care of her for a week, especially my mother, who was usually so calm and composed about everything. It was clear that she was full of secret resentment against Michaela, and even suspected that she would not return when she had promised to. But I reassured her. Michaela always kept her promises, and since it was only because of my insistence that she had agreed against her will to return to Israel instead of extending our stay in London, I could hardly object if she permitted herself one last little fling: two weeks on her own to enjoy her liberty and independence to the fullest. After putting Shivi down in the crib my father had borrowed from a young colleague at his office and giving my parents detailed instructions about feeding and bathing her, as well as telling them a little about Lazar's successful surgery and my own prospects at the hospital, I went to bed early and immediately fell into a deep sleep, which for some reason was so haunted by recurrent nightmares that I got up before dawn, said a whispered good-bye, and set out for the return journey to Tel Aviv and to my first day of work at the hospital as a permanent, albeit half-time, member of the medical staff.

Since I had given the keys to the English girls, I was forced to stand outside banging on the door of the apartment until one of them, in short pants and a blouse that barely covered her breasts, woke up and let me in. They had misunderstood my instructions and unrolled their sleeping bags in the bedroom instead of the living room, but apart from this mistake I saw that they had not disturbed anything in the apartment and had left the kitchen clean and tidy. Nevertheless, I urged them again to go down to the desert and enjoy an experience which they could never have in England. At close quarters, I saw that they were not as young as I had imagined them to be at the airport. They were my age, and in the spare, athletic build of their bodies they reminded me of Michaela, whose depression when she landed in Israel in two weeks' time I could already imagine. I drove to the hospital, and since I didn't yet have a parking space, I had to park a long way off and walk. Although autumn had officially begun, the morning light was still so bright that I had to put on my sunglasses so my eyes could make the transition from English to Israeli light. First I went to the anesthesiology department, to introduce myself to its head, an energetic middle-aged woman with a sharp, ironic tongue, whom Lazar had informed of my appointment a week before and who was ready, although the official confirmation had not yet arrived, to fit me into the night shifts in the operating rooms. Strange, I thought, that here too I was beginning with night duty, as in London, but I accepted her offer, not only to cut my contact with the English girls down to a minimum but also to enable me to keep an eye on Lazar and perhaps alleviate his loneliness. In the cafeteria I came across Nakash and asked him about Lazar. His recovery was proceeding as expected. He had already been disconnected from most of the equipment and transferred to the ninth floor, to a private room in Levine's department, where Levine could also take an active part in treating him. In three or four days' time he would be able to go home. There you are, I said to myself, what were you so frightened of? But I refrained from going up to visit him, knowing that the room would be crowded with visitors from the hospital and from outside. I decided to postpone my visit until the evening, before my night shift began.

I returned to the apartment in the hope of finding my two visitors already gone, but it seemed that they had just woken up,

and, wearing bathrobes over their bathing suits, they asked me
the way to the beach and invited me to go with them. I was
about to refuse, but suddenly I said to myself, Why not? Perhaps
a soothing dip in the sea was just what I needed to banish the
oppression from my heart. I began to look for my trunks, which I
had not worn for ages, and which, judging by the amused looks
of the English girls, had indeed gone out of fashion long ago. It
was a strange feeling to find myself walking down the busy Tel
Aviv street in the middle of the day in a pair of trunks and a light
summer shirt, like a teenager, in the company of these two
strange English girls, who turned out to be cousins who liked
traveling the world together. "Have you been to India?" I asked.
No, they hadn't been to India yet. I immediately urged them to
go. Yes, they heard praises of India everywhere, including, of
course, from Michaela. In fact, they were considering joining us
when we went, to help us look after dear little Shivi. We entered
the sea, which was warm and gentle, without any waves. For a
moment the smell of the water reminded me of the smell of the
amniotic fluid in the London apartment, perhaps because there
was an amniotic element in the algae constantly breaking up in
the water. But the smell didn't stop me from enjoying diving into
the water and racing one of the English girls. Now I began to feel
lighter, as if whatever had been weighing on me since Lazar's
operation had been swallowed up and dissolved inside me. After
emerging from the sea and drying myself, I invited the English
girls to join me for hot corn on the cob. On the beach I found
Amnon playing ball with an intelligent-looking boy. "Now I
know why your thesis is stuck," I couldn't help saying, scolding
him, but I immediately regretted it. However, he did not seem
hurt by my remark, and he was very interested in the two girls.
"Ah," he said with a bitter laugh, "now I know why you were in
such a hurry to get me out of the apartment." I had a hard time
convincing him that they had descended on me without any
warning, and feeling the need to make some kind of gesture, I
didn't object when he suggested returning to the apartment with
us. It was now four o'clock in the afternoon, and Amnon and the
girls, still in their swimsuits, began putting together an improvised meal. "I'm sorry, but tomorrow you'll have to leave the
apartment," I warned the girls again, this time without mentioning the desert. "Because it looks as if I'm going to bring the baby

back tomorrow, and she needs peace and quiet," I suddenly added, in order to provide a logical-sounding pretext for the evacuation order. Amnon immediately invited them to go and stay with him, and they accepted the invitation gladly. They didn't look like promiscuous women to me, but perhaps their blood relationship gave them a boldness and confidence to embark on secret adventures together that ordinary girlfriends wouldn't have had. They weren't pretty, even though their bodies were smooth and appealing. Taken separately, neither of them seemed particularly attractive, not even to a man like me, who hadn't slept with his wife for over two weeks now, but the sudden thought that perhaps Amnon would go to bed with both of them at once immediately aroused me, even though the fantasy of making love to two women at once was not among my favorites.

I called my parents to hear how they were getting on with Shivi. Everything was going smoothly, although my father had had to come home early from work to help my mother, who sounded, despite her calm, reassuring voice, rather strained. I had already noticed that ever since the severe influenza she had come down with in Scotland, she seemed frailer, and I promised myself that as soon as Lazar recovered and Michaela returned to Israel, I would go up to Jerusalem for a day or two to check up on her health. In any case, my parents did not disguise their profound enjoyment of their granddaughter, who had already demonstrated a number of cute tricks. I said good-bye to Amnon and the two English girls, who were still eating the meal they had prepared, and set off for the hospital. It was six o'clock. First I went to intensive care unit to announce my arrival. I took my beeper and turned it on, and then I went up to the ninth floor to internal medicine to look for Lazar. He wasn't hard to find. At the end of the corridor I saw a few doctors and members of the administrative staff, who evidently couldn't wait to visit the recovering director, and peals of happy laughter, immediately recognizable as Dori's, rang out in the distance. I turned back, not wanting to be part of the crowd, and only returned two hours later. Now it was quieter. Dori was sitting on a bench in the corridor. Their son was sitting on one side of her, and her mother on the other.

I greeted them all and asked how the patient was feeling. Dori went very red and for a moment she was speechless, as if she were in love with me too, but the granny, who was delighted to see me, said that her son-in-law was doing well, and Professor Hishin, who had changed his dressings in the morning, was very pleased with the rate of his recovery. Dori regained her composure and smiled brightly and introduced her son to me. He nodded indifferently, no doubt sick and tired of the constant introductions to the stream of visitors making the pilgrimage to the ninth floor. I reminded him that we had already met for a moment almost two years before, when I had gone to their house on that first evening to talk about the trip to India. He raised his eyes to examine me. "Yes, it's the famous Dr. Rubin," repeated his mother, avoiding the use of my first name. They were all waiting outside, it seemed, because Professor Levine was examining the patient and changing his dressings. Although I knew that my intrusion would annoy Levine, I couldn't resist the opportunity to get a look at the place where I had seen the chest being rapidly sawed open, and I knocked lightly on the door and went inside. Professor Levine, who was busy smearing iodine on the long line of brown stitches running down Lazar's chest, glared at me angrily as I entered the room, which surprised me with its size, the stunning view from its window, and the multitude of flowers filling it. But the warmth of Lazar's greeting prevented him from objecting aloud to my entry. "Where did you disappear to?" cried Lazar—his eternal cry to me, which had first been sounded in India, although it was they, not I, who had disappeared in the train station at New Delhi. "I'm right here," I said with a smile, "I've been here all the time." I asked him how he was feeling and he immediately said that he was feeling fine, as if he wanted to please me too, along with the rest of the doctors who had participated in his operation, at which for some reason he insisted on thinking I had played an active role. Levine, who had finished smearing the stitches with ointment, now began to bandage the wound with the unpracticed hands of the head of an internal medicine department. I picked up the patient's charts, which were pinned together at the foot of the bed, and looked at the temperature, the blood pressure, the EKG, and the results of the blood and urine tests which had been run on Lazar over the past few days. Maybe the fact that I had taken part in the surgery gave me the nerve to draw Levine's attention to the acute irregularities to be seen in a number of the EKG strips, which showed premature ventricular beats, sometimes even in couplets or triplets, whose origin was unclear to me. "Isn't there a danger of ventricular tachycardia here?" I asked. At first Levine tried to ignore my question, but since I stubbornly repeated it, he decided to say something, perhaps in order not to worry Lazar. "Yes, Dr. Rubin," he said rapidly and rudely. "We saw that too. We're not blind, you know, and we're perfectly capable of drawing our own conclusions. We don't need every doctor in the hospital sticking his nose in here, even if the patient is the director. No doubt you have work to do elsewhere. Why don't you get back to it and let us worry about Mr. Lazar?"

But I couldn't stop worrying, and four hours later, late at night, I knew that I would have no rest until I went up again to the ninth floor, already in darkness except for the nurses' station, which, in my doctor's gown, I had no problems passing. I stopped outside the closed door of Lazar's room and listened, but all I could hear was the television. I knocked lightly, careful not to burst in without an invitation. But the fact that there was no answer did not make me turn away and only increased my anxiety. I opened the door. Apart from the moonlight pouring into the room through the open window and the glare of the television, the room was in darkness. Dori was curled up in a big armchair, sleeping with her legs tucked up underneath her, one hand clutching her glasses and the other holding the outstretched hand of Lazar, whose little eyes were fixed on the television suspended from the ceiling next to the screen of his monitor, which was turned off. Ever since the trip to India, when I had first become aware of the strength of the bond between them, I had not felt the unique nature of their intimacy so strongly. After a whole day at his side, she couldn't leave him to his own devices for a while and go home to be by herself. Suddenly I felt a shiver of pain running through me for the way I had betrayed him. And I wanted to take a vow that after Lazar recovered I would never try to touch her again, not even if she asked me. If it really was an impossible love, then everything about it should be impossible and unreal. Lazar regarded my entrance in the dead of night as completely natural, and he greeted me with a friendly wave. I went up to him, and since his eyes were slightly glittering and his cheeks flushed, I put out my hand instinctively to feel his forehead, which he offered me obediently, as if from the moment he had crossed the lines in his hospital he had become the patient of every nurse and doctor in it, who were all at liberty to touch him as much as they liked. He had a slight temperature, which was natural and expected after the brutal shock his whole system had suffered, but which might also be interpreted as a warning sign. He told me that the nurse had discovered the fact that he was febrile a short time before but had decided to wait until morning to consult Professor Levine. "I'll get you a pill to bring your temperature down," I said simply. Because Lazar had been "stolen" from cardiac surgery and taken under the personal wings of the heads of two different and even contradictory departments, and the master surgeon who had operated on him had disappeared into thin air, he was essentially abandoned in this attractive private room, which was still full of the smell of flowers although all the vases had been removed for the night. Our whispers had awakened Dori, who opened her lovely eyes, which immediately filled with her brilliant, happy smile as if nothing untoward had happened in her world. "Well, Benjy, how does he look to you?" she asked, and it was hard to tell if she was asking me as a physician or a friend. "He looks fine," I said with a smile. "But with all these important professors looking after him, I'm afraid he might get a little lost between them," I added, and immediately regretted it, because I saw that her anxiety for him was so great that any expression of doubt or concern coming from outside could upset her equilibrium. "What do you mean?" she asked. "Nothing, really," I said, trying to reassure her, "but I just dropped in by chance and discovered that he has a temperature, and it turns out that nobody's given him a pill to bring it down because they don't want to wake Professor Levine, as if no other doctor is allowed to touch him."

"But why? Can't you give him a pill?" she asked with a naïveté that touched my heart, which was still excited by the sight of her eyes—eyes that I had seen without their glasses only when I had made love to her. "Of course," I said confidently. "Why not? Even if it's only a slight temperature, why should he suffer?"

But I was not worried about Lazar's temperature. My thoughts turned stubbornly around the possibility of ventricular tachycardia, which could suddenly turn into ventricular fibrillation. The charts at the foot of Lazar's bed contained the records of a considerable number of EKGs that had been done since his operation. I picked them up to examine them in the full moonlight of the autumn night and immediately noticed longer runs of a rapid, ectopic beat, five to six in a row, whose shape was obviously different from the regular and dominant sinus rhythm, which made me think they were of ventricular origin. Imperfect as it was, my knowledge of cardiology was enough to arouse my fears and give me a powerful urge to photograph these EKG strips and take them with me to the library tomorrow to study them, or even to go up to Jerusalem after my night shift and show them to Professor Adler, to hear what the master had to say. Perhaps for the first time since I had begun work at the hospital, I felt so powerfully convinced of something that it was only my youth and inexperience that prevented me from getting in touch with Professor Hishin right then, in the middle of the night, and expounding my interpretation of the data to him, an interpretation that was so obviously right that only it could save us from the catastrophe threatening to descend. But I had left my post in the emergency room for some time and was concerned that I might have been missed. I went to the nurses' station at the end of the corridor and signed an order for two paracetamols for Lazar and one 5 milligram of Valium for his wife, and after seeing them swallow the pills I left them with the promise to come again tomorrow afternoon, because I knew that in spite of the confidence they felt in their professor friends in the hospital, they had also developed a kind of hidden dependency on the young doctor who had accompanied them to India.

Therefore, after waking up late the next morning, I did not drive to Jerusalem as I had promised to help my parents with Shivi, who, although my mother assured me she had been no trouble at all and was giving them a lot of joy, was still a handful for two older people to look after by themselves. I phoned them and apologized profusely. And since I didn't know how to explain, even to myself, the nagging anxiety I felt about Lazar and the need I felt to stay close to the hospital, and I didn't want to lie to them, I told them the truth without going into any medical details, and these two rational and realistic people had to be content with mysterious premonitions and to rely on the trust that they were accustomed to having in me. Six hours before my shift began I was already back at the hospital, where I went to the library to consult the EKG and arrhythmia teaching manuals used by nurses in cardiac intensive care courses. But no clear conclusions emerged from my reading. It appeared that there were atrial beats which could look like ventricular beats. The uncertainty only increased my anxiety, whose source was now less clear than ever. I went to the coronary intensive care unit and looked at the EKG strips of patients with acute myocardial infarction taken over the past few hours, and when there was a quiet moment I asked the doctor in charge to show me EKGs showing clear runs of ventricular tachycardia. Equipped with these strips, I went up to the ninth floor to see how Lazar was doing. In the cafeteria I had already heard from two psychiatrists who had visited him that morning that he looked and acted "like a man-eating tiger," and that tomorrow or the next day he would probably be sent home, and the week after that he would presumably be back in his executive chair with his hands once again on the reins.

The two psychiatrists spoke about him with anger and bitterness, for Lazar had turned their well-meaning visit into a power struggle over his new initiative to do away with the psychiatric department in the hospital and turn it into an outpatient clinic— a community mental health service. "Let them take their mental illnesses somewhere else, we don't need them here," he said, smiling from his bed, when I told him about the psychiatrists' angry reaction to his ideas for their department. The private room, which I had last seen bathed in moonlight, full of the intoxicating scent of flowers, had already been transformed into a kind of office, with two telephones on the floor and a pile of files next to his food tray. Levine was still trying to keep the stream of visitors at bay, but Hishin, who was standing next to Lazar's bed as large as life and twice as tall, was perfectly satisfied with the new energy displayed by his patient. Lazar's temperature had gone down, the bandages had been removed, and through the hospital pajamas the straight row of neat stitches was clearly visible. Dori was sitting in the corner, listening smilingly to Lazar's secretary's chatter. She was heavily made up, wearing an elegant suit and high heels; it seemed that she had already spent a few hours in her office and had also done some shopping, judging by the plastic bags heaped at her crossed feet. I suddenly turned to her, rudely interrupting the secretary. "Are you going to spend the night here again?" She nodded her head in surprise, as if I should know that she preferred the discomfort of sleeping in an armchair to being separated from her husband and spending a lonely night in her bed. A consoling thought crossed my mind, light as the touch of a feather. In spite of everything, there had not yet been one ugly moment between us. And a powerful wave of love swept over me for this middle-aged woman, who boldly took out a cigarette and lit it in the closed room, to the horror of Professor Levine, who came into the room at that moment and held out both his hands to her in an imploring gesture, to stop her from poisoning us all.

❧❦❧

Was it possible that in the depths of my heart I wished for Lazar's death? This secret thought, which held a certain sweetness, and which had been stubbornly simmering inside me ever since the flight home from Rome, now seized hold of me again and forced me to go out to the little balcony and bend over the railing as if I wanted to spew it out of me once and for all. Levine drew Hishin onto the balcony to show him the results of some tests which had just arrived, including the left ventricular function using a technetium radioactive scan. Hishin took off his glasses and ran his eyes rapidly over the results. He looked completely calm. "It's so predictable," I heard him exclaim in his loud, confident voice. "You don't need to be a cardiac surgeon to know that the heart muscle is still stunned from the surgery and the prolonged use of the cardiopulmonary bypass machine. That explains the poor function." But Levine, whose voice was too low for me to hear his arguments, appeared to be insisting on something. Hishin listened attentively, but without appearing to be convinced. "All right," he said, "we'll keep him until the end of the week and repeat all the tests in ten days' time. And if the cardiac function is still unsatisfactory, we'll take him to Jerusalem to Bouma and see what he has to say." Levine nodded, but he didn't seem satisfied. Suddenly he fixed his blue eyes on me standing in the corner of the balcony, the EKG strips in my hand, and trying not to look as if I were dying to intervene in their conversation. Levine beckoned me to approach. I took a few steps, and to my astonishment he touched my arm in a friendly gesture, and in his deep, serious voice, his eyes on the strips in my hand, he said to Hishin, "Listen to what Dr. Rubin has to say, Yosef. You were the one who was so impressed with him that you chose him out of all the residents in the hospital to go to India. Tell Professor Hishin what you think about Lazar's arrhythmia." I was so overwhelmed by Levine's gentle touch on my arm and by the friendly tone in which he spoke that at first I was confused and stammered incoherently, but gradually I organized my thoughts and even added a few new elements I had picked up a couple of hours before in the coronary intensive care unit. Hishin listened to me with a paternal smile, but he seemed to be enjoying the vigor with which I expounded my views rather than following what I had to say. "And you let a resident like Benjy slip through your fingers?" he said to Levine when I had concluded my argument. "It wasn't up to me," said Levine in tone of real regret. "It was up to him." And with this the medical debate ended before it had even begun, just as Lazar's two children, Einat and the boy, now a soldier in uniform, entered the room and were enthusiastically greeted by all those present.

It turned out that Einat, who hugged and kissed her father with a certain hesitation, had just arrived from the United States, and her brother had met her at the airport. As she turned to her mother, who came up to hug her, she caught sight of me and waved. I shook my finger at her in mock reprimand. "You sleep at our house and leave without even saying good-bye?" She blushed, laughing and apologetic, and then explained to her parents how rushed she had been during her short stopover in London. I felt surrounded by warmth. In the room crowded with the Lazars' family and friends, I felt as if I were planted deeply among them. The unexpected reconciliation with Professor Levine added to my joy. But I didn't have much time to bask in these good feelings, for everyone was in a hurry to go somewhere except Einat, especially the rather sad and alienated son, who kept his distance from me. He had to get back to his base, and his mother had to drive him to the bus station and then rush home to prepare herself for another night at the hospital with her husband. Now she stood next to his bed to say good-bye and make various arrangements, and as she patted her hair lightly into place and asked him what to take home and what to bring back with her, I noticed that his hand, still blue from the hematoma caused by the infusion needles, was groping for hers, which was stroking his hair, both in order to stop her from caressing him in public and to draw it to his chest, perhaps to hint at a new, nagging pain which he was loath to trouble his doctor friends with.

And so we all parted from the administrative director except for Einat, who looked exhausted from the flight but insisted on believing, according to the biological clock inside her, that it was still morning. We went out into the corridor, where a clear and wonderful light poured through the big ninth-floor windows directly from the sea, streaming toward us over the roofs of the houses—the soft, pink autumn light of the afternoon hours, when the whole hospital was taken over by the visitors who crowded the elevators and flooded the rooms of the wards, who used the flowers, the fruit, the evening papers, and the boxes of chocolate which they strewed about them to banish the medical staff with their instruments and medications and instill new hope into the hearts of the sick people huddling beneath their blankets. Although Dori had her son on one side of her and her husband's secretary on the other, I still hoped that I would be able to snatch a word or two with her in private, but I was prevented from doing so by Hishin. I had sensed that he wanted to talk to me in Lazar's room, as if the information I had gathered and expounded to him and Levine on the balcony about the irregularities in the EKG had led him to believe that I had succeeded in finding a new lead to the wayward heart of Lazar, which apparently had him worried as well. Perhaps he even regretted letting me go so easily. In any case, he signaled me to wait for him, went over to the nurses' station, and held a short telephone conversation with the head nurse of his department, who in spite of his pleas refused to let him off an operation that had already been postponed from the morning. Then he turned to me and asked me in a friendly way if I was going home before my shift. I looked at my watch. It was half-past four, and my shift began in two hours' time. If I'd still had my motorcycle I wouldn't have hesitated to go home in order to take a shower and rest before the long night ahead of me, and especially to call my parents again. But crawling along in the Tel Aviv evening traffic and finding parking for the car was another matter. "In that case," he said firmly, as if he were still my patron, "come and keep me company in an operation that won't take long but can't be postponed any longer. Lazar tells me that in the hospital in London they let you operate as much as you wanted to. The English apparently like cutting up their patients slowly and delicately." He winked at me and laughed loudly. I laughed too, not only because of the friendliness he had displayed toward me since my return from London but because of the feeling of victory and self-esteem that had filled me ever since the sudden reconciliation with Professor Levine. Who knows, I said to myself, the wild thought popping into my mind, perhaps Amnon was right and one day I will be the head of a department here, or perhaps even the director of the hospital. Thus, wrapped in premonitions of greatness, which sometimes carried me away, I generously agreed to begin my night's work then, in that clear and rosy hour of the afternoon, and followed Hishin down to the surgical wing. I took the last green shirt and trousers left on the cart, and while the anesthetist began the preparations for the "takeoff" of a very young woman who looked at us sadly and accusingly, I succeeded in persuading the switchboard operator to give me an outside line to call my parents. They had been trying to get in touch with me to tell me about a call from Michaela, who had phoned that morning from Glasgow, where she had spent the night at my aunt's with Stephanie on their way to the Isle of Skye. It was surprising and annoying to know that while we were all steeped in worries and cares, Michaela found the time to go off on a jaunt to Scotland and visit the places my mother had known as a child. I asked them about Shivi, and they said that she had vomited twice in the morning and they had called in old Dr. Cohen, the pediatrician who had taken care of me, and he had examined her and prescribed some medication but mainly reassured them. They read the name of the drug to me over the phone and asked my permission to give it to Shivi. Although she was apparently feeling better, it was obvious that they were nervous and wished that I would come and get her.

I promised that I would drive to Jerusalem first thing in the morning, as soon as my night shift was over. As I entered the changing room, I saw Dr. Vardi, my short and sturdy rival-friend, standing in a blood-soaked green uniform, with the mask still tied around his neck emphasizing the burning seriousness of his eyes as he looked at us. Hishin asked him about the operation that had just been concluded, and Vardi began to answer with his usual compulsive thoroughness, until Hishin seemed sorry that he had asked. He appeared distracted and troubled, as if his mind were somewhere else. "Do you want me to assist you?" asked Vardi, who seemed upset by my sudden presence at the side of his patron. "No, there's no need. You've done enough today, you can go home," said Hishin, and laid his hand on my shoulder. "I've got Benjy here, as both a former surgeon and a present anesthetist, and as a friend, and that's quite enough." We went into the operating room, washed our hands, put on gloves and masks, and suddenly he asked me if I could manage the anesthesia alone. I answered confidently in the affirmative, although formally speaking I was not yet supposed to be the only anesthetist present at an operation. He told the anesthetist that he could go, after getting some necessary information from him, and turned to the white stomach of the woman, which as always gave rise to tender feelings of compassion in me. With a swift and precise movement he cut a thin, firm line from her navel to her pubic hair, which for a moment seemed on fire in the ray of light filtering through the round porthole in the door. Although the bypass operation I had witnessed a week before by far surpassed the abdominal surgery now being performed by Professor Hishin, who suddenly seemed a little like a butcher, in its medical-technological complexity and even its aestheticism it was impossible not to admire his precision and skill, and also the human warmth and intimacy of his long fingers as they felt their way among the tissues opening up in front of him, not only to see but also to sense what needed to be done.

There were three of us in the operating room, Hishin and I and a new nurse whom neither of us had seen before, with a face as fresh and pure as an angel's. After half an hour, when the critical stage of the operation was approaching, the internal telephone fixed to the wall rang. I went to pick it up and immediately recognized Levine's voice, asking urgently to speak to Hishin. At first, in the wake of the reconciliation between us, I wanted to identify myself, but Levine sounded so agitated that I decided against it and confined myself to saying that I didn't think Hishin would be able to come to the telephone now and would call back as soon as he could. But Levine insisted, and Hishin, who was listening with half an ear to the conversation, asked me to find out what was the matter. Still without saying who I was, I said that Hishin couldn't come to the phone now and wanted to know what the trouble was. A note of hesitation came into Levine's voice, and he asked who was speaking. After I identified myself, his agitation increased, and he said in a deep voice, "I think that you were right, Dr. Rubin, about Lazar's arrhythmia. His condition has deteriorated—at the moment he's being mechanically ventilated. There's a cardiologist from coronary intensive care with him now. He's diagnosed ventricular tachycardia and is considering an electric shock, but it's very important to me for Hishin to come up here at once to see him, because he knows his general condition better than anyone else." And he put the phone down. From the tone of his voice I realized that Hishin's presence was important to him not for the reason he gave but because he wanted him by his side in this emergency in order to share the responsibility for any catastrophe. I immediately filled Hishin in on the picture. He froze in his place and raised his two bloody hands in the air as if he wanted to hold his stunned head between them. He knew that Lazar was now fighting for his life upstairs, and he knew that there was no way he could leave the operating room. He couldn't even send me to find out what was going on. Suddenly I saw that his hands were trembling, and I sensed that he was losing his intense inner concentration. He tried to go on working, but immediately stopped and asked me to go out and see if Vardi was still around to take over from him, and when he saw that I was hesitating, unwilling to abandon the anesthesia machine, he added angrily, "Don't worry, I'll look after it while you're gone."

It was breaking every rule in the book to leave the operating room now, but I knew that if I could find Dr. Vardi, Hishin would be able to go upstairs, and with his courage, his resourcefulness, perhaps he would be able to save Lazar's life. But the wing was empty except for a couple of nurses in the intensive care unit. Suddenly the twilight turning red around me intensified my feeling of dread, and in the absolute silence I could sense my heart beating. Hishin was absorbed in the woman's stomach, and nobody was watching the anesthesia machine. But I pressed the button of the main door of the wing nevertheless and hurried out into the bustling corridor to see if I could find some other surgeon to take Hishin's place. In the distance I saw Nakash's brown suit. He was on his way home, but the minute I told him what was up he hurried back into the surgical wing with me, although he wouldn't enter the operating room itself in his ordinary clothes. In my absence there had been another phone call from Levine. "But what does he want?" cried Hishin, his face gray. "How can I leave the operating room now?" In the meantime the rumor of the administrative director's deteriorating condition had apparently spread through the hospital like wildfire, and two doctors from cardiothoracic surgery had already hurried upstairs, as Dr. Levine called desperately for help in all directions. With a pang I saw that Hishin's hands were trembling again. He stood still for a moment, closed his eyes in concentration, and then returned to work at the proper tempo, refusing to give way to the temptation to hurry things up.

The quiet, fresh-faced young nurse, who had not yet opened her mouth, could no longer restrain herself and asked, "Who's Lazar?" Hishin didn't answer, but I began to tell her much more about Lazar than her innocent question warranted, as if I wanted by my words to strengthen his soul as it hovered between life and death. The telephone rang again. It was Nakash, who announced that he had succeeded in persuading Levine to bring the still unconscious Lazar down to the cardiothoracic surgery intensive care unit, which was close to us in the surgical wing. Hishin nodded his head. The hour of his most terrible test was upon him, under the watchful eyes of the entire medical staff of the hospital. Would he really be able to save his friend? But he went on cauterizing the blood vessels to prevent bleeding. From time to time he would offer his forehead to the nurse for her to wipe away the perspiration. The sound of loud, excited voices reached us as Lazar was brought into the wing, but Hishin didn't budge from his place and he signaled me too not to move. Nakash came into the room, wrapped in the green operating room uniform, a plastic cover on his head and his face hidden behind a mask. In his quiet, noble way he offered to help so that Hishin could leave as soon as possible. All he could tell us about Lazar was that his heart was still fibrillating in spite of the electric shock he had received. Suddenly Levine burst into the room in his ordinary clothes, with a strange, rather mysterious expression on his face, looking as if his psychiatric leave had already begun. But Hishin stopped him immediately. "For God's sake, David," he said in a stern tone, "let's try to keep our heads here. I have to finish the operation. And this young woman too deserves to get everything we can give her." He bent over the gaping stomach, steadily continuing his work, and when it was all over and she was ready to be sewn up again, I could no longer hold back and offered to complete the suture for him. Hishin gave me a hard look, his little eyes burning in his pale face; he thought for a minute, and then he said, "Right. Why not? Nakash can take over the anesthesia." He put the scissors down on the tray, held out his hands to the nurse for her to remove his gloves, and hurried from the room.

I began stitching the big incision, straining my ears to hear what was going on in the intensive care unit, even though I knew that the heavy doors would prevent any sound, encouraging or otherwise, from reaching us. I suggested to Nakash that he pop out to see what was happening, but he waved a dark hand in firm refusal and said, "No, Benjy, let's wait. We don't want to disturb them now," as if he too were afraid to see what was happening next door. And so I continued neatly and carefully suturing the surgical wound, doing my best to ensure that the scar on the young woman's stomach would be as unnoticeable as possible.

At last I was able to give Nakash the signal to bring our patient around and to ascertain from the state of her pupils, before he got dressed and hurried home, whether she had indeed returned to the land of the living. Outside in the corridor I felt the full weight of the weariness and the anxiety that had accumulated inside me. I decided to sit down for a moment on one of the little chairs, to fill in the anesthesia form and to ask the nurse with the face as pure as an angel's to find out what was happening in the intensive care unit at the end of the corridor. She came back immediately and said, "I'm sorry, Dr. Rubin." I jumped up and hurried there myself. My eyes were immediately drawn to the bed crammed between the various instruments, between the respirator and the big old defibrillator. His body was covered with a white sheet, but over his face there was a green sterile cloth, which for some reason brought back in a flash the picture of the two of them in the textile bazaar in New Delhi, standing next to a stall selling silk scarves, where she'd tried on one scarf after another and he'd watched her with an expression of weariness and boredom and had tried to move on; and then she'd held out a green silk scarf, and before he could resist, she'd put it on his head and adroitly tied the ends under his chin, like a granny's handkerchief, and stepped back to contemplate his embarrassed and amused expression before bursting into peals of jubilant laughter, in which she was momentarily joined by the passersby. And now he was dead. The pain clutched my heart. And his good friends Hishin and Levine would not be able to escape the duty of going, stunned and eaten up with guilt, to give the terrible news to the woman who couldn't stay a single day by herself. Nakash was now standing beside me in his suit and tie. For a moment he hesitated, and then his curiosity got the better of him and he went up to the dead body lying between the medical instruments and lifted the green cloth off, to look at Lazar's face and perhaps to say good-bye to him too. In spite of everything Nakash had come to us from the East, and despite his great expertise in anesthesiology and his thorough knowledge of medicine, in the depths of his soul he remained a fatalist, and when death descended on someone close to him, he accepted it completely, without question, without complaint, and above all without trying to blame anyone.

He also did not want to hear my diagnosis, but calmly took his leave of Lazar and of me and went home, switching off the light behind him with his usual economy and casting the entire wing into gloom. I decided not to change my clothes but to hurry as I was to the emergency room, not only because my shift had already begun but also because I was sure that somebody there would be able to tell me what had happened. But the two young surgeons I found there, who had been with Hishin and Levine and the others when they tried to resuscitate Lazar, were still so stunned and upset that despite their eagerness to explain and interpret everything, as eager young doctors will, it was difficult to get a clear picture from them. All I learned was that after Lazar had been declared dead, Levine and Hishin had rushed off

to treat Einat, who went into shock when she heard of her father's death. At first they had wanted to co-opt me to join the
delegation bearing the bad news to his wife, but since I was still
busy in the operating room, they had called on Lazar's secretary
instead, who went into hysterics and began to scream and cry.
Again, unlike the usual practice, the young doctors did not try to
blame anyone. Not even Levine, who had been with Lazar when
the fibrillation began. Nobody could have expected it—only two
hours before an EKG had yielded completely normal results. Arrhythmia was characteristically elusive—it came and went as it
pleased. I decided to keep my peace, since nobody could possibly
know just how deep my ties with the Lazars went, and I busied
myself with the work of the emergency room, which was particularly intensive, with the knowledge of the death of the hospital
director breaking over us in wave after stunning wave as we
worked into the night. At two A.M., I was called to the surgical
wing to assist with a local anesthesia. As soon as it was over I
went into the little instrument-packed room again, as if to be
certain that the body had indeed been transferred to the hospital
morgue, where I had for some reason never been before.

"How do you get there?" I asked the man at the information
desk in the entrance lobby, who told me what I wanted to know
but insisted that at this hour of night the place was locked and
there was nobody there. "Don't talk nonsense," I said angrily,
"people die at night too," and I went down to the basement. On
the stairs I met three doctors, whom I immediately recognized as
Dr. Amit, deputy head of cardiothoracic surgery, Dr. Yarden, the
anesthetist who had taken part in Lazar's operation, and the elderly pathologist Dr. Hefetz. I knew that they were coming from
the place that I was going to. To my surprise, they not only
recognized me but did not seem surprised to see me there, as if it
were only natural that I should be going down to the morgue at
two in the morning. "Were you there when it happened?" they
asked immediately, as if looking for someone to blame. "No," I
said, "but ever since the operation I haven't been able to stop
thinking about the possibility of ventricular tachycardia." Dr.
Amit shook his head. He didn't agree with me; perhaps the immediate cause of death had been the arrhythmia, but he suspected that the deterioration in Lazar's condition stemmed from
an infarct caused by an occlusion in one of the bypasses. All

three of them seemed very depressed by what had happened. "This death won't do the reputation of our hospital any good," pronounced Dr. Hefetz, who agreed to come down with me and show me the body. "But there isn't much left to see," he warned me as he turned back down the stairs—for Lazar, like the rest of us, had donated his organs to the hospital research laboratories. It seemed strange to me that the pathologist agreed without any hesitation to my request, as if he, too, understood that I had some special rights here. Had he heard about the trip to India? He opened the door leading to the two adjoining basement rooms. In the center of the room stood a large refrigerator with rows of big iron drawers. He pulled one of them out. I saw a smaller, shrunken Lazar, crudely stitched up after the removal of his internal organs. "Did they take his heart too?" I asked. "Of course not," Dr. Hefetz answered in surprise.

I suddenly felt calm and wide awake. I knew that I shouldn't wake my parents at this hour of the night, but I felt that I had to share my feelings with them. I called them up and told them about Lazar's sudden death. Like all kindhearted people on such occasions, they were shocked and saddened. Again and again they wanted to know how and why it had happened, as if from their home in Jerusalem they could understand what important professors at the hospital like Hishin and Levine had failed to understand. Suddenly I wanted to console them and tell them not to grieve, for Lazar's soul had already been reincarnated in me, but I knew that they would think my sorrow had driven me out of my mind, and so I only asked them for my aunt's telephone number in Glasgow so I could get in touch with Michaela. I took a beeper from the emergency room, switched it on, and stole into the administrative wing, which I was sure that the secretary had forgotten to lock up in the commotion. I was right. The door to Lazar's office was open, and I didn't even have to put on the light, because there was enough moonlight for me to see the numbers on the telephone. I found Michaela and Stephanie with my family in Scotland. I told Michaela about Lazar's sudden death and asked her to cut her trip short and come home. There was a silence on the other side of the line. "Look," I said aggressively, "I know you're entitled to another week in Britain, but it wouldn't be right to leave me to cope with the baby alone now in the new situation that's arisen."

"What situation are you talking about?" asked Michaela in surprise. For a moment I was angry that she couldn't understand by herself, but I tried to stay cool. "I'm asking you, Michaela." I spoke quietly but firmly. "It's not only Shivi who needs you; I need you too. You're the only one I can talk to about what's happening to me. Because nobody else would believe that Lazar's soul has entered my body." There was a profound silence on the other end of the line again. But it was no longer the silence of resistance. It was a new, different silence. And I knew that what I had just told her would capture her imagination and excite her curiosity so much that she would cancel her trip to Skye and fly home.

PART FOUR

Love

Sixteen

Twice during the week of mourning I paid a condolence call to the Lazars'. The first time alone, the day after the funeral, and the second time with Michaela, who returned to the country four days after our midnight telephone conversation. I might have paid a third visit, with my parents, who vacillated between going to the funeral and paying a condolence call until I persuaded them that their relations with the Lazars did not justify either of these measures and it would be enough to send a sympathy letter, which I helped them formulate over the phone. So that I could perform the overt and covert duties imposed on me by Lazar's sudden death, I asked my parents to keep Shiva with them until Michaela arrived. The overt duties were clearer than the covert ones, and involved the funeral itself, which was scheduled for the day after his death so the hospital administration and his many friends there could organize a dignified ceremony and try to rehabilitate the hospital's reputation in the wake of damaging rumors about a failed operation and an incorrect diagnosis. I myself was careful at first to maintain medical confidentiality, precisely because I felt that I would be a more reliable source of information than Professor Levine, who was so stunned and grief-stricken by the death of his friend, which had taken place not only in his department but under his personal care, that he retired into a corner and delegated some of his authority to his deputy as a kind of private punishment for himself. In this way he succeeded in diverting most of the darts of criticism from himself to Professor Hishin, who had "stolen" the operation from cardiothoracic surgery and brought in an expert from another hospital. True, patients occasionally died after bypass surgery in the cardiothoracic surgery department too, but these were considered "internal" deaths, while Lazar's was "external," brought from outside in an act of treachery. Since I was still convinced that the cause of Lazar's death was not connected to the surgery but stemmed from a mistaken diagnosis, when the criticism intensified I felt I had to break my silence and defend Professor Hishin from his detractors in the hospital, among them people I hardly knew—physicians, nurses, and members of the administrative staff—who began buttonholing me in the corridor the day after Lazar's death and questioning me about what had really happened. Dr. Nakash, who chanced upon one of these corridor conversations, immediately took me aside and warned me, with uncharacteristic sharpness, to stop letting my mouth run away with me. At the funeral too, which began in the plaza in front of the hospital, I sensed that he and his wife were deliberately keeping close to me and discreetly trying to prevent me from joining the inner circle of mourners, family and intimate friends now surrounding Dori, who was standing at a careful and fearful distance from her beloved husband.

Mourners were packed into the plaza—their numbers exceeded all my expectations, and many appeared to be truly grieving, for throughout the crowd I saw tears sparkling in the eyes of men and women as they listened to the eulogy delivered by the medical director of the hospital, a gray, retiring man who began by reading in a low clear voice from the notes he had prepared about Lazar's life history. Lazar had been born and brought up only two or three streets away from the hospital. In his youth he had studied medicine, but in his second year he had had to abandon his studies because of his father's illness and go to work to support his younger brother and sister, recognizable in the circle surrounding Dori by their physical resemblance to their brother. From a distance it seemed that the two of them were careful not to get too close to Dori, as if they feared that this pampered, vivacious woman's rage at being left alone by her husband might be greater and more violent than her grief. Even her mother kept her distance, standing with her grandchildren on either side of her, the three supporting each other. Only Hishin, perhaps by virtue of his medical authority, which in the eyes of the Lazars was absolute, dared to approach Dori and take her arm as she stood steadily on her straight legs, her left foot even at this difficult time in the lax, slightly out-turned position I always found so appealing. Hishin had honored the occasion by wearing a

black suit, but instead of a skullcap he wore an old black baseball cap on his head, which gave him the air of a sorrowful bird.
As someone who had stood at his side for many hours next to the
operating table and learned to sense every shift in his mood, I felt
even from a distance the tremendous tension in his movements,
as if he were about to whip out a knife and operate on himself. I
did not yet know that he had claimed the right to eulogize Lazar
at the graveside and that he was going over the first sentences of
his speech in his mind as his little eyes scanned the hostile audience. Dori's eyes too wandered over the people around her, but it
did not look as if any sentences, or even words, were coming into
her mind. She was so stunned by the catastrophe that she didn't
even realize how her eyes, encountering the familiar faces of her
friends, lit up, even at this terrible time, in the old, friendly smile,
although the light was so dim and weak that I thought my heart
would break.

The next day in the Lazars' apartment, among the many people filling the large living room—Dori wearing the black velvet
jumpsuit I remembered, her face pale and free of makeup—I
heard her asking about the eulogies that had been delivered outside the hospital, admitting that she had been unable to take in
what was being said. But although the people surrounding her
tried their best, none of them could remember the details. When I
could no longer restrain myself, I intervened from the other end
of the room and repeated almost word for word not only Lazar's
biography as sketched by the medical director but also the emotional phrases of the mayor, who had obviously felt both affection and respect for Lazar in spite of the bitter financial disagreements between them. But there was no need to repeat Professor
Hishin's words next to the freshly dug grave to her, both because
she, like everyone else there, could not forget their power and
eloquence and because Hishin himself was now sitting beside her
with the strange young woman who was his mistress or perhaps
already his wife and who lived for most of the year in Europe.
During the week following the funeral he went to see the Lazars
twice a day, partly to give his support and protection to the
widow of his good friend, who was a beloved friend in her own
right, and maybe partly to confront, if necessary, any complaints
against him then and there. So it was only natural that in the
quiet stir of people coming and going he would not overlook my

presence. Even though I was sitting in a remote corner of the room, far away from him, I could feel his eyes returning to me, trying to guess if I intended to surprise Dori with something she did not yet know. But I had no desire to surprise anybody. The heaviness I had felt inside ever since Lazar's death, accompanied from time to time by a slight dizziness, as if I had no control over what was happening inside me, had banished any complaints from my mind, especially any complaints against Hishin, who could never have guessed that the pity that flooded me at the sight of Dori's and Einat's tearstained eyes was accompanied by a great and paralyzing joy, which made me forget my manners, and instead of getting up to take my leave after half an hour and giving my seat to one of the other people who kept streaming in through the open door, I stubbornly sat where I was, nodding somberly to acquaintances from the hospital, as if I too were one of the mourners here.

While I could not count myself as a member of the grieving family, I felt that I secretly belonged here in this apartment, although I had only briefly visited it twice before, including on the eve of the trip to India, and from the moment I crossed the threshold I felt warmly and intimately at home. Ever since the return from India it had been the scene of my constant fantasies, and now the wounded spirit of the master of the house, which had been compassionately gathered into my soul, enabled me not only to get up and go into the kitchen without asking permission to pour myself a glass of cold water, but even to advance down the hallway and peep into the bedroom where I had given Lazar and his wife their vaccination shots before we left for India. After all, Dori, who had invaded the bedroom of a strange house in London, could hardly rebuke me for standing mesmerized in the doorway of her large, elegant bedroom, where the soft autumn twilight turning the big windows red only intensified my distress at the sight of the female clothes thrown onto the bed and the chairs, the scattered shoes, the drawers left open in a kind of chaos, which to the best of my knowledge would have infuriated Lazar. No wonder I jumped at the light touch on the back of my neck. It was Hishin. His tall body had seemed slightly stooped during the last few days, and his little eyes were tired and bloodshot. Was he looking for something too, or had he simply followed me here? He stood silently next to me, as startled as I was at the sight of the chaos created by the despairing and perhaps also angry widow. "Have you ever been here before?" He surprised me by the strange question. "A long time ago"—I blushed—"before the trip to India." Suddenly it occurred to me that he wasn't referring to the apartment but to the bedroom itself, and I continued hesitantly, "I vaccinated both of them here before the trip." He nodded his head. There was something profoundly attentive in his manner toward me. Ever since Lazar's death, and despite the great difference in our status, I had felt that there were unanswered questions between us, connected more with medical ethics than with medicine itself. But since I had never seen him so vulnerable before, I was careful to avoid saying anything that might upset his confidence in the natural course of events leading to the death and in the impossibility of preventing it. My curiosity on one point, however, was so intense that I couldn't stop myself from asking: how did Professor Adler, who had performed the operation, explain what had happened? "Bouma?" cried Hishin angrily, and the childish nickname seemed intended now to shrink the Jerusalem master back to his natural human dimensions. "He doesn't know anything about it. He left the country right after the operation and he won't be back until next week. But what can he tell us, Benjy, that we don't already know? You know yourself that the ventricular tachycardia had nothing to do with the surgery, which you saw succeed with your own eyes." A warm surge of happiness welled up in me to hear Hishin using my diagnosis as if it had now been confirmed as the absolute, undisputed truth.

Glowing with the excitement of this unexpected triumph, I went on looking at the bedroom, which suddenly filled with rose-tinted shadows that swallowed up the chaos left by the woman with whom I had fallen impossibly in love, and I decided to reward Hishin, who, although he had not found a place for me in his department and preferred my rival to me, had nevertheless seen me as the ideal man to send to India. I began to praise the eulogy he had delivered at the cemetery. "Your eulogy was terrific," I said, "if that's an appropriate word in this context." He closed his eyes impatiently and bowed his head modestly in acknowledgment as he listened to the footsteps of the people going in and out of the front door. Although he had already received a lot of compliments on his speech, it seemed that my response was important to him. "I feel so sorry for her," I added, unable to restrain myself. "What will she do without him?" Hishin gave me a quick glance, somewhat surprised, as if he considered it inappropriate for a young man like me to speak in a tone of such concern about people who were almost as old as his parents. "She's incapable of staying by herself for a minute," I added in a resentful voice, which included a note of despair. "In what sense is she incapable of staying by herself?" he said in surprise, as if by this cunning denial of a well-known fact he might be able to obtain some secret knowledge hitherto hidden from him. But I realized that I had better be careful, precisely because the events of the last few days had drawn us closer together, and the devastating guilt which continued to tear him apart, even if he didn't admit it, would sharpen his awareness of the abyss gradually opening up inside me. The words of the eulogy he had delivered between the Kaddishes were still echoing in my mind. Had he prepared them in advance, or had they really welled out of him spontaneously with the grief and the tears breaking out all around him as the grave was filled? When I saw the men lifting the stretcher to slide the body into the grave, I had eluded the invisible grip of Nakash and his wife in order to break into the inner circle, and I had seen Hishin supporting Dori, whose legs suddenly gave way beneath her as she began to sob. He waited until she steadied herself and only then opened two buttons of his black suit, exposing a tie that was surprisingly red, as if he had wanted to tear a symbolic wound in his own chest, and delivered his astonishing speech, whose gist I repeated to Michaela on the way back from the airport. And although Michaela would no doubt have preferred to hear first about Shivi, who had recognized her mother immediately in spite of the long separation and was now lying serenely in her lap, she restrained herself and listened attentively as I repeated Hishin's words to her, for she knew that if I thought something that had been said there was important to me, it was important to her too. Hishin began his speech with the unequivocal statement that the hospital director had been worthy of the title "the ideal man"— not as a cheap romantic compliment, but on the grounds of a realistic examination of the personality of the deceased, who, although he had been forced to abandon his medical studies in his youth as a result of his parents' difficulties, had never abandoned the vocation of medicine in the wider sense of the word and had joined the administrative staff of the hospital, where because of his energy and talent he had soon risen to a position of power and authority. Here Hishin straightened himself up next to the fresh grave and began to describe in an almost critical tone the nature and extent of the power that Lazar had accumulated as the administrative director, secure and permanent in his position while the medical directors changed every few years. He went on to describe the way in which Lazar had used his power to serve the medical staff efficiently and well, on the condition that they put loyalty to their patients first. His power, explained Hishin, was built on two principles: "knowledge of the details, and acknowledgment of limits." There wasn't a detail in the life of the hospital, from the numbers of doctors absent on leave to a broken cogwheel in the dialysis machine, that Lazar considered beneath his notice, and the moment he knew something he turned it into his responsibility. But the vast scope of the responsibility that Lazar was prepared to take on himself, continued Hishin, had never blurred his awareness of the precise limits of his authority, especially with regard to the medical staff—he respected the doctors in the hospital and never interfered with their professional judgment.

❧❧

Michaela listened quietly and patiently, apparently sensing that if I felt it was so important to repeat Hishin's eulogy to her even before she reached home after being away for a year, something more personal, touching on me and her, was bound to come. And indeed, the real excitement came only after Hishin abandoned the tone of general praise for the "ideal man" and began talking in a tender, intimate tone about Lazar's reactions to his trip to India two years before, in order to illuminate a different, hidden aspect of the soul of the efficient administrator who had left us for another world. The many mourners, standing scattered among the white headstones in the afternoon light of an autumn that was already anticipating the first winter rains, began quietly coming closer in order to hear Lazar's impressions and thoughts about India, as quoted by Professor Hishin—not only to my own astonishment, but also, as I sensed immediately, to that of Dori, who wiped her tears and looked questioningly at the speaker. Even though Lazar had been shocked and horrified by what he had seen on the dusty streets of India, said Hishin, and especially indignant at the sight of the sick and maimed lying abandoned in their poverty and filth, he had not avoided honestly facing the question of whether the great gap between our own world and theirs granted us a spiritual advantage too. Could we claim with any degree of confidence that our happiness was any greater and more real than theirs? "And perhaps," Hishin went on to ask on behalf of Lazar, who could not rise from his grave to deny the strange thoughts attributed to him, "perhaps it is just the contempt and indifference shown by the people of the world whom we call 'backward' and 'undeveloped' for both details and limits—perhaps it is just they who can give us a truer sense of the universe through which we pass so quickly, and help to assuage the longings we all feel for immortality, especially at painful moments of parting like this, when we bury those dear to us." Then, looking around at the faces of the mourners listening to him attentively, Hishin straightened the black baseball cap on his head and went on to speak of the night Lazar had spent with a retired Indian clerk in the little compartment of a train traveling from New Delhi to Varanasi, and of Lazar's amazement at this Indian clerk's calm confidence in his ability to ensure his rebirth by dint of a correct immersion in the waters of the Ganges. It was strange to hear Hishin talking about that night in the train as if Lazar had been all alone in the compartment, but then I remembered that Hishin was right and Lazar *had* been alone that night, sitting awake in the dark and looking at the three people sleeping next to him. And Hishin continued in a voice full of pain, as his eyes came to rest for a moment on me, "Can we deny that we too, people as completely modern as we are, sometimes dream of being born again, especially as we stand before a freshly filled grave? But how can we console ourselves with the idea of rebirth when it becomes clearer from day to day that there is nothing to be born again? For there is no such thing as a soul and never has been." Now a murmur of protest passed through the crowd, but Hishin continued undeterred. He himself, he announced, had spent his whole life prying into the most secret corners of the human body, and he had not yet come across any traces of a soul; and his brain-surgeon friends argued that everything they found and touched was pure matter, without a hint of the existence of any informing spirit, until they were as convinced as he was that one day it would be possible to reconstruct the whole thing artificially, and certainly to transplant parts of the brain. Just as today we implanted artificial devices and donor organs in the body, the day would come when it would be possible to implant or inject into the brain devices or substances that would expand our memories, sharpen our intelligence, or intensify our pleasure. "And so," Hishin concluded with a surprising turn, "I can't console myself with the immortality of Lazar's soul, from which I could ask forgiveness, but only with the memory of what I received from the flesh-and-blood man himself and what I gave him. And if, indeed, a mistake was made, it was only because of my great love for him."

A faint, ironic smile crossed Michaela's lips. It was impossible to tell whether it was occasioned by Hishin's words themselves or by my efforts to quote him word for word. "So that's how he thinks he'll get out of it," she said softly, without explaining what she meant, and her great eyes tried again to meet mine, which had been avoiding her ever since I met her at the airport and which were now scanning the familiar streets around our apartment, looking for a parking place. In the apartment too, where I had not yet rearranged the furniture moved by Amnon, Michaela went on trying to meet my eyes, to make me repeat the dramatic announcement I had made in my excitement when I had called her from Lazar's office a few hours after his death, an announcement that was so important that without a second thought she had cut her stay short, canceled her trip to the Isle of Skye, and returned home. But I went on avoiding her eyes, and she put Shivi down in the little playpen my parents had bought her the week before and followed me into the kitchen, where I was standing in front of the sink, and put her arms around me and kissed me, not only with the lust aroused in her by every change in location—and the apartment could be considered a new locale after a year's absence—but also in order to let me know that the bizarre and mysterious message I had conveyed to her that night was both credible and attractive to her. A new warmth and sweetness began streaming into me from Michaela's strong arms clasping me to her body and from the long tongue licking my face. And the desire that I had forgotten in the anger of our parting and in the drama and distress of Lazar's illness and death surged up in me with such force that I almost choked in my enthusiasm as I tried to swallow her tongue and to cover her eyes with kisses, if only to hide the penetrating look she still beseeched me with in order to hear again the wild confession which had compelled her to hurry back to Israel. I picked her up in my arms, and while Shivi raised her head to follow our movements, I carried her into the other room, which because of Amnon's love for the sea had turned from the grandmother's bedroom into the living room. I laid her on the narrow couch, and without stopping to open it up and double its size, I took off her clothes and knelt down to caress and kiss her private parts, trying to find some sign of her unfaithfulness to me in England or Scotland. But I found no such sign, and I stood up and lay down next to her and made love to her at length, pleasurably and generously, as on that night in the desert, overlooking Eyal's wedding. And we only stopped when Shivi's whimpering turned into a demanding cry.

"Did I make love to Lazar too?" she asked me with a hint of laughter in her eyes when she came out of the shower, shaking her wet hair. She watched me affectionately as I fed Shivi, who was sitting in her high chair facing the glow of the sunset in the kitchen window. Her air of amusement made it easier for me to answer her question. "You've just made love to a lot of people, alive and dead," I said quietly, "and among them perhaps—why not?—Lazar too." And in the darkness of the evening descending on us, next to the baby listening and playing with her empty bowl, I told Michaela the whole story of the drama of his death: the diagnosis, the surgery, the recovery, and the sudden collapse. I spoke not as a doctor intent on proving the superiority of his diagnosis but with the profound emotion of a young man who had seen the steadfast heart of his friend open like a book and did not want to leave him alone even after it had ceased to beat. "You didn't want to leave him alone?" said Michaela in surprise, with a note of disappointment in her voice, as if she had expected something more definite but also more mysterious. "Exactly," I said, wondering whether to switch on the light in the kitchen, which was already full of shadows. "That's what I meant. What did you think I meant?" I laughed lightly. "That I really thought Lazar's soul could migrate into mine?"

"Why not?" replied Michaela almost in a whisper, and she began delicately stroking Shivi's forehead in the area between her eyes in a caress she had evidently perfected during the two weeks she had spent alone with the baby in London, which Shivi appeared to enjoy as if she were a cat. "If you succeeded in incorporating the midwife's soul on the night of the birth, why shouldn't you incorporate Lazar's soul too?" She was treading a fine line between irony and profound seriousness, as always when trying out an idea that held a hidden educational intention. "The midwife's soul?" I laughed. "Who said so?"

"She did," replied Michaela. "Don't you remember? When we were all admiring the way you delivered Shivi so perfectly?" I was silent. It gave me a kick to hear her call my delivery of the baby perfect, but I didn't want to go on discussing Lazar, who in any case couldn't rise from his grave to betray me.

The next day I took Michaela to pay a condolence call on the Lazars. I insisted that she come with me to console Einat, who had almost been an eyewitness to her father's death. We didn't know if it was proper to take a baby to a house of mourning, but we took Shivi with us anyway, since we did not yet have a baby-sitter and I didn't want Michaela to go without me to the apartment I visited so often in my imagination. Again I found the living room full of people, many of them familiar faces from the hospital, who had put off their condolence calls to the last days of the week of mourning. They could not possibly have all been in daily contact with Lazar, but they had all felt themselves to be under the shelter of his eagle eye, and now that the shelter was gone, they wanted to examine the extent of the gap yawning over their heads. I found Hishin there too, sitting in the same place as before, at Dori's right hand. The shabby black cap that he had worn to the funeral was perched on his head again, like a symbol of his private mourning. His young companion, whom he had brought back with him from one of his trips to Europe, had been replaced by a short man, rather sloppily dressed in sportswear, who from a distance seemed familiar. When I went closer, it turned out, to my surprise, to be Professor Adler, the Jerusalem master surgeon. Although it was not the usual thing for a surgeon to pay a condolence call on a family mourning the death of his patient, Hishin had insisted on bringing him here, in order to prove to everyone that in spite of the unfortunate outcome, he

was convinced that his friend had performed the surgery successfully. He had brought him directly from the airport, on his way
home to Jerusalem. With the baby hanging on Michaela's stomach in her sling, we hesitantly approached Einat and Dori, who,
free of her husband's reprimanding eye, was smoking one slender
cigarette after another as she listened, without concentrating and
without smiling, to Professor Adler's patient and methodical ex-
position of his guiltless role in her catastrophe. Einat, whose face
was very pale, rose immediately to greet Michaela, and she
hugged and kissed her so warmly and lovingly that Shivi was
almost crushed between them. Dori stopped listening and transferred her attention to her daughter, who was weeping around
Michaela's neck. I was alarmed to see a silent tear rolling down
her cheek and the ash of her cigarette almost falling onto the
carpet, and I instinctively bent down to move the ashtray closer.
Now Professor Adler recognized me and smiled at me encouragingly. Would he also remember the ventricular tachycardia? I
wouldn't be surprised, for judging by the direct, intelligent look
in his eye, it seemed that if he had not been in a hurry to get back
to Jerusalem then, he would have listened with patience and respect even to the words of an insignificant junior physician like
me. Accordingly, when Einat took Michaela and Shivi into her
room, I sat down boldly in the place she had vacated, next to the
two professors and Dori. As if my presence had the power to
soothe Dori's pain and distress, I saw the old, involuntary smile
flashing dimly in her eyes again—a smile she may have felt the
need to justify, for she immediately told Hishin and his Jerusalem
friend how fond Lazar had been of me, while I, who felt not only
his fondness but also his love like a leaden weight inside me,
bowed my head like a young boy listening proudly but also impatiently to his mother praising him in front of strangers. Then,
unable to restrain myself, I turned to Professor Adler and asked
him how he explained what had happened to Lazar's heart after
the surgery, which I myself could humbly testify had succeeded.
But although he tried to explain, and even sketched the heart that
had failed and died on a large sheet of paper, it seemed that the
expert surgeon who had so briskly and firmly sawed Lazar's
chest open was not capable of producing even one convincing
reason for his sudden death, but only of piling one lengthy explanation on another in an attempt to disguise their essential weak-

ness. Dori tried to listen to him, but the arrival of a delegation of her colleagues, judges and lawyers in black gowns, distracted her. And who could blame her? Even if the real cause of her husband's death was discovered, it would not bring him back to life.

From her point of view she was right, of course, but not from the point of view of a doctor, especially a young one, for whom an unexplained death is intolerable. Therefore I kept on at Professor Adler, trying to make him clarify, not only to me but to himself, what had really happened. And he seemed ready to respond patiently to my challenge and to saw through Lazar's chest in order to open again the book on the heart which had failed, and to probe Koch's triangle, the place where the real threat lay hidden. But here Hishin interrupted his friend, who in his zeal to prove his point had forgotten the fact that he had just arrived back in the country a few hours before, and reminded him that it was getting dark and that his wife was expecting him in Jerusalem; a new wave of visitors had arrived too, and we all felt that it was time to get up and vacate our places. Professor Adler stood up and said good-bye to me in a very friendly way, and also invited me to come to Jerusalem and continue our conversation there. "That would be great," I said immediately. "My parents live there, you know," and I escorted the two professors to the door as if I too had moved in for the duration of the mourning period, like Einat and like the granny, who was standing in the kitchen in a clean apron making tea for the visitors. She seemed delighted to see me again.

Clearly my beloved, who could not bear to be alone at the best of times, could not be expected to rely solely on the presence of her soldier son—from whose room the sounds of a lively adolescent conversation could be heard, accompanied, if my ears did not deceive me, by rock music played very softly—but required her mother and her daughter as well. They had both come to stay with her, at least for the week of mourning. But what would happen in the future? I thought anxiously, as if it were up to me to find a solution, and I gave the bedroom door a little push and saw, to my relief, that the chaos raging here two days before had disappeared, as if the troubled spirit of Lazar had returned to establish order. Was it really my responsibility now to see that she wasn't left alone? I asked myself. Although I had spent two weeks traveling with her and gone to bed with her twice, I still knew very little about her. Seeing her now surrounded by friends and well-wishers, hugged and kissed until her bun came loose and her hair fell around her face, hiding not only her tears but also her wonderful smile, which not even profound sorrow and grief could extinguish, I asked myself, had the time really come to take this burden upon myself, simply in order to go on devoting myself to the impossible love which had suddenly become possible?

❧❧

But was it really possible? I thought excitedly as I entered Einat's room, my face burning, to take Michaela and Shivi home. As soon as I saw the curious but anxious look in Einat's eyes, I suspected that Michaela had said something to her about the transmigration of a certain soul, for Einat was strongly drawn to India in her own right, and during the weeks that she had spent lying helplessly in the monastery in Bodhgaya she may have been exposed to the beliefs of the people taking care of her, and she might be very willing to believe in all kinds of extreme ideas. I quickly smiled at her and touched her arm reassuringly, as I had touched her when I was her doctor and she was my patient. But this time a shiver seemed to pass through her at my touch. Has Michaela got so much influence over you, it was on the tip of my tongue to say in protest, that you're prepared to believe that an alien entity could invade the boundaries of my personality? But I said nothing, and I sat down silently on the bed and quickly stretched out my arms for Shivi, whose body arched in tension, as if a stranger had picked her up and not her father. Einat looked drained. She had witnessed her father's death throes for only a few minutes, until Professor Levine had sent her out of the room, but those minutes had left their scar. "A real scar that she won't give up easily," said Michaela on the way home, "a scar she can show to people who love looking at scars, or to anyone who just loves her. A more spiritual scar than the one left by the hepatitis, in spite of the dramatic blood transfusion you gave her in Varanasi." It was impossible to tell by her tone if she was being sarcastic or not. I had already noted that things I thought Michaela said in malicious sarcasm turned out later to have been said in all seriousness and innocence. I therefore hesitated to reply. The memory of the blood transfusion in Varanasi now seemed, after Lazar's death, to have taken place in a dream and not in the real world, which was currently filled with drops of fine, fresh rain that turned the lights of the cars in front of us into trembling diamonds. Shivi sat up on Michaela's lap, drawn to the movement of the windshield wipers starting and stopping again. I noticed that Michaela had left Shivi's sling in Einat's room. But I said nothing, not wanting to turn back and preferring to return later in the evening to see who was going to stay with Dori during the night. "Did you say anything to Einat about me?" I asked, without going into detail, but Michaela knew right away what I was talking about. "No," she said immediately, her great eyes shining with a secret smile. "If she doesn't realize what's happened for herself, what good will my words do?" And then she added in a whisper, "Didn't you see how she trembled when you came into the room?" I slowed down and closed my eyes for a couple of seconds. Did she have any idea of what she was leading me into with this kind of talk? "I see you're trying to fan the fire," I mumbled, gripping the steering wheel tightly and wondering at the word "fire," which had slipped out of my mouth. "But the fire's already broken out, Benjy," said Michaela in a quiet, steady voice. "That night when you phoned and asked me to come home and you weren't afraid to admit what you felt, you rose in my estimation to the level of a Brahmin, and that's why I didn't hesitate to interrupt my trip and come home, even though I suspected that you would try to deny later what broke out of you then with such spontaneous beauty and power." I kept quiet, smiling in astonishment at Shivi, who turned her eyes from the wipers and gave me an inquiring look, as if wondering why I didn't respond to Michaela, who was now in the grip of real enthusiasm as she tried to persuade me to stop denying what had happened to me. She had no intention of belittling my medical understanding, she said, which was in no way inferior to that of my professors, including the little Jerusalemite, who in spite of all his expertise was blind to the approaching death of Lazar, lying open before him on the operating table. She said she knew that I had already sensed Lazar's death in England, knew it was the reason I had hurried back, like a man seeing the flicker of flames on the horizon of a distant field who hurries toward the fire, not to put it out but to obtain inspiration from it, for it is a sacred fire in which the dead are burned and the soul is liberated from the body. Michaela knew how powerful that fire was, how its attraction can call the widow to throw herself atop its blaze.

"The widow?" I whispered, surprised and amused by the wealth of Michaela's Indian associations. But Michaela, it turned out, wasn't just talking—she had actually seen a widow being burned when she was in India, and she would never forget it as long as she lived. Although this rite was forbidden by law and took place rarely and clandestinely, and even though strangers were never permitted to approach it, the sidewalk doctors and their helpers in Calcutta had gained the confidence of two Indian ethnologists who wanted to reward their devotion to the sick and maimed by showing them something that was not only shocking and horrifying but that went to the very heart of the national identity. Not all the doctors and nurses invited were enthusiastic about the idea of traveling for two days on rough roads to a remote village, which for all its primitiveness had already been invaded by a miasma of tourism and commercialism. But nothing would have prevented Michaela from taking advantage of the opportunity to see this ancient ritual, which the British had done everything in their power to stamp out, for she knew that anyone who shrank from the sight of death in India was resisting the true spirit of the place and had no business being there. The ceremony took place on the outskirts of the village, in a hidden hollow, and all the spectators had to keep their distance, especially the strangers among them. The widow was a woman of about fifty, supple and strong, who they were assured had chosen of her own free will and in perfect faith to be burned alive. The memory of the bright, distant flame slowly consuming her would never be forgotten by Michaela or by Einat, whom she had persuaded to accompany her. "I'm constantly amazed to discover how much time you spent together," I said to Michaela, who was carrying Shivi upstairs and had still not felt the absence of the sling, which I would soon "remember" so I could set out once more, full of happiness and excitement, for the home of another widow, whom no one would ever ask to throw herself on a funeral pyre in order to show the world what an honorable woman she was and how much she had loved her husband.

"Yes," said Michaela, shaking the raindrops from her hair and entering the apartment, "we hung around a lot together, but our reactions were always very different. Even though it was terrible to watch, I left that place with a feeling of elation, just like the Indians who had taken us there and who you can be sure were no less sophisticated and modern than you and me. But Einat was so upset and shocked, so confused and horrified and even angry with me for taking her, that I think it began then."

"What began then?"

"Her illness. The hepatitis. The deterioration."

"But in what sense?" I pressed her, excited by the thought that I was close to identifying the source of the mystery that had been disrupting my life. "I don't know." Michaela shrugged her shoulders. "Maybe her immune system was weakened when she saw a middle-aged woman like her mother slowly going up in flames. And once that happens, in all that filth, it's easy enough for some vicious virus to take hold in you." When Michaela saw how interested I was in the ritual widow-burning, she promised to look for a couple of photographs that one of her friends had managed to take in secret before a number of soldiers had arrived to disperse the crowd. But they had been unable to save the woman, who had already turned to ashes.

The doorbell rang. It was Amnon, who had come to welcome Michaela home before his night shift began. We were both glad to see him and insisted that he stay for supper, after watching us bathe Shivi, which, he said, might even tempt him to have a baby of his own. In order to suppress the excitement mounting inside me at the thought of returning to the Lazars' apartment, I demanded his help in putting the furniture back where it belonged. Michaela tried to dissuade me at first, on the grounds that the present arrangement was worth a try at least, but I held on my opinion that it might be okay for a bachelor but not for a married couple, and the front room should be reserved for guests, not converted into a bedroom. Neither of them was convinced, but I, as "the original tenant who signed the lease, and therefore as the true representative of the landlady," insisted on restoring order, and we dragged the big bed back into its place and set the narrow couch opposite the big window from which it was possible to catch a glimpse of the sea, but certainly not on a night like this, which was full of fog and rain. Considering the weather, and how late it was, Michaela was very surprised when I insisted

on going to get the forgotten sling, as if we could not do without
it until the following day.

Was Hishin's guilt really so great that on his way back from
Jerusalem he had returned to visit the grief-stricken family again?
I wondered anxiously when I recognized his car parked next to
the Lazars'. I ran up the stairs and knocked lightly on the door,
rehearsing a short sentence of apology, which I delivered to the
granny, who greeted me with a welcoming smile, fresh and neat
in a white blouse and a tailored tartan skirt. The apartment,
which a few hours before had been crowded with people, was
now empty and a little dark, and the many chairs, which had
apparently been borrowed from neighbors, were scattered without order all over the room, expressing the mourning that had
descended on the house better than any words could have done.
Without wasting words, the granny led me down the dark hallway to Einat's room to look for the forgotten sling while Dori's
sobs, coming from the direction of the kitchen, pierced me like a
knife. The open door of her dark bedroom revealed renewed
chaos. There was a light on in the soldier's room, but it was
empty except for a rifle leaning against the wall. The door to
Einat's room was closed, and the granny first knocked lightly,
and when there was no reply she carefully opened the door.
Einat, who was curled up, fully dressed, asleep on her bed, with a
little reading light shining on her face, opened her eyes immediately, as if she had been expecting my return, and pulled Shivi's
sling out from under the bed. "I'm sorry," I whispered, and
stepped forward to take it from her hand. She smiled and nodded
her head. "Give Shivi a kiss from me," she said, and curled up
into herself again like a sad fetus, limply allowing her grandmother to take off her shoes. I retreated into the hallway, refusing to resign myself to leaving the apartment without catching a
single glimpse of Dori. It occurred to me to ask the granny, "Are
you sleeping here?" "No," she said in an apologetic and slightly
embarrassed tone. She spent all day here, but at night she went
back to the retirement home to sleep. At her age it was hard to
get used to a strange bed. Now she was waiting for her grandson,
who had gone out for a breath of fresh air with his friends, to
come and drive her home. I kept quiet, slowing my footsteps and
keeping my ears cocked for Dori's tearstained voice as she spoke
to Hishin in the kitchen. "I can take you," I offered immediately,

leaning forward to examine the granny's face in the dim light. "Thank you very much," she replied without hesitation, careful not to let the offer slip through her fingers after her exhausting day. "But is it on your way?" she asked. "I'll put it on my way," I said decisively, and followed her into the kitchen to inform Dori and Hishin that I was taking her home. They were sitting at the kitchen table in a pool of sad neon light. Among the dirty cups and glasses on the table lay Dori's eyeglasses and several crumpled tissues. Her eyes were as telling as when I had made love to her, but now they were red and swollen. For the first time since the death I was able to grasp the depths of pain to which she had sunk. Hishin sat at a little distance from her, his face gloomy and thoughtful, his long legs stretched out in front of him. The black baseball cap was lying on the table. In front of him was a plate containing the remains of his supper, and between his long fingers was one of Dori's slender cigarettes, which he was apparently smoking in a gesture of solidarity with her sorrow and despair, for I had never seen him smoke before. They both looked up at me without any surprise or question, as if it were only natural that I should be wandering around the apartment at this late hour. Dori made no attempt to hide the traces of her weeping, but instead she lifted her head as if to show me her tearstained face and demand from me too some clear, strong word of consolation or hope, so that she could restore herself, if not her husband.

"May I take your mother home?" I asked her, my face flushed, as if the old lady's authority were not enough. "Of course," Hishin replied for her, "you'll be providing an important service." In an intimate tone he said to Dori, "The boy must have forgotten himself with his friends." She nodded her head and took a sip of tea. I stood hesitating in the kitchen doorway, the straps of Shivi's sling over my shoulder, and behind my back in the hallway, where the lightbulb had apparently burned out, I heard the granny quickly getting ready to leave. "It's raining outside," I warned. "But it isn't cold," I added reassuringly as I saw Dori reaching out to take another cigarette. Suddenly I felt an uncontrollable urge to stop her, as if I were being prompted by Lazar, who always tried to prevent her from smoking, and I stepped quickly forward and reached for the pack of cigarettes. At first she was astonished, as if the dead man's hand had come

back to life. But she immediately recovered, and assuming that I
too, like Hishin, wanted to try one of her slender cigarettes, she
offered me the pack with a generous, heart-wrenching smile, and
I had no option but to take a cigarette and bend down to get a
light from her, mumbling something about the strangeness and
confusion of the last few days, while Hishin looked at me affectionately and nodded his head. As soon as we were outside, I
threw the cigarette away and ground it out with my foot. The
light rain, which had freshened the air, made Dori's mother
happy, as if only changes in nature could bring some comfort to
people so overcome with grief. "Your baby's not only sweet,
she's also very well behaved," she announced as I showed her
how to buckle the seat belt. "Your Michaela apparently knows
how to handle her," she added. "I do too," I said, unable not to
claim my share of the credit as a devoted husband and father.
"You too, of course," the old lady agreed, although she seemed
to have more faith in the inner serenity of Michaela, about whom
she now began to question me. But I didn't want to waste the few
minutes of the short drive on pointless chatter about Michaela or
Shivi, or even myself. I wanted to talk about Dori and how she
was going to manage in the future, and even how she was coping
in the grim present, and in this context I mentioned Hishin's
constant presence in the apartment. "Yes, Hishin never leaves
us," she said. "It's very difficult for him too, of course; he feels
guilty about transferring Lazar's operation from the department
where it belonged and bringing in a strange surgeon from outside." Once more I found myself defending Hishin and his acts,
as if his guilt were liable to rub off on me. She listened sympathetically to what I had to say, nodding her head encouragingly
as if she too would like to clear Hishin of any guilt and be convinced of the inevitability of her son-in-law's death. "Of course,
for a doctor, no death is completely unavoidable," I said, trying
to convey a more complex thought to her. "How can that be
possible?" She sounded astonished, as though I were trying to
persuade her of the possibility of everlasting life. "Because if we
accepted some deaths as inevitable, we would lose the element of
positive competition among doctors," I explained. Now she
seemed really worried by my words. "Is the competition among
you really so fierce?" she asked. "Why not?" I replied. "We're
only human. To give you an example, when I changed a couple

of the medicines Professor Levine had prescribed for you, I admit I felt a little triumphant."

"But in the meantime he's changed them all back again," she said sharply, and smiled with obvious enjoyment at my discomfort.

The old folks' home was in darkness, even though it was only ten o'clock at night, but the old lady didn't seem in the least upset. She thanked me warmly, allowed me to extricate her from her seat belt, put on a white beret to protect her head from the persistent drizzle, and stepped carefully out of the car. I got out too and offered to accompany her inside. In her excellent physical and mental condition, she was in no need of an escort, but with her sharp wits she sensed that I was eager to continue the conversation, and she therefore thanked me gratefully, as if I were doing her a great favor. We walked slowly across the deserted terrace. I asked her a question or two about the place, and she answered briefly. Now we were standing in front of a big glass door, behind which the doorman was sitting opposite a television screen on which the two of us flickered like a couple of ghosts. Suddenly she shivered, as if she too had finally recognized the lost soul of her son-in-law in some movement of my head or hand, or even in the tone of voice that I had just adopted. The glass door did not open immediately. The old lady looked straight at me, but without realizing that it was my very presence which now forced her to speak of him. "Poor Lazar, my heart aches for him," she said sadly, and she tugged at the white beret to protect at least one side of her face from the blustering wind. As if she wasn't sure whether I shared the intensity of her emotion, she added, "Do you know how fond he was of you, and how well he spoke of you?" I nodded my head painfully, as if everything I had felt since my return from England had now been confirmed. "But what's going to happen to Dori now?" I asked. She shrugged her shoulders. "It will be very hard for Dori. Very hard."

I saw that she still hadn't grasped the crux of the matter. "But how will she stay by herself?"

"How?" Dori's mother sighed, still not understanding what I was getting at. "I don't know how. She'll have to find a way. It will be very hard for her. As it is for everyone else."

"But what way? In what sense?" I pressed her, refusing to let her evade the issue. "She's incapable of being on her own for a minute. It's impossible for her." I saw that my insistence was beginning to confuse her. Her eyes wandered, and she hugged the door for shelter, afraid to meet my eyes lest she admit that I knew something nobody was supposed to know, something that even she refused to acknowledge. But I pressed on, oblivious to her discomfort in my fervor. "How, for example, will she stay by herself at night? Who'll be there with her?" Finally she understood that she could no longer evade my questions, which sprang from a deep inner source, perhaps prompted by Lazar himself. "Don't you worry your head about that," she said, smiling in relief. "She'll find a way not to be by herself. She'll find someone to be with her. Even when she was a child and we sometimes left her alone in the evening, she would run to find some little friend to spend the night with her. She always knew how to find people to look after her, so that she wouldn't have to stay by herself for even a minute." I was flooded with sweetness at the thought of the little girl running in the pleasant evening streets of childhood to find a little friend to spend the night. I suddenly felt as if the worry had been removed from my heart and, more significantly, as if a new horizon had opened before me, full of a reassuring promise. I pressed the button next to the door and asked the doorman over the intercom to open it. He checked his list for the old lady's name, and after he found it he pressed the buzzer and I left her. But I didn't leave the place before calling Michaela on a pay phone to apologize for my lateness and to tell her that I was on my way home.

Michaela was indifferent to this announcement, but Amnon, who was still at the apartment and eagerly waiting for my return, wasn't. Nevertheless, I couldn't resist passing Dori's house again, and after checking that Hishin's car was no longer there, I climbed softly up the dark stairs, and stood holding my breath outside the door, with my hand on the lock, to give my beloved the feeling that even if her mother had already gone home and her daughter was asleep in her room and her son had not yet returned, she was not alone.

Seventeen

Has the time come to reflect on love, so that what was impossible will become possible? The solitary bird—which broke into the room in the dead of night and underneath the bed, among the clay fragments of the broken statuette, pecked crumbs from the heart of an ancient sandwich, which had been prepared for a school lunch and for some reason had found its way there and been forgotten—may spread its great wings at dawn and fly away to find where she has disappeared to, the curly-haired little girl in the blue uniform with the school badge fastened to her chest with a safety pin, who was left to do her homework at the kitchen table many years ago.

❧

After the official mourning period was over, I found myself drawn to the administrative wing to find out if Lazar's heir had already been designated. This was, of course, a pointless and ridiculous project, not only because it was only a week since he had died, but also because Lazar was not one of those executives who chose an heir-apparent during their lifetime, but believed that his true heir would have to make it on his own, after stiff competition with his peers. Nevertheless, when I walked down the corridor on my way from the surgical wing, in my green uniform, with the mask still hanging around my neck, my feet would lead me to the administrative wing and I would hesitantly advance toward Lazar's office, whose door still bore, as if nothing had happened, the bronze plate inscribed with his name and office hours. In those days I would find the office quiet, with none of the feverish activity that had always characterized it, as if most of the urgent administrative problems demanding his attention had solved themselves with his death. The two secretaries who had always been there had disappeared, replaced by a young Anglo-Saxon typist who appeared not to be typing documents or letters but to be slowly copying material from a thick old medical textbook, presumably for one of the clinical seminars held in the hospital. The absence of Miss Kolby, Lazar's faithful personal secretary, who had always treated me with particular affection, struck me as strange. I say "absence" and not "disappearance" because sometimes I would find traces of her in her room—a handbag, or a coat hanging on a hook. But when I tried to find out where she was, the secretaries in the adjacent rooms would shrug their shoulders, unable to give me a clear answer. "She's wandering around" was the best answer they could come up with, referring to the confines of the administrative wing, to other parts of the hospital, and to a space beyond its geographical limits. "She's *still* wandering around," a friendly secretary tried to explain when I came back to the wing after my day's work was over, illustrating not only the extent but also the rhythm of this wandering with a circular motion of her arm.

The truth is that I too had been infected by this aimless wandering. The women apparently realized this, and accordingly did not bother to ask exactly what I wanted from Lazar's secretary, or whether I wished to leave a message. They seemed to sense that I had no explicit question or request but only an abstract desire to hang around in one of the many empty spaces left in the hospital by the death of the administrative director. For I had a lot of spare time now, not only because Michaela's return took Shivi off my hands, but also because I was employed at the hospital only on a half-time basis and the private work in Herzliah had not yet been renewed. After my year in London and all the experience I had gained at St. Bernadine's it seemed beneath my dignity to apply for night shifts at the Magen-David-Adom station, but until Michaela found a job and we knew where we stood, at least financially, I had no choice but to request a few night shifts there at the end of the month. Lazar's departure had deprived me of the administrative patronage I still required. The permanent half-time job I had taken was more administrative than medical, the fruit of Lazar's manipulations, which were intended to compensate me for some undefined injustice done me, in India or here. And although the permanency of the position was an achievement that most of my peers could only dream about, its partial nature left me in a situation of disturbing ambivalence, so that sometimes I wished I had the guts to give it up altogether and look for a full-time job, even on a temporary basis, in the surgical department of some other hospital. Because of this, my search for Lazar's personal secretary was intended not only to give me a chance to rub up against one of the intimate voids left by the energetic director but also to clarify my position and prospects at the hospital as she, an experienced secretary, saw them.

More than ten days had already passed since the week of mourning, and I decided to go and look for the wandering secretary again. I was already dressed in my ordinary clothes and on my way home. In the darkness of the corridor her room looked deserted like the others, but I tried the handle of the door anyway, and found her sitting alone at her desk with a pile of accounts in front of her. I took the faint scream uttered by the pale and wilted Miss Kolby as more than met the eye. True, I had come upon her unexpectedly, at an hour of the evening when the administrative wing was empty and most of the office doors had long been locked. We both apologized immediately, I for bursting in without knocking and she for not having contacted me after hearing that I had been looking for her. She stood up and gripped my wrist, speaking directly and with deep emotion. "Yes, after what happened here I can't settle down. I keep wandering around and thinking, why weren't we more careful? Why didn't we pay more attention? And why did we fail to read the obvious signs? Every day I feel guiltier for not being firmer."

"Firmer with who?" I asked. "With everyone. Including Dori, who gave in to them in the end. But above all with him. Because he's definitely to blame as well."

"He?" I pretended not to know who she was talking about, because I wanted to hear her say his name. "Yes, Lazar is definitely to blame too," she said, going on bitterly and bravely with her accusation. "Why shouldn't he be to blame? I warned him against the designs of Professor Hishin, who in the end thinks of nothing but himself and his department. And you?" She fixed her eyes on me. "You too, Dr. Rubin, are to blame, because you knew and you kept quiet."

"What did I know?" I said, my face red. "Everything," she

replied without hesitation. "Although it's true that you may not have had the power to stop them. But let's sit down." She opened the door to Lazar's room and led me into it in the most natural way in the world, as if Lazar were sitting there and waiting for us in order to set his administrative seal on the collective guilt that had led to his death.

What did I know, I wanted to ask her again, but I stopped myself, both because I didn't want to get into a confrontation with her now about the depth of my knowledge and because I felt a need to take on some of the guilt that this good woman was dishing out so liberally. She switched on the light in the large, elegant room, which, apart from the fact that the big sofa had for some reason been removed, taking with it some of the room's previous coziness, was exactly the same as before. The soil in the big planters was dry and cracked, but the plants themselves were still green. Miss Kolby sat down, with a proprietary air, in the armchair opposite the big desk, her usual place when she took dictation from Lazar, after bringing up one of the chairs standing against the wall for me. But when she saw that she had underestimated my height, which forced her to look up at me from below, she changed her mind, rose from her chair, and with a dry, businesslike air wheeled Lazar's big executive armchair out from behind his desk so that I could sit not only more comfortably but at her eye level. "It's all right, it's all right," she said, encouraging me to sit in the armchair, although I had not shown any signs of hesitation. In contrast to her pale face and tired eyes, her movements became brisker and more alert, as if with my appearance the death had turned from a fait accompli to a kind of misadventure, which decisive intervention might still be able to correct. And thus, while a shock of happiness surged through my being, her eyes began to focus intently on mine, as if to prevent the soul already trapped inside me from slipping away. As expected, she began to talk about the deceased and the interest he had taken in me. Even though he had not succeeded in persuading Hishin to keep me on in the surgical department, at least he had found a way to secure my place among the anesthetists. Again I saw how Lazar's affection and concern had sheltered me over the past two years, like a kind of invisible insurance policy hovering over my head, whose value I was only able to appreciate now that it had been lost. She too, of course, had lost her insurance policy, and her position as the secretary attached to the source of power in the administrative wing was now in danger of collapsing completely. Nevertheless, she did not appear depressed but rather in the grip of an inner enthusiasm—the enthusiasm of a woman no longer young who suddenly discovers that the borders of despair, which she thought she had long ago crossed, have moved.

"But where have you been all the time?" I allowed myself to ask in a mildly rebuking tone, despite the difference in age between us. "Where? With Dori, of course," she answered immediately. "Somebody had to help her organize things."

"What things?" I asked, a thrill of pleasure running through me. It turned out that she meant very ordinary, simple things, such as bank accounts, Lazar's insurance policy, the papers for the car, and various bills which Miss Kolby had taken it upon herself to settle, for who knew as well as she did that Lazar's wife was utterly helpless in such matters? "What do you mean, helpless?" I protested, leaping to Dori's defense. "She's a partner in a big legal firm."

"Precisely," said Miss Kolby. "It's a big firm with a whole battery of accountants and secretaries, who take the practical side of things off her hands. And at home Lazar would take care of everything, of course."

"And the children?"

"The children are gone," she announced briskly. "Einat went back to her apartment, and the boy went back to the army. Someone has to help her."

"She's alone now?" I whispered, my anxiety mingled with a hint of pleasure. Miss Kolby looked at me curiously, to see if I was aware of the deeper implications of my words, and then she admitted that for the last three nights, ever since the soldier had returned to his base, she had been sleeping in the apartment with Mrs. Lazar. "You're sleeping there!" I said with a feeling of relief. "And it doesn't inconvenience you?"

"What if it does?" she replied evasively. "Someone has to help her, until a more radical solution is found."

"Radical?" I sniggered, for the word seemed extreme to me, and it was indeed inappropriate for the simple solutions imagined by the secretary, such as Dori's mother coming to live with her, or Einat agreeing to return home for a while, or Dori renting a room to a student until her son completed his military service in six months' time and decided if he too, like his sister, wanted to travel to distant lands. "I thought you had something more radical in mind." I lowered my eyes and released the catch under the chair so that I could rock slightly to and fro. "Yes, that would make things easier for everyone," Miss Kolby replied, to my surprise, without hesitation or hypocrisy, in the practical spirit she had gained from Lazar during all their years of working together. But she immediately added a reservation: "But it would have to be with someone like Lazar. Someone who knows how to pamper her and take care of everything for her, so that she can keep her spirits up and go on smiling good-naturedly at everyone and listening to everybody's troubles. Because even you wouldn't believe it if I told you how she can sometimes behave like a frightened little girl, but obstinate too, and how helpless and almost stupid she can be when she has to deal with anything technical, even something as simple as a household appliance." She stopped for a minute, hesitating about whether to confide the secrets she had discovered over the past few days to me. "Even I, who knew them both well, had no idea of how much Lazar took care of everything for her. Would you believe that she doesn't even know how to work her own washing machine?"

৯৲৫

Miss Kolby burst into astonished laughter at the new task she had taken on herself, as if the ghost of her ex-boss were still issuing a stream of domestic instructions to her now that the administrative instructions had ceased. I joined warmly in her laughter. I was delighted with this conversation about the touching helplessness of the beloved woman who from hour to hour was becoming more possible for me. And the thought that maybe at this very moment on this chilly autumn evening she was home from the office and wandering around the apartment alone, helpless and despairing before the washing machine and the big dryer, and also the stove, which refused to light, and the stereo system, which refused to play, did not give rise in me, as in Lazar's secretary, to pity mixed with something like disgust or disbelief, but to powerful longings. For a moment I was tempted to throw caution to the wind and confess my stubborn, mysterious love to the worried secretary, and thereby notify her that another shoulder was ready and willing to share the burden. But even though I was prepared to expose myself, I wasn't sure that I had the right to expose Dori too, not even to this close family friend. "Are you going to sleep there tonight as well?" I asked carefully, unable to control the slight tremor of desire in my voice. She hadn't decided yet. Dori insisted that she no longer needed a constant companion, since the worst was already behind her and she was recovering and coping on her own, and perhaps it would be for the best and for her own good to leave her to her own devices, but on the other hand she had caught a cold two days ago and yesterday she had even had a fever, and this being the case, Miss Kolby thought that she should drop in to see how she was managing. Not to sleep there, but just to check up on her. In fact, she was going to get in touch right now.

Although as a physician-friend I could have stolen in through this loophole, I held my tongue and did not ask to speak to Dori. Ever since the night when I had stood silently outside her front door, I had been determined that the signal to renew contact should come from her, not me. Now that the natural protection bestowed on her by Lazar was gone and she was left exposed and vulnerable and by herself I had to restrain myself severely and be attentive to her wishes only, not to mine, as if it were incumbent on the alien soul that had taken up residence inside me to protect her from the longings and passions of its host. Thus, while Miss Kolby spoke to Dori on the phone, I went over to the window and lifted the curtain and stood behind it, half listening to the conversation and drinking in the clear autumn light bathing people who were now streaming out of the hospital with empty hands and a feeling of relief after visiting the sick. Throughout the conversation I was careful to remain in the background, so that the secretary would not feel obligated to mention my name and give Dori the impression that I was trying to get to her through her friends. She had to feel free, precisely because any contact between us now was apt to be fateful. When I emerged from my hiding place behind the curtain, before I could ask how Dori was feeling, the secretary turned to me with a serious expression and said, "She's looking for you." As if she suspected that I had not grasped the importance of the summons, she repeated emphatically, "Dori's looking for you," as if this were the gist and conclusion of the conversation between them. "So why didn't you call me to the phone?" I asked with a smile of surprise. She shrugged her shoulders and maintained an embarrassed silence. Accustomed for years to protecting Lazar and keeping his presence in the office a secret from callers until she had his express permission to reveal it, she had left it up to me to decide if I wanted to reply or not. Even the pencil poised between her fingers seemed to be waiting for some clear instruction from me.

But did I have any clear instructions for this faithful secretary, who had surprised me by her sensitivity, since I didn't know myself if this was indeed the signal I was waiting for or simply a call from a woman with a bad cold to a physician who had acted for a short time as her family doctor? Because if it was the signal calling me to come to her, it had arrived more swiftly than I could have imagined, though that was understandable in a woman incapable of staying by herself. I nevertheless found it startling. Was I ready for her call? I asked myself frantically as I hurried home, where Michaela was waiting for me to take her to the movies. I didn't get in touch with Dori, and we went to an early show, where I watched the vicissitudes of the love affair on the screen and tried to see if the solutions proposed by the director would suit my case. But my thoughts kept straying to the woman waiting for me to get in touch with her and prevented me from studying these solutions, which did not seem to suit the characters in the movie either, so the director had to pervert and contort every plausible and natural feeling in order to bring his movie to a satisfactory conclusion. "Completely idiotic," pronounced Michaela when the lights went on, and she took the glasses off her beautiful eyes and put them away in her pocket. "Like an Indian movie, but there at least the kitsch is open and unabashed, without these sophisticated tricks." I agreed with her, and told her about the movie I had seen in Calcutta. She was astonished to hear that I had wasted my few hours in Calcutta on a silly Indian movie, a few of whose colorful scenes had nevertheless remained in my memory. "You're right," I admitted, "but Calcutta made me panic, and I was afraid of getting lost." I told her about the dream I had had more than two years before on the flight from Bodhgaya to Calcutta, and I described the details so vividly that I seemed to have just woken up from dreaming it again in the darkness of the movie theater. "But it's impossible to get lost in Calcutta," said Michaela, and she began to describe the unique construction of the city, which made it very easy to find its center. I was unable to follow the thread of her words, not only because of the ethereal note she often struck when she was talking about India but because I was preoccupied by the thought that Dori was ill and suffering and perhaps still looking for me.

Indeed, our baby-sitter, a cute and intelligent little girl of about twelve who was the daughter of Hagit, Michaela's girlhood friend, and an unknown father, whose tender years caused us to go to the first show instead of the second, informed us as soon as we came home that "Lazar's wife is looking for you."

"Lazar's wife?" I repeated in surprise. "Is that how she referred to herself?"

"Yes, that's exactly what she said," the child replied confidently. Michaela gave me a look of mild astonishment when she saw that instead of going at once to the telephone, I started examining and even correcting the arithmetic exercises in our baby-sitter's notebook, and while she dug into the dish of multicolored ice cream sprinkled with flakes of chocolate that Michaela set before her—the only payment her mother permitted her to take from us—I also arranged her schoolbag for her, in place of her absentee father, smoothing out the creased papers and disposing of an old sandwich as I waited for her to say good-bye to Shivi so I could take her home. "Aren't you going to call Mrs. Lazar back?" Michaela finally asked, when I was standing at the door. "There's no need," I answered immediately, without even raising my eyes. "I know exactly what she wants. She's sick and she's looking for a doctor," and I told her about the conversation with the secretary who had taken Dori under her wing and was sleeping in her apartment. "If she's already taking to her bed," said Michaela sadly, straightening the collar of the little girl's windbreaker and making faces to amuse Shivi, "we can expect the mourning to be a heavy, long-drawn-out affair."

"Heavy, yes, that's only natural," I agreed, "but long-drawn-out? I'm not so sure." Michaela listened to me attentively, still trying unsuccessfully to catch my eye. "What do you intend to do about the phone call?" she pressed me before I shut the door behind me. "You can't just ignore her."

"I know," I reassured her, and I promised that I would drop in on her on my way home. When I went back inside and took my medical bag out of the closet, Michaela looked relieved.

I didn't call Dori, mostly because I was afraid that if I did, she would content herself with asking a couple of questions and reject my offer to go over and examine her. I was determined not to allow my role as doctor to replace my true role, which was becoming more possible from minute to minute, and which so flooded me with anxiety and desire that I didn't even wait for our baby-sitter to wave to me from her window, but drove off the moment her curly head disappeared into the stairwell, in a hurry to arrive before something inside me could subvert my decision to interpret Dori's phone call as the true call for which I had been waiting. Accordingly, I decided to leave my medical bag in the car, and as I soared to the top floor in the elevator, I knew that I needed no external confirmation in order to go in to her. I was impelled forward by the presence that had been stirring inside me ever since the death of Lazar, and as I stood in front of the door, surrounded by blossoming plants, I actually put my hand into my pocket to look for the key. When no key was forthcoming, I pressed the bell. It immediately uttered a shrill, piercing, birdlike whistle, but nobody seemed to hear it or to pay any attention to it. There was silence. The door was one of those heavy, opaque security doors, and left no crack to reveal if there was a light on behind it. I again pressed the bell, which the Lazars must have installed after they returned from India, for I didn't recall such a piercing whistle the first time I visited them, and during the week of mourning I had had no opportunity to hear it because the door had been left open to accommodate the constant stream of visitors.

In the distance I could hear her footsteps hesitating. And rightly so, for how could she have guessed that I would turn up unannounced on her doorstep at an hour like this? But when I sensed her hesitating on the other side of the door, unable to make up her mind whether to ignore the visitor or to ask who it was, I pressed the whistling doorbell again and called out, "It's only me." And in order not to let her off the hook, I added, "You were looking for me?" Then the door opened, and she stood there clumsily attired in a flannel nightgown and a thick green sweater of Lazar's. Her hair was disheveled, and by the red spots on her cheeks and the dull glitter of her eyes I could see that she had a real temperature, which actually reassured me, for even if it turned out that no love-call had been or could have been intended, it was still a good thing that I had come. "They've left you alone!" This strange cry escaped my lips, intended only as an exclamation of astonishment, but it also, to my surprise, contained a note of pain. "Who left me?" she asked with a frown, an expression of resentment crossing her face, perhaps because she sensed that in the depths of my heart I still insisted on thinking of Lazar as someone who might not have left her alone. "I mean," I stammered, "Einat, or . . ." and I couldn't remember the name of her son. But she immediately understood and leapt to his defense. "He had to return to his base," she said, still without a single smile, almost with hostility. Was it possible that she was angry at me? I felt a thrill of happiness, accompanied by a shadow of fear, as I identified the note of impatience with which she had sometimes addressed her husband in India. "Were you looking for me?" I repeated stubbornly, without even mentioning her obvious illness, in order to force her to address me as a young lover whose way was suddenly clear before him, not as a doctor on house call.

"Yes, I was looking for you," she admitted somberly, also ignoring the illness that had her in its grip. As if it were now my job to be at her beck and call, and she added resentfully, "Where have you been hiding from us?"

Outraged by the light shed on my situation by the last word in this short sentence, I did not hesitate, and with the feeling of confidence that had been swelling inside me ever since the first sign I had received from the secretary at the beginning of the evening, I clasped her to me in a firm embrace, her heaviness feeling curiously weightless in my arms. Whether it was the ardor burning in her limbs which gave her this new lightness or the strength of Lazar's soul bursting out of me, it was impossible to tell. Now, when I touched her, I realized that her fever was high and worrying, and that she herself was apparently unaware of how high it was. Her skin, which was very dry, without a trace of perspiration, seemed to show signs of a viral infection, which no antibiotic, including those in my bag downstairs, would be effective against. In spite of Lazar's heavy sweater wrapped around the upper part of her body, she was shivering, and I knew that if I insisted on removing it now and taking off her nightgown, the shivering would increase. I therefore knelt down in front of her and put my head on her stomach in the hope of kindling her desire.

But she didn't want any part of it, and with a savage gesture she pulled my hair as if to raise me to my feet and demanded clear protestations of love from me, as if she were no longer prepared to put up with the panic-stricken silence of our last encounter in bed. Because her feverish weakness gave this unexpected demand strength, I began, without releasing my grip on her, kissing and stroking her face and her hair and groping my way down the hallway to the bedroom, which seemed to have been taken over by chaos again, I began to seek and also to find new words, not only to describe my impossible love for her but also to try to tell her of the passionate desire aroused in me by the new obligation I felt not to leave her alone. "I know why you're looking for me. I know exactly why," I repeated in my emotion, and I helped her get back into the big bed, torn between the natural desire of a doctor to cover her with the blanket and balance the inner heat of her body with the heat of the air around her and the impulse to go on exposing her flesh, to undo the buttons of the thick old sweater so that I could pull up the nightgown and look at the strong breasts resting peacefully and abundantly above that round, pampered belly. And for the first time since my arrival, I saw a weak smile crossing her face, and although she seemed willing to postpone covering herself with the blanket, she was not ready to allow me to make love to her before I told her how much I loved her or explained my attraction to her in the light of the deepest secret of her being.

"It was Lazar." I couldn't resist betraying her dead husband as I went on stroking and kissing her arms and her bare legs. "Right at the beginning, when I wanted to know the real reason that you insisted on coming with us to India." She tried to open her eyes, heavy with both sickness and desire. "Even though he spoke about it complainingly, it was interesting to see how attracted he was, too, by your fear of abandonment." I went on talking, gradually lowering my body onto the big double bed to bring my head closer to her and slowly slide it down between her thighs, to be engulfed by the source of warmth itself. She was surprised to hear that Lazar had spoken about her so intimately to a stranger, even before the beginning of our trip. But now she understood too why sometimes at train stations I had tried to help him by staying with her in his place, not understanding that for her there was no difference between "being left alone" and "being left without him."

"So what's going to happen now?" I asked, carefully and gently moving my lips down her body. Her head froze on the pillow and she did not reply. "Has it always been this way?" I raised my head for her response, and beyond the white hill of her belly she nodded in confirmation, her eyes closed, swooning in the intensity of her passion and the heat of her fever. I advanced my lips to the glowing coal of her vulva, and with the last vestiges of her strength she began to move on my tongue, moaning with pleasure, but also pleading for mercy and warning me that I was going to be infected with her germs.

Before her illness could interfere with our lovemaking, over which the threat of my failure in London was still hovering, I hurried to get up and switch off the light, leaving only the little reading light on, and with the practiced speed acquired in the changing room next to the operating room, I took off my clothes and gently but firmly undressed her too, while continuing to shower her with the words of love and affection she desperately and stubbornly demanded, so that I could penetrate the core of her dread and calm the terror of her loneliness. And only afterward did the doctor and the lover join together in one man, who not only hastened to cover her with two big blankets but also turned his attention to her dry, barking cough. "Now I'm going to be your doctor too," I assured her, thankful that the illness had not been the pretext for her call. She lay curled up in the fetal position, limp and exhausted. I got dressed quickly and went downstairs to fetch my bag. I took the key from the door and put it in my pocket so she would not have to get out of bed to let me in. In spite of how late it was, the boulevard was full of gray-haired, elegantly dressed couples, evidently subscribers to the Philharmonic, whose concert must have lasted longer than usual. I hurried to the pay phone on the corner, behind which I used to hide to spy on the Lazars' comings and goings. Who would have guessed then that a night would come when the key to their apartment would be stowed in my pocket and she would be lying in their double bed alone, sick and helpless, waiting for me to come and help her as if we were an old married couple? I pushed the phone card into the slot and waited for the number of units I had left to be displayed. Did I really have to call Michaela now? I asked myself, and if I did, what should I say to her? If she were given to worrying about my lateness, I could have reassured her with a few words. But Michaela felt very secure in the world; she was not in the least prone to anxiety or panic, about me or anyone else, and she was always surprised when she heard that anyone had succumbed to an attack of anxiety about her. I knew that when she picked up the phone she would not ask where I had disappeared to or when I was coming home. She was far more likely to ask if I had already turned into a Brahmin.

❧❦

The little green screen on the telephone showed that I had three units left on my card, plenty for a conversation with my parents in Jerusalem, whom I had forgotten to phone earlier in my excitement. But my mother, whom I got out of bed, was very surprised to get my call, since only half an hour before she had spoken at length to Michaela, who told her about Shivi's exploits of the day, and mentioned that I had been called out to treat the sick Mrs. Lazar. "I'm sorry, I didn't know, I haven't been home yet," I explained. "So where are you phoning from now? Are you still there?" she questioned me anxiously. "No," I hastened to reassure her, careful at the same time not to tell a lie. "I'm speaking from a pay phone in the street. I simply remembered that I forgot to phone you today as I promised."

"Oh, you shouldn't have," said my mother, even though she was evidently touched by my concern. "When we speak to Michaela it's the same as if we spoke to you. But how come you're only through there now? What's the matter with her? Is it really something serious, or just a false alarm?"

"I don't know yet," I said, scrupulously avoiding a lie. "She has a high temperature but no other symptoms. It looks like a viral infection. I hope the Indian hepatitis hasn't returned through the back door," and I laughed a strange, brief laugh, surprised to see that despite how late it was the screen already showed two units less, leaving me only one unit to call Michaela. "But why did she call you?" my mother said with some annoyance. "Where are all their friends?"

"I don't know, Mother." I tried to cut the conversation short. "She asked me to go, so I went. What could I do? Refuse? Look, I'm in a hurry. We'll talk tomorrow. Good night." But when I inserted the card into the slot to call Michaela and give her, in the metaphor she favored, the first flicker of the flame that would soon burn our house down, the last unit had vanished into thin air. If only the white-haired symphony-goers had still been strolling down the street, I would have shamelessly approached one of them and offered to buy his telephone card at its full price, never mind how many calls were left on it. But the boulevard was already deserted except for one young man, who could only offer me a telephone token, which was useless on this phone.

Suddenly I felt a strong temptation not to go back to her, not even to return the key, but to leave it in the mailbox and disappear, in order to stop my impossible fantasy from turning into a real love affair, full of suffering and disappointment. Could a woman like her really love me? I asked myself despairingly. Would she really want to take me in? And what would her children say? Her mother? Hishin? What would my parents say? And what kind of love could she give me, a woman who had a little girl inside her, abandoned by her parents in a dark empty house, running in the street to look for a little friend to come and spend the night with her? It was only because I had fallen in love with her that she was clinging to me like this. Perhaps I should warn Michaela that something bad was going to happen in the story in which Lazar's sudden death was only the beginning. But when I went to the car and opened the door, I felt again a vague stirring inside me, which was not only the result of my weariness after a long day's work but also the longing of a lonely, tired soul who wanted to go home, now that the key was within his grasp. I took the little medical bag my parents had bought me for my graduation from medical school out of the trunk and went upstairs, and while I pressed the bell lightly with one finger—to warn her of my arrival with the shrill, birdlike whistle—my other hand opened the door with the key, and I asked myself if it would be worth waking her up if she had already fallen asleep.

But there was no need to wake her. In spite of her exhaustion she could not settle down, and she had gone to take a shower, after which she had changed Lazar's old sweater for the black velvet jumpsuit, put on white socks to warm her feet, and stuck

bits of cotton wool in her ears, and thus attired she sat down on
the sofa in the living room to smoke a cigarette, sunk in her fear
of abandonment as if it were the fear of death itself. When she
saw me come in she flashed me her old involuntary smile, watching silently as I put my bag down on the low glass table, where a
map of India had been spread the first time I met her. But then
the smile faded and she asked me sadly, "How long does it take
you to take a bag out of your car?" I didn't reply but only
smiled, pleased but also agitated by the thought that she was
already becoming dependent on me. And in order not to sweep
away all the boundaries between us, I asked her if Michaela had
phoned to ask for me. "Here?" she asked in surprise. "Does she
know that you're here?"

"Of course," I answered immediately, and by the decisive tone
of my voice I wanted to let her know that now that Lazar had
died, there would be no more need to lie to anybody in the
world. She seemed somewhat confused by this reply, and looked
silently at the medical instruments I removed from the bag, most
of which were still new and gleaming, since I had no private
patients so far and I used the clinic's equipment when I paid
house calls during my night shifts at the Magen-David-Adom
station. I took a chair and drew it up to the sofa, and with a
quick, light movement I whipped the cigarette from her fingers,
something which even Lazar had not dared to do. I put it out in
the ashtray, said firmly, "You shouldn't do that," and took her
wrist to feel her pulse, which was rapid but not as rapid as I had
expected, as if her temperature had gone down a little during my
absence.

Her blood pressure was normal, even low for her age, the diastolic less than eighty, and her heartbeat, which was rapid because of the fever, sounded soft and clear. In the narrow beam of
light from the otoscope I looked into her throat and ears. There
were no obvious signs of infection, only a redness due to excessive dryness. "You must have something hot to drink," I said.
But it turned out that her electric kettle had broken down a few
hours before. I interrupted my examination to go into the kitchen
and see what was wrong. Standing among unwashed cups and
glasses on the gray marble counter was the electric kettle, which
had nothing wrong with it apart from the fact that the plug had

come loose from the socket. I showed her the source of the problem. "Is that all?" She smiled incredulously. "I don't believe it."

"That's all," I said firmly. "How come you didn't see it for yourself?" But she was apparently incapable of seeing anything. Miss Kolby had already told me how she shrank from electrical appliances as if they were capable of harming her. But now, when the red light on the kettle went on and she was convinced of the insignificance of the "breakdown," she decided to trust me and showed me the toaster, which had also stopped working a few days ago, hoping that here the problem would prove equally easy to fix. In fact one of the screws had come loose, and with the aid of a kitchen knife I soon returned the red glow to the coils. And then, for no apparent reason, while the electric kettle began to whistle in the silence of the night, tears suddenly welled in her eyes, as if only now she realized the depths of the new abyss of dependency into which she had been cast by her husband, who had abandoned her for the world of the dead. I stood still and didn't make a move toward her. The sorrow and the pity in my heart prevented me from touching her, and she returned slowly to the living room and sat down in an armchair to finish her sad, soft weeping for the catastrophe that had suddenly become concrete. In the kitchen I poured two cups of tea and added a few cookies which I found in one of the drawers. I found the sugar bowl, and cut a few slices from an old melon I found in the refrigerator. I went into the living room and put the tray down on the glass table next to my stethoscope. Was she really a woman who would have to be taken care of all the time? I thought in a sweet panic, remembering how Lazar had danced attendance on her in India, and how naturally she had accepted his services, as she now accepted mine, nodding her head in thanks and picking up a teacup and beginning to sip the hot lemony brew gratefully, until I asked myself if this was already the dependency I hoped for, which would make it impossible for her to send me away.

"But how can you leave Michaela for so long?" she rebuked me, her eyes still red from crying. "She must be worried."

"No, Michaela isn't the worrying type," I said, and I respectfully described her independent spirit and inner serenity, and how she was at her best on occasions like this. "She isn't waiting up for me. I'm sure she's been fast asleep for hours." But I wasn't sure at all. Just the opposite—I thought that Michaela might have stayed up, if only to strengthen me with her thoughts from a distance, so that I could rise to the demanding occasion she knew was before me. And if she hesitated to call, it wasn't on her own account or mine but only out of her concern for Lazar's wife, whose grief might turn into panic and terror owing to a careless move on my part. Michaela did not yet know that before Lazar's death there had been a bond between us, which even if it did not cause the death at least prepared us for it. If she had known, she would have been as sure as I was of the trust the woman sitting here put in me. For instance, after she finished the last drop of tea, while she was wondering whether to ask for another cup, I stood up and put the stethoscope around my neck to conclude the interrupted examination. And without hesitating, she stood up submissively, and at this deep hour of night she pulled down her jumpsuit and stood facing me, half naked, white and heavy in the breasts and arms, exposing the secret map of beauty spots on her shoulders, and although she seemed slightly embarrassed, she showed no trace of fear that her young doctor would turn into a passionate lover again. As the diaphragm of the stethoscope began to warm up between my fingers, I listened carefully first to her heart and then to her lungs, which seemed a little congested but without any suspicious wheezing, and accordingly left me without a clear diagnosis, since I had no desire at this time of night to draw blood, as I had in Einat's little room in the monastery in Bodhgaya, in order to run tests. Since I was not in the habit, like some of the young doctors on night shifts in the emergency room or the Magen-David-Adom station, of throwing out sly psychological hints to people who thought they were ill, I stopped myself from making some critical remark to this beloved woman about the deceptions of the mind and only advised her to get back into bed and give both body and mind some rest. And although she was now alert and even a little vivacious, like a lot of patients who need no more than a doctor's examination to free them of their feelings of illness, she accepted my suggestion and only asked for another cup of tea before she went to bed, and she even went to put the kettle on herself, in order to make sure that nothing else was wrong with it, waiting to break after I left. But I had no intention of leaving her, not only because I knew that in the depths of her soul she couldn't stay by herself, but also because I was certain that Michaela, if she had indeed succeeded in staying awake, would both accompany me in her thoughts and actively support me in the attempt to return the soul that had invaded my body to its proper home and bed.

Dori obediently swallowed the two pills I gave her to bring her temperature down and went to take off her clothes and put on a fresh, flimsier nightgown. Then she got straight into bed, asking me only to cover her with three blankets and put the light on in the hallway before I left. But I didn't want to leave yet, certainly not before I heard the deep breathing of her sleep. I remained in the hall next to the open bedroom door, looking through the dark windows at the new restlessness of the treetops, constantly buffeted by the autumn wind. And as my eyes returned to gaze quietly at the contours of the figure buried beneath the mountain of blankets, I kept asking myself how I would be able to leave her. Even when her breathing became deep and rhythmic and was joined by a faint snore, which I remembered from the night in the train compartment with the Indian clerk, I still could not bring myself to leave. Waves of love and desire began swelling in my double soul, and a thrilling new pleasure kept me rooted to the spot. I could have gone into the bedroom and sat down for a while on the edge of the big bed without waking her, but I went on standing in the hallway, leaning against the doorjamb, keeping myself awake thanks to long experience on night shifts and hours of standing next to the operating table. But when the faint snoring became loud and coarse, because of the position of her neck on the pillow or congested sinuses, I remembered Lazar climbing onto the upper bunk in the train racing to Varanasi to take hold of her and make her stop. I went into the bedroom to follow his example, but my hold must have been too strong, or lasted too long, for she woke up, and with her eyes closed and her hair wild she sat up in bed and cried in alarm, "You?" I let go of her and retreated, because I knew that she meant *him,* and only *him,* as if through the touch of my hand she had felt the dead man's hand. But all this lasted no longer than a second, and by the expression of pain on her face I knew that the illusion had already been shattered. She groped for the switch of the reading light, but quickly gave up the attempt, dropped her head, and curled up into herself again, to seek the even rhythm of her breathing. But she did not find it, and she woke up and opened her eyes.

"I'm bothering you," I whispered when I saw her putting on her glasses to see me better. "No," she said at once in a clear, wakeful voice, as if she had not been sleeping for the past hour. And when I kept quiet, as if I thought she was only being polite, she raised her head from the pillow and said, "You've never bothered me." Then, as if to reinforce her words, she added, "You never bothered Lazar either. Before the trip we were wondering whether to take a doctor with us, because you know how it was with us, always together, wanting to be alone together. But already on that first evening, from the minute you came in, we felt that we would be able to get along with you. And we weren't wrong. Throughout the trip we marveled at how you always managed to be at our side without bothering us. Is it all due to the English manners you learned at home? The British temperament you inherited from your family? Is that what keeps you from getting on people's nerves, from pushing yourself forward, even though you too want to go far?"

"Far to where?"

"Very far." Her voice rose clearly in the silence of the night. "Very far?" I snickered. "Yes, very far," she repeated without hesitation. "Lazar always used to say about you, That's a man who wants to go very far, and he'll get there too, but quietly, the way I like." She fell silent for a moment, her eyes closed, as if she were about to go to sleep again. "But go where?" I insisted, a new fear stirring inside me. "Far to where?" She bowed her head patiently, like a mother facing a son who demands explanations for things that can't be explained. "Far, the way he saw himself going far." "You mean in the hospital?" I demanded with a tremor in my voice. "Yes, in the hospital too, of course," she said. "That's why he insisted on fixing you up with a permanent job, even if only half-time. When Hishin let you go, he was afraid that you would leave and go to another hospital. Because like him, you not only notice things that other people don't notice, but you also know how to absorb them and contain them in yourself, so that when you need them they'll always be there, without your having to worry about it."

"Without my having to worry about it." I echoed her words in excitement, not actually understanding what she meant. "But what made him talk about me at all?" She straightened her pillow behind her head and smiled. "Perhaps because right at the beginning, when Hishin suggested you, he said, 'This is the *ideal* man for you,' and Lazar, who was influenced by Hishin, began to believe it, especially after you confronted us at the airport and forced us to interrupt our flight and insisted on going to a hotel and giving Einat that blood transfusion, which even after all the clarifications we never really understood. But Lazar always said, Never mind, let it be arbitrary, let it even be completely mysterious. I know and feel that it saved her life." I had already heard Einat speak about her father's positive attitude toward the blood transfusion I had given her, but the explicit word "mysterious," uttered now in the darkness in the name of the dead director, filled me with happiness, in spite of the contempt it might have implied. And I felt a pressing desire to hear this word repeated in Lazar's name, until I was unable to contain myself any longer and I stepped forward, and without warning, in a trance of exhaustion, I lifted the blankets to join myself to the warm source of the mystery. At the first touch I knew that the two pills I had given her to take before she went to sleep had done their work; her body temperature was normal. If I really had another soul inside me, I thought feverishly, it needed its turn too, and I began passionately embracing and kissing Dori once again. She was startled and began to struggle, but even in the depths of my fatigue I was stronger than she was. And again she pleaded with me not to be silent, to speak of my love, as if making love in silence, and in the stillness of the night, was the worst kind of betrayal. I repeated the words I had said at the beginning of the evening and felt her ripe, mature body relaxing between my hands.

In the end she fell into a deep sleep, and I lay behind her back with my arms around her stomach, in the same position in which I had seen the Lazars sleeping in the hotel room overlooking the Ganges. I thought about Michaela, asking myself if she had stayed awake up to now to accompany me in her thoughts or if she had given up and gone to sleep. In either case, there was no need for me to hurry home. Even though I knew that I must not lose control over my conscious mind in this most intimate place, lying where the dead director lay, I could not overcome the deep impulse to go on holding her sleeping body in my arms, if not to sleep, then at least to dream a little, perhaps the very same dream I had dreamed in the big old propeller-driven plane flying from Gaya to Calcutta. But I couldn't remember the dream, only the interior of the plane, with the many Indians crowded into it. Then I tried to remember the movie I had seen with Michaela at the beginning of the evening, but it had evaporated from my mind. Thus I had no option but to surrender to the sleep overpowering me. But not for long. About three hours later, at five o'clock in the morning, I woke up in the same position in which I had fallen alseep, wide awake, as if this short sleep had satisfied me completely. I carefully disentangled my arms, slid off the bed, got dressed, and left the room, closing the door behind me. I felt light and spiritual, relieved of the inner weight that had been oppressing me for so long. In the living room windows the first lines of light were visible, and I wandered around the silent rooms, trying to identify the source of the anxiety threatening the woman I now had to leave alone. At seven I had to be at the hospital for my shift, and before then I had to go home to shave and change my clothes. But I didn't want to go home to Michaela like this, sticky and rumpled from the long night, and I was also afraid that I might have caught Dori's virus, if it was a virus, in the course of our lovemaking. I went to the bathroom, planning just to clean myself up with a washcloth. But the water heater was boiling, and I gave in to the temptation, got undressed, and took a shower. Lazar's toilet aricles were still scattered over the shelves, and his presence made itself felt in all kinds of things: his toothbrush, his shaving kit, his aftershave lotion, his bathrobe hanging behind the door. He had been right about my talent for noticing insignificant details and absorbing them into myself, for I now found myself recognizing many of the things he had taken with him to India, easily distinguishing them from the articles belonging to other members of the household. This being the case, I unhesitatingly, and without any feeling of strangeness, wrapped myself in his bathrobe, shaved myself with his shaving gear, and brushed my teeth with his toothbrush. I felt no need to say good-bye before leaving the apartment, for I was determined to return to Dori as soon as possible. I even took the key.

How strange it was, after such a night, to emerge into the bright Tel Aviv morning, which held not one single hint of mystery. I looked at the broad, familiar boulevard, at the cars covered with wet leaves torn from the trees by the tempestuous winds of the night, the crates full of milk standing outside the little supermarket, the newspaper boys, their rounds over, racing down the street on their Vespas. If only I too could race straight to the hospital, which was waiting for me now no less than it had once waited for Lazar. But I knew that even though I had already bathed and shaved, I had to show myself to the woman waiting for me in the kitchen, and to my surprise not alone, but with sweet little Shivi, who had already woken up and was sitting in her high chair, her mane of hair wild and a red third eye painted between her eyes—a sure sign of her mother's surging longings. And when Shivi saw me enter the room she put her two little hands together on her lips in the Indian greeting, as Michaela had taught her, in order to welcome the new Brahmin who had risen from the underworld.

Eighteen

And it quickly finds her, no longer a little girl in a wrinkled school uniform but a tall, attractive young woman standing in her kitchen in the morning, a red apron around her waist, stirring porridge with a big wooden spoon for her three children sitting in chairs of different heights according to their age, and gazing in astonishment at the windowsill, where a big bird has just landed and is pacing up and down before them like an agitated, preoccupied schoolmarm. The children's glee is very great at the sight of the boastful, brightly colored tail, wagging to and fro like the pendulum of a living clock. But the young mother standing behind them knows that in spite of the general merriment, she must be quick to calm the youngest of her children, for otherwise he will soon burst into tears for fear of the winged creature, which now stands still and stares at her with a single piercing green eye. She picks the little one up, cuddles and kisses him to comfort him, and hands him to the mystery that enters the room, her balding husband in a smart suit, with the gold-rimmed glasses on his eyes. And the mystery takes the child with such a bright, cheerful smile that we may presume he has already recovered from his insanity, and no longer goes about insisting that the world stands still and every hour is final and sufficient unto itself and nothing is ever lost in the universe.

✿✿✿

But was it wise to drop in on her now, or should I have gone straight to the hospital? The pallor of Michaela's face and the redness of her eyes bore witness to the fact that she had not been indifferent to the events of the night. Had she followed them in full consciousness, or in the fog of sleep? She smiled at me welcomingly when I came into the kitchen, as if she bore me no grudge for my absence and was even surprised at my hurrying home. Did I really have to confess everything that had happened last night, I asked myself, and tell her about the impossible infatuation that was turning into a possible love before I left for the hospital? Or did I have the right to silence? At first I only bent down to give a tender fatherly kiss to Shivi, and also to Michaela, from whose fingers I gently took the spoon in order to go on feeding the baby so she was free to prepare a hasty breakfast, which would include, if possible, a small bowl of the sweet baby cereal to which I had recently become addicted. I tried to eat my breafast in silence, but I soon saw that not only was Michaela demanding that I give an account of myself, but even Shivi had stopped eating to stare at me expectantly with all three eyes. This being the case, I began carefully, gradually selecting from the night's events a few of the essential details, concentrating mainly on the physical and spiritual health of the new patient who had imposed herself on me, slightly exaggerating her helplessness in everything from her domestic arrangements to her electrical appliances, and mockingly describing the obscure but real dread that descended on her when she was left alone. Although after Lazar's death I had resolved to try to avoid telling lies, at this moment I did not want, in the short time at my disposal, to drop the bombshell of the lovemaking into the bright morning air of the little kitchen, and I decided to make do with a description of the psychological support I had given the widow. But Michaela, who seemed fascinated by every word that came out of my mouth, insisted on confirming what she in any case sensed in her heart, and when she asked me in so many words if I had also slept with Lazar's wife, I could not deny her the full enchantment that my story seemed to arouse in her.

Thus, with my eyes fixed on the big clock hanging on the wall above the many-armed statuette we had received from Einat, which was standing on a high shelf, safely ensconced between two vases, I began to describe economically not only the first bout of lovemaking but also the second, to show how serious my battle with the soul inside me had been. I may have gone too far, for suddenly Michaela's face went very red and she seemed stunned, not so much by the sex itself as by its repetition, which was a clear sign of the profound change awaiting us all. "If so, he's got a strong grip on you now," she pronounced, contemplating me with a mixture of pity and admiration. "Instead of entering some lifeless, inanimate object in order to animate it and be reborn, he's latched onto a living human being in order to cling with all his strength to his previous place." And when I maintained my silence she added, "Be careful, Benjy, that in the end you don't lose your soul."

"But I've apparently already lost it, Michaela," I whispered with a very glum smile, shrugging my shoulders and taking my plate to the sink. And I took the key to the Lazars' apartment out of my pocket, as if to prove to her the concrete reality behind the bizarre metaphysical exchange we were conducting, half in earnest, half in jest, over our kitchen table—a reality that for all its pain was also one which might thrill her. For before her very eyes an ethereal idea from the India she so adored and longed for was being incarnated, not by a Hindu but by a rational, practical Western doctor, a moderate man trapped in the mystical seam between body and soul, where even Stephen W. Hawking had floundered, paralyzed. My heart contracted now at the sight of Shivi's eyes raised in deep attention to the words of the adults standing over her head. I had already noticed the peculiar attention she paid the conversations between her parents, an attention full of an inexplicable inner excitement, which led her now to rub her finger unconsciously on the perfect circle of the third eye which Michaela had painted on her brow and to turn it into a smudge spreading over her entire forehead. I looked at the clock. There were only a few minutes left before I had to leave for the hospital. I saw from close up that Michaela's beloved statuette was covered in dust and even had delicate spiderwebs clinging to it. Michaela looked with a smile at the key I showed her. "Now do you understand the profound wisdom behind the custom of burning the widow on her husband's funeral pyre?" she asked, and there was a malicious gleam in her eye. "No, I don't understand it," I answered honestly, a faint tremor of anxiety passing through me. "She has to be burned so that the yearning soul of her husband won't steal into her through a stranger's body. They don't burn the widow to punish her for remaining alive, but only to protect the soul of some weak, innocent stranger who is prepared to lend his body to the husband's eternal love." I nodded my head, and with a certain absentmindedness, because it was already time for me to leave, I took the statuette down from its shelf and lightly removed the lacy covering of spiderwebs, examining it to see if there was any coordination among its six arms. "In that case," I said, smiling, "do you think Dori should have been burned too?"

"Of course," she answered unsmilingly, in a provocative tone, her face flushing. "If she made Lazar love her so much, let her follow him to the grave." And with a new thought flickering in her great eyes: "And if she can't do it by herself, she can be helped." These last words, which had surely been said in a joke, struck terror into my soul, but I went on smiling, bending over Shivi, who seemed so interested in the statuette in my hand that I gave it to her. But she wasn't ready to receive the unexpected gift, and the statuette slipped out of her little hands and fell to the floor, scattering its six clay arms in various directions, and after a moment detaching itself from its head as well. A cry of pain burst from me, but Michaela remained composed, as if she had been prepared for an act of revenge after what she had just said. She crossed her arms on her chest to ensure the restraint she had imposed on herself, showing no intention of kneeling down with me to pick up the pieces of the little statue so dear to her heart, nor any intention of answering my ridiculous question as to whether it might be possible to mend it. With satisfaction and a note of triumph in her voice she said, "Now I'll have to go back there to find another one." And when she saw that I wasn't taking her seriously she added: "The only question we'll have to think about is whether I'm going to take Shivi with me right away or whether I should leave her for the time being with you, or your mother, or, why not, with Lazar's wife."

But there was no time to discuss this question now. The operation in which I was to participate as an anesthetist was scheduled to begin in half an hour. Surprisingly enough, in spite of the sharp words we had exchanged and Michaela's explicit announcement that she was going back to India, I did not feel that a real rift had taken place between us, and I left for the hospital feeling excited, and even a little happy at the idea that Michaela was giving me permission to continue my affair without throwing me out of the house. When she asked me just before I left if I would leave her the car in view of the rainy weather and the chores she had to do, I agreed immediately, since I had no idea

that she meant chores connected with her trip to India. Surely the
broken statuette alone could not have been enough to make her
get up and leave immediately for the Far East. Nor did I believe
that my infidelity had shocked her. A woman as free-spirited as
Michaela wasn't outraged by infidelities, hers or anyone else's.
No, it made more sense to think that what was happening to me
had simply reawakened, with great intensity, her old longing for
the spiritual climate in which she felt, as she had repeatedly explained to me, free and liberated, in a place that only seemed so
wretched and defeated. But was it really only her old longing for
India? Perhaps there was a new yearning behind it all, not for the
great subcontinent but for herself, as the true source of what was
happening to me, since more than two years before it had been
she who had come back from India in order to tell the Lazars
about their daughter's illness. Now, just as I too was being swept
up into an ill-fated karma, she felt that in order to rescue me she
had to return to the starting point, and to take my baby with her,
so that she might draw me back to the place where wise and
understanding forces would come to my aid, working through
those who needed me urgently—in other words, the truly sick
and maimed of the world, waiting on the sidewalks of Calcutta
for volunteer doctors to come to them from the world that called
itself free and happy. But I only began to understand all this
when Michaela finally decided to take Shivi with her, after Stephanie in London agreed to join her on this trip to India. On the
morning in question, in the operating room, feeling slightly dizzy
as I stood behind the anesthesia machine, I was thinking neither
of Michaela nor of myself but of the woman I had left sleeping in
the spacious apartment, either sick or well, who would soon
wake up and find herself alone and begin to worry about when I,
or somebody else, would come to keep her company.

❧

When I reached the hospital I wanted to go straight to the administration wing to tell Lazar's secretary that I had responded
to the call she had referred to me in the fullest possible way, and
to find out indirectly if she had already received any reports from
the other party. But there was no time. So I waited until after the
"takeoff" had succeeded and the patient had begun to sail gently

along his appointed course before slipping into the anteroom to call her and tell her that I had made a house call and there was nothing to worry about. She thanked me gratefully. "I know we're being a bit of a burden to you," she said, glibly including herself with the woman who was constantly in my thoughts, "but I saw that Mrs. Lazar was a little lost, without knowing exactly who to turn to, because Lazar used to put the whole hospital at her disposal. And although everyone'd be happy to help her, after what happened, everybody thinks that someone else is taking care of her."

"Yes," I said, "I thought that Professor Levine had taken her under his wing. He's more or less their family doctor, isn't he?"

"He was," she corrected me emphatically. "He was in the past. But now he's angry with her because she refuses to put all the blame on Hishin. He isn't satisfied with what I keep telling him, and what I told you too—that we're all a little to blame, me, Dori, her mother, and even Lazar himself. But no—that crazy, stubborn man, who was forgiven so many times by Lazar, wants to set up a kangaroo court to sentence Professor Hishin. He's not like you, Dr. Rubin, and refuses to take responsibility for himself. Yesterday, after you left, I felt a little bad about including you in my accusations."

"But why?" I reassured her. "You're right. We're all guilty, morally at least. Me too. No less than Lazar himself." But there was no time to elaborate on the moral guilt for Lazar's death while the patient I had left on the operating table could implicate me in criminal guilt as well. I therefore hurried back to make sure that the numbers flickering on all the monitors were compatible with the smooth continuation of the flight, leaving Miss Kolby with the promise that I would get back to her during the day for a firsthand report on the quarrel that had flared up between the two friends. This secretary was proving herself to be a pillar of support on which we could all lean in the confusion left by her boss's death. But how much support would she give me, I wondered, when sooner or later she found out about my relationship with his widow? I decided to go on investing in her, for I very much wanted this loyal and lonely woman on whom Lazar had depended, like many powerful executives depended on their secretaries, to be my ally not only in the little battles of the hospital but also in the great battle that had commenced this morning.

At the end of the operation, after I saw the clear gleam of consciousness in the pupil of the anesthetized patient's eye, which
meant I could leave him with the nurses in intensive care, and
after I received no reply when I called the Lazars' apartment, I
bought two sandwiches in the cafeteria instead of joining the
surgeons for lunch and hurried to Lazar's office.

Miss Kolby flushed with pleasure, not just because of the
cheese sandwich I offered her but mainly because I wanted to eat
my lunch in her company. "Lazar used to do that sometimes,"
she said, and the sweet light of memory touched her delicate,
faintly lined face. "When he saw that I was staying in the office
because of the workload and refusing to go to the cafeteria for
lunch, he would get annoyed with me, and in the end he would
go and get me something to eat."

"Someone who's become accustomed to taking care of one
woman is apparently drawn to taking care of other women too."
I laughed affectionately at the thought of the energetic director,
who was probably suffering torments of frustration in his grave
because of his inability to take care of things. "He used to take
care of me too," I recalled. "On the trip to India, on the flight
from Rome to New Delhi, when I fell asleep and missed supper, I
woke up and found a sandwich and a chocolate bar in the pouch
of the seat in front of me." Lazar's secretary bowed her head in
sorrow. Grief for her patron was apparently welling up in her
again, especially in view of the changes that had taken place in
her office since yesterday, as if the many administrative problems
that had seemed to vanish along with the administrative director
had not found anyone else in the entire hospital to take care of
them and had come back to flood the office in the form of stacks
of files piled on and around her desk. Was an heir about to appear and take over? Judging by the arrival of an unfamiliar secretary, who had replaced the vanished typist, it seemed so. This
new secretary had apparently been brought in from outside the
hospital, and although she had not known Lazar, she listened
avidly to every word Miss Kolby and I exchanged, a secret,
faintly mocking smile occasionally crossing her face. When she
saw that Lazar's secretary was ignoring her and not troubling to
introduce me to her, she waited for a break in our conversation
and introduced herself and asked me my name, which I knew she
would not forget but would file away for future reference, like all

ambitious secretaries. Then she offered to make me something to drink. But Miss Kolby dismissed this offer and took me into Lazar's office, both to give me the treatment a member of the inner circle of the previous director's friends deserved and to escape the curiosity of this woman, who might have been hired not only to assist her but to replace her.

When I entered the big room I saw that the sofa which had been missing the day before had now been returned, apparently after undergoing some minor refurbishment or repair. The dry soil in the planters had been watered. Here too stacks of files awaited the attention of the new director, signs of whose imminent arrival were apparent everywhere. "Do you know who it's going to be?" I asked Miss Kolby, who was putting on the electric kettle. "No." She shrugged her shoulders. "I haven't the faintest idea. I don't even know if they've decided on anyone yet. But I can already feel him in the air."

I suddenly felt a twinge of envy, as if the man who was going to replace Lazar and run the hospital were superseding me too, for I was both willing and able to make decisions regarding these files, one of which I even picked up and paged through, to the evident disapproval of Miss Kolby, who said nothing. "What does the administrative director actually do all the time?" I asked when I saw that the file in my hands was a personnel file, with the photograph of a young woman attached to it. "Personnel problems?"

"Not just those, of course," she replied, "but they did take up a lot of Lazar's attention. He was attracted to them. Yes, he took satisfaction in secretly controlling people's lives." I took the cup of coffee she offered me and sank onto the sofa with a deep sigh, overcome by exhaustion after standing on my feet for six hours during the surgery, on top of the nearly sleepless night I had spent at the Lazars'.

But this secretary was so devoted to the Lazar family that it didn't surprise her at all to hear that I had spent the whole night there. The only thing she couldn't understand was why I had remained awake. "That's going too far," she rebuked me, as one who had accumulated a few nights' experience in keeping vigil over the loneliness of Mrs. Lazar herself. "It would have been enough for her to know that you were there, sleeping on the sofa in the living room." She settled into an armchair next to me, crossing her extremely thin legs and speaking as if she thought it likely that I might be called on to spend the night again this evening, and other nights to come too. A wave of pleasure flooded through me, and a wish to confess what had really happened. Why should Michaela have the right to spread the news in her Indian version of events while I was sentenced to silence? And the woman sitting next to me wasn't just a secretary, but a bosom friend of the Lazars. In the depths of her soul she must have realized who was really sitting beside her, because when she saw me yawn and sink back into the cushions, she suddenly suggested that I remove my shoes and use the sofa for a short nap before my next operation, in only half an hour. "Sometimes I used to arrange things so that Lazar could take a short nap between appointments without anyone's noticing. You deserve a rest too. Why not?" she declared warmly. And while I was hesitating over whether to accept this tempting offer, she drew the curtains to darken the room, took a thin blanket out of one of the bottom drawers, and disconnected the battery of telephones, after which she left the room, saying, "Even fifteen minutes will help to make up for the sleep you missed last night, and in the meantime I'll phone to find out what's going on and where Mrs. Lazar disappeared to." There was no doubt, I reflected with an obscure satisfaction, that Lazar's sudden death had turned this usually correct and refined woman's head too, if she could suddenly invite me to take a nap on his sofa. The idea of sleep seemed impossible, excited and intoxicated as I was by the previous night's events. But I closed my eyes and withdrew like a snail into my thoughts, and wrapped myself in Lazar's blanket, which was too thin to provide any warmth and apparently intended only to protect him symbolically from the world constantly knocking at his door.

In the stillness of the room I suddenly became aware of the steady dripping of the rain, and it began to oppress me, as if it too were joining in the general hostility that would confront me as soon as Michaela's departure for India and my love affair became known. But if, in addition to taking Lazar's place with the woman who was only a few years younger than my mother, I was called upon to fill his chair, which I could see looming behind the desk, and to administer the hospital in his place, the hostility might be seriously diminished. And why not? I might be only a young doctor, but I felt that I had the ability and the strength to make decisions. With my medical education, I would even be able to improve the quality of the decisions taken in this room. Prompted by a sudden urge to examine the file I had previously glanced through, I got up and walked over to the desk in my stocking feet, only to discover that the picture of the young woman on the cover had misled me and that the file belonged to the head nurse in the surgical department, who had written to ask Lazar to postpone the date of her retirement and added a recommendation from Hishin. But while I was deliberating over what I would say if the decision were up to me, Lazar's secretary, who had overheard the rustle of the papers in the next room, knocked on the door and came in to announce the good news that Dori was at home, her temperature had gone down, and she was feeling fine. She had gone out to do some shopping and was about to go in to her office for a few essential meetings. She sounded altogether more cheerful, and tonight her son the young soldier would arrive for a few days' leave, so we could all relax. "Didn't you tell her that I was here?" I asked. But, faithful to her principle of never betraying anyone's presence without their explicit permission, she immediately replied, "Of course not. We've already given you enough trouble. Now her son's with her, and Hishin has also promised to get in touch with her. You've already done more than enough."

With this confirmation, I left the administrative wing for the surgical wing, where I was scheduled to assist Dr. Joubran, who was soon to replace Nakash as anesthetist in the intensive care unit, in a thyroidectomy. But when I arrived, there was nobody there except for the patient, an elderly man with a lot of red hair, who had just been brought down from the ward to the operating room. In spite of the premedication he had been given in the ward, he was still very alert, sitting up restlessly on his bed in a short white open gown, his naked legs swinging in the air, listening to the sound of the storm raging outside, his eyes wide open and terrified. I went up to him, introduced myself, and urged him to lie down. I gently rubbed his neck and shoulders, as if I were calming a frightened animal. His medical file and the brown envelope with his X-rays were lying at the foot of his bed, and although it was not my duty as the assistant anesthetist to study them, I took out all the documents and X-rays and spread them on the bed and examined them one by one. Then I asked him a few questions about himself. He was a quiet, modest man of about seventy, a member of a kibbutz in the Jordan Valley, who was proud not only that he still worked six hours a day in one of the regional factories but also that his son, who had brought him down from the ward and was now waiting outside in the waiting room, was also a loyal member of the kibbutz. I talked to him a bit about his illness and asked him to tell me how he felt and where it hurt. He said that he had hardly any pain, and his main feeling was fear at being left alone in the operating room. His face was flushed and his breathing heavy and noisy. I decided to examine him, in order to pass the time and also to set my mind at rest. First I measured his blood pressure, which as I had suspected was alarmingly high, and totally unsuitable for the lengthy surgery he was about to undergo; his pulse and heartbeat were irregular too. It was impossible to tell if these findings were temporary, caused by the panic raging inside him, or if there was some organic cause which nobody upstairs had noticed. I called the internal medicine department and asked to speak to one of the doctors. When they put me through I recognized the voice of Professor Levine. At first I wanted to put the receiver down, but he had already recognized my voice and called me by my name. Ever since Lazar's death we hadn't exchanged a word, and so I tried to be as careful as possible and to give him only the dry facts, without interpretations or suggestions. He listened to me attentively and did not try to belittle any of the details I mentioned or dismiss my speculations. Instead he inquired, with a very uncharacteristic anxiety, what I would recommend doing, as if I, not he, were the true source of authority here. "I thought maybe one of your people could come down and discuss it with the surgeons," I suggested cautiously. "There's no point in talking to the surgeons," he said with inexplicable anger. "Once they've got their hands on the patient, they won't let go. No, the best thing would be for you to get him out of there right away and bring him back to the ward, and after that perhaps we'll decide what to do together." Now I knew that I had made a mistake by interfering. The terror of the patient, and the anxiety that had been floating around inside me since the morning, had already fanned the flames of Levine's paranoia. But I had no option now, and I went out into the corridor to look for the patient's son, a sturdy kibbutznik who was sitting and reading a newspaper, to ask him to take his father back upstairs. I refrained from accompanying them, not only because I had to wait for the operating team to explain the disappearance of their patient, but also because I didn't want to meet Professor Levine, who I knew wasn't interested in discussing the patient's condition but in denouncing Professor Hishin and his role in Lazar's death. The surgeon soon arrived, and as I had imagined, it was none other than my old rival, Dr. Vardi. I told him dryly about my examination of the patient, my phone call to Professor Levine, and the decision to postpone the operation. He listened quietly to my explanations, his blond head slightly bowed. I knew that he was dying to come out with some crushing remark about the strange new collaboration between myself and Professor Levine, but he restrained himself and said nothing, as if he realized that I was not myself and did not want to upset me any more. Finally he shrugged his shoulders and said, "In that case, we can all go home."

✻✻✻

Since I didn't have the car with me, I thought of getting a ride part of the way with Dr. Vardi, but when I stood in the entrance to the hospital and realized how heavy the downpour was, I was overcome by a desire to wash away all the tension and tiredness that had accumulated inside me with the pure water filling the air. I said good-bye to him and went out into the storm, occasionally taking shelter under a store awning or in the entrance to a building, vacillating between the need to go home and rest and the intense desire to go to Dori's office in the south of the city and see for myself if she was as well as she said she was. But my problem was solved when a deluge soaked me to the skin, forcing me to go home and change my clothes. The apartment was empty, and judging by the few plates in the rack over the sink, Michaela and Shivi had not even come home for lunch. I switched on the hot water heater and got undressed and into bed, where I covered myself completely with the quilt. The thought of sending the red-haired patient back to the ward without his operation now filled me with remorse. Who would have imagined that the mere sound of my voice would throw Levine into confusion? If he was really tormented by guilt over Lazar's death, I would have to be particularly careful in any future contact with him. The telephone rang. For a moment I was afraid to answer in case it was a summons to return to the operating room, but it was only Hagit, Michaela's childhood friend and the mother of our young baby-sitter. She was looking for Michaela, who was supposed to have arrived at her place with Shivi an hour before. "They must have been held up by the rain," I said, without feeling worried, and I asked her to tell Michaela that I had come home early from the hospital. "Do you want her to call you when she gets here?" she asked. "Only if she wants to," I replied, and after I put the phone down I called my parents. They weren't at home, but they had installed a new answering machine, which I knew they had been considering buying. My father's slow, excited voice answered first in Hebrew and then in English and asked the caller to leave a message after the beep. I congratulated them on their new acquisition, which was intended to improve communication between us without making it too burdensome, for ever since Shivi had arrived in the country their craving for daily contact had increased. I added something about the storm raging in Tel Aviv, told them how their granddaughter had accidentally smashed the Indian statuette to smithereens this morning, and promised to call again during the evening. Now that I had fulfilled all my duties to the world, I snuggled up under the granny's big down quilt and dove into my soul to discover what remained there.

At last, a dream bathed in light rose quickly in the darkness of my closed eyes. And clearly the dream was mine and nobody else's, for my father was supposed to be present in it, since I had gone especially to meet him in a rural settlement next to a lake which lay hidden in the gentle fold of a pleasant hill whose slopes were covered with plots of land so well tended that they looked like flourishing gardens. Although it was a fine spring day, vestiges of the long, hard winter were still floating at the edges of the sky, scraps of gray cotton wool sailing past the stone window of one of the houses, which consisted of nothing but one narrow room. In it a handful of silent farmers, their reddish hair proclaiming them to be blood relations, were sitting around a long narrow table full of knives and forks, waiting for the last guest so they could begin their meal, which an invisible woman was cooking in a lean-to kitchen. Maybe they're waiting for me to bring him to them, I thought, and I went out to search for my father among the narrow canals of water winding between the houses, and as I walked I thought not of him but of the old car he had given me. Where had it disappeared to, I wondered, where had I parked it? Was it possible that I had driven up the narrow dusty paths through the flourishing fields covering the slopes of the hill? The hill was so easy to climb that I effortlessly reached its summit and looked down at the large lake surrounded by empty wasteland, and I went down the other side, and as I walked I felt full of distress that I was here all alone and there was nobody to help me drag the old car out of the grim gray water of the lake, into which I had apparently absentmindedly allowed it to roll. But then I was awakened by the ringing of the telephone, which immediately rescued me from my distress. It was Hagit, phoning to tell me not to worry, because Michaela had called to say that she and Shivi were on their way to her house.

"Thank you. But I really wasn't worried," I explained affably to this good friend, who apologized for waking me up in her eagerness to reassure me. "I always have complete faith in Michaela. Soon you'll see just how much I trust her, when you hear about her new plan to return to India, this time with Shivi."

"So you gave in to her in the end?" cried Hagit, who sounded upset at the idea of parting from her friend, even though she knew how Michaela longed for India. "And you? Are you going too?"

"How can I leave everything here? You tell me," I demanded. Then I added, "Maybe I'll go in the end to bring them back." And with this thought I also reassured myself when shortly afterward I heard how much Michaela had already accomplished in preparation for the journey. It was as if to compensate for the dismemberment of her beloved statuette she had decided to grow another head and two more pairs of hands during the few hours of my absence so she could transform her return to India into a fact from which there was no turning back. She had been to several travel agencies to compare dates and prices of cheap flights and make notes of possible alternatives, and she had visited the Indian consulate that had recently opened in Tel Aviv to apply for a visa, and of course she had not forgotten to go to the Health Bureau to find out whether a baby of Shiva's age could be vaccinated. Since all this wasn't enough for her to feel that her trip was becoming a concrete reality, she had made her way in the pouring rain to a number of used-car lots to find out how much she could get for our car, which she had decided to sell to pay for her trip, and at the same time to inquire about a second-hand motorcycle for me so as not to leave me without any means of transport after she was gone. All this had been preceded, of course, by a long telephone conversation with Stephanie in London, to warn her of the imminence of the date of departure. She told me all this on the phone as soon as she arrived at Hagit's place, as if she were afraid that I might have changed my mind during the day and would try to prevent her from taking Shivi, whose participation in the trip she regarded as absolutely essential, especially now that Stephanie had agreed to go along.

Michaela's voice was full of excitement; it was evident that the day of running around in the rain to prepare for the trip had filled her with joy, as if the possibility of a great love had opened up today not for me but for her. Darkness had already descended on the apartment in spite of the earliness of the hour, and the rain which had been falling all day was still pouring down, as if the winter so often promised by the weather forecasters had finally burst forth in full force. I had taken a shower and changed into clean, warm clothes, and when Michaela called I was in the middle of wondering whether to go to Dori's office to find out where I stood after the night before. It was even dark in the kitchen, which was usually full of light in the afternoons, and only a single ray of light succeeded in escaping the sunset hiding behind the clouds and weakly penetrating the window above the sink. To Michaela's credit, I have to say that her great happiness did not prevent her from sensing my somber mood, which was due not only to the return of the soldier-son and my growing uncertainty about my position but also to the thought that I would soon have to travel around on foot. After repeating her assurance that she would not have Shivi vaccinated without first consulting me, Michaela suddenly took pity on me and said persuasively, "You remember how amazed I was the first time we met, at Eyal's wedding, that you hadn't taken advantage of your free trip to India to stay on for a while by yourself? If you regret what you missed then and you want to join us, why don't you come along? We'll welcome you with open arms and accept you just as you are, whatever the state of your soul." And her laughter burst out, free and uninhibited, just as it had always done in London. For a moment the thought crossed my mind, Why not? Perhaps this was my chance to escape from the snares in which I was getting increasingly entangled. Maybe in the place where the gorgeous silk of my infatuation had gradually been woven, my love might slowly unravel and dissolve into the mystery that had given birth to it.

But Michaela was not able to penetrate my thoughts any further, nor to take advantage of my momentary indecision and sweep me along with her. And perhaps she didn't want to. She immediately took my silence for a refusal, and without asking me what I was going to do for the next couple of hours she said good-bye, without telling me when she was coming home—as usual. I switched on the light in the kitchen, not only in order to banish the gloom but also to look for my old crash helmet in the storage space between the kitchen and the bathroom. I wasn't angry with Michaela for selling the car to finance her trip; I knew there was no other way we could pay for it, and although my parents had given the car to me to replace my motorcycle, it was still our joint property, like everything else we possessed. Her offer to buy me a motorcycle with part of the money she got for the car seemed fair to me too, and I even liked the idea, although I knew that seeing me on a motorcycle again would upset my parents, whose continued absence from their house on a day like this surprised me. When I heard my father's excited voice on the answering machine again, I was careful not to say anything, in order not to alarm them by leaving two messages in a row, and I quietly replaced the receiver and put on the black helmet, which during the year and a half of lying in storage had absorbed the bitter smell of mold brought by winds from the nearby sea. In the mirror I saw my previous self, young and carefree. Wouldn't the motorcycle make things more difficult for me in the battle I had commenced today with the world around me? Naturally I couldn't expect a woman of mature years to put on the second helmet like Michaela and ride behind me to visit my parents in Jerusalem. But it was quite possible that on some hot summer evening when the streets were jammed with traffic and parking places were hard to find, she might be persuaded to mount the pillion in order to arrive at the movies on time. The mere thought of this filled me with yearning to see her now, and although it was not a hot summer evening but a rainy winter one, I couldn't bear to stay in the apartment alone any longer, and I took an old umbrella that the granny had left in a corner with the mop and the broom and went outside.

There was no doubt that the big black umbrella had belonged not to the dainty little granny herself but to her husband, and I was glad to see that in spite of long disuse it opened easily and gave me plenty of protection from the rain. I decided to continue by foot, remembering with a smile the Indians who never parted from their umbrellas, rain or shine, by day and sometimes even by night, as if the black shelter above their heads were intended not only for physical protection from the elements but also for spiritual elevation. Indeed, I too felt elevated when I arrived almost completely dry at Dori's office, which I found very crowded and busy at this early evening hour. The lights were on in all her colleagues' rooms, and there were a number of people in the waiting room. I had to wait until one of the three secretaries opened Dori's door to usher in two clients who had been sitting conspicuously apart in the waiting room, and then I let her know I was there and asked her how she was feeling, in my capacity as a fussy family doctor. Even if she was embarrassed and confused by my sudden appearance, she maintained her composure and greeted me with the old automatic smile, as if I were one of the clerks here. A silver-haired gentleman in an elegant suit who looked like a lawyer drew his chair up to hers, apparently to equalize their positions vis-à-vis the two clients who entered the room, presumably for the purpose of reaching a compromise. She took advantage of the brief pause and came over to me, confident that I would not try to draw her into a long discussion just now. She was wearing black, as she often had before Lazar's death. But this time I did not recognize her outfit, which consisted of a black sweater with a high collar and a slightly too-tight skirt, which made her stomach stick out with an ugliness than even her long shapely legs, in high-heeled boots, did not make up for. Was she really better? I asked myself. Or maybe she had never been ill? But the night before I had felt her fever in every part of my body. She evidently had no intention of introducing me either to her colleague, who was obviously wondering who I was, or to the unfamiliar secretary who tried to bar my way and find out whether I wanted Dori or one of the other partners. I did not want to get involved in a long discussion either, but only to tell her my big news: that Michaela knew, that she was going abroad, and that very soon I would be free to make myself entirely available to Dori until . . . who knows? Even marriage was possible. But it was impossible to say any of this in the presence of so many strangers, so I stuck to the role of the devoted doctor dropping in on his patient on his way home from work to ask if the medication had helped. "Everything's fine. The fever's gone down completely," she said, smiling in embarrassment, and when she saw that I was not content with such an optimistic report, she added, "It's just that I've started to cough. I'll try to pick up something on my way home. Symphocal, or something like that."

"Symphocal is good for children," I responded quickly, even though it was effective with adults too. "I'll bring you something better. When are you leaving here? Because I haven't got the car." She touched my arm lightly with her fingertips to bring me to my senses. She didn't have a car either. Someone from the office would take her home, or perhaps Hishin would pick her up, because he wanted to come over and look for some papers Lazar had taken home with him. "So if not here," I said, retreating, "I'll take it around to your apartment." And with those words I took the keys out of my pocket, to show her that I was serious.

Upon seeing them, she uttered a strange cry of relief, as if she had been looking for them everywhere, and reached out and snatched the key ring nimbly from my fingers. In spite of her patience with me, in the face of the growing irritation of the other people in the room—and her confidence that my youth would prevent the inquisitive secretary from guessing the nature of our relationship—she wanted to restrain me and draw clear limits, which I immediately showed myself willing to accept, and in spite of my disappointment at having the keys taken away from me, I said good-bye pleasantly and left. Outside, the rain had stopped, but I opened the umbrella anyway. I soon found a pharmacy, where my physician's card enabled me to obtain a powerful cough medicine from the restricted-medicines cabinet, a drug that Nakash liked to use to nip colds and influenzas in the bud. Although I could have gone back to Dori's office and left the cough medicine with her secretary, I felt a strong urge to return to the Lazars' apartment. Seeing that the lull in the rain was continuing and the radiant, sparkling air was bringing many people out to walk happily in the streets, even though they had to negotiate between the puddles, I decided to continue on my way, taking a shortcut across town and thinking of the letter I would leave for my love along with the medicine. Soon, as if I had been coming home here for years, I could recognize in the white light the distant silvery tops of the trees in the boulevard next to the house, and even though the slot in the Lazars' mailbox was big enough to accommodate the package, I folded my umbrella and took the elevator to the top floor, knowing that perhaps in doing so I was entering a battle for my love against its most fanatical, if still unknown, opponent.

❧

But he had not yet come home from the army. The door was opened by Einat, with the sound of the washing machine spinning in the background. She had come home to do her laundry, and she now stood in the doorway, surprised and even a little alarmed to see me holding the medicine bottle in my hand, not only because she did not know her mother had been ill but also because she had thought that her father's death would put an end to my relations with the family, not the opposite. Now that her face was so pale and her beauty had faded, I noticed a resemblance to Lazar that had not been evident before, as if the painful memory of seeing her father die before her eyes had carved his image secretly on her face. She was sloppily dressed in a greenish sweater and a pair of jeans that were too big for her. When she took the bottle hesitantly from my hand, careful not to touch me, I was afraid that in her distraction she was liable to send me away. I asked her if I could call the hospital. Without a word, still fearful, she showed me the way to the living room, which was now perfectly clean and tidy—no doubt the work of the maid. Einat went into the kitchen and shut the door behind her, ostensibly to give me privacy but actually to quickly finish eating the improvised meal I had interrupted. I phoned the internal medicine ward to ask about the patient whose surgery I had prevented at the last minute. Although I didn't know his name, the nurse immediately knew whom I was talking about, not by the details of his medical condition or his age but by his red hair, which had apparently made an impression on her too. It turned out that he had been returned to the operating room after a heated argument between Professor Levine and Professor Hishin, who had suddenly appeared in the ward and insisted that the operation take place. "So they did it anyway," I said softly, thinking remorsefully that my excessive anxiety had led to a renewed outbreak of the rivalry between the two friends. "Did they mention my name, by any chance?" I asked. "Yes, Dr. Rubin," said the nurse. "They're angry with you and with Dr. Vardi for playing hooky."

"Playing hooky?" I giggled at the use of this childish term. But was there any point in trying to explain my real motives? I put the phone down and went to ask Einat, who was sitting at the kitchen table polishing off a carton of cottage cheese, if I could make another phone call. The kitchen too was clean and tidy, and between the flowered curtains on the big window I saw that it was beginning to rain again. Einat smiled shyly. "What a question! As many as you like. Make yourself at home," she said, and as I turned back to the phone to call Hagit and ask Michaela to come and pick me up here and take me home, she asked if I had time for a cup of coffee before I left.

I was of course happy to accept her offer. In the first place I intended to wait for Michaela to come and pick me up anyway, and, more to the point, I still hoped to see the mistress of the house when she came home. I wanted to try to get to know Einat a little better, and also her soldier brother, who suddenly arrived, soaking wet. Since I had last seen him in the corridor of the internal medicine ward he had exchanged his khaki uniform for the pale gray of the Air Force and his gun for a small, light submachine gun, no doubt thanks to the intervention of influential friends of the family, who had succeeded in getting him transferred to a service unit close to home and his widowed mother. Despite his surprise at my presence, which bordered on hostility, I tried to be nice to him. When I told Einat about Michaela's plans to return to India, it was as if this simple announcement transformed her, rousing her from her apathy and even restoring a little of her previous beauty to her delicate face. "I knew it!" she cried enthusiastically, although she also ex-

pressed some doubt about how much fun it would be to wander
around India with a baby. But when I told her that a good friend
from London would be accompanying them, she was reassured.
A good friend could be a great help. If only she could, she too
would gladly join them, but nobody would give her permission
to go now, especially after what had happened. It was impossible
to tell whether she meant the hepatitis or the death of her father.
"You need permission?" I cried in astonishment. "Whom from?
Your mother? I'll give you permission." And although I didn't
say in whose name I was giving her permission, she understood
that it was in my capacity as a doctor, and her eyes lit up with a
rare, provocative gleam. "And if I get sick again," she asked,
"will you come by yourself to fetch me?"

"You won't get sick again," I said confidently, "and if by any
chance something does happen to you there, don't worry. We'll
come to the rescue again. Why do you still want to go there,
Einat? Wasn't the first time enough for you? What draws all of
you so much to India?" She was surprised at my question. "I
thought Michaela had already infected you with the India bug."

"Michaela is a lost cause. She's already half a Hindu herself," I
replied. "That's why she's incapable of explaining anything to an
outsider like me." Einat looked at her brother, who was standing
in the doorway listening to our conversation and eating a thick
slice of bread. Then she bowed her head, trying to meet the challenge of finding a convincing explanation for the fascination with
India. In a quiet, halting voice she began to formulate her
thoughts. "A lot of things are attractive. But the most compelling
is the sense of time. Time's different there—it's free, open, not
harnessed to some goal. Without any pressure. At first you think
it's unreal, and then you discover that it's the true time, the time
that hasn't been spoiled yet." When she saw that I had not succeeded in understanding the depths of this other sense of time,
she added, "Sometimes it seems there that the world's stopped
turning, or even that it never started turning in the first place.
And every hour there is enough in itself, and seems final. So
nothing ever gets lost." A faint sneer now crossed her brother's
face, but when he saw that I was nodding my head in profound
agreement, he crammed the rest of the bread into his mouth and
went to pick up his submachine gun and duffel bag, which were
lying in the middle of the living room floor.

But the shrill whistle of the front door bell interrupted him, and he opened the door to his wet, shivering mother, both of whose hands were full—one with a cake box and the other with a shopping bag and a dripping umbrella. Although she knew that her son was due to arrive, she broke into loud cries of joyful surprise and hurried to put down her packages and embrace him as if he had just come home from the wars, forgetting that there were other people present. In the end she gave Einat a quick kiss too and asked her to help her unpack her bag. When at last she turned her attention, with a suspicious smile, to the medicine I had brought her, the bird-cry pierced the air again, and Hishin appeared at the door in a heavy, waterlogged coat and with the old baseball cap once more on his head, carrying another shopping bag. He too was glad to see the soldier, slapping him on the shoulder and saiding, "I see we pulled it off" as if he had had a hand in the boy's transfer. Without asking permission from anyone or taking any notice of me, as if I were some kind of ghost, he took off his coat and hurried over to the big desk standing in the corner of the living room. This was apparently the true purpose of his visit, for within a few minutes he had succeeded in identifying the documents he was looking for and separating them from the rest of the files and papers. Then he announced to Dori, with a satisfied look, "Now I can rest easy." A violent attack of coughing prevented her from reacting, and when all her smiles did not succeed in calming the spasms racking her, she picked up my medicine and showed it to Hishin, who said nothing except that it was a strong cough medicine favored by Nakash, which did nothing to recommend it to Dori. "Wait, don't go yet," she said to her old friend, who showed no signs of intending to leave. "Let's all have tea." And after asking Einat to put the electric kettle on and see that the plug wasn't loose, she went into her bedroom to take off her wet, muddy boots, to which a few autumn leaves were sticking. Hishin finished reading what was written on the label of the bottle and without saying a word sank into an armchair, the files in his hand, still ignoring me pointedly, as if I really had turned into a ghost. During the past month he had grown a little thinner, and there were new lines on his face, which still, in spite of everything that had happened, fascinated me. From the bedroom the sound of Dori's coughing reached us. Hishin stopped reading and listened, a faint smile crossing his face, as if he did not believe there was an organic cause for her cough. His eyes finally met mine, and he suddenly said in a natural tone of voice, as if he were continuing a conversation that had already begun, "What happened this afternoon with Levine? What exactly did you discover that made you phone him from the operating room?" But before I had a chance to answer he silenced me with a rude wave of his hand. "Never mind. Never mind. Don't start reciting numbers again. I know. You're right. You're always right. But for God's sake, leave Professor Levine out of it. What do you want from him? Why did you call him?"

"I didn't call him," I said to defend myself. "I called the ward, and he picked up the phone and told me to send the patient back upstairs."

"Okay, okay." Hishin waved his hand again and continued in a harsh voice, "Forget it. But in future leave him alone. He's having a very rough time at the moment. He's afraid of his own shadow, let alone the faintest hint of criticism from anybody else, especially you."

"Me?" A cry of amazement escaped me, which in spite of its genuineness held the knowledge that Levine was now afraid of me. "Yes, you, you," said Hishin impatiently, even angrily. "What have you got to be surprised about? Ever since the operation and what happened, with all the diagnoses flying around, you somehow managed to get stuck inside his head, and he can't stop thinking about you. So until he calms down, do me a favor and just leave him alone. Don't talk to him about anything, medical or anything else. Just keep out of his way. He's completely out of control. We had a terrible fight today."

The excitement that gripped me now was so great that I didn't know where to begin. Alongside the intense embarrassment Hishin's words caused me, I also felt pleasure and satisfaction. I should have protested against Hishin's strange outburst, or at the very least been astonished, but given his serious expression I knew that he'd appreciate it if I held my tongue. We both turned to Dori, who now entered the room still coughing, as if everything she had choked back when she was with her clients were now coming out. She had changed and was dressed in a strange assortment of garments: a white embroidered blouse and thick woolen trousers, old slippers on her feet and a muffler around her neck, as if she did not yet know what to expect from the evening or the people now gathered, who were dear and close to her. I rose from my place, flushed with lust and love, impatient to begin my battle here and now, but I was surrounded by people who were obligated to protect her and send me away. I waited for Michaela to join us, which she soon did, with Shivi in her sling, alert and curious in spite of her long, active day, as if she had already begun the trip to India. Michaela's great shining eyes scanned the room and looked so penetratingly at Dori that I was afraid she was about to make a public declaration of my love, and suddenly I felt terrified and wanted to get out of there as quickly as possible. Einat urged Michaela to sit down and have a cup of tea, but I firmly declined her offer. "Enough. We have to go. Shivi's been away from home all day, and your mother should be in bed." I looked at Dori, who broke into a cough again but still obstinately refused any medicine. Einat would not take no for an answer, however, and implored Michaela, almost tearfully, not to leave. Was it only Michaela's intention to set off for India again that so excited Einat and drew her to my wife, or was it something else? There was something that wrung my heart in the way that Einat took Shivi out of her sling and began rocking her in her arms. Michaela was in a quandary. She was perfectly willing to accede to Einat's pleas and sit down for a cup of tea, especially since it would give her an opportunity to satisfy her curiosity about the woman I had made love to twice the night before. But she sensed my agitation and my unwillingness to remain at their home. Since she was so happy and satisfied with her preparations for her journey, she decided to be nice to me and gave in to my demand to leave at once. And I was right to insist, for when we got home and I removed Shivi's diaper, I saw that the long day had left its mark in a red rash between her legs and around her tender little groin. I decided to bathe her myself, and when I had finished getting her ready for bed and Michaela was sunk in a profound reverie in the tub, I picked up the phone and called my parents. It was intolerable that twenty-four hours should have passed since I had issued my challenge to the world, and nobody had yet noticed it.

Since it was relatively late, I was surprised to find my mother alone in the house. My father had gone to a general meeting of the employees of the Agriculture Ministry. His absence encouraged me to begin my confession immediately. Without beating around the bush, to the sounds of Michaela splashing in the bathtub, I went straight to the heart of the matter. I had something to tell them. Michaela had decided to return to India with Shivi. Yes, with Shivi. Stephanie was coming from London to join them. I was staying here. In the meantime. Not only because I had nothing to look for in India, but also because I had found what I looking for right here. I had found love. An old-new love for a married woman, now suddenly made possible. Possible in the sense that her husband had died. She's older than I am, much older, and you can guess who she is. Yes, you can guess. Yes, you know who she is. If you don't know, I'll tell you. So you do know. Yes, it's serious, and yes, I'll have the strength to cope with it. How do I know? I know because the dead man is supporting me too. The dead husband. In what sense? In a mysterious sense, which you'll never be able to understand, because I don't understand it myself, but I don't have to understand, because I can feel it inside me. My mother now sank into a silence so stern that I had to move the receiver away from my ear. In the end she was brief. She was too intelligent to try to argue with me now, especially since she could feel my tremendous agitation. She only asked me to promise her one thing: that I wouldn't say a word about it to my father. I promised her at once. But she wasn't satisfied by my promise, and for the first time in my life she asked me to swear to her. And I swore by the life of Shivi, who was soon to set out on a long journey.

Nineteen

For now, after the mystery finishes eating the porridge served him by his young wife and enjoying the sight of his three laughing, frightened children throwing crumbs at the windowsill to appease the impudent, obstinate bird, he rises to his feet, picks up the new briefcase given him by his wife, and with sweet solemnity takes his leave from his family to go to his daily work. Although judging by his status as a subsidized ex-patient of a reputable institution for the mentally ill, no real work is waiting for him, when he emerges into the bright, sunny morning his body, which is as supple as a dancer's in its elegant suit, is still bursting with energy, and his furled, folded umbrella begins to wave vigorously in the air as if an entire orchestra were following in his wake. And even though we can assume that he has not disclosed his destination to anyone, the second bird, circling faithfully above his head, precedes him to the windowsill of the travel agency, where he is warmly welcomed by the travel agents, eager to know at last where he is bound.

Yes, the earth has suddenly begun to move, he admits with a shy smile shining in his black eyes, now clearly visible behind the polished lenses of his gold-rimmed glasses. But the mystery of its movement, he continues, is no different from the mystery of its stillness. Is there really any need to travel to all the fascinating and seductive places whose pictures are hanging on your walls, he asks, when if we only rise a little above time, trying to sweep us along like a strong river in its current, where we want to go will come to us wherever we are, thanks to the revolutions of the earth itself. If you don't believe me, please be so good as to ask the bird tapping on your windowpane.

Is a new sense of humor budding here to replace the one that was withered? wonder the travel agents, whose computers

*stopped working as soon as he entered the office. If so, maybe
there is hope that an unconscious too can be implanted, to replace the one that was amputated.*

✿✿✿

It was only when my head was already heavy with sleep on the
pillow, while the calm breathing of Michaela—who had no ob-
jection to sleeping in the same bed next to me—murmured in my
ears as I tried to close my eyes and mobilize the darkness inside
me to overcome the splinters of light constantly coming into the
house from the outside world, that I realized I had made a mistake. I should never have agreed, certainly not on oath, to my
mother's request not to say anything to my father, for in this way
I indirectly admitted that there was something perverse about my
love, which was apt to upset my father so much that the whole
thing had to be hidden from him in order to spare his feelings.
How else was I to understand my mother's request? My parents
had always been scrupulously open and aboveboard with each
other, especially in everything concerning me, not necessarily because the bond between them was particularly strong but out of
fairness and loyalty, which were the guiding principles of their
lives—and now my mother was suddenly breaking the rules and
betraying my father. Did she think that she would be able to
convince me to give up Dori without his help? Or maybe the
opposite—was she afraid that in the battle that had already begun between us, he might cross the lines and become my ally? In
the feverish confusion of my thoughts I could not come to any
clear conclusion about what my mother might do or how she
might react, but I was sure that tonight she wouldn't sleep a
wink, and she might not even go to bed. I felt sorry to think of
her suffering alone, awake in the night. If I were really a good,
sensitive son, not only in the superficial manner in which I fulfilled my obligations, I would call her and tried to comfort her
and reassure her, or at least give her an opportunity to express
her anger, in words or silence. But since I knew that my father
might pick up the phone instead of my mother, or during the
course of our conversation, I did nothing. If she had decided to
engage me in single-handed combat, she would have to do so
without the solidarity of their marriage.

From that moment on, this principle ruled the relations between my mother and me. I was silent, and any initiative for further clarification was in her hands, just as the initiative for setting the date for the journey to India was in Michaela's hands, and the only initiative left to me was in the pursuit of my relationship with Dori. But while my mother and I seemed to have been struck by a slight paralysis, Michaela continued her preparations energetically and efficiently, until the trip to India was drawn tight as a bow and all that had to be done to deliver the arrow was touch the string. Deliver in the sense of redeem, for Michaela's devotion to the dream of the return to India was so great that it gave her journey a spiritual, almost religious status. Not redemption from me, of course, but from the materialistic and achievement-oriented reality around us, which Michaela was not yet resigned to spending the rest of her life in. And her joy was intensified by the fact that she was enabling others to benefit from the journey too. Not only Stephanie, who was calling us almost every day from London, but even Shivi, whose tender mind Michaela believed would absorb impressions that would last for the rest of her life.

In order to prepare Shivi for the journey, Michaela painted a third eye on her forehead every morning, red, blue, or green, which made her look adorable and increased her excitement over their departure. I tried to spend as much time as possible with her, picking her up whenever she held out her little arms to me. Michaela often could not take her along when she went about the business of preparing for the trip, since the car had already been sold, half the proceeds going to the trip and the other half to buying a motorcycle for me, not as big and strong as my old one but quick and light enough to be effective on the flat, clogged roads of the city. When Stephanie arrived on a charter flight from London in the middle of a clear winter's night, I saw no problem in taking the motorcycle to the airport to pick her up, for her luggage consisted only of a backpack, which even my modest little motorcycle could take with ease.

Indeed, there was a kind of lightness hovering over all the preparations for the trip. The date had been set, and since Michaela had chosen to fly from Cairo, which could be reached by a cheap bus ride, the tickets turned out to be exceptionally inexpensive, especially in view of the fact that Shivi was not yet one year old and was thus entitled to fly for free. This was Michaela's reason for refusing my mother's request to postpone the flight until after Shivi's first birthday party, which might have consoled them a little for the separation from their granddaughter, the bulletin of whose doings was the high point of their day. Although they relied, as I did, on Michaela's resourcefulness and experience and her grasp of the mysteries of the Indian mentality, the fact that the trip was open-ended naturally caused them profound anxiety, which Michaela tried to assuage to the best of her ability, not only because she was fond of them but also because she had learned to respect and appreciate them when they had visited us in London. Accordingly, she found the time to take Shivi to Jerusalem and spend a day with my parents to say goodbye and set their minds at rest with a detailed and practical discussion of the solutions to all kinds of problems that might crop up. In order to reassure them even further, she took Stephanie with her, to remind them of the solid common sense of her friend from London, who would act as both her traveling companion and a substitute mother for Shivi if, God forbid, something happened to Michaela, or if she simply felt like taking off for a couple of days to places unsuitable for small children.

As I could have predicted, my mother succeeded in persuading Stephanie to accompany my father and Shivi on a walk in the park so that she could remain alone with Michaela and tactfully try to find out what had really happened between us and whether there was any substance to my declaration of love for the "older woman," whose name my mother still refrained from mentioning, even though she knew very well who she was. Michaela's replies to her questions astounded her, not only because they were frank and explicit, for which she may have been prepared, but because they were given in terms of reincarnation and the transmigration of souls, as if the trip to India had already begun and Michaela were sitting with her friend on the banks of the Ganges, not in a Jerusalem neighborhood opposite a woman whose mind was as uncompromisingly clear as the Israeli light coming through the windows. My mother had grown used to Michaela's rather obscure and esoteric manner of analyzing human situations in London, and as long as it concerned other people, usually unknown to her, she could react with tolerance, but now they were talking about me, her only child, and my marriage, which was in danger of breaking up completely. But my mother understood that the infidelity was only a pretext for Michaela to realize her dream of going back to India, a dream that had been hovering over our marriage from the first day. In the middle of the conversation she therefore changed her tactics, suggesting to Michaela that her trip with Shivi was not something that must necessarily deepen the rift in our marriage but rather something that could open the way to a future reconciliation. Michaela agreed immediately, perhaps because she suddenly pitied this stoic woman who was longing for reconciliation and suffering torments of guilt over my behavior. And in order to gain my mother's support for her trip, she explained how her and Shivi's absence for the next few months could help me to extricate myself from a situation that would probably lead to suffering and misery. She believed that my feelings, if only for Shivi, would take me to India too, where it would be possible to strengthen me, precisely because reincarnation and rebirth were a natural part of daily existence there. "The two of you are welcome to come with him," added Michaela in complete seriousness. "We'll be happy to have you." And her great light eyes were radiant with generous hospitality, as if the expanses of India were rooms in her private home. "It would be really wonderful to meet there, as we said we would in London."

My mother hurried to report this conversation to me before Michaela, Stephanie, and Shivi returned to Tel Aviv. She even went out to buy another carton of milk, and called me from a pay phone on the way so that my father would not overhear. Her anxiety was no longer for my endangered marriage, nor for my love for Lazar's wife, which she still saw as a passing and unrealistic fantasy. Her anxiety was now focused on Shivi, for this was the main thing she grasped in all Michaela's confused eloquence: that Michaela wanted to use Shivi as bait to draw me, and perhaps my parents too, after her, even at the price of dragging Shivi irresponsibly around India, in places full of sickness and suffering. And so she suddenly demanded, in a tone that was almost hysterical, that I put a stop to the trip immediately, or at least prevent Michaela from taking Shivi. "It's impossible, Mother, to prevent a mother from taking her baby with her," I replied quietly, trying to maintain my composure, my heart aching at this display of irrationality on the part of so rational a woman. But I promised her that I would make arrangements with Michaela so I could send for Shivi if I decided at any stage to do so. In spite of my sorrow at the idea of parting from her, which grew as the date of their departure drew closer, it was not of Shivi that I was thinking now but of another baby, whose helplessness, which Lazar had tried to make light of and conceal, only fanned the embers of my desire, which had remained alive and burning ever since the unexpected lovemaking on her sickbed. If my mother had really succeeded in persuading Michaela to leave Shivi with me, I would have lost my freedom and flexibility in the battle for my love, which kept returning to its starting point and leaving me at square one again, especially since Dori had once more succeeded in surrounding herself with loving companions so she would not have to be alone. Not only had her son found a way of coming home every night from his base, but Hishin too was a frequent caller in the evenings, and who knew if she hadn't succeeded, with the power of her ingratiating smiles, in persuading even her mother to stay over from time to time, in order to introduce a little structure into the accumulating chaos that gathered in her bedroom and close the open drawers behind her.

❧❦❧

When the day of departure actually dawned, my heart was flooded with sorrow, as if I only now realized that I was going to be deprived of the affection and company that surrounded me without having made sure of even a fraction of the love for which I hoped. And the parting from Shivi was made even more painful by the fact that it took place at midnight, the strange hour chosen by the cheap travel agents to take the busload of young backpackers directly to the airport in Egypt for their flight. When I saw Shivi strapped into her carrier like one more pack next to Michaela's and Stephanie's big backpacks, I realized that my tolerant attitude toward the trip might not have been completely responsible. Although I had vaccinated the baby myself with the dosage prescribed by two reputable pediatricians in the hospital, I could not avoid the thought that I should have made them postpone their departure to make sure there were no complications. Shivi looked healthy and happy, though, as she gazed curiously at the faces of the young backpackers bending

over her with admiring cries and showing their worried parents
the baby with the third eye painted on her forehead as encouraging evidence of a traveler who was even younger than they were.
I still felt guilty over Michaela's irresponsibility and my own, and
I swore to myself that the moment my situation became clearer, I
would find a way to bring my daughter back to her natural place.
But until that moment arrived, her "natural place" would presumably be on sidewalks and train platforms; after all, she was
beginning her trip on two Tel Aviv paving stones, with damp
sand creeping out between them, while her mother was busy embracing her friends, who were far more numerous than I had
imagined and so loyal that not even the lateness of the hour had
prevented them from coming to say good-bye. Even Amnon had
deserted his night watchman's post and hurried here in order not
to miss the moment of farewell to Michaela. I overheard him
promising to go and join her if he received a postcard inviting
him, even though I knew that he would never abandon his parents and his retarded brother, who needed him so much.

Finally it was my turn to say good-bye, and after showering
kisses on Shivi's face and looking deep into her eyes so she would
not forget me, I took Michaela aside to warn her once more to be
careful. Although I had avoided touching her since the morning
when the statuette had been broken, in order not to cause any
embarrassment, I no longer shrank from contact with her, and to
reinforce my words I took her into my arms, held her tightly, and
placed a long kiss on her lips. Her great eyes remained open,
shining in the darkness of the night, and her fingers lightly
stroked my hair, which was something she never did, as if she
knew that the danger hanging over my head was graver than any
of the possible dangers threatening her on her trip. Before joining
Stephanie and Shivi, who had already disappeared into the bus,
she did not forget to say, "If you get into bad trouble, just leave
everything and come to us. We'll all be glad." And while I joined
my hands and held them to my face in thanks for this generous
gesture of reconciliation, she let slip this final, surprising sentence: "Nothing's worth dying for, Benjy." Without giving me
the chance to reply, she hurried into the bus, which was apparently waiting just for her and now lit its little red lights and
silently, as if it had already joined one of the great rivers awaiting
the young travelers, sailed out of the narrow alley, leaving behind

it a crowd of friends and relations who suddenly realized that there was not much left of the night.

Accordingly, they did not hurry home but hung around exchanging telephone numbers and addresses in an attempt to tie a web of connecting threads to their loved ones, whose disappearance into the night turned even the joking words of parting they had just uttered into a suddenly painful memory. Only now did I notice Einat, who was standing next to Amnon's pickup truck wearing a long black coat that emphasized the fairness of her hair, which she had brutally cropped as if in an act of self-mutilation. Had she just arrived, or had she been trying to avoid me? A shy smile crossed her face as she hesitated about whether to accept Amnon's offer of a ride home on the condition that she climb into the back, for the seat next to Amnon was already taken by Hagit and her daughter, who had insisted on coming to say good-bye to her little charge. I quickly went up to Einat, for even if she guessed what had happened between her mother and me, this was no reason to avoid her. In fact, it was an opportunity to try to turn her into an ally. In spite of her embarrassment and resistance, I persuaded her to give up Amnon's pickup for the pillion of my motorcycle, and with my own hands I put the helmet on her head and gently buckled the strap under her slender chin. Although I was used to the fear of first-time pillion riders, I had never come across anxiety as intense as that coming from Einat. Like a terrified animal, she clung to my leather jacket, occasionally breaking out into a scream, as if I were going to roll her into some terrible, hostile abyss instead of simply taking her home, driving barely above the speed limit through the still, silent streets of the city. As we neared her building, located in a pretty seedy quarter of the city, I asked about the terrible anxiety that had taken hold of her. But she was not embarrassed by her hysterics during the ride, nor did she laugh them off. She acted as if her panic had been natural and completely justified, if not because of the motorcycle then because of the driver. Now too, with the bike silent beside us and my hands removing the strap from beneath her chin, she seemed to be afraid of me, pale and shivering with cold, ready to give me her telephone number as I requested, as long as I would release her into the dark stairwell, where she disappeared with such celerity that she neglected to put on the light.

Did she really know about my love for her mother? And did this love, I asked myself, with not a little pain, seem to her so alarming, so outrageous and repulsive, that she couldn't even stand for a moment next to the man who had gone to the ends of the earth to rescue her and whom she had trusted far more than her parents to save her life? Even if she thought that this love deprived her of her due, she could still have respected its mystery, which had begun in the hotel in Varanasi when I took blood from her mother to revive her. These reflections continued to trouble my thoughts on my way home and added distress to the sorrow of returning to the apartment, which in spite of Michaela's efforts to leave it neat and tidy was still full of traces of the baby, the memory of whose sweet face brought tears to my eyes. And although my parents had told me not to hesitate to wake them up to tell them about the parting, I refused to burden my already sorrow-filled heart with the anger and disappointment of my mother, who knew that I had agreed so casually to their going so I could devote myself entirely to the insanity of the love I had so perversely chosen. I therefore not only refrained from calling Jerusalem but disconnected the phone, darkened the apartment, and got into bed hoping not only to sleep but to lose consciousness completely.

But my sleep, which did indeed begin with a full loss of consciousness, was soon violently interrupted by something like an electric shock passing through it. As if by someone's hand on an invisible switch, it not only was interrupted but disintegrated completely, and from its ruins something seemed to fly up and disappear. And in spite of my soul, which was feverish with exhaustion, and my body, which was sinking heavily and limply into the bed, my conscious mind had taken control of me again and knew that there was no more hope of sleep. However tightly I closed my eyes, I found no consolation in the darkness, only a bus with little red lights, racing now, after crossing the border, on a desert road not far from the sea in the silvery moonlight, with Shivi sleeping on Michaela's lap and Michaela probably sleeping now too, perhaps leaning on the shoulder of her friend Stephanie, who was chatting with one of the young backpackers. And for the first time I felt a pang of the anxiety of abandonment squeezing my soul, as if I were not looking at the lights of the bus which held my wife and daughter receding into the distance not from the breadth of this double bed but from the opening of a little pup tent, alone and abandoned in a desolate wilderness. Suddenly I was exposed to the incomprehensible indifference of the universe, and I had to switch on the reading light, although it did not restore my composure. Instead, it only increased the pain of my envy for all those who are able to sleep, connected to each other by their bodies or their dreams. It was then that I thought, I have not been liberated but abandoned. And even the soft sound of the rain falling outside could not soften the new dread of loneliness stealing into the walls of the house. I felt as if the blood coursing through my veins were not enough to sustain me. When I shifted restlessly underneath the quilt and threatened myself with getting out of bed in the hope that my weariness would overcome me and return my lost sleep, the bed itself seemed to cast me out, as if my touch on the pillows and bedclothes were a burden to it. And a little like a sleepwalker I emerged from the circle of light in the bedroom into the darkness of the living room, trying to attach myself to a less alienating version of reality, the one contained in the shabby floral upholstery of the sofa, which immediately aroused my longing for the plump, laughing woman who sat on it with her legs crossed, frozen in alarm but also in delight at the young man's declaration of love. But was such a longing, which might warm the heart with a sweet sorrow, enough to make me take off my pajamas and with limp heavy movements put on layer after layer of clothes? No. Something more real and powerful forced me to switch off the lights and go out into the rainy night with my helmet in my hand, in order to seek human contact. As if now that Lazar's soul had left me, my abandonment had doubled.

If it had been even six o'clock in the morning I might have called my parents and avoided this weird nocturnal expedition. However, I could not have unburdened myself to my mother in my father's presence or spoken of everything weighing on my heart—the parting from Michaela and Shivi, our plans for the future—though sharing these feelings would have eased my sudden sense of abandonment. But it was three o'clock in the morning, and since I never had had time to become acquainted with the Tel Aviv pub scene, let alone with the all-night discos, I could not seek human contact at this hour with anyone but those who were always prepared to give it—in other words, those at the hospital, where I knew that even at this still, secret hour, absolute and eternal vigilance held sway over even the remotest corner in the building, wrapping staff and patients alike in a blanket of security, whether they were tossing in their beds or asleep in their chairs or dead in their iron drawers. I knew that after getting over the surprise of my sudden arrival at the wrong time, one of the anesthetists in the emergency room might try to coax me into changing places with him, so I decided to go to one of the other parts of the hospital. It seemed much darker than usual. I asked one of the security guards about the darkness. He too was aware of the difference and concerned by it—if darkness reigned over the entire hospital, it meant that it wasn't just a coincidence or an accident but the result of a new directive from administration to save electricity. And then it dawned on me, like a flash of lightning: they had found a successor to Lazar, and he must be someone from outside, if his first instruction was to dim the lights. I decided to go up to the pediatric ward, where there were always parents awake, sitting in vigil. But first I went down to my locker in the intensive care unit, to leave my helmet and leather jacket and put on the coat with my name embroidered on it and hang a stethoscope around my neck. Thus protected by the neutral identity of a doctor on night duty, I went up to the pediatric ward. As I had guessed it was humming with activity, not so much because of the concern of the parents, some of whom were sleeping in corners while others paced the corridors red-eyed with despair, but thanks to the wakefulness of those children whose as yet undiagnosed illnesses gave them the right to demand unremitting attention. I too wanted attention, but the parents who surrounded me did not see that I was no less exhausted than they were. Although I repeatedly explained that I was not a pediatrician but an anesthetist and I had only come up here to look for someone, they clung even to this passing medical authority and showered me with questions of a medical or bureaucratic nature, which I answered patiently but in a general, ambivalent, evasive, and noncommittal way, as if the source of authority which had always given strength and clarity to my responses and diagnoses were slipping away from me. It was not surprising that after a while even the most insistent of the parents turned away from me, and with my whole being crying out for the sleep that had been denied me, I walked down the corridor and peeped into the rooms full of bright posters and toys, to soften my burning eyes with the sight of the sleeping babies, some of whom were no older than Shivi, now lying in the warmth and safety of Michaela's arms, or perhaps Stephanie's lap. Even after I had gone downstairs, firmly resolved to go home, get into bed, and drown the inexplicable anxiety that had taken hold of me in sleep, I nevertheless made one last effort, going outside, still in my white coat and stethoscope, oblivious to the wind raging in the little stand of trees behind the main building, and into the annex that housed our small psychiatric department, which Lazar's death had perhaps saved from extinction. Although I had never been there before, I knew very well that no concerned relatives would be wandering around its corridors. And even if they were, it was not them I was seeking but the doctor on duty, to ask his advice.

The doctor on duty was sound asleep. Still, I found someone to talk to in the person of an old acquaintance, none other than the ex–head nurse of Hishin's surgical department, whose application to have her retirement postponed for a year had been rejected and who was doing night shifts as a substitute nurse in various departments of the hospital in order to supplement her modest pension. "But who rejected your application so quickly?" I exclaimed sympathetically, and I told her that I had seen her file on Lazar's desk a few days before. "If Lazar were still alive, he would never have rejected a request from Professor Hishin to leave you with him for another year," I added confidently, for like other people working in surgery, I had felt the greatest respect for her, even though I knew that she too preferred Dr. Vardi to me. But the white-haired nurse sitting in the cold, deserted nurses' station, wrapped in a thick winter coat with a little electric heater at her feet, was not at all sure how Lazar would have treated her request if he had been alive. "Sometimes he could be rigid and almost cruel in his obstinacy," she pronounced, and when she saw that I was astonished by her words she added, "Don't imagine, Dr. Rubin, that just because you spent a couple of weeks with him and his wife in India, you knew all the sides of his personality." There was a slightly aggressive note in her voice, and I expressed my surprise that even though two years had passed she still remembered my trip to India. "But how could I forget?" She laughed. "I still remember you coming in all confused with that big medical kit you got from Dr. Hessing and asking me to inoculate you. You looked so pressured and so angry and bitter about the whole business that Professor Hishin had forced you into." I suddenly was overcome with affection for this noble elderly woman, uncomplainingly doing the job of a substitute nurse to take a few more shekels home every month. I also remembered how I had dropped my trousers in front of her that evening, behind an improvised screen, so that with a light and steady hand she could inoculate me with the two shots I had brought from the Health Bureau. "It's strange that we're meeting again today," I said, unable to control the little confession that had been burning inside me ever since I had arrived at the hospital, "because my wife and baby left tonight on a trip to India. Only a few hours ago I took them to the bus to the airport in Egypt, and when I got home, tired out, and went to bed, I suddenly woke up after an hour or two. I couldn't go back to sleep again. In fact, I can hardly stand to be on my own, something that has never happened to me before."

❧❧

She listened quietly to my complaint with a serious expression on her face. I knew that she didn't have much imagination, but she had a lot of common sense and sympathy for any human distress, as long as she was convinced that it was genuine distress and not just a passing mood. She offered me a cup of coffee, but I refused. "No, I still want to try to sleep," I explained. "I have to go back to bed. In less than eight hours I have to be on my feet in the operating room." Like everyone else on the hospital staff, she was surprised at the strange half-time post Lazar had created for me, and she asked me if I thought the arrangement would last now that he was dead. "Why not?" I asked with some annoyance. She shrugged her shoulders. Perhaps they'd find a way to eliminate irregularities committed in the name of friendship, things that weren't strictly according to the letter of the law, she said—it all depended on the new director. "But is there a new director already?" I asked. "Has anybody seen him? Has Hishin said anything?" It appeared that she knew nothing, and neither did Hishin. But her guess was that somebody had already been appointed to the job, maybe even two or three people. Lazar had

had a lot of power in the hospital, and perhaps the time had come to spread it around a little. That, at least, was what Professor Hishin thought should be done. "Yes," I reflected quietly, "Hishin's going to miss Lazar a lot." She nodded her head. Her conclusions were graver than mine. Hishin was afraid of the new director's revenge, and that was why he was demanding that his powers be divided. In spite of his eulogy at the graveside, he was well aware of the damage he had caused, not because of overconfidence in his medical decisions, as many people thought, but out of jealousy, for fear that some other doctor in the hospital would take charge of the case and get close to Lazar and usurp his favored position. That was why Hishin was still tortured by guilt, both toward the deceased and toward his wife, because everybody knew how close a couple the Lazars had been and how they had always done everything together, and anyone who loved one of them loved the other one too. For a second my blood froze. "In what sense, love?" I smiled, and my heart filled with despair at the possibility of the guilt and the love uniting into a powerful emotion that nothing would be able to withstand. "In what sense?" Hishin's old nurse, taken aback, tried to think of an appropriate answer. "In the sense that he'll stay close to her now and take care of her until he's sure that she isn't angry with him and she doesn't hate him. Because the truth is that Hishin is peculiarly attracted to people who're angry with him or who hate him," she said. For many years she had been sharpening her perception of the head of her department, just as Miss Kolby had done with Lazar. "But how can he stay close to Lazar's wife now that he's got a woman of his own?" I objected. "Only one woman?" she retorted. "Hishin has a lot of women that he's attached to. He'll have no problem adding another one to the list."

A brief but wild scream now rose from one of the rooms, and a chorus of muttering immediately broke out from the other patients, as if they had been waiting up all night for one of their fellows to have a nightmare. The nurse cocked her head in the attentive gesture I remembered from my year in the surgical department, to see if they would all settle back down or if further intervention would be necessary. I felt a pang of pity for this hardworking woman, who as the head nurse in the surgical department had been accustomed to thinking in the drastic terms of knives and incisions, sutures and infusions and wounds to be dressed, and who now had to cope with mysterious mental illnesses by means of the little colored tablets lined up on the shelves of the cupboard behind her back. She was definitely disturbed by the freedom with which I went up to examine her stock. Although she knew that as a physician I was entitled to treat myself, she insisted that I could not take anything without the express permission of an authorized psychiatrist. In spite of this slight, I felt that she was right, for by dint of her strictness and her unimaginative honesty she was forcing me to try to calm my troubled spirit, torn between exhaustion and panic, by spiritual and not material means. For instance, a phone call to my parents, whose ability to judge my mood by the tone of my voice soon succeeded in locating the source of the pain and putting it into perspective. Even if my mother had distanced my father from me by refusing to allow him to know about my love for Dori, his natural, kindly patience could still be of value in a crisis. But it was five o'clock in the morning, and it was impossible to think of calling them before six, even if one of them happened to be awake and prowling around the house, as sometimes happened at this hour.

I said good-bye to the nurse, and to show her that I didn't bear a grudge against her for refusing to let me help myself from the bottles of pills on her shelves, I promised to come back and visit her on one of her shifts. I returned to the main building, looking up at the cloudy sky and wondering whether Michaela too, in the heart of the desert, was searching the sky for the first stain of dawn. I went down to the intensive care unit to return my gown to its place, put on my leather jacket, and take my helmet, but instead of going upstairs I punched the code that opened the door to the surgical wing. It was a simple code, the first three even numbers, which hadn't been changed since I started at the hospital, and it occurred to me that here was a job for the new administrative director—to change the code, because as things were there wasn't a worker in the hospital who couldn't open the door. As always in the hour between shifts there was no activity, but the darkness was new. The order to save electricity had succeeded in penetrating to the holy of holies of the hospital, and the operating rooms, always flooded with light coming from a separate and independent source, were all shrouded in darkness except for one little room. Although I spent a lot of time in the wing, since Lazar's death I had not had any particular reason to visit that little room, which was full of instruments and medications used in cardiac surgery, first and foremost the cardiopulmonary bypass machine, with the white plastic tubes dangling from it like a great octopus's arms. It wasn't the big machine that attracted my attention, however, but the cupboard of anesthetics, most of which I knew not only by name and function but also by their pharmacological composition. With a giggle I thought of the strict nurse, who had refused to give me one little tranquilizer from her stock, whereas I was now standing before a cupboard full of powerful, expensive drugs, and without asking anyone's permission, on my own initiative, I could easily prepare a little cocktail that I could inject into my vein and that would soon put me completely to sleep: a sleep without sensation, without consciousness, without movement or dreams. A sleep from which nothing would wake me.

But strangely enough, as I stood alone in the dark, empty surgical wing among dozens of sophisticated instruments capable of taking a man apart and putting him together again in an improved version, I felt none of the panic and anxiety that had interrupted my sleep and sent me rushing out of the house. It was as if what threatened me were connected not to the outside world but to what lay within the familiar walls of my own house, which had been abandoned by those closest to me. Was it possible that my love sought to embrace both the woman herself, and her inability to stay by herself, for fear of something that might be without form or shape but was sexual and infinitely malevolent in its intentions, not only hiding in the little storage space near the bathroom or the dark corner next to the kitchen where the brooms were kept but spreading through the little spaces between the closet shelves, pervading the drawers with the socks and underwear with a musty, invisible smell, until they turned to spiderwebs and skeins of dust underneath the bottom drawers where she kept her high-heeled shoes? Was this the smell she tried to sniff out in the hotel rooms where it was proposed that she should sleep? And suddenly this surprising new understanding of what was happening to me cheered me up so much that I switched off the light and left the surgical wing without taking a single drop of a sedative or analgesic or muscle relaxant, because I didn't want anything material and external to calm my spirit, just the belief that whatever was disturbing me tonight would in the end strengthen me in my efforts to get closer to her and engulf her totally now that I was free of the yoke of my little family. On my way home I turned into the broad avenue next to her house in order to make sure that Lazar's big car was parked in its usual spot, under the pillars of the building. I didn't get upset when I spied an unfamiliar little car blocking its exit, because a little bit of imagination was all it took to realize that they must have bought it for the soldier, to make it easier for him to come home every night to be with his mother.

The minute I walked into my apartment, I could feel the agitation of abandonment stirring again in the ruins of my exhausted soul, as if only here, between these walls, this familiar furniture, lay the real world, substantial and secret, which immediately exposed one's weakness and inability to remain and contend with it alone. Although the hands of the clock had not yet reached six, I didn't want to wait and I phoned my parents to tell them the story of my parting from Michaela and Shivi and at the same time receive an encouraging word. My father was the one who picked up the phone, and he also conducted the conversation with me, asking questions and demanding details. He did not seem able or willing to give me any encouragement or comfort, for he more than anyone felt the loss of Michaela and Shivi, as if all the progress I had made in the past two years had gone down the drain with their departure. The rustle and echo accompanying the conversation told me that my mother was listening in on the phone next to her bed, but to my surprise she did not join in, as if she didn't want to talk to me. I knew that her anger was deeper than my father's, and also more justified, but her silence began to worry me, and when I felt that my father was about to bring the conversation to a close, I asked to talk to her. She interrogated me dryly and even coldly about where I was calling from, if I was at the hospital or at home. When I told her that my shift only began at noon, she wanted to know why I was calling so early. Did I wake up early, or couldn't I fall asleep? "Both—I woke up and I couldn't fall asleep," I explained, and I told her a little about my night of wandering and added, "I seem to be having difficulty in getting used to staying by myself again." For some reason a silence now fell in Jerusalem, and I heard the sound of my father putting his receiver down, as if now that my mother had taken over the conversation, he could express, in his shy but decisive way, his disapproval of me, for he never cut short a telephone call with me of his own volition. Then my mother's voice softened a little, as if she too had understood the meaning of my father's action, and she asked if I meant to come to Jerusalem for the weekend. When I said yes, she asked me not to use the new motorcycle but to come up by bus, as if the separation from Michaela had made my existence more dangerous and vulnerable. "And if you want to visit your friends, you can use your father's car," she added to encourage me to agree, and quickly put the phone down, as if from the distance she could feel me trembling on the brink of sleep.

I disconnected the phone, in part because I had already spoken to my parents, but also because I knew that if Michaela called before her flight, she'd call my parents and not me; she knew that their sorrow was greater than the sorrow she left behind in her own apartment, where I now began to draw the curtains to prevent any ray of light from sabotaging the sleep that almost had me in its grip. I was convinced that the more I blotted out the world around me, the less severe my anxiety would be. Indeed, a deep sleep, frightening in its power, overcame me at last, and nothing succeeded in penetrating the leaden curtain that came down on me, as if I were not lying on my bed on a noisy, busy Tel Aviv day but in an iron drawer in the hospital morgue. The hospital was also blotted from my mind for the first time since I had begun working there, for after nearly twelve hours of sleep I woke to discover that it was already six o'clock and long past the hour I was supposed to begin my shift. They must have tried to get in touch with me from the operating room, and given up in despair owing to the disconnected phone, and found someone to take my place. The thought that someone had taken my place did not increase my guilt, as might have been expected in someone as reliable, dutiful, and punctual as myself, but only gave me a sense of relief. As if not only Michaela and Shivi had disappeared from this reality, but I had too.

True, there was a clear contradiction between the pleasure I felt in this disappearance and the agitation and anxiety caused by my solitude. But I knew that there was one person in the world capable of understanding my situation perfectly. Accordingly, I did not switch off the little light, which was revealing more and more of the threat looming in the known and familiar world of my apartment—a threat that made me feel again as if I didn't have enough red blood cells in my body—but in great excitement I got up to reconnect the phone, in order to call her office and demand the right to talk to her not, only as a lover and occasional doctor but also as a tenant calling on his landlady for help. Dori had just left to go to a café with one of her friends, and her secretary, who couldn't tell me exactly when she would be back, asked me very civilly who I was and what I wanted. I couldn't tell her what I wanted, but I agreed to tell her who I was, and asked her to have Mrs. Lazar call me back. "My wife and daughter left last night for India," I told the secretary. And when I sensed by her silence that she didn't know what to make of this announcement, I added in a hoarse voice, "And I'm sick in bed." This strange lie, slipping so glibly from the lips of a man who had always been taught to tell the truth, began to depress me so much that I felt the need to disconnect the phone again, so as to spare myself the necessity of reinforcing the first lie with additional ones. Once I had announced my illness, I was sure that she would get in touch with me, but what I wanted from her now was not duty but love. I realized that the lie I had just told might poison whatever was between us, just as it would have poisoned my relations with the hospital if I phoned them now to excuse my absence on the same grounds. The fear of infection, even an imaginary illness, in an operating-room doctor was always taken very seriously and I felt it would be wrong to take the easy way out, playing off their justified anger aroused, no doubt, by my failure to show. If a replacement had already been found for Lazar, let him call me into his office and warn me about the consequences of another disappearing act—like the one I was contemplating right now, at six o'clock in the evening, while the outside world pulsed and throbbed in a tumult of activity and people who had just finished a successful and rewarding day's work went from shop to shop and bought things to help them relax and spend a pleasant evening at home.

I got up and switched off the light so that I could disappear into
the darkness and shut out the intimate world where the threat of
loneliness grew greater the farther my wife and baby receded into
the distance. But I was so saturated with sleep that I couldn't
even close my eyes in the utter darkness I had succeeded in creating around me, let alone sink back into slumber. After spending
hours on call and growing accustomed to sleeping and waking
quickly, I had lost that innocence of youth which allows itself to
be engulfed in sleep without rhyme or reason. Quite the opposite:
after ten hours of uninterrupted sleep my mind had begun to
acquire the pure and lucid quality of an angel gliding through the
sky, so that even hunger and thirst did not trouble me. I felt the
stubble that had grown on my chin since the previous morning
and asked myself whether Dori would come to look for me here.
If I were really sick in bed, it wouldn't be in the hospital or in my
parents' home but right here in this apartment, which she had
signed the lease for, even though she wasn't the actual owner.
That didn't of course oblige her to love me but it did oblige her
to remember that here she had agreed to hear my declaration of
love, which she had listened to without interrupting and in the
wake of which she had gone to bed with me. Since my mind
continued to accumulate clarity and lucidity, I began to believe
that I had it in my power to influence from a distance not only
her thoughts but also her plump, pampered body, whose sweet,
secret map of beauty spots I had not yet finished studying. And
thus, after her last client has left, she will stand up, wrap herself
in her blue velvet tunic, scatter her smiles to everyone she is
leaving behind in the office, and even if there is no real rain in the
air but only a few solitary drops shaken by the wind from the
trees, she will stop to open her umbrella over her head, even for
the few yards between the office door and the big car parked
carelessly and inconsiderately in the little side street. After smiling again into the rearview mirror as she checks to see if the road
behind her is clear, perhaps she will remember the strange message I left for her and with her little foot on the brake, she will
sigh and take her makeup out of the big bag lying on the seat
beside her and draw a narrow line around her eyes and powder

her nose and cheeks. But instead of painting a third eye in the middle of her brow, the better to perceive the reality around her, she will only flash another smile at the little mirror in front of her, in the hope that it will smile back and cheer her up. Only then will she relax her foot on the brake and sail into the middle of the street, very slowly but also with total indifference to the cars behind her.

Maybe she hopes I won't hear her, knocking so softly on the door? For she is not only hesitant about entering this place she knows so well, which was taken over almost two years ago by her lover, she is also worried that none of her family or friends know that she is about to be swallowed up in a vortex of intense and demanding love, from which nobody can save her but herself. Maybe she hopes that the light knock on the door won't be heard so that she can turn around and go downstairs with a clear conscience at not having deserted me in my illness, even if she's sure it isn't serious. But my soul, which I sent to accompany her here in the big car crawling through the dense early evening traffic, the soul that waits for her when she stops to buy a cake and fruit at the stores I recognize from the times when I followed her and Lazar home on my motorcycle, the soul that blows on her face through the air vents next to the dashboard to persuade her to make a detour and see what the meaning of this silence is on the part of one who left so clear a message about himself— this soul is also attuned to catch not only her lightest knock on the door but even the sound of her breathing if she decides to stand there, without moving, on the other side of my door, as I once stood outside her door.

Is it any wonder, then, that I sprang out of bed, trembling with excitement but protected by the darkness, to open the door to the woman illuminated by the dim light of the stairwell, her umbrella in one hand, her key ring and a little bunch of flowers in the other, and a new hat on her head, which suited the shape of her face and announced to the world by its black color that she still considered herself to be in mourning?

Only then, as she entered the apartment, did I dare switch on a single light, to dispel the darkness and reveal the shadows in the room and discover how exaggerated and even childish my fears were, if they could be so quickly banished. Although I was supposed to be ill, with my hair matted, my face pale and unshaven, my body dressed in a pajama top, she did not ask me how I was but looked around as if she had only now remembered that she was also the landlady, entitled to check up on the nature and extent of the changes made by her tenant in her apartment. Judging by the way the smile vanished from her lips, she was not only surprised but also annoyed by the many changes that Michaela and I had made, wittingly and unwittingly, in her mother's cozy, well-cared-for apartment. But she refrained from comment and just took a step toward the crib standing in the corner of the living room, and as she looked at the crumpled sheet and the furry teddy bear, which was too big to take to India, I wondered whether Shivi was missing him now, as she crawled down the aisle of the airplane. Anxiously inspecting the woman who was much older than I was, I saw that the new hat was only one sign of the change that had taken place in her appearance: gone was the tailored suit tightly encasing her body, the high heels which were so flattering to her legs, replaced by plain, sturdy comfortable flat shoes and a loose suit with pants, which, even though it completely concealed her stomach, transformed her into a shorter, squarer woman, although, strangely enough, also a younger one. Then at last she turned to me and asked in an inquiring and slightly mocking tone, "Are you really sick?" I bowed my head a little so that she wouldn't see the faint blush spreading over my cheeks but would be able to hear my halting words of apology for the lie that had brought her to the only place which truly belonged to both of us, as well as the only place where we could now be free of the judgment of the third eye. But she interrupted me in a maternal tone, which also contained a new note of impatience. "Never mind, don't apologize. I knew you weren't." As if to soothe my guilty conscience, she handed me the modest bunch of anemones. I filled a blue vase with water in the light of the quiet flashes of lightning flickering in the window over the sink, and raised the flowers to my face to search their scent for the scent of her body, trembling at the certain knowledge that these flowers were meant not to bring us closer but the opposite, to say good-bye. After I put them in the vase and saw that she was already sitting in the same place on the couch where she had sat two years before and listened silently to my confession, I was flooded by a wave of pain. Did I really have to begin again from the beginning every time I met her? Was

everything that happened between us so contrary to nature and
divorced from life that it evaporated from meeting to meeting, as
if it didn't have the strength to sustain itself for our benefit? If
only she had been able to believe, as Michaela believed, that her
husband's soul had been reincarnated in me, it might have set her
mind at rest. I didn't have to wait for the plane to land in India in
order to offer her everything an ardent young man had to offer,
so she wouldn't have to stay by herself anymore.

But it was apparently precisely because she sensed what I was
about to offer her now that she had answered my call and made
a detour on her way home after a long day's work. It wasn't my
supposed illness that had drawn her here but the fact of
Michaela's and Shivi's departure, which had taken place with
such speed and which she now realized wasn't just an idle threat
made in anger on the night when I had not come home. The fact
that I had cooperated in this adventure of Michaela's, and agreed
to let her uproot the baby from her home and set off on a
backpacking trip with no definite limits in time, in strange places
filled with filth and sickness, just so that I could be as free as she
was—this worried Dori and alarmed her with the obligations it
sought to impose on her. When she could no longer contain herself, she blurted out a strange and surprising question—"But
who are you?"—even before she asked me what I wanted. Perhaps this was the question I had long been waiting for, for without hesitating I began to tell her, the mere glint of her glasses
now filling me with excitement, about the other river, the fifth
river, which had flowed alongside me throughout our trip to India: the love and closeness between herself and Lazar. If at first I
had been disturbed and put off by the intensity of the relationship between them, which was so different from anything I had
known at home between my parents, in the end I was powerfully
drawn to it. While I had been careful to wet only the tips of my
fingers in the four real rivers flowing between New Delhi and
Calcutta, in this fifth river I had bathed my whole body, and as if
that weren't enough, I had also drunk from its waters, which
now, after the death of Lazar, were bursting from me until I was
no longer sure who I really was. And although I knew that the
disparity in age between us made us impossible for each other, I
also knew that only I could guarantee that she would never be
alone again.

"But I want to be alone." The surprising answer came in a whisper but with great vehemence, and a gleam of anger flashed in her eyes before it died and disappeared, together with the lights, which now went out not only in the room and the apartment but in all the windows of the buildings surrounding us. And from the entire neighborhood, in which the power had suddenly failed, a faint, muffled sigh rose, a mixture of sorrow and excitement, leading me to pronounce with a smile, which held a little pity too, "But you can't."

"Because I never really wanted to before," she replied with a curious confidence, as if the unexpected darkness that had descended on us enabled her to explain her entire life as if it were purely a matter of will. No wonder then that when I got up to look for a candle or a flashlight, she said, "What for? Leave it. The light will come on again soon anyway." She took a slender cigarette out of her bag, and with its tip burning in the darkness around us, which seemed to be trying to produce light from every pale object in the room, even from the white smoke curling up from her cigarette, she spoke not only of the need to part from me but also of the obligation to do so, just because we had both lost the protection of our mates. Now that the man whose heart had failed to keep up with the intensity of his desire to dominate her was dead, she felt that the secret relationship that had come into being with me, which had been meant to give her some relief from the suffocation of his boundless and domineering love, was quickly turning into the same kind of demanding love, until she could almost believe, with me sitting in front of her in the dark, that Lazar's soul had been reincarnated in me.

When I heard this sentence coming explicitly from the mouth of the person who had been closest to him, I could no longer restrain myself and I rose from my place, transported by the heady knowledge that I was now free to realize all my hopes, not only with regard to her but also about the hospital and wherever else I wanted to go. As if not only the city, the country, and the world were opening up before the spirit which bore my darkest and most secret desires, but even the universe itself, where the most beautiful stars were now shining in the continuing darkness around us. But Dori too apparently felt the power of the terrible freedom seeking to engulf her, and she stood up, angry and frightened, and said with a hysterical sob in her voice, "No. Don't come any closer. You mustn't touch me. I won't allow you. It's impossible. Einat already knows about us. It's horrible. You have to let me go. Say to yourself, She's gone. She's gone to join her husband in the land of the dead."

Twenty

On the Friday evening of a dry, clear winter's day, the journey on the top of a double-decker bus going from Tel Aviv to Jerusalem seemed not quite real to a motorcyclist used to riding low on the ground—like a gentle sail, rocking the hills and woods and rolling them up like a bolt of soft fabric. Now I was pleased that I had kept my promise not to make the trip on my bike, although I wanted to test its pull on the steep street leading to my parents' house. This gentle journey, with its pleasant memories of riding on English double-decker buses, seemed to ease and soften the despair of my thoughts. I had lost the battle for my love. As quick and generous as she had been in her response to my first declaration of love, so sharp and stubborn was she now in her refusal to allow me even to approach her, as if she were fighting for her life. Even the darkness of the long power failure seemed to help her in her efforts to evade me. And when I insisted, in spite of her objections, in taking down a dusty candelabrum which had remained on the shelf from her mother's days, and lit the stubs of the two thick red candles, I was alarmed to see in the light of the crimson flame that her face was hard and burning, as if the struggle to separate herself from me were using up all her strength. A feeling of pity for her stirred in me. And I kept quiet, to make it easier for her to leave me.

When I reached the central bus station on the outskirts of Jerusalem, I saw that nobody was waiting at the stop for my parents' neighborhood. It looked as if I had missed the last bus. Although I could have called and asked my father to come and get me, I preferred to take a bus to the center of town and walk from there, perhaps in order to postpone the difficult meeting awaiting me. Since the evening when I had blurted out my confession to my mother, I had not met her face to face, and our telephone conversations had become brief and businesslike. Even Michaela and Shivi's parting from my parents had taken place without me. Perhaps for the first time in my life, I felt apprehensive about going home.

I slowed down deliberately and tried out a number of new shortcuts in the little streets, which I had not frequented for many years as a pedestrian, wondering at the sight of the many worshipers in heavy coats disappearing into the doorways of private houses which on Friday evenings turned into song-filled little synagogues. Once more I realized how from year to year the Sabbath was tightening its grip on the city, not like Tel Aviv, where it descended like a filmy veil of silence, touching first the tops of the trees, like the ones I saw from Dori's windows. Although she believed in her heart that if she persisted she would succeed at last in staying by herself, after death had released her from the yoke of love, I knew for certain that at this darkening moment, as dusk descended, she was not alone but surrounded by members of her family—her mother, the soldier, and maybe also Einat, with whom I would have to make my peace—and in the brightly lit apartment they were all helping her prepare dinner. Full of longing for the city I had left behind me, I entered my parents' home, looking at the remains of the Sabbath candles smoldering in the two old silver candlesticks standing, as always, very far from each other on the dinner table, which in recent months had been surrounded by five chairs, including Shivi's high chair. But this evening the table had returned to its state during the days of my bachelorhood—three chairs opposite three drearily familiar pale blue plates. I knew I was tense and worried in anticipation of the meeting, and that my parents too were afraid of the anger in their hearts. Since they didn't know if I would keep my promise to come by bus, my lateness had added a new worry to the anxiety that had been hovering in the air here since Michaela's and Shivi's departure. Although a first announcement of their safe landing in India had been recorded on the answering machine, it was too brief to satisfy my father, who was far more concerned about Shivi than my mother. Because he was shy and reserved and careful not to burden others with his feelings, the anxiety secretly gnawing at him had built up into a new and unfamiliar aggression toward me for so lightheartedly allowing his beloved little granddaughter to set out on this irresponsible adventure. And although my mother—who was not an emotional woman, and whose attitude to Michaela and Shivi was always more matter-of-fact and balanced—might have been able to calm his fears a little by speaking to him logically, she did not do it. The gloom and depression that had descended on her with my astonishing confession, whose contents she had decided to keep from my father at all costs, seemed to prevent her from coming to my support in the simple argument that I now repeated to my father—that Michaela was entitled to take her child wherever she wanted to, including India. But this argument did not relieve the gloom around the dinner table. Nor was it dispelled by my parents' restraint and good manners, nor by the obligatory humor which was part of every Englishman's birthright. I was especially disturbed by a new phenomenon: my mother persistently and deliberately avoided looking me in the eye. Even when she spoke to me, she averted her face. She did not yet know that my love had been rejected and now caused me nothing but suffering. Seeking my father's eyes, which met mine unhesitatingly but in total silence, I thought bitterly of the injustice of it all. When I challenged him for not answering my questions, he admitted with a embarrassed smile that he couldn't stop thinking of what was happening to Shivi in India, what she was eating, where she was sleeping. "Stop worrying," I said to him, "nothing will happen to her. Michaela has a special talent for finding her way around in the most questionable places." My father listened and nodded his head, but he did not seem reassured.

At the end of the meal he asked my mother to help him find his prayer shawl, for it appeared that the old janitor in his office had invited all the staff to his grandson's bar mitzvah, which was to take place the next day in a synagogue in one of the new suburbs that had grown up at some distance from the city. "But do you really intend to go?" my mother said in surprise. "Why risk getting lost? I'm sure nobody really expects you to go." But my father insisted. He was sure the invitation was genuine. It was important to this good, simple man for my father to honor his grandson's bar mitzvah with his presence. Uncharacteristically, my mother went on trying to talk him out of going. And then a strange idea occurred to me. She was afraid to remain alone with me in the house, exposed against her will to the story of my love affair, which apparently still filled her with indignation and shocked her to the depths of her being. This being the case, despite my exhaustion after all my sleepless nights, I decided to spare them my painful presence, and soon after dinner I took my father's car and went to visit Eyal, whom I hadn't seen for ages. He and his wife had gone to live with his mother, whose condition had deteriorated. Even though I knew that living with her must be difficult for Hadas, I thought that the saving of rent had probably consoled her. Hadas opened the door and kissed me warmly and immediately asked for news from my "Indian women." Eyal had apparently been delayed at the hospital, and Hadas would soon take the car to pick him up. In the meantime we chatted. She had put on weight and looked placid and serene, as if married life suited her. We spoke about Michaela's trip to India. "It was only to be expected," said Hadas. "Ever since she came back, she never stopped announcing her intention to return. When we wondered at the speed with which she agreed to marry you, she said, Benjy's a doctor, he'll always find something to do in India." She didn't even mention Shivi, as if she were simply a part of Michaela's body. And when I began to complain about how much I missed the child and how sad it made me to look at her empty crib, it was suddenly time for her to drive to the hospital to pick up Eyal. Before she left, she woke Eyal's mother, who knew that I was coming and had asked Hadas to receive me. She didn't get out of bed but invited me into her bedroom, in which nothing had changed since my childhood except for a wheelchair, which was standing next to her bed and which filled me with surprise and concern. She reassured me, a faint blush spreading over her bloated face. She didn't need the wheelchair, she only used it out of laziness, because her legs found it hard to bear the weight of her body. Indeed, since the last time I had seen her, she had put on even more weight. She was very glad to see me and began telling me all kinds of stories about her son and daughter-in-law, but my heart, which was shriveled up in its own pain and sorrow, was not interested in hearing stories about other people, even if they were good friends. My weariness and the excitement of the past week were also beginning to take their toll. Since I was now deep in the old brown velvet armchair opposite her bed, breathing in the familiar smell of the big bedroom, my eyes began to close of their own accord as she spoke. She smiled to herself. In the light, fitful slumber that descended on me, I saw her getting up, vast beyond belief, wrapping herself in her robe, sitting down in her wheelchair, and riding over to me to place a blanket on my knees, and then gliding out of the room, whose warmth and coziness combined with my depression to make me want to disappear or be absorbed into my surroundings.

When Eyal and Hadas arrived after a considerable delay, the three of us were unable to enjoy the reunion as we had hoped. Even though Eyal was very tired from a hard day at the hospital, he didn't want to talk about anything not connected to medicine and his work. He was particularly interested in finding out what had happened in Lazar's open heart surgery, and if anything in my position could change for the worse now that the director who had taken me under his wing had gone. But still a little dazed and slow from my unexpected nap, I answered in general terms, which did not satisfy Eyal, eager for gossip about dramatic confrontations between doctors to rouse his overworked soul from its lethargy. Only his mother was now wide awake, and she even got out of her wheelchair to give us a little midnight snack, including warm cookies fresh from the oven, which I polished off despite how late it was. When I reached home after midnight, I did not make for the kitchen as usual to look for something before I went to bed, but sat for a while in the dark living room, brooding about the fact that although I knew my mother was lying awake in bed, she did not dare to come out to me as usual, as if she were afraid of facing me. I myself would not have objected to holding the impossible but essential clarification between us right now, in the middle of the night. My father's prayer shawl, which was lying on the table, ironed and neatly folded, testified to the fact that his determination had overcome her fears of being alone with me, and tomorrow, whether we wanted to or not, his absence would force us to confront one another. This being the case, I averted my face when I walked past their open bedroom door, so I wouldn't see her lying there awake, and went straight to bed. And in complete contrast to the torments of insomnia that I had suffered in recent nights, even before I could curl up in the fetal position to look for help in the memory of that primal sleep, the flicker of consciousness went out, as if the presence of my parents in the next room, even though they were hostile to me at the moment, acted on my nerves like a shot of dormicum.

Perhaps because sleep came to me so immediately, I felt no pleasure on waking but only a sudden oppression, exacerbated by the sound of my mother's soft but unquiet steps pacing around the house. It was very late, and the fact that my mother had failed to wake me before my father left was a sign not of her consideration for my tiredness but of her fear of listening to my story. To make things easier for her, I didn't go straight to the kitchen to have breakfast. Instead I went to the bathroom to take a shower and shave and then back to my bedroom to get dressed, and only then, washed and dressed, as in the movies, where the perfectly groomed appearance of the hero at the breakfast table is a declaration of his decency and stability, I looked into the living room, which was bathed in the quiet light of a winter Sabbath in Jerusalem. She was sitting in the corner of the sofa, upholstered with green floral fabric that they had bought on their last visit to England. She was holding her book at a great distance from her upright head, which was as sharp as the head of a sad, tired bird. Vocal music full of emotion was pouring out of the radio, interrupted by the conceited voice of the director of the Saturday morning musical quiz. She sensed my presence immediately, and she looked straight at me, although from a distance, and said, "Everything's ready on the table, Benjy. Eat first and then we'll talk." This strange and definite separation between breakfast and the conversation about to take place was a clearer indication than anything else of her fear that talking about my love would dirty us. I stopped in my tracks, and despite the dryness in my throat and my craving for coffee, I walked into the living room and said, "Never mind. I'll eat later. Father might be back at any moment. Let's talk now." I switched off the radio, and for no apparent reason, without asking her permission, I shut the book which she had placed open on the table—an English translation of a Hebrew novel she had mentioned admiringly at dinner last night. Then I lowered myself slowly into an armchair and asked, "Are you angry with me?" Before she had a chance to answer I added, "If you're angry or worried, there's no more reason for you to be. The relationship I told you about has already been broken off. And anyway, what did you think? That there was any chance for a love like that?" It was possible to

sense the deep shock that passed through her at the sound of the
word "love" coming from my mouth. "What are you talking
about?" she asked, as if she could hardly breathe. "About my
love for that woman," I replied firmly and quickly, trying to fix
her eyes on mine and not let her evade me anymore. "But how
can it be possible?" She dropped her eyes with a forgiving smile,
as if struggling with the strange obstinacy of a child. "It's possible," I stated in a voice that was quiet but full of anger. "I'm
telling you so. Listen to me. I'm very unhappy, because I fell in
love with that woman with all my heart and soul." My mother
clenched her hand and raised it to her mouth in a gesture of
obvious distress. A long silence ensued. "But when did it begin?
This love of yours?" she asked in the end, and a very thin,
twisted smile passed over her lips, as if only by twisting them
could she force her lips to pronounce the word in whose reality
she had up to now refused to believe in—perhaps for herself as
well. "When?" I was at a loss, because it suddenly seemed to me
that we were talking about something very ancient. "Apparently
on our trip to India. But not at the beginning, only toward the
end. At first she got on my nerves. But at the end my feelings
underwent a transformation. Maybe they took a young doctor
with them so that he would fall in love with Einat, but I fell in
love with her instead." My mother listened to me with concentrated attention, nodding her head slightly. "But what do you
want now?" she asked gently, the shy little girl's fist still by her
mouth. "What you always want when you love somebody. Everything," I answered calmly, suddenly feeling that only the
whole truth, that truth which had always been a supreme value
in this house, would protect me from her disgust, even if I revealed everything that had happened over the past two years to
her. "Yes, everything," I repeated firmly, "because I already had
everything. Because I've already been with her. Even before Lazar's death. Even before my marriage to Michaela, but afterward
too. A few times. In England, for example, when you were away,
in the house where you stayed—but not in your room, in another
room further inside the house." My mother's face now turned
very red, as if the indication of the exact spot made the act so
powerfully real that it made her giddy. She averted her face, in
profound agitation but not in anger. Did she think that what had
happened a few feet from the room where she had stayed with

my father had caused Lazar's death and compelled Michaela to take Shivi and escape to India?

But even if such harsh thoughts crossed her mind, she repressed them and said nothing, perhaps in the hope of stopping the spate of my confession and not giving me any more opportunities to reveal further details about the love that aroused such antipathy in her. The minute I grasped the power of the truth in my hands, I took pity on her and kept quiet. "But now, Benjy, you say it's all over?" she suddenly asked with great delicacy. I bowed my head in confirmation. "But why? Now that Lazar's dead?" asked my mother in surprise, logical to the end in spite of her revulsion. And something like a faint smile began breaking inside me, as I tried to explain the woman who wanted to test her ability to be a self-sufficient, independent human being. Even her response to me had only resulted from her wish to lighten the burden of her husband's suffocating love, which because of her inability to be alone had twined about her like a strong, stubborn vine. My mother's thin mouth parted a little in amazement as she listened to me, and it was now possible to discern, beneath the wrinkles on her face, the straight and delicate features of the naive Scottish girl she had once been. "But I thought . . ." she stammered. "So did I," I interrupted without letting her finish her sentence, without knowing what she wanted to say—trying with all my strength to avoid her small, slightly bloodshot eyes. "And maybe that's the reason I'm so miserable and confused. Because now that I feel his love forcing me to dominate her too, I know she's right." A deathly pallor spread over my mother's face, as if the mysterious and absurd thing I had just said was far more dangerous in her eyes than my lost love for the woman who was only nine years her junior. And then my mother, the epitome of restraint and composure, couldn't sit still any longer, and she jumped up in a storm of agitation, her stooped back turning her into a dangerous bird, her braided bun coming loose without her being aware of it and falling onto her shoulders, and with her arms folded on her chest, perhaps in order to muffle the pounding of her heart, she began pacing up and down the big room, looking all the time at the clock on the wall, until she recovered her self-control and stood before me in a calmer frame of mind and suggested that I go and have my breakfast, as if the egg, the cheese, the coffee, and the toast would do more than any words at her command to return me, and perhaps her too, to the only reality she considered worthy of the name.

❧❧❧

When she saw me hesitate, she added, "Come on, I could do with a cup of coffee too." I stood up and followed her into the kitchen, sat down in my usual place, and looked at the piece of butter beginning to melt in the black pan. She broke an egg, dropped it into the pan, and surrounded it with pieces of salami. Should I take pity on her and stop now? I asked myself. Or should I remain faithful to the truth? The egg began to bubble; the slices of salami began sinking into its edges. She sliced bread and put it in the toaster; then she dished up some of the Quaker Oats my father had prepared for himself before setting out early in the morning, to fortify himself for the long hours in the synagogue. She put the bowl of oats in front of me without asking if I wanted it, apparently in the belief that the traditional breakfast of my childhood would bring me back to my senses. But the pleasant smell of the cinnamon strewn over the wrinkled white surface of the oats, the smell of the childhood of an only son, who knew that whether he liked it or not, in the course of his life he would become the be-all and end-all of his parents' existence, made me so profoundly sad that my eyes suddenly darkened. I put the spoon down, feeling that all I wanted was to go back to bed and sink into a long sleep. My mother noticed the spoon slipping from my hand, and without saying anything she moved the bowl away carefully and smiled at me. In spite of everything, the news of my breakup with Dori had appeased her and brought her some relief. But her relief only sharpened my pain, and I felt my hunger vanish, and without looking at her I pushed away the big plate she now placed in front of me, with the fried egg surrounded by the red salami, which in my childhood I saw in my imagination as the huge eye of a prehistoric beast, and I started to talk to my mother frankly, to warn her of what was happening inside me. Even though I had always accepted her teachings about not wasting time on the impossible and always doing only the right and proper thing, now, after Lazar's death, I saw that what had once seemed fantastic and impossible might be real and possible. Without deciding the question of whether the soul as such existed or there was no such thing, as Hishin had argued in his eulogy next to Lazar's grave, I felt that whatever had taken possession of me, real or imaginary, had turned my love into the only thing worth living for, and without it life would be bitter and lonely, frightening and superfluous. Now that Michaela had gone and taken Shivi with her, I felt that I was losing my ability to stay by myself, an ability that I had always had and that I could always rely on. For a number of nights now I hadn't been able to sleep. And I felt nervous and exhausted all the time. I knew that I could easily put myself to sleep, just as I put other people to sleep every day on the operating table. Without pain, in a state of complete relaxation—the absolute sleep that a doctor could bestow on himself in exchange for all his years of study and experience.

She turned off the gas under the boiling kettle and poured herself a cup of coffee. Her head was bowed and her face was so mournful that I asked myself whether she saw my thoughts of death, which I had thrown at her simply to show her how miserable I was, as an actual possibility. Did she recognize a catastrophe inside me of which I myself was not yet aware? Without consulting me, she took the plate I had pushed away, slid the wounded eye back into the frying pan, and asked me, "Is it possible that you're really thinking of it?" I saw that she didn't have the courage to say the word itself, and I asked her, "Of what?" in order to force her to say it. And she said it, holding the cup between her hands, careful not to touch it with her lips, as if death had settled into the black liquid. "Yes, Mother," I answered calmly. "Already in India I was drawn to the riverbanks to see the cremation of the dead, for even if death seems more natural and less tragic there, it is very far from being empty." My mother's face was now so grave that she really seemed to be taking my threat seriously. And the thought suddenly flashed through my mind, Why couldn't I have used the same threat with Dori? At least when I had insisted on accompanying her down the dark stairs to her car, which was parked in a nearby street whose darkness was interrupted by the flickering light of oil or gas lights. They reminded me of the dim lights in the ring-shaped street in New Delhi where I had gone around in circles on my way back from the Red Fort, without arriving at the hotel where she lay dozing, not because she was tired but out of loyalty to her husband, who had fallen exhausted onto his hotel bed after spending a sleepless night on the plane. I had pointed the lamps out to her and reminded her of New Delhi, but she smiled without remembering. Her flat shoes made her look shorter and clumsier, but also younger, perhaps because the new black hat was no longer on her head but at her nape, tied around her neck with the ends of the scarf dangling from it. I should have done it then, in the dark Tel Aviv street, which was full of a real, powerful mystery; I should have threatened this woman who wanted to cut herself off from me and stay by herself. If it had been the opposite, if I had wanted to leave and she had asked me to stay, I would not have hurt her as she was hurting me. But I said nothing then, for I knew that she would smile and dismiss my threat like dust. Only my mother, who knew me better than anyone else, knew that I had never, not even when I was a small child, uttered a threat that wasn't real to me. And as she stood now with the cup of coffee between her hands, she did not have to wonder whether the threat was real or imaginary, but only to say in a low voice, "How dare you even think of such a thing? There are people who depend on you."

"Not you," I replied quietly but vehemently. "Certainly not you. The only person who depends on me is Shivi, and she's got Michaela, who'll always take care of her because she sees her as part of herself."

My father's footsteps were now heard, and judging by the speed with which the front door opened and the way he called my mother's name, I guessed that he had come back cheerful and content, if not with the ceremony at the synagogue, at least with his own good deed, and perhaps also at not having lost his way. His face was blotched with red, a sure sign that he had been drinking wine. "You came back so soon?" said my mother, getting up quickly and going to meet him in the hallway, to prevent him from coming into the kitchen, presumably to give me time to recover and wipe the glum expression from my face. "Why soon?" said my father in an offended tone, as if he had forgotten his worries during the morning's little adventure. "I left the house at seven o'clock this morning, and how long can they drag out their prayers?" It turned out that he had found his way without too much difficulty, and since he was the only one of the office staff to put in an appearance, he was greeted with respect and enthusiasm and also given the honor of reading from the Torah. "It was important for me to go," he affirmed, if not to us then at least to himself, and he took off his hat and entered the kitchen. When he noticed the primeval wounded eye, which had shriveled a little in the pan, he said, "Is that for me?"

"Yes," said my mother, "if you want it. Benjy didn't feel like eating this morning." He sat down immediately and ate my breakfast with relish, even though he had had refreshments at the synagogue too. He realized from our silence that something important had been said between us during his absence, but he was too full of his own experiences to try to find out what it was, and I soon left to wander around the neighborhood until lunch and breathe the dry, cold air of the radiant Sabbath morning. Strange how rarely I had set out on foot in recent years, I thought, and a sweet melancholy descended on me with the memory of the rainy evening when I had walked across Tel Aviv holding a big black umbrella over my head. But how different the Jerusalem streets were from the straight, open streets of Tel Aviv. Where could you find in the whole of Tel Aviv a steep narrow lane like this, running along the wall of the Lepers' Hospital and suddenly opening out into the plaza fronting the Jerusalem Theater? What a pity that I couldn't test the true power of the new motorcycle on an incline like this, I thought regretfully, as if I were about to leave the place forever. And thus, with a feeling of parting, perhaps genuine, perhaps imaginary, I continued along the street of the foreign consulates, which I had taken every day to school, examining the familiar facades of the houses and stopping to read the signs on the gates. Among them were many brass plates with the names of physicians, mentioning degrees and specializations, and I was surprised to see how many of them I still remembered from my schooldays, such as the big old sign bearing the name of the famous cardiologist Professor Siegfried Adler, and next to it a small new one, PROFESSOR AVRAHAM ADLER, CARDIAC SURGEON. So this is where Bouma lives, I said to myself, the master-surgeon who came down from Jerusalem to Tel Aviv to kill the administrative director and send his soul flying into mine in order to ruin my love affair. And all the arguments Bouma had piled on top of each other hadn't torn off the veil of mystery surrounding that death.

I felt an urge to go inside and see the house. After all, I had promised Professor Adler to drop in to see him when I was in Jerusalem, so we could continue our discussion about Lazar's sudden cardiac fibrillation. He seemed like a serious doctor who was interested in hearing the questions and observations of a younger colleague. It was almost noon. Even the laziest people were already up, and the most industrious could afford an hour of idleness at this time of day on a Saturday. Was it possible that the son, the successful professor, stayed in the same old apartment as his father? I wondered when I saw that there was only one entrance to the house, with an old sign simply saying ADLER, without any first names on the door. I was sure it couldn't be where my Adler lived. But since the music pouring out of the house had a welcoming sound, I knocked on the door, and a sprightly old German Jew in a sporty sweater opened it. I explained not only who I was and who I was looking for, but also why. It turned out that Adler Junior did not live here but in Ein Karem, near the hospital; only his clinic was here, next to his father's clinic and residence. In the meantime Professor Adler's mother came out too, a stout, confident German who had bequeathed her plumpness to her son. What a pity, exclaimed both Adlers, who seemed very suited to each other; they would have phoned their son at home to ask if he could see me, but he had flown to a conference in England yesterday and would only be returning in a few days' time. "A pity," repeated the pleasant old man, the well-known cardiologist. "I'm sure he would have wanted to talk to you, Dr. Rubin, about Mr. Lazar's operation, which we were all very sorry about. I know who you are; he mentioned the fact that you were present at the operation and that you thought of the ventricular tachycardia. He spoke to me a lot about that operation, and although it wasn't his fault, he was left with an uneasy feeling about the whole thing. True, it isn't exactly his specialization, it's more my specialization, but he wants to go into the subject more deeply, in order not to be taken by surprise . . ." He laid his gnarled old hand on his sweater in the area of the heart, as if he felt a pain there. "I know," I interrupted him, "Koch's triangle." The old man's face lit up, and his brown eyes, full of humanity, gave me a warm look of acknowledgment. "Yes, Koch's triangle," he repeated happily and in an intimate tone, as if he had been personally acquainted with the learned Koch, who had identified the tiny invisible command post of the heart. He invited me in. But the conversation with Professor Adler Senior, which continued for a whole hour in his big study, where the somber library consisted mainly of history and literature rather than medical books, did not help to solve the mystery of Lazar's death but only increased it. During the course of the conversation I discovered that this famous cardiologist, who had been one of the great names of Hadassah Hospital in his day, was not really interested in the cause of Lazar's death, having never met the man. His only aim was to protect the reputation of his son, and with this in mind he began to tell me about all kinds of cases of sudden ventricular fibrillations that he had come across in the course of his long career and tried to connect them to Lazar. His wife, who sat next to us and listened attentively to our conversation, interrupted from time to time to mention patients of her husband's whom she recalled. Although it was very pleasant to sit there between the two kindly old people, protected from the bright midday light outside, and to impress them with both my knowledge and understanding and with my interest and questions, I could not keep my parents from their lunch any longer.

❧❧❧

I hurried home, and although I was only half an hour late I saw by the dread on my mother's face that she had taken my threat with alarming seriousness, and after lunch I decided not to go out again but spent the afternoon dozing in my room, in anticipation of the sleepless nights awaiting me now that I was unable to stay by myself in the empty house. My father too, still tipsy from the wine they had plied him with at the synagogue, sank into a deep sleep. My mother sat up trying to read her novel, but in the end she couldn't help herself and came into my room to make me swear not to divulge a word of our conversation to my father. Why make him any more miserable than he already was? She didn't say anything about my threat, as if talking about it added to its reality. But in the evening, when I was already back in Tel Aviv, she took advantage of a brief absence on my father's part to call and ask how I was feeling now. My vague and detached answers, and especially my fear of not being able to sleep, increased her anxiety, and she suggested that I come back to spend a few days in Jerusalem. "But how can I? I'm expected at the hospital tomorrow." She thought for a moment and then said that perhaps she or my father, or both of them, could come to Tel Aviv for a day or two. To her surprise, I didn't turn this offer down immediately. "We'll see," I said. "Let's think about it." But she persisted, and suddenly she began speaking haltingly in English, which she never spoke to me. If I was thinking of doing anything drastic, I should warn her, at least. "Don't take us by surprise," she whispered over the phone, turning the vague threat I had presented her with that morning into something real and alive. "You have no moral right to keep even the thought from me," she added. "I've never hidden anything from you." And she was right; neither she nor my father had ever hidden anything from me, nor did it seem as if they had anything to hide. "But why are you in such a panic?" I said with grim humor, lying on the sofa with my eyes closed, laying the side of my face on the exact spot where Dori had sat with her legs crossed, listening with excited sympathy to the declaration of love bursting out of me. "Not that I'm really thinking of harming myself, but if you believed in reincarnation, you would find the world less alarming. Because if anything happens to me, I'll leave you my soul, at least." But she was in no mood now to understand irony or witticisms on my part.

In the middle of the night the phone rang, shattering the remnants of my brittle sleep. It was Michaela, calling as the dawn rose in Varanasi. Her voice was warm, clear, and joyful. "Varanasi?" I cried in astonishment, and with a note of envy. "I thought that this time you wanted to go to places you haven't been to before." "Right," admitted Michaela, who sounded happy and relaxed, but how could she deprive Stephanie of the chance to touch the open heart of India? Even I, the superficial tourist, knew that the heart was there, in the ghats and temples lining the banks of the Ganges. "And Shivi?" I cried. "What about Shivi?" Shivi too could not fail to be impressed by the spiritual power of Varanasi, because she was now happy and contented after a little restlessness in New Delhi, perhaps because of the diarrhea, which was already clearing up. "But what was it?" The strange cry that escaped me was not only the cry of a father and physician, too far away to save his child, but also the cry of someone in need of salvation himself. But Michaela, who even in her joy grasped my pain, quickly reassured me. I could rely on her. When it came to Shivi there were no compromises. In any case, in a few days' time they would be in Calcutta, where they would be surrounded by excellent doctors and good friends. "Calcutta again?" I exclaimed in surprise, and the suspicion entered my heart that the doctors of Calcutta were as much an attraction to her as the mystery and fascination of India. "And Shivi?" I couldn't help bursting out again. "How are the Indians treating her?" And this strange question, which had broken out of me in the hallucination of nighttime, was greeted with excitement. Even an "expert" on India like Michaela would never have imagined that Shivi would arouse such interest and affection among the Indians, who were not accustomed to seeing such a small representative of the West; in her tininess, she exposed the humanity common to us all. When Michaela told them her name, their interest turned to real enthusiasm. "They're not annoyed that you gave her the name of one of their gods?" I cried, with a tumult of feelings flooding me. But it appeared that not only did they feel no anger, they expressed only joy and admiration at seeing the little creature with her light blue eyes bearing the name of the stern and dangerous god, the destroyer of the world—so much so that people sometimes followed her around. "Be careful, Michaela, for God's sake, be careful," I began to shout into the receiver as her voice grew fainter as if it were being carried away in a gale. Then it was completely lost.

I couldn't go back to sleep after this conversation, and I had to be at the hospital very early in the morning anyway, since all the operations had been moved up to the first half of the day because of the farewell party for Dr. Nakash, which was to take place at lunchtime. Nakash himself appeared in the operating room as usual on this, his last day of work, to stand with his famous serenity next to the anesthesia machine, his smooth bald head gleaming darkly through the plastic of his cap. No wonder the speakers at the farewell party in the little auditorium next to the administrative wing were full of sincere praise for the devoted loyalty of this man, who in forty years of work had never missed a day. Hishin also made a speech in honor of his faithful anesthetist, but ever since Lazar's death he had lost his confidence and humor, and his speech soon became boring. The ceremony was conducted by a young man of about thirty, who was introduced as one of the two directors who were taking over Lazar's job. "I see," I said with some emotion to Miss Kolby—who came to the party not because she knew Nakash but because she was still at loose ends after having been removed from her position in the administrative director's office—"that one man isn't enough to fill the void left by Lazar." Indeed, it needed more than one man to overturn some of the decisions taken by the former director, such as bestowing a permanent a half-time position on a young doctor. My job was canceled that very day, right after the party, when I spoke with the new man, who was my age and who apologized profusely and tried to appease my obvious depression, which was caused not by the cancellation, which I had expected, but by the youth of the man now rocking in the chair of the previous director, whose soul had rapidly departed from my body.

Until a new post was found for me as a regular resident in the anesthesiology department, I could only be grateful to Dr. Nakash, who invited me the next day to act as an assistant anesthetist in a private operation at the hospital in Herzliah. During the entire course of the lengthy operation, removing malignancies and metastases from the patient's abdomen and chest, Hishin was unusually quiet and sad, and when I saw that he was deliberately avoiding my eye, it occurred to me that he had heard either directly or indirectly about my affair with Dori. But after the operation was over, when we were getting dressed in the changing room, I discovered the real reason for his hostility. Professor Adler had told Hishin about my visit to his father. "What exactly are you up to, Dr. Rubin?" He pushed me into a corner. "Are you really only interested in discovering the truth?"

"Yes," I replied immediately and unhesitatingly, trying to hide my naked legs from his eyes, "that's all. Nothing else. And I would keep it to myself as well. What did you think? That I would go and tell Dori?" His little eyes scrutinized me in silence, believing and not believing. Then he continued sternly, "I hope so. I certainly hope so. . . . I hope you won't get it into your head to go to her and involve her in your truth. It's time you grew up, Dr. Rubin, and realized that there are mysteries in medicine too. That's its fascination. We deal with living human beings, not inanimate objects." I couldn't resist asking, "But how is she? How is Dori? Is she getting over it?" Now Hishin couldn't help smiling a faint smile of satisfaction. "Can you ever really tell?" He spread his hands out in a questioning gesture. "But at least we've succeeded in persuading her to go on a trip to Europe. We've already made a date to meet her in Paris next week." Because of his obscure marital status, there was no knowing whether there was another woman behind his use of the first-person plural or he was referring only to himself. In any case I couldn't restrain myself. "She's going to Europe already?" I burst out in a cry of pain. The old ironic gleam returned to Hishin's eyes. "I trust you don't have any objections?" He leaned over and gave my shoulder a friendly pat. My heart beat painfully. Was she already capable of taking a trip on her own, whereas I found it more difficult from minute to minute to stay by myself?

When I recognized Dr. Nakash standing quietly at the bus stop, I braked and offered him my crash helmet if he would agree to let me take him home. Nakash had had his driving license suspended for three months for speeding. "You, speeding?" I marveled as he put the helmet, still warm from my head, onto his own bald head. "And I always see you as the most stable person in the world."

"Is that what you see?" Nakash grinned and got onto the pillion. He confessed that he had never been on a motorcycle before, but I felt no current of fear behind my back; instead, his hand, which sometimes seemed to put patients to sleep and wake them up by its touch alone, lay lightly on my shoulder, somewhat calming my anxiety about the lonely night ahead. I took him home and gladly accepted his invitation to go up and have something to drink in his small apartment, which in contrast to my expectations was rather chaotic; the living room was filled with scientific journals, and the equipment of a small, improvised laboratory dominated half the room. Nakash and his wife were testing the possibilities of combining anesthetics, analgesics, and muscle relaxants used in the operating room into tranquilizers for everyday use. "Only tranquilizers?" I asked, willingly giving Mrs. Nakash my cup for another round of coffee, which had a good but unfamiliar taste. "Or more than that?" They exchanged looks, as if wondering how far they could trust me. They were both very dark and skinny, as alike in their ugliness as identical twins.

They naturally avoided giving me a full and unequivocal answer, but it was evident that they wanted to give me a hint, mentioning that their own end would be quick and gentle, and above all free of the arbitrary decisions of self-righteous doctors, sanctifying the suffering of life. In order to show me concrete proof of their success, they gave me a little bottle containing a few sleeping tablets, the product of their home laboratory, which differed from the usual sleeping pills prescribed by family doctors not in the heaviness or duration of the sleep they induced but in the speed with which it descended, and perhaps also in the ease and pleasantness of waking from this sleep. Even though I felt more prepared to face the night with the little bottle in my pocket, I decided not to hurry home, and in spite of the gale-force winds blowing, it occurred to me to keep an old promise and go to visit Amnon at his place of work. He was so surprised and pleased to see me that he could hardly bring himself to let me out of his bearlike embrace. "And I was beginning to think that you were getting fed up with me because of that damn thesis," he blurted out—a strange but accurate complaint, which gave me a guilty pang. "But I'll finish it, Benjy, you'll see. If I'm a little stuck, it's only because I don't want to chew over the same old stuff as everybody else, I want to say at least one thing that will be absolutely original." And this original idea he sought not only by day, at home or in the library, but also by night at his watchman's post, especially now that he had been promoted and no longer had to walk around the perimeter of the factory, but sat with a walkie-talkie and telephone in the little hut, which was full of his books and papers. But before talking about himself and his plans, he wanted to hear about all the women I had sent to India. Had they already reached their destination in Calcutta? Michaela had promised to phone him from there, directly to this hut. If Michaela had revealed to him what she had hidden from me, I said to myself, perhaps he knew other things about her too. And to my astonishment I discovered that Amnon did indeed know things about her, and about me, that nobody had told him but that he had grasped through his own intelligence and intuition, and especially through his immense curiosity, dating from our high school days, about his friends and acquaintances.

❧❧

"Did you guess about my impossible love affair too?" I couldn't resist asking him, without looking him in the eye, my head bent over the papers strewn on the table in an attempt to identify something familiar in his equations and charts. He was surprised by the unexpected confidence I was placing in him. No, he admitted honestly. He had heard about it for the first time from Michaela when they said good-bye. He had guessed that something which affected me deeply had happened in India, but he thought it was connected with Einat and not her mother. Yes, at first he had sensed that something had opened up in me when I came back from India, but on the way back from Eyal's wedding, when we had stopped on the little hill on the road from the Dead Sea to Jerusalem and I had begun holding forth about my own private theory of the contraction of the universe and how spirit was going to shrink matter until there was nothing left of it, he had begun to worry about me. I had always been the good friend whom nobody had to worry about, the successful student who homed in steadily and accurately on the target his parents had set for him. But when he saw the speed with which I decided to marry Michaela—whom, if I didn't mind his saying so, I didn't really love enough—he began to feel that I might be following in his footsteps and losing my way. Even now, if I had come to visit him here in the middle of the night, it meant that I wasn't in the greatest shape. While he himself was stuck and buried in the ground, maybe because of his brother—yes, because of his poor little brother—I, who had always seemed to him the ideal, well-balanced man, had turned into a kind of spaceship which had gone out of orbit and was now spinning aimlessly among the stars. But a spaceship that could be brought back on course. I myself must have seen how astronauts left their shuttles to return straying objects to their original course. Because that was the great advantage of space—nothing crashed there.

For a moment he was silent, astonished at himself for having blamed his failure on his retarded brother. And then, as if unable to contain his emotion, he stood up and hugged me warmly again, pressing the revolver on his belt against my chest until I too had to stand up and return his hug. Thus we stood embracing in the little watchman's hut, listening in the silence to the wind howling outside, accompanied by the unearthly whistles of the walkie-talkie. Although my heart genuinely ached for him, I felt repelled by the sentimentality that had been overpowering him of late. God save me from deteriorating into this kind of pain and self-pity, I thought with increasing disgust. Better to be detached—not depression but Nirvana, which is the end of all incarnations. I was already thinking of Nakash's sleeping pills, which would sweeten the night for me. You can always rely on Nakash, Hishin used to say. The news that Dori was going to travel to Europe by herself continued to astound me. Was it possible? I thought in anger and envy. Mightn't it be dangerous? And a new thought came into my mind. I had to find Einat and talk to her. Gently but decisively I extricated myself from Amnon's emotional embrace, and although I had the telephone number of Einat's apartment, I asked him if he knew what she was up to. He hadn't bumped into her since the night of Michaela's departure, but he thought she was still working as a waitress in the same pub where she had worked before.

In spite of his detailed explanations, I did not find the place easily. The savage wind buffeting the motorcycle led me astray in the little streets close to the sea in the north of the city, and it was a long time before I found myself standing in front of the red-painted wooden door with the name of the pub emblazoned on it. It was a small place, apparently not very popular, for even on a night like this only a handful of people had taken refuge in it, and even they were sitting in a noncommittal way, as if they were still making up their minds whether to stay. The music was not too loud and pleasant enough, and I didn't have to look far for Einat, in jeans and a red tee shirt with the name of the place printed on it, collecting glasses from one of the tables. Remembering her panic on the night I took her home after we said good-bye to Michaela, I didn't go up to her at once, but only waved to her from a distance and sat down in a quiet corner where we would be able to talk later. Although she must have realized that I had gone there looking for her, she didn't come up to me but sent the second waitress to take my order while she went to stand behind the bar, as if to place an additional barrier between us. She knows everything, I thought fearfully. After I had traveled to the ends of the earth to take care of her, and may have saved her life at a certain moment, could she really want to sever all contact with me? Even now I could remember the results of her blood tests, and my hands still remembered her swollen liver. I couldn't help myself. I took my beer from the waitress and carried it over to the bar, to sit opposite her and force her to listen to what I had to say. But Einat, who had obviously been watching my every move, hurried to a remote corner of the pub and began talking to the people sitting at one of the tables. The few people and low music made it impossible to force her to face me and listen to at least one question without arousing attention. I therefore remained standing at the bar, sipping my beer slowly, knowing that sooner or later she would have to come back. But instead she disappeared. I asked the other waitress where she had gone, but she said she didn't know. I waited a few minutes and then asked for my glass to be refilled and returned to my table. But Einat didn't come back, and since no new customers showed up, the second waitress did not seem bothered by her disappearance.

Half an hour passed. One of the customers requested rock and roll, and the second waitress immediately complied with his wishes. I closed my eyes. I wasn't used to drinking, and the two beers had made me slightly light-headed. I decided to leave, but not before visiting the bathroom. It was deserted, but next to it was a door leading to the little neon-lit kitchen. I saw her immediately, sitting in the corner next to a big refrigerator and holding a glass of milk. Presumably it hadn't occurred to her that I would pursue her, for when she saw me she turned very pale, as if she had seen a ghost, jumped up from her chair, and held her slender hand up to stop me with a desperate, pathetic gesture, which I immediately respected. She looked frantic, afraid to meet my eyes, her fingers nervously pleating the edges of the big red tee shirt, hoping against hope that someone would come in to save her from confronting me. But nobody came in, and the savage new music grew louder inside the pub.

"Tell me, Einat, did I make a mistake when I fell in love with your mother instead of falling in love with you?" I asked her in a quiet voice, without beating around the bush. Her face, which looked even purer than usual against the gaudy background of the colored bottles on the wall, turned bright red. She shook her head quickly, as if trying to repulse me, and mumbled, "No, you didn't make a mistake."

"Your mother and father took me to India to fall in love with you, and I behaved like a doctor," I went on. "Was I wrong? Tell me, was I wrong?" She went on shaking her head with a tormented expression on her face and said, "No, you weren't wrong. You couldn't have behaved any differently." Now a deep calm descended on me, as if I had received her approval for the oblivion I sought. But she didn't know what I intended to do, and fearing a continuation of the conversation, she slipped nimbly past me like a little squirrel, taking great care not to touch me. She hurried up the steps and just as she was, in the thin tee shirt, opened the wooden door, letting in a wild gust of wind, and disappeared, perhaps into the pub next door.

In the stairwell I heard the telephone ringing as I arrived home. It can only be Michaela, I thought, and I began running upstairs. But the ringing stopped before I could open the door. On the little bottle Dr. Nakash had given me was a label listing all the ingredients of the home-produced drug he had concocted. Should I take a whole pill? I wondered, and broke one of the little tablets in two. I swallowed one of the halves, and judging by the speed with which my eyes drooped, I realized that the minute quantities of a distilled poppy extract which the experienced anesthetist had added to the usual ingredients had produced a knockout sleeping pill. But I couldn't allow the wonderful heaviness to overpower me, because in the depths of my mind I was waiting for the phone to ring again. Which it soon did. But it wasn't Michaela, it was my mother. "Where have you been? Where have you been?" Her voice rose complainingly in my ear, as if I owed it to her to be at home when she was looking for me. It turned out that Michaela had called my parents from Calcutta early in the evening and had a long conversation with them. "So what do you want?" I responded sulkily to this information, hanging on to the thin, slippery thread of wakefulness trying to slip away from me. "Couldn't it have waited until morning?" But my mother had a definite aim in mind. Michaela and Shivi had arrived safely and found rooms in a hostel where some of the volunteer doctors were staying, but Shivi had not yet recovered from the diarrhea that had started in New Delhi, and she had a slight fever too. Ever since this conversation my parents had had no peace. Didn't I think it was time for me to take a firmer line with Michaela? They had succeeded in getting the phone number of a store near the hostel where it would be possible to leave a message for her. While I struggled against the thick blanket of sleep that was now wrapping itself around me, I tried to reassure her. Diarrhea was endemic in India, especially in newly arrived tourists. Lazar had suffered from it throughout the trip, and nothing had happened to him in the end. But the main thing—which they seemed to have forgotten—was that Michaela was now in the company of real, Western doctors, and they would help her overcome all of Shivi's problems. I didn't know if I had succeeded in dispelling my mother's anxiety, but the shock effects of Nakash's half-tablet made it impossible for me to say anymore, and I rudely cut the conversation short, perhaps even without saying good-bye.

The next day in the afternoon, when I began disconnecting my patient from the anesthesia machine before checking his pupils in the narrow beam of my flashlight, one of the nurses from the intensive care unit came up to me and told me that there was a woman waiting for me in the waiting room. To my surprise I found my mother sitting among the relatives of the people undergoing surgery, probably listening as usual to other people's troubles without saying anything about her own. Had she identified herself as the mother of one of the young doctors standing next to the operating table, or had she kept quiet in order not to appear boastful? Even from a distance she looked very tired and tense, like someone now fighting alone on two fronts without knowing which was the most important. She was wearing her gray wool suit, which I remembered from my high school graduation ceremony, and although last night's gale had swept the clouds from the sky and left it a sparkling, polished blue, she had not forgotten to bring her umbrella, like the native of the British Isles she was. I touched her shoulder and bent over her tenderly. She interrupted her conversation and looked up, confused to see me in my green operating-room uniform. Then she introduced me to the woman sitting next to her, who immediately asked me if I knew anything about her husband's operation. I apologized to her for not knowing anything, and without asking my mother what had brought her to me, I lifted her to her feet and offered to show her around the operating rooms, which she had never seen before. She was surprised and pleased by my offer, and only wanted to know first if I had permission to take her inside. I told her that I didn't need anyone's permission and took a white gown from one of the trolleys and helped her on with it. Then I secured a plastic head-cover over the thin, childish braid coiled on the nape of her neck. Naturally I didn't take her into the room where an operation was underway, but into the one that had just been vacated, to show her the various instruments and especially the anesthesia machine and to tell her the names of the different anesthetics, pointing out the little colored bottles. She listened attentively to my explanations, and although she didn't appear to be taking in too much of what I said, she didn't ask any questions, as though some new and menacing thought were preoccupying her and paralyzing her mind as she gazed at all the lethal possibilities at my disposal.

Since I was due to participate in another operation shortly, we had no time to dawdle, and I took her up to the cafeteria to hear the real reason for her unexpected visit. It was hard to get anything clear out of her. First of all, she protested, she hadn't made a special trip to see me. She had been to visit my father's aunt in the old folks' home, the grandmother of his niece Rachel, who had been so nice to them in London, she and her husband Edgar. And afterward it had occurred to her to drop in on me in the hospital, to talk to me about Shivi. My reassurances the night before had not succeeded in putting her mind to rest. She wanted to give me the phone number in Calcutta where I could get in touch with Michaela again. If Michaela wanted to endanger herself, let her, but she had no right to put the baby at risk. Altogether, my mother was surprised at me—how could I be so indifferent to my own child? I wanted to make a crushing reply, but I said nothing, trying unsuccessfully to imagine Shivi in Calcutta. While I was drinking the last drops of coffee, I looked into her bloodshot eyes and tried to figure out what it was she wanted from me. She, who never lingered over partings, was now finding it difficult to part from me, and after I accompanied her to the exit, she turned around and followed me back to the surgical wing. "Don't worry about Shivi," I repeated before pressing the numbers of the code that opened the big glass doors. For a moment I wanted to add, You should worry about me instead, but I didn't, and I disappeared from her view into the bright corridor opening out in front of me.

❧❦❧

The next evening, after I had eaten my supper, despairingly aware of how my new dread of being alone was creeping up on me even in the early twilight hours, I decided to return to the hospital and explore the possibilities available to me in one of the empty operating rooms. The thought of going to sleep on the operating table and never waking up seemed increasingly attractive to me. But at seven o'clock my father phoned from Jerusalem. It appeared that when he came home from work that afternoon my mother wasn't at home, although the insurance agency where she worked as a secretary was closed on Tuesday afternoons. He had found a vague note saying, "Gone out for a while, don't worry."

"Then why are you worried?" I said impatiently. "She'll probably come back soon." But about two hours later he phoned again, to say that there was no sign of her and nobody knew where she was. "You know I'm not a hysterical type," he said, trying to defend himself, "but I don't know where she could be." We arranged to talk again in an hour, but after fifteen minutes he phoned again. It was after nine. He had conducted a little search of the house, and it seemed to him that the new suitcase which she had bought in London was missing. Perhaps she had lent it to somebody without telling him. "Surely she couldn't have gone anywhere without giving me any warning?" he asked, and now he spoke in English, without even an occasional word in Hebrew, as if he had made up his mind to cling firmly to his mother tongue, which alone was capable of anchoring him in the chaos swirling around him. I asked him if he wanted me to come to Jerusalem. "Not yet. But if I have to go and report her missing to the police," he added in a humorous tone, "you should come with me." I promised him that I would stay near the phone, sensing how my father's new anxiety, streaming to me from Jerusalem, was making me forget my own anxiety, which quickly turned to astonishment when he phoned with the update. Not only was the new suitcase missing, but her favorite summer dress was also gone. "Could she have suddenly taken it into her head to take a trip somewhere? But where?" he asked himself more than me, without any note of complaint or anger against his wife for leaving him without a word. "See if you can find her passport," I suggested to him at ten o'clock at night. He went to look for it immediately, and fifteen minutes later he announced that he had found her Israeli passport, but the British passport, which was always in the same place as his, was missing. Could she have taken it with her? But why? "I'll give you an answer soon," he promised with a peculiar confidence in his voice, and half an hour later he phoned to say that he had just concluded a long conversation with my mother's sister in Glasgow, and even though she had been astonished and also a little amused by his announcement and couldn't give him any leads, he had the feeling that she wasn't as worried as she should have been. Did she know something that she was hiding from him? Or were the Scots just more phlegmatic than the English?

It was now clear to both of us that my mother had undertaken a mysterious journey to an unknown destination. If my father had been more familiar with her wardrobe, he might have been more able to find out what was missing, but he was indifferent to such details, and it was hard to get anything specific out of him. His concern, however, evaporated the minute he realized that my mother had gone on a trip. Now he began to see the whole thing in a different light. Although people might disappear in the course of a journey to an unknown destination, at least a journey progressed in a definite direction; a rational woman like my mother would never set off without a goal, and this notion calmed him. "I'm turning into Sherlock Holmes in my old age," he said with a chuckle at one o'clock in the morning, astonishingly wide awake, and he reported on private investigations of her belongings in the secret corners of unfamiliar drawers. At five o'clock in the morning, between one fitful doze and another, I tried to call him, but there was no answer. I left a message with the hospital switchboard to say that my mother had disappeared, I had to go to Jerusalem at once to help my father look for her, and I wouldn't be coming to work. Why couldn't I have lied and said my mother was sick? I castigated myself as I sped along the expressway to Jerusalem in the teeth of an east wind that had blown up, watching the rays of the sun forcing their way through the haze. Luckily the key to the house was always on my key ring, and I was able to walk inside and find my father sleeping soundly in his bed.

"I want to keep calm," he said, his face pink with the pleasure of sleep in spite of the vicissitudes of the night. "I know that she's a sensible woman, with logical goals. But I'm sure that this disappearance of hers is directed at you, not at me. I've sensed for a few weeks that something wasn't right between you. That she was angry with you for something you did. But however hard I tried to get at the truth, she wouldn't give me even a crumb. Perhaps you can tell me now what happened between you." But I had vowed to my mother, who was now trying to direct my life by remote control, that I wouldn't tell my father anything. And I certainly didn't intend to add to his troubles now. Soon he would have to decide how to excuse his absence from work. Would he too feel that he had to tell the truth about his wife's disappearance to his colleagues and make a laughingstock of himself? But at half-past seven the phone rang. It was my aunt, talking excitedly from Glasgow. My mother was on her way to Calcutta to bring the baby back. She would land there in a couple of hours. Michaela knew that she was coming. It seemed that my aunt had not been able to rest all night long, and eventually she had succeeded in getting the details of my mother's sudden flight out of Edgar, our pale, thin London relation, for he was the only one my mother had trusted enough to confide in.

With the news of my mother's flight to Calcutta a profound calm descended on my father, and he got dressed and went to work. "If you find out something new, phone me at the office," he said as he left the house. And I stayed alone in my parents' apartment as in the days when I stayed home sick from school. I didn't call the hospital. Since I had made the bizarre announcement of my mother's disappearance, I might as well give it time to sink in and take on the menacing dimensions it deserved before I canceled it. But since I had remembered to slip the little bottle Nakash had given me into my pocket before leaving for Jerusalem, so that I would have something to give my father to calm his anxiety, I took the second half of the little sleeping pill and swallowed it, saying to myself as I did so, Now that my mother's flying over India to bring the baby home, I'll need all my reserves of strength for her return, when she will undoubtedly lay the whole burden on me.

When my father returned in the early afternoon he found me sleeping deeply, and he didn't wake me, for unlike my mother he had always respected my sleep. He let me go on sleeping even when he received another phone call from my aunt in Glasgow, who until my mother's return from India served as the go-be-

tween for us and Edgar, the strange relation whom my mother
had rightly chosen to guide her on his journey because of his
connections with firms doing business in India; through telephone calls, telegrams, and faxes, he was able to guide her safely
to her destination by means of faithful Indian clerks who waited
for her at airports and train stations, making modest but respectable arrangements for the comfort of an elderly woman traveling
alone and returning with a slightly feverish infant, straight there
and back, without looking right or left at the glorious and terri-
fying abundance of life that surrounded her.

My mother left on Tuesday morning and returned on Friday
evening. Her whole trip took seventy-seven hours. For about
twenty-six of them she was in the air, and for about six she
traveled by train. Since I returned to work in the hospital on
Thursday and I didn't want to complicate things for my colleagues with another absence, I didn't go to the airport to meet
them but let my father go instead. I took off from the emergency
room as soon as I could get away, and as dusk began to fall I was
already racing to Jerusalem on my motorcycle, with my visor
raised so I could enjoy the scents of the wild grasses and early
blossoming of the almond trees. In my parents' house the lights
were on in all the rooms, and I quickly saw that there were new
lines on my mother's exhausted face, but also a new radiance.
Shivi, whom my mother now insisted on calling Shiva, like
Michaela's Indian friends, was really in pretty bad shape, though
not at all critical. She was thinner and browner, and in her little
yellow sari, with the third eye (which my mother had not wiped
off during the entire journey home) shining between her eyes, she
reminded me for a moment of the Indian children who had run
after me when I went down to the Ganges. In our time apart, she
had learned to walk, and since she now recognized me immediately—not like the time at the airport when the two English girls
had brought her back from England—she began tottering toward
me. I swept her up into the air and clasped her little body tightly
to my chest. All this time I had thought of her as being a part of
Michaela, and I hadn't realized how much she was also a part of
me. It appeared that Michaela had agreed to let my mother have
her without any arguments. She was a realistic woman, and she
knew that there were risks for a small child in India. In the short,

stormy night my mother had spent in Calcutta, she had received the impression that Michaela's spiritual attraction to India was reinforced by the simple human experience of working with the sidewalk doctors, which gave her a feeling of worth and led the Indians to regard her as almost a doctor herself, even though she had never graduated from high school. Nevertheless, my mother believed that she would soon return. "But will you be able to take her back?" she asked, still not looking me in the eye. "Because if not, you'll have to come back to Jerusalem."

"Did you remember to get vaccinated before you left?" I asked my mother, who now realized that she may have endangered her health by her journey. But my father was overjoyed, getting down on his knees to watch the movements of the little girl, whom I now set down gently on the floor to continue her tottering investigations. He did not seem to bear my mother a grudge for her disappearance; in fact, he was very proud of what she had done. Had he kissed or hugged her, I wondered, when she emerged from the airport terminal? I had never seen them kiss or embrace in my presence or in the presence of others; sometimes I wondered how I had been born at all.

※C※

At last the door opens, and slowly they wheel the mystery's bed out of the operating room on its way to the intensive care unit. It is sunk in a deep sleep and wrapped in white bandages, connected to infusions and flickering instruments, but none of the nurses waiting in intensive care knows what to do for it or how to help it, for no knife or saw has been brandished over it, no tube or needle inserted to implant what was amputated at the dawn of time. Even if no drop of blood was shed, it is still suffering torments after a long night of stubborn delving into a black and riven soul. And perhaps they do well to bring a big cage in which two wild birds are chained together into the room full of morning light. Perhaps the birds will relieve his suffering with their song. Indeed, for the first time a smile breaks on his face. Has the first tender young plant already taken root? ask the nurses clustered around his bed. Among them is the little girl left behind in the kitchen in her school uniform, who has grown tall and beautiful and stolen in unobserved, disguised as a nurse, to take care of him. But the ray of light shattering on the emerald of her eyes betrays her. And then I can't stop myself any longer from bursting into this dream. My darling, I whisper to her, my darling, my love.

Harvest in Translation

THE THUNDER KEEPER

"Coel has obvious respect for the land and people who populate it . . . She creates dense and compelling characters in complex stories to entertain her loyal fans." —*The Denver Post*

"Coel gets the atmosphere just right. She is on original and interesting ground." —*Publishers Weekly*

THE SPIRIT WOMAN

"Intriguing Arapaho and Shoshone history and realistic treatment of contemporary Native American issues make this cozy a winner." —*Library Journal*

"A well-drawn tale. Margaret Coel changes the direction of the series so that there is an added freshness that doesn't lose the essence of the Wind River mysteries." —*Midwest Book Review*

"Gives the readers a rare look into the lives of the Arapahos, and they can feel the pain of a nation forced to live by the white man's standards. This is one of those books that keeps the blood pumping. Tight tension keeps it moving at an accelerating pace." —*Rendezvous*

THE LOST BIRD

"A truly touching story . . . the whole book is infused with the spirit of the Arapaho community." —Sarah Smith, author of *The Knowledge of Water*

"Among the best mysteries of the year. She writes vividly about western landscapes and Native American customs . . . Coel is clearly at the top of her game." —*Booklist* (starred review)

"An engrossing mystery and a great read. Margaret Coel manages to have enjoyable characters and a super mystery—not an easy task." —*The Literary Times*

continued . . .

The Story Teller

"Vivid western landscapes, intriguing history, compelling characters, and quick, tight writing that is a joy to read . . . Holden is a unique mix of the modern and the traditional. One of the best of the year."

—*Booklist* (starred review)

"All the strengths of this fine series are present here: Coel's knowledge of and respect for western history, a solid mystery with a credible premise in Indian lore, and the struggles of Holden and O'Malley with their powerful, but so far unconsummated, attraction to each other."

—*Publishers Weekly*

The Dream Stalker

"Seamless storytelling by someone who's obviously been there."

—J. A. Jance

"Critics who have called Coel a 'female Hillerman' are right on the mark."

—*The Boulder Daily Camera*

"Murder, romance, a nuclear storage facility, and Indian lore blend appealingly in this third mystery . . . Another coup for Coel."

—*Publishers Weekly*

THE GHOST WALKER

"Margaret Coel guides us mystery lovers on another of her gripping tours of evil among the Wind River Arapahos."
—Tony Hillerman

"Coel is a vivid voice for the West, its struggles to retain its past and at the same time enjoy the fruits of the future."
—*The Dallas Morning News*

"A corking good read . . . Excellent . . . An outstanding entry in a superior series."
—*Booklist* (starred review)

"A tautly written, compelling mystery, grounded in and sympathetic to the Arapaho culture."
—*Milwaukee Journal Sentinel*

THE EAGLE CATCHER

"Margaret Coel's account of dastardly deeds among the Arapahos on the Wind River Reservation shouldn't be missed by anyone interested in either new trends in mystery writing or contemporary American Indian culture. She's a master at both."
—Tony Hillerman

"An uncanny sense of dialogue . . . Coel merges her grasp of history with the mystery genre. The result is so successful, you wonder what took her so long."
—*The Denver Post*

"Insightful commentary about Arapaho culture, well-drawn characters, and a lively pace."
—*Publishers Weekly*

❮ The ❯
Shadow Dancer

Margaret Coel

BERKLEY PRIME CRIME, NEW YORK

THE SHADOW DANCER

A Berkley Prime Crime Book / published by arrangement with
the author

PRINTING HISTORY
Berkley Prime Crime hardcover edition / September 2002
Berkley Prime Crime mass-market edition / August 2003

ISBN: 0-425-19127-3

Berkley Prime Crime Books are published
by The Berkley Publishing Group,
a division of Penguin Group (USA) Inc.,
375 Hudson Street, New York, New York 10014.
The name BERKLEY PRIME CRIME and the BERKLEY PRIME
CRIME design are trademarks belonging to Penguin Group (USA) Inc.

PRINTED IN THE UNITED STATES OF AMERICA

10 9 8 7 6 5 4 3 2 1

Acknowledgments

Many people read all or parts of this manuscript and contributed the expertise and good judgment to make the story much better than it otherwise would have been. I am very grateful. My sincere thanks to:

Thomas D. Lustig, senior staff attorney, Rocky Mountain Natural Resources Clinic, National Wildlife Federation; Thomas Dougherty, senior advisor, office of the president, National Wildlife Federation; Mike Pease, bomb disposal officer, Boulder Police Department; J. David Love, Ph.D., retired research geologist, U.S. Geological Survey, and Jane Love, friends and excellent advisers, as are Swede Johnson, attorney, and Elizabeth Girard, M.D.; Elaine Long, author of *Jennie's Mountain*, a friend and writer whom I've long admired; Arthur Long, expert on many subjects, including dynamite; John Dix, my nephew and the best baseball player I know; Carl Starkloff, S.J., and Anthony Short, S.J., valued friends and consultants, both formerly of St. Stephen's Mission on the Wind River Reservation; Beverly Carrigan and Carl Schneider, also valued friends and sharp-eyed readers; Karen Gilleland, another excellent friend and gifted writer;

Virginia Sutter, Ph.D., member of the Arapaho tribe, long-time friend who has taught me much about the Arapaho Way; and Kristin Coel Henderson, my daughter, and George Coel, my husband, the best consultants and toughest critics of all.

Dedicated to

Eleanor Margaret Henderson

Father, the morning star!
Look on us. We have danced until daybreak.
We have danced until daybreak.
Take pity on us.
Take pity on us.
Hi'i'i'!

Stand ready!
Stand ready!
So that when the crow calls you,
You will see him.
You will see him.

— ARAPAHO SONGS

‹ 1 ›

My relations, stand ready, stand ready. I bring you the words of the father himself, Hesuna'nin. The father sent the lightning that cleansed and burned me into the ground. He took me to the shadow land, where I saw the ancestors: Black Coal, Sharp Nose, Yellow Calf, Little Raven, Medicine Man, Left Hand. I saw the beautiful women standing tall and proud and the children running and playing with hoops and sticks. The father told me to tell you that the new world is coming. Already crow is flying on the clouds and bringing the ancestors back to us. They come with the mighty herds of buffalo, deer, and elk. Once again the white lodges will spread beneath the cottonwoods. Green grass will cover the plains. There will be wild fruits and vegetables, and the rivers will run clean. The father will keep his promise to us. The new world will slide over the old, like the right hand over the left.

From a half-mile down the road, Father John O'Malley could see the small, white house reflecting the late afternoon light, stark and solitary in the empty expanse of the plains. The second act of *Faust*, "*De l'enfer qui vient*," rose from the tape player beside him and mixed with the sound of the wind over the half-opened windows of the Toyota pickup. It was the last Monday in May, the Moon When the Ponies Shed Their Shaggy Hair, in the Arapaho way of marking the passing time. For a week, the temperature had been setting record highs.

He turned into the bare-dirt yard and stopped next to the concrete stoop at the front door. The curtains in the front windows were half-closed against the sun, making the house seem inviting, a shady oasis. A twenty-year-old sedan with the rear bumper bent at one end was parked next to the house. He let the tape play a moment, then hit the off switch and got out, giving the door a hard slam that sounded like a rifle shot in the quiet. Anybody inside would know he'd arrived.

He leaned against the pickup and pulled his cowboy hat down against the sun. It was not polite to bang on the door and call attention to yourself. If someone wanted to see you, he'd come out and say so. Beyond the house, the plains ran into the dun-colored foothills of the Wind River mountains. The white peaks lay along the blue sky like a serrated knife.

In his eight years at St. Francis Mission on the Wind River Reservation, Father John had come to love the quiet vastness and the way the plains revealed their secrets when you happened upon them unexpectedly—the swell of a bluff, the cut of an arroyo, the patches of sagebrush and pink, blue, and yellow wildflowers. So different from Boston, where he'd spent most of his forty-eight years. He was an Irishman, from a long line of Boston Irish with the same red hair and blue eyes and white skin that always looked flushed in the sun.

He'd been a drunk in Boston, alone in his study, grading papers for his American history classes at the Jesuit prep school, sipping whiskey—a harmless relaxation after the long day, he'd told himself. He'd found so many ways, dozens of ways, to hide from the truth there, until the day the Superior had confronted him. He'd spent a year in Grace House, and afterward—still recovering, always recovering— no one had offered him a job. Except for Father Peter at an Indian mission in Wyoming that Father John had never heard of. Three years later, Father Peter had retired and Father John had become the Superior. You couldn't hide here, with the earth stretching into the sky. He was grateful for that. Your shadow was always alongside you.

"There you are, Father." Minnie Little Horse stood in the opened door, patting at the white apron draped over her pink housedress. The sound of her voice surprised him. When had the door opened? She was in her seventies, with tightly curled gray hair that matched the pinched look on her dark face. Squinting into the sunshine, she waved him inside.

"How are you, grandmother," he said, using the term of respect. He followed her into the L-shaped living room that extended into the kitchen in the rear. Another elderly woman—this would be Minnie's sister, although she looked frailer and more sunken into herself than the last time he'd seen her—sat on the sofa: needle in one hand, white thread dangling over a piece of tanned deerskin in her lap, an embroidered design of colored beads taking shape on the skin.

"You remember Louise," Minnie said.

"Yes, of course." Father John walked over, and the old woman slipped her free hand, small and rough as bark, into his. Her face was crosshatched with wrinkles, the thin hair only partially concealing patches of pink scalp. She looked up at him out of ancient eyes, like the eyes of grandmothers in the Old Time, staring out of the bronze-tinted photos.

"Eat, eat," Louise said, removing her hand. "We got cold chicken in the fridge. Minnie'll get you a plate." The other woman was already starting for the kitchen.

He had to laugh. The people were always trying to feed him. A habit from the Old Time, he knew, when Arapahos fed everybody who wandered into the villages.

He thanked the sisters and said he'd take a raincheck. The afternoon was wearing on, and Elena, the housekeeper at St. Francis, served dinner at six. It was Monday. That meant stew. Elena ran the residence like a drill sergeant. She expected promptness, and he was usually late. He would be late today, but his new assistant, Father George Reinhold, in all his German exactitude, would no doubt be on time, which, Father John knew, would only partially mollify Elena.

"Cup of coffee, then?" An impatient let's-get-this-over-with note seeped into Minnie's voice.

"Coffee would be fine," he said. He took the chair across from Louise, set his hat on the side table, and made small talk for a few moments: the hot weather, the wild grasses burned brown in the sun. The old woman smoothed the deerskin in her lap. What's it gonna be like in July, when the real summer heat comes on? They oughtta move to Alaska, she said. Finally she laid the deerskin on the cushion beside her.

"I been saying to Minnie," she began again, and he knew this was what the sisters wanted to talk about, "we can't keep our worrying all bottled up. We gotta call Father John."

The call had come this morning. Minnie's voice, breathless and hurried. She didn't want to bother him, but she didn't know what to do, and he, being a white man . . . Could he come over? He'd glanced at his daytimer. A married couple due in for counseling in thirty minutes, social committee meeting this afternoon, parish council meeting tonight. And he wanted to finish writing the annual report for the board of directors meeting next weekend.

He dreaded the annual board meeting—the bishop himself from Cheyenne and seven Jesuits from around the country, all scrutinizing the financial and spiritual conditions of St. Francis Mission. And always the possibility that the board would decide the mission had outlived its purpose—a nineteenth-century anachronism adrift in the twenty-first century—and recommend to the Provincial that it be closed.

He'd told Minnie he'd try to swing by about four-thirty or five.

Minnie was back with two mugs of coffee—one for him, the other for her sister. She sank onto the far side of the sofa, clasped her hands over the white apron, and drew in a long breath, composing something inside her head. Finally she said, "Louise and me, well, we been real worried about my grandson, Dean." The words came in a torrent, as if a dam had burst.

"What's going on?" Father John could still see Dean Little Horse running around the bases after he'd hit the ball into left field, long legs stretching out to take him home. Another score for the Eagles, the baseball team Father John had started his first summer at St. Francis. Dean was fifteen then, tall and thin-limbed, with black hair that fell over his forehead and dark eyes lit with curiosity and intelligence. He'd gone off to college three years later, and the last Father

John had heard, he'd landed a job with a software company in Lander.

Minnie bit at her lower lip, then she said, "We can't find him, Father."

"What do you mean?" Father John set his mug on the table next to his chair. The house was stitched with tension.

"Four days now, since last Thursday. Ain't that right, Louise?" Minnie glanced over at her sister. "We been calling and calling. He don't answer the phone. I went to his apartment in Lander yesterday, but nobody was there."

"What about his office?"

"That's just it, Father." The woman sat perfectly still, frozen with anxiety. "I went to his office, and they said he didn't come to work Friday and didn't show up today."

Father John leaned forward. He set his elbows on his thighs and clasped his hands, trying to fit what the woman had said into some kind of logical context. Dean Little Horse might have decided to get away for a few days. Maybe he went fishing or decided to take a trek into the mountains.

He didn't believe it. No Arapaho would just leave without telling his family. And Minnie and Louise were Dean's family. They'd raised him from infancy, from the day after his father, Minnie's only child, had died in a car accident. Dean's mother, seventeen years old and terrified, had shown up at the front door. Twenty below zero outside, Minnie once told him, snow so deep that the girl's footprints across the yard looked like post holes, and she'd handed Minnie a bundle wound in blankets and said, "Your grandson. I can't take care of him."

Minnie had tried to get the girl to come inside, but she'd turned and run back through the post holes, hopping through the swirling snow on one leg, then the other. Minnie had begun unwrapping the hard, still bundle, shaking with fear that the baby—God! She hadn't known about the baby!—was already dead, frozen to death.

"Have you contacted the police?" he said finally.

Minnie was shaking her head, eyes closed against the possibility. "We don't want the police, Father." She opened her eyes and gave him a look that pleaded for understanding. "Dean's a good boy, never had trouble with the police. Louise and me, we don't want the police to know his name. Far as they're concerned, Dean Little Horse don't exist, and that's how we want to keep it. They hear he's missing, they're gonna classify him with the losers and drunks that hang out at the bars."

"Fort Indians," Louise said.

Father John understood. The drunken Indians who, a hundred years ago, had hung out at the forts, trading their buffalo robes and their women, everything they had, for another drink of whiskey. Oh, yes, he understood. He'd traded his career for whiskey.

"Dean was twenty-three last March." Minnie scooted to the edge of the sofa. "He's got himself a college degree, knows all about computers, You're a white man. You tell me where he might've gone off to."

Father John had to glance away from the raw fear in the women's eyes. They both knew that Dean Little Horse could have gotten into serious trouble—a reservation Indian, making his way in the outside world. There were people who'd run an Indian off the road if they saw him. He'd been in the backseat of a van once, on his way to speak at a luncheon for local businessmen. The Toyota had been sputtering, in need of new spark plugs, and they'd offered to pick him up. Four white men and the Indian priest, careening down the highway toward Riverton, and an Indian standing alongside the road, waiting to cross.

"Let's see how high he jumps," the driver called out.

"Yeah, go for it." The others whooped and hollered. The van veered toward the Indian, who jumped back, stumbled, and fell into the ditch.

"Stop!" Father John had shouted. Even the memory brought the heat into his face.

"Hey, Father." The driver's head had swirled around, as if he'd forgotten who was there. "No harm done. Just a little joke."

"Let me out," he'd said.

"Hey, what about your talk?" One of the businessmen seemed to realize what had happened. "Lots of people gonna be disappointed."

They were a quarter-mile down the highway when the van finally pulled over. He'd crawled past the brown-trousered legs, freed himself, and slammed the door. The van had squealed into the traffic and he'd run back to find the Indian, but the man was gone.

He felt his skin prickling. *Dean was like that Indian. He could be lying in a ditch somewhere.* He said, "I'll have a look around Lander."

"Oh, would you, Father?" The fear in Minnie's eyes dissolved into a look of such trust and expectation that he could almost feel the weight of it settling over his shoulders.

He said, "I'll need some information. Dean's apartment. The name of his company." He pulled out the small notepad and pencil he always carried in the pocket of his plaid shirt.

Minnie recited the addresses, telephone numbers, all from memory.

Father John wrote quickly. "What about his friends?"

"Friends?" Minnie was quiet, and he glanced up. Her dark eyes were like stones. "Kids he went to high school with on the rez, lot of 'em moved away. Far as I know, Dean was making new friends. He never had trouble making friends. Everybody likes Dean."

"I think he had a girlfriend," Louise said, her voice small and tentative.

"Oh, Louise." Minnie gave the other woman an impatient look. This was well-trodden ground. "We don't know that for sure."

"Too busy to come for dinner last few Sundays," the other woman persisted. "Only normal a good boy like Dean would find himself a nice girl to spend Sundays with."

"Any idea of who she is?" Father John said.

Minnie squared her shoulders and drew in a long breath. "Dean never said anything about a girlfriend. I think . . . I really think he would have told us."

Father John slipped the notepad and pencil back into his pocket, then got to his feet. "Look," he said, taking in both women. "We'd better only give this one day. If I don't find him, I want you to promise to file a missing persons report."

Minnie pushed herself out of the sofa. "Louise and me, we feel a lot better already." She glanced around at her sister pressed against the cushions, as if to ward off a blow that only she saw coming.

"Tell Dean to call us right away, Father," Minnie said. "Tell him how we been awful worried."

Father John jammed down on the accelerator. The pickup thumped over the hard-packed dirt and onto the road. An uneasy feeling set like a rock in his stomach. Nobody dropped off the earth for four days. Something had happened. He should have insisted that Minnie go to the police immediately, but he knew it wouldn't have done any good. No amount of reasoning could break through the logjam in the woman's eyes. He was going to have to try to find her grandson. He had to get as much information about Dean Little Horse as he could, and he had to get it fast.

‹ 2 ›

The sun had burned hot all day, and now the heat pressed down over the flat, open stretch of plains on either side of Blue Sky Highway. Vicky Holden eased up on the accelerator. Ahead a line of traffic waited to turn into the graveled parking lot in front of the Arapaho tribal headquarters. She stopped behind a white pickup, her turn signal clicking in rhythm with the flashing light on the pickup. The air seemed hotter than on the highway at sixty miles an hour with the breeze blowing through the Bronco.

She didn't mind the heat, the smell of dry sage in the air. Reminders that she was home again after four months at Howard and Fergus, her old law firm, trying to convince herself she belonged in a steel-and-glass skyscraper on Seventeenth Street in Denver. She belonged on the Wind River Reservation, where not every foot of earth had been paved over and there were still the open spaces and sky that had always sheltered and comforted her people.

The traffic inched forward. Vicky could see what was causing the bottleneck: a dozen men and women—all Indians—circling the entrance to the parking lot, waving placards and shoving baskets at the vehicles that slowed past. They looked young, early twenties, she guessed, with calm expressions that might have been painted on the dark faces. The women wore long, white gowns that brushed the tops of their moccasins; the men, white shirts and trousers with fringe dipping over the shoulders and running down the arms and legs.

A semi slowed past, the driver gawking out his window. Then the white pickup swung into the turn and Vicky followed, bouncing over the gravel past the Indians. The men's clothing was made of buckskin, like the clothing of the warriors in the Old Time. The women's dresses were muslin. Now she could make out the painted symbols on the clothing: blue bands for her people, whom the other plains tribes called the Blue Sky People; yellow circles and crosses for the sun and the morning star; red thunderbirds for the eagle, the messenger of the Creator, and squiggly lines radiating from the eyes, the symbol of lightning.

A placard thrust itself across the windshield and Vicky stomped on the brake. Red block letters said: HESUNA'NIN IS THE WAY. PREPARE FOR THE NEW WORLD.

The placard slid past, and for a second, she caught the eye of a tall, muscular man with black braids that hung over the designs painted on his shirt. His features—the knife-edged mouth, narrowed eyes, and fleshy nose—seemed to sink into his flat face. He thrust a basket into her opened window. A few coins lay in the bottom. She pushed the basket away.

The man—Pueblo, Ute, Cheyenne, Lakota, she wasn't sure, but he didn't have the sculptured face of the Arapaho—stepped back and glanced around, the narrowed eyes issuing orders to the others. Then he started across the parking lot toward a black truck, a hopping motion, as if his left leg worked independently from the rest of his body. The others moved out of the circle and marched behind him like a precision drill team. He waved the placard overhead and shook the basket in a slow, jerky rhythm.

Vicky had no idea who the Indians were, and the realization made her feel as if she'd happened into an alien place, not her own place at all. Even the moccasin telegraph had failed to reach her since she'd returned to Lander. Had she remained on the reservation, where she belonged, instead of living and working in town, she would know. She would be connected.

She tried to push away the sense of being adrift. She was back home, after all; Lander abutted the southern boundary of the reservation. She swung right and parked in front of the squat brick building, once a school, now the tribal offices. She grabbed her briefcase from the passenger seat and crossed the sidewalk to the glass door.

A blast of cool air rushed over her as she stepped into the dark-tiled entry: receptionist's desk against the opposite wall, plastic molded chairs along the side walls. Two elders had pulled their chairs forward and were staring out the door. One of them grinned at her. "We was bettin' on whether they was gonna let you pass," he said.

Vicky smiled at the elders, then walked over to the receptionist, a strikingly pretty young woman who leaned sideways around the computer monitor with the poise of an expert rider turning her pony. Vicky gave her name and said she had an appointment with Norm Weedly.

"He's waiting." The woman's eyes switched to the corridor on the right.

Vicky found the office: third door on the left, TRIBAL

WATER ENGINEER printed in black letters on the pebbly glass. She was about to knock when the door swung open. Weedly gripped the edge. Tall and wiry, with ropelike muscles in his neck and forearms, wearing blue jeans, yellow plaid shirt, and hiking boots. Arapaho, in his early forties, Vicky thought, close to her own age.

"Come on in." Weedly ushered her into an office not much larger than an outsized closet. Two chairs and a metal desk with papers and folders sloping across the top took up most of the space. Motes of dust hung in the column of sunshine that slanted through the window. Tacked on the walls were maps of the reservation and aerial photos of the major rivers—Wind River, Little Wind River, Popo Agie— that spilled out of the mountains and into a spidery system of irrigation canals. Other photos showed views of the main reservoirs: Diversion Dam up north and, to the west, Bull Lake Dam, an earthen wall paved with concrete that contained a lake the color of turquoise.

"How ya doing?" Weedly threw the question over one shoulder as he walked around the desk. He sank into the swivel chair, picked up a folder, and motioned for her to take the straight-back chair next to the door.

Vicky sat down, settled the briefcase on her lap, and fielded the small talk about the weather, the heat spell— early this year—all the polite preliminaries to the real purpose of the meeting.

Finally, the water engineer cleared his throat and said, "So, what's your opinion on our problem with the Wind River, counselor?"

Vicky felt a little flush of satisfaction. Her people had finally asked for her opinion on an important matter—the ongoing damage to the Wind River and to the fish and wildlife from the inadequate stream flow. There were a lot of lawyers in big-name firms with more experience on water issues and Native American rights than she had, and yet Weedly had called her—a fresh look at the problem, he'd said. Whatever she suggested, he'd promised to take to the JBC, the Joint Business Council, which represented the Arapahos and the Shoshones, the two tribes that shared the reservation.

Vicky raised the flap of her briefcase and extracted the clear-plastic-covered report she'd spent the last two weeks writing. "We have to go back to court. We don't have a choice." She handed the report across the desk.

Weedly flinched. She might have handed him a firecracker about to explode in his face. He stared at the plastic cover. "Not gonna happen, counselor. JBC's had decades of lawsuits over water, enough to satisfy anybody's litigious nature, and when it was all done, State Supreme Court gave the state the right to control the amount of water in the rivers."

"But the U.S. Supreme Court affirmed our treaty rights to the water." Vicky heard the stridency in her voice.

"All well and good, but the state still decides how that water can be used." The engineer jumped up and turned toward the photos behind his desk. "State has a lot to say about the amount of water in the reservoirs and irrigation canals," he said. He might have been talking to himself. "And every year, after the spring runoff piles up silt against the dam headworks, the local irrigation district decides to release walls of mud into the Wind River." He turned back to her, a mild look of surprise in his expression, as if he'd just remembered she was there.

"I was hoping you'd find some legal loophole for us to

keep the Wind River from dying." He shifted his gaze above her head, as if the river itself had suddenly come into view. "This summer . . ." He halted, then stumbled on: Hot weather. Silt. Evaporation. River dies, might never be able to reclaim it.

Vicky got to her feet—she always thought better on her feet—and walked over to the window. Outside, the black truck was gone. Only a few pickups and her Bronco stood in the lot. She felt shaky with a sense of futility and helplessness. What had he expected of her? A miracle? Was she supposed to find a loophole that had just happened to slip by the scrutiny of other lawyers?

She turned back to the man standing ramrod straight behind the desk. "Bull Lake Dam is the key," she said, gesturing toward the photo of the thick turquoise finger of water crooked into the green mountains. "One hundred and fifty thousand acre-feet of water. Everything below the dam"—she swept her hand over the map of the reservation—"depends on the water stored here." She held the man's gaze. "I suggest we file a federal lawsuit based on our rights as a sovereign nation to regulate water quality in the rivers. We ask the feds to impose water quality standards, which would ensure a better stream flow and cleaner water. A limited lawsuit."

"No such thing. We'd be opening up the whole complicated water issue again. Last thing the state's gonna want to see." He leaned over his desk and flipped the edge of the plastic cover, as if he should open it but didn't want to, and Vicky wondered if he would ever read the report.

"You said yourself the river will die."

"JBC won't go for it." His fingers scratched at the report.

Vicky drew in a long breath. "I'd like to get on the agenda for the next JBC meeting."

"I'll give the council your report." Weedly pushed the plastic across the desk. "You lawyers," he said, a lighter tone now, "never give up hope the courts can settle everything. Problem is, Vicky, we have other issues with the state. We might be sovereign, but take a look." He gestured toward the map of Wyoming, the reservation a large block of red in the center. "We're surrounded. We depend on the state for maintenance on state roads across the rez, money for schools, welfare programs. Let's say we file another lawsuit on the water issue and the federal court says, yeah, Indians got the right to regulate water quality in our rivers. You think the state won't make us pay in other ways?"

"That shouldn't happen."

"Yeah? Aren't you forgetting something? The Indians lost the war."

Vicky got to her feet. She gripped the briefcase hard; the leather felt flimsy and wrinkled in her hand. Did everything have to be filtered through a prism of the past? Would her people always be immobilized by the old fears?

She said, "What about the agenda?"

"Won't do any good."

"I'd like to try."

Weedly was quiet a moment. In his eyes, Vicky saw the smallest flicker of possibility. "I'll see what I can do," he said finally. Then he started around the desk and stretched out a sinewy hand for the tan cowboy hat on the coattree in the corner. "Past quitting time. I'll walk out with you."

Vicky led the way across the deserted lobby, the receptionist's chair pushed into the desk, the two plastic chairs angled toward the door. Outside, the late afternoon heat lay

over the parking lot like an invisible ceiling. The sun was
high above the mountains, a red-orange flare that cast blue
shadows over the foothills in the distance. An engine
thrummed out on the highway. Except for the Bronco and
a green Ford pickup—Weedly's vehicle, she assumed—the
parking lot was empty.

"The Indians took their placards and baskets and left,"
she said.

"Good news." Weedly kept in step across the sidewalk.
"Last week they were up at Fort Washakie disrupting traffic.
Did the same over at Arapaho. Mostly, people ignore them,
so they go back up into the mountains to wait for the end
of the world."

"What's it all about?"

The man threw her a sideways look. "Where you been?"
There was a hint of amusement in his voice. He knew she'd
been working in Denver.

"On another planet." She'd been back only a month, hardly enough time to settle into a new office in Lander and
write the report Weedly had asked for. She still had a sense
of displacement, as if she'd stepped out of herself for a while
and now had to get used to her own skin. There was so
much to catch up on.

"James Sherwood, you know him?" Weedly gestured with
his head toward the entrance to the lot where the Indians
had been circling about.

"Sherwood family used to run a ranch in the mountains
west of Fort Washakie." Vicky walked around the Bronco,
inserted the key, and opened the door. A blast of heat hit
her.

"That's the family." Weedly remained on the sidewalk,
hands jammed into the pockets of his blue jeans. "Old peo-

ple died, rest of the family moved off the rez. All that's left is James. Calls himself Orlando. Lives up at the ranch with his so-called followers, the shadow dancers. Every six weeks they put up what they call a shadow dance that lasts four days. Dancers claim they go into the shadow world and commune with the ancestors, who, they say, are on their way back to earth. Gonna be Indian heaven here soon. Maybe all our water problems'll solve themselves."

He gave a shout of laughter and shook his head.

"I didn't see Sherwood here," Vicky said.

"Never leaves the ranch. Too busy communing with the ancestors. Real sad, I'd say. James Sherwood was a bright kid at Indian High. One of the best and the brightest." Weedly stared across the empty lot. "God help us if that's what becomes of the best and brightest."

"What happened?" Vicky said.

"Heard he moved to Denver, went to college, got to be a computer whiz kid. Landed a good job, then bam! Went on a hike in the mountains one day and got hit by lightning. Spent time in a coma. Says he died and went into the shadow world. Met up with Wovoka himself."

"The Ghost Dance prophet," Vicky said, reaching into her memory for what she'd heard about Wovoka. Bits and pieces started to come: Paiute Indian, started the Ghost Dance religion sometime in the 1880s, gathered followers from tribes across the West, her own people among them. Now she had it: Grandmother had told stories about how the Ghost Dance had given the people hope in the bad time when they were sent to the reservation and the buffalo was gone and the children were crying with hunger. Father, was what Wovoka called himself. Hesuna'nin.

"Followers come from all over," Weedly was saying.

"Probably some Arapahos at the ranch." He let out a guffaw. "Orlando says the new world's coming on the last day of one of the dance sessions, just like Wovoka prophesied. All the followers got to do is keep dancing. If the new world doesn't get here after one dance session, they wait six weeks, then hold another. One of the Indians out here told me the dancing's gonna start up again tonight."

Vicky was quiet a moment. "What do the Four Old Men say about it?" The spiritual leaders had the final word on Arapaho beliefs, an authority that Sherwood, or Orlando, seemed to have taken to himself.

"I suspect the Four Old Men are thinking that sooner or later Orlando's followers are gonna give up, just like Wovoka's followers did when they kept dancing and dancing and the new world never came. Pretty soon Orlando's gonna be sitting up at his ranch all by himself, one lonely prophet."

Weedly shrugged. "Orlando's harmless. Big nuisance, sending the followers out to block traffic and make converts, but harmless."

The man gave her a little wave and started across the lot toward the green pickup. "I'll get back to you about the JBC," he called.

Vicky was already behind the steering wheel, pulling the door shut. She backed out, lowering the windows as she went, then shot forward onto the highway, the wind hot and scratchy on her face and hands. She checked her watch, conscious of her muscles tensing. She'd agreed to meet her ex-husband, Ben, for dinner at the Peppermill in Lander at six-thirty. She was going to be late. Ben hated it when she was late.

‹ 3 ›

The sun seemed stuck in place over the mountains when Father John turned into the mission grounds and drove through the tunnel of cottonwoods, branches drooping in the heat. *"Gloire immortelle"* swelled around him. He swung onto Circle Drive beyond the trees, and the vistas opened up. White clouds shot through with reds and oranges hung motionless, like clouds painted on a blue canvas.

He checked his watch. Almost seven. The quiet interlude between the end of the day's activities and the beginning of the evening's. The buildings around Circle Drive had a vacant, abandoned look: the yellow stucco administration building with his office in the front corner; the church with the white steeple towering over the mission grounds; the old gray stone school, now the Arapaho museum; the two-story red-brick residence. Between the buildings he could see the faint shadows beginning to spiral onto the plains.

He parked in front of the residence, turned off the opera, and hurried up the sidewalk. From out on Seventeen-Mile Road came the scream of a truck taking the curve too fast.

The minute he let himself in the front door, the three-legged golden retriever, Walks-On-Three-Legs, bounded into the entry and stuck a wet nozzle into his hand. He patted the dog's head and promised they'd have a game of Frisbee soon. Then he set his cowboy hat on the bench next to the door. From the kitchen down the hall—past the stairs, the door to his study, the archway to the living room—came the odor of meat and vegetables simmering in tomato sauce.

" 'Bout time you got home." Elena stood at the end of the hall, a short, squared figure silhouetted in the white fluorescent light that shone through her cap of gray hair, electrifying the strands. She wore a shapeless dress cinched at the waist by a blue apron, which she smoothed across the middle, as if she were laying a tablecloth. Her face was in shadow, eyes black slits of irritation.

The old woman had been keeping house for the priests at St. Francis now for . . . nobody knew how long. Every time he'd asked, he'd gotten such answers as: since the snows piled up to the eaves, the pastor got a used blue Chevy, the grass dancers won the biggest prize in the powwow. He'd finally understood. The number of years wasn't important. The mission had been passed down to her from the ancestors, along with dark brown eyes, a caramel complexion, and a world infused with spirits and wonders, not always meant to be analyzed and counted. She lived in a tiny house two miles away with her husband and an assortment of grown kids and grandkids, but St. Francis Mission was also home.

Father John followed the squat figure into the kitchen, the golden retriever bounding beside him. Father George was at the table, elbows scrunching the red-checkered tablecloth, an empty bowl with traces of stew pushed to one side. The new priest had short, sandy hair above a prominent brow that made his gray eyes seem deep-set and shadowy. He wore a yellow polo shirt, and the opened collar spread around his thick neck. There was a solidity about the man, a certitude, Father John thought, that seemed to draw people to him, the way a shelter on the plains might draw people in a windstorm. Father John could imagine someone in trouble coming to Father George and going away comforted and assured, reined in against a wall of stone.

His assistant lifted a mug of coffee in greeting. "Missed a great feast," he said.

"Drove like Mario Andretti to get here." Father John walked over to the cabinet, took out a bag of dog food, and shook the kernels into the dish on the floor. It was a pattern they'd developed, he and Walks-On. When he came home, he fed the dog, even though, he knew, Elena had already fed him. He set the bag back on the shelf. "Turned down chicken dinner at Minnie and Louise Little Horse's."

"Good thing." Elena was ladling chunks of potatoes, carrots, and meat into a bowl. "Those old ladies don't know the first thing about cookin'. Could've poisoned you by mistake." She set the bowl down hard on the table. Thick brown liquid washed over the rim and dripped onto the tablecloth.

Father John sat at his place across from the other priest, said a silent prayer, then took a bite of stew. It was delicious, and Elena had kept it hot, the way his mother had kept dinner for him all those years ago when he was late coming home from baseball practice.

"Much better than chicken," he said, glancing up at the housekeeper standing next to the table, hands on hips, gray head tilted in an attitude of expectation.

"You got that right."

She gave him a dismissing wave, but he could see in her

expression that he'd worked his way back into her good graces. He smiled up at her, then took another spoonful of stew.

"As I was saying to Father George before you come in the door . . ." She was untying her apron, folding it in half, hanging it over the metal bar on the stove. "I got a baby shower for my granddaughter tonight." She started down the hallway. "Leave the dishes," she called. "I'll get to them tomorrow." The usual parting instruction, and usually he rinsed out the dishes and stacked them in the rack.

"Parish council meeting's been canceled," Father George said.

Father John held his spoon suspended over the bowl. The front door slammed shut, sending a tremor through the floorboards. He'd been counting on tonight's meeting, the last meeting with the Arapahos on the council before the board of directors arrived.

"Two guys with the flu. Three people out of town. One woman had a family emergency in Casper." The other priest shrugged. "Had no choice but to call the other members and cancel the meeting."

"Maybe we can reschedule before the weekend," Father John heard himself saying. He'd call the Arapahos on the parish council tomorrow. He wanted to go over the annual report with them before the board meeting this weekend.

What was it about the annual board meeting that had him so on edge? "Important matters on the agenda, John," the Provincial had said last week when he'd called. But there were always important matters on the agenda. It was what wasn't on the agenda that bothered him, followed him like a shadow—that this was the year the board would recommend that the Jesuits close St. Francis.

He ate some more stew and tried to ignore the uneasy feeling. It defied logic. The Jesuits had run St. Francis for more than a century. Why would the Society close the mission now?

"Don't count on the parish council having much influence on the board," Father George said, as if the man had seen into his head. "The board will look at data, John. Clear, quantified data. Types of liturgies and programs, numbers of participants, and most important, results."

"What's going on?" Father John pushed the bowl of stew aside. He was no longer hungry. This new man, his assistant, here only two weeks, seemed to know more about the agenda than he did.

The other priest gave a snort of laughter and set his mug down. Threads of coffee ran down the sides. "What makes you think I'm privy to the board's thinking?"

"You know the new members." There were seven directors, including the bishop. Three—still a minority, he reminded himself—were new: a philosopher, a college president, a former Provincial—all Father George's colleagues. His assistant had been a Provincial himself once—that was the year Father John had spent at Grace House. He winced at the memory, the juxtaposition of their careers.

Father George flattened both hands on the table. "Isn't it obvious that the board has to consider whether we're making the best use of our limited resources and manpower?"

Father John didn't say anything. This wasn't going to be the usual meeting, with black-suited, white-collared men nodding over the annual report, eager to get back to college classrooms and administration jobs and leave the management of an Indian mission to John O'Malley. The uneasy feeling churned inside him like an old engine trying to kick over.

"And another matter." Father George was just warming up. "You have to wonder—do you not?—about the depth of the people's Catholic faith, with a cult operating on the reservation. What does that cult leader call himself? Orlando!" The priest snorted. "Says he's a prophet. People can be taken in by such rubbish, you know. All it takes is some charismatic man and a lot of people—people who don't have anything else to believe in—will follow the leader into fire or flood. Don't forget what happened to the poor people who followed Jim Jones to Guyana. Cults can be very dangerous, John. We have to speak out against Orlando and the shadow dance from the pulpit."

Father John stared at the man across from him a moment. Somehow they'd veered off the subject. "You see the irony here, don't you?" he said finally.

"Irony?" Father George sat back in his chair, a relaxed air of expectation about him.

Father John hurried on. "The early Christians were also considered a cult. The Jesus followers were crucified and beheaded. Everybody thought they were mad. Some people still think we're mad, George. And priests like us are the maddest of all. We walk away from what everybody else considers normal." He threw his head back toward the hallway, the front door, and the world beyond. "We live far away from our families and everything else that other people hold dear, and we follow a charismatic leader."

"So now you're comparing Orlando to Jesus Christ?"

Father George raised his eyes to the ceiling and shook his head. Father John was quiet a moment. "I'm saying that the Indians at the shadow ranch are believers, George, just as we are, but we believe in a different messiah." His own belief, he was thinking, stabbed at him at times like a sharp knife and fixed him in place. He was always free to walk away, he knew, but then he would be left with the wound, open and gaping like a void.

"You're playing the role of devil's advocate," Father George said. "Frankly, John, we don't have the time to play intellectual games."

The other priest pushed himself to his feet, and Father John wondered if his assistant was referring to the shadow dancers or to St. Francis Mission. Which one was running out of time?

"The shadow dance is a cult," Father George went on, "and we must speak out against it."

Father John said, "I want to talk to the elders before we say anything about the dance."

"The elders? I can't imagine they'd have anything to do with a self-proclaimed prophet."

"The shadow dance is a revival of the old Ghost Dance religion . . ." Father John began to explain, but the other man had raised his hand, like a traffic cop.

"From the 1880s! Times were different then, John. Indians were drawn to the prophet, Wovoka, because he promised them a better life, which, incidentally, never came about. The opposite occurred. The Seventh Calvary—Custer's regiment, I believe—killed the last of the Ghost Dancers at Wounded Knee in 1890. Custer's revenge, some historians call the massacre. Correct?"

Father John nodded. It didn't surprise him that Father George had already looked into the history. His new assistant was thorough, a stickler for detail. He took in a long breath and started again to explain: The Ghost Dance religion was part of Arapaho tradition, and the elders guarded the tradition. Since Orlando seemed to have patterned the shadow dance after the old religion, he didn't want to say anything about it until he'd spoken to the elders.

"The board's going to decide whether to continue the mission, isn't that right?" he said, steering the conversation back on track.

Father George looked away for a moment. Walks-On, snuggled on his rug in the corner, snored into the quiet. Finally the other priest brought his gaze back. "I wouldn't expect a peremptory decision, John. They're reasonable men. They'll discern the best option."

Father John got to his feet and started stacking the dishes in the sink. He turned on the hot water, squeezed the bottle of yellow detergent, and watched the liquid churn into suds. Behind him, the other priest's footsteps moved across the vinyl floor and into the hallway.

"Where do you stand, George?" Father John glanced over his shoulder at the other man's back.

"What?" Father George swung around. In the backward tilt of the sandy head, the thrust of the jaw, Father John saw the truth. The Provincial had sent George Reinhold here to gather information—quantified data—for the board of directors. George Reinhold was the Provincial's man on the scene, the objective observer.

"I doubt my opinion will matter."

"What is your opinion?" Father John picked up the towel flung over the drainboard and faced the man.

"My opinion? I think we should close this place, sell the land, and use the money to better advantage. Offer more college scholarships to Arapaho kids. My opinion? That would produce a greater benefit over time than fielding a baseball team and trying to sober up a bunch of alcoholics. There are other places Arapahos can go for those programs."

He started backing into the hall. "I'm sorry, John," his voice softer. "The directors are aware of your fondness for the mission, but we have to be practical." He turned and continued down the dimly lit hall, grabbed the knob on the bannister, and swung himself onto the stairs. Each step sent a muffled thud reverberating into the kitchen.

Father John tossed the towel onto the drainboard. So, he was unexpectedly free tonight after all. He walked down the hall and, scooping his cowboy hat off the bench, let himself out the door.

‹ 4 ›

No sign of Ben.

Most of the tables in the Peppermill were occupied. The subdued sounds of music and laughter floated from the bar that adjoined the dining room. Vicky waited inside the door while the hostess threaded her way past the tables toward the front: tall, attractive woman in her thirties, with brown hair pinned back into a bun, the ends sticking out like feathers around her head, and thick, black eyelashes that deposited little flakes of mascara on her cheeks. Below the collar of her black dress was a tiny white name tag: MARY SEELS. She reached for the menus stacked on a small table.

Vicky said she was meeting Ben Holden.

The woman's hand stopped over the menus. A barely concealed look of surprise came into her expression. She seemed to look at Vicky for the first time: the black hair parted on the side and smoothed slightly back; the blue linen dress and silver necklace; the high-heeled sandals. Finally she said, "Mr. Holden hasn't arrived yet, but your table is ready. Follow me." She turned abruptly and led the way through the dining room to a table with a stiff white cloth and places set for two.

Vicky wondered if the woman was another one of Ben's conquests. There had been many over the years. Indian, white, Hispanic. Ben's appeal was universal.

She pushed the thought away—it no longer mattered—and studied the menu. Then she stared through the plate-glass window at the pickups and sedans crawling down Main Street, the people hurrying along the sidewalk, dodging pieces of paper tossed in the breeze. The conversation with Weedly played over and over in her mind, like the cracked phonograph records in her grandmother's house when she was a child. Had he really expected her to come up with some strategy that hadn't occurred to any other tribal lawyer in the last decade?

She smiled at the idea, so typical of her people. The Sioux and Cheyenne, they had taken up guns and bows and arrows and hatchets and gone out to right the wrongs, but the Arapahos said: Let's eat and talk and smoke the pipe together. They would stay at the bargaining table, looking for some way out of an impasse, even when the soldiers were surrounding the villages.

Madness. You couldn't negotiate with people who didn't want to negotiate. You had to fight white people with their own laws. The federal courts, she was sure, would support the tribe's right to clean water in the Wind River. But before she could convince a federal court, she had to convince her own people.

She spread the white napkin across her lap, then took a drink of the ice water the waitress had poured. Laughter erupted over the buzz of conversation from the nearby tables.

Still no sign of Ben. She was beginning to wonder if she'd gotten the right day. He'd been calling since she'd returned to Lander. Morning and afternoon calls to her office, and she, training a new secretary, installing the fax machine—a thousand details. Calls in the evenings to her apartment. *I have to see you.*

He'd called this morning, his voice tense, rushed. He was going to be in town. Dinner at the Peppermill? Six-thirty? "Fine," she'd said, managing to squeeze the word past the tightness in her throat. Ben was the father of her children, Lucas and Susan. The ties between them, she knew, would never be completely severed.

He was striding through the restaurant now with the purpose and confidence of a warrior, tall, still-in-shape, dressed in blue jeans and a starched white shirt that she knew instinctively he'd worn for her. She recognized the bolo tie with the silver eagle clasped below the opened collar. She had given him the tie on their tenth anniversary. The sight of him—when had she seen him last? four months ago?—sent a shiver running through her.

"Sorry." He yanked the chair from the table so hard that it floated free from the floor, like a piece of driftwood in his hand. Then he squared it a couple of feet from the table and sat down, not taking his eyes from her.

Vicky felt her mouth go dry. The memories came, unasked for, unwanted: Ben slamming into the house, shouting at the kids, kicking at the dog. And the smell of whiskey permeating the air, and she in the kitchen, standing over the sink, retching with the odor and the fear.

She made herself take a sip of ice water and tried to detect the odor now. Only the slightest whiff of aftershave.

"It's okay, Ben," she said, falling back into that other time. *It's okay, honey. Take it easy.*

"Business problem. Took longer than I thought." He waved the waitress over, a short, slim woman probably in her thirties with the stooped shoulders of someone much older and black, curly hair that emphasized the lines of fatigue in her face.

"Couple juicy burgers and some coffee, Lucy," Ben said.

Vicky started to change her order—a bowl of soup and a salad had sounded good—then stopped. It was barely perceptible, the silent acknowledgment between Ben and the waitress, as if they shared some secret. The woman nodded, then moved away.

Ben took a drink of water. He was gripping the glass hard. She could see the white peaks of his knuckles poking through the brown skin, and she felt her own muscles tighten with the effort—curious how familiar it seemed— to position herself somewhere out of the line of his anger.

"Goddam busiest season." He spat out the words, as if they'd been talking for the last hour. She couldn't remember when they'd last talked. The hurried telephone calls—she'd been in a hurry to end them—hardly counted.

She tried to concentrate on what he was saying about the Arapaho Ranch, where he was the foreman: shorthanded as hell right now, moving the herds to the high pastures, blasting out new roads, a couple of ponds. "Hell of a time for two Lakota bastards to rip me off." He shifted his gaze to some point across the restaurant, as if he wanted to reel the words back in.

"Rip you off?" she said.

Ben jerked back against the chair. "Forget it." He locked eyes with her, and she felt herself becoming small. "Those slimy bastards didn't reckon on who they're dealing with. I caught up with them a couple hours ago. This time tomorrow, there's not going to be any problem."

A chorus of laughter and the sound of clinking glass floated over from the next table. Ben turned and glared at the two couples. "Jesus, what I wouldn't give for a drink right now," he said, locking eyes with her again. "That's over. You know that, don't you?"

"I'm glad for you," Vicky said after a moment.

The waitress set two mugs of coffee on the table, then delivered the plates of hamburgers with french fires piled on the side. "You and me, Vicky. We've got unfinished business," he said after the waitress had stepped away. He was shaking the ketchup bottle over the fries.

Vicky held her breath. She knew the rest of it. It was as familiar as a wound that refused to heal, always there, festering. "Listen, Ben . . ."

"First thing we have to do is get Susan home." Ben lifted his hamburger and took a bite.

"Susan?" Vicky hadn't anticipated a discussion about the kids. "What are you talking about?"

He swallowed quickly, his Adam's apple bobbing in his throat. "Eat." He nodded toward her untouched hamburger. "You don't eat enough. You're too thin. You need to get some meat on your bones."

Vicky took her knife and sawed the hamburger in two, then picked up the smaller piece. Going through the motions now. She had no appetite.

"Lucas is working in Denver," Ben went on. "Not the same as living here, but Denver's only seven hours away. You finally came to your senses and moved back. Now all we gotta do is get Susan here, and our family'll be together again."

Vicky set the hamburger down. There was no family to reclaim. There were only individuals trying to make their way, and Ben, determined to round them up into a corral, the way he rounded up the herd on the ranch. "Susan has a good job in Los Angeles," she heard herself saying. "She has friends. She has a nice apartment."

"She can work at the ranch. I need another bookkeeper, and she's good at computers."

"You expect Susan to live on the ranch? A hundred miles from anywhere, surrounded by a bunch of cowboys?"

"Any of the bozos touch her, he answers to me."

"Ben, for godssake."

"Listen to me, Vicky." He leaned over the table. "We gotta start somewhere, you and me."

"We're never going to start again."

"Lucas can drive up on weekends."

"My God, Ben."

"We'll be together," he went on, and Vicky realized he was talking to himself, repeating what he probably told himself in the middle of the night, like some madman, unhinged from reality. "We'll go to the celebrations and the powwows, like we used to. Remember? You and me and the kids. We had a great time. We'll go out to my brother's place for dinner. Get to know one another again."

Vicky threw her napkin on the table and got to her feet, aware of the other diners craning around to watch. "I'm going to call Susan and tell her to stay in Los Angeles where she's happy," she said. "I'm going to tell her she can't live out your fantasy of the perfect family that we never were."

The color drained from Ben's face, something changed

behind his eyes. He laid his hands flat on the table and pushed himself to his feet, rising toward her, his chest heaving with the gulps of breath. Instinctively she drew back, the restaurant swam around her. She felt sick.

"You don't care about the family." He drew out the words until they hung between them like black smoke. "All of us broken apart like these here dishes." He grabbed a fistful of the white tablecloth and yanked it off the table. Plates, mugs, glasses lifted into the air, then crashed onto the carpet in a crumpled heap of white cloth, hamburger, fries, ketchup, shards of glass. Coffee and water pooled over the table and gathered into creamy puddles on the chairs.

"You listen to me." He took hold of her shoulder. His fingers dug into her flesh. She was aware of the stunned silence around them, the diners leaning toward them. "I've had enough of people taking what belongs to me. Susan's coming home. Lucas is gonna come home sooner or later. We're gonna work everything out between us, Vicky. You and me."

He let go of her so abruptly that she staggered backward, groping for the edge of the table to steady herself. Ben was already heading toward the front, a sure and unhurried pace, as if the most serious negotiations had just been settled. The hostess moved sideways as he shouldered past, and then he was out the door. The restaurant was quiet.

Vicky fumbled in her bag for a couple of bills, which she tossed on the table—they fluttered into a pool of water—aware of the waitress frozen in place a few feet away, staring at the mess strewn over the carpet. Outside the window, Ben's brown truck screeched into the street, black clouds fuming from the exhaust pipe. Out of the corner of her eye, she saw a dark truck pull in behind.

"I'm sorry," she mumbled toward the adjacent tables. Then she made her feet carry her through the dining room. Outside she kept close to the brick building, her legs shaking beneath her. She turned the corner and crossed the parking lot to the Bronco. Gripping the keys in the bottom of her bag, unlocking the door. She sank gratefully into the front seat and made herself take a deep breath. She had to be calm. It was only a scene—there had been others. And she knew the next scene: the ringing phone, Ben's voice at the other end. He was so sorry. Didn't know what had gotten into him. Could she ever forgive him?

No, she could not. Whatever talent she'd had for forgiveness was gone.

She turned the ignition and drove out of the lot, aware of the other diners inside the restaurant, mannequin heads turned toward the street, eyes following the Bronco.

She continued north, then turned west, driving aimlessly, eating up the time until Ben was out of town before she returned to her apartment.

‹ 5 ›

My relations, the ancestors are crying for the pain you have endured. They stumble and fall with their tears as they walk through the clouds. They cry because the evil people want to stop our dancing and prevent the new world from coming, just like in the Old Time. I say to you, the evil ones must not prevail. We must dance on and on.

Father John parked in front of the apartment building, a flat-roofed, red-bricked, two-story affair with arched windows and a glass entrance that, with the exception of the enormous blue spruce over the front sidewalk, probably hadn't changed in fifty years. The sun had begun to slip behind the mountains, sending layers of red, orange, and violet through the sky. A few vehicles slowed past; a car door slammed down the street.

Father John let himself into the small entry. A bank of metal mailboxes lined the wall on the right. He found DEAN LITTLE HORSE among the typed names in the windows. Apartment 2D.

He took the stairs on the left two at a time, came out

through a steel fire door, and started down the corridor. The bronze fixtures dangling from the ceiling cast an eerie shade of yellow over the beige walls and worn beige carpet. The black numbers were barely visible on the doors. New Age music, soft and melodious, drifted past one of the doors. A baby was crying behind another.

He knocked on 2D. Silence. He rapped again, louder this time.

He waited a moment, then rapped on the door across the hall. Another moment passed before the door opened. A stocky, blond-haired man in his mid-twenties with fish eyes that blinked at him from behind thick glasses, wedged himself next to the frame.

Father John said he was looking for Dean Little Horse.

"You got the wrong place, partner."

The door started to close, and Father John placed his hand against the panel. "Look," he said hurriedly. "I'm a priest at St. Francis Mission. I'm trying to find the man across the hall. How long have you been here?"

The door opened wider. Interest flashed in the fish eyes. "Honey?" he called without looking away. "When we move in? Thursday? Friday?"

"Thursday." A woman's voice came from inside. Beyond the man's thick legs, Father John could see the stacked cartons, the plastic bubble wrap scattered over the green carpet.

"Ain't seen nobody over there," the man said.

Father John felt a knot tighten in his stomach. Dean had been missing since Thursday.

Father John thanked the man and started back down the corridor. The door slammed behind him, creating a kind of vacuum that trapped the muffled sounds of flutes, the faint smell of onions.

He stopped at 2B and knocked. Beyond the door, the scrape of footsteps. Finally the door inched open, held in place by a brass chain that bisected the face of a tall, good-looking woman with curly red hair. The sound of flutes rose around her.

"What is it? She peered under the chain and ran her fingers through a tangle of curls.

He told her his name, and she leaned into the opening, her gaze traveling from his cowboy hat to his plaid shirt, blue jeans, and cowboy boots. "Priest?"

He ignored the skepticism in her tone—it wasn't the first time he'd encountered skepticism—and told her he was looking for Dean Little Horse, who lived down the hall.

"Indian guy."

That was right. Did she have any idea where he might be?

"He's an okay guy." The woman visibly relaxed against the edge of the door.

"When did you last see him?"

She shrugged. "Haven't seen them around for a while."

"Them? Who else lives there?"

The woman fastened her eyes on the chain for a moment. "Some Indian woman. Never got her name. She was weird, you ask me. Came and went around here like a shadow. Kept to herself. Wouldn't even say good morning. Not like Dean. He was real friendly. Helped me dig my car out of the snow last March."

"Any idea where she might have worked?"

The woman gave a little shrug and went back to pulling her fingers through her hair. "From the way she looked, I'd say check the bars."

Father John was quiet. Louise Little Horse was right. Dean had a girlfriend. He said, "Where can I find the manager?"

The woman pulled a red curl toward the stairway. "First floor, first door on the left."

Father John made his way back through the steel door and down the stairs. He tried the manager's door, waited a few seconds, then knocked again. A phone was ringing inside—four, five rings—and then it stopped.

He headed outside. A middle-aged man in blue jeans and a white T-shirt, with a thick chest and a stomach that bulged over his belt buckle, was looming up the sidewalk. "You lookin' for somebody?" he called.

"Dean Little Horse." Father John dodged around the branches of the Blue Spruce. "You the manager?"

"One and only." The man squared his massive shoulders. "What happened? Girlfriend couldn't find him, so she sent you around?"

"What are you talking about?"

"Who the hell are you?"

"Father O'Malley from the reservation."

"Oh." The man chewed on his lower lip a moment. "Heard'a you, the Indian priest. Well, I don't like them Indians around here. Nothing but trouble every time I rent to 'em. Got the correctness police now, swooping down if I say I ain't renting to Indians, so I got to be careful. Dean, he seemed like a good guy, so I took a chance on him. Bad mistake. He takes off last Thursday. Girlfriend comes around, gets hysterical. Says she's gotta find him."

"When exactly was she here?"

The man rolled his eyes to the sky. "Last night. Yeah, Sunday night."

"You know her name?"

"That's a problem I got with Little Horse." The manager kept his eyes on the sky. "Never told me there was gonna be two of 'em in the apartment a lotta times. I charge more for two people. More wear and tear on the building, you know what I mean? Took a while before I figured out the girl was staying over a lot. I told Dean, your rent just went up, buddy."

"Her name." Father John spoke through his teeth.

"How should I know? Wasn't like she was official here. Kept to herself. Didn't like nobody getting friendly with her, know what I mean?"

Father John wondered how friendly the manager had tried to get. He said, "If you hear from Dean, ask him to call me at St. Francis Mission."

The man shrugged, then shouldered past, stepping off the sidewalk into the dirt and throwing aside a branch as he went.

Father John got into the Toyota, took the notepad out of his shirt pocket, and wrote: *Last seen, Thursday. Girlfriend: Indian. Looking for Dean Sunday night.*

The manager had disappeared inside the entrance when Father John started the engine and pulled into the street, but he could feel the eyes watching him through the slats that covered the corner window on the first floor. He headed toward Main Street.

The streetlights had flashed on, and little circles of white light shone into the dusk dropping over the cars parked at the curbs. Father John eased on the brake, trying to make out the numbers on the flat-faced brick buildings. Finally he caught an address illuminated by a neon sign blinking in the plate-glass window.

He took the next intersection on the yellow light and pulled up in front of a white stucco building with a pair of plate-glass windows on either side of the blue paneled door. Painted across the top in large black letters were the words BLUE CROW SOFTWARE. He got out and walked to the door. Locked.

In the shadows beyond the windows, he could see the rows of cubicles, computer monitors, and keyboards on the desks. A cone of light shone over the center of the office, where a man in a white T-shirt with sleeves rolled to the shoulders, earphones clasped over his head, and hips swinging side to side, steered a vacuum cleaner about, as if the machine were a stiff, unwilling dance partner.

Father John waved, but the man kept pushing—pushing and dancing—lost in the rhythms probably blasting in his ears. He swung around in an awkward tango, and Father John waved again. This time, the man looked up, his round, pinkish face frozen in a mixture of surprise and fear. He let go of the vacuum, pointed to his wristwatch, and shook his head.

Father John gestured toward the closed doors in the shadows beyond the light. Some poor, overworked manager might still be in the office. But the man waved him away, then turned around and curled his back over the vacuum cleaner.

Back in the pickup, Father John made a sharp U-turn in front of a truck, which sent out a loud blast. The noise reverberated off the parked vehicles. He waved in the rear-view mirror at the driver, who was giving him the finger. Five minutes later, he was on Highway 789 heading north, a profusion of stars popping like firecrackers in the sky. The spiky shadows of junipers passed outside the passenger window, and outside his window, the Popo Agie River reflected back the stars, like a long, narrow mirror.

He slowed past the steak houses in Hudson, then turned left into the shadows of Rendezvous Road, his thoughts still on Dean Little Horse. College degree, good job, grandmother and great-aunt, and a girlfriend looking for him as recently as last night. A man like that didn't just step off the earth. First thing tomorrow, he decided, he would pay another visit to the Blue Crow Software Company.

Ahead, around a wide bend, blue, red, and yellow lights flashed into the gray dusk. Father John could see the vehicles blocking the road, men moving in slow motion, flashlight beams crisscrossing the flashing lights. Shards of broken glass glistened on the blacktop.

He stopped next to a policeman in the navy blue uniform of the BIA and leaned out the window, craning to see past the vehicles. "Anyone hurt?" he said.

"That you, Father John?" The officer moved closer and shone a flashlight in his face. Colored balls of light exploded in his eyes for half a second. "Chief Banner'll want to talk to you." The policeman turned the flashlight on three officers standing next to the dark truck parked ahead of the police cars.

Father John inched ahead a short distance, set the gear in park, and got out. The breeze was warm, laced with the odor of manure and something he couldn't identify for certain. Smoke? Voices, subdued and serious, mixed with the crackle of police radios. In the lights swinging over the white cars, he saw Art Banner, the Wind River police chief, coming toward him.

"How'd you hear?" The chief was only a couple of feet away, but he sounded like he was shouting through a bull horn. The lights alternated over the round, dark face.

"Hear what? What's happened?" A single-vehicle accident, Father John was thinking. Besides the police cars, the only other vehicle was the dark truck.

It was then he saw the shattered windshield and the figure slumped over the steering wheel, as still as death. It hit him like a sledgehammer in the chest: he'd found Dean Little Horse.

"We got a homicide." The chief tilted his head toward the truck. "Looks like he might've stopped to help somebody. Trying to be a good Samaritan." He stared for a moment at the plains extending into the shadows beyond the road. "Took a bullet in the head for his trouble. Anonymous call came in from one of the steak houses in Hudson about forty minutes ago saying somebody was dead out here. That's a fact. He's dead, all right."

"Who, Banner? Who is he?"

For a moment, the chief stood motionless in the flashing lights. Then he took off his cap and drew a fist across his brow. "Thought you must've heard already, John. Thought that's why you showed up here." He took in a long breath, as if he were trying to get enough air to expel the name: "Ben Holden."

‹ 6 ›

Father John stepped past the police chief and walked over to the truck. He had a sense of unreality, as if he had stepped into a nightmare of darting lights and hushed, disembodied voices. The brown Ford truck was solid and clear, real. Inside, collapsed over the steering wheel, was Ben Holden: the humps of his shoulders beneath the blood-soaked shirt, the head falling against the steering wheel. His temple was smashed, bloody.

He couldn't remember when he had last seen Ben Holden, what they had talked about. It made no difference. The unspoken subject between them had always been Vicky.

A flashbulb went off behind him, suffusing the slumped body in the yellow light that exploded in the shattered windshield. The police photographer moved in closer and took a couple more shots, then backed away.

Father John reached inside the window and began tracing the sign of the cross over the man's head. "May God have mercy on your soul, Ben," he whispered. "May He take you to Himself and grant you peace." He was startled by the grief that hit him, like a cold blast out of nowhere. He and

Ben were alike—they might have been twins—battling the same demon, loving the same woman, in need of forgiveness and redemption. Redemption took time—a lifetime. Someone had robbed Ben of his time.

Out of the corner of his eye, Father John saw the shadowy figures converging on the truck. The breeze swept off the plains and swirled little bits of dust and twigs over the blacktop.

"This is gonna be the FBI's case." Banner's voice behind him. Father John turned slowly. "Agent Gianelli's on the way. Meantime we've got the weapon. Twenty-two-caliber pistol tossed in the barrow ditch over there." He gestured toward the ditch a few feet beyond the truck. "Lab'll pick up the fingerprints," he went on, a new confidence in his voice, as if his professional duties were the only thing of which he was sure. "Gianelli'll run a trace on the gun, see if he can identify the owner. My boys'll lift tire prints, if we find any."

Father John realized the chief had been hit by the same wave of grief that had hit him. Ben and Art Banner went back a long time. They'd grown up together, served in the Army at the same time, married the same year. There was the shock of it, the death of a man who had always been around.

The chief said, "Family's got to be notified."

"What about Vicky?"

"Just about to send White over to tell her." Banner glanced at an officer standing behind the truck. "I'd go myself, but the fed's . . ."

"I'll tell her," Father John said. His shirt felt moist against his back. This was the toughest part of being a priest, bearing the bad news that no one wanted, like a ragpicker appearing at the door with a burden of trash. And with the trash—words, that was all he had. Weak, indistinct, inexact words to try to convince the family that God would not desert them.

He started toward the pickup, then turned back. "You have her address?" They hadn't spoken, he and Vicky, since she'd returned to Lander. But she'd been on his mind. He'd picked up the phone—how many times?—wanting to know how she was, wanting to hear her voice. Each time he'd set the receiver down. There'd been no legitimate reason to call her: no parishioners thinking about divorce, no one picked up for selling pot or driving drunk. The moccasin telegraph kept up a running account of her new office, new apartment, but she hadn't called.

A faint look of surprise crossed the chief's face. There was an awkward beat of silence, and Father John wondered about the gossip on the moccasin telegraph that never reached St. Francis Mission, at least not his ears.

"Hold on." The chief nodded to the officer behind the truck, but the man was already thumbing through a notepad. He leaned into the flashing lights and read off an address.

Father John knew the place, a two-story apartment building with white railings around the second-floor balconies—a New Orleans building plunked down on the plains. He started for the pickup; the chief's voice trailed behind, ordering White and another officer to drive out to Spring Valley Drive and notify Ben's brother.

Father John backed across the road, then headed south the way he'd come, saying the same prayer over and over: "Lord, have mercy on the Holden family."

• • •

The apartment was warm and stuffy, and even though she'd stood in a hot shower for twenty minutes and wrapped herself in her white terry cloth robe, Vicky couldn't shake the cold that gripped her. What had she been thinking? That she could return to Lander and go on as before? That Ben would be on the other side of Blue Sky Hall at tribal get-togethers. Across the aisle at powwows. How was she doing? Oh, fine. And he? Just fine. A woman at his side, strikingly beautiful, clinging to him for her very breath. And Susan and Lucas on the phone: You hear what Dad's up to? They'd relate how Ben had increased the herd and accomplished other amazing feats to make the Arapaho Ranch the most successful in the state.

But he wouldn't be in her life.

She'd been wrong. Ben would never leave her alone. What did she have to do to be free? The iciness inside her, she knew, was anger as distilled and pure as crystal. She would be free when one of them was dead.

She sat down on the sofa, tucked her legs under her robe, and tried to concentrate on the report she'd given to Weedly this afternoon. She had to build a strong case, if she was going to convince the JBC to go back to court over the Wind River. It was important. The river was dying. They had no choice.

An insistent knock sounded at the door. She froze, her heart pounding in her ears, her breath trapped in her lungs. Some part of her had been waiting for Ben to come to the apartment. The Bronco in the parking lot, the light filtering at the edge of the drapes—he could see that she was here.

The knock came again. She got up, went to the door, and

peered through the peephole. On the other side: the tall, handsome man, the blue eyes, the red hair glinting under the ceiling light. A wave of warmth and surprise washed over her. Then she realized that John O'Malley would never come here unless something had happened. She yanked the chain free and opened the door, her hands shaking. Something terrible had happened.

"I have to talk to you."

"Susan?" she said as he stepped inside, his eyes never leaving hers. "Something's happened to Susan? Lucas? What? An accident? You've got to tell me." She was struggling not to scream. She knew how it went: An accident somewhere. The police called the mission, and Father John O'Malley drove out to deliver the horrible news.

"It's not your kids, Vicky," he said. Taking her hand, he led her to the sofa.

His voice had seemed to come from far away, the words seeping into her consciousness a half-second after he'd spoken them. She was still shaking, an involuntary motion that worked its way into the muscles of her arms and legs.

She took a deep breath and tried to calm herself. "Who, then?"

"It's Ben, Vicky. He's dead."

She stared at him, unable to summon a response. There were no words to contain the reality. Two hours ago, she and Ben were having dinner at the restaurant. They'd argued. He'd pulled off the tablecloth, sent their dinners flying over the floor, and stomped out. There must be some mistake. She could still see the wrinkled back of his white starched shirt.

"Accident?" Her voice sounded low and cracked in her

ears. She realized John O'Malley was holding both of her hands in his.

"He was shot on Rendezvous Road," he went on, his tone punctuated with sorrow. Something about Ben stopping to help someone. The police getting an anonymous call.

She couldn't understand. Nothing was making sense. She withdrew her hands and pulled back against the cushion. She was drowning, she thought. Wave after unfathomable wave of disbelief and confusion crashing over her.

She realized that John O'Malley had gone into the kitchen. There were the sounds of a faucet squeaking open and water splashing into the sink. How odd to be drowning, she thought, when the inside of her mouth was as dry as a bone.

He was standing over her, handing her a glass. She took a long sip of cool water. Then, steadying the glass in the folds of her robe, she looked up at him. "I'm responsible," she said.

"Vicky . . ." he began, but she put up one hand to silence him.

"We were supposed to have dinner this evening. Instead we had another argument. It was terrible. Ben . . ." She hesitated, blinking at the scene burned into the back of her eyes. "Ben stomped out, and I thought, *I thought,* the only way I would ever be free was if one of us was dead."

"No, Vicky." His voice cut through the fog in her head. He sat down beside her. "Whatever you thought, it didn't make it happen. It didn't kill Ben. That's magical thinking." She felt his hand covering hers again. "You must try to be rational."

She yanked her hand away. She knew all about white man's rationality. She'd sat through their logic classes and studied their laws. What did they mean? What the elders taught, that was the truth.

"You don't understand." How could he understand? "We must guard our thoughts. We must send only good thoughts into the world, because once they exist, they become real. They become *reality*. I'm responsible . . ." She dropped her head into one hand. The tears were coming, a dam bursting, for the man she'd once loved and for the way things should have been.

"I'm so sorry." He took her glass of water and set it on the coffee table. Then she felt his arms slipping around her, pulling her close. She leaned against his chest, feeling as if time had stopped. She could hear his heart beating. How fitting that John O'Malley was here. Of course he would come to her. Curious, she thought, that in the new world she'd tried to carve for herself since she'd divorced Ben, this white man had become so necessary.

There was a thud on the door. A second passed before John O'Malley settled her back against the cushion and got up. "Ted Gianelli," he said behind her. "He may have more information."

"Give me a minute." Vicky lifted herself to her feet. She made her way down the hall to the bedroom—shaky, dizzy. She untied her robe, tossed it over the bed, and pulled on a pair of blue jeans and a white cotton blouse, her fingers numb as they worked the tiny front buttons. The male voices floated from the living room like the low rumble of drums.

In the bathroom, she splashed cold water on her face, then stared at the woman in the mirror: mussed black hair; dull, black eyes; face blanched of color, like someone who had been ill a long time. Her ancestors would have chopped off their hair, slashed their arms and legs with knives—a fitting expression of the enormity of death.

She ran a brush through her hair and put on some lipstick. The woman in the mirror was transformed, a rational look about her, like an attorney, a white woman. She went back to the living room.

"Rotten news, Vicky. I'm very sorry." Ted Gianelli, the local FBI agent, was standing next to Father John, twin pillars of solemnity caught in the light from the table lamps. The agent was dressed in a dark sport coat and light trousers with knifepoint creases, a red paisley tie knotted at the collar of his light blue shirt, as if he'd dressed for the office and this was just a routine part of the day. His short black hair lay tightly against his head; his fleshy face remained as immobile as a mask.

"What happened?" Her voice sounded shaky. She dropped onto the sofa, and Father John walked over and sat down beside her.

"We don't have all the facts yet." The fed pulled a side chair over and perched on the edge. "Looks like Ben stopped voluntarily. There's no sign of skid marks. Could be somebody was in trouble."

Vicky nodded. That made sense. The reservation was Ben's place. He was perfectly at ease there. If someone needed help, Ben would stop. A chief was responsible for the welfare of his people.

"What was it? A robbery?"

Gianelli shook his head. "He had a hundred dollars in his wallet. Some very expensive tools in the lockbox in the truck bed. No sign that anyone tried to break in."

"The killer could have been scared away," Father John said. "Maybe he saw headlights coming down the road. Banner said somebody passed by and called the police."

Gianelli leaned forward, rested his elbows on his thighs, and clasped his hands between his knees, as if he were considering the possibility, his face still unreadable. Finally he said, "Police got an anonymous call from a pay phone in Hudson. Caller said he didn't see anything except a guy sloped inside the truck. But we've got the gun. Twenty-two-caliber pistol. Should tell us something." The agent turned toward her, anticipation working into his face muscles. "Ben Holden was a strong and powerful man. Men like that make enemies. What can you tell me, Vicky?"

She closed her eyes. The scene at the restaurant reeled through her mind in slow motion. She saw clearly now, all the details, nuances, and shadows she'd missed the first time. Ben wasn't angry with her. He was angry before he came to the restaurant. She was the catalyst that caused the explosion. She had always been the catalyst: the ranch equipment broke down, the kids misbehaved, she said something wrong, and the explosion burst forth.

She looked at the agent. "Ben was angry when I saw him."

"You saw him this evening?" Something changed behind Gianelli's eyes.

"We met at the Peppermill." Vicky paused, gathering the details. "He said two ranch hands—Lakotas—had ripped him off."

"Ripped him off? You mean stole something? Embezzled money?"

"He didn't say. He'd talked to them this afternoon. He said he'd straightened everything out."

"Where do I find the Lakotas?" The fed was jotting notes in a notepad he'd fished from the inside pocket of his sport coat.

Vicky shook her head.

"What time did he meet you?"

"About seven-fifteen."

"When did he leave?"

The scene was still rolling across her mind. She tried to calculate how long it had taken the waitress to deliver the hamburgers, how long they had argued. "It must have been close to eight." Then she added, "We had an argument."

"Mind telling me what it was about?"

"Come on, Ted," Father John said. She could hear the irritation in his tone. "What difference could it possibly make? You heard what Vicky said. Ben was angry at two Lakotas who ripped him off."

The fed tapped the pen against the notebook, the new element still in his eyes. Vicky said, "Ben thought we should be a family again."

Gianelli jotted something down. Then he said, "Eight-thirty, Ben would have been on Rendezvous Road. Did he say where he was going?"

Vicky shook her head. She'd feared Ben would stay in town and show up at her apartment. She'd thought it was Ben when John O'Malley had knocked. "He must have been on his way back to the ranch," she said.

The fed agreed that was possible. Then, as if he were talking to himself, he said, "Shouldn't be too difficult to get a line on the Lakotas. Stick out like sore thumbs. Every Arapaho and Shoshone on the res'll know where they're hanging out."

But they won't tell you. Vicky glanced at Father John and saw in his expression that he'd had the same thought.

The fed got to his feet, the quick, assured movement of the linebacker he'd once been for the New England Patriots.

"If you think of anything, Vicky, anything at all, call me. Oh, and Vicky . . ." He made it sound like an afterthought, a clumsy attempt. She clenched her fists and waited for the rest of it. "I probably don't have to tell you to stick around. Don't leave the area. I'll want to interview you again in the next couple days."

"What are you inferring?" Father John was on his feet. "You can't think Vicky had anything to do with Ben's murder."

"I'm not sure what to think at the moment. The investigation's just gotten started. Fact is, Vicky was the last one to see Ben alive."

"Wrong, Ted," Father John said. (It was as if she wasn't in the room: strange, having her own life discussed.) "The killer was the last."

There was an awkward silence before the fed brought his eyes to hers. "Like I said, Vicky, stay where I can reach you." Then he walked across the room and let himself out, closing the door softly behind him.

Vicky felt as if she was going to be sick. She, a suspect in Ben's murder? It was ridiculous. Surely the fed didn't believe her capable of killing the father of her own children?

The realization came over her like a slow-moving fever. It was exactly what he believed. She was the last one to see Ben alive. And Gianelli *knew*. He knew about the past. He knew why she had left Ben all those years ago.

"My God," she said.

"Listen to me, Vicky." Father John leaned over and set a hand on her shoulder. "You're not guilty. You're not responsible. Gianelli'll trace the gun and find the killer."

Vicky struggled to control the panic leaping inside her. She set her own hand on his. A moment passed before she felt steady enough to get to her feet. "I have to call Susan and Lucas," she said.

"I'll get you the phone." Father John started toward the desk.

"Not from here." She couldn't call from here. She had to go home to her people where the spirits of the ancestors could strengthen her. Her mother had been dead five years now, but Aunt Rose was still alive. Her mother's sister, which meant, in the Arapaho Way, that Aunt Rose was also her mother.

"I have to go to Aunt Rose's."

"I'll take you." Father John's voice was soft and matter-of-fact. Rational. He understood. She always went to Aunt Rose's when the world shook beneath her and she couldn't get her balance.

"It's okay. I'll drive the Bronco," she said, starting toward the hall. She had to pack a few things; she didn't know how long she'd want to stay.

"I'll follow you, then," he said.

❖ 7 ❖

The screen door clacked into the silence that spread over the dirt yard behind the little white house. Vicky rearranged herself in the webbed chair and tried to shake off the sense of unreality that clung to her like a new skin. She watched Aunt Rose coming toward her: thick legs paddling forward, brown shoes raising little spitwads of dust. The morning sun blazing behind her made her pink housedress look as faded and gray as her hair. She held out a mug like an offering.

"You won't eat," she said. "Least you gotta drink something."

Vicky thanked the old woman and took the mug. The smell of fresh coffee came at her like an aroma breaking through a dream. She took a sip. She'd been sitting out in the yard since before dawn, watching the sun float up out of the darkness and turn the sky violet and red. Gradually the colors had melted into a crystalline blue. She had asked the spirits to guide the father of her children to the ancestors.

Aunt Rose unfolded the chair leaning against the house,

dragged it over, and sat down next to her. Vicky steeled herself for the urgent, well-meaning pleas for her to pull herself together, think of the kids. The old woman had been fussing over her since she'd knocked on the door last night.

She'd been expecting her, Aunt Rose had said. The moccasin telegraph was buzzing with the news. Vicky had waved at John O'Malley, his headlights washing over the Bronco, and stepped into Aunt Rose's arms. It was over now. She and Ben were over.

It had taken a while before she'd felt in control enough to call the kids. First Lucas. He was the stronger. He didn't speak for a moment. The sound of his breathing, irregular and forced, had filled the line. Finally the questions had begun, like the questions of a warrior trying to determine the cause of an ambush. How? Why? Who?

She told him what she knew, and he'd asked more questions. She didn't have the answers. After a while, the call had ended, and she'd rung Susan. Silence again, followed by screams that pulsed down the line. They'd talked only a few minutes, a breath of time, and there had been so much Vicky had wanted to say. But Susan had slammed down the phone, a punctuation, Vicky knew, to the anger her daughter harbored toward her—*she* was the one who had left the girl's father—anger that had exploded in an inarticulate blame for her father's death.

Susan was flying to Denver this morning, and she and Lucas would drive to the reservation. They'd be here this evening.

Aunt Rose's voice droned beside her, something about the old religion. "Do you good to hear the preaching," she said. "Take away some of the pain. Get your mind on the new world that's coming."

Vicky shifted sideways and gave the woman her full attention. "What are you talking about, Auntie? That cult in the mountains? Have you gone to the shadow dances?"

"Not the dances themselves." A defensive note crept into Aunt Rose's tone. "Only the Indians living up at the ranch take part in the dances. Every six weeks they dance for four days, like the Ghost Dancers in the Old Time. Wovoka gave Orlando all the instructions when he was in the shadow world. He promised that if the Indians dance, good things'll happen. We're gonna have our own land with plenty of trees and water and no whites telling us what to do. There's gonna be all Indians in the new world, like Wovoka said."

Vicky reached over and took the old woman's hand. "Surely you don't believe this nonsense."

Aunt Rose flinched. "Nonsense? The Creator give us the Ghost Dance a long time ago. Sent Wovoka to show us the new way of praying. Now Wovoka's sent Orlando. We gotta start praying again like in the Old Time, or the good things won't happen."

"Orlando is James Sherwood." Vicky kept her voice measured and calm. "The Sherwoods were always"—she hesitated—"different. Remember? James's father shot himself. His mother left the rez and died in a mental hospital in Denver."

Aunt Rose was quiet a moment. "Orlando died, too," she said finally. "He stayed in the shadow world a long time. He was with Wovoka and the ancestors. He's a holy man."

"Oh, Auntie." Vicky stopped herself from saying that James Sherwood was crazy, *Nokooho*. She could still see the white-clothed dancers circling the parking lot, shoving collection baskets at motorists, and people dropping in coins. People like Aunt Rose, naive and trusting. She was always taking people into her home. How many times had Aunt Rose taken *her* in? No place to go? Rose White Plume always had room. The tribal social services, the police would drop off people for a few days. Nothing official. It was just that everyone on the rez knew that Rose White Plume had a good heart.

"Promise me," Vicky said, "that you won't give the shadow dancers any money." She could imagine the old woman, entranced by the preaching, snapping open her pocketbook and dropping a few precious dollars into the baskets.

"Now, Vicky, I got enough. What I don't need . . ."

Vicky reached over and took the old woman's hand. "You already give away what you don't need. How many people have you fed in the last month?"

Aunt Rose tilted her head back and studied the sky. "Young couple with a baby drove up here from Oklahoma and got stranded. Couple kids fighting with their folks. Social services said they needed some cooling-off time." She paused, still searching the sky. The list was growing, Vicky thought. "Two, three girls stayed for a couple days."

"See what I mean, Auntie?" Vicky said, but she was talking to herself. Aunt Rose had shifted her attention toward the front of the house, and Vicky turned in her chair.

Her heart jumped.

For an instant, she'd thought the man coming toward them was Ben: tall and fit-looking, hair as black as slate, narrow sun-browned face, sharp, handsome features. And the same eyes, shining with anger. His boots kicked up swirls of dust. Vicky set her mug, still half-full, on the ground, stood up, and faced Hugh Holden.

"I want to talk to you, Vicky." He was a couple of yards away now.

"Hello, Hugh," Aunt Rose said, a scolding note ringing in her tone. The Arapaho had ignored the proprieties and launched immediately into business.

Hugh Holden glanced at the old woman, but there was no recognition in his eyes, no deviation from his purpose. He came closer. Vicky could smell the sour mixture of coffee and cigarettes on his breath.

"What happened last night between you and Ben?" The man stood with fists clenched at his sides, white knuckles straining against the brown skin. He was like Ben.

Vicky stepped backward, a reflexive motion. The chair wobbled against her leg. "I don't understand . . ."

"Bullshit. The fed says you and Ben had dinner. How come, Vicky? How come you were willing to have dinner with somebody you hated? Walked out on without so much as a go-to-hell. Broke up his family. Broke him up bad. Then, when he tried to get you to come back, all you could think about was some priest. That priest . . ." He drew in a long breath that flared his nostrils. "John O'Malley's the reason you turned against Ben. What'd you decide? To get Ben out of the way so you and the priest can have your little romance?"

"That's crazy, Hugh." Vicky tried to keep her voice calm. She'd had this conversation before, but it had been with Ben. Ben had believed the same, and she had never succeeded in convincing him that there was nothing between her and John O'Malley, except friendship. He was her closest friend, that was all. He was a priest.

"God knows I never understood what kind of spell you put on my brother," the man went on as if she hadn't spoken.

"Years he carried the torch for you, sure you were gonna come to your senses and go back to him. Even made plans to add rooms on the cabin up at the ranch. Room for Susan. Room for your office." He gave a snort of derision. "You being a lawyer were gonna want an office."

"Hugh, listen to me," Vicky began, struggling to wrap her mind around the magnitude of the fantasy world in which her ex-husband had lived. "Ben had trouble with a couple of ranch hands."

"You're the only trouble Ben had," he said, spraying her face with pinpricks of spittle. "Why a restaurant in Lander, Vicky? So he'd be sure to drive across Rendezvous Road? You knew he was gonna be out there alone. You set him up."

"What?" Vicky reared back. "How dare you!"

"I know what happened." The man's mouth twisted sideways. "You might fool everybody else, but you don't fool me. You hated my brother. You didn't want him bothering you, showing up in Lander, messing up your life. You wanted him dead."

Aunt Rose stood up. "You've said enough, Hugh Holden. You'd better go."

"How'd you arrange it, Vicky?" The man kept on. "Who'd you hire to shoot my brother? Skin? White man?"

"For godssakes, Hugh," Vicky said.

"I swear on my brother's grave you're not gonna get away with it. I'm gonna be all over that FBI agent until he gets you convicted, and if the law doesn't get you, Vicky, I swear I will."

"I said, get going, Hugh Holden," Aunt Rose shouted. "You ain't welcome at my house anymore."

Vicky made herself hold the man's eyes until he'd turned

away and started back along the side of the house. He was almost to the front when he stopped and looked back. "One more thing. The family's gonna make the funeral arrangements, you got that? We're gonna bury my brother like an Arapaho warrior. His kids are gonna be with the family where they belong, but you better not show your face. That's a warning."

Vicky felt as if her muscles and bones had fused together. She couldn't move. Her eyes stayed locked on the Indian until he'd disappeared around the house. She was barely aware of the warmth of Aunt Rose's hand on her frozen arm.

"You come inside now," the old woman said. "I'm gonna get you some more hot coffee." An engine growled into life, tires squealed. Vicky saw the blue pickup peel down the road ahead of a cloud of dust.

"He thinks I killed Ben," she said. *She had thought . . .*

"Man's crazy with grief. Don't know what he's saying." Aunt Rose lifted her chin and locked eyes with her. "You are my sister's daughter and you are my daughter. You had nothing to do with this terrible thing. You are not a murderer."

Vicky felt the tears coming. The contours of the old woman's face, the shape of her shoulders and arms blurred in the sun. She ran a hand over her cheeks.

"Let's go inside," she said, but Aunt Rose was staring toward the front of the house.

"Looks like we got another visitor."

Vicky followed the old woman's gaze. A white Blazer was slowing for a turn into the yard, a white man behind the wheel. The Blazer swung out of sight. She heard the engine cut off, the door slam shut.

"Well, it's to be expected," Aunt Rose said. "People

gonna be dropping by all day. You go on inside. I'll tell 'em you ain't up to seeing folks just yet."

"It's okay, Aunt," Vicky said. "It's the fed. He could have news." She started down the side of the house through the sunlight reflecting off the painted wood, aware of Aunt Rose hurrying behind her, gasping for air.

In the front yard, Gianelli was standing on the stoop, one fist in the air, as if he'd just knocked and was about to knock again. "Vicky," he said, glancing around. "We have to talk." Then, to Aunt Rose, "How are you, Mrs. White Plume?"

"You'd better come in." Aunt Rose made her way to the stoop, brushed past the agent, and pushed the door open. "Come on, come on," she said, beckoning the man inside.

Vicky followed. The living room was cool and smelled of coffee and the bacon and fried eggs that Aunt Rose had tried to get her to eat earlier.

"Sit down." The old woman kept moving toward the kitchen. "I'll get some coffee."

Vicky sat down on the sofa. "What have you found out, Ted?"

The agent didn't say anything for a moment. He was still standing, glancing around, the helplessness about him almost comical: white man in polished, tasseled shoes and blue sport coat, surrounded by a sofa and chairs that might collapse under his weight, a rabbit-eared TV, sunlight glinting on the glass that covered photos of the ancestors.

After a moment, he took one of the wood side chairs and fumbled for the notepad inside his blue sport coat.

"Not a whole lot," he said finally. "I want you to tell me again what happened last night."

Vicky felt the muscles in her throat constrict. What exactly had she told him? How would he compare what she'd said then with what she said now? How would he construe her words? This was how suspects felt, she thought. She went through the story again: Ben preoccupied and angry, arriving late. They argued. He stomped out.

The fed looked up from the notepad. "You didn't say anything last night about him throwing the dishes on the floor."

Vicky was quiet a moment. "Obviously you've talked to people at the restaurant."

"About a dozen witnesses saw the whole thing. All of them say Ben was out of control, but you didn't tell me how bad it was. Why didn't you?"

"We'd had similar scenes in the past." *God, she was on the witness stand. She was the defendant.* "You know about the beatings, Ted. You know why I left Ben fifteen years ago. Everybody on the res knows. What are you getting at?"

"Witnesses say something else, Vicky." The agent drew in a long breath and tapped his ballpoint on the notepad. "They say you were pretty angry, too. They say you followed Ben out of the restaurant. They say your Bronco followed his brown truck down Main Street. A good prosecutor might conclude that, over the years, you'd accumulated a lot of reasons to want Ben Holden out of your life permanently. A good prosecutor might think you followed him to Rendezvous Road."

Vicky jumped to her feet. "You've known me for five years, Ted. We've worked together on cases. Do you really believe I'm capable of shooting someone?" She stopped. She had shot a man last year to stop him from killing John O'Malley. She had been capable.

She rephrased the question: "Do you think I'm capable of premeditated murder?" Out of the corner of her eye, she saw

Aunt Rose in the doorway to the kitchen, eyes widened in fear, two mugs of coffee shaking in her hands.

"I think anybody might be capable, if they're pushed hard enough." The agent stood up and faced her. His eyes were as still and opaque as stone. "Do you own a pistol?"

Aunt Rose let out a little groan.

"Of course not." Vicky made her voice hard to match his eyes.

"Where did you go after you left the restaurant?"

"I drove around for a while and went home."

"Anyone see you? Friend? Neighbor?" He was shaking his head in answer to his own questions. "Look, Vicky, I want to help you. Give me someplace else to look."

"I told you, Ben'd had trouble with two Lakota ranch hands. He met with them just before he came to the restaurant."

"Roy He-Dog and Martin Crow Elk." The fed nodded. "Ben's assistant says the Lakotas left last week. They're probably at Pine Ridge by now."

"Ben said they were still here."

"He could've been mistaken, or . . ." The agent hesitated. "Maybe you misunderstood."

"I'm telling you the truth."

Gianelli let out a long sigh; his shoulders sloped forward. "I have to ask you again not to leave the area."

"You're saying I'm under suspicion for homicide."

"Everybody's under suspicion, this point."

"That's not true."

"Vicky—" he began, but she cut him off.

"From now on, if you want to talk to me, you'll have to contact my lawyer."

"You're a lawyer."

"Right. A fool has herself for a lawyer."

The fed pulled his lips into a thin line above his squared jaw. "That's the way you want it." He slipped the notepad back inside his sport coat, and walked to the door.

She turned away. The sound of the door closing came like a shot behind her.

"That white man's crazier than Hugh Holden." Aunt Rose sounded quiet and determined.

Hugh Holden. Vicky could feel her heart knocking. Ben's brother knew how persistent Ben had been. Hugh would confirm everything the fed already suspected. She had a motive to kill her ex-husband; she had no alibi.

She said, "I have to get back to Lander, Aunt."

◀ 8 ▶

It was half past seven when Father John drove out of the mission grounds and turned onto Seventeen-Mile Road. Blue Crow Software opened at eight, and he wanted to be there. Before he'd left, he found Father George in his office at the rear of the administration building—down the corridor lined with the tinted pictures of past Jesuits at St. Francis Mission—and told the man he'd be back in a couple hours. The pale gray eyes had flickered up from the computer monitor. One hand rose in acknowledgment.

"There'll be a lot of phone calls." He'd tried to warn the other priest. Everyone on the rez had probably heard about Ben Holden's murder by now. The moccasin telegraph was efficient. The phone would be ringing off the hook with people wanting to talk, trying to figure it out.

He'd offered Mass this morning for Ben Holden. *Lord, give him your peace.* He'd prayed for Vicky and for the family. *Give them your strength.* The few old people scattered about the pews had joined in the prayers, voices rumbling through the quiet. The early light streaming through the stained glass windows played over the wrinkled brown faces lifted

toward him. They made him a priest, he'd thought, the
people who needed him. Just as sick people made someone
a doctor and people in need of justice made someone a lawyer. He drew his priesthood from the people.

Then let me be the kind of priest they need.

After Mass, he spent a half-hour at his desk going over
the annual report, checking the quantified data that Father
George and the new members on the board would be scrutinizing. He totaled the numbers of participants in the programs that Arapahos couldn't find elsewhere, at least easily:
religious education, baptism, confirmation, marriage preparation. The numbers looked good. But good enough for
reasonable men charged with recommending the best use of
limited resources?

Dear God, he hoped so.

Just before he'd left, he'd dialed the number of Amos
Walking Bear, the president of the parish council. The elder
had answered, his voice clear and sharp. He'd probably been
up for hours. They spent ten minutes talking about Ben
Holden's murder, and Amos had broken the news: The family wanted an Arapaho ceremony. The funeral wouldn't be
at the mission.

Father John had stopped himself from asking why the
Holdens didn't want a Catholic funeral. The answer hovered
at the edge of his mind. When Vicky hadn't gone back to
Ben in the past, the man had blamed him. The Holdens
probably also blamed him. He and Vicky were friends. Just
friends. And yet, the truth was—he couldn't hide from the
truth—she was important to him. He had never meant to
love her; it had just happened. He had the odd feeling that
Ben and the Holden family had seen a part of him that he'd
tried to hide, but it was like his shadow. It was visible.

Father John realized that the elder had switched to the subject of the parish council. "Might get some of the members to a meeting tonight," Amos said.

That was great, he'd said. Then he'd told the elder that he'd see him at seven o'clock and pushed the disconnect button. For a moment, he thought about calling Vicky. She'd been on his mind all night—there in his dreams, small and vulnerable, looking at the fed with wide, questioning eyes, as if she were struggling to comprehend what the fed had just told her: Stay in the area.

He'd replaced the receiver. It was still early. Aunt Rose was probably up, but Vicky might still be asleep. He hoped so. She needed the rest, and Aunt Rose wouldn't want him disturbing her. He tried to ignore the unsettling feeling that always came over him when she went to her people on the reservation, as if she'd gone into another world through a door he couldn't enter.

Now he turned south on Rendezvous Road. The plains opened around him, a rough cut of brown bluffs and hidden arroyos that swallowed up the thin strip of blacktop stretching ahead. Scattered clumps of sagebrush bent sideways in the wind. In the far distance, the mountains emerged through the white haze.

He rewound the tape in the player beside him. The machine clicked and whined and finally spilled out the opening notes of *Faust*. After a few miles, he slowed around a wide bend. The road looked different in the daylight, but this was the spot where Ben Holden had been shot, no doubt about it. Tiny yellow and blue wildflowers poked through the brush in the barrow ditches on both sides of the road. There were no other vehicles in sight, no houses, no sign of human life, only the sweep of the plains and, on the west, the foothills striated yellow and blue in the sunshine.

The yellow police tape stretched down the other side. He hit the stop button on the tape player, pulled across the pavement, and got out. A bee was droning over the ditch, and somewhere a crow was cawing. The breeze was already hot, and the tape fluttered between the metal poles stuck in the dirt at the edge of the blacktop. Beyond the tape was a rectangle of flattened brush and wild grasses where the truck had been parked. A faint trace of tire tracks led to the flattened area. No sign of skid marks. Gianelli had been right. Ben had intended to stop.

Father John walked about thirty feet down the road to the end of the tape, his eyes hunting the ground for other patches of flattened grass. The breeze swept along the ditch. Nothing looked disturbed.

He crossed the road and hunted his way back. No indication of another vehicle off the road. He crossed back over to the pickup and slid behind the steering wheel, trying to form a picture in his mind of what had happened. Brown truck looming out of the dimness, headlights scraping the blacktop. The truck slows, pulls off the road, stops. No engine trouble, no flat tires, no reason to stop. Unless there was something up ahead, larger than a person standing by the road. A vehicle stopped in the road.

Father John started the pickup and turned back into the southbound lane. Vicky said that Ben had gone looking for two Lakotas yesterday. They'd ripped him off, and Ben Holden was the kind of man to take matters into his own hands. The Lakotas could have guessed he'd take the shortcut across the reservation on his way back to the Arapaho Ranch. They could have been waiting. A truck parked across the road could block both lanes.

Gianelli was a good investigator, Father John told himself, slowing down the main street of Hudson. The agent would put it all together. He'd probably found the Lakotas by now, taken them in for interviews. Unless . . .

He gripped the wheel hard. The Lakotas were in South Dakota, swallowed up in the emptiness of a reservation like Pine Ridge. The FBI might never find them, which meant that Ben's murder might never be solved and Vicky . . . Suspicion would cling to her like a black shadow the rest of her life. He swallowed back the dry knot of anger in his throat. He and Vicky had worked together to help so many people, and now she was the one who needed help. He had to find a way to help her.

He passed the semi on the straightaway outside of town and leaned onto the accelerator, eating up the miles into Lander. Twenty minutes later he found a parking space a half-block off Main Street and walked back to the office of Blue Crow Software.

At the desk inside the door was a young woman with a dusting of freckles across her pale cheeks and dark hair that fingered the shoulders of her blue blouse. He was looking for Dean Little Horse, he said.

The welcoming smile froze in the pale face. "Dean Little Horse." She enunciated each syllable as if she were testing a foreign language. Then she flattened her hands on the desk and levered herself to her feet.

"What'd you say your name is?"

He hadn't said. Now he told her his name and said he was the pastor at St. Francis Mission.

She nodded. That made sense. Indian priest looking for an Indian. "One moment." She sidled around the desk, then took off almost at a run across the green carpet, down an aisle between rows of cubicles. She knocked on a door in the rear and slipped inside.

Father John waited. The clack of keyboards sounded through the low electronic buzz that permeated the air. Two men in T-shirts and khakis emerged from one cubicle and crossed into another, heads bent together, voices hushed and tense.

Finally the woman came back across the office. "Tom can see you now." She nodded toward the door. Standing in the opening was a short, dark-haired man in a blue shirt with sleeves rolled up to his elbows and blue jeans.

Father John made his way down the aisle and took the man's extended hand.

"Tom Miller. People around here call me boss, but not to my face." He gave a forced laugh that ended on a high note. The man probably hadn't hit thirty yet. He ushered Father John into a small office with a desk perpendicular to a window that looked out on a parking lot next to an alley.

"Have a seat." Miller nodded toward the red plastic bucket chair in front of a filing cabinet. He sat down behind the desk, lifted one hand, and started rubbing his shoulder, the corners of his mouth turned up in discomfort. "Hardball. Pulled the deltoid. Thanks to spending way too much time in front of computers since I started the company. We make the software that keeps your water flowing out of the faucets." Pride seeped into the man's voice. "It's our software that opens the gates at Bull Lake Dam and lets out the right amount of water. So you're looking for Dean Little Horse."

Father John took the bucket chair. He removed his hat, hooked it over one knee, and said that was right. "When's the last time you saw him?"

"That would be . . ." Miller stopped rubbing his shoulder

a moment and stared at some invisible calendar behind his eyes. "Thursday. Left work early. About four, I'd say. Hasn't shown up since."

Father John took a couple of breaths. "Has he called? Offered an explanation?"

"Nada." The man's fingers carved a circle into his shoulder. "One day he's in his cubicle writing code, next day he doesn't show up. I figure it's some Indian thing. You know, somebody dies, so he has to go to the ceremonies, take care of family business."

"Has Dean not shown up for work before?"

Miller dropped his hand and settled back against the chair, forehead scrunched in concern. "Come to think of it, can't say that's the case. Dean's a reliable guy. When his grandmother started calling here, I decided he's got himself into trouble. Too bad. Dean's a genius at problem solving, and him taking a powder leaves us in the lurch. We're developing software for dams in five states. We gotta push the product out the door."

"What do you know about his girlfriend?"

"Girlfriend?" The man gave another snort of laughter. "Best advice my old man ever gave me—he ran a Fortune Five Hundred—was, stay out of your employees' personal lives. I don't ask, and they don't tell."

"Dean have friends around here?" Father John nodded toward the door.

Miller shrugged. "Shares cubicle space with Sam Harrison. Not in yet. You might catch him later."

Father John stood up and thanked the man, who had started to his feet before gripping his shoulder and sinking back. "Maybe you should see a doctor," Father John said.

"Doctors. What do they know?" He lifted a couple of fingers in farewell.

Father John let himself out and walked back down the aisle, aware of the eyes swiveling toward him from the cubicles. The receptionist's desk was vacant.

Outside, the street was nearly deserted. A couple of vehicles moving past, two businessmen making their way up the sidewalk, briefcases brushing the sides of their pressed blue jeans, a young woman pushing a stroller, hugging the shade under the store awnings. He turned the corner and jaywalked to the pickup across the street. He was about to get behind the steering wheel when a man darted out of the alley behind the software offices.

"Hey!" The man waited for a couple of pickups to pass, then started across the street. "You the guy looking for Dean Little Horse?"

Father John slammed the door and stepped into the lane. "You a friend?"

"Sam Harrison. Just drove into the parking lot out back. Boss said you wanted to see me." The man looked like a college kid, with curly brown hair, an eager, handsome face, and questioning eyes behind the round glasses with thin wires clipped behind his ears. He was dressed in khakis and a striped beige shirt. A gold chain glinted around his neck.

"What can you tell me about Dean?" Father John was thinking that Harrison must have come in the office from the back parking lot while he was exiting the front.

"You up for a cup of coffee?" The man glanced toward the corner. A pickup came down the street, honked, veered around them, honked again.

"Let's go." Father John led the way across the street. They walked in silence down the sidewalk and around the corner to the coffee shop with the pink saucer and cup painted on the plate-glass window, blue steam rising from the cup. The man insisted upon paying for a couple of mugs of coffee at the counter. They sat down on the metal ice cream chairs at a round table with fake marble on the top.

" 'Bout time somebody got serious about finding Dean," Harrison said. Behind the round glasses, questions and concern mingled his eyes.

"Where do you think he is?" Father John took a sip of coffee.

The man shook his head and cradled his mug in both hands. "I thought we were friends, you know? Dean and I got along real good. First Indian I ever got to know. That's something, isn't it? Lived next to the rez all my life and never got to know one of the Indians." He took a drink of coffee and seemed to contemplate this. "Maybe I got it wrong, about us being friends. Maybe he didn't trust me after all. Me, being white. If he was in trouble . . ." He let the words drift over the table.

Father John set his mug down. "You think Dean's in some kind of trouble?"

"Maybe. He got real quiet the last few weeks. Real short tempered, which wasn't like Dean. Bit my head off a couple times. He was working on upgrades for the software at Bull Lake Dam. Boss says I gotta take over the project now."

Father John worked at his own coffee again. Then he set the mug down and pulled the notepad and pencil out of his shirt pocket. "I hear Dean had a girlfriend. Any idea who she is?"

"Janis some Indian name." The man shrugged.

"Arapaho?"

"Yeah, but not from around here. Oklahoma Indian, Dean

said. Came up here last winter. He met her at a party on the rez. Man, she must've been something. Gorgeous, Dean said. A real fox, you know what I mean? Dean was in love for sure. Said she was real spiritual. I asked him once what he meant, and he said, 'Part of our tradition. You wouldn't understand.' "

"What do you think he meant?" Father John prodded. Something stirred in the back of his mind, remnants of gossip, and then he had it. Indians from other places were coming to the rez to join the shadow dancers.

Harrison pushed his mug aside and stared out the painted window. "Come to think of it, Dean said something about some ranch in the mountains she went to live on. She'd come to town now and then, and he'd be real happy. Then she'd go back to the ranch, and he'd be a bear. Afraid he was never gonna get her back. Worrying all the time about Janis." He snapped his fingers. "Beaver, that's her name. Janis Beaver."

Father John jotted down the name, then slipped the notepad back into his pocket, drained the last of his coffee, and got to his feet. "If you hear from Dean," he said, sliding the metal chair into place, "ask him to call me. Doesn't matter what kind of trouble he's in."

Harrison tilted his head back and gave him the kind of solemn, focused look he used to get from the best students in his American history classes.

He walked quickly back to the pickup, checking his watch as he went. Almost ten. Time to drive up to the shadow ranch and make it back to the mission before the Eagles practiced at four. He slid behind the steering wheel, flipped open the glove compartment, and pulled out the cell phone a couple of his parishioners had given him a few weeks ago. He seldom used it, and when he tried, he found that, more often than not, it didn't work on the reservation.

Now he punched in the numbers for Information, then called Eldon Antelope, one of the dads who helped coach the baseball team. An answering machine picked up. "If I'm late for practice," he said. "Take over, will you?"

‹ 9 ›

L AW OFFICES OF VICKY HOLDEN.

The old-fashioned sign on the front lawn mimicked the house, with curlicue posts that matched the gingerbread trim on the eaves. Vicky parked at the curb and hurried up the sidewalk. After four months in a Denver skyscraper, she could hardly believe her good luck to find a bungalow zoned for offices on the corner of a quiet, residential street. On the front door, below the beveled glass, was a bronze plaque engraved with her name. She let herself inside.

"Oh, my!" Esther Sundell, the secretary she'd hired two weeks ago, rose from behind the desk in what had once been the living room. Her hands fluttered a moment, then clasped together. She was in her fifties, with dark brown hair fading into gray, cut just below her ears. About her own height, Vicky guessed, five-foot-six, but stouter, with broad shoulders and a thick waist concealed under the oversized blouses that she favored.

The day Vicky opened the office, Esther had appeared at her door. She was related to Laola, she'd said, Vicky's former secretary, although Vicky still wasn't sure how she was related. She needed a job, and Laola had told her that Vicky needed a secretary. She'd hired the woman on the spot.

"I didn't think you were coming in," Esther said, a trace of anxiety in her voice. She was still nervous about getting everything just right.

"I'm not in." Vicky opened the French doors to her private office in the former dining room. She'd called early this morning and left a voice mail, knowing she wouldn't be able to concentrate on work. That was before she'd realized she was at the top of Gianelli's suspect list.

"Then I *did* get your message right?" There was obvious relief in the woman's voice. "You've had about twenty calls. I said you were out for the day. I canceled your appointments for this afternoon."

Vicky thanked the woman, dropped her bag on the desk that straddled the space between the window and the French doors—a dining table would have stood here—and adjusted the white, horizontal blinds. Slats of sunshine shot across the walls and gray carpet.

"I just wanted to say . . ." The secretary was standing in the opened doors, hands gripping the knobs. "Well, I heard about your ex-husband. It's all over the news. Radio, TV, big headline in the morning paper. If there's anything you need, all you have to do is ask."

Vicky perched on the leather chair she'd hauled from Lander to Denver and back to Lander again, under the impression that she could haul a piece of home around with her, and gave the secretary a smile that she hoped would end the conversation. She reached for the phone.

Esther remained between the doors. "Ben Holden must have been a wonderful man. Foreman at the Arapaho Ranch!

And my, so handsome in the newspaper picture. Like one of the Indians in the movies."

Vicky gestured with the receiver. "An important call," she said. *God, even in death, Ben could attract women.*

"Oh, of course." The hands fluttered upward like birds scared out of a nest. Then the woman backed into the front office, pulling the double doors with her until they clicked shut. Her shadow moved across the glass panes.

Vicky tapped out the number for Howard and Fergus, her former firm in Denver, and asked for Wes Nelson, the managing partner.

There was a brief silence, then the familiar voice at the other end. "Tell me you've had enough of small-town practice and you're ready to come back to the big time."

Vicky was struck by the irony. She'd wanted to come *home*, and yet, if she'd stayed in Denver, she wouldn't be a murder suspect now. "Something terrible has happened," she said. Then she told him about Ben, spilling out the details of the scene at the restaurant, the shooting on Rendezvous Road, the fact she did not have an alibi.

"Whoa, Vicky," he interrupted. "You telling me the feds think you had something to do with this?"

She said it looked that way and forced a little laugh.

"You need a good criminal lawyer, Vicky. We have the best in the region. Who do you want? I'll send anybody you name."

Vicky stared at the piles of papers on her desk. No Seventeenth Street criminal lawyer would want to set aside a mountain of work, drive three hundred miles to Lander, and hold her hand through a ridiculous investigation. She said, "I'm thinking about a couple of lawyers in the area." She gave him the names. Wes had connections throughout the region. "Who would you recommend?"

"You think one of the firm's lawyers wouldn't jump at the case?"

"There isn't a case," she said, striving for more confidence than she felt.

"Not yet, but it could go hard on you. I want to make sure the FBI agent plays by all the rules." Wes was quiet a moment. "What about an attorney who *used* to be at the firm? UCLA grad. Hated to lose him, but like you, he wasn't cut out for city life. Has firsthand experience dealing with federal agents on Indian reservations."

A memory stirred somewhere in the back of her mind. Indian lawyer at the firm two or three years ago. Substitute the University of Denver for UCLA and the lawyer's résumé sounded like her own.

"Adam Lone Eagle," Wes was saying. "Lakota. Hails from Pine Ridge."

Lakota! One of the seven branches of the Sioux Nation. The largest tribe on the plains, fierce, warlike. They couldn't be ignored. Her people had tried to stay out of their way, but there were times—after the massacre at Sand Creek for one—when Arapaho warriors had gone over to the Sioux to fight the whites.

"Curious," she said. "Ben had trouble with a couple of Lakota ranch hands before he was killed."

"Fed picked them up yet?"

"He thinks they've already gone back to Pine Ridge."

"All the more reason you're going to need Adam Lone Eagle. If they've gone into hiding, he might know how to smoke them out."

"Adam Lone Eagle." Vicky let the name roll over her tongue. "Where do I find this warrior?"

"Practically in your backyard. He's with Grant and Bovee in Casper now."

That Indian lawyer. Vicky vaguely remembered the news flashing across the moccasin telegraph a year ago. Another Indian lawyer in Wyoming. Lakota. She'd put it out of her mind. Her people weren't likely to hire a Lakota. She smiled at the irony. She was the one who was going to hire him.

"How soon can you get to Casper?" Wes asked.

Vicky glanced at her watch. Almost eleven. Casper was about a hundred and fifty miles away. "I can be there by two," she said.

The roofs of Casper twinkled in the sun ahead. She passed the turn to the airport and drove toward downtown through streets laid out more than a hundred years ago, wide enough in which to turn wagon trains. She found a parking place a block from the redbrick building with the white sign on the front: GRANT AND BOVEE, LAW OFFICES. Then she walked back, edging past a group of men in suits, two abreast, talking, laughing, gesturing, as if they owned the world, which they did, she was thinking. And Gianelli was like them.

She pushed open the heavy wooden door and stepped into the cool, spacious reception area, all marble floors and over-stuffed chairs and tables with bouquets of fresh flowers. A middle-aged woman with a head of tight black curls and thin black eyebrows penciled above her eyes glanced up from behind the half-moon desk. Vicky gave her name and said she had an appointment with Adam Lone Eagle.

"Oh, yes." The eyebrows rose in two perfect arches. "Mr. Lone Eagle's expecting you."

‹ 10 ›

Vicky followed the secretary down the corridor to the door with ADAM LONE EAGLE written in black letters on a wooden plaque. The door was half-opened, and the secretary ushered her inside. Standing by the desk across the room was a man probably in his forties, close to six feet tall, with muscular shoulders and chest that filled out his blue-striped dress shirt. His black hair was cut long and combed back, shiny in the light. He had a narrow face with prominent cheekbones, a long nose with a bump at the top, and a full mouth above the strong chin that curved into a little cleft. Handsome, she thought, with the golden brown complexion of a man who lived in the sun, like a warrior in the Old Time.

"Vicky Holden!" He seemed to rear back, the dark eyes appraising her. She saw the flash of approval in his expression. He started forward, took her hand, and led her into the office. "About time we met," he said, not letting go of her hand. His grip was warm and firm. She could feel the strength in the man, and it gave her a measure of comfort and security that she hadn't felt in so long, she'd almost forgotten they existed.

"Thanks for seeing me on such short notice," she managed, taking in the office around them: the soft gray carpeting and slatted blinds that blocked most of the sunlight, the polished desk that reflected the fluorescent ceiling lights.

The man directed her to the chair in front of the desk, then walked around, taking his time—a signal, she thought, that there was nothing to worry about—and settled into the brown leather chair on the other side.

"Funny thing," he began. (Ah, the polite preliminaries would be observed. It increased her feeling of comfort.) "Wes has often mentioned you. Said we should meet. I was planning to drive over to Lander one of these days and introduce myself. Couple of Indian lawyers oughtta know each other, don't you think?"

He pulled a yellow pad across the desk and plucked a gold pen from a holder. His fingers were long and well-shaped; his nails trimmed and neat. He wasn't wearing any rings. "Sorry to hear about your ex-husband." He held her eyes a moment. "Terrible thing. Must've been quite a shock. Wes tells me you and Ben had dinner together before he was murdered."

"It was an attempt to have dinner," she said. "It turned into a row."

"Not the first time, I take it." He left his eyes on hers, and she saw that Wes had filled him in.

"Now Ted Gianelli thinks you had something to do with the homicide."

Vicky relaxed into the chair. She was in competent hands. "He isn't the only one," she said. "Hugh, Ben's brother, thinks I hired someone to kill Ben." She paused. "I want you to know before we go any further. I did not murder my ex-husband."

"I didn't ask you." Adam was jotting something on the pad. "Frankly, it doesn't matter."

"Doesn't matter?"

"We don't have to prove your innocence. Gianelli and the U.S. attorney have to prove your guilt. That's their job. My job will be to make sure they stay within the legal boundaries while they look for evidence."

"There isn't any evidence, Adam." Vicky stood up and walked over to the window. She pulled the slats apart. A column of sunshine lay over the street and sidewalk. A businessman hurried past, and at the curb, a woman was lifting a child out of a car seat in a van. An ordinary day, Vicky thought, except that the earth was shifting beneath her.

"Why does that upset you?" There was a surprised note in the lawyer's voice. "You know how the system works. You know I have to shield you from an indictment."

Vicky made herself take several slow breaths before she turned back. Adam Long Eagle was on his feet, fingers tapping the desk, dark eyes on her. "So, do we go forward?"

She nodded and walked back to the chair.

"We both know innocent people can be indicted and prosecuted," he said. "All it takes is enough circumstantial evidence to put together a logical case. You're in a precarious position. Abused ex-wife. You spent ten years married to Ben Holden, ten years of abuse. You've been divorced for . . ."

"Fifteen years," she said.

"Wes said Ben wouldn't leave you alone, always wanted you back. That true?" The man hurried on without waiting for an answer. "You have no alibi for last night, and any dim-witted prosecutor can make the case that you had a motive."

Vicky walked back to the window. It was disconcerting hearing her own story from a stranger. "They found the weapon," she said, looking back. "A twenty-two-caliber pistol. There might be prints. The gun can be traced."

The lawyer sat down and filled a couple of lines on the notepad. "Don't count on it," he said finally. "Killers don't leave behind traceable guns with prints, unless they're certifiably stupid."

That was true. Vicky pushed open the slats again and stared at the pickups and sedans passing outside. The pistol would probably be a dead end.

"You own a gun?"

She whirled around. "No."

"What about access?"

"Access? I can buy a gun at any gun shop."

"Easy access. Anybody you know . . ."

"Ben owned guns. Every rancher on the rez owns a gun. There are lots of people I know with guns. What are you getting at, Adam?"

The lawyer stood up and came around the desk. "I don't like it. Gun left at the scene." He shrugged, but there was something forced in the gesture. "It might be traceable," he said, a lack of conviction in his tone.

"Yes." Vicky heard the same tentativeness in her own voice. They both knew that whoever had waited for Ben on Rendezvous Road was clever and determined. Why, then, had the killer left the weapon?

"From now on," the lawyer was saying, "you do not talk to Ted Gianelli or any other fed, police officer, sheriff's deputy, or detective. You talk to nobody about the homicide. Got it? When Gianelli calls, and he will call, your secretary will tell him to call me. All communication goes through me. And another thing, you don't talk about the homicide to anybody else. Not friends or family. Nobody. I don't want Gianelli picking up random bits of information that he might use against you. Is all this clear?"

Vicky walked back to the chair, then to the window again. "So your strategy is to sit tight and act guilty," she said. "That's crazy. Ben argued with a couple of ranch hands. Lakotas." She stopped pacing and locked eyes with the man.

The lawyer reached back and dragged the yellow pad across the desk. "Names?" He gripped the pen and glanced up at her.

"Roy He-Dog. Martin Crow Elk." The names that Gianelli had given her were imprinted on her mind. "The fed claims they went back to Pine Ridge last week, but he's wrong. Ben met with them yesterday."

"I know the families." The gold pen moved over the notepad. "I'll make a few phone calls to Pine Ridge and tap into the news. If they're on the rez, I'll hear about it." He looked up. "You think they shot your ex-husband?"

That was the problem. She'd been so sure. It *had* to be the Lakotas who followed Ben to Rendezvous Road. But she didn't have any evidence. And Gianelli was right about one thing. Ben was a powerful man; he could have made other enemies.

Vicky folded her arms and stared out the window. It was clear now—hadn't she known all along? No one could know whether the Lakotas were guilty or innocent until they were found. And if they were still in the area, she was the one who would have to find them.

She glanced back at the lawyer. "I'm going to ask around . . ."

"Haven't you heard a word I said?"

"We're talking about my life, Adam."

"Let Gianelli do the asking around."

The office was quiet. Outside a truck geared down.

"He won't find the Lakotas."

The lawyer slapped the notepad down hard on the desk. It made a sharp, crackling noise. "If you want me to advise you, you have to play by my rules. That's the first rule: Play by my rules." He allowed the words to fill the space between them. "I have to know everything about you. How you spend your days. Who your friends are. That's the way it has to be if I'm going to shield you from a murder indictment."

He reached back and withdrew a business card from a metal card holder. After jotting something on the card, he handed it to her. "My home number. You can call me anytime, day or night."

"In the meantime, what exactly am I supposed to do? Hibernate in a cave?"

"Do what you normally do. Go to the office. Take care of clients. You must have work to do."

She told him about the report on the Wind River for the JBC. God, how could she concentrate on the report?

"Good. Finish the report. See your friends and family. Go to Ben's services."

"I'm not invited."

He stared at her a moment, as if he had to bring a new image of her into focus. "So Ben's family really does think you're responsible." He drew in a long breath. "What they think doesn't matter. We'll stick to our plan."

Vicky slipped the card into her black bag. "What about your fee?"

"The fee's taken care of. Wes's instructions were: 'Don't worry about the tab, just keep her safe.' You're going to be all right, Vicky. Trust me."

‹ 11 ›

Father John drove north out of Lander, the highway curving toward the foothills, then running straight into the parched, empty plains. Traffic was light: a couple of RVs with out-of-state plates, pickups with two or three Indians in the front seat. Father John squinted past the sunlight reflecting off the hood. *"A moi les plaisirs"* blared over the thrum of the tires on the road, the noise of the wind. He'd been drawn to *Faust* lately, the soaring, plaintive music and the story of a man who gave up his soul—and for what? What could be more important than your soul?

He turned west out of Fort Washakie and started winding up a narrow ribbon of concrete. Below, the reservation crept toward the horizon, golden in the sun and peaceful, with small houses scattered about and roads that carved the land into large squares. Cottonwoods and willows marked the paths of the Wind River on the north and the Little Wind on the south. Where the rivers met, just east of the mission, was a cluster of greenery. He could see the church steeple rising among the cottonwoods.

And then the road headed into a canyon. The pavement

ended, replaced by a two-track with weeds and brush that
scraped at the undercarriage. A thin forest of ponderosas and
junipers sprouted on the slopes. He negotiated another turn.
The high peaks, still covered in snow, came into view behind
the ridge ahead. A barbed wire fence on the right ran to a
small, log shack.

Father John eased on the brake and guided the pickup
into the turnoff next to the shack. He stopped at the metal
gate across a dirt road that wandered up-slope into the trees
and turned off the tape player. The wind hissed in the trees.

A short, compact Indian with a rifle gripped in both
hands stepped out of the shack and walked to the center of
the gate. The round, flat face was turned toward him. Pueb-
loan, Father John guessed, dressed in white buckskin with
fringe running down the outside legs and across the chest.
The partially laced V-shaped opening of the shirt exposed
the thick tendons in the man's neck. An eagle feather rose
over his head, held in place by a woven headband that
wrapped around his forehead and kept the long, black hair
close to his head. He wore beaded moccasins that made a
shushing noise against the packed dirt.

"No outsiders allowed." The guard hunched over the top
rail and lifted the rifle, squinting in the sun.

Father John leaned out the window and tried to ignore
the rifle. "I'm here to see one of the dancers."

A look of incomprehension came into the stone black
eyes. "Afternoon dancing's going on now. Dancers don't see
nobody."

"Janis Beaver," Father John persisted.

"Nobody means you, white man. Back up and get on
outta here." The Indian knocked the rifle against the top
railing. A blue vein pulsed in his temple.

"What's going on?" Another Indian emerged from the trees and started toward the gate. He walked with a jerky motion, as if one leg was slightly shorter than the other. His buckskin suit looked like the guard's—an old woman somewhere, a traditional, might have made the clothing for both men, even beaded the moccasins. Black braids swung over the front of the man's shirt.

The guard threw a glance over one shoulder. "White man's lookin' for somebody. Told him to get goin'."

The other Indian lurched to the gate and grabbed hold of the top rail, as if to steady himself. The buckskin shirt wrinkled around the bulky shoulders and biceps. His eyes were so deeply set they looked like charcoal smudges on the flat face. He was several inches taller than the guard—a Plains Indian, maybe Lakota.

"Who are you?" His voice was high-pitched, tentative.

Father John got out of the pickup and slammed the door. The sun burned through his shirt. He gave his name and said he wanted to talk to Janis Beaver.

"Nobody here by that name."

Father John locked eyes with the man. "She's here, all right. I'm looking for a friend of hers, Dean Little Horse. I think she can help me find him."

Both Indians were quiet, faces unreadable. Finally the Lakota turned to the guard. "I guess Orlando's gonna want to see him," he said, his high voice trailing into a whine.

The faintest look of incredulity came into the other man's expression. He hesitated, then gestured with the rifle toward a clearing next to the shack.

"Park over there," he said. "No vehicles allowed in the village. Nothing here made by white people."

Father John parked where the guard had indicated, then

swung himself over the gate and hurried to catch up with
the Lakota, who had started up the road, dragging his left
leg, his shoulders and head bobbing as he went. The wind
blew through the trees, as dry and hot as the wind off a fire.
Father John pulled the brim of his hat low against the sun.
His throat felt dry and scratchy. His shirt was clinging to
his back. No telling how far they had to go. He wished he'd
brought a bottle of water.

The Lakota started around a bend, past the clump of trees,
and Father John sprinted ahead to catch up.

"Where we going?"

"To the village."

"Village? There's a village on Sherwood's ranch?"

"Name's Orlando." The man stopped and pivoted toward
him. "You oughtta show respect for the prophet." He threw
his shoulders around in an awkward motion and started out
again, as if he didn't want to waste any more time.

Father John followed. The road narrowed into a steep path
that switched back and forth up the slope. Strange, he
thought. There was no sound of drums or rattles, and yet
the guard had said the dancing was in progress.

"How long have you been with Orlando?"

Silence. Except for the breeze in the pines, the Indian's
moccasins scraping the hard ground, and the sound of his
own breathing loud in his ears. Below, Father John could
see the canyon he'd driven up, a winding chasm in the earth
tossed with boulders and brush. The top of the ridge was
about thirty feet above, he guessed. The switchbacks were
shorter, the angles sharper. With each turn upward, he had
the sense that he was climbing farther away from the ordinary, familiar world below.

The Indian came around a switchback, and Father John

saw the man's jaw muscles twitch, as if he were silently testing the answer. Finally he said, "Hospital in Denver, after I got my leg broke. I seen him die, and I seen him come back to life. He was different when he come back 'cause he'd gone to the shadow world. He started preaching right there, up and down the corridors, telling the rest of us Indian patients what we gotta do. Soon's he got out, the people started asking him to come to their homes and tell 'em how to get saved. He said we gotta start living like the new world was already come, even if it ain't come yet. Some of us come with him to the ranch." He stopped talking a moment, then hurried on: "Lot more comin'. People here gonna be saved from the event."

He took another switchback and bent forward up the incline. Father John could see the calf muscles of the man's right leg bulging through the buckskin. The left leg was stiff and thin, like a stick dragging beside him.

"What are you talking about? What event?"

The Indian glanced around, eyes slit in confusion and anger, as if he'd been goaded into saying more than he wished. "Don't concern white people." He braced himself against a boulder, then hurled himself upward with his shoulders before taking a final jump onto the top of the ridge. He set both hands on his hips and stood motionless, gazing out into the distances, black hair and white buckskin clothes gleaming in the sun.

Father John dug his boots into the ground to keep from sliding backward and, bending forward, his breath a hard knot in his chest, pulled himself over the boulders until he was standing next to the Indian. He took in a couple gulps of air. "Who are you?" he said finally.

The Indian was still staring across the space that opened

below. "I am the prophet's disciple," he said, the high voice almost lost in the wind sweeping over the ridge. "My ancestors followed the messiah, Wovoka. Now I have heard the messiah's words from the prophet."

He turned and started across the bare strip of ground that curved away like the rim of a volcano, then disappeared down the other side.

Father John ran a hand over his face, wiping away the perspiration, still breathing hard in the thin, hot air. The wind smashed his shirt against his chest.

He walked to the opposite side. A cluster of ranch buildings stood in the meadow below: small, frame house, barn, two smaller structures, weathered-looking and run-down. A couple of horses paced in the corral next to the barn, and beyond the corral, a small herd of buffalo grazed in a pasture.

On the other side of the meadow was a village of about twenty tipis, arranged in a circle, white canvas lit by the sun. Inside the circle were the dancers, dressed in white, holding hands and moving clockwise in a slow, silent motion around a lodgepole set upright in the earth. Next to the pole, someone was seated in a chair that faced the east. A large man stood behind the chair, arms folded across his chest, watchfulness in his manner. From somewhere in the distance came the caw-caw sound of a crow.

Father John gazed at the scene below for a moment. His assistant was right. They couldn't ignore Orlando and his followers. This was a cult with its own messiah, its own prophet, isolated from the rest of the world. He should have spoken with the elders about the shadow dance and warned his parishioners. He wondered how many of his parishioners had already followed Orlando here.

He started after the Indian, who was working his way

down the narrow footpath in a hop-hop motion. Dropping closer to the village, Father John could see the bark on the clusters of poles that poked through the tops of the tipis. The sloped canvas walls shimmered in the breeze. The faint smells of manure and garbage floated toward him. The dancers were still circling about. He could still hear the crow—a frantic note in the sound now—but he couldn't see the bird.

"How many people are here?" he said to the Indian's back.

"You ask a lot of questions." The Indian glanced around, then slowed his pace, as if he were waiting until Father John caught up. "The saved are here. That's all you need to know. We're gettin' ready for the new world. Won't be nothing of white people then. Nothing made by whites. Everything we need is gonna be Indian. There's gonna be plenty of buffalo meat, roots, vegetables, berries. Everybody's gonna wear skins—all the women and children, just like the men. This way." He plunged ahead across the grassy area at the base of the slope, then they worked their way past the tipis. The crow had stopped cawing.

"We wait," the Indian said when they had reached the edge of the dance arena.

The dancers shuffled past, holding hands, silent except for the noise of their breathing—in and out like tiny bellows—as if they were in some kind of trance. Father John counted: twenty, twenty-five men and women, with the round, flat faces of the Navajo and Puebloans, the broad faces of the Sioux and Cheyenne, the narrow, defined faces of the Arapaho, none older than thirty, all dressed in white. Men in buckskins, women in loose, flimsy dresses that swayed about their legs. Across the shirts and dresses, painted in bright colors, were symbols of the Plains Indians: blue bands for the sky, yellow circles and crosses for the sun and the morning star, and red thunderbirds for the eagle that flies to the Creator.

As the dancers came around, they faced the rail-thin Indian who slumped in the webbed folding chair in the center, fingers spread over the knees of his buckskin trousers. Painted on the front of his shirt was a large, red crescent moon. He looked about thirty years old, with black hair cut just below his ears and intense, deep-set eyes that made his face appear skull-like. He was surprisingly pale, like a man who had been ill for a long time. As the dancers circled around, he held the gaze of each one for a long moment, and Father John could almost feel the electric charge that passed between them.

James Sherwood, he thought. A prophet who called himself Orlando.

The large Indian with shoulders like a bull, stationed beside the chair, was probably not much older than Orlando. He was also in white buckskin, arms folded across his chest, black hair pulled back into a ponytail, gaze fixed on the dancers passing by. He had a nose that curved like a beak, cheekbones that jumped out from beneath the brown skin, and fleshy lips. A vivid red scar ran from the edge of his mouth to the tip of his ear.

The crow screamed again. Now Father John saw the bird, perched like an outsized black beetle on top of the lodgepole behind Orlando. Strips of brightly colored fabric wound around the pole, the ends flapping in the breeze. The bird turned its beaked head side to side, shiny eyes on the dancers below, then tilted its head upward and screamed into the sky.

Father John shifted his gaze to the dancers. He had no idea what Janis Beaver looked like. Arapaho from Oklahoma, Sam Harrison had said. "A fox, you know what I mean?" She could be any one of a half-dozen women swaying past, but his eyes kept coming back to the girl dancing between two muscled young men. She was very pretty, with brown, almond-shaped eyes, finely shaped nose and cheeks, rounded lips that she brought together in a small circle. Her black hair was parted in the middle and combed back. It hung like a veil to her waist. A white rope cinched her dress, emphasizing the full breasts and curved hips.

Out of the corner of his eye, Father John saw Orlando shift in his chair, then lift both arms in a kind of benediction. The dancers stopped immediately. The crow pivoted on its perch and cawed.

And then it was very still. Even the breeze died back. After several seconds, a deep, baritone voice broke the quiet. "My relations, hear my words. I have returned to you from the shadow world in the west. I have seen crow leading the armies of ancestors. The regeneration will come before the spring passes away. We will dance for two more days. Wovoka does not forget his promise."

The prophet got to his feet and started across the arena. The crow let out a scream and swooped down, perching on the man's thin shoulders. Walking close behind him like a bodyguard was the large Indian with the red scar that pulsed in his cheek. The dancers formed a long corridor through which they passed, Orlando lifting his hand, blessing those on the right, then on the left. He stopped in front of the tipi that faced the east, set apart from the others, then ducked inside, the crow still clinging to his shoulder. The bodyguard followed.

"Wait here." The Lakota beside Father John started loping toward the tipi.

Father John headed across the arena, through the dancers milling about. Several men came toward him, then parted, like water flowing around a rock, as if they hadn't seen him, and continued toward the northern curve of tipis. The women huddled together in small groups, moving toward the southern curve. They looked alike; he couldn't find the pretty girl with almond eyes.

Then he saw the Lakota coming along a diagonal path toward him, one shoulder thrust forward, left leg slightly behind. His eyes blazed with anger. "You got no right walking around," he said. Then he drew in a long breath. "Orlando'll see you now."

❮ 12 ❯

Father John ducked into the tipi. It was cool inside. The sun streamed down from the opening overhead and cast a mixture of light and shadow over the straw mats on the floor and the buffalo robes draped over the hay bales around the periphery. Daylight glowed through the canvas walls. He was aware of the Lakota and several other men crowding behind him, the rapid gasps of their breathing.

Orlando sat on a bale on the far side of the tipi, facing the east, the crow still on his shoulder. He looked straight ahead, but the dark, intense eyes seemed to take in the entire tipi. There was a half-smile about his mouth, an unhurried sense in the way he shifted forward on the hay bale. And something else: the shadow of fatigue in his pale face and the kind of transparency that Father John had seen in hospitals when patients were close to death.

The Indian with the scar on his cheek sat a few feet from Orlando, far enough away, Father John thought, to show respect, yet close enough to throw himself between the prophet and any danger.

"Down on your knees." Father John felt the jab of the

Lakota's fist in his back. "You are in the presence of the prophet."

Father John shrugged away and moved into the column of light, locking eyes with Orlando. "I want to talk to Janis Beaver," he said.

Orlando didn't say anything for a moment. His mouth moved silently, then the baritone voice burst across the tipi: "Why do you suppose someone called Janis Beaver is with us?"

"She's one of your followers."

"I have many followers." The man lifted both arms toward the village in a kind of benediction. "They've come here to be free of the white world. Soon the world will be cleansed and purified. We will have all that we need. Plenty of buffalo, wild vegetables and fruits. We will bend our own bows, straighten our arrows, and carve the tips from the finest flint. The women will tan the skins and sew beautiful garments. We need nothing from white people. Go away. You have no right to disturb us."

"I believe Janis can help me find her friend, Dean Little Horse," Father John persisted. "It's important that I talk to her."

Orlando lifted his hand and waved at the Lakota, who was now standing at attention beside Father John. "Leave this unbeliever with us," he said.

The Indian bobbed backward. There was the sound of the flap being pushed aside, moccasin feet slapping the ground. The crow lifted its head and gave three short cries.

"You know this man, Little Horse?" Orlando said.

"I know his grandmother. She can't sleep nights worrying about him. She raised him from the time he was an infant. He's like her own son."

"He has defiled our village." The baritone voice deepened. "He is an unbeliever. We do not want him here. We told him to go away. You must also go. Leave us."

"As soon as I talk to Janis," Father John said, "I'll be on my way."

"Why do you ask for these people?" Orlando started to his feet, then lurched backward. The Indian with the scar jumped up, took hold of his arm, and steadied him. "Janis!" Orlando flapped his free arm in the air. "I know no one by this name. Why do you white men come here and disturb our dance, looking for people we don't know? This morning, an FBI agent"—he enunciated each syllable, horror in his tone—"came to our village looking for Lakotas, interrupted our dancing, demanding to check the followers' IDs. And now you! You interrupt our afternoon dance. Shall we have no peace?"

He started forward, the guard holding one arm, the other still flapping in the air. The crow lifted off his shoulder and flitted up toward the poles tied at the top of the tipi. "What is it you want? To stop our dancing? Is that it?" Orlando was shouting now, spraying tiny flecks of spittle into the column of light between them. "I know you white people. You don't wish the new world to come. You want to stop it, just like before."

An absent look came into the dark eyes, as if some other scene had started playing out before him, demanding his attention. He flinched away from the other Indian's grip and lifted both hands overhead. The crow had started circling the tipi, screaming, flapping its black wings. "Here are the soldiers," Orlando shouted to the bird. "I see them on the horizon. I see the breaths of their horses in the morning frost. It is so cold. The snow is deep. I hear the hooves pounding in the snow. They are coming, coming."

Father John stared at the man. My God. It was as if Orlando were reliving the massacre of the last Ghost Dancers at Wounded Knee more than a hundred years ago.

"Run, run," Orlando shouted again, his voice raw with fear. "We must run through the snow. Everyone run!"

The other Indian placed an arm around the man and started to lead him backward toward the bale. "Medicine man!" he shouted. "Get the medicine man."

Orlando bent forward, coughing and crying out—a long wail of grief—gasping for breath. The crow perched on the bale of hay close by, head wobbling on its humped shoulders.

As Father John started toward the man, he felt a fist slam into his ribs. He stumbled sideways.

"Don't touch the prophet!" The Lakota lurched past and threw himself toward Orlando. He took the prophet's other arm, and the two Indians pulled him back onto the hay bale.

Father John heard the footsteps pounding outside, then dancers began plunging through the opening, two, three at a time. They gathered around Orlando, a deliberateness in their movements, as if they'd practiced the routine many times before, and each dancer knew exactly where to go.

Someone passed a bucket of water through the flap. The bodyguard with the scar on his face scooped a glass of water and held it to Orlando's lips.

He pushed it away and started coughing again, still bent in half, head dropping between his knees. Water dripped from the long fingers.

"Medicine man!" the bodyguard shouted again.

Another Indian stooped low into the tipi and the others

began peeling backward, clearing the way. Father John slipped outside.

He ran to the first tipi on the south and knocked against the canvas flap. "Janis!" he called.

There was no response. He pulled the flap aside. The inside was bare, except for the straw mats on the floor. Daylight pooled in the center. Beyond the light, three women lay curled on the mats, white dresses bunched around their bare feet. They looked half asleep, drugged, Father John thought, and whatever drug they'd taken hadn't yet worn off. The pretty girl wasn't there. An odor of exhaustion mixed with the smells of canvas and dried straw.

"Where's Janis Beaver?" he said.

One woman flopped over, turning her back to him. The others looked away, expressions as blank as sheets of paper.

He dropped the flap and ran to the next tipi, conscious of the commotion behind him, the footsteps pounding through the village, voices shouting. The crow was screaming from the top of the lodgepole.

He went through the same routine again: calling out, waiting, pulling the flap aside. There were four women lying in the shadows inside, shoulders touching. They might have been marooned in a blizzard, he thought, dependent on one another for warmth. "Janis Beaver?"

Heads shaking, eyes studying the straw mats. He'd started to back away when one woman gave him an almost imperceptible nod to the east. She lifted a hand and ran three fingers over her cheek.

He closed the flap and ran east past one tipi, then another. He stopped at the third and glanced back at the crowd of men pressing around Orlando's tipi. The cawing of the crow ripped through the air.

He leaned into the flap. "Janis," he said. "I have to talk to you about Dean." He waited a moment, then pushed back the flap and stepped inside.

The interior resembled Orlando's, with straw mats, hay bales, a buffalo robe draped over one bale. A woman was curled up on the floor, hands thrown over her head in exhaustion. On the right, propped against a bale, the pretty girl with knowing, almond eyes, face drained of color, long strands of black hair that fanned over the shoulders of her white dress. A red crescent, like that on Orlando's shirt, was splashed on the front of her dress.

She stared up at him a moment, then began scooting sideways, pushing herself with her bare feet, a frantic kind of fear and confusion in her expression.

"I won't hurt you." His voice was calm. He told her his name and said he was from the mission. "What can you tell me about Dean? He's been gone for five days. His grandmother's crazy with worry."

"You shouldn't've come here." Her voice had the flat, dead quality of an automatic machine. The almond eyes darted about the tipi.

He squatted in front of her and tried to hold her attention. "You must tell me what you know about Dean. You went to his apartment on Sunday looking for him, didn't you? Where is he?"

"It's forbidden for men to come to the women's tipis." She looked up, then to the side. Finally she began studying the edge of the hay bale.

"Please tell me, Janis." He could hear the voices outside coming closer.

"Only the prophet comes here." She was trying to dig a finger into the hay.

"What? Janis, try to concentrate. Where's Dean?"

"The prophet will choose the new people for the new world."

"What are you talking about?"

And then he knew. He felt his stomach turn over. "You mean children."

"Holy children," the woman said, her voice still on automatic. "We will bear the holy children for the new world."

He let out a long breath. God. He wondered if the women were already pregnant. Orlando! A man gasping for breath, and yet, he had seemed assured and confident gazing at the dancers, buoyed, Father John suspected, by their adoration.

"Listen to me, Janis," he said. "Is this what you want? You don't have to stay here." He glanced around at the other woman and wondered if she was really asleep. "You can both come with me. We'll get out of here." He could still see the guard at the gate with the rifle gleaming in the sun. He had no idea how they were going to get out.

She didn't answer for a moment, as if she were trying to remember something important. Finally she said, "The prophet was sent by Wovoka. He speaks only truth. I want to go into the new world."

"Do you have any family?" Father John tried another tack. "Do they know you're here? I can call them for you."

She was quiet; the almond eyes still darting about.

"What about Dean? He's in love with you, Janis."

For the first time, her eyes met his. "I tried to tell him, but he wouldn't listen. The prophet . . ." She hesitated, then crossed her arms over the red painted symbol on her chest. "The prophet is my life now. I could never love Dean the way . . . the way . . ." She struggled over the words, leaning back against the bale, as if searching for shelter. "He wouldn't listen. He went away."

"Where? Where did he go? His grandmother has the right to know."

Janis leaned back into the hay and began rolling her head, her eyes following the motion. "Lost. Lost. Lost. Tell the old woman to forget about him."

"What are you talking about?" Something moved at the corner of his eye—a disturbance in the atmosphere. The column of light through the opened flap widened.

"On your feet, white man." The Lakota's voice behind him, the man's grip, like a vise, on his shoulder.

Father John stood up. "Come with me now, Janis. I'll take you to the mission. You can call your family," he said, but she was staring beyond him, unseeing, as if she'd gone into another place that his voice couldn't reach.

"Out, white man!" A second hand took hold of his other shoulder. Father John swung around, wrenching himself free. The man with the scar stood next to the Lakota. Father John walked past them and stooped through the opening. The crowd was still gathered in front of Orlando's tipi. He started across the arena.

"You white men"—the Lakota was hopping beside him; the crow flapped and screeched overhead—"think you can do anything you want, stop our dancing, stop the new world . . ."

"You lied to me." Father John wheeled toward the Indian. "You said Janis wasn't here. What about Dean Little Horse? Are you hiding him someplace? Out on the ranch? In a shack? A cave? Where is he?"

"You heard what the prophet said. He's gone from here."

Father John held the man's gaze a moment. Then he

turned around and walked past the tipis and across the grassy area. He started climbing up the slope, the Lakota breathing hard behind him, like a pony snorting and scratching at the ground.

They crossed the top of the ridge and followed the footpath down. The roof of the guard's shack poked through the trees below; the bumper on the pickup flashed in the sun.

Father John cut through the trees and took a diagonal route down the slope, the Indian still behind him. He could see the guard inside the shed as he climbed over the gate. "I'm going to find Dean," he said, facing the Lakota again. "You might as well tell me where he is."

The Lakota met his eyes. "You're a foolish white man, priest. Go back to wherever you came from. You and your mission are not wanted here."

"Is that a threat?"

"You have heard the words." The Indian kept his gaze steady.

Father John felt the skin on his arms prickle. Had Dean threatened Orlando when he learned about the prophet's plans for Janis?

He got into the pickup, slammed the door, started the engine, and backed past the Indian standing on the other side of the gate. Then he slipped the gear into forward and jammed down the accelerator. The pickup skidded out onto the road, dust spattering the rear window. In the side mirror, he caught a glimpse of the guard framed in the doorway of the shack.

Father John reached Fort Washakie, pulled over, and punched in Gianelli's number on the cell phone. An answering machine clicked on at the other end; the agent's voice, disembodied and matter-of-fact, floated down the line. "I have to talk to you," Father John told the machine. Then he left his numbers: the cell phone, the office. "Call me," he said.

He drove back onto the street, turned left, and parked in front of the redbrick building with the sign in front: WIND RIVER LAW ENFORCEMENT. He waited in the small area inside the entry while the woman behind the glass pane disappeared into a hallway. After a few moments, she returned.

"Chief Banner says to come on back." She spoke into the round metal grate in the glass. A buzzer sounded, and he walked through the door on the left and down the corridor. The whiff of stale smoke and floor wax hung in the air. The chief was coming from the opposite direction, waving a sheaf of papers. He motioned him into an office with stacks of folders and papers toppling over the desk and file cabinets, an array of family photographs tucked among the stacks.

"You come about Ben's murder, we're doin' all we can." The chief dropped into the chair behind the desk and tossed the papers on some folders. Father John pulled over a metal-framed chair and sat down.

"This is fed business," the chief went on. "We're cooperating. My boys lifted prints and tire tracks. We been all over the rez looking for a couple of Lakotas Vicky says that Ben met with Monday afternoon." He shrugged. "No luck. My guess is, those skins are out of here, laying low up at Pine Ridge 'til this gets settled."

"I just came from the shadow ranch," Father John said. "There are thirty Indians there from a lot of other tribes."

The chief nodded. "Number one on our list of places to look. Gianelli went up there himself this morning." The chief opened a file folder and consulted a typed sheet. "Roy He-Dog and Martin Crow Elk. Nobody by those names at the shadow ranch." He shifted forward, the navy blue uniform shirt wrinkling over the broad shoulders. "You ask me, it's not looking good for Vicky."

"You can't be serious."

"I'm not saying she shot Ben. I'm just saying, it's not looking good. She's got motive." He paused. "We both know how Ben treated her. She had opportunity and . . ." Another pause. He cleared his throat. "Vicky shot a guy last year."

True. All true. Father John set an elbow on the armrest, and blew into his fist. A perfect example of logic that added up to nonsense. "She didn't shoot Ben," he said.

The chief threw out both hands. "Let's hope the evidence proves her innocent. Gianelli's tracing the gun now. Should have the results tomorrow."

"You've got to find the two ranch hands Ben had trouble with," Father John said. "They could be calling themselves something else. Sherwood calls himself Orlando."

The smallest shade of doubt came over the chief's face. "The fed checked IDs on all the dancers. You got evidence those Lakotas are hiding at the ranch? We'd need evidence to get a search warrant." He raised an eyebrow and gave him a look of caution. "Something more than just a gut feeling, John."

Father John shook his head and glanced toward the window. The afternoon sunlight looked gray in the dust-smeared pane. He didn't have any evidence. Just a gut feeling that things were wrong at the shadow ranch.

"We been watching the place for two months." Banner crossed his arms over his chest. "Ever since Sherwood came back. He's probably harmless. Brilliant kid, once upon a time. You ever know him?"

Father John shook his head. He'd never seen him at Mass. And eight years ago, when he'd organized the Eagles, Sherwood would have been too old for the team.

"Walked away with a lot of honors at Indian High. Went to college in Denver. Became some kind of computer whiz, I heard." The chief raised one hand and snapped his thick fingers. "Hiking up around Boulder and gets hit by lightning. Spends a month in a coma and becomes a new man. Calls himself Orlando now. God knows why. Never heard of any Arapaho Orlandos."

"He has an armed guard at the gate and at least two other guards around the village. The followers all look drugged."

This brought the chief forward. He picked up a pencil and began stabbing at a folder. "You talk to people up there?"

Father John nodded. "A couple guards. Orlando himself, and an Arapaho girl from Oklahoma, Janis Beaver."

"Anybody tell you they're being held against their will?"

"No." The girl had wanted to stay, he was thinking. She could have left with him—he would have found a way— but she was in love with Orlando.

"Well, that's a problem. We've got consenting adults up there. Point is, John. There's no proof otherwise, and folks have the right to live as they please, long as they don't break the law. The American way, right?" A mirthless smile came into the man's face. "They want to live in a mountain valley with some nutcase, well, that's their right."

Father John was quiet a moment. The click, click sound of computer keys came from down the corridor. "How do they live?"

"We asked the same question when Indians from other tribes started showing up on the rez asking for directions to the shadow dancers. Said they heard about Orlando on the Internet. So I drove up and paid a visit to Orlando. Turns out, he got severance pay from his company and disability insurance. He sends the dancers into Ethete and Fort Washakie every week. They preach and pass the collection baskets. Get a little money that way. Adds up to enough to feed people. They say they're gonna be self-sufficient, soon's the new world gets here. Got some buffalo. Planted a garden."

Banner shrugged, then went on: "Man didn't seem like the kid I remember, but I gotta admit, there's an intensity about him, and he's got that deep voice that sort of mesmerizes people. He claims he visited the shadow world. That gets people's attention. How come you went up there?"

Father John sat back and closed his eyes a moment. He'd assured Minnie Little Horse that he wouldn't talk to the police about Dean, and yet . . . Dean was missing; he'd been at the shadow ranch; and someone there—Janis? Orlando?—knew where the young man had gone.

"I'm trying to find Dean Little Horse," he said. He'd explain to Minnie later.

The chief tilted his head back and stared at him. "Dean's missing? We don't have a report."

Father John told the chief what he knew. Dean had been missing since last Thursday. He'd never had any trouble with the police. Minnie didn't want his name in the police files.

"Shit, John." Banner slammed a fist down, scattering a stack of papers. "Indian's missing, and nobody's looking for him except you? Minnie's got to get in here and file a report.

I'm gonna need everything she knows. Hell." He pulled a blank sheet of paper toward him. "I'm gonna start things rolling right now. What have you learned?"

Father John gave him the address of Dean's apartment and the Blue Crow Software Company, and the names of everybody he'd talked to, including Janis Beaver.

The chief's black scrawl covered half the page.

"Dean was at the shadow ranch recently," Father John went on. "I'm pretty sure Janis knows more than she was willing to tell me. She was looking for Dean on Sunday." He was quiet a moment. "Dean could be in danger."

The chief was still writing. "Ben Holden gets killed; Dean Little Horse goes missing. Two good men, John." He shook his head and laid the pen across the notepad. "Let's hope Dean's still alive. Maybe we'll get something out of Orlando, we lean on him enough. The shadow dancers are gonna get more attention than they want."

Father John got to his feet. He felt uneasy. Too much attention, and Orlando and his followers could feel threatened. There was no telling what a man who believed himself a prophet might do, if he felt threatened.

‹ 13 ›

The late afternoon sun beat down on the baseball field. The air was bright. In the distance, the white-peaked mountains rose against the sky like furious waves in the ocean, but the sky itself was as still as blue glass. The end of a perfect summer day, Father John thought, except that summer was officially a couple of weeks away. He stood behind third base, dripping with sweat. The Eagles looked good. The batters connecting, Howard Night knowing when to throw a fastball, when to throw a curve ball, the infielders chasing down grounders, and the outfielders shagging fly balls. Charlie Moss had hit a drive up the middle and sprinted to first, and Father John motioned up the next batter, his eye on Charlie. The kid was quick and smart. He had a good feel for the pitcher's delivery; he knew exactly when to run.

He was running now, head down, short legs pumping. Howard threw to the second baseman, but Charlie had already dived for the base.

"Safe." Eldon Antelope was on the side line, waving both hands overhead.

The batter struck out, and Father John motioned up the next kid. The breeze felt like a hot blow dryer on his arms and face. The sky was a brilliant blue, falling to the earth around them. Sometimes he had the illusion here, on the plains, that he was moving through the sky.

Out of the corner of his eye, Father John saw Vicky hunched on the bench behind home plate beside two of the mothers. Staring across the field, something different about her, something new mingling with the aura of bereavement, so that, even though she was only inches from the other women, she seemed completely alone. *Hisei ci nihi.* Woman Alone, the grandmothers called her.

How long had she been there? He'd been so intent on the game, he hadn't seen her arrive. He felt the same mild sense of surprise and gladness he'd felt the first time she'd appeared. Out of nowhere, standing in the doorway to his office: a slim figure; dark complexion and black hair smoothed away from her face; dark blue suit and white blouse; black bag hung over one shoulder.

The Arapaho lawyer, he remembered thinking, the subject of the gossip among the grandmothers at the senior women's meetings in Eagle Hall. Divorced a fine man like Ben Holden! Went off to Denver to become a *ho':xu'wu:ne'n.* Now she was back.

They hadn't said she was beautiful.

The batter sent the ball to center field and sprinted down the baseline. Charlie was heading home, head down, and then he was safe.

"All right!" Father John called. "That's it for today."

The kids hopped up and down, then started off the field in a run. They were good, and they knew it. "Listen up," he called, and began gathering a circle of brown faces with teeth too big for the mouths. "Practice on Thursday. What're we going to do Saturday morning?"

"Whip the Riverton Rangers."

"You got it."

"Clean up!" Eldon called. The man had already started stuffing the bats into green canvas bags, and the kids scattered about, gathering helmets, gloves, balls. Then the two mothers began herding several kids across the field to Circle Drive, where a line of pickups and old sedans were parked.

Father John walked over to Antelope. "Mind putting away the gear?"

The Indian glanced at the woman waiting on the bench, then motioned over two boys running across the field. "Nah. We'll take care of it, Father."

"Good practice," Vicky said when he sat down beside her. He wondered if she had taken in any of it.

"Any news?"

"Looks like Gianelli has a suspect." She kept her eyes ahead, and he followed her gaze across the deserted field, the path between second and third base worn into a gray line through the brown earth. The Indian man and boys dragging bags of equipment across Circle Drive headed toward the storage shed behind Eagle Hall. He wondered if she was registering the fact they were there. "Hugh Holden thinks I'm guilty," she said.

Now he understood. Hugh Holden had probably had a long meeting with Gianelli. Father John didn't say anything.

"Battered ex-wife, couldn't make a complete break from her ex without killing him," she went on, the words clipped and sharp.

"Gianelli doesn't have any evidence." He heard the counselor's note in his own voice, but it sounded slightly off-key, his own concern leaking through.

"You don't understand, John. Ben was shot with a twenty-two pistol. Anybody on the rez could own the gun. It could be traced to someone who knows me."

"Look," he said after a moment. "Gianelli will work out what really happened. You have to be patient."

She tipped her head back and gave a tight laugh that sounded like a cry. "You and Adam Lone Eagle," she said. "White man and Lakota on the same side."

"Who are you talking about?"

"The criminal lawyer in Casper I just hired." She tossed off the information absentmindedly, then rose from the bench and walked to the end. Her heels scraped at the dried ground.

"What does Lone Eagle say?"

Vicky wheeled around and stared at him, as if she were trying to recall whom they were talking about. Then she said, "Be patient. Sit tight, as if nothing has changed. Everything has changed, John. Whoever killed Ben could have intended to make it look like I'm guilty. I can't sit tight."

"Listen to me, Vicky," he began, but she interrupted.

"I have to find the two Lakota ranch hands. They're involved, John. I don't know how, but they're involved, I'm sure of it." She was pacing, back and forth, back and forth. "Ben was mad enough to kill them. I'm sure he threatened them in some way. Gianelli thinks they took off for Pine Ridge last week, but he's wrong. They're hiding somewhere." She gestured toward the plains rolling into the far distance.

"Arapahos aren't going to hide two guys involved in Ben Holden's murder."

"Whoever's hiding them doesn't believe they had anything to do with the murder. They'll be protected. Nobody's going to turn two Indians over to the FBI. Gianelli will never find them."

He stood up and set a hand on her arm, stopping her in place. Then he told her about the shadow ranch and about the possibility—he was acutely aware of the fact that he had no proof—that the Lakotas could be hiding there under assumed identities. He explained that he'd gone there looking for a young man who was missing, Dean Little Horse, and told her about the guards and the village and the dancers. He said he'd talked to Orlando himself and to one of the followers, Dean's girlfriend, an Arapaho from Oklahoma named Janis Beaver.

"Shadow ranch. I saw some of the followers in front of the tribal offices." Vicky was staring at some image in her mind. Finally she locked eyes with him again. "The Lakotas are cowboys, John. Why would they get mixed up with a crazy Indian like Orlando?"

"Gianelli went to the ranch this morning. He didn't find them . . ." Father John paused. He was already regretting telling her about the shadow ranch. The guard at the gate had a rifle.

"Listen, Vicky," he went on, still holding her shoulder. "I've talked to Banner. He's starting a search for Dean, and he's going to check on the shadow ranch again. If the Lakotas are there, Banner'll find them."

"I have to find them," she said. Then she started down the base line toward Circle Drive.

He caught up with her. "No, Vicky. Let Banner and Gianelli handle this. You don't know what the Lakotas had against Ben. You get close to them, they could come after you."

"You don't understand, John." She kept walking. "They killed Ben, and they're going to get away with it unless I find them. They're hiding on the rez somewhere. Ben found them. I can find them, too."

"It's not your investigation." He took hold of her arm and turned her toward him. It was then that he saw the moisture in her eyes.

"Ben was my husband once," she said. "And this is my life."

"Vicky." He held her name on his tongue a moment. "Then let me help you."

She pulled away from his grip and stepped backward, shaking her head. "You can't, John. You can't help me. Promise me you won't get involved."

"What are you saying?"

"Hugh Holden, all the Holdens think the same as Ben did. The only reason I didn't go back to Ben was . . ."

In her hesitation, he understood. He looked away a moment. Dear God, how obvious had his feelings for her been on the reservation? Had everyone seen his shadow self?

"Lucas and Susan will be with the Holdens," Vicky was saying. "They'll listen to all the lies Hugh tells them. If you help me, if we're seen together, my children will believe the lies."

Father John brought his eyes back to her. What she said was true, and he could see the force of it in the steady way she looked at him.

"You must promise me, John." Her voice was so soft that he had to bend toward her to hear.

He waited a moment, then he said, "I don't want anything to happen to you, Vicky. If you won't let me help you, then you have to promise me you won't put yourself in danger."

She smiled up at him. "Then we have a deal?" When he didn't say anything, she turned and started toward the Bronco. He walked alongside her, feeling a sense of helplessness. She was so small and vulnerable, and he knew her so well. Nothing would stop her from finding the cowboys who had killed her ex-husband.

They reached the Bronco, and he opened the door. He waited until she'd slid behind the wheel and started the engine. Then he closed the door and watched the Bronco spin out into the drive, rear tires spitting back sprays of gravel. The vehicle plunged into the tunnel of cottonwoods and turned onto Seventeen-Mile Road.

Gracious God, he prayed. Keep her safe. He felt a pang of regret as sharp as a pain over the promise he'd given her. If she were in danger, he knew, he would have to break the promise.

Vicky drove back to Lander through the quiet heat settling over the asphalt. She avoided Rendezvous Road, taking Highway 789 south, the long way, reaching Lander with the sun blazing over the mountains and exploding in her windshield.

A red sedan sat in her parking space behind the apartment building. She parked beside it and hurried up the outside stairs to the second floor. Here and there, lights twinkled behind the windows of the apartment building across the street.

From thirty feet away, she could see the door slightly ajar

at the end of the corridor. Hushed, familiar voices drifted through the opening.

She found Susan and Lucas slumped on the living room sofa, leaning back into the cushions for support, hands clasped in their laps. Vicki had asked the manager to let them in, should they arrive before she returned. She'd expected to be here first. Lucas must have held the pedal to the floor all the way from Denver.

He jumped to his feet and came around the coffee table toward her. It always took her breath away, the first time she saw her son, even if it were after an absence of only a few hours. He was so like Ben: tall and muscular and striking looking with chiseled features and black hair trimmed a little long. He wore faded blue jeans and a sporty gray shirt with the collar opened and sleeves rolled back, exposing thick brown forearms and capable hands.

And yet he was different from Ben, more at ease in the world that extended beyond the reservation. The corners of his mouth turned up in a smile, but he was looking at her out of deep-set brown eyes that still held the shock of his father's death.

"Hi, Mom," he said, encircling her in his arms.

When he let go, she turned to Susan, who was starting to get up, reluctance in the way she moved, her face rigid with grief and contempt.

Vicky reached out, took the girl's hand, and led her around the coffee table. Then she grasped her other hand and stood back, taking her in. She was looking in a mirror; the image that reflected back was her own, a lifetime ago. Her daughter had the same black, shoulder-length hair, parted in the middle, one side tucked behind her ear. Honey-colored skin, eyes like black agates shot through with light. Susan stood quite still, chest rising and falling beneath her pale blue T-shirt, hostility crackling about her. And yet, beneath the hostility, Vicky recognized the vulnerability, the *unformedness*. A chill ran through her at the thought of a man—a man like Ben—honing in on the unformedness and taking Susan over.

She pulled the girl closer—she was small and thin; the knobs of her spine poked through her shirt—not wanting to let her go, but Susan slipped free and dropped back onto the sofa. "It's the end of our family," she said, "now that Dad's dead. He was the only one trying to hold us together. He was the only one who cared. We don't have a family now."

"That isn't true," Vicky said. She was thinking, We have a sad, hurting family.

Lucas sat down beside his sister. "Do you know yet what happened?" Emotion surged beneath the calm surface of his voice.

She began explaining: The local FBI agent was handling the investigation. She was sure he'd make an arrest soon. (God, she could be the one arrested.) She pulled over a small side chair and sat across the coffee table from her children— hers and Ben's—twenty-two and twenty-four years old now. "Your father"—she chose the words carefully—"had a very important job running the ranch. He had a lot of responsibility. He was a strong man. He could have made enemies."

"You think somebody from the ranch killed him?" This from Susan, the anguish so palpable around her that Vicky had to check herself to keep from reaching out to shove it away.

"It's possible."

"The fed's checking on everybody Dad worked with?" Lucas, now.

Vicky nodded. She hoped that was the case.

Susan shifted forward until her knees knocked against the edge of the coffee table. "Uncle Hugh says you saw Dad just before he was killed."

Vicky was quiet a moment. "I don't know what Hugh might have told you, but . . ." God, the lies Hugh could have told her children.

"You got in a fight with Dad!" Anger and shock laced Susan's voice. "The last night of his life, and you were shouting at him in a restaurant."

"Hugh's very upset." Vicky held her daughter's eyes. "He's looking for someone to blame."

"You hated Dad! You wanted him dead!" Susan propelled herself to her feet, and Lucas rose beside her, an arm going around his sister's shoulders.

"Take it easy, Susan," he said, a soothing tone, rational.

Vicky stood up. She felt as if she were stumbling, being driven through an endless field. It was true. She had wanted Ben out of her life. Some part of her, a shadow that she didn't want to acknowledge, had willed him dead—and the truth of it lashed at her like a whip.

"Listen, Mom." Lucas waved his other hand toward her. "We'd better be going. We can talk later."

"Going?" she managed, the word clinging to her tongue. "I thought you'd stay here. There's an extra bedroom, and Susan can sleep in my bed." She'd thought Susan could sleep with her. "I'll take the sofa."

"I wouldn't stay in this place . . ."

"Enough, Susan," Lucas said, a new firmness in his tone. "I think you've said enough." He guided his sister around the coffee table and across the room. Glancing back, he said, "I'll call you tomorrow, Mom." Then they were through the door, the sounds of their footsteps receding down the carpeted corridor.

Vicky sank back into her chair. She felt that she would choke on the acid in her mouth. The kids would go to Hugh. Her children, absorbed into the Holden clan, Ben's people, blaming her, blaming her. And Gianelli. She'd always thought of the agent as a good investigator. She laughed out loud, startled at the sound; it was like a cry. A good investigator who would turn everything Hugh Holden said against her.

‹ 14 ›

Father John stood at the window in his office and listened to the buzzing sound of a phone ringing across the reservation. In the last five minutes two pickups had come around Circle Drive and stopped near the alley between the administration building and the church. Three members of the parish council had climbed out and headed down the alley toward Eagle Hall. Now a rusted orange pickup swung in alongside the others. The door opened and a knobbed stick, cut from a tree branch, stabbed the ground. Amos Walking Bear gripped the top of the stick and swung his massive weight out of the cab. Bent over, slowly picking his way with the stick like a blind man, he started down the alley.

The phone stopped buzzing.

"Hello?" It was Minnie Little Horse. She sounded out of breath, distracted.

He told her he'd talked to a few people about Dean. The exclamation of joy and relief that shot through the line made him wince. He didn't have good news.

"Listen, Minnie." He said that he'd already talked to Banner and that the chief had started a search for Dean.

Silence shaped by fear and grief filled the line. Finally the woman said, "We didn't wanna bring in the police."

"It's time, Minnie," he said. It was past time, he was thinking. He wanted to assure her that Dean had gone someplace, was hiding for some reason, but he didn't believe it. Instead, he told her that the chief was going to need her help.

He heard the sigh at the other end. Then the woman agreed to call Banner, and he set the receiver in place, a sense of inevitability pressing around him. Five days now. No one had seen Dean Little Horse in five days.

He dialed Gianelli's office again and left another message. Then he dialed the man's home. They'd been friends once. He thought of the agent as a friend. He'd had Sunday dinner not long ago at the agent's home. Spaghetti and meatballs and everybody talking at once—Ted and his wife and four little daughters who had somehow become teenagers—and he and Ted trying to stump each other on opera trivia. He hated to admit that Gianelli probably knew more about opera than he did.

"Agent Gianelli." The familiar voice was on the other end.

"I've been trying to reach you," Father John said. Then he told him about his visit to the shadow ranch. "The Lakota ranch hands could be hiding there," he said.

"We checked everybody's ID this morning. Nobody there named Roy He-Dog or Martin Crow Wolf."

"They could be using other names."

"We've got every law enforcement agency in Wyoming and South Dakota looking for those two Lakotas. We'll get them, John, and when we do, we're probably gonna find out that . . ." He paused.

"What?"

"That they left the rez before Ben Holden was killed. If they had trouble with Holden, it wouldn't have been smart for them to hang around."

"Vicky says they were still on the rez—"

The agent cut in. "That's what she'd like us to believe. I got the Holden clan on my tail. Hugh Holden thinks he knows who killed his brother."

"For godssake, Ted. Vicky didn't kill Ben."

Gianelli cleared his throat, a low, rumbling noise. "I don't want to think so. I have to go wherever the evidence takes me."

"The shadow dancers are on some kind of drugs," Father John said, trying another tack. "Dean Little Horse was there a few days ago. Now he's missing. Look, Ted . . ."

"No, you look, John. You think we aren't keeping a close eye on Orlando and the rest of the nuts up there? We can't go swooping down and close up the place without hard evidence. We find evidence they're harboring two Lakotas we want to talk to about a homicide, we find evidence they've got illegal drugs, we'll be all over them. Stick to your pastoring, John, and let me do my job."

The line went dead. Father John set the receiver in the cradle. His muscles felt tense and cramped. He knew the pattern. Gianelli: proceeding in a rational, logical order. And all the time, Vicky, out there alone somewhere looking for two killers. Dear God, he thought. She could find the killers before Gianelli did.

It took a few minutes to get his thoughts back to the mission. He collected the stapled copies of the annual report, the notes he'd made this morning. Then he turned off the desk lamp and walked over to Eagle Hall.

Seated on straight-back chairs arranged in a semicircle were four members of the parish council: Elvira and Justice Burns, Dave Buck, Amos Walking Bear. Four out of ten, Father John thought. Not even a quorum.

"Just about to start the meeting without you." Father George sat a few feet apart, facing the others, gripping a stack of papers.

Father John hooked a chair and pulled it over next to Amos, who turned stiffly and extended a bear-paw hand. "How ya doin', Father?" he said. His other hand cupped the top of the walking stick. He was in his seventies, with wispy gray hair and a broad face with hooded black eyes and heavy jowls. Behind the man's flat expression, Father John caught a look of reassurance. His assistant was wrong; the meeting wouldn't have started without the pastor. Nothing started until the time was right and everyone was ready.

Father John handed the reports to Amos, who removed the top copy and passed the others. Father George had already started copies of the financial reports from the other end. Minutes passed. Eyes floated over the stapled pages. The hall was quiet, except for the occasional sound of rustling papers.

"I believe it's clear"—Father George snapped his copies against one thigh—"the mission's debts have risen steadily over the past year. Income is sporadic. Last quarter, donations fell by half."

"Donations usually increase in the summer with tourists

coming to Mass," Father John began, but the other priest was shaking his head.

"The point is, we never know when the money might come in. We can't rely on miracles."

Father John stopped himself from saying that St. Francis Mission had operated on miracles for more than a hundred years. It was not the argument he needed for the board of directors this weekend.

"Excuse me, Father." Amos placed both hands over the stick and hoisted his shoulders forward toward Father George. The others turned, watching the elder. "Could you tell us what you're getting at?"

Father George cleared his throat. "The board of directors must consider the complete financial picture. It would be irresponsible to overlook the numbers. We may have to reallocate our resources."

"You mean close the mission." The old man sat back and glanced at Father John. "What do you say, Father?"

"I don't want to close St. Francis." *Dear Lord, how could we close the mission?* He glanced at the other council members: two men thumbing through the pages, as if they might discover better numbers; Elvira looking straight ahead, lips drawn into a tight line. "I won't have the final say," he managed.

Amos kept his gaze on him a moment, then turned back to the other priest. "Where the kids gonna get Catholic instruction? Where's the AA gonna meet? Who's gonna visit when we get sick? Where we gonna have Mass?"

"There are fine Catholic parishes in Lander and Riverton," Father George said.

Silence. The Indians were staring at the other priest. Finally, Elvira said, "This is our mission, been here since the

Old Time 'cause that's the way the chiefs wanted it."

"Look," Father John began. He could almost smell the tension. "You're welcome to come to the board meeting. You can tell them about the programs."

"The directors know about the programs," Father George said.

"We're gonna be there." Justice nodded toward the others. "Trouble is, rest of the council's got a lot going on right now."

One by one, the Indians rose to their feet, Justice and David retrieving cowboy hats from vacant chairs, tucking folded reports in jeans pockets; Elvira gathering up the floppy bag she'd set on the floor. Only four council members to speak up for the mission, and this, a number's game.

Father John took Amos's arm to help steady the old man and walked him to the door. The stick thumped on the hard floor. Behind them, he could hear Father George folding and stacking the chairs.

Outside, Father John said, "Do you have a few minutes?"

The hooded eyes glanced sideways at him. The old man nodded, and they turned around the corner to the administration building.

Amos Walking Bear *inhabited* the side chair: thick legs spread apart, forearms covering the armrests, one hand curled over the top of the walking stick. "That white man"—he gestured with his large head toward the rear office—"ain't the first thinks he's gonna close this place down. Him and those directors coming here from other places don't understand. Good things come down to us from the past, we gotta hold on to 'em."

Father John hoped that would be the case. He moved the other chair around and sat down facing the old man. "Couple of things I'd like to talk to you about, grandfather." He heard the suppliant tone in his voice. Here, in the office, he counseled other people; now he needed counseling.

The old man nodded. "I seen the worry following you around like a shadow. You thinking about Ben Holden's murder."

"Vicky could be indicted."

"Holden clan turned against her long time ago." The old man hunched over and shook his head. "They don't like to admit Ben Holden might've made himself some enemies. Sure, he got respect 'cause he handed out a lot of jobs. But he got to strutting around like he owned the rez. Ordering folks about. Not our way." He shook his head. "Somebody could've gotten fed up."

Somebody else, Father John thought. Not Vicky. He said, "Vicky says he had trouble with a couple of Lakotas who stole something from the ranch. She thinks they could be involved, but the fed says they left the rez a week ago."

Amos threw his head back and guffawed. "Only time the fed probably got it right. They stole from Ben Holden, most likely they lit out of here like lightning before he could get a hold of 'em."

Father John glanced toward the doorway. A shaft of light from the desk lamp flowed into the corridor, pushing through the shadows. Vicky was so certain Ben had seen the Lakotas yesterday. And this afternoon, at the shadow ranch— so many Indians from other places. And yet, Gianelli had gone to the ranch. He hadn't found the Lakotas.

Father John drew in a long breath. He was chasing shadows. He told Amos about his visit to the ranch and said he'd been trying to find Dean Little Horse.

"I hear he went missing." The old man sat very still. "You think he's following Sherwood?"

He said he didn't think so. "Dean's girlfriend is at the ranch. She called him an unbeliever because he refuses to accept Orlando as a prophet."

Amos began tapping out a steady rhythm on the floor with his cane. He was quiet a moment, then he said, "Wovoka, now he was a prophet, and the Ghost Dance he brought to the people, that's a good part of our tradition. Helped the people back in the Old Time when we didn't have nothing. Gave people hope."

Tap. Tap. Tap. "Wovoka came along and said if people do the Ghost Dance every six weeks for four days, the old world will come back like it was. Now Sherwood comes along. Says he died, went into the shadow land, and become Wovoka's spiritual son. Says Wovoka give him a new name, Orlando, and told him to go back to this world and preach the old religion." He paused, and in the creases of the old man's face, Father John saw the geography of pain passed down through the generations. "Maybe Indians up at the shadow ranch don't have nothing else to hold on to. Maybe they need hope for a little while, just like the people in the Old Time."

"They have armed guards at the ranch," Father John said. "The woman are being used sexually."

The cane knocked harder on the floor. "Indians won't put up with it for long. Soon's they see the new world ain't gonna be in this world, they're gonna find a way to get out of there." The old man shifted toward Father John. "Ghost Dance religion ended soon's people lost heart. They seen nothing was gonna change in this world, and they stopped dancing. Same thing's gonna happen with the shadow dancers. Let 'em be, Father. Sometimes people need a little hope, even if they're gonna be disappointed."

Father John walked the old man out to his truck, the last vehicle still parked in front of Eagle Hall. He waited until Amos had climbed behind the steering wheel and turned on the engine. Puffs of black smoke belched from the tailpipe as the truck made a U-turn, then lurched along Circle Drive. He started up the front stoop, the taillights blinking like red fireflies through the cottonwoods.

The building had settled into evening, shadows splayed over the corridor and across the office. In the silence, a dripping pipe, the creak of old wood. Father John searched the bookcase behind his desk, pulled out a large red-bound volume, with *History of the Plains Indians* printed in black across the top.

He sat down and opened the book. The pages were worn and dog-eared, marked with stick-ons and torn pieces of paper. There were checkmarks penciled in the margins alongside paragraphs that he'd wanted to be able to locate quickly. He flipped to the index, found "Ghost Dance," and turned to the page indicated.

Across the page: the photograph of a middle-aged Indian, with a frowning, somber expression seated on a chair draped in a buffalo robe. The camera flash had laid down a strip of light, like an interrupted halo, across his black hair, which was parted to the side and cut straight below his ears, like Orlando's. He wore a black vest buttoned over a white long-sleeved shirt. An arm band above his right elbow held an eagle feather that rose toward his shoulder. A white scarf was tied at his neck. Beneath the photo, in bold type: WO-VOKA, 1889.

Father John skimmed through an excerpt from *The Ghost Dance Religion*, written more than a century before by James Mooney, an anthropologist:

> *Sitting or lying around the fire were half a dozen Paiute, including the messiah and his family, consisting of his young wife, a boy about four years of age, of whom he seemed very fond, and an infant. It was plain that he was a kind husband and father.*
>
> *He had given the dance to his people after he received his great revelation. He fell asleep in the daytime and was taken up to the other world. Here he saw God, with all the people who had died long ago engaged in their oldtime sports and occupations, all happy and forever young. It was a pleasant land and full of game. After showing him all, God told him he must go back and tell his people they must be good and love one another, have no quarreling, and live in peace with the whites; that they must work, and not lie or steal; that if they faithfully obeyed his instructions they would at last be reunited with their friends in this other world, where there would be no more death.*

Father John skimmed the following pages. The Ghost Dance religion had spread across the plains. Cheyenne, Lakota, Arapaho, all the tribes crowded onto reservations, a vast expanse of the prairies gone, the buffalo slaughtered, the warriors dying, the children hungry. For two years, the people danced in hope of the new world and then—as Amos had said—they had given up hope and stopped dancing.

Except for Big Foot's band.

He thumbed through the pages until he came to the section on the massacre at Wounded Knee, South Dakota, in the freezing December of 1890. The last of the Ghost Dancers, led by Chief Big Foot, trying to outrun the Seventh Cavalry—Custer's regiment, bent on revenge, shouting, "Remember the Little Big Horn!" When the Hotchkiss guns were finally silent, more than two hundred people lay dying in the snow.

There were photos. He studied the grainy, black and white pictures for several minutes: brown humps of human bodies scattered across the frozen prairie, the narrow trench where the bodies were buried, stacked like cordwood. A priest, a Jesuit, had been with the band. He had gone among the dead and dying, blessing them, comforting them, until he had lost consciousness from his own wounds.

Father John closed the book and sat for a long time, staring into the shadows. The Ghost Dance religion had ended in catastrophe. And now, Orlando, calling himself the prophet, the son of Wovoka, was preaching his own version of the old religion.

He couldn't shake off the feeling that it would end the same way.

The morning seemed unnaturally still, the sun burning yellow through the blue sky, the day's heat already settling in. There were few vehicles on the highway, and Vicky eased up on the accelerator and leaned into the curves alongside the Wind River. Past Boysen Reservoir, north into the Wind River Canyon. Rock-strewn hills with thin stands of pines and sagebrush rolled past. The river dwindled to a narrow creek, stained brown by the muddy sludge beneath the surface.

She'd left instructions with Esther to call Norm Weedly at the tribal offices and arrange for her to meet with the JBC later. Later. The idea stabbed at her like a needle. The Wind River could dry up in the hot weather. She should be in the office now, refining her arguments for the tribal council, carrying on as if nothing had changed, the way Adam had advised.

She slowed through Thermopolis, then turned west along the edge of the Owl Creek mountains. She could imagine the gossip buzzing over the moccasin telegraph, dredging up her past—hers and Ben's. How could she talk to the business council about cleaning up the river? The council members, seated behind the curved desk on a platform—nodding, nodding—wondering if she was a murderer. As long as Gianelli and everybody else suspected her, Ben's killer would be free. She swallowed back the knot of tears in her throat. Ben—the man she'd once loved, the father of her children—Ben deserved justice.

Through the filters of junipers, she glimpsed the log bunkhouse at the Arapaho Ranch, the peaked red roof burning in the sun. She let up on the accelerator, turned right, and thumped across the cattle guard, then followed a narrow road another half-mile. Dust rising from beneath the tires laid a thin gray film over the windshield.

She parked close to the bunkhouse. A cowboy—black cowboy hat pushed back—stood on the narrow porch that ran along the front, eyes squinting in the sunlight, one thumb hooked into the belt of his blue jeans. His other hand cupped a cigarette backward, so that the smoke curled along the sleeve of his blue shirt.

She got out and walked up the wood steps. "Where can I find Don Redman?" she said.

"He don't wanna see you." The man's voice was raspy, smoke-filled. He hadn't taken his eyes off her.

Vicky gestured toward the barns and ranch offices beyond the bunkhouse. "He in the office?"

The cowboy lifted the cigarette to his lips and took a long drag. Then he blew the smoke in her direction.

"Look," Vicky said, "whoever you are . . ."

"Friend of Ben's. He's got a lotta friends here. You better not hang around."

The screened door banged opened. Redman, Ben's right-hand man, stepped onto the porch and gave her a nod of recognition. He was big, middle-aged, with the slumped shoulders of a man who'd spent years in a saddle and permanent squint lines around his eyes from staring into the wind. A year ago, Ben had brought Don Redman to her office. She couldn't remember the reason, only that Redman had sat in the waiting room while the Ben she'd hated at times had railed at her in the private office about something she'd done or hadn't done. And that—how ironic, she thought now—was when she had believed that she and Ben might get back together.

She asked if she could have a few words.

Redman hesitated, arms dangling at his sides, brown hands clenching and unclenching. Finally he opened the door. "Inside," he said, the thin lips barely moving.

She crossed the porch, walking past the cowboy, and followed Redman into the spacious room that ran along the front. On the left, sofas and chairs draped with Indian blankets and a big-screen TV. On the right, kitchen cabinets that wrapped around a long table with scrub marks across the top and chairs pushed against the sides.

The manager nodded toward a chair and waited until she'd sat down. "Men are pretty torn up about Ben's murder," he said, taking the chair across from her. "Best foreman we ever had. Knew how to run the ranch, all right. Bought quality bulls, crossbred the stock, and produced calves with heavier wean weights. Not to mention, he grew the herd to the highest number ever. Put the Arapaho Ranch on the map, you might say. Got a reputation for being one of the best in Wyoming. Men are gonna miss Ben."

He pulled his mouth into a disapproving line and shook his head. "Fed come around yesterday, asking a lot of questions. Lot of questions about you."

Vicky felt a knot tighten in her stomach. *She did not have to defend herself. She was not guilty.* "I'm trying to find the ranch hands Ben fired last week," she said.

"He-Dog, Crow Elk." The man tapped a stained finger on the table top. "Only mistake Ben might've made, hiring those bastards, but we needed the extra hands. Ben had a lot of work lined up, what with you and him getting back together. Started building a couple rooms onto his cabin." He tossed his head in the direction of the cabin tucked among the trees. "Blasted out a new road and was gonna blast out some more trees for a pond. Said you were gonna keep a pony up there. Said you were gonna have your choice of the best pony in the corral."

"Where are the Lakotas?" She ignored the invitation in the man's eyes to keep the conversation on Ben.

Redman let out a short breath. "Pine Ridge, my guess. Took off with the bank bag . . ."

"They stole money?" Ben hadn't mentioned money.

"Cash and checks. Ben had 'em ready to take to the bank in Thermopolis. Bag was on the desk, time he told the Lakotas to pack their gear and get off the ranch. Didn't turn his back more'n a minute, and the bag was gone. So were the Lakotas."

A sense of relief washed over her like a cool blast of air. Vicky leaned back against her chair. So this was why Ben had been so angry. The ranch hands had stolen the bank bag from under his nose. He would have tracked them down, threatened to report them to the fed. But he wouldn't have *wanted* to report other Indians. He would have handled the matter himself. Return the money, he would have told them. No questions asked. Case closed. If they didn't—they would have understood—he would smash in their faces, then report them.

It made sense. It explained why the ranch hands had waited for him on Rendezvous Road.

But there was another possibility. Vicky looked away. The knot in her stomach felt like lead. It could also explain why the Lakotas would have left for Pine Ridge before Ben was shot.

And yet . . . Ben had met them that afternoon, she was sure. He had known where to find them.

She felt a path opening ahead, if she could only reach it. She clasped her hands over the table. "What else can you tell me?"

"Forget it, Vicky. Those guys are gone. They got the money and took off." Something caught his attention— boots clumping across the porch—and he scooted his chair back and glanced out the front window.

Vicky followed his gaze. Men in cowboy hats, backlit by the sunlight, moved like shadows beyond the glass. She was aware now of the low murmur of voices. She said, "Did the Lakotas have relatives on the rez?"

Redman shifted back toward her. "You and the fed ask the same questions. Possible, I guess. They came and went as they pleased around here. Couldn't depend on 'em. Maybe visiting relatives. How do I know?" He shrugged. "Ben didn't like their ways. Had a couple arguments, gave 'em warnings. Trouble is, we were shorthanded. Finally he decided to let 'em go. Not soon enough, you ask me. Nobody liked 'em. Kept to themselves. Acted high and mighty, like they had some special power nobody else had. Lakotas!"

"They shot Ben," Vicky said after a moment.

Redman looked skeptical. "That's what you want the fed

to think." He glanced over his shoulder at the window. The sounds of boots pounding and scraping the floor and the murmur of voices drifted through the log walls.

Vicky kept her eyes on the man across from her. "I want the fed to find Ben's murderers."

Redman stood up and leaned over the table. "I don't know what went down out on Rendezvous Road." He hesitated. "But I know you had reason . . ."

Vicky jumped to her feet and locked eyes with him, daring him to recount her life to her: Ben's drinking, the beatings, the day she'd finally mustered up enough courage to take the kids to her mother and drive to Denver in a rusted-out Chevy with the reverse gear shot.

The man glanced away. "Ben getting involved with that white woman and all."

"What!" She felt as if she'd taken a blow in the face. "What white woman?"

He laughed and shook his head. "Don't tell me you don't know."

She started laughing, too. She had to hold her hand over her mouth against the rising sense of hysteria. How like Ben! Pleading with her to come back to him. *We'll be a family again.* And all the time, there was another woman.

"What's the woman's name?" She didn't care, she told herself. "She might know about the Lakotas."

Something different came into the man's eyes, as if he'd caught an unexpected glimpse of her, and in that glimpse had seen the determination to find Ben's killer. "Came to the ranch once. Blond hair, real pale face, big blue eyes. She's a looker. Stayed with Ben up at his cabin."

Vicky crossed to the window, struggling to calm the mixture of irony and grief that churned inside her. The little cabin nestled in the pines. Quiet and remote. *We'll be a family again.*

She stepped back. Outside, cowboys were shouldering together on the porch, crowding the steps. A couple of cowboys ran across the open field toward the bunkhouse, carrying coils of thick rope. All the hands gathering, all convinced of her guilt.

She turned back to the man watching her from across the table. "Her name, Redman. I have to know her name."

"Nobody around here poked into Ben's business."

"Did you tell the fed about her?"

"Wasn't his business. I ain't saying nothing that hurts Ben's reputation. He was a good man."

He was a bastard, she thought. A handsome, charming, manipulative bastard, but . . . She closed her eyes and took in a long breath. He didn't deserve to be murdered.

She started for the door.

"Hold on." The man's footsteps scraped the floor. He stepped between her and the door. "Let me see what's going on out there."

He cracked the door open. The voices outside went quiet. And then, someone shouted: "Where is she? Bring her out here. What's she got to say for herself?"

Redman slammed the door. "Looks like we got ourselves a lynch mob."

The room started to close in around her, hot and bright and airless. The buzz of voices came from far away. Her mouth felt dry. "I can't hide here forever," she said. "They think I killed Ben. I have to convince them they're wrong."

"You don't get it." Redman kept one hand flattened against the door, as if he might prevent it from bursting open. "Ben was the chief. We respected him. We would've followed him into fire, and now he's dead. They're riled up enough to kill whoever did it."

He lowered his head, a bull gathering strength for the charge. "Wait here." He flung open the door, stepped outside, and slammed the door behind him. His voice sounded hollow and distant through the log walls. "We don't want no more trouble around here. Ben's killer is gonna be arrested and convicted. He's gonna pay in the regular way."

"*She's* gonna pay our way." It was the raspy voice of the cowboy on the porch when she'd arrived. What had he done? Run back to the barn and office? Shouting, *She's here! Ben's killer!*

Vicky yanked open the door and stepped onto the porch.

"There she is!" the raspy voice yelled.

‹ 16 ›

Vicky stared at the wall of cowboy shirts and blue jeans blocking her path to the steps and the Bronco below. The air crackled with hostility. Masculine smells of leather, perspiration, and tobacco clogged her nostrils. Most of the cowboys looked Arapaho. Her own people! A few familiar faces among them. Dark eyes stared back at her from beneath the brims of cowboy hats. Expressions were fixed, unreadable. The men seemed to breathe in unison, with long exhalations that sounded like the air hissing out of tires.

"Let's make room." Redman shouldered his way into the crowd, but the cowboys closed around him.

"Let me pass." Vicky started across the porch, aware of the stifling heat, her blouse damp against her back. The cowboy with the raspy voice blocked her way.

"Why'd you kill Ben?"

She looked up into a brown face ignited with hatred. The silver snaps down the front of his yellow shirt glinted in the light.

"How dare you," she said, fighting for the implacable

courtroom voice that masked the sense of being on a precipice, the abyss yawning around her.

"Tell us the truth." A bassoon voice emerged from the shadows by the railing. "You hire somebody to shoot him?"

"Get out of my way." Vicky tried to sidestep the yellow shirt.

"Let her through," Redman shouted from over by the steps, but his voice was lost in the roar of voices that pressed around her.

"Ben wouldn't be dead, weren't for you."

"What happened, Vicky?"

She tried again to dodge past the heavy male bodies, but they formed a phalanx in front of her. She stepped back, trying to clear a little space. "I know Ben was your boss," she began, choosing the words, adjusting the inflections by the faintest twitch in the brown faces, the way she delivered a summation to a jury when her client's future depended on the impact. "You respected Ben. You loved him." She paused, giving them time to absorb the idea, reconnect with some lighter part of themselves. "I loved him, too," she said.

"You're lying." The yellow shirt leaned toward her. She could feel little pricks of spittle on her cheeks.

"I loved him once," she said. "You're forgetting Ben was the father of my children. I did not kill the father of my children." There, she'd said it again. She'd vowed she would not defend herself from something she hadn't done, but she'd said it.

A half-second passed. No one spoke. The breathing seemed quieter, resigned. The cowboy in the yellow shirt stepped to the side. "Time we head out for Ben's wake," he said, his voice cracking with smoke.

One by one, the other cowboys rearranged themselves on

either side of the porch until she could see down a narrow corridor to the top of the steps where Redman was beckoning her forward.

She kept her eyes straight ahead, not wanting to unhinge the brief pardon she'd received, and followed the man down the steps to the Bronco. Her hand shook over the door handle, the ignition. Finally the engine burst into life, and she drove toward the ranch entrance, vaguely aware of the shadows moving in the rearview mirror.

Not until she'd crossed the cattle guard did she feel her heart begin to return to its regular rhythm. She sped east, her thoughts on the white woman. She would be beautiful. Young and beautiful, that was certain. There had been a beautiful twenty-something in Ben's life a couple years ago. Another thing was certain: The white woman lived somewhere in the area. Ben never liked too much inconvenience with his affairs.

The roofs of Thermopolis shone through the trees ahead. She slowed through town, then sped up again on the highway south. Ben's wake was at Blue Sky Hall this evening. You're not welcome, Hugh Holden had told her. But Lucas and Susan would be there and, she resolved, so would she. The kids might need her.

It struck her that the white woman might also be there.

Father John reached across the desk and picked up the phone on the first ring. He felt a stab of impatience at the sound of a man's voice—another parishioner wanting to know about Ben Holden's wake. Father John told him what he'd heard. Blue Sky Hall, eight o'clock. No, he wouldn't be

holding the service. The family wanted a traditional ceremony. Amos Walking Bear was in charge.

A trace of bewilderment worked into the voice at the
other end of the line. Ben Holden. Such a big man. He'd
expected a man like Ben Holden would be buried from the
mission.

So would the board of directors, Father John thought,
setting the receiver in place. He was already steeling himself
for the questions and the sly comments masked as criticism.
Explain, Father O'Malley, how you expect to attract Arapahos to Catholicism when a leading man, like Holden, is
buried in the traditional manner? Should we, perhaps, direct
our resources to places where we may expect a higher degree
of success?

Father John went back to work on the changes he'd made
in the annual report. He'd added a new section on the programs he hoped to start: day care and senior care; tutoring
center for elementary kids; lay ministry for the sick and
shut-ins. Above the section, he'd written: *St. Francis Mission
in the Future.* Now he drew a black line through the title.
Too grand and hopeful. He didn't want to alienate the directors. He wrote: *Proposals.*

He stuffed the loose sheets of paper inside the file folder,
then picked up the phone again and dialed Minnie Little
Horse's number. He'd been trying to reach the old woman
all morning and hoping each time the phone rang that she
was calling with news about Dean.

The buzzing noise continued. Minnie and Louise were
probably at Banner's office, still providing names, addresses—which meant, he realized, that there was no news.
Day six now, and Dean was still missing.

He grabbed the folder and strode down the corridor toward the source of computer keys clicking in the quiet. Father George was hunched over the monitor. The other priest glanced up, then sat back in his chair and began flexing his hands, like a pianist before a concert. "How's the report?"

Father John set the folder on the desk. "I think it's finished." He hoped he'd included everything, every possible reason to continue St. Francis Mission.

"Not a moment too soon."

His assistant had that right. The bishop would be pulling into Circle Drive at any moment; the directors would arrive tomorrow. The opening meeting was set for tomorrow night, and the tone for the weekend would be established.

Father George went on: "I'll make the changes and print out copies." His eyebrows came together in a concentrated line, and Father John realized that the man loved playing the keys, bringing the words to life on the screen, like a conductor calling forth the notes of the symphony in his mind.

"I must say, John"—now the other priest was rotating his shoulders and rolling his head—"you've advanced some strong arguments on behalf of the mission. However . . ."

Father John raised both hands. He didn't want to hear again about allocating resources and quantifying data. He pulled a metal chair next to the desk, straddled it backward, and rested his arms over the top.

"You were right about the shadow dancers," he said. "I went to the ranch yesterday."

The other priest's eyebrows shot up. "You went up there?"

He was looking for somebody, Father John said, tossing off the explanation. He didn't want to elaborate. Looking for a missing Arapaho probably wasn't the kind of thing the directors thought the pastor of St. Francis Mission should be doing.

He nodded toward the monitor. "Can you find the website?"

"If it's there, I can find it." Father George shifted forward and moved the mouse around the gray pad next to the keyboard. The screen began to change; columns of figures gave way to a maze of graphics and text with icons across the top and down the sides. Click. Click.

"Here we go," he said. The screen started to scroll and a photo of Orlando came into focus: long, white robe; straight black hair cut below the ears; eyes uplifted; hands outstretched.

Father John leaned closer and read the text.

Prepare yourself for the new world. The great event will sweep away all evil and destroy the oppressors of Indian people. The ancestors will walk among us once again. I, Orlando, the son of Wovoka, have gone into the shadow land and heard the words of my father. What Hesana'nin has promised will come to pass.

"How many followers so far?" Father George clicked on the mouse.

"About thirty, I'd guess." Another photo flashed onto the screen. Father John recognized the Charles Russell painting of a village in the Old Time. White tipis rising against the clear blue sky. A mountain meadow with streams carving through the wild grasses. Buffalo grazing in the distance. Children playing a stick game; women tending to iron kettles hung on tripods over the campfires; men lounging by the tipis, carving arrowheads, bending branches into bows.

A lodgepole stood in the middle of the village, a black crow perched on the top.

"So this is paradise." Father George clicked the mouse again. A map of the Wind River Reservation covered the screen. A black line traced the winding road into the mountains, a black circle outlined the ranch. Another click and the map was replaced by a photo of Orlando seated cross-legged inside a tipi, arms outstretched. The banner across the top read: JOIN THE SAVED AT THE SHADOW RANCH. COME TO ME.

"There's your strong, charismatic male leader." Father George tapped the screen. "Preaching an apocalyptic religion organized around core beliefs. Believers are cut off from families and friends in a secluded area." He swiveled toward Father John. "The classic attributes of a cult, just as I've been telling you. I say we denounce Orlando from the pulpit on Sunday."

Father John stared at the photo on the monitor. Orlando looked younger, more robust, a larger version of the frail, sick man he'd seen doubled over in a fit of coughing.

He said, "I spoke with Amos Walking Bear. The elder thinks the followers will drift away when they realize the new world isn't coming, just as the Ghost Dancers finally lost heart."

Except for Chief Big Foot's band, he was thinking, trudging through the snow, still clinging to Wovoka's message, with the horror moving toward them, like a storm darkening over the mountains.

"We have an obligation to guide our parishioners . . ." Father George hesitated. "As long as we're here."

The other priest was right. The armed guards, the women huddled in the tipis, and Dean Little Horse, the unbeliever, were missing. Father John couldn't shake the unsettled feeling that had clung to him since he'd driven out of the ranch, as if some nameless force were approaching that couldn't be turned back.

"I'll talk to Amos about calling a parish meeting."

"Meeting?"

"Amos and the other elders can explain the old Ghost Dance religion and the fact that Wovoka preached peace and forgiveness. They can help the people understand the difference between a man like Wovoka and . . ." He swallowed hard. "A prophet like Orlando."

Father George sat back in his chair, rested his elbows on the armrest and steepled his hands together under his chin. "Maybe I'm missing something," he began, "but it seems to me that Wovoka proclaimed the end of the world, just like Orlando. Sounds like the same apocalyptic message."

"Not the same, George. Wovoka urged Indians to live good lives and work hard for their people while they waited for the new world. Orlando . . ." Father John glanced away a moment, the images of the shadow ranch imprinted in his mind. "Orlando has armed guards on the ranch. The dancers looked drugged, and he's taking advantage of the women. Wovoka believed a new and better world would come eventually. Who knows what Orlando might do to hasten the coming."

Father John stood up and swung the chair back into place against the wall. "You're right, George. The man could be dangerous."

The other priest was nodding. "We have to take a strong stand in the pulpit."

"We have to work with the Arapaho elders," Father John said.

• • •

It was midafternoon when Father John heard the tires skittering over the gravel on Circle Drive. He got up from his desk and went to the window. A blue sedan slowed past the administration building, then turned into the alley. Before the sedan disappeared past the corner, he caught a glimpse of the dark-haired, young-looking man with the round face and the fleshy chins folding over the white clerical collar.

He hurried out of the office, around the building, and down the alley. The sedan was parked in front of the guest house. Bishop Lawrence McCall was hauling his stocky frame out of the front seat. He shut the door and headed to the trunk, the top of which was rising in the air.

"Bishop, good to see you," Father John called.

The man swung around, set his left hand over his forehead, like the brim of a hat, and peered through the brightness. The breeze pulled at the front of his black suit coat and smashed his trousers against his thick legs.

"Father O'Malley," he said, extending his right hand. "Didn't see any reason to bother you. I know my way to the guest house."

Father John shook the man's hand. He had a firm grip, at odds, somehow, with the smooth, clean-shaven face, the round, reddish cheeks. A couple of times a year, the bishop managed to escape, as he put it, from the telephones and endless meetings in Cheyenne and spend a few days fishing on the reservation. He always stayed at the guest house.

"Let me get your bag." Father John lifted the small black bag from the trunk. Then he ushered the bishop toward the door and followed him inside. The one-room house was cool and drenched in shadows.

"Just what I need." The bishop spread his arms, as if the sofa bed, table, lamp, and closet-sized kitchen were his congregation. "Peace and quiet for twenty-four hours." He gestured toward the black suitcase. "Peaceful morning on the river, just me and the fish. Good mystery novel. And don't plan on me for dinner tonight. I'll be meeting friends in Riverton. In fact, don't plan on seeing me until the meeting tomorrow night. When do you expect the other directors?"

"Sometime tomorrow," Father John said.

"Good." The bishop gave him a conspiratorial look. "Don't tell them I'm here."

Father John smiled. "Enjoy fishing," he said. He let himself out, closing the door behind him, and headed back to the office.

The moment he sat down at his desk, he checked his phone messages. No word from Gianelli. Nothing from Vicky. He'd tried to call her all day, leaving messages with her secretary—*Ask her to call me.* And what is this about, Father? the secretary had wanted to know. Just ask her to call me, he'd said again. He wanted to hear her voice and know that she was safe.

‹ 17 ›

icky could hear the rhythmic sound of the drums as she threaded her way among the parked pickups and sedans in front of Blue Sky Hall. She slipped past the solid wood door and stood next to a group of men leaning against the back wall. The hall was jammed: families crowded into the rows of folding chairs on both sides of the center aisle, other people standing along the walls. Most were Arapaho, although a few white people were scattered about.

The opened casket stood at the far end of the aisle. She could make out the crown of Ben's head, the black hair against the shiny white fabric inside the casket. Her heart lurched. An immense sadness and regret mixed with the flood of memories that washed over her. She'd seen Ben for the first time at a rodeo at Fort Washakie. She was seventeen, and she couldn't take her eyes off him. The way he'd hung on with one hand to the bronco bucking out of the chute, the other hand waving his cowboy hat overhead. Whooping with the sheer madness of it, shouting into the sky, and she'd fallen in love with him then. Then—she'd been so certain—he was everything she wanted.

He'd seen her, too, because after he'd slid off and the Bronco was bucking its way around the arena, Ben had walked straight over to her and said, "You and me, girl, we're gonna get together." Later, after the first time they'd made love, he'd told her he was whooping and shouting out of that chute because he'd spotted her over in the stands.

She pressed her fist against her mouth. From the front of the hall came the slow, deliberate beating of the drum that matched the rhythm of her heart. The singers' voices rose in the same song of grief that the ancestors would have sung for the fallen warriors.

She could see the Holden clan in the front: Susan and Lucas seated in the first row, next to Hugh, Ben's brother, which meant he was also their father, in the Arapaho Way. The realization made her flinch.

The air was stuffy. Fluorescent lights shone through a kind of fog that hung below the ceiling. The faint odor of coffee mingled with the smells of roasted meat and sugary cakes.

She'd missed the food. A couple of men beside her were still sipping from Styrofoam cups. Plates and boxes of left-overs were stacked on the tables in the back corner for people to take home to family members who hadn't been able to come. "We always eat first," she remembered her grand-mother explaining. Years later she had understood. In the Old Time, the people never knew when they might eat again. They ate when they had the opportunity, then did whatever else they had gathered to do.

The song ended. Amos Walking Bear rose from the front row and, leaning on his cane, made his way to the casket.

The hall was quiet. The old man stood with head bowed, light glinting in his gray hair, black bolo tie pulled tightly against the collar of his white shirt. And then his voice boomed into the hall. *"Ani'qu ne'chawu'nani, Ani'qu ne'chawu'nani."*

Vicky set her head back against the wall, closed her eyes, and let the comforting sounds flow over her. She'd never learned to speak Arapaho—her parents were progressives—but she recognized the style. Formal and correct, the style in which the chiefs had addressed the villages. She caught snatches of words and phrases. The elder was calling the people to peace and forgiveness.

The voice stopped, and she opened her eyes, conscious of people turning in the chairs toward her, then looking away. The whispers sounded like the rush of the wind. Several men leaned out from the wall and craned their heads in her direction.

Amos was coming down the aisle, tapping his cane. Smoke curled over the top of the iron pan he held in one hand. Inside the pan, she knew, were smoldering chips of cottonwood and dried sage. He lifted the pan, allowing the smoke to drift over the people, to comfort and cleanse. Heads began to bow, and for a moment, Vicky felt free of the unwelcome glances.

The elder reached the end of the aisle. He stopped and held out the pan toward her. The sweet odor of sage floated over her. She felt a surge of panic. She wasn't sure if he was condemning her or forgiving her. Either way, her people believed she was guilty.

As he started back up the aisle, Vicky saw the thick-set man, muscles bulging beneath his denim shirt, striding down the side aisle toward her. One of Ben's cousins—she recognized the sway of his shoulders, the set of his jaw. He planted himself in front of her. His breath had a sour smell. "Hugh wants you out of here," he said, making no effort to lower his voice.

She moved sideways along the wall, aware of the rough concrete catching at her blouse. Heads turned again in her direction.

She gasped. Lucas had come up behind the man, and for a moment, she'd thought he was Ben. Ben, twenty years ago. He took her arm. "You stay if you want, Mom," he said, looking hard at his father's cousin, who shrugged his shoulders and started back toward the front.

"You can sit with me."

Vicky shook her head. "Not with the family."

Lucas stepped back and nodded toward someone farther down the wall. A moment passed before two folding chairs were pushed toward them. He guided her to one and took the other. Gradually she felt the gazes move away, like a breeze shifting in another direction.

The singers' voices rose over the beat of the drum. The elder was leaning over the casket now, applying the circles of sacred red paint to Ben's forehead and cheeks, marking him as one of the people so that the ancestors would recognize him in the shadow world.

Vicky closed her eyes and searched for the words to pray for Ben Holden. *Have mercy on him,* she managed. Then she said the prayer silently over and over again like a mantra. After a moment she opened her eyes and glanced about.

She saw the woman at once—when had she come in?— standing along the wall on the right, in a black, long-sleeved dress with a black scarf framing the pale, beautiful face and nearly obscuring the strip of blond hair along her forehead.

She looked vaguely familiar—a white woman from the area, no doubt. Vicky had the feeling that she should know the woman, and yet she couldn't remember any occasion in which they might have met. She'd never known a lot of white people in the years she'd spent married to Ben. Their life had revolved around family, powwows, rodeos, celebrations—all on the reservation. Occasionally white faces had appeared in the crowds, but no one she knew.

Now she was with white people every day: her office was in a white town, her apartment a few blocks away. She'd opened her office in Lander almost six years ago. Still she couldn't place the woman. Client? Opponent? The woman was nowhere in her life.

But Ben knew her, Vicky was certain. The truth of it sat like a weight against her heart. This was Ben's woman.

She was aware that the painting ceremony had ended; the drumming and singing had stopped. Quiet settled over the hall for a moment. Then, chairs scraped the floor and people started to their feet, grabbing purses and jackets, lifting sleeping toddlers. Groups of people surged into the center aisle.

Lucas stood up and leaned toward her. "Susan and I"— he hesitated—"and Uncle Hugh are going to stay with Dad."

Vicky nodded. Someone always stayed with the body through the night, until the burial in the morning. She kept her eyes on the woman in the crush of people at the side door.

"Do you want to see him?"

"What?" Vicky turned to her son.

"You know, to say goodbye."

Vicky glanced back toward the woman. She was about to

slip outside and into the oblivion from which she'd come, taking with her anything she might know about the Lakotas.

"Yes," she said, getting to her feet and pulling her eyes toward the casket almost hidden behind the groups of people making their way out of the rows and down the aisles. "I'd like to say goodbye."

Lucas took her hand and led her against the crowd flowing toward the entrance. A reverent quiet lay over the hall, broken by the shuffle of footsteps, the occasional hushed voice. Vicky saw the eyes turn away as she passed.

The Holden clan—two rows deep—remained seated, barely concealed anger rippling in the muscles of their clenched jaws. Hugh Holden sat ramrod straight, eyes locked on the far wall.

Vicky went to the casket, Lucas still beside her. Her breath jammed in her lungs. Ben was dressed in a blue, Western-cut jacket, and white shirt with a bolo tie—the tie she'd given him on their tenth anniversary. A white satin pillow had been arranged around his right temple where, she knew, he'd been shot. His hair was parted on the left, neatly combed and fanned over the edge of his shoulders. There were red circles painted on his forehead and cheeks. He looked like Ben and yet, not-Ben. Smaller, sunken, diminished by death.

She ran her fingers along the cool edge of the metal casket, then along the rough fabric of his sleeve. "Go in peace, Ben," she whispered. "Go in peace."

She felt Lucas's arm slip around her shoulders, and she leaned against him a moment. Then she stepped over to Susan in the front row. Her daughter lifted her chin and stared at her out of eyes clouded with incomprehension.

Moisture glistened on her thin cheeks. Vicky took her face in both hands, leaned over, and kissed her forehead. The dampness clung to her lips as she hugged Lucas a moment, then made her way past the rows of empty chairs and trailed the last of the crowd outside.

The white woman was nowhere in sight. Vicky waited in front a few moments, watching the parade of vehicles turning into the road. Finally she crossed through the beams of headlights to the Bronco.

She knew how to find Ben's white woman.

Thirty minutes later, Vicky parked in front of the Peppermill Restaurant and let herself through the double-glass doors. Faint odors of onions and spices floated into the quiet in the entry. A few couples were lingering over cups of coffee and half-eaten plates of dessert in the dining room. The waitress from Monday evening was carrying a tray loaded with dirty dishes toward the swinging doors in the rear.

"One?" The brown-haired hostess with her hair pulled into a bun beckoned her toward the dining room.

Vicky followed the woman past several other tables littered with dirty plates and coffee-rimmed cups. She felt a sense of relief when they passed the table where she and Ben had sat.

"Coffee?" The hostess laid the menu on a small table near the swinging doors that concealed the kitchen.

"That would be fine," Vicky said, taking the chair that faced the dining room. There was a low hum of conversation from the nearby tables, the sound of clanking dishes and gushing water behind the swinging doors.

The hostess returned and set a cup and saucer on the table,

then poured a stream of coffee from an aluminum pot. "The waitress will take your order in a moment," she announced before heading toward the front.

The doors pushed open. The waitress stood between them a moment, balancing a tray of dinner plates, black hair curled around the wary expression on her face. She pulled her gaze away, crossed the restaurant, and began distributing the plates in front of three men. Another moment passed before she came over, her gaze fixed on the small pad in her hand.

"What can I get you?" she said, a peremptoriness in her tone. "Kitchen's about to close."

"You recognize me, don't you?" Vicky said. "You saw me here Monday night with Ben Holden."

The woman didn't say anything. Vicky could see her throat muscles working as she swallowed. "Why'd you come back?"

"I want you to give me the name of the white woman Ben brought here."

"Don't know what you're talking about . . ."

"Yes, you do," Vicky said. She'd seen the quickly covered-up surprise in the waitress's face when she'd found someone else with Ben. She'd seen the conspiratorial look he'd given the woman.

"It's important," Vicky hurried on. "I have to talk to her."

The waitress glanced over her shoulder toward the hostess. Someone let out a long laugh that lingered over the muffled clanking of dishes. "I don't wanna get involved in murder," she said finally. "I don't need the cops in here asking me questions." She leaned over the table. "What I need is this job," she whispered. "I got a kid to take care of."

"I have two kids," Vicky said. "A lot of people think I killed their father. The white woman may know something that will help me."

The woman stood up straight and began flipping through the notepad. "You better give me your order." She held a pencil over the pad, as if she were already writing.

"Bring me a bowl of soup."

"We got creamy potato, vegetable—"

"It doesn't matter. Who is the woman?"

"Only time I ever seen her is when she come in here with"—she hesitated—"your husband."

"Ex-husband."

At this, the waitress gave her a smile of recognition. "I got me two of 'em," she said. "Roving eyes, both of 'em. I sure know how to pick 'em."

"Do you know her name?"

"I'll get your soup." The waitress stepped back, then disappeared behind the swinging doors.

Vicky took a sip of the coffee. Bitter, barely warm. This was a mistake, she thought, a long shot. How many white women lived in the area around the reservation? Ten thousand, at least. The waitress couldn't know them all.

The woman was back. She set down a bowl of butter yellow soup and an oblong dish stuffed with cellophane-wrapped crackers. "I heard him call her Marcia once," she said, positioning the dish in the center of the table.

"Anything else?" Vicky prodded. Marcia, she was thinking. There was something familiar about the name.

"I don't make a practice of listening in on my customers' conversations." She moved the dish closer to the bowl, and Vicky took a package of crackers.

"Of course not."

"She might've been a rancher. I'll get you some more coffee." The waitress hurried to the serving table, lifted the coffee server, and headed back, stopping to refill cups at another table, throwing quick glances over one shoulder toward the hostess in front.

"What makes you think the woman's a rancher?" Vicky asked, watching the brown liquid rise in her own cup.

"I heard them talking about ranch stuff, you know, cattle prices, best kind of hay, that kind of thing. One night . . ." She hesitated.

"What? Tell me, please."

The waitress drew in a breath. The rim of her nostrils inflated. "I heard her going on about her daddy dying and leaving her the ranch, like it was this big burden, and I'm thinking, I wish my daddy'd left me something other than a shit pile of bad memories, and Ben, he was giving her all kinds of sympathy, saying he sure knew how hard it was for a lady like herself to run a big ranch like the—" She stopped, eyes widening into circles of memory. "The Bishop Ranch, is what he said."

Vicky sank back against her chair. Marcia Bishop. Of course. The woman ran one of the biggest ranches in Fremont County. Vicky had never met the woman, but she'd seen photos of her in the newspaper, awarding trophies at the county rodeo, donating antique ranching gear to the historical society. She was blond and beautiful.

She started to thank the waitress, but the woman had turned away. A pink flush worked its way along the back of her neck, like a visible wave of regret at having said too much, having gotten involved.

Vicky fumbled with the cellophane wrapper, nibbled at the cracker, and took a few bites of the thick, lukewarm soup that tasted like congealed buttermilk. She threw a couple of bills on the table, enough for a large tip, and made her way back across the restaurant.

"How was everything?" The hostess's head snapped around.

"Just fine," Vicky said almost to herself. She was thinking that, first thing tomorrow, she was going to visit one of the most prominent white women in Fremont County.

‹ 18 ›

My relations, Wovoka has spoken to me a great truth. It is Wovoka's spirit that dwells within me. I am he, my relations. I am Wovoka come back to you. He has given me his great powers. I can control the elements. I will make the thunder and lightning. I will call forth the great cleansing waters. Oh, listen to me, my relations. The time approaches. You must dance and dance. There is nothing that will stand in our way. Together, we must prepare for the ancestors.

The AA meeting was about to get under way. Lights glowed through the oblong windows of Eagle Hall, and several pick-ups stood at various angles in front. From the alley, Father John could see a few people scattered about the rows of straight-back chairs. He'd considered canceling tonight's meeting—the AA members would probably go to Ben Holden's wake. Then he'd thought better of it. There might be someone who needed the meeting.

He needed the meeting; that was the truth of it. He'd wanted a drink all day. Each time the phone had rung, he'd thought it was Vicky, and he'd grabbed the receiver, reaching for her voice, a sense of premature relief flooding over him that she was safe. But it was never her voice on the line, and he'd felt the old tension grip his muscles. A sip of whiskey, that was all he needed. The tension would dissolve. He could remain calm and rational.

He stuck his head in the doorway and told the Indian woman in the back row that he'd be there in a moment. *He had to be there.* Then he walked through the darkness to the guest house and rapped on the door. The blue sedan stood a few feet away.

A moment passed, and he rapped again. The door swung open. Bishop McCall peered out over the half-moon glasses perched partway down his nose. He held a paperback book opened against his light-colored shirt.

"Everything all right?" Father John said.

"Ah, more than all right." The bishop stepped outside. "Would you look at that." He tilted his head toward the stars sparkling in the darkness overhead. "Peace, quiet, a good steak dinner with old friends, God's own beauty, a twelve-inch trout waiting for me in the morning." He pounded the book against his chest. "And a crackling good mystery novel tonight."

He lowered his head. Shadows sliced across his round face. "I understand there's a wake this evening. Well-known man murdered, is that true?"

"Ben Holden," Father John said.

"You have no part in the services?"

"The family wanted a traditional burial." The moccasin telegraph had reached the bishop's friends, Father John was thinking.

"Still a fair amount of tradition here." The man pushed the glasses up over his nose. "I understand there's a revival of the Ghost Dance religion on the reservation."

Father John said that was right.

The bishop was quiet a moment. Unspoken between them, the thought that somehow Father John had failed. The Arapahos still clung to the old ways. "Well"—the bishop glanced up at the stars again—"it'll be a shame to close this place. We both love it here, John, but . . ." Dropping his head now, staring into the darkness. "We mustn't think only of ourselves."

"The mission belongs to the people, Bishop."

The man gave him a sideways smile, and Father John could see a flash of white teeth. "Don't lobby me, O'Malley. I'm on to all the tricks. Every pastor thinks the world will end if his bailiwick's closed."

Father John was aware of the sound of his own breathing in the evening quiet. He could almost taste the whiskey on his tongue—Dear God, would he never forget the taste? He'd been right. The board was planning to recommend the closure of St. Francis. Even the bishop knew about the plan. Everyone seemed to know except the pastor.

Out on Circle Drive, an engine screamed and accelerated, tires skidded in a burst of gravel. Father John wheeled about, expecting a truck to careen down the alley and slam to a stop at Eagle Hall. Someone was shouting: "Get outta here! Whites outta here!"

A dark-colored pickup sped past the end of the alley, kicking out a cloud of gravel, then was lost behind the church, the engine roaring into the night. The pickup came around the far side of Circle Drive. A man raised himself through the passenger window and pointed the barrel of a rifle into the sky. "Sonsobitch!" he shouted.

"Get down!" Father John grabbed the bishop around the

shoulders and pushed him to the ground, then dropped down beside him. The gunshots were coming faster, recoiling around them, punctuating the noise of the truck, the sound of glass shattering, and the shouting and laughing. He could feel the bishop shaking under his arm. People were spilling out of Eagle Hall, running about, screaming and shaking fists into the air.

Father John lifted his head and shouted, "Go back," but his voice was lost in the crackle of gunfire. The pickup careened past the alley on two tires, and he threw himself across the bishop's head and shoulders.

He counted the seconds. At twenty, he realized the roar of the pickup was farther away, and an eery kind of quiet was moving across the mission, like the quiet following a whirlwind. He waited another ten seconds. The pickup was gone.

He scrambled to his feet, then helped the bishop upright. "You okay?" he said.

The man was still trembling, and Father John kept an arm around his shoulder and walked him back to the guest house. His face looked white in the lamplight. He tried to adjust his glasses, both hands shaking against the frame, a perplexed look in his eyes. One of the lenses was shattered.

"Stay inside," Father John said. Then he left the man standing next to the sofa bed and ran outside, past the paperback book tossed under the sedan's bumper, down the alley. Two vacant parking spots yawned in front of Eagle Hall. Three women stood outside the door, one towering over the others. "You all right, Father?" she called.

"Get back inside!" He pushed his hand against the air. "They might be back."

"Bastards won't be back," she yelled, her voice edged with

hysteria. "Joe and Lou chased 'em outta here."

Father John could taste the acid in his mouth. Dear God, they might have been killed. "Are you all right?" he shouted.

"We know rifle fire when we hear it." The tall woman raised a fist. "We hit the floor."

He gestured toward the hall. "Call the police," he shouted, then he ran past the church, through the grassy area in the middle of Circle Drive to the Toyota pickup in front of the residence. He gunned the engine and, pulling the door shut, wheeled out onto the drive, then onto the straightaway, glancing both ways on Seventeen-Mile Road before running the stop sign and heading west. He drove into the darkness, his thoughts collapsed into a single intention: He had to catch the pickups chasing the gunmen before somebody was killed.

‹ 19 ›

They were nowhere. Father John kept the accelerator to the floor and peered into the darkness beyond the headlights. Shadows rushed past the windows. And then, around a wide bend, taillights blinked in the distance. He stomped harder on the accelerator, aware of the chassis and doors shaking around him, the pickup bed bouncing behind.

He drew up behind the taillights: an old sedan doing about forty, tiny head barely visible above the front seat. But there were headlights in the oncoming lane ahead. A light-colored pickup drove past, then another. He hit the brake and made a U-turn. The pickups had already pulled over, and he stopped alongside the first.

"We lost 'em, Father. Sorry." Lou LeBois was leaning out the window, one of the breeds on the reservation, descended from an Arapaho woman and a French trader.

"You guys okay?"

"No problem."

"They could have shot you." He hadn't meant to chastise them.

"We was prepared." The breed lifted a rifle off the front seat.

Father John squeezed his eyes closed a moment against the feeling washing over him that some horrible event had been averted. "Mind coming back to the mission," he said. "The police will want to talk to you."

"You got any idea who them bastards are?" The Indian in the other pickup leaned out his window and crooked his head back.

"Yeah," Father John said. "I know who they are."

"Who'd want to do this?" Ted Gianelli said.

Father John stood at the window in his office. Three BIA police cars were parked in Circle Drive, blue and red lights blinking on the roofs. Several officers were walking about, stopping from time to time to scoop up something. The office window had been blown out, and a warm breeze blew past the jagged pieces of glass hanging from the frame.

He turned around. Shards of glass littered the carpet and winked on the papers strewn over his desk. The FBI agent sat on one of the side chairs, a matter-of-fact look about the man, dressed in the usual blue sport coat and tan slacks, balancing a small notepad on one thigh. His thick fingers wrapped around a gold pen.

Father George slumped in the other chair, elbows locked at his sides, chin dropped onto a fist. Father John had found his assistant standing in the middle of Circle Drive, talking to the officers. The other priest had broken away and walked over to the pickup. "God, what's going on around here?" he'd said. Then he'd explained that he'd been in the kitchen, he and Walks-On. He dove under the table and pulled the dog—howling and shaking—with him.

Father John walked over and leaned back against the edge of the desk across from the fed. "I told you. I had a run-in with one of the guards at the shadow ranch. He warned me to leave the reservation."

The fed dipped his head and scribbled across the notepad. Then he looked up. "Good time to shoot up the mission. Everybody else is at Blue Sky Hall tonight for Holden's wake. Can you ID the shooters?"

Father John shook his head. He'd already told the agent that he hadn't even gotten the make of the truck. Lou LeBois thought it was a Ford, but he wasn't certain. Nobody had gotten the license.

Father George jumped to his feet and announced he was going to check on the bishop. The man had quite a fright, he said, shaking his head. He crossed the office and started down the corridor, his heels clicking on the wood floor. The front door slammed shut.

Father John swept up another pile of glass specks. George and the bishop. That was great. Tomorrow they would be recommending that St. Francis Mission be closed before somebody was killed.

He realized the fed had asked again about the shadow ranch. "Start at the beginning," he said. "Give me all the details."

Father John walked back to the window. The scene below was the same: blinking lights, shadowy figures moving about. He told the fed about the armed guard and the two other guards. About Orlando and Janis and Dean Little Horse. "They know where Dean is."

"What makes you so sure?"

"I think Dean went to the ranch Thursday night after he left work. Maybe he stayed for a while, trying to talk Janis into leaving with him. He was gone by Sunday evening, because Janis Beaver went looking for him then."

"That's it?" Gianelli got to his feet and stuffed the notepad back into the inside pocket of his sport coat. "Jesus, John. You're jumping to a hellava lot of conclusions. All you got from your snooping was a visit from a couple of trigger-happy hotheads who don't happen to like whites. Lucky nobody was killed." He started toward the corridor, head down, a linebacker coming off the bench and into the action.

Father John followed the man outside. "Wait a minute," he said.

Gianelli was partway down the steps. He turned and glanced up. The lights threw blue and yellow stripes over his face. "Make it quick. I want to get to the shadow ranch while the tires on any truck in the vicinity are still hot."

"What do you have on Holden's murder?"

The fed looked away, his gaze following an officer coming down the drive, picking up something, slipping it into a Ziploc bag. "I have to go where the evidence takes me," he said.

"Vicky didn't have anything to do with it."

"I hope that's true." He met Father John's eyes again. "I expect to have a report on the murder weapon tomorrow."

"Then you'll have the killer."

Gianelli started down the steps. "We'll have an indictment," he called over one shoulder. Then he walked over to the officer, who held up the plastic bag.

"We've found six shells," the officer said.

"Get a hold of Chief Banner," Gianelli said. "I need a

couple of BIA cars at the shadow ranch." He brushed past the officer and walked over to the white Blazer in the middle of the drive.

"Might want more than a couple," the officer hollered. Then he went over to the squad car behind the Blazer, leaned inside, and lifted out a black radio. "That's a tight community," he called over the static and whining noise. "Don't like outsiders, especially cops."

The Blazer was already pulling around the squad car. It sped out of the mission toward Seventeen-Mile Road.

Father John crossed the alley and walked along the front of the church, searching the shadows that washed over the white stucco for signs of damage. There was one small chip near the door. He walked down the far side, then circled back and made his way down the alley, checking the walls and windows. The stained glass windows were intact, for which he gave silent thanks. Two windows shot out at the administration building, another two at the residence. A warning, this time.

He spotted Lou LeBois sitting on the stoop outside Eagle Hall, holding a cigarette off one knee. The end glowed orange. Father John walked over and sat down next to the Indian.

"You okay?"

The Indian nodded. "Why do you stay here?"

The question caught him by surprise. "This is home," he said.

"Them Indians want to run you off."

"We don't run off easily." He hoped that was true.

The man laughed, then took a long draw on the cigarette and blew a gray plume of smoke into the shadows. "Indians like that don't make rules for the rest of us."

"I'm glad to hear it."

"Can't live backward. Past is dead. Every day's new." He threw his head back toward the hall. "So they say in AA."

"Hey, Father." Leonard Bizzel, the caretaker at the mission as long as Father John had been there, emerged from the alley and walked over. A group of men in blue jeans and cowboy hats crowded behind him. "We been lookin' for you. We got a lot of warriors on the way over. We're gonna hang around tonight."

"It isn't necessary." Father John pushed himself to his feet. The last thing he wanted was an armed guard. "The police will keep an eye on the place."

"We got a pickup out at the entrance," Leonard went on, as if he hadn't heard. "Another pickup's gonna be parked by the church. That oughtta discourage the bastards. They're gonna figure we got guns."

"Look," Father John began. *God, somebody could get shot!* "I appreciate it, but the cops—"

The man interrupted. "This is our mission, Father. We're not leaving."

"Okay," he said after a moment. "It's your mission."

‹ 20 ›

Vicky drove down the long driveway, through the ponderosas and junipers, and parked in front of the two-
story, log ranch house. A tall, slender woman with
large blue eyes and an oval face framed with curly blond
hair that looked white in the sunlight stepped onto the
porch, almost as if she'd been watching from behind the
curtain at a front window.

"You must be Vicky," she called, moving to the railing
with the litheness of an expert horsewoman whose muscles
flowed in rhythm with those of the horse.

Vicky came up the wood steps. "And you must be Marcia
Bishop," she said. The woman was even more beautiful up
close.

"We might as well get this over with." Marcia Bishop
wheeled around and stepped back into the house. Vicky
followed her through the door and down a hallway into a
spacious room. Blocks of sunlight lay on the overstuffed sofa
and chairs and winked in the large, glass-topped coffee table.
A wall of windows overlooked a meadow with a barn and a
corral where a couple of ponies nuzzled the fence, and be-

yond, the rock-bound slopes of the mountains west of
Lander.

The woman planted herself in the center of the room.
"Something to drink?" she said, as if politeness required her
to ask. She was dressed in a tan, silky blouse, unbuttoned
in a long V that exposed her slim neck and pale skin, and
brown jeans that hugged the smooth curve of her hips and
made her look comfortable and at ease.

Vicky shook her head, acutely aware of the stiffness of her
lawyer clothes: the linen dress and high-heeled sandals that
cut into the tops of her feet.

"Sit down, please." Marcia Bishop gestured toward the
sofa behind the glass-topped table. She waited until Vicky
settled herself, then sat in the flower-printed chair across
from the table. "I've been expecting you, I must say." She
spoke in a precise manner that seemed natural and easy, like
a long-accustomed habit.

"Ben was . . ." She drew in a long breath; her nostrils
flared. "A lovely man. Ben was a lovely man."

Vicky had to glance away from the cold certainty in the
blue eyes. She could imagine what had attracted Ben to this
woman: her beauty and position. It would be like coming
home from the rodeo with the championship trophy, and
Ben was always the champion.

But what had attracted this white woman to Ben?

She knew. Oh, she knew. She and Marcia Bishop had
fallen in love with the same man—the handsome, charming,
confident Indian chief. The difference between them was
that Vicky had fallen out of love with him.

"Did you know him long?" she said after a moment.

"Eight months. We met at the county rodeo last fall. Sure
I can't get you something to drink?"

"A glass of water would be nice." Vicky tried for a smile. Her tongue clung to the roof of her mouth. The air felt close and warm.

The woman rose from the chair and let herself through the door at the far end of the room. A few seconds later she crossed the room and handed Vicky a crystal glass filled almost to the brim with water and ice and a slice of lemon. She sat back down. "It's only fair you should know that Ben and I were going to be married," she said.

Vicky took a long drink. She could still see Ben across from her, hear his voice begging her to come back to him. And after all the years, she finally understood. Ben was a chief, and a chief needed his wife and family and respectability. All of that had nothing to do with the parade of women through his life.

She was barely aware of the white woman prattling on about how the Holden clan hadn't approved, she being a white woman. Didn't want her at the wake last night. Well, Vicky must know all about that because they didn't want her there either, but they'd both gone, hadn't they? And Ben was being interred at this moment, on the Holden ranch, and think of it, neither of them were welcome on the ranch.

She drew in a long breath. "We would have been married by now, if you hadn't returned to Lander."

Vicky tried to focus on what the woman was saying. "What possible difference could my return have made?"

Marcia laughed and shook her head. "You're very clever, Vicky. You think I don't know? Ben told me everything: how you could never accept the fact that it was over between you; how you insisted on getting back with him. He wanted to, shall we say, let you down easy. You were the mother of his children, he kept reminding me, and he hoped to remain on good terms for the kids' sake. So naturally I agreed to postpone our plans. He was very fond of you, Vicky, I'm sure. I don't mean to be cruel, but you must accept the fact that it was over between you."

Vicky made herself take a sip of water. "I didn't come here to discuss my relationship with Ben," she managed. "I'm trying to find the Lakota ranch hands he fired last week. I'm hoping you can help me."

"Are you certain that's what brought you here?"

"I don't understand," Vicky said.

A dilemma seemed to be playing out behind the blue eyes, as if the woman couldn't decide whether to press on. Finally, she said, "You should know that the FBI agent has already called. He's bound to come around soon. I was hoping you'd show up first."

Vicky set the glass on the table and waited.

Finally, the woman said, "Ben and I were in Cheyenne at a horse show when he got an e-mail. Some emergency, he said, so we drove back Monday morning. I've been waiting to hear your explanation." Mockery seeped into the woman's tone. "Naturally you'll want to convince me that you know nothing about the e-mail and that the so-called emergency had nothing to do with Ben's murder before I speak with the fed and tell him everything. I'm surprised you didn't show up sooner."

"You're mistaken if you think I had anything to do with Ben's murder," Vicky said. "You must tell Gianelli the truth."

"The truth?" Marcia lifted her chin and stared at her out of half-closed eyes. "That you were insanely jealous? That you couldn't stand the idea of Ben with a white woman?

That if you couldn't have him back, no one would have him? I intend to tell the truth. You can count on it."

For a moment, Marcia Bishop seemed to blur into the bright light at the windows, and Vicky realized that Ben had convinced everyone—this blurred woman, Hugh Holden, even Lucas and Susan—that *she* was the one who had tormented him. He had given her the perfect motive.

Beyond the blurred woman, Vicky could see the cottonwood branches moving in the breeze, a colt trotting after a mare in the corral. She felt like a wild animal caught in a trap on a normal, peaceful day, the iron jaws tightening around her. The harder she tried to escape, the more she howled into the wind, the tighter the jaws became.

She blinked and tried to bring the woman back into focus. "What about the ranch hands?" she said. "Where are they?"

"They had nothing to do with his murder."

"How can you be certain?"

Vicky instantly regretted the question. How could the Lakotas have killed Ben when *she* was the murderer? She hurried on: "Ben saw them before he was killed."

"That's what you'd like the FBI to believe, I'm sure."

"Please, Marcia," Vicky said. "They stole money from the ranch and Ben went after them. He might have said something—please try to remember—about where they were hiding."

"Ben was right. You really never understood him."

"What?"

"You think he cared about the money?" She leaned forward. "It was the dynamite, Vicky. A hell of a lot of dynamite. Enough to blow up the reservation."

"Dynamite! No one at the ranch mentioned dynamite."

Marcia Bishop propelled herself upright, walked to the

window, and stared outside. "No one else knows. Ben kept control of the dynamite. He's the only one who knew the amount in the magazine."

Vicky got to her feet. A picture was emerging in her mind, like blocks of color scrolling onto a monitor. It was Ben who had the permit to buy dynamite to blast out tree stumps, build new roads and ponds. Ben who kept the dynamite in the magazine, locked and secure. He wouldn't have wanted anyone to know it had been stolen.

"You have to tell Gianelli." Vicky heard the stunned note in her voice.

"I have no intention of telling anyone." The other woman turned toward her. Light shone through the white-blond hair and flashed in the blue eyes. "I'll deny everything I've said. I'll say you made it up out of desperation to save yourself. Let the Lakotas blow the reservation into the dinosaur age. What do I care? You killed Ben. You destroyed everything. You deserve whatever happens."

‹ 21 ›

The road wound down the mountain slope through sparse stands of evergreens. An occasional branch scraped at the side of the Bronco. Lander lay in the sunshine below, gray ribbon streets and roofs floating through trees. To the north, tiny, blocklike houses and clumps of buildings dotted the open spaces of the reservation. And somewhere, two Lakotas with dynamite. *God. God. God.*

She felt the rear tires skid in the gravel. Dust floated in the rush of air over the half-opened windows. It was so like Ben to take charge. He wouldn't have wanted the moccasin telegraph spreading the news that Lakotas had stolen dynamite from the Arapaho Ranch. He would have gone after them. He would have gotten the dynamite back. He was a chief. He protected the people. He gave his life . . .

It made sense, except . . .

Except for something else in the woman's eyes—the dark shadow of hatred, pure and unrelenting. Vicky couldn't get it out of her mind. She had a sense—odd, she thought—that Marcia Bishop loved and hated Ben at the same time.

Promising to marry her, yet calling his ex-wife and taking *her* to dinner. The woman could have followed Ben to the Peppermill. All her suspicions—surely, she'd had suspicions—would have been confirmed. The woman could have seen her with Ben.

Possible, Vicky thought. Marcia had known what she looked like. "We were both at the wake," the woman had said, and she'd called Vicky by name this morning.

Vicky slowed through the residential neighborhood on the west side of Lander, allowing this new picture to develop in her mind. How else could Marcia have known her? Unless . . . The picture still emerging, taking on a new and unexpected shape. Unless Ben had carried her photo.

It could be true, and the realization brought new waves of sadness and regret at the way things had turned out. My God, Ben might have been still carrying her photo after all the years.

She gripped the steering wheel, steadying herself. Her nails dug into her palms. She would call Gianelli the minute she reached the office. The agent had to convince Marcia Bishop to tell everything she knew. And Gianelli could check the dynamite records at the ranch. He'd see that there were other people with motives to kill Ben Holden.

She pulled into the curb in front of her office and watched the green Chevrolet truck in the rearview mirror draw in behind her. Adam Lone Eagle loomed in the windshield a moment, then ducked out the door. He walked toward her as she was getting out of the Bronco.

"Vicky, we have to talk," he said. His tie was loosened below the opened neck of his light blue shirt. The cuffs were rolled back, exposing the hard line of muscles in his forearm. His eyes were as black and opaque as pebbles in a river.

Vicky shoved her door closed and told herself to stay calm. The lawyer had made the two-hour drive from Casper when he might have called. Her heart was pounding. She felt as if a flash flood had roared over her.

"We can talk inside." She started around the front of the Bronco, but the pressure of his hand—hard and definite—stopped her, and she turned toward him.

"There's a place I always like to visit when I'm in the area," he said. "It's beautiful, calm, and peaceful. Do you mind if we go there?" He turned without waiting for an answer and walked back to the truck.

She followed and let herself into the passenger seat. The minute he turned the ignition, the sounds of Count Basie surrounded her, the rhythms low and insistent. "You like jazz," he said.

"Is that what you came here to talk about?"

"No."

"Then, what?"

He threw her a sideways glance, a little smile. "Be patient," he said. "Wait for the right time."

Vicky left her eyes on the man a moment. She liked that in him, the patience. It called her to the old ways and to herself.

She turned and looked out the window. The rhythm of drums and blare of saxophones occupied the space between them, like another passenger. Outside the downtown storefronts blurred past, the sun winking in the plate glass windows. She understood that he would tell her what he'd come to tell her when the time was ready.

They were out of town now, heading east. Count Basie gave way to Ella Fitzgerald. The sign alongside the road read: ENTERING THE WIND RIVER RESERVATION. A couple of miles passed, then another sign: SCENIC VIEW. Adam turned into the wide pullout.

The minute the truck stopped, Vicky got out and walked across the gravel to the horizontal metal bar that marked the drop-off. The plains stretched below—vast, quiet, and secluded. Buttes and arroyos melded together in shadows that created a sense of flatness and sameness that, she knew, was not the reality, only the shadow of reality.

"Makes you think of the ancestors." Adam gripped the metal bar next to her and leaned into the view. "You can almost see warriors riding out on the hunt. Problem is"— he turned toward her—"the warriors are gone, and so is the buffalo. The people aren't in charge anymore. We have to live by their rules." He gestured with his head toward the dark blue shadow of Lander in the distance.

"You'd better tell me what happened," Vicky said. The sun burned through her blouse, but her skin felt cold and clammy.

"I talked to Gianelli this morning. He has the report on the twenty-two pistol that killed your ex-husband. He's linked the murder to you."

"What!"

"The gun was registered to the deceased Lester White Plume."

Vicky felt frozen in place, her mind trying to absorb what she'd heard. Uncle Lester's gun. She could see the black gun cradled among the white socks and underwear in Aunt Rose's dresser drawer. When was that? A month ago, after she'd gotten back from Denver? "You don't have to worry about me none," Aunt Rose had assured her. "I'll be just fine. I still got Lester's gun."

"There's more, Vicky," Adam said. "The gun was obviously wiped clean, but the lab picked up a partial fingerprint on the barrel. It's yours."

Vicky looked around for someplace to sit down, but there was no place except the graveled earth rising toward her. She was only half aware of Adam's grip on her arm.

"Well, Gianelli has everything now," she managed. "Motive, opportunity, gun, fingerprint. I'll be indicted." This was why Adam had brought her out here. To give her the news in a place of the ancestors, where she could draw the strength she was going to need from their spirits. A sense of gratitude toward the man mixed with the fear and anger that clasped her like a vise.

She turned toward the shadows moving over the plains. "Someone wanted me to look guilty. Whoever killed Ben stole the gun from my aunt, then left it on Rendezvous Road knowing it would be traced to me."

"Who, Vicky? Who could have taken the gun?"

"Dozens of people." Vicky pushed back from the metal bar and walked over to the truck, then back to the bar. Back and forth, back and forth, kicking at the gravel. "Aunt Rose took in all kinds of people. Teenagers in trouble, people just out of jail. Her heart's as big as that." She waved toward the space below. "Gianelli has to check out her recent houseguests."

"He thinks he has the murderer." Adam's voice was low.

She stopped pacing and faced him. "And you, Adam? What do you think? Oh, forgive me." She threw up one hand. "I forgot that you don't care whether your client is guilty or innocent as long as you win the case."

Adam reached out and took her arm. "I think the fed is full of shit, and I told him so. I told him there has to be another explanation." His fingers dug into her flesh. "Listen to me, Vicky. It's likely the grand jury in Casper will indict you. Maybe tomorrow, maybe the next day. If it happens, I've asked Gianelli to let you surrender. I don't want him bursting into your office, handcuffing you, and dragging you to the county jail. He agreed. If you have any unfinished business, you should take care of it. I'm sure I can get you released on bond, but—"

"Stop it, Adam." Vicky ducked free of his hand and turned away. She crossed her arms, struggling to contain the terror and confusion coming at her like a storm blowing over the plains. She'd stumbled into another reality, incomprehensible. Beyond the metal bar was the real world—the world of the ancestors in another time, another life. A part of her—the part untouched by the white world—would have been at home there.

A crow flapped over a butte and cawed into the wind.

She had to think! The Lakota ranch hands had a motive; they'd stolen the dynamite. But other people could have wanted Ben dead. Marcia Bishop? The white woman could have stalked Ben and shot him in a fit of jealousy.

She locked eyes with Adam and told him about Marcia Bishop and the dynamite.

"Dynamite!" The lawyer's eyebrows cocked upward in an arch of surprise.

"Ben was determined to get it back. He would have made trouble for the Lakotas."

Adam was shaking his head. "They've taken off, Vicky, disappeared into thin air. I talked to some folks at Pine Ridge. Nobody's seen them. He-Dog's aunt thinks he could sill be on the Wind River Reservation, but there's no sign of him here."

Vicky stared out at the plains. She prayed silently to the spirits of the ancestors. "Help me."

Then she turned back to the lawyer waiting a few feet behind her. "There are Indians from other tribes at the shadow ranch. The Lakotas could be hiding there."

"Thirty Indians . . ." Still shaking his head. "Gianelli has IDs on every one. They aren't there, Vicky." Adam leaned closer. She could smell the trace of aftershave, the faint whiff of perspiration. "Let's say you're right. How did the Lakotas get your aunt's gun? She's an old woman, right? Is it likely that she took in a couple of male Lakotas?"

Vicky didn't think so. And yet, if they had stayed at the house, they would have heard about her and Ben. Aunt Rose: passing the time of day over a cup of coffee, making small talk. Her niece had been married to the foreman at the Arapaho Ranch, did they know? A very important man. Would have been a chief in the Old Time. Had a bad breakup, those two.

"What about Marcia Bishop?" Vicky heard the desperation in her voice. Nothing was making sense. "She could have gotten a hold of the gun somehow."

Adam didn't say anything, and she knew he'd heard the desperation.

"Take me back to the office," she said, starting for the truck. She flung open the door and got inside.

Adam came around the other side and crawled in behind the wheel. "Listen, Vicky, I want you to take care of your own affairs."

"This is my affair."

"I'm your lawyer. Let me handle this." He hesitated, some new idea taking shape behind the black eyes. "I'm going to lay it on the line, Vicky. You've got a reputation for getting involved in matters you have no business getting involved in. You've put yourself in dangerous situations. You had to shoot a man."

Vicky flinched. She felt the warm flush in her cheeks, the stab of pain that always came with the memory. She tried to concentrate on what the man was saying: If the Lakotas got wind that she was looking for them, they'd come after her. She should concentrate on putting her affairs in order. Didn't she have a report on Bull Lake Dam to finish for the JBC? She should do normal things. He would take care of the rest.

He started the engine and wheeled back onto the road. Gravel peppered the undercarriage for several moments.

"I'm dead serious, Vicky." He glanced at her out of the corner of his eye. "You do things my way, or you find another attorney."

‹ 22 ›

"Bastards had it in for us." Leonard Bizzel kicked at the glass shards that winked in the morning light, then positioned the metal ladder below the window space in Father John's office. The Arapaho knew the grounds and buildings—the location of every hammer, box of nails, and cleaning fluid. He took the attack personally.

"Don't you worry, Father. I'll have the windows fixed in no time, and we'll be back to normal." He started toward the shed around the corner where he kept his tools. "Oh, almost forgot." He looked back, eyes shadowed with concern. "Warriors are gonna hang around the mission, case those bastards decide to show their ugly faces again." He threw a brown fist toward the cottonwoods.

Father John followed the man's gesture. Parked in the trees along the drive was a green pickup. Two men inside the cab, as still as mannequins, cowboy hats pulled forward. He took in a deep breath. The warriors would have a rifle stashed between them, and he didn't want anybody killed. On the other hand, he doubted that last night's shooters would drive past the pickup. A part of him, he had to admit, was glad for the guard.

"Tell them thanks," he called to Leonard, who was out of sight. He could hear the man jiggling the door of the shed.

"They don't need thanks, Father," the Indian shouted. "Just doin' their job."

Father John started up the front steps, his eyes on the truck. He wondered if the men were parishioners. It didn't matter. They were warriors protecting what belonged to the people.

He shoved open the heavy wood door and stepped inside. The building felt cool, the night air still clinging to the stucco walls. The quiet amplified the thud of his boots on the floorboards. He could see the door at the far end of the corridor. Father George had left an hour ago for the Riverton Airport. At any minute, Father John expected the other priest's sedan to roll around Circle Drive and disgorge the three new members of the board of directors, all former colleagues of his assistant, who would help decide the future of St. Francis Mission.

The hot breeze blew through the open space in the window and rustled the papers on his desk. He sat down, pulled the phone onto a stack of paper, and dialed Gianelli's office. He listened to the mechanical voice that barely resembled the agent's, then left his name. Gianelli would know he was calling to see if last night's shooters were in custody. And the agent would know if the BIA police had anything new on Dean.

There was something else: By now Gianelli would also have the report on the twenty-two used to kill Ben Holden.

Both Vicky and Dean had been on his mind all night, threading their way through crazy dreams that made no sense: the dark pickup chasing them across the mission grounds, fire bursting through the windows, and he, trying to run after them, wanting to protect them, his legs paralyzed, two stumps frozen into the ground.

He woke in a tangle of sheets and perspiration, and he'd offered Mass this morning for them both. *Let them be safe.*

He held down the disconnect button half a second, then dialed Vicky's office. The clank-clank sound of a chisel burst through the window opening.

"Vicky Holden's office." The woman's voice was still unfamiliar, still tentative. The new secretary in Vicky's new office. Everything seemed new and unfamiliar since she'd returned from Denver, as if she'd stepped into a life in which he had no part. No, Ms. Holden wasn't in today. What was this about?

To reassure her, he supposed, and reassure himself that she was okay. He said, "Ask her to call Father O'Malley."

She repeated his name, emphasizing each syllable, as if she were still trying to comprehend the purpose of his call.

"When do you expect her?"

"I really can't say."

He hung up and walked over to the window opening. Leonard was bent over a folding wood table he'd dragged from the shed, fitting a pane of glass into the frame. The ladder was still against the wall, the pickup still parked in the trees.

A blue sedan turned into Circle Drive.

Father John came down the front steps as his assistant sprang out of the sedan and opened the rear door. A tall angular man with a full head of white hair that framed a composed, aristocratic face unfolded himself from the backseat. Father Niles Johnston, president emeritus of two Jesuit colleges, dressed in black clericals and starched white collar. The man looked like an older version of the photos Father John had seen in the Jesuit magazines. It was Niles Johnston who had written him a letter insisting the board scrutinize the "long-term goals"—he'd ended with a question mark— of St. Francis Mission.

Father John walked over and shook the man's hand. "Good to meet you," he said.

Two other priests, also in clericals, were climbing out of the other side: Father James Bourne, an old friend from the seminary who'd taken a straight path, with no detours for treatment at Grace House, and was now a college vice president. Father John didn't recognize the other man: Father Allen Beckner. Short, rotund, with a horseshoe of black hair laid around a pink scalp and alert, penetrating eyes behind the rimless glasses that rode partway down his bulbous nose. He looked like the artistic renditions of Thomas Aquinas. Fitting, Father John thought, for a philosopher and Thomistic scholar.

Father John walked around the sedan, shook hands, and welcomed the priests to the mission.

"What's going on?" Father Niles was staring at Leonard clambering up the ladder.

"An unfortunate incident—" Father John began.

Father George cut in: "Four windows shot out last night."

"Shot out, you say?" The philosopher stepped forward.

"Yes, well—" Father John began again, groping for the words that might allay the bewilderment in the philosopher's eyes. There was no room for such incidents in the cool, logical contemplation of the higher truths. "We had a little trouble last night . . ."

Father George took hold of the philosopher's arm. "A

pickup with two crazy men sped through the grounds. There was a lot of rifle fire. Fortunately, no one was hurt."

"Well, well." Father Niles threw his white head back and straightened his thin shoulders, as if the suggestion, implied in his letter that St. Francis had outlived its usefulness, had just been confirmed.

The phone had started ringing inside the office, a faraway sound, oddly insistent. Father John started toward the steps, but the ringing stopped. Either the answering machine had picked up, or Elena had answered in the residence.

"Windows'll be fixed by tomorrow," Leonard called from his perch on the ladder. He was adjusting the new frame into the space. "Won't be any more trouble with the warriors here." He nodded toward the cottonwoods.

Father John saw the other priests turn in a precise maneuver and stare fixedly at the green pickup, their expressions dissolving from curiosity to dismay. "You have warriors here?" Father Niles said.

"What happened, John?" Father James, his old friend from the seminary, came around the sedan toward him, sympathy in the man's eyes.

Father John started to explain that a cult had gotten started and the followers wanted whites off the rez. He stopped. It was complicated, and the sun was beating down on the bare heads and black clericals of the other priests, who were blinking in the brightness in an obvious effort to understand what in heaven's name he was talking about.

He said, "Why don't we go to the residence. You look like you could use a cool drink."

The other priests threw each other a look of relief, then started trudging single-file down a path through the field of wild grasses in the center of the drive, Father George in the lead.

Father John started after the others. He caught snatches of the small talk: mission looked pretty much as they had imagined. Fewer windows, Father Niles observed. Everybody laughed.

They were crossing the far side of the drive when Elena burst from the residence and propelled herself down the steps, arms flapping ahead. "Father, Father," she yelled, fear and hysteria in her voice.

Father John darted around the others and ran to her. "What is it?"

"They found him." She was shouting, her chest heaving with the effort.

"Take it easy." He laid a hand on her shoulder. "Who are you talking about?"

The other priests were pressing around, heads bending toward the housekeeper.

"Amos called. Says they found Dean Little Horse in the foothills west of Fort Washakie. He's been shot, Father."

The other priests jumped backward, as if she'd cracked a whip in their direction.

She let out a long wail: "Somebody shot him to death."

‹ 23 ›

A phalanx of official vehicles stood at the side of the dirt road: five white Ford sedans with the blue and yellow insignia of the Wind River Police; Gianelli's white Blazer; a paneled truck with FREMONT COUNTY on the side. A dozen blue-uniformed police officers and several men in slacks and sports coats milled through the trees about fifty feet off the road.

Father John parked behind the paneled truck and started through the trees. Pine needles snapped under his boots. He'd left Father George and the others staring after him and driven out of the mission. They were probably seated at the kitchen table now, sipping iced tea, discussing homicide on the reservation and last night's shooting. He could hear the gravelly voice of Father Niles Johnston: *We really must consider . . . In view of everything . . . A dangerous place.*

Now he could see Ted Gianelli and two uniforms leaning over a dark object that looked like rags, a pile of bones. The agent broke away and came toward him. "Coroner's about to bag the body," he said. "You want to offer a prayer?"

Father John nodded and kept walking. The uniforms and

sports coats stepped back, and he saw the mud-caked blue jeans and yellow shirt and brown flesh in a heap on the ground. He went down on one knee and caught his breath. The body had been hollowed out. Where the stomach and abdomen had been was a jagged hole with torn masses of flesh and intestines. The plaid shirt was bunched and ripped, the chest matted with brown blood. He pulled his eyes to the face smeared with dirt, the hollow eye sockets, and the expression frozen in fear and shock.

He made the sign of the cross. "May the good and merciful Lord remember you, Dean, forgive you your sins, whatever they may have been, and grant you the peace and love you longed for here."

He tried to swallow back the knot of revulsion and anger in his throat at the senselessness, the absence of reason—there was no reason. The two men from the coroner's office began smoothing a gray plastic bag across the ground a few feet away. Father John got to his feet and turned back to the agent.

"What happened to him?"

Gunshot wound in the chest. Bullet probably hit his heart. We'll know after the autopsy. Coroner says he's been dead several days. Killer tried to bury him." He nodded toward clods of earth around a shallow trench several feet away. "Mountain lion probably dragged him out, started at him. Tom Hizer lives up the road. He spotted the body this morning."

Father John looked away a moment, trying to force his thoughts into a logical sequence. He turned back. "What kind of gun?"

The agent was rubbing his fingers into his temple, squinting in discomfort. "Have to wait for the autopsy, but . . ." He paused.

"It's a small wound."

"A twenty-two? Like the gun that killed Ben Holden?"

"Don't get your hopes up there's any connection, John. We have the murder weapon in the Holden case. We know the owner. Registered to Lester White Plume, deceased husband of Rose White Plume." He drew in a long breath that expanded the chest of his navy sport coat. "Look, John . . ." He paused. "We got a fingerprint off the barrel. It matches Vicky's."

The implications hit Father John like a fist in the chest. The physical evidence, the final piece that would tie everything together and convince a grand jury to indict Vicky.

"There has to be some explanation," he said. "Vicky's not capable of murder."

"She killed a man once."

"Give me a break. That was in defense of human life." *Defense of his life.* "Now we're talking about premeditated murder."

"I don't like the idea any more than you do." Gianelli was digging his fingers into his temple again, as if to rub out some invisible pain.

"What if it turns out the same twenty-two killed Holden and Dean?" Father John pushed on. "Vicky didn't even know Dean."

"So you're trying to tell me that two Lakotas shot Ben, then shot Little Horse? Put your famous logic to work, John. How the hell did they get the gun from Rose White Plume? And what beef would a couple of cowboys have with some guy like Dean, spent all day writing computer software. Where the hell's the connection?"

Father John glanced away. Two sports coats struggled toward the road with the bulky gray plastic bag between them. They dropped the bag onto a gurney, then shoved the gurney into the paneled truck. There had to be a connection. What was the connection?

A new idea flitted like a shadow at the edge of his mind. Two men, Dean and Ben, Arapahos, born and raised on the rez. They belonged here. Two Lakotas, outsiders who might not care about the rez or the people. The idea was coming into focus, assuming logical order. The outsiders posed some kind of threat, created some kind of danger. Dean and Ben had tried to stop them. They'd been killed.

He said, "Dean stayed at the shadow ranch. The Lakotas could have been there at the same time."

"Shadow ranch again." Gianelli shook his head and glanced away a moment. Then he said, "Look, John. Let me do my job, okay? I'm gonna push Orlando and his bunch real hard. If there's some connection, I'll find it."

"What about the guys that shot up the mission? Have you found them?"

"No vehicles at the ranch. Village was lit up with bonfires. The followers were doing their dance, dressed in white, circling around, holding on to one another. We interviewed Orlando himself and about a dozen others. They claimed they didn't know what we were talking about. Without evidence . . ." He shook his head. "You want to give Dean's grandmother the bad news?"

It was probably all over the moccasin telegraph, Father John was thinking. Minnie and Louise would have heard by now. He said, "I'll stop by the house."

‹ 24 ›

"You bless the boy?" Minnie said.

Father John scooted his chair close to the sofa where the old woman sat with her sister, their hands intertwined. The living room was crowded with Arapahos seated on the other chairs, huddled in the corners. The low buzz of conversation ran like an electric current through the air.

He told the old women that he had blessed Dean's body.

The information seemed to give them some degree of comfort, as if Dean could now start on the road to the shadow world.

Someone handed him a mug of coffee and Father John took a sip. Then he told them he'd found Dean's girlfriend. "She said Dean had been at the shadow ranch."

Both women were shaking their heads. "That's an untrue story," Minnie said. "Dean wouldn't stay with those Indians. They think the world is gonna end."

Louise said, "I knew he got himself a girlfriend. He might've gone up there to see her."

"I suppose." Minnie patted her sister's hand. "He

would've been worried about her, if she took up with that cult. But he wouldn't have *stayed* there. He had a future, that boy. He was going someplace." Her voice began to crack, and she paused. "He didn't think the world was ever gonna end."

Father John didn't say anything for a moment. Then he asked if Dean had known Ben Holden.

The two women stared at him out of eyes round with surprise. "Ben Holden? Everybody knew Ben Holden. He got murdered a few days ago. What's that got to do with Dean getting murdered?"

"Did he ever work at the Arapaho Ranch?"

"What're you saying, Father?" A rail-thin man sat down on the sofa armrest. "You think the same bastard shot 'em both?"

"I don't know," Father John said after a moment. "I'm trying to figure out if there's a connection."

Louise waved away the idea. "Dean never took to ranching. He was a thinker, that boy. Stayed in school. Used his head. Nothing in common with Ben Holden."

"Hell," said the man on the armrest. "Ben was a whiskey man. Dean didn't even drink."

He was chasing shadows, Father John thought. Connections that didn't exist. He tried to focus on the conversation: Minnie and Louise saying that Dean had to be buried within three days—buried at the mission, Father—so that his spirit could find the way to the ancestors, and he trying to explain the mysterious workings of the white bureaucracy. First, the coroner had to release the body. He promised to hold the funeral as soon as possible.

Then he got to his feet and made his way to the door, shaking hands, clasping shoulders as he went, trying to corral the sadness running inside him. He should've insisted that Minnie go to the police when he'd first talked to her—why hadn't he insisted? And yet, what good would it have done? Dean was already dead by then.

Outside, the sun glistened on the open spaces. He climbed into the pickup and headed south. It would take most of an hour to get back to the mission. The other members of the board of directors had probably arrived by now. The first meeting would get under way in a couple hours. He was going to be late.

The offices of Blue Water Software had the vacant end-of-the-day look, but a light glimmered through the front window and the door opened when Father John tried the knob. A wall of refrigerated air hit him. The hum of an air-conditioning unit mingled with the click of computer keys.

The receptionist looked up from the papers she was arranging into neat stacks on the desk. "We're about to close, Father," she said.

He asked if Sam Harrison was still there.

The woman picked up the phone and pressed a key. "The priest from the other day," she began, bringing the thin-penciled eyebrows together.

"Father O'Malley," he said.

"Yes, of course. Father O'Malley's here to see you."

A second passed before Sam Harrison emerged from the maze of cubicles. "Come on back, Father," he said, waving him into the aisle.

Father John followed the young man past vacant cubicles with monitors gleaming with iridescent images of mountains and lakes and dams. They turned into a cubicle with two desks set at right angles. A long, fluorescent lamp emitted a glow of light over the papers and the computer monitor on one desk. The lamp on the other desk was turned off; the monitor was dark.

"I heard the news," Harrison said, brushing his brown curly hair off his forehead and sinking into a chair in front of the monitor filled with tiny words and numbers that seemed to make no sense. Father John took the chair in front of the blank monitor.

"Dean! Man, I can't believe it," Harrison said. "Just yesterday, a police officer was here, asking questions, nosing into Dean's files." He nodded toward the blank monitor. "Why'd anybody want to kill him?"

"I need your help," Father John said.

"Anything, Father. You name it, and I'll do it." Harrison scooted his chair forward.

"Did he ever mention an Arapaho named Ben Holden?"

The young man tilted his head toward the ceiling. "Not that I can recall." He looked back. "Wait a minute. Isn't that the Indian got shot the other night? Big man on the rez?"

Father John said that was the man. "What about the Arapaho Ranch? Dean ever talk about the ranch?"

Harrison was shaking his head. "Dean wasn't the cowboy type. He was a desk jockey." He gave another nod toward the monitor. "Liked putting computers through their paces. What're you saying, Father? Dean's murder has something to do with the murder of the big guy?"

"I'm not sure." Father John got to his feet. It was a long shot; he'd been grasping for some connection. Nothing tied Dean Little Horse to Ben Holden, except for the fact they'd been shot by a twenty-two. "Look, Harrison," he said, "if you think of anything . . ."

"Hold on, Father." The young man jumped up, pushed back the chair that Father John had just vacated, then sat down in front of the blank monitor. He flipped a switch; blue, red, and yellow icons began to form in the white light. Harrison leaned closer and clicked on the mouse by the keyboard. Black boxes of text replaced the icons. He tapped on the keys, and tiny x's appeared in one box.

"Dean and I, we worked pretty close," he said. "Troubleshooting glitches in our software. You know, gate doesn't open at the dam way it should, we find out what the computer's ordering and tell it to order something else. He had my password. I have his. Made life simpler."

A column of names began scrolling downward. "Police officer printed out Dean's contacts. Mostly clients, looks like. Dam operators. People we work with every day. Hold on." He hunched forward and clicked the mouse. The scrolling stopped. "Whatd'ya say the big man's name was, Ben Holden? Here we go." A blue line highlighted a name and e-mail address that began with BH.

"Let's see if Dean saved the messages he sent out." Harrison clicked again. "Here we go. Good old Dean. Saved everything."

Lines of text started to form. Father John leaned around the young man and peered at the monitor. "Urgent!" appeared in the subject box. The message read: "I'm a Rap like you. Must talk to you immediately. I know about the day box."

The e-mail had been sent on Sunday at 8 P.M.

"I'll get a printout." Harrison was on his feet, striding into the corridor.

So there was a connection, Father John thought. Dean had tried to get a hold of Ben Holden. But he didn't know

Holden—he'd had to explain that he was also Arapaho. He'd wanted to give Holden some information: he knew about a day box. It was urgent. Urgent enough to get them both killed.

Harrison stepped back into the cubicle and handed him a printed sheet of paper. "Hope this helps find whoever shot Dean."

Father John thanked the man and made his way back down the aisle and into the late afternoon heat. He walked back to the pickup, fished the cell phone out of the glove compartment, and left another message for Gianelli: "I've found the connection."

‹ 25 ›

Vicky kept her eyes on the belt of gray asphalt rolling under the hood of the Bronco and struggled against the feeling that the sky and the plains were closing in on her. She'd checked her messages when Adam dropped her off at the office. Four or five calls from Aunt Rose. Two calls from the mission priest, her secretary's term for John O'Malley. Oh, and a call from Norm Weedly. The JBC had decided to pursue other avenues concerning the Wind River and Bull Lake. Thank you very much for your efforts. Your fee will be mailed shortly, his exact words, the secretary said.

Vicky tightened her grip on the wheel and turned onto Blue Sky Highway. She understood. Gianelli thought he'd solved Ben's homicide, and the JBC had decided not to retain a lawyer about to be indicted for murder. No matter what Adam said, she intended to find out how the Lakotas or Marcia Bishop or whoever had shot Ben had gotten Aunt Rose's gun. Adam wouldn't approve. He was the type of lawyer—it was obvious—who expected clients to follow his advice. She was the same. She wouldn't keep a client who didn't follow her advice. It hit her that tomorrow she'd probably be arrested, and she wouldn't have a lawyer.

She eased on the brake and turned into the bare-dirt yard in front of Aunt Rose's house. The old woman was already at the door, as if she'd been waiting for the sound of the Bronco. She looked disheveled, sleepless. Her eyes were bruised red from crying.

"Oh, Vicky." She reached out, took Vicky's hand, and pulled her into the house. "I don't know what happened. I don't understand." She started sobbing and taking in great gulps of air.

Vicky hugged the old woman. She could feel her trembling beneath her cotton dress. "We'll figure it out, Auntie." She guided her to the worn upholstered chair, then perched on the ottoman and waited until Aunt Rose had dug a tissue out of the front of her dress and dabbed at her eyes.

"The fed was here first thing this morning." She waved the wad of tissue at the door. "What's the FBI want with an old lady, I said. He said, what do I know about Ben Holden getting himself shot? He wanted to know if I got a gun. I seen clear as day what he was up to. You got it all wrong, white man, I told him, but he kept wanting to know if I owned a gun. I said no. Well, that was the truth, 'cause Lester was the one that owned the gun. So the fed said, your husband had a license for a twenty-two pistol. So what if he did, I says, and then he told me that Lester's gun killed Ben Holden."

The old woman paused. Moisture glistened in the creases of her brown face. "I went back into the bedroom to get the gun and prove he was crazy; the fed was right behind me. I opened the dresser drawer and . . ." She dabbed at the tears, smearing the moisture across her cheeks. "Maybe I put the gun somewheres else, I said. I started looking everywhere, pulled out the drawers, looked in the closet. I'm telling the fed how I'm an old woman, and maybe I got forgetful and put the gun someplace I can't remember. But it's nowhere."

Aunt Rose dropped her face into her hands and emitted a soft, wailing noise. Her shoulders shook. Vicky patted her hand and said it was okay, everything would be okay. She wished she believed it.

"You're wrong, Vicky." Aunt Rose glanced over the wad of tissue. "The fed thinks you shot Ben. He wanted to know all the times you been here." Her features rearranged themselves into a look of defiance. "I told him, I'm not talking to you no more without a lawyer."

Vicky smiled at the image of Aunt Rose standing up to Ted Gianelli. "You may have to answer the question in court." She made her voice matter-of-fact. "You'll have to tell the truth."

The truth, she was thinking: She'd come to Aunt Rose after Ben was killed; she'd spent three days here after she'd returned from Denver. She always came to Aunt Rose when she was off-balance. But there was another truth. Somebody else had taken the twenty-two.

"Would you like some coffee?" she said after a moment.

The old woman nodded, and Vicky went into the kitchen. She found the coffee canister, measured out the grounds, filled the glass container—going through the motions, her thoughts on Gianelli. He would have talked to the neighbors down the road. Arapahos paid attention; they knew who was visiting who. It kept the moccasin telegraph humming. He would know the exact dates she'd been here.

She stared at the brown liquid dripping into the glass container and tried to breathe slowly. She could feel her ribs squeezing her heart.

After a moment, she poured a mug of coffee, then found a notepad and pencil by the phone and went back into the living room. Aunt Rose lay with her head tilted back against the chair.

Vicky set the mug on the table next to the chair and dropped back onto the ottoman. "Listen, Auntie," she said, "have any whites stayed here? Anyone connected to the Bishop Ranch?"

Aunt Rose locked eyes with her, surprise mingling with disbelief in the woman's expression. "What're you talking about?"

"Marcia Bishop, Ben's girlfriend. Has anyone stayed here who knew her?"

In the way that the old woman shrugged, closed her eyes, shook her head, Vicky knew she was clutching at shadows. It wasn't Marcia Bishop who had found her way into Aunt Rose's bedroom and taken the gun.

She said, "How about any Lakotas, Auntie? Two Lakota ranch hands stole dynamite from Ben. They might have been looking for a place to hide out."

"Lakotas? Lakotas took dynamite? What're they gonna do? Blow up our reservation?"

"Roy He-Dog. Martin Crow Elk. Do those names ring a bell?"

Aunt Rose sat very still, like a child searching for the right answer to please the teacher. Finally she shook her head.

"What about Indians from other tribes," Vicky pressed on.

"I know Lakotas when I see 'em. Even if they said they was some other tribe, I'd know 'em."

Vicky felt the vise clamping in her chest again. "Let's

start with the most recent visitors and work back."

Aunt Rose shifted her gaze to some point across the room. "Two girls social services sent last Saturday. Stayed the night."

Vicky wrote Saturday. Two days before Ben was killed. Then she made a note to check identities with social services.

"Week before," Aunt Rose went on, "Mark Shield stayed a couple days. Dad goes on a drunk once in a while, and Mark comes over. He's a good boy."

Vicky wrote down the name. She knew the Shield family. Mark was about fourteen. "Before Mark," she said.

"Well, that'd be, about a month ago. Let me see—couple girls stayed one night. They were from Montana."

Vicky held the pencil over the notepad and waited.

"Come here to join up with the shadow dancers. Seen all about 'em on the Internet. Cop stopped them late at night on 287 for driving too fast and they told him where they were going. So he tells them to come here first, get some sleep and food, before they headed into the mountains. Maybe he was thinking they might change their minds, but soon's they woke up in the morning, they took off."

"Did you get their names?"

"Sue and Mary. They was sisters. Last name was Buckle."

Vicky wrote down the names, then shadow ranch. She felt a little surge of excitement.

"Gun was here when they left," Aunt Rose said.

"Are you sure, Auntie?"

"Oh, I'm sure. I was doing some spring cleaning. Gun was right there in the drawer where Lester kept it. Let me see, there might've been somebody else . . ."

Vicky dropped her head into her hand. It was impossible. The truth was, anyone could have walked into Aunt Rose's house and taken the gun. No telling how many people knew about it. People worried about Rose White Plume taking in strangers, and Aunt Rose assured them, just as she'd assured her. No need to worry. I got Lester's gun.

"Janis . . ."

Vicky dropped her hand. She felt her heart turn over. John O'Malley said he'd talk to a girl named Janis—what was her last name?—at the shadow ranch.

"Stayed here couple weeks ago. Oklahoma girl."

Oklahoma girl! Vicky felt as if the gears had suddenly snapped into place. The girl was from Oklahoma.

"Come to the rez last winter," Aunt Rose was going on. "Seen the shadow dancers at Ethete and decided to join 'em. Met Orlando himself. Oh, she wanted to live up at the ranch in the worst way, but her boyfriend, well, he didn't want her to go. So she showed up at the door." She paused, as if she were groping for the memory. "Wanted to know if she could stay a little while. Needed a place to think. I don't know how she heard of me."

Vicky didn't say anything. Everybody's heard what a soft touch you are, she was thinking.

"All she talked about was Orlando," Aunt Rose went on. "How he's the son of Wovoka. How the new world didn't come before, but now it was gonna come. No more trouble and suffering, no more kids getting kicked around. I figured she'd been kicked around plenty, poor girl, and sure enough, one morning she gets up and says she had a vision. Orlando was calling her, and she had to go. Last week, her boyfriend comes looking for her, and I had to tell him she went to the ranch. Dean Little Horse. Seemed real nice. Too bad what happened to him."

Vicky stared at her aunt. "What happened?"

"You don't get the moccasin telegraph in Lander?"

She heard the news on the radio this morning, Vicky was thinking. Nothing earthshaking. And this afternoon, Adam was playing a jazz CD, and she hadn't turned on the radio on the drive to Aunt Rose's. She could think better with the noise of the wind crashing through the Bronco.

"What, Auntie?" she pleaded.

"Found his body out in the foothills. Shot to death, like Ben."

Vicky sprang to her feet. "What else have you heard, Auntie?"

The old woman shook her head and looked up at her. "Last I heard—Josephine Cleary called just before you drove up—they don't know who shot him. He'd been dead three, four days."

Vicky started pacing. The door. The window. The ottoman. She sat back down. "Think, Auntie. Could Janis have taken the twenty-two?"

Aunt Rose's lips moved silently a moment. Then she said, "Can't say for sure. Maybe it's what happened."

It was what happened. Vicky could feel the truth of it. The girl named Janis had taken the gun to the shadow ranch, which meant the Lakotas had been at the ranch. They'd brought the dynamite to Orlando! Ben must have gone to the ranch and confronted the Lakotas Monday afternoon. They'd grabbed the gun—a perfect weapon, registered to someone else. They probably didn't even know it was registered to the uncle of Ben's ex-wife. They'd followed Ben to the restaurant, then to Rendezvous Road.

Vicky jumped up and began carving out another circle over the braided rug, conscious of Aunt Rose's dark eyes following her. There was more. Dean had probably gone to the ranch and tried to get Janis to leave. Probably caused trouble, and someone—the Lakotas?—had shot him. They could have used the same gun.

And yet . . . Gianelli had already checked the ranch. The Lakotas weren't there, but . . . *they had been there.* She was going to have to convince the fed to get a search warrant. She had to get some evidence.

It hit her like a clap of thunder. The dynamite could still be at the ranch. If she could get a photo . . .

"I'm sorry, Auntie," she said, starting for the door, grabbing her black bag from the table as she went. "I have to go."

Aunt Rose's voice behind her, as if she'd seen into her head: "You're not goin' to the shadow ranch! The dancing's going on. Outsiders aren't allowed."

Vicky opened the door and turned back. "What did Wovoka preach, Auntie? How was the new world supposed to come?"

Aunt Rose stood very still a moment, as if she were trying to grasp a memory. Then she staggered backward into the table. The mug turned over and a stream of coffee ran onto the floor. "He preached . . ." She hesitated, then swallowed and started again. "The new world's gonna come after the great event. The Ghost Dancers was supposed to dance for four days. Every six weeks they danced for four days. They was supposed to keep dancing until the great event happened. There was gonna be an explosion and a great flood that would wash the earth clean. They didn't know when the event was gonna happen, but it was gonna be on the last day of the dance."

Vicky stood very still, trying to pull from her memory what Norm Weedly had said: *They're starting the dance today.*

That was Monday and this was Thursday, the fourth day.

Today was the last day!

"I'll call you later, Auntie." Vicky wheeled about and ran outside to the Bronco. She jammed her key into the ignition and shot onto the road, past Aunt Rose standing on the stoop, gesturing with both hands, as if she could pull her back.

‹ 26 ›

It was almost six when Vicky reached Lander. Offices and shops had closed an hour ago. She left the Bronco in the lot behind her apartment building and ran up two flights of stairs. In the living room, she leaned over the desk, struggled to catch her breath, and played back her phone messages. Adam Lone Eagle's voice: They had to talk. It surprised her that the man was still in town. She deleted the message.

Two calls from Lucas. He and Susan were leaving tomorrow. Could they get together tonight? Call as soon as you get in. He left the number. They were still at Hugh's house.

She picked up the receiver. The familiar longing clung to her like a worn dress. She'd hardly seen the kids since they'd arrived for Ben's funeral, and tomorrow Lucas would be starting for Denver, Susan for L.A. How would they hear that she'd been indicted? From the radio? Somewhere between Laramie and Cheyenne? She had to talk to them first, prepare them. God only knew what Hugh Holden had told them.

She tapped out the first three numbers, then stopped, her

fingers numb against the keys. The shadow dance would end tonight. Whatever great event Orlando had planned would happen tonight.

She dropped the receiver, went into the bedroom, and stripped off the lawyer clothes—the linen dress, the hose and sandals she'd worn all day. If everything went okay, she'd be home by ten. She'd call the kids and arrange to meet them for breakfast tomorrow before they left.

She pulled on a pair of blue jeans and a black T-shirt and jammed her feet into her sneakers. Then she tied her hair in a short ponytail. Rummaging through a closet shelf, she found a black waist pack and walked back through the apartment, gathering up the items she might need: screwdriver, tiny flashlight that fit in the palm of her hand, metal nail file. She pulled her cell phone and apartment key from her bag. Then she found her camera in the desk drawer and inserted a new roll of film. She jammed the items into the waist pack, except for the small key, which she stuck in the pocket of her jeans where she could find it without rummaging through the pack.

Ten minutes later she was driving north onto the reservation, trying to recall everything John O'Malley had said about the shadow ranch. Armed guard at the entrance. Dirt road over the ridge into the village, guards around the periphery. When she was a child, she'd gone to the ranch with her grandfather to buy a bull. There was no guardhouse then, no village. Just a log ranch house where she'd sat at the kitchen table and licked at the sucker Mrs. Sherwood had given her. Through the window, she'd watched her grandfather and Mr. Sherwood leaning onto the top rail of the fence, the black bull pawing at the ground on the other side.

She turned west at Fort Washakie and began winding up a graveled road. Dusk was moving down the slopes like a storm. She tried to fix the map of the ranch in her mind. Ranch house, barn and corral, a couple of shacks. The dynamite would be in one of the shacks, away from the house.

She turned right where the road branched into a Y and continued climbing. The gravel road stopped, and the Bronco bounced along the dirt two-track that cut through the boulders and scraggly pines spilling down the slope. Around a bend, in the gray light, a small wood structure with a peaked roof came into view.

She turned off the headlights, let up on the accelerator, and crept forward. The guardhouse was coming closer.

And then she saw the clearing outside the passenger window. She maneuvered out of the two-track, across a narrow ditch, and through the clearing. She set the Bronco under a canopy of branches, the bumper nosing against a boulder, and cut the engine. The guardhouse was about a hundred feet away.

She waited, not breathing, half-expecting the guard to appear in the rearview mirror. The wind hissed in the trees around her. She was alone. She tried to locate her position on the map in her mind. The road to the ranch cut over the ridge on the south. Guards could be patrolling the road. She had to stay north and work her way upward around the trees and boulders.

She got out and, keeping her eyes on the guardhouse, buckled on her waist pack. Then she ducked low and started through the trees, her sneakers crunching the pine needles. The air was clogged with odors of pine and dried earth. She moved from shadow to shadow, plotting the route as she went, staying close to the branches that scratched at her hands and pricked at her T-shirt and jeans.

The line of trees gave way to another clearing with patches of grass and scrub brush at the base of the slope. On the left, the two-track intersected with the dirt road that curved out of sight. The guardhouse was close; she could see a shadow moving inside.

She moved back into the trees. A large man filled the doorway, then stepped outside. The white buckskin shirt and trousers, the flat, round face and ponytail—she took all of it in, but her gaze fastened on the rifle in his hands. He walked down the two-track, glancing in the direction she'd come, then swung around and started into the clearing.

She held very still, watching him come closer. The rifle, a black cannon pointing toward her. He stopped, turned around, and went back into the guardhouse. A light flickered on, and the guard hunched over a shelf, as if he were writing something. He was making out a report!

She ran across the clearing and, still running, started up the slope. Darkness was coming on fast. It was getting harder to see. The ground rose steeply beneath her; she could feel the pull in her calf muscles.

She leaned onto the cold surface of a boulder and gasped for breath. A wall of rock loomed above, too high to climb. She edged along the base until she came to a place where the boulders looked manageable. Jamming one foot into a crevice, she propelled herself upward, the air burning in her lungs. She steadied herself and lunged for a higher boulder.

And then she saw the flash of white as another guard came along the top of the ridge, rifle slung over one shoulder. She held still, the edge of the boulder cold and jagged against her palms. She could feel the guard's eyes on her.

The seconds crawled past. It was a long time—a lifetime—before she heard the shush of footsteps rocking away, as if the man were limping. She edged along the boulder until she could see the white suit silhouetted against the gray sky, the dark head bobbing. Then she pulled herself onto the top and, crouching low, darted across the flat, treeless ridge.

Directly below, sheltering in a stand of cottonwoods, was the dark shadow of a log ranch house with dim lights twinkling in the windows. Behind the house were the shadows of the barn and two small sheds. In the meadow to the left was the village: about twenty tipis arranged around a clearing filled with white figures circling silently around the bonfires. The orange flames licked at the white clothing.

A crowd was milling about the tipi that stood apart from the others, facing the east. Orlando's tipi, she realized. The tipis of the leading men were always set apart. People ducked in and out of the opening, a deliberate intensity in the motion. She was wondering if Orlando himself might appear, when, out of the corner of her eye, she saw the flash of white again moving toward her on the ridge.

She slid down the slope and crouched behind a boulder, still watching the guard. Coming closer. Then he turned and started back the way he'd come. He was dragging his left leg.

Vicky began working her way downward, slicing off the slope in dog legs. She reached the bottom and sprinted through the cottonwoods toward the house. She stopped next to the porch that extended across the front, watching the windows for some movement inside. There was nothing.

After a moment, she walked up the steps and peered through one of the windows. Pushed against the living room wall were several tables covered with computers and monitors with white, ghostly lights shining into the shadows. Odd, after all these years, how she remembered the interior: living room, dining area, and kitchen on the left; bedroom on the right. But the wood-framed sofa and chairs, the crocheted doilies over the backs, the braided rug were gone.

She moved past the door to the other window. She could make out a cot and a small table. There were no sounds. The house was vacant.

She stepped back and tried the door. To her surprise, it opened and she went inside. There were no cabinets or chests in the living room, nothing in which to store dynamite. She pulled her flashlight out of her pack, went into the kitchen, and started flinging open the cabinet doors. The tiny beam played over paper plates, a can of coffee, and in one cabinet, stacks of brown prescription bottles. She focused the beam on one of the labels: James Sherwood. Valium. Take two pills daily for muscle spasms. The beam moved to another label: James Sherwood. Vicodin-ES. Take two pills daily for pain.

She ran the light over the other labels: the same prescriptions from different pharmacies. Some pharmacies were in Denver, others in Riverton and Lander. It struck her that Sherwood had been stockpiling the drugs. She shook several bottles. They were empty.

She retraced her steps through the living room to the bedroom. The closet was empty. She checked under the cot. Nothing.

She went back into the living room, leaned over a monitor, and tapped a key. The white light dissolved into a blue background with rows of brightly colored icons. She clicked on the e-mail program—there could be something, some hint of what Orlando was planning. Even that might prove the dynamite was here.

She waited until the white blocks outlined in black began to take shape. Thirty new messages flashed on the in-box, all with similar subjects: "We love you, Orlando." "Pray for us, Orlando." "My offering."

She opened the last message. "I'm sending two hundred dollars to you for your preaching. I want to join you in the new world." She opened another and another. They were like the first. She wanted to laugh. Orlando, preaching a return to the old Indian ways, using the Internet.

She clicked on bookmarks. A list of website URLs popped up. She was about to select the URL for the shadow ranch when her eyes fell on the line below—the address for the Bureau of Reclamation, Bull Lake Dam. She highlighted the box and brought up the site. A color photo of Bull Lake, like the photo in the tribal engineer's office, rolled onto the monitor. The lake wrapped into the mountain slopes, as quiet and blue as the sky.

Black lines of text started forming below. She slid into the chair in front of the monitor, not taking her eyes away. She was reading the specifications for the dam! Height, ninety feet. Materials, earth covered with concrete on the inside and boulders and rock on the outside. Capacity, 156,000 acre-feet of water. Enough—the realization made her cold—for a great flood. She scrolled back to the photo of the lake and the dam. With sickening clarity, she understood why the Lakotas had brought the stolen dynamite to the shadow ranch. Orlando intended to blow up Bull Lake Dam.

Voices, a snatch of conversation, broke into her thoughts. She glanced at the window. Shadows were moving across the porch toward the door.

❮ 27 ❯

Vicky slid off the chair and moved into the kitchen. The scuff of her sneakers was like drumbeats on the plank floor. Behind her, the front door creaked open. She lunged for the back door. The knob froze in her hand. The orange and yellow lights from the bonfires reflected in the window next to the door. It was then that she saw the man dressed in white standing out back.

She stepped away from the window, heart thumping, legs shaking, and glanced about the kitchen. Cabinets too small to hide in. Table. Three chairs. Stove. Refrigerator in the corner.

"I tell ya, somebody's here." A high-pitched, nervous voice bounced through the quiet. Light burst on in the living room and spilled into the kitchen.

"Check the bedroom." There was an edge of anger in the second voice. "I'll get the kitchen."

The sound of footsteps rose toward her. Vicky darted past the table and squeezed into the corner on the far side of the refrigerator. The footsteps stopped, and a fluorescent bulb staggered into life overhead. She blinked in the brightness and pressed against the cool, smooth surface of the refrigerator. The man outside plastered his face against the window, his breath making a gray smudge on the glass. The slightest turn to the left and he would be looking right at her. She stopped breathing.

The man in the kitchen stood near the table. She could see a slice of him: the thick shoulders and thigh beneath the buckskin suit, the brown fist at his side. A maroon scar seemed to pulse in his cheek. An odor of male perspiration floated toward her. The sound of his breathing was quiet and controlled, like that of a wolf stalking its prey, ready to lunge at the smallest movement.

"Bedroom's clear." The high-pitched voice from the living room broke through the quiet.

The man with the scar relaxed his shoulders into a flabby mound. He gave a wave toward the window, switched off the light, then moved out of sight, and the footsteps, steadier, more relaxed, receded into the living room. "Called me in here for nothing," he said. The living room light went off. "Get back on the ridge. This ain't the time to get nervous."

The guard outside was still peering through the window, shining a flashlight beam over the kitchen. The slim beam shimmered over the countertops and the table. Coming closer. Vicky slid back along the refrigerator until her shoulder and arm jammed into the wall and the plug in an electric socket scraped her leg.

"I seen somebody running across the ridge." An aggrieved, squealing sound came into the high voice. "I know what I seen, and I ain't seein' shadows."

"Yeah? Nobody's here."

"Hold on." The high voice again. "Looks like somebody's been messin' with this here computer."

Oh, God. She'd left the website on the monitor. She pressed her face into the smooth, cold refrigerator and tried to swallow the bile rising in her throat. She was going to be sick.

"What the hell?" The light switched on again in the living room, and now the kitchen window reflected the image of the broad-shouldered man with the scar standing next to a shorter man with one shoulder lower than the other. They bent over the monitor.

"Tol' ya somebody's—"

"Jesus, Martin," the big man interrupted. "Orlando must've sent somebody over to check the dam, that's all. We don't want no mistakes. All the same, I don't want nobody in here I don't know about." He drew himself upright and moved out of view. Vicky heard the sound of a key rattling in the front door. Then, his reflection in the window again, moving toward the kitchen. The shorter man fell in beside him, walking in a jerky motion.

Their reflections were gone from the window, and they were in the kitchen now. Vicky had a clear view of them in the shadows at the door. The man with the scar uncurled his fist, inserted a key in the lock, and yanked the door open.

"You giving orders for the prophet now, Roy?" the other Indian said.

Roy. The man with thick shoulders and the maroon scar was Roy He-Dog. The short, limping man was probably Martin Crow Elk. She was close enough to reach out and touch Ben's killers.

"Nobody's gonna bother the prophet," He-Dog said, stepping outside. "Medicine man's taking care of him. All we gotta do is follow our instructions. Can't have any mess-ups."

The door closed with a force that rattled the windowpane and ran through Vicky like an electric shock. There was another jingling noise, and she realized that He-Dog had reinserted the key and was locking her inside.

They were gone. She could hear the voices receding toward the village. She crept to the door and grabbed the knob. Rigid. Struggling against the waves of panic that flooded over her, she moved to the window. There was no one outside; the guard must have left with the others. The tipis glowed through the trees, and light from the bonfires striped the ground and sides of the barn. The perfect ad for a dude ranch, she thought: Come experience the Old West. She gave a burst of laughter that sounded like a cry.

The window was the old-fashioned type with two vertically sliding panes. She turned the lock in the center, then gripped the metal handle at the bottom and pulled. The window held fast. She examined the thick globs of paint around the edges and realized the window was painted shut. She made her way around the periphery of the house. All the windows, painted shut.

She pulled the cell phone out of her waist pack and punched in 911. The Lakotas were here now; she'd seen them. The police, Gianelli, somebody had to get here. The phone felt inert in her hand, and she stared at the tiny green letters in the readout: NO SERVICE. A sense of unreality floated over her. She was in an unreal world, far from the normal, everyday things.

She went back to the kitchen, took the screwdriver out of her waist pack, and started chipping at the frame. Little specks of paint pricked her hands. She cringed at the noise, then tried the window again. Still stuck. She stepped back.

She could keep chipping—maybe it would work—but the noise could attract the guards.

Think! she told herself.

The big man had locked the doors with a key, which meant the other guards could also have keys, and that meant an extra key might be stashed somewhere. She raised herself on her toes and groped along the top of the door frame until her fingers ran over a small piece of metal, cool and jagged, wedged in the crack. She managed to coax the metal over the lip of the frame. The key dropped at her feet.

She picked it up, unlocked the door, and ran outside, down a path to the barn, still gripping the key, trying to stay in the shadows. About thirty yards away, the tipis wrapped around an arena filled with the orange and red light of bonfires. A large crow perched on top of the pole in the center. The dancers were wheeling in slow motion through the flickering light, their long shadows moving over the tipis. At the entrance to the tipi that faced the east, a guard stood motionless, one hand gripping the black barrel of a rifle.

Vicky climbed through a log fence behind the barn, ran to a small shed, and tried the door. Locked. She moved sideways until enough light fell over the door that she could see the keyhole. She jabbed in the key, hoping the same key would fit all the locks on the ranch buildings. The lock remained rigid. Glancing back at the tipis, she inched around the corner to the window. It was black inside. She dug out her flashlight. The light beam fractured in the black glass, then spread over the shelves inside crowded with stacks of folded blankets, bolts of white cloth, industrial-sized cans of food. The labels weaved in the light: BEANS. STEWED TOMATOES. CHICKEN SOUP. In one corner was a pile of logs and branches, the kind Grandfather always kept to start campfires.

She let the light rest on each shelf for a moment. No sign of dynamite. The dynamite would be in the other shed, as far away as possible from the food and computers.

Switching off the flashlight, she picked her way past the pine branches toward the flat-roofed shed outlined against the gray sky. Through the trees, she saw the guard coming along the periphery of the village. She stood still until he was out of sight, then hurried to the door.

It was also locked, and she tried the key, but it stuck in the keyhole. She had to yank hard to disengage it. She walked around the outside. There were no windows. She could imagine the oily, pungent odor of dynamite in the darkness.

She found her nail file in the waist pack, then knelt in front of the door, shone the flashlight in the keyhole, and probed the gears with the file. It was an old lock, cast in bronze, the kind Grandfather had used on the barn. She could hear the gears clicking over.

She shoved the door open and slid inside, closing it softly behind her. Then she ran the light beam over the walls: metal shelves crowded with spurs and bit chains and folded saddle blankets. An old saddle thrown over a wooden saddle horse, and a small white box in the far corner. She moved closer and focused the beam on the black letters stamped on the side: ARAPAHO RANCH.

She set the flashlight on the dirt floor and took out her camera. The light flickered over the ceiling. Her hands shook, her fingers fumbled for the correct buttons, then she raised the camera, located the dynamite crate in the lens, and pressed the top button. Another picture, then another, moving in closer now, going down on one knee, the flash sizzling in her eyes.

The door snapped open behind her, and smoky air rushed into the small space. She felt something hard—fist? boot?—crash into her back, and she sprawled forward over the hard dirt floor. She was breathing dirt. Dirt in her nose. The gritty, bitter taste of dirt in her mouth. Another blow sent a white hot flash of pain through her ribs, and she drew in her legs and curled into herself. Before the blackness, she was aware of the low, confident voice of He-Dog floating above her: "Goddamn. A woman!"

‹ 28 ›

Father John turned off Seventeen-Mile Road into the mission grounds, the sun lost behind the mountains, the sky layered in reds and violets. He checked his watch. Almost eight-thirty. The board of directors had been meeting for thirty minutes. Father George was a stickler for starting on time.

He followed the blinking red taillights of a truck through the tunnel of cottonwoods, past the green pickup with the two Arapahos, cowboy hats pushed back, seated in front. He waved to the guards and turned onto Circle Drive. Several pickups and old cars were parked in front of the church and administration building. He stopped alongside an orange truck just as the driver's door swung open. Amos Walking Bear gripped the top of the door and lifted himself out. Another elder, Clarence Wilbur, was climbing out of the passenger seat.

"Good to see you, grandfathers," Father John said. He walked over and clapped Amos's shoulder.

The elder reached inside the cab, grabbed his cane, then waved the cane toward the alley leading to Eagle Hall.

"Okay if we come to this here big meeting?"

"Absolutely." Father John smiled at the two old men in plaid shirts and blue jeans and cowboy hats outlined against the fiery sky, faces creased in shadow. He'd been hoping Amos and some of the parish council members would attend the board of directors meeting.

He ushered the elders down the alley, Clarence hunched forward, Amos tapping the cane ahead. Old warriors more accustomed to riding than walking over the dried, hard earth. He left them at the entrance to Eagle Hall.

Then he walked back to the concrete steps in front of the administration building and took them two at a time. Cool shadows stretched across the corridor into his office. The new windowpane glowed red in the sunset. He flipped on the desk lamp and checked his messages. No message from Gianelli.

He lifted the phone. He had to warn Vicky. There was some connection between Ben and Dean, something that had gotten them both killed. And they had both gone to the shadow ranch. Vicky might stumble on the connection—he knew her; she wouldn't stop until she'd found Ben's killer. She could be sucked into the vortex of a madman.

He tried her office first: "You've reached the law office . . ."

He hit the disconnect button, tapped out her home number, and listened to the ringing. Pick up. Pick up. An electronic voice told him to leave a message.

"Call me as soon as you get in," he said to the machine. "This is John," he added.

He pressed the disconnect again, wondering how he was going to convince her to be careful, not take risks. Not take risks? That was a laugh. There was no telling what risks she might take. He stared at the phone in his hand a moment before dialing Gianelli's office. Another answering service. "I have to speak to you right away, Ted," he said. "It's urgent."

Urgent. That was how Dean Little Horse had termed the message he'd sent to Ben Holden. He replaced the receiver and headed for the meeting.

Two long tables where the parishioners usually sat for feasts or for donuts and coffee after Sunday Mass had been pushed together at the end of Eagle Hall. Seated on the far side were the directors: Father George and the bishop in the center. The three Jesuits who had arrived this morning sat on the left, and on the right, five other Jesuits who had trickled in during the afternoon, heads bent over copies of the annual report. Amos, Clarence, Leonard Bizzel, the caretaker, and half a dozen other Arapahos were scattered around the folding chairs in front of the tables, holding up copies of the report, squinting in the bright, fluorescent light.

"Sorry to be late." Father John took the vacant chair at the far end, next to Father Niles Johnston, who nodded his white head and continued running a finger down the column of figures on the page in front of him. Amos was in the front row, and in the elder's eyes, Father John recognized the fear that had been gnawing at his own insides the last couple of weeks. There was no denying the truth in the financial report.

A stapled packet of papers was handed down the table to him. "We've been going over the finances," Father George said.

Father John left the packet unopened. He'd written the

report, totaled up the columns again and again in the quiet of the night, hoping that each addition would yield a different sum, but it was always the same. Expenses exceeded income.

"We don't understand . . ." Father Niles hesitated, then cleared his throat and, like the university professor he'd been for thirty years, launched into a discourse on the impossibility of operating a business with accounts in the red. Indeed, no business—he was warming to the subject now—could consider being in the red *normal*.

"St. Francis is not a business." Father John set his elbows on the table and clasped his hands. He was the superior here, he reminded himself. The officer-in-charge, in the military hierarchy of the Jesuits—officer-in-charge of a backwater post—but in charge nonetheless. Not his assistant, not the directors, not even the bishop, who was leaning forward, looking at him along the line of black coats. They were advisers. They would probably advise the Provincial that the mission should be closed, but they would do so without the acquiescence of the Superior.

"What this report doesn't take into account"—Father John had waited until the other priest stopped for a breath—"are the random acts of generosity."

"Random acts?" One of the priests at the far end spoke up, making no attempt to hide the contempt in his voice. Rumbling noises of disdain erupted down the line and the other priests shifted over the table, like soldiers ready to charge.

Father John went on: "Donations always arrive when we least expect them." The little miracles, he almost added. He'd depended on the little miracles for the past eight years. He was aware of the other priests' eyes on him, the expressions of disbelief in their pale, flushed faces. But the Arapahos sat straight-shouldered, nodding, smiling. From outside came the sounds of tires on gravel, and Father John felt his muscles tense. Dear God, don't let the shooter return.

"Surely, John, you can't expect the mission to operate . . ." The dead ringer for Thomas Aquinas presenting a logical, reasoned argument. "It's foolish to presume . . . Random donations cannot be counted upon . . . Bankruptcy . . ."

The door opened and six Arapaho men filed inside. They moved silently into the last row, sat down, and dipped their heads in respect to the elders seated ahead.

"Welcome," Father John said. "We're discussing finances."

The Indians nodded.

Father Niles lifted his white head and said, "Without either an endowment or a reliable source of income—and may I inject that St. Francis has neither—how do you intend to meet the current bills?"

"That would appear to be one of the great mysteries of the universe," said the Thomistic scholar.

Father George cleared his throat. "As it happens, Father, two checks arrived in today's mail." There was a note almost of apology in his tone. "They should cover the month's expenses."

The Arapahos exchanged sideways glances. Warriors, Father John thought, watching for the next skirmish.

It came at once. "We must not ignore the other issues." Father James, his old friend from the seminary, always wanting to take the broad perspective. "The Society is stretched thin, as we know. Universities, colleges, high schools, missions, and not enough priests to fill the positions. We have to reevaluate each situation."

"You've seen our schedule of programs," Father John began.

"Yes, yes, yes." Father Niles gave an impatient wave. "Despite the programs, it appears that not everyone on the reservation would like the mission to continue."

There was a slight change in the atmosphere, a stillness falling over the hall. Finally, Father John said, "The shooting last night was an isolated incident."

"Isolated!" The bishop gave a bark of laughter. "You say it's isolated, and yet two guards are posted at the entrance to keep out other riflemen. Please, Father."

The door squealed open again, and more people crowded inside: two, three, four families, several grandmothers and elders. They filled up the remaining chairs. Leonard jumped up and began unfolding other chairs stacked along the back wall.

Amos Walking Bear got to his feet and leaned forward on the cane. "Can I speak, Father?" he said, locking eyes with him.

"Of course, grandfather." Father John could feel the impatience bristling along the table. Father Niles let out a long exhalation of breath.

"Long time ago," Amos began, the dark eyes moving along the row of priests, "hundred and twenty years ago, the chiefs made a pact with the Jesuits. You come here and teach our children and we'll give you land. We'll put up buildings and take care of the place. So the Jesuits—they was all white men—said they'd come and help the people. They kept their word, and that surprised us." There was a little undercurrent of laughter in the audience; heads started nodding. Several other Arapahos were filing through the door, finding places along the back wall.

The elder went on. "Now you come here from some other places and you say you're gonna do like the rest of the whites and go back on your word. You say—"

"I believe," the bishop interrupted, "that you're talking about the past. We have to consider the state of the mission now."

"Excuse me, but I'm talkin' about now, Bishop." Amos kept his tone polite, steady. "Mission's still here. People still need help. You gonna go back on your word?"

People were still crowding into the hall, a sea of dark faces pressing toward them. Leonard was backing through the door, dragging four chairs.

"If you insist upon looking at the matter in those terms," another Jesuit at the far end spoke up—an historian. "It would seem that, after all this time, the Society has certainly . . ."

Leonard hurried past the crowd standing along the side wall and leaned over the table. "Important message, Father," he whispered. "Phone was ringing when I went to the office for more chairs. Rose White Plume says it's an emergency." He pushed a slip of paper scribbled with a telephone number across the table.

Father John got to his feet. "Excuse me," he said, interrupting the historian in the middle of explaining the relationship between the Jesuits and the Plains Indians in 1874. "There's an emergency. Please continue." This last he directed to Father George.

Then he hurried through the crowd in the side aisle and nearly collided with another group coming through the door. He waved them inside, then broke into a run down the alley, around the corner of the administration building, up the concrete steps. He turned on the light in his office and dialed the number.

Aunt Rose picked up on the first ring. He could feel the fear vibrating through the wires.

"Father John, grandmother. What's happened?"

"Oh, Father. I didn't know who else to call."

"Tell me what it is," he said, trying to soften the bite of impatience in his tone.

"It's Vicky."

"Is she all right?"

"I don't know. I don't think so. That's why I called you. Somebody's gotta find her."

"Find her? What are you talking about?"

"She's not home. She's not at her office. I been callin' and callin' and nobody answers. I tried callin' her boy, Lucas. He's over there with the Holden clan, but nobody answered there, either. She says she had to find a couple of Lakotas that killed Ben. She could be in trouble, and nobody around to help her!"

"Where did she go, grandmother?"

"Up in the mountains to see the shadow dancers."

"The shadow ranch?" God, she went alone to the shadow ranch. "When did she leave?"

"Four hours ago. Should've called me by now. She says the Lakotas have the dynamite. They're gonna blow up something."

Father John heard his own gasp of air, sudden and disembodied. The day box Dean had wanted to tell Holden about contained dynamite! It was probably the day box that Holden—or the Lakotas—would have used to carry sticks of dynamite to someplace on the Arapaho Ranch where they intended to blow out tree stumps or build a road or pond. Vicky must have found out that the dynamite was at the shadow ranch.

And so were the killers.

He tried to remember what he'd read about Wovoka: The event would occur on the final night of a dance session. Tonight was the final night of the current session.

"Listen to me, grandmother. I want you to call the fed."

"I already did. He's got his answering machine on."

"Call him again. Leave a message. Tell him everything you've told me. Tell him he has to get up to the shadow ranch, that Vicky's in danger."

There was a sharp gasp at the other end.

"I'm going up there right away," he said. Then he said, "Try not to worry." He was talking to himself, as well as to the old woman.

He hung up, rummaged in a bottom desk drawer for a flashlight, then grabbed a jacket from the coat tree and ran for the Toyota.

It was only when he drove past the guards still parked under the trees and sped toward Seventeen-Mile Road that he remembered the board meeting. The fate of St. Francis Mission could be settled tonight, and he wouldn't be there.

‹ 29 ›

From far away away came the sound of drumbeats calling her back to life. Vicky struggled to fight her way up through layers of blackness, dimly aware of the vibrations pulsing through the ground beneath her. Her arms and legs felt stiff, dead. She couldn't dislodge whatever was jammed in her mouth. It was foul and tasted of gasoline. It made her retch.

The drum beat faster, the sound crashing through the blackness. Footsteps thudded nearby. Men were shouting and, over the shouts, the sound of women wailing.

Vicky snapped into consciousness and blinked in the dim light. Something was going on outside. The village had been enveloped in silence, and now—drums, shouting. She tried to raise her head. Pain shot down her neck and into her shoulders. She realized she was tied up—trussed up like an animal carcass—arms pulled back, wrists looped together, ankles and legs squeezed tight. She twisted her fingers about until they grasped the rough surface of a rope—the same rope crossing over her arms and chest and squeezing her ribs against her lungs. Her head was throbbing.

She maneuvered around in a half-circle, trying to get her bearings. She was still in the shed. In the thin thread of light that traced the edges of the door, she could see the metal shelving on the right and the crate of dynamite. The dynamite was still here! That gave her an odd sense of hope. Whatever Orlando intended to destroy, he hadn't destroyed it yet. There was still time.

She had to get out of here. By pulling sideways, she could see her waist. The waist pack was gone—the screwdriver, nail file, flashlight, every piece of metal she might have used. She searched the shadows on the floor. The pack wasn't here.

The drums beat harder, cutting through a cacophony of panic—shouting and wailing—that matched her own. Her eyes raced around the walls looking for a nail, a hook, a piece of metal, something sharp, that she could reach. There was nothing, except the metal shelving that held the containers of insecticide and rodenticide.

She scooted toward the shelves, rolling her hips and shouldering herself sideways, panting through her nose, fighting back the gorge in her throat. Finally she managed to back up against the vertical metal frame.

She tried to lift herself on one hip, fingers running up the frame, searching for a sharp edge. Her fingertips brushed a crack in the metal. A loose piece jutted out, but it was too high. She couldn't get a grip on it. The rope pulled her legs, keeping them straight, like two dead stumps attached to her body. Her knees wouldn't bend; she couldn't get any leverage.

She maneuvered around, flipped onto her stomach, and lifting her legs, thrust her feet at the frame, trying to push the broken strip downward. The rope cutting into her flesh made her retch with pain. She kicked again. The frame shivered, but the broken strip stayed in place.

She lay with the side of her face pressed into the dirt floor, exhausted, breathing in dust mixed with the smell of chemicals and her own perspiration and fear. Outside people were shouting and running about. She could feel the frenzy vibrating through the shed. God, what was going on? The dance must have ended. *They*—the Lakotas, Ben's killers— would come for the dynamite. They'd come for her.

She flipped to her side and slid upward along the frame. The hard, rounded edge bit into her spine. Her fingers curled around the metal, and she pulled herself higher, wincing with the pain that ripped through the sockets of her arms. Her eyes blurred; the tears burned on her cheeks. She strained upward, forcing her fingers to climb higher— an inch, a half-inch. Something warm and wet—blood— ran along her hand.

She'd found the broken metal. She pulled as hard as she could until she felt the strip give way and bend downward, the edge cutting into her fingers. It was as sharp as a knife.

Suddenly she was aware of the silence. The drumming and shouting—when had they stopped? She was enveloped in silence, as if the shed had been deposited in the middle of the plains surrounded by the endless stillness of the sky and something else: the stillness of a tornado before it touches down.

She thrust the rope around her wrists into the sharp edge and started sawing. Up and down, pain ripping across her shoulders, numbness flowing down her arms. The tears were coming fast, blurring the shed in the dim light, until she felt as if she were moving under water. Up and down. Up and down.

There was a barely perceptible loosening, a slackening so slight she feared she'd imagined it out of her own desperation. She kept sawing, buoyed with new hope and strength. She wondered if the drums and shouting had been as frightening as the silence outside.

The rope gave way. She could raise one wrist above the other and managed to slip one hand free. She yanked at the rope until it dangled loosely around her chest and she was able to reach one arm around and rip the rag out of her mouth—the stinking rag! She took in hugh gulps of air, then tore away the rope, spasms racing down her arms.

She was scrambling upright when she heard the thud of footsteps outside.

"Get a grip on yourself." It was He-Dog, the confident voice, sharp with anger. "We got work to finish."

Vicky tugged at the rope still around her legs, then started rolling—propelling herself—across the shed to where they'd left her. Then she remembered she'd left the gag by the shelving.

"But Orlando . . ." The high, whiny voice of the man with the limp.

"Shut up!" Something blocked the light around the door, and the shed plunged into blackness.

She scooted back to the frame and threw herself facedown, hands scrambling over the dirt trying to find the gag.

"He said he was the messiah," the whiny voice went on. "He said nobody was gonna die in the new world . . ."

"I said, shut up, you fool!"

Her hand clamped over the soggy cloth. She jammed it into her mouth and started scooting sideways, pushing herself with her hands.

"We gotta keep going. Do just like we promised, so the

new world can come." The door burst open, orange-tinged light flooding into the shed. Vicky slid downward and tried to make herself small, part of the shadows.

"He's waiting for us." The boots stomped past her, as if the men had forgotten about her. "He's bringing the ancestors."

"I don't know . . ."

"Get the box. The trucks are coming up." Then, in a softer tone, "You heard what the messiah said. We gotta go on."

The men crossed back to the door as He-Dog kicked it wide open, then stepped aside and waited for the other man to haul the box outside. There was the low rumble of a truck engine cutting back.

Vicky shut her eyes; she could feel He-Dog's gaze burning into her. Then, the boots clumped out the door, and her eyes snapped open. She could see the men pushing the box into the bed of a truck, then slamming the tailgate. Someone stood by the door, the end of a cigarette glowing red in the orange light.

"Take care of the woman," He-Dog said.

"You hit her pretty hard." The high-pitched whine again. "She's dead."

He-Dog walked alongside the truck and lifted a gun out of the rack at the rear window. He handed the gun to the other Indian. "Make sure. We gotta get to the dam before somebody comes looking for her. We can't take any chances." He nodded toward the shed. "Do like I say."

And then the man with the limp stood in the doorway, blocking the light. Vicky could hear the engines revving up behind him, the tires spinning against the earth as the black barrels of the rifle turned toward her.

• • •

In the half-light of the moon breaking through the clouds, the trees on the uphill slope looked like a wilderness of spirits. Another mile, Father John guessed, before he reached the guardhouse. He'd turned off the headlights a mile or so back, and the two-track disappeared ahead in the grayness.

As he came around a curve, he saw the glow of light through the trees. He slowed down and inched forward until he spotted the narrow clearing. He jerked the wheel right, drove into the trees, and stopped a few inches behind a bumper that glinted in the dim light. Vicky's Bronco. She'd done exactly what he planned to do: avoid the guardhouse and hike over the ridge.

He found the flashlight under the seat, got out, and shone the light into the Bronco. It was stamped with her absence. The pines around the vehicle glowed in the light beam. He switched off the flashlight and gave himself a moment for his eyes to adjust in the moonlight that filtered through the branches. Gradually the darkness seemed to lift, and he walked back to the pickup.

A gunshot reverberated overhead. The retort rolled through the trees and echoed off the mountainside.

Father John dropped down alongside the pickup and waited for the next shot. A guard on top must have spotted him. Except for the wind in the trees and the sound of his own heart, an immense silence closed around him.

He waited. Only one shot. He tried to think logically. The sound had been close, yet muffled, which meant it hadn't come from on top. It must have come from the valley on the other side. From the village. Where Vicky was.

Dear God, he prayed, the only prayer he could manage. Dear God, Dear God.

He plunged into the trees, dismissing the idea of checking the toolbox in the back of the pickup for a wrench or screwdriver. There were no weapons to match a rifle.

He'd gone about thirty feet when he spotted the clearing, moonlight running like a river between the trees and the upward thrust of the ridge.

He stopped at the edge. To the left was the guardhouse, a black shadow straddling the earth a dim light inside. Something was different, he could sense it. No sign of movement. The guardhouse was deserted.

Father John stayed in the trees, trying to decide what to do. He could work his way to the guardhouse, then take the main road into the village—the shorter route. But the guard might have just stepped away for a moment, gone to check on the rifle shot. And he ran the risk of meeting other guards on the road.

He was about to cross the clearing when headlights flashed across the guardhouse. A truck roared past and turned onto the two-track. Another truck squealed out behind. Through the trees, Father John could see the headlights streaming in the direction of the reservation.

He stared after the trucks for a couple seconds, trying to grasp the logic. There was no one in the guardhouse, and the other guards could have just driven off. Something had happened, and whatever it was, it was not good. And Vicky was still at the ranch.

He plunged back into the trees, crashing through the branches that scratched at his face and hands. Then he backed the pickup onto the two-track, rammed the gear into forward, and drove for the guardhouse, headlights blazing ahead. He thumped past the opened gate and started climbing up the switchbacks that he'd taken with the Lakota two days ago.

At the summit, the road narrowed, then started downward. Father John hunched forward, gripping the wheel tight, trying to keep the tires from slipping sideways down the slope on the tight turns. An orange light glowed from the center of the village below. There were no other vehicles in sight, no sign of movement, and the absence of human activity created a void that struck him as more ominous than a phalanx of guards. It was the void at the end of the world.

He bounced across the meadow past the log house and hit the brake. The pickup was still rolling forward when he grabbed the flashlight, jumped out, and ran toward the village. Bonfires were scattered about the arena, casting orange and red shadows over the white tipis.

He was thirty feet away when he saw the large white mounds, like mounds of snow, among the bonfires. He stopped. He was breathing hard, his heart was thumping. The reality came to him in fragments, small enough to absorb one at a time, until he understood. The crumpled bodies in white, the naked arms and legs, the hands splayed in the dirt, the bare feet and stray moccasins flung about. Gray smoke that smelled like charred cottonwood hung over the arena. He had a sense that he'd stepped into the past, and the heaps of bodies lying around the bonfires, locked in the silence of death, were Chief Big Foot's followers. That the massacre at Wounded Knee was still taking place.

He made himself go to the nearest body—a young woman. He dropped down on both knees beside her, grabbing for her wrist and probing for a pulse. Where was the pulse? Her eyes were closed, as if she'd dropped into a peaceful sleep. It was a couple seconds before he could feel it: the almost imperceptible rhythm of her blood coursing through her veins. He saw the slight movement of her chest. She was breathing! He knew instantly that she was drugged—drugged, but alive—and he felt almost sick with relief.

He got to his feet and went to the next body. A round-faced, pudgy man, his eyelids flickering, his breath slow and quiet. Dropping down again, Father John felt the steady pulse in the thick neck. Then he got to his feet and went to the next dancer and the next, working his way around the arena, some part of his mind keeping count: five, six, seven. A total of twenty-six dancers, drugged and unconscious. Alive, thank God, alive.

He looked around. Vicky had to be here somewhere. In the house, the sheds. He'd started across the arena when he saw the flap thrown back on Orlando's tipi and candles inside flickering over the canvas walls. He ran over and stooped inside. Across from the opening, Orlando lay on a buffalo robe spread over three hay bales. He was dressed in white buckskin, arms crossed over his chest, bare feet emerging from the trousers, black hair spread out like a fan. Three small candles at his head gave off a yellowish light and the faint smell of wax and sulfur.

Father John walked over and lay one hand on the cool, soft wrist, trying to detect some sign of life. The flesh was inert, the man's chest was still. "May God forgive you," he said.

Then, with a sickening clarity, he realized the man had been *laid out*. He must have died earlier, and then what? Had the dancers wanted to follow him into the afterworld? It must have been part of a plan. The dancers were supposed to die, like Orlando. The guards had probably distributed whatever drugs they'd taken, but something had gone wrong and the drugs hadn't worked the way Orlando had intended. But the guards had already sped off.

And Vicky could be with them.

He wanted to believe, but a part of him knew that if they'd found her here, they would never have allowed her to live. The sound of the rifle shot screamed through his mind. They'd shot her. Left her somewhere in the village. In one of the tipis, in the ranch house or the barn or the sheds. He would search every inch of the shadow ranch until he found her.

He lurched through the opening and started toward the other tipis. The breeze was hot and smoky, reeking of death.

On the far side of the arena, beyond the prone figures of the dancers and the bonfires, almost imperceptible but present nonetheless: a moving shadow. He ran toward it, then stopped. Vicky emerged from between two tipis, face blanched, eyes wide in shock.

‹ 30 ›

She walked into the arena as if she hadn't seen him, arms extended, gaze darting around the drugged dancers. The bonfires glowed orange and red on her face.

"Vicky!" Father John shouted, but she kept walking. He shouted her name again, then grabbed her by the shoulders, stopping her in place. He turned her toward him, aware of the warmth of her, the reality of her, in his hands. "Are you all right?"

She tilted her head back and blinked up at him, as if she were trying to bring into focus some specter that had materialized in front of her. He felt her trembling beneath his hands.

"Orlando killed them!" Vicky strained toward the white mounds.

"They're unconscious, Vicky," he said. "We have to get help. They've been drugged."

"Drugged!" She let out a little cry and cupped one hand over her mouth. Then she said, "My God, John. It's started. They've gone into the shadow world to welcome the ancestors. The new world is coming. The Lakotas are going to blow up Bull Lake Dam."

He could read the truth in her eyes, as if fragments had arranged themselves into a coherent whole that he could finally grasp. Before the new world could come, the old world had to be washed away. The Lakotas had stolen the dynamite for Orlando. Bull Lake Dam! The water would crash down over the reservation. Ethete, Arapaho, Riverton—St. Francis Mission.

"We have to get to a phone," he said, taking her arm and guiding her through the tipis toward the pickup.

Father John drove down the two-track and onto the graveled road, taking the bends on two tires, Vicky tapping at the buttons on his cell phone. "No service," she screamed.

They were careening toward Fort Washakie when the sound of sirens rose like a wall of granite down the road, then the red, blue, and yellow lights flashed into the night. Father John pulled onto the shoulder as three BIA police cars sped by.

"They're on the way to the ranch." He could hear the feeling of relief in his voice.

"How . . . ?" Vicky turned toward him. She was gripping the phone in one hand. A residue of yellow light washed over her.

"Aunt Rose called them," he said, pulling the pickup back onto the road.

She started tapping the buttons again. "It's working," she cried. Then, into the phone: "Vicky Holden." She was shouting. "Get medical help to the shadow ranch. The dancers are unconscious. They've been drugged." She hesitated, then plunged on. "They took Valium and Vicodin. I saw the empty prescription bottles. And now, two Lakotas are on the way to Bull Lake to blow up the dam. That's right. They have dynamite."

Vicky was quiet a moment, then she clicked off the phone. "There's an officer on patrol in the area. He's on his way."

Dear God, Father John thought, let the officer get there in time.

Father John slowed through Fort Washakie and turned north. Highway 287 lengthened into the darkness beyond the headlights. There were no other vehicles. He jammed down on the accelerator. Black shadows of trees raced by outside his window.

"Orlando has everything planned," Vicky said. "He wants to make sure his prophecy comes true. He's going to destroy the reservation."

"Orlando's dead, Vicky." Father John glanced over. She was staring at him, pinpricks of light flashing in her eyes.

"I don't understand. He was waiting for the new world. Why did he die and not the . . ." She halted, as if another thought had intercepted the one she'd been following. "The prescriptions were his," she said. "He must have built up a tolerance, so he took more pills than the dancers. He must have taken an overdose."

Possible, Father John thought. The man was sick. He'd probably been using the drugs for some time. He could have taken a lot to make sure they worked.

Father John eased up on the accelerator and guided the pickup around a bend. The road cut through a shadowy landscape of treeless bluffs, the flat surfaces soaking up the moonlight. He was acutely aware of Vicky beside him, her profile outlined in the moonlight.

He looked at her. She was alive; thank God, she was alive. "I was afraid they'd killed you," he said. "What happened?"

She began slowly, then hurried along, the story spilling out: the climb up the ridge, the house, the guards, the dynamite box, the shed. He could feel his muscles tense as she talked. They'd knocked her unconscious in the shed; she could have been killed.

"They came back for the dynamite." Her eyes were still on him. "After everything got quiet, they came back. They took the box outside, and I heard He-Dog say, 'Shoot the bitch.' Crow Elk came back into the shed." Hysteria had begun to seep into her voice.

He reached over and took her hand. "You're okay, Vicky. You're safe."

She gripped his hand in both of hers. "He was pointing the rifle at me, John. I could see down the barrel. It was a long, black tunnel. It was very still. And then I saw the fear in his eyes. He was looking at something he'd never seen before and it was horrible, and that's when I knew he couldn't do it. He jerked the rifle up and everything exploded around me, and he ran out. I heard the trucks drive off."

Father John was quiet for a long time, watching the road ahead, unable to imagine a world in which she did not exist. He tried to follow what she was saying: how Orlando must have sent the Lakotas to the Arapaho Ranch to steal the dynamite. There would be dynamite on the ranch to clear out stumps, build roads, create waterholes; Orlando would have known that.

"Ben could have called Gianelli," Father John said.

"Admit somebody had stolen dynamite from him? You didn't know Ben."

"I knew him." Recovering alcoholic. Determined to get *everything* back that belonged to him, including Vicky.

"He went after the Lakotas himself." Vicky paused. "I don't understand how he knew they'd gone to the shadow ranch."

"Dean Little Horse," Father John said. "He was there for three days, trying to get Janis to leave. He must have seen the dynamite, and . . ." A new idea shoved its way into his mind. "He wrote the operating software for the gate at Bull Lake Dam. He must have guessed what Orlando had in mind. If Orlando blew up the dam, he would cause the flood he'd been prophecizing. Dean left the ranch on Sunday, went to his office, and e-mailed Ben Holden."

Neither spoke for a few moments, then Vicky said, "They were alike, Dean and Ben. Dean had his own reason for not going to Gianelli. He was probably trying to protect the girl. He didn't want the fed to go to the ranch, not with Janis still one of Orlando's followers."

It made sense, Father John was thinking, except for one thing. Dean must have begged Janis to leave with him, but she hadn't gone with him. And yet, she went to Dean's apartment on Sunday evening, looking for him. Maybe she'd decided to leave the ranch after all. But it was too late by then. The Lakotas had already found Dean. And she'd gone back to the ranch, back to Orlando.

He tried to follow what Vicky was saying, something about Janis Beaver staying with Aunt Rose and stealing the gun. "The perfect weapon," she said. "It could be traced right back to me." The sound of her laughter was forced and tight. It drifted over the thrum of the tires on the asphalt.

They were climbing now, the pickup bouncing over the narrow road. The slopes on either side blocked out the moonlight, so that only the headlights shone through the darkness. He could still see Janis Beaver, huddled in the tipi, the pretty face hard with certitude. Dean had come for her. He'd loved her, but in the end, she'd chosen Orlando. And now she was lying unconscious—God, let the ambulances be there!

Father John wheeled through a sharp curve, trying to remember. Where was Janis lying? There were several young women close together by one of the bonfires. Had she been among them? In another group? A solitary mound in front of one of the tipis? Had all the faces simply blurred together in his own shock?

The road was climbing along Bull Creek; the trees were sparse now, crowded out by clumps of willows that looked black and grotesque in the moonlight. He eased on the brake and peered ahead for the turnoff into the area of Bull Lake.

He steered around another curve, then spotted the break in the willows. He turned left. The willows crept close to the sides of the pickup, the tires chattered on the gravel. He could see the dam ahead, a black wall rising out of the earth, backlit by the moonlight. The road veered to the right, climbing toward the top of the dam. Another quarter-mile, and he could see the lake, an enormous body of black water. A metallic sheen rippled over the surface.

A white Wind River police car, a kaleidoscope of lights whirling over the roof, blocked the road ahead. The driver's door hung open. Father John jammed down the brake pedal. In the headlights, he could see the bulky figure slumped next to the door.

‹ 31 ›

Father John got out and ran to the prone body. A hole as big as a crater gaped in the officer's chest and a pool of oil-black blood was soaking into the fragments of his blue uniform shirt. The holster on the black belt was pushed back, the flap still snapped over the gun handle. Father John lay a hand against the man's neck. It was as inert as leather.

He looked up through the whirling red and blue lights at the sky. It was immense, a vast and impersonal darkness with moon-edged clouds moving eastward and breaking up at intervals to reveal a scattering of stars that flickered in the void. They were too late. The Lakotas were here, and when the officer had tried to stop them, they'd shot him. It was a moment before he could summon a prayer: "God, have mercy on us."

He got to his feet. Stepping around the body, he reached inside and grabbed the black radio. He fumbled with the buttons a moment. A shrill noise mixed with static, then a woman's voice. "Go ahead."

"This is Father O'Malley," he managed. "The officer at Bull Lake . . ." The name, what was the man's name? He leaned over the body, unable to read the blood-smeared badge. "He's been shot. Get some other officers up here. The dam's going to be dynamited."

"Cars are on the way, Father." The woman was shouting at the other end. "Father, you better get out of there."

He replaced the radio and turned to Vicky. The blue and red lights washed intermittently over her face and black T-shirt. "The Lakotas are at the spillway," she said.

She was right, he knew. There was no movement along the top of the dam, no sign of anyone, only the flat concrete surface that held back the lake from the darkness dropping away below. The Lakotas would plant the dynamite deep inside the spillway; the dynamite would blow a hole in the base; the water would surge through and bring down the dam. And the flood . . .

"Listen to me," he said. "This whole place is going to be obliterated. Get the flashlight out of the pickup. Start climbing. Climb as high as you can. Please, Vicky."

She stared at him in disbelief. "For goddsakes, John. We have to get to the spillway." She shouldered past and threw herself into the passenger seat.

He got in behind the wheel, and started maneuvering the pickup backward into a narrow clearing. There was no time to argue, and it wouldn't do any good. She would never run away. They hurtled down a narrow path that angled along the side of the dam.

In the gray light, he could see the boulder and rock face of the dam rising higher and higher outside Vicky's window as they dropped toward the creek below. The sound of running water grew louder, and then the creek came into view, a narrow funnel of silver pouring out of the concrete spillway that resembled the entrance to a tunnel. The cuts of other service roads converged through the brush and rock.

Vicky leaned forward, braced her hands on the dashboard, and stared down at the roads. "They've already left," she yelled. "The trucks are gone!"

Father John tightened his grip on the wheel. The roads below were vacant. He felt a stillness settling over him— the stillness of death. The Lakotas had already set the dynamite and gotten out of there. The dam would blow at any moment.

They were close to the creek now; he could feel the cool moisture in the air. He turned right, and the pickup lurched to a stop in a clump of willows. "Wait here," he said. "Let me take a look around."

"It's my world that's about to be destroyed, John." Vicky threw her door open and started to slide out.

He took hold of her arm. "Listen to me, Vicky. I need you to stay here. Watch for the trucks, do you understand? You can see the roads from here. The Lakotas might not have finished setting the dynamite. They could come back."

It was a moment before she nodded. He grabbed the flashlight from under the seat, got out, and started through the willows, moving at a diagonal toward the edge of the spillway, sweeping the flashlight beam ahead. The squish of his boots in the muck mixed with the sounds of the creek. He was breathing in the damp spray.

He reached the base of the dam and started edging along the sloped rock-faced wall. At the entrance, he grabbed the rough corner and swung himself around. It was pitch black inside. The flashlight beam was no more than a thin strand of light penetrating the darkness. He waved the beam along the wall, then across the opposite wall. Webs of green moss crawled over the concrete and glistened in the light. Deep inside, almost lost in the blackness, was the faint metallic sheen of the gate. Water ran beneath and spilled out into the creek, sending up little jets of spray.

He was about to start up the spillway when the light beam hit the dynamite. Twelve sticks taped together, dangling from some kind of hook embedded in the concrete. Extending from the middle tube were two thin leg wires—one blue, the other yellow. They ran above the surface of the water, then angled out the entrance.

He kept the light beam on the wires: along the creek, into the willows. Suddenly they disappeared. He stooped close to the ground and pushed aside the branches until the beam found the yellow wire, thin and stiff, running in a straight line into an area of trampled grasses. He traced the wire toward the small metal object glinting in the light.

He moved closer. A clock, he could see it clearly now: the black numerals circling the white face and the yellow wire attached to the hour hand. A black wire ran from the minute hand. He struggled to pull from his memory everything he'd ever heard about dynamite. The tiniest electric spark—that much he knew—and it would detonate.

He went down on one knee and shone the light over the wiring, conscious of the sound of his own breathing against the water lapping over the rocks. The hour hand was on 12; the minute hand was a little more than one minute before 12. One minute, and the hands would touch, and when they touched, an electrical charge would shoot through the wires to the dynamite.

Something had to deliver the charge—a battery. That was it! The blue wire he'd lost in the willows was attached to a battery; so was the black wire on the minute hand, making a complete circuit. He had to detach the wires.

He reached for the clock, then drew back his hand. The minute hand was a hair's breath from 12. The wires so close, he could accidentally jam them together and set off the dynamite. He had one minute now to find the battery.

He started following the black wire from the minute hand, crouching low, stumbling through the bramble, throwing back the willow stalks, counting off the seconds. The flashlight flickered off, then on again.

Twenty-five seconds, twenty. The wire twisted through the brush and disappeared in the undergrowth. He stepped backward, picked up the trail again, then lunged into the brush. He had it now, the tiny black wire snaking close to the ground. He kept the light on top of it all the way to the oblong black box set on a bed of willow branches.

Ten seconds. He threw himself toward the box and fell on his knees. The wire from the minute hand looped over the positive pole. The blue wire attached to the dynamite was twisted around the negative pole. He yanked at one wire, then the other. They strangled the poles, refusing to let go. He threw down the flashlight and fumbled for the end of the black wire and started unwinding it, his mind still ticking off the seconds.

Six. Five. Four.

"Come on," he shouted, yanking as hard as he could. The wire popped free, and the recoil sent him backward into the mud and trampled branches. He lay still for several minutes, gasping for air, his heart pounding against his ribs.

He didn't see the shadow until it flickered across the beam of light.

‹ 32 ›

"What the hell . . ." a voice shouted.

Father John felt something hard crash against his ribs and he flipped sideways. His face pushed into the wet, mushy earth and sharp roots. The crash came again and again, his shoulder this time, then his back. A jagged line of pain ran down his spine and into both legs. The pain seared his lungs. He couldn't breathe.

He clawed at the ground and managed to get enough leverage to raise himself up so that he could see the large, broad-shouldered Indian standing over him, the white buckskin trousers splashed with mud. Moonlight splayed across his dark face, and Father John could see the scar carved into the man's cheek. Orlando's body guard, a rifle gripped in one hand.

"It's that damn priest," the man hollered to a shadow on the other side of the creek, half-hidden in the willows.

"What'd he do? Pull one of the battery wires?" Another Indian started wading toward them, boots slapping at the water. He climbed onto the bank, slipped backward, then caught himself and stumbled forward, dragging his left leg.

Mud covered his buckskin pants almost to his knees.

"We gotta kill him, Martin," the man with the scar said.

Martin Crow Elk, Father John thought, the Indian who'd taken him over the ridge to the shadow ranch. The other man was Roy He-Dog, Orlando's bodyguard. He wondered what kind of fake IDs they'd used to convince Ted Gianelli they were not the Lakotas he was looking for.

"Don't see it makes any difference how he dies," Crow Elk said, his voice high-pitched with the whine of an adolescent. "He oughtta die like the rest of the evil ones." He leaned over and examined the battery. "All we gotta do is put the wires back and reset the clock, and they're all gonna die."

He-Dog seemed to consider this a moment, then he wheeled around and started back into the willows. "I'll take care of the clock. Ten minutes'll be enough for us to get out of here." His voice trailed behind him like a shadow, and Father John understood. The two men had set the clock and given themselves enough time to drive up one of the roads on the other side of the dam. When the dam didn't explode, they'd raced back.

Crow Elk stooped over, his left leg outstretched, his moccasin slipping in the marshy earth. He picked up the wires.

"Hold on," Father John shouted. It took all of his breath. He gasped for more air. "This isn't what Wovoka wants."

"What!" The Indian looked up. "What right you got, talk about Wovoka. What'd you know?"

"I know what Wovoka preached to the Ghost Dancers. Live a good life, live in peace."

"Yeah? Well, that changed after the soldiers came and killed Big Foot's people, dumped the bodies in a trench, the last believers. Nothing but filth, those white troops. Earth's gonna be cleansed of filth in the regeneration. Wovoka give Orlando the instructions on what to do."

"No, you're wrong." Father John raised himself against the pain until he was sitting upright. He wrapped an arm around his ribs and fought for another gulp of air. "Wovoka was a holy man. He knew about the massacres that had happened before, but he still preached peace. He never wanted innocent people to die."

"Shut up." The Indian bent over the wires.

"You dynamite the dam," Father John managed, "and hundreds of people will die. Innocent people, Martin. Both Indians and whites. I don't think you want to kill innocent people. You could've shot Vicky, but you didn't. Who killed the officer up there?" Father John tilted his head toward the top of the dam. "It was He-Dog, wasn't it?"

The Indian glanced between the wires and the battery. "Righteous people gonna live in the new world, soon's the flood's gone and the earth's clean. Orlando's gonna come back. He's gonna bring Wovoka."

"Wovoka will condemn you," Father John said. The pain ratcheted through his voice.

The Indian threw his shoulders back and shouted. "You don't know what you're talking about."

Father John could hear the break in the man's voice, like a spidery crack in glass. He started to his feet, coughing with the effort, aware of He-Dog crashing back through the willows.

From somewhere in the darkness came the faint wail of a siren.

"Clock's set," He-Dog shouted. He held the rifle low along his thigh and bent his head in the direction of the siren. "Fix the battery. Let's get outta here."

"Think of Wovoka, Martin." Father John was almost upright now. He dug his boots hard into the soggy ground to steady himself. "You blow up the dam, Wovoka won't want you with him. You'll be an outcast. You'll be alone."

"Shut up, white man!" He-Dog's voice sounded like the howl of a wild animal. He raised the rifle and hunched forward, a slow, deliberate motion. His top lip rolled back; the scar pulled taut across his cheek.

Father John had a sense of time collapsing around him, compressed into a finite moment of consciousness.

"Drop the gun!" Vicky stood up in the willows, pointing a long-nosed handgun at Roy He-Dog. "Now," she yelled, moving forward and planting her feet apart. "I'll shoot you."

Father John kept his gaze on the gun in her hands. She must have climbed back up the road. He could still see the gun inside the officer's holster. Now she held it steady, not more than three feet away from the back of the Indian's head.

He-Dog reached down and set the rifle in the mud.

The next thing Father John saw was Martin Crow Elk lurching sideways, pulling the wires toward the battery. Father John leapt forward and crashed against the Indian, knocking him to the ground. He rolled over, grabbing his stiff leg and sobbing.

Father John took hold of the wires and, stumbling to keep his balance, ground them beneath his boots until they disappeared into the mud. Then he picked up the battery and hurled it as hard as he could in the direction of the creek, grunting out loud with the pain that seared his ribs.

He walked over and unpeeled Vicky's fingers from the gun. The sirens were coming closer, a distinct, sharp sound that banked against the concrete dam.

He-Dog stood motionless. "You're gonna pay, white

man," he said. "You and this white woman that used to be Indian are gonna pay. You got no right . . ."

"Get down." Father John waved the gun.

The Indian shot him a look of hatred, then began folding himself downward. Onto his knees, his hands. Finally he stretched out, the side of his face against the mud.

Father John picked up the rifle. Then he slipped the officer's pistol into the back of his belt.

He went over to Vicky and slipped his arm around her shoulders. "It's over," he said.

She slumped toward him, as if she'd finally understood what she was staring at: Crow Elk sprawled on the ground, still grasping his leg. He was sobbing quietly, a kind of relief in the sound. He-Dog lay on the ground as still as stone.

"I saw two men wading across the creek," Vicky said, her voice choked with tears. "I was so afraid for you. I ran up the road to the officer's body and . . ."

"I know," Father John said. She was shaking beneath his arm.

It was then that Father John heard the low rumble of an engine kicking over. Then, headlights flayed the darkness on the other side of the creek. There was the sound of tires skidding in gravel. He saw a dark pickup plunging up a track at the far side of the dam. The pickup reached the top of the ridge, then taillights winked up at the sky as the truck dipped south, toward the reservation.

He sensed Vicky tense next to him. "There were others," she cried. "They're getting away."

"The police'll be here any minute. They'll stop them." He hoped that was true. "We'll wait."

• • •

Vicky listened to the tires humming on the asphalt. A soothing sound, she thought. She lay her head against the back of the seat and watched the stripe of orange light widening in the sky. John was quiet beside her, lost in his own thoughts, she guessed, his gaze locked on the road moving toward them.

It hadn't been a long wait at the dam. Ten minutes at most before the sound of sirens had filled the air and headlights shone through the pines. And then, crouching shadows darted toward the spillway, like troops moving into a village occupied by the enemy, flashlight beams bouncing in the air. One officer had reached the spillway and started inside, moving through a bubble of light. Other officers materialized on the slope above.

"Drop the rifle and raise your hands."

She'd watched Father John lay the rifle on the ground and lift his arms before putting her own hands into the air. The officers were swarming around He-Dog and Crow Elk.

"Father John!" An officer stepped past the others and shone a flashlight toward them. The light had blinded her a moment.

"You wanna tell me what the hell went on around here?" He threw a glance back at the officers handcuffing the two Indians, then holstered his own gun.

Vicky remembered sinking down into the willows, grasping at the stalks for balance, and all the while, John's voice above her, explaining, explaining. After a while—time had lost meaning—she realized that Gianelli's white Blazer and a line of Fremont County sheriff's cars were parked near the spillway. The explanations had started again and—odd, when she thought about it now—she'd been riveted by the way Gianelli's thick fingers had maneuvered a pen across a tiny pad in his fleshy palm.

At some point, John O'Malley had leaned over, taken her arm, and guided her to her feet. One of the sheriff's deputies would retrieve her Bronco and bring it to Lander tomorrow, he'd told her. He was going to take her home.

Now John O'Malley's voice floated through the quiet. Was she all right? He must have asked before, because he wanted to know if she was *sure.* In the dim light of the dashboard, she could see the concern in the set of his shoulders, the tight curve of his hand on the wheel. She assured him that she was fine.

"It takes a while for shock to wear off." He reached over and touched her hand, keeping his eyes on the road.

"I would have killed them," she said after a moment.

"But you didn't."

The small space, the close air, the priest a few inches away: she felt as if she were in the confessional. "You don't understand. I *wanted* to kill them for what they'd done to Ben."

He didn't respond. The trees passing her window stood out in relief against the pale early-morning light. She was thinking that he wouldn't want anything more to do with her, now that he'd seen the shadows of her life.

"There will be a reckoning, Vicky," he said finally. "He-Dog and Crow Elk will be looking at charges of murder, and Gianelli will probably come up with a lot of other charges. They'll spend the rest of their lives in prison."

"What about the guards in the other truck?" None of the officers had mentioned the other truck.

"They'll find them. Every officer in the county's looking for them. They'll be held accountable."

"And Orlando? What about his accountability? He escaped. He's dead."

"He'll answer to God."

Vicky turned to the window and combed her fingers through her hair. Outside the pines were changing from black to dark green. John O'Malley was a priest. He believed in justice, if not in this world, then in the next. A powerful reason to believe in an afterlife, she thought, since there was seldom justice here. She found herself straining to believe along with him. Justice had to exist somewhere.

The pickup took the curve into the northern reaches of Lander. The street lamps along the curbs looked yellow and faded in the early light. There was a sense of unreality to the brick bungalows, the parked cars, the store fronts that reflected the glow of headlights as they passed. Other headlights blinked in the opposite direction, then turned at an intersection, leaving them moving alone through a shadow world.

They turned into a parking space in front of her building and stopped at the double glass doors. She could see the lobby, dimly lit and one-dimensional, like a photo.

She struggled to hide the tremor that pulsed through her. It was over, she told herself. Ben's killers were in custody. The guards in the truck would be arrested. Orlando was dead. *Over.* The tremor remained, as if her body refused to accept the reality.

John got out and walked around the front. She could see that his shirt was caked with mud, and dried mud clung to his jeans.

Her door opened. "I'll walk you in."

She slid out beside him and started up the walk, her legs wobbly beneath her. He reached past and opened the glass door. They took the stairs to the second floor in silence.

In silence, down the corridor past the closed doors with brass numbers high in the center, 4B, 3B, 2B.

Vicky stopped in front of 1B and fumbled in her jeans pocket for the slim key. "I can put on some coffee," she said, but she knew, even before he began shaking his head, that he would decline.

"It's almost morning. I have to take the six o'clock Mass."

She turned toward him. "You came after me. Thank you."

"Aunt Rose was worried about you." He paused. "So was I."

Auntie, she thought. The old woman had probably been awake all night, pacing the floor, worrying about her. She had to call Aunt Rose right away.

Vicky was about to thank him again when he placed both arms around her and drew her to him. She allowed herself to relax in his strength a moment and to savor the feeling of being at home.

"It'll take time to get over Ben's death, Vicky," he said, releasing her. She felt suddenly adrift again, on her own.

"If you ever want to talk, you know where I'll be," he was saying. In any case"—trying for a smile now that she sensed was hard and off the mark somehow—"I'll be here for a while."

She understood. John O'Malley was only at St. Francis Mission for a while.

Vicky watched him walk back down the corridor and disappear behind the door to the stairs. Then she inserted the key in the lock and grasped the knob. It didn't move. She jiggled the key again. This time the knob turned, and she realized that she'd locked the door on the first try, which meant it had been unlocked. Curious, she thought, as she stepped into the living room and closed the door behind her. She always locked her door in town.

The apartment was still. The shadows of the furniture—sofa, chairs, desk, bookcases—stood out against the dim light glowing through the windows.

A musky odor, like the odor of a wild animal, hit her. And something else—the faintest noise of a breath stifled in mid-gasp. For a moment, she didn't move. Then she stepped to the table lamp and turned on the switch.

The lamp burst into life and the shadows retreated to the edges of the room. On her left, in front of the bookcase, stood a small, pretty girl, with darting black eyes and black hair that hung in tangled ropes over the shoulders of her white gown. A red crescent moon leaped out from the bright blue stripe painted on the front. The skirt was splashed with mud. In an instant, Vicky knew that it was Janis Beaver, aiming a rifle at her heart.

‹ 33 ›

"**G**et ready to die, bitch."

The girl raised the barrel until Vicky could see the notches of the rifling. The picture came to her with great clarity now, as if the scene were playing out in front of her. It was Janis who had driven the truck up to the ridge on the other side of the creek. Janis who had guarded the dam while the two men set the dynamite. Janis—my God, it must have been the girl—who had shot the officer.

"Why didn't you shoot me at the dam?" Vicky felt completely focused and calm. Survival was all that mattered. Everything else faded into the shadows at the periphery of the room. She had to keep the girl talking and watch for the chance to distract her.

"Why, Janis?" she pushed on. "You must've had a clear shot."

Confusion. Regret. A mixture of emotions came into the narrow, finely formed face. "You think I didn't wanna kill you and that priest, after I seen what you did to He-Dog and Crow Elk? Everything was ready; the new world would've been here by now. We was almost to the top of the ridge, and the dam was supposed to blow. But nothing happened. So He-Dog says, something must've went wrong, and he and Crow Elk drove back down. Good thing I decided to go down there after them, else I wouldn't've seen what happened. But I seen how you and that nosy priest ruined everything. I heard the sirens coming and got out of there."

She stopped a moment. A look of wonder came into her eyes. "All them cop cars racing up to Bull Lake," she said, "and they never seen me pulled over in the trees. After they went by, I drove back to the rez, and all the way, I said to myself, they're gonna pay. The ex-wife of Ben Holden and that priest, they're both gotta pay."

"How did you know where I live?" Vicky tossed out the question. *Talk. Talk.* A moment's distraction was all she needed. She kept her eyes on the girl, but her gaze was taking in everything in the space between them: the sofa, the little table with the brass lamp, the light glowing through the white shade. There was no weapon, nothing she might grab and fling.

"Know where you live?" Janis repeated. "It didn't take a law degree. Your auntie, she talks about you all the time. She must've told me two, three times about your new apartment. I seen your name on the mailboxes downstairs."

"I locked my door this morning."

"No kidding." The girl was enjoying this, playing with her.

"Don't need a law degree for that either," Janis said. "Just some wire and a plastic card I found in the glove compartment. Worked just fine."

"You're very clever."

This seemed to please the girl. She gave a smile of acknowledgment, then lifted the rifle a couple inches, her finger curled around the trigger. From somewhere outside came the sound of an engine turning over, and Vicky realized John O'Malley was pulling out of the parking space. She was alone. *Hi sei ci nihi.* She would die here, alone. Just as Ben had died out on Rendezvous Road alone.

"Ready to join your ex?" Janis rolled her head and emitted an eerie sound, somewhere between a laugh and a wail. "Oh, he was something else, your ex. 'Need some help, ma'am?' A real gentleman. Never even seen the pistol. Never knew what hit him."

Vicky felt her muscles seize and turn to stone. Her breath came in a sob. She'd gotten it all wrong. It wasn't the Lakotas who had followed Ben to Rendezvous Road. It was Janis Beaver.

She was alone with Ben's killer.

Her mouth was dry. Her tongue felt swollen. She stumbled with the words: "Why, Janis? Why did Orlando leave the killing to you? First Dean, right? Then, Ben." It was making sense. Janis was the one who had taken the twenty-two from Aunt Rose's house. She had used the gun to kill both Dean and Ben. "Why did you have to do the dirty work? Wasn't Orlando man enough?"

Janis rocked backward, an agitated, defensive motion. "Dean wouldn't listen. Kept trying to get me to come with him. Said all kinds of lies about Orlando. How he was a phony. The messiah, a phony! I covered my ears. Don't tell me filth, I said. But he kept saying phony, phony, phony. Then he went snooping around the ranch and came back to the tipi shouting how the crazy guards must've stolen dynamite from the Arapaho Ranch and what the hell did they think they was gonna do? He guessed everything. He heard what Orlando said about the old world getting cleaned, and he knew all about the dam. He was going to stop the great event."

The rifle tilted toward the floor, almost as if the girl had forgotten about it. Vicky reached for the lamp, all of her energy focused on the switch. *She had to turn off the light.*

"Stop!" The rifle jerked upward. The girl seemed to muster her forces, remembering her intention. "I said, don't move."

Vicky stood very still, one hand still outstretched. She was barely aware of the soft orange light creeping through the window. It would be daylight soon. People would be up and about. Doors slamming, footsteps pounding down the corridor, car engines turning over outside, all the ordinary sounds of life that might distract the girl. She had to keep her talking!

"I think you're lying," Vicky said. "Dean was shot in the mountains west of Fort Washakie, miles from the shadow ranch."

The girl's chest started to quiver, and a low rumbling noise, like a stifled laugh, came out of her throat. "Orlando said, if you love me, you gotta take care of the problem. I went to Lander Sunday after Dean left. Found him outside his office. Told him I'd changed my mind; it was just gonna be me and him. Oh, he bought it, all right. We drove up to this real peaceful place. It was a good place for him to die."

Her body was shaking now, her head bobbing back and forth. "The problem was taken care of, everything was gonna be fine, like Orlando wanted. Then next day Ben Holden shows up and tells He-Dog and Crow Elk to turn over the dynamite, or he was going to the FBI. When he left, Orlando said, 'You know what to do, Janis, if you love me.' He knew I loved him. So I followed Holden down to Lander and waited 'til he come outta the restaurant. I followed him to Rendezvous Road. I passed his truck, then stopped. I figured he wouldn't think anything about stopping for a woman with car trouble. Now you're gonna die, just like he did."

Janis raised the rifle and hunched her shoulders over the barrel.

"Janis," Vicky shouted. "Orlando's here!"

"He'll come back with the ancestors."

"He's here now, Janis. He's bringing the ancestors now! Look!" Vicky threw both hands toward the orange glow in the window.

Janis stood very still, some argument playing out behind the black, fixated eyes. Then she rolled her head toward the window.

Vicky lunged for the cord and yanked it out of the socket. The lamp skittered over the table and crashed onto the floor. Except for the orange glow, the room was swallowed in shadows.

"You tricked me!" It was a howling noise, the cry of a trapped animal.

Vicky dropped down next to the sofa and crouched at the end, her heart thudding in her ears. She could hear the girl moving toward her, then she caught a glimpse of the dark figure passing the window.

She inched toward the coffee table and stopped, all of her senses on alert. Janis was heading toward the table. One step, two steps. Vicky held her breath. One more step, and she could maneuver herself behind the girl, throw her weight against her, grab the gun.

The air exploded.

The sound of a gunshot bounced around the walls and furniture. Vicky drew herself in and huddled close to the carpet. She stopped her breath. The rifle fired again and again. A whizzing sound passed over her head, followed by the thuds of bullets breaking plaster and splintering wood. Then another shot, and she felt something sharp, like a knife, slice across her shoulder. She winced with the pain and jabbed her fist into her mouth to stop the scream welling in her throat. Something wet and sticky was trickling down her arm. She could smell her own blood. She pulled herself into a tight stillness. *The mountain lion is still*—her grandfather's voice in her head—*it waits for its enemy to come.*

From far away came the sounds of footsteps hammering and men shouting. A pale morning light had begun to seep across the room. Vicky felt the slight displacement in the air, like the displacement when a bird flaps past, and she realized the girl had moved along the coffee table and was standing a few feet away, aiming the rifle down at her.

"Vicky!" A voice in the corridor, and someone pounding on the door. Janis flinched, and in that nanosecond, Vicky flung herself upright at the girl. Then they were falling together against the hard edge and the leg of the coffee table. Vicky was aware of the rifle skittering across the carpet and the pain that locked her left arm. She jammed her right elbow into Janis Beaver's chest as they hit the floor together. The girl was coughing and spitting. Vicky felt the sharp nails raking her face.

From behind came the noise of the door slammed back against the wall and someone shouting—John O'Malley's voice!—"Vicky! Vicky!"

She was aware of people pouring around them. Someone

started pulling her upright, away from the screaming girl crawling toward the rifle. And then the rifle was snatched away, and she realized a large man had grabbed the girl, lifted her to her feet, and was pinning her arms to her sides.

And John O'Malley was helping her to her feet.

The ceiling light came on. The coffee table and sofa, the rest of the room swam around her. She grabbed a fistful of John O'Malley's shirt to steady herself. The girl had started screaming obscenities, kicking out at the man trying to hold her, and then she went quiet and limp. Another man had picked up the rifle and stepped back. Others—who were they? neighbors?—burst through the door, shouting: "What's going on? Anybody hurt?"

She could see the crowd in the corridor—women with disheveled hair and sleepy eyes, robes flung over night-gowns, a man in a white T-shirt and boxer shorts.

Father John was leading her over to a chair. She sank into the cushion, aware of his finger tracing her shoulder. Her blood felt warm and sticky on her arm. "You've been hit. Were you hit anywhere else?"

She shook her head. People were filling up the room.

Father John made his way through the crowd. Vicky watched him pick up the phone from the floor next to the desk and tap the keys. There had been a shooting, he said into the mouthpiece. Send an ambulance and the police. Over the sound of his voice, she could hear the sirens in the distance.

He disappeared into the kitchen a moment, then he was back, pushing through the crowd that stood in silence, frozen in shock. He dropped down on the armrest and set a cold towel against her shoulder. Her skin went numb; the pain began to subside.

"You came back," she whispered. "I heard you drive away, but you came back."

"I spotted a black truck parked down the street," he said. "I thought I'd better check and make sure you were okay."

They were quiet a moment. Then Vicky said, "She killed Ben."

Father John didn't say anything. The sirens blared from the street below, then cut off. Red, blue, and yellow lights flashed across the window.

Janis was still. She looked like dead weight in the large man's arms, black hair wet and matted against the narrow face. The sirens cut off, and in another moment the building vibrated with the crash of footsteps in the corridor.

‹ 34 ›

Vicky stood at the window over the kitchen sink and marveled at how time always slipped into a slower rhythm at Aunt Rose's house. In the brush shade outside, Susan was working her way around the table, arranging plates, knives, forks, napkins. Lucas sat across from Aunt Rose, giving the old woman his full attention. She was telling a story, her hands darting like birds between them, her face lit with pride, the same pride, Vicky thought, that the grandmothers in the Old Time took in the young warriors.

Aunt Rose must have finished the story, because Lucas threw back his head and laughed into the sky. Vicky felt a stab of pain. Everything about her son—the tall, muscular body; the handsome, golden-brown face and black agate eyes; even his laugh—was so like his father's.

She turned back to the counter and began mixing the potato salad. Her arm was still stiff and sore, but the bullet had only grazed her shoulder. There was still a bluish-red mark that looked like a burn.

A warm fug of onion and pepper odors filled the air. Grease popped from the frying chicken. This would be their last dinner together, she was thinking. Lucas, Susan, Aunt Rose, almost everyone she loved. Tomorrow, the kids would leave.

They'd been with Aunt Rose almost a week. Susan and Lucas had canceled their plans to leave last Friday. She was grateful. She could never have asked them to stay, not when they had begged her to stay all those years ago—two black-haired children with large, sad eyes—and she had driven away, promising to make things right one day. A promise she had never kept.

It had been a hectic week. The phone had rung almost nonstop, until Aunt Rose had pulled the plug and created blissful silence. Reporters and TV crews had knocked on the door, but Aunt Rose had told them to go away. Vicky had made trip after trip—half a dozen-trips—to Fort Washakie and Lander for interviews with the police and Gianelli, going over the same details and dodging reporters in the hallways. When she finally fell into bed at night, her head spun with the details, and she found herself sitting upright, hugging her pillow and staring into the darkness, trying to wrap her mind around the fact that Ben was gone.

Tomorrow, after the kids left, she would return to her own apartment, her own office. Normal life. Norm Weedly had called. The JBC had agreed to hear her arguments for filing a federal lawsuit. She intended to do her best to convince them to go forward. The people deserved clean water.

Vicky finished the potato salad and started to arrange the fried chicken on a platter. The screen door opened. Susan stepped inside and leaned against the counter. Her face was flushed with the sun, her hair shone.

How she loved this girl that she had lost, Vicky thought. It was like an arrow lodged in her heart. A couple of nights ago, they'd sat on the bed and talked a little before Susan had darted away. But it was a start, Vicky felt certain. A small step toward finding her daughter again.

"It's not the same here without Dad," Susan said, so much sadness in her tone that Vicky dropped the tongs she'd been using, crossed the little kitchen, and took her daughter in her arms.

"I know you miss him," Vicky said, running one hand along Susan's silky hair. The faint smell of shampoo mingled with the humid, spicy odors that filled the kitchen. She didn't know what else to say. That *she* also missed Ben? In a way, it would be the truth. He'd been endlessly patient, tolerant, and accepting with the kids, and she was grateful for that, even though he had never been that way with her. It was as if Susan and Lucas were always more than he felt he deserved, and she was never enough. He had stayed close to the kids. *That* was the memory of Ben she would hold on to. The other memories, she would let go.

The screen door banged open, punctuating Aunt Rose's voice: "Got some company." She stood on the stoop and held the door back. "Bring out another plate."

Susan pulled away and started rummaging in the cabinets. "Just like Aunt Rose to find somebody in need of dinner," she said. She was smiling.

John O'Malley, Vicky thought, aware of the pure, glad rush moving through her. She'd caught sight of him at the interviews, but he'd been questioned in one room, she in another. She'd wanted to thank him again for coming back to the apartment. If he hadn't called her name and knocked when he did . . . All week, she'd been trying to block the thought of what would have happened.

She handed Susan the bowl of potato salad, then picked

up the platter of chicken and, backing through the screen door, followed her daughter outside. Halfway across the yard, she stopped. The man in the brush shade—hands jammed into the pockets of his khaki trousers, dark blue polo shirt outlining the muscles across his back—was Adam Lone Eagle. Chatting and laughing with Lucas, as if they were old friends. In a way, they were, she guessed. Lucas had gone to Lander with her for the interviews, and Adam had been there. They had seemed to hit it off.

"Vicky!" The lawyer looked around, then walked over. "Let me give you a hand," he said, taking the chicken platter.

"You fry this chicken?" There was approval in the sideways glance he gave her as they stepped into the shade. He set the platter on the table.

"Nice to see you, Adam." She tried to keep the disappointment out of her voice. If John O'Malley hadn't come to her, well, tomorrow, she resolved, she would go to him. There was so much that had been left unsaid between them.

"Sit down. Eat, eat." Aunt Rose dropped into the webbed folding chair at the end of the table. "Give thanks to the Creator," she said when everyone was seated. "We have good food to sustain our lives, a good house to shelter us. We been blessed with the good people the Creator sent us." She paused. Lucas and Susan both bowed their heads, taking a moment, Vicky knew, to absorb again the reality of their father's death.

"So now we eat," Aunt Rose said. An order meant to be obeyed, just as her own grandmothers and great-grandmothers had been obeyed when they ordered their families and visitors to eat. No one left an Arapaho village hungry. She passed the chicken and motioned for Susan to start the potato salad.

The polite preliminaries took up most of the meal: the hot weather, the powwow next week, the new convenience store about to open. Adam Lone Eagle was observing the Arapaho tradition, Vicky knew. He understood it wasn't yet the time to discuss what they all knew had brought him here.

After Lucas had delivered mugs of steaming coffee, and she and Susan had distributed the rhubarb pie that Susan had baked that afternoon, and the sky had softened with the sun edging below the mountains, the Lakota cleared his throat. Everyone else became quiet. The breeze clattered softly on the brush walls.

"I met with Gianelli and the U.S. attorney this afternoon. Janis Beaver has confessed to the murders of both Dean Little Horse and . . ." He hesitated. "Ben," he said softly. "The grand jury has indicted her on two counts of first-degree homicide. He-Dog and Crow Elk are looking at twenty-six counts of attempting to assist a suicide; conspiracy to commit murder; conspiracy to destroy public property; theft of an explosive substance . . ." He threw up his hands, as if the list were too long to enumerate.

Aunt Rose shook her head. "The shadow dancers went wrong," she said. "Lost their way. Wovoka never preached the stuff Orlando preached. Orlando got it all wrong. Too bad. He could've been good for the people, brought us closer together, given us back some of the old way."

"Unfortunately, the followers believed in him," Adam said. "They found his website on the Internet and came here to be saved. There's no evidence they were coerced into taking drugs. They all told the same story. They had a final celebration, worked themselves into a frenzy, then took the drugs so they could join the ancestors coming after the flood. Orlando had the same intention. But he'd been taking the drugs so long, he knew he had to take more than usual. Before he swallowed the pills, he'd ordered He-Dog and Crow Elk to blow up the dam. Afterward, they were supposed to return to the shadow ranch, take the drugs themselves, and wait for the ancestors."

Adam took a long sip from his mug, working out something else in his mind. Finally he said, "Orlando could count on the two Lakotas to blow up the dam. He understood that . . ." He paused again and gazed out over the yard. "We have an old wound that still festers, an old grudge that was never settled."

"Wounded Knee," Vicky heard herself saying. In the man's expression, she glimpsed the kind of sorrow that her own people carried through the years, like a bundle of broken arrows that had belonged to the ancestors.

Adam nodded. "Orlando knew how to use the massacre. He preached about how the soldiers had killed Big Foot's band and stopped the Ghost Dance before the new world could arrive. He convinced the followers that no one could be allowed to stand in the way of the new world this time. Not Dean Little Horse or Ben Holden. He even sent He-Dog and Crow Elk to St. Francis Mission to warn away Father O'Malley. Those Indians would've killed him, if they'd seen him."

He paused. "You're lucky, Vicky, that they didn't kill you."

Susan gasped. "No more risks, Mom. Promise you won't take any more risks."

Lucas leaned toward her and thumped the table. "We

don't want to worry about you all the time." He hesitated. "The way Dad did."

A new kind of quiet, uncomfortable and heavy, gripped the brush shade a moment before Vicky said, "Believe me, I prefer a nice, quiet, normal life." She glanced around the table, and beyond to the expanse of open land lying hot and quiet under the red-flamed sky. This was normal, she thought.

"I like the same kind of life," Adam said, and she realized that, for the last several moments, he had not taken his eyes from her.

The phone rang again—at least the tenth call this morning, Father John guessed. He looked up from the notes he was making for tonight's parish council meeting. The click-click sound of Father George's computer keys down the hall punctuated an aria from *Falstaff* that emanated softly from the tape player on the bookshelf behind him. Yesterday, both he and Father George had said the funeral Mass for Dean Little Horse. They'd blessed the young man's grave in the mission cemetery.

His assistant was a hard worker, he had to admit. The man had practically run the mission by himself all week.

Father John was tempted to let the phone ring. Gianelli or Banner wanting to talk to him again, another reporter wanting an interview.

Finally he reached over and lifted the receiver. There was always the chance the caller was someone in need of a priest.

"Father O'Malley," he said.

An unfamiliar voice sounded on the other end, a reporter from a newspaper in the Midwest somewhere. Would he answer a few questions about the shadow dance cult? Did all those people intend to commit suicide?

No, they had not intended to commit suicide. Not exactly. It was complicated. They'd believed they were going to the ancestors and would return immediately to a new and better world. He said he'd already given a statement to the press that explained everything. Why couldn't they get it? He had no other comment.

He hung up. It was the last thing he'd needed, after the board of directors meeting last weekend, for his name to be splashed across the national news: JESUIT PRIEST INTERVENES IN MASS SUICIDE. The Provincial was not pleased. Two minutes after CNN had broken the story, the phone had rung, and Father John had known, before he'd answered, who was on the other end.

"My God, John, what is going on out there?" Father Bill Rutherford, an old friend from seminary days, two young men full of promise, great things ahead, which had been true in Rutherford's case.

Father John had started to explain, but the Provincial had interrupted.

"Am I clear on this? The board of directors is attempting to ascertain whether the society should continue to support St. Francis Mission, and you leave the meeting to go to a place called the shadow ranch, where there are one dead man and twenty-six unconscious people. Then you drive to a dam that's about to be blown up?"

He was clear, Father John said. Then he said that he didn't regret what he'd done. There was every chance several of the dancers would have died if the medics hadn't gotten there when they did. Several were still at Riverton Memorial, although most of the dancers, according to the moccasin telegraph, had left the reservation and gone back to wherever they'd come from.

The line had gone quiet for a moment. "Yes, it was fortunate you arrived in time," Father Rutherford said, a quieter tone, less agitated, the tone of the priest, not the administrator. Then, the administrator again: "CNN says you and that woman lawyer are heroes. You placed your own lives in danger. I'd hoped you wouldn't continue making a practice of this kind of activity. Surely the police can handle such emergencies."

Of course, Father John had said. No, he didn't plan to make a practice of this kind of activity.

"Good. I'm glad to hear it." The Provincial didn't sound reassured. Then—a lighter tone—he said: "I don't want to turn on the TV and see your Irish face on the national news again."

His Irish face had been on the national news for six days, a burden, he imagined, that the Provincial was clenching his teeth and trying to bear, just as he was. Especially since his name was continually linked with Vicky's.

He hadn't been able to stop thinking about her. He'd tried calling her at Aunt Rose's, and finally given up. They must have unplugged the phone. Why wouldn't they? He wished he could do the same. He'd passed her in the halls at the interviews, asked how her shoulder was. He'd been relieved when she waved her arm and assured him she was fine. But she'd looked fatigued and tense, with bluish scratches on her face and dark circles rimming her eyes, as if she hadn't been sleeping. He probably looked the same, he thought. He hadn't been sleeping either.

He'd gone back to his notes when he heard the sound of a vehicle turning onto Circle Drive, then the motor cutting off. His fingers tightened around the pen at the thought of another reporter poking his head through the door. He'd get rid of him as fast as possible.

A moment passed before he heard the footsteps on the concrete steps and the swoosh of the front door opening and closing. He recognized the footsteps crossing the corridor and got to his feet just as Vicky appeared in the doorway.

"How are you?" he said. She looked more rested, more the way she'd looked the first time she'd appeared in his doorway, except that now she wore jeans and a white shirt.

"That's what I came to ask you." She stepped inside and dropped into one of the side chairs.

"Your shoulder?" He walked around the desk and sat against the edge.

"The only part of me that isn't brown," she said. "It's red and blue."

He tried to push away the thought that had nagged him all week: The bullet that grazed her shoulder had come within inches of her head. *Her head.*

"I never got the chance to thank you again for coming back to the apartment," she said. "You got there just in time."

Thank God, he was thinking.

The clacking of computer keys floated from the rear office. Then Vicky smiled, as if a new thought had pushed to the forefront of her mind. "What about the mission?"

"Why do I get the idea you already know?"

She shrugged. "The moccasin telegraph is a wonder of technology. It continues to operate even with the phone unplugged. I heard how the pickups and cars were parked all the way out to Seventeen-Mile Road, how Eagle Hall was jam packed and people stood outside, chanting and praying, how speaker after speaker got up and told the board they had no business closing the mission. And Amos spoke for thirty minutes. In Arapaho!" She threw back her head and laughed. "I wish I could have seen the board members' faces. They must have felt like the cavalry surrounded by Indians."

He laughed with her. "The board left first thing the next morning."

"I hear the mission stays," she said.

"That was the consensus before the board left."

"I'm glad, John." She got up, walked past him to the window, and stared quietly outside a moment. "My family doesn't want me taking any more risks."

"Smart people, your family." Father John paused. The Provincial didn't want him taking risks either, and he had promised to try to refrain. But he would go, he knew. He would always go if someone needed him. And so would Vicky. They were alike, he thought.

She turned toward him. The sun glinted in her hair. "John," she said, "there's so much I want to say to you."

He felt his heart knock against his ribs. "Don't, Vicky," he said. "Don't say anything."

She was shaking her head. "Ben and his family were right, you know. For a long time, I'd been hoping . . ."

He put up his hand to stop her, but she went on.

"But I understand now. This is your place. This is where you belong." She lifted both arms toward the mission and beyond, and he knew that she was not referring only to the place, but to what he was, a priest. "But this is also where I belong. It's my land, my place. I can't keep going to Denver. I can't run away from this place again, but the thing is, I don't think I can stop loving you."

"Oh, Vicky, don't." He shook his head. "Don't love me."

He would never stop loving her. "There will be someone——"

She cut in and hurried on, as if she were delivering a speech she'd memorized. "The fact is, we're both here, and I want us to be friends, John. I really need you to be my friend, but I have to make room in my life for something else."

She pivoted around and looked out the window. He walked over and placed his arm around her. "You deserve to be happy," he said. She seemed small next to him, and he could smell the faint odor of sage in her hair. Outside the sky was blue and clear as glass. A crow was circling above the cottonwoods. Walks-On lay on his side in the sun in front of the residence. All the buildings looked peaceful, rooted to the earth.

She was right. This was his place, this was where he could be the priest he wanted to be. Still, he felt as if something hard had been laid on his heart.

"I want you to be happy, Vicky," he said, letting her go.

She was quiet a moment, her gaze fixed on the mission grounds beyond the window. Finally she said, "It's like the new world that Wovoka promised would come someday. The mission is beautiful and peaceful. The ancestors left this for us, like a sign, something to strive for and hope for. No wonder the people turned out for the board meeting. It wouldn't be the same here without this place."

"You sound like the pastor."

She laughed, and there was something free and light in the sound of her voice that made him glad.

"Oh, no," she said. "There's only one pastor at St. Francis Mission, John O'Malley."

NEW YORK TIMES BESTSELLING AUTHOR OF
THE SHADOW DANCER

MARGARET COEL

KILLING RAVEN

BERKLEY PRIME CRIME

MARGARET COEL

THE SPIRIT WOMAN

Coel returns to her bestselling mystery series featuring Arapho lawyer Vicky Holden. A missing archaeologist echoes a similar disappearance from twenty years earlier—and both are tied to the legend of Lewis and Clark's guide, Sacajawea.

❏ 0-425-18090-5

THE EAGLE CATHER

When Arapaho tribal chairman Harvey Castle is found murdered, the evidence points to his own nephew. But Father John O'Malley doesn't believe the young man is a killer. And in his quest for truth, O'Malley gets a rare glimpse into the Arapaho life few outsiders ever see—and a crime fewer could imagine...

❏ 0-425-15463-7

THE GHOST WALKER

Father John O'Malley comes across a corpse lying in a ditch beside the highway. When he returns with the police, it is gone. Together, an Arapaho lawyer and Father John must draw upon ancient Arapaho traditions to stop a killer, explain the inexplicable, and put a ghost to rest...

❏ 0-425-15961-2

THE DREAM STALKER

Father John O'Malley and Arapaho attorney Vicky Holden return to face a brutal crime of greed, false promises, and shattered dreams.

❏ 0-425-16533-7

THE STORY TELLER

When the Arapaho storyteller discovers that a sacred tribal artifact is missing from a local museum, Holden and O'Malley begin a deadly search for the sacred treasure.

❏ 0-425-17025-X

THE THUNDER KEEPER

The apparent suicide of a young Arapaho on sacred ground shocks the populace of the Wind River Reservation. But strange events following the death lead Vicky Holden and Father John O'Malley to suspect foul play.

❏ 0-425-17025-X